SEASON
OF
SHADOWS

ALSO BY MARY MACKEY

The Kindness of Strangers
A Grand Passion
The Last Warrior Queen
McCarthy's List
Immersion
The Dear Dance of Eros

SEASON OF SHADOWS

Mary Mackey

BANTAM BOOKS
New York ♦ Toronto ♦ London ♦ Sydney ♦ Auckland

SEASON OF SHADOWS
A BANTAM BOOK

All rights reserved.
Copyright © 1991 by Mary Mackey.
Book design by Chris Welch

No part of this book may be reproduced or transmitted in any form or by any means, electronic or mechanical, including photocopying, recording, or by any information storage and retrieval system, without permission in writing from the publisher.
For information address: Bantam Books.

PUBLISHED SIMULTANEOUSLY IN THE UNITED STATES AND CANADA

Bantam Books are published by Bantam Books, a division of Bantam Doubleday Dell Publishing Group, Inc. Its trademark, consisting of the words "Bantam Books" and the portrayal of a rooster, is Registered in U.S. Patent and Trademark Office and in other countries. Marca Registrada. Bantam Books, 666 Fifth Avenue, New York, New York 10103.

PRINTED IN THE UNITED STATES OF AMERICA

For A.W.

ACKNOWLEDGMENTS

Once again I owe a debt of gratitude to novelist Sheldon Greene, who with unfailing patience read every version of this novel in manuscript. His suggestions and criticisms were invaluable. Special thanks also to Angus Wright, Viola Weinberg, Heather Hafleigh, Barbara Lowenstein, Coleen O'Shea, Steve Rubin, and Gene Young.

This book is a work of fiction. Except for a few well-known characters such as Indira Gandhi, all names, characters, places, and incidents are products of the author's imagination or are used fictitiously. Any resemblance to actual events or locales or persons, living or dead, is entirely coincidental.

SEASON OF SHADOWS

PROLOGUE

The Kingdom of Patan

June 1966

*I*n *the early dawn*, the Himalayas were dark and brooding. Towering over the valley of Sindhala, they rose up and up, resting against the bleak gray sky like giants. They were very old and very holy. Before the first people appeared in this part of the world, their slopes were already worn down by the rains of countless centuries; when the Buddha himself passed this way on his return to India, they had offered him shelter. There was very little they had not seen of human desire and folly; now, in the first pale light of the new day, they were silent, shrouded in their own mystery.

Then suddenly everything was glitter and heat and dancing shadows; crystals of ice sparkled on the tips of the highest peaks; the glaciers shone like great solar mirrors, unbearably bright and blindly beautiful. To the east, a twisting ball of orange flame thrust itself over the horizon; it was the sun, dressed in the same colors as the monks in the temples below who were swaying over their cups of buttered tea, chanting prayers for the prosperity of the prince and the royal family. For this was an auspicious day: a wedding day. In the great valley, the red and gold prayer flags were already fluttering from every housetop, and the smoke from a thousand cooking fires was rising into the air. Everyone was getting up early this morning to see the wedding procession.

Outside the temples the younger monks were putting the finishing touches on the great shrines that would be carted through the streets of Sindhala. The painted eyes of the buddhas looked down on them benevolently from beneath their golden crowns: blue, dreaming, compassionate eyes that saw everything and desired nothing. Here, mounted on a wooden platform, was a dragon god three stories high, garlanded with flowers, dancing on sheaves of rice so that the bride would be fertile; over there, a dreadful black Kali trampled the plaster bones and skulls of her enemies, showing her great red tongue as she lapped up the last bits of evil that might threaten the ceremony.

The children of Sindhala were half-crazy with delight at the sight of these preparations. They ran back and forth in their new clothes like flocks of small, agitated birds, ignoring their mothers' pleas to come inside and finish their breakfasts, for who could eat on a day like this? Besides the shrines, there were going to be soldiers and bands and big black foreign cars with rich strangers in them. There were going to be real elephants with jeweled houses on their backs called *howdahs*, and inside one of them the bride would be sitting, concealed behind red silk curtains. She was blond with skin like milk, and she came from America, that fabulous land where everyone ate meat three times a day, and there were no lepers, and Chubby Checker sang "Let's Do the Twist" just the way he did on the radio. The children twisted a little, for old movies came here occasionally, years after they had been popular in the West, shown outdoors on projectors run by bicycle generators. Then the children broke into some of the ancient, traditional dances of Patan, their hands and arms swaying gracefully. On the great wall that surrounded the city, the same dances could be seen, carved into the stone over a thousand years ago. *"Andu baka ta Patan!"* the children sang. "Nothing ever changes in Patan!" For this was the pride of their people: to be eternal and unchanging and different from all other people in the world.

Lucy Constable, the Radcliffe graduate who was soon to become the princess of Patan, certainly would have agreed with the children if she had had time to listen to their song. She might even have taken a few of the littlest ones on her lap and tried to explain what it felt like to visit their country for the first time. "Patan," she might have told them, "is a kingdom of dreams. I keep expecting to wake up back in my own bed in the dorm, with Cassie snoring across the room and the radiator huffing in the corner, but instead I feel as if I've climbed into a time machine and gone back to the thirteenth century."

But Lucy was far too preoccupied with her own problems that morning to tell the children stories. She had other things on her mind, some of them sober, as befitted a woman in her position, and some of them . . . well, some of them could only be called surreal. A kingdom of dreams can sometimes be a kingdom of nightmares, especially if you don't know the basic rules, especially if you're a stranger and a princess-to-be both at the same time. The idea that going to Patan was like getting into a time machine was all too true; she had been in the country only a week, and already she had encountered problems that seemed exotic, incomprehensible, and altogether medieval.

On this, the morning of her wedding day, Lucy stood in the central courtyard of the royal palace next to her best friend, Cassandra Quinn, looking at the elephant they were supposed to ride to the ceremony. The elephant was a relic from another century when royal brides and their attendants had ridden above the peasants like goddesses, and custom required—*demanded*—that she and Cassie climb into the jeweled howdah on its back and join the procession to the temple. All of this had seemed quite wonderful and romantic when Prince Mila, her husband-to-be, had explained the ceremony to her back in Cambridge, Massachusetts, but here in Patan, confronted with the real elephant, Lucy was having second thoughts.

She straightened the folds of her gold embroidered wedding sari and frowned at the elephant who seemed to be in a foul temper. He had been flown in only two days ago from the lowland jungles, and since he was now a good six thousand feet above sea level he was probably suffering from altitude sickness. She turned to Cassie. "Well, what do you think?" she said, gesturing at the elephant. "Is it safe to climb up on that beast, or is it suicide?"

"No, it's not safe, definitely not." Cassie shook her head so hard her earrings trembled. "But what choice do we have? They're all waiting for us. Look, I think we can handle this elephant. It may be bigger than we are, but we're definitely smarter."

"Are you sure?"

"Positive. It doesn't stand a chance against us."

They stood for a few moments, staring uneasily at the elephant, which continued to make threatening gestures. Lucy was wondering if Cassie was really as sure as she sounded, and Cassie was thinking that Lucy had really gotten herself into a mess this time, which was unusual because under ordinary circumstances it was Cassie who got into scrapes and needed saving.

They were an interesting pair of women, physically different in almost every possible way. Cassie was tall and skinny, with watery gray eyes, a flat, frankly ugly nose, and curly black hair that seemed to live a life of its own. Her green sari hung awkwardly over her large breasts, making her look a little like an ear of corn, a rather fitting comparison when you considered that she was, after all, a botanist. Lucy, on the other hand, looked like nothing so much as a tongue of flame. Dressed in bright red silk, she was short, blond, and pretty, with quick blue eyes, delicate hands, and a compact body that radiated inexhaustible energy.

Lucy, who had just gotten her B.A. in psychology, was perhaps the smarter of the two. Her mind worked with a quickness that took people by surprise, and her thoughts came out in an orderly fashion as if she were keeping everything neatly filed under some system of her own invention.

Cassie, on the other hand, was less organized and far more impulsive. Lucy had always thought that it was a miracle she had made it through Radcliffe without being expelled. Even though she was a scientist, Cassie made her way through life as if she were an artist, working more by instinct than reason. Often she thought that she should have *been* an artist, a photographer to be precise. When Cassie had a camera in her hand, she was like a painter who had found the right brushes. Then she was quick like Lucy and bright and passionate and sometimes almost beautiful, but most of the time she seemed to live in a darker world. All of which is simply to say that Cassie was more vulnerable and less secure than Lucy.

Yet despite their differences, the two friends had much in common. Both were well educated, witty, loved to talk, and had a wicked sense of humor; both were fiercely loyal; both cared more about people than money; and both were just a touch insecure about what it meant to be so very smart and female in what was still very much a man's world. Add to this the fact that they had both lost their mothers at a tender age, had been sent by their respective fathers to the same progressive boarding school in Colorado when they were in their early teens, had roomed together there for two years and then for four more years at Radcliffe, and knew each other inside out, and you had the basis for a friendship that was already well into its sixth year.

Cassie was the first to break the silence. "Time is running out," she observed.

"You're right," Lucy agreed. "You're absolutely right." Gripping each other's hands, they took a cautious step forward. As they did so, a murmur of encouragement rose up behind them. It was soft and musical like the buzzing of a hundred bees, and it was all in Patanese.

At the sound of the voices, Cassie and Lucy froze in their tracks. Without letting go of Cassie's hand, Lucy turned around and inspected the anxious throng of ladies-in-waiting, courtiers, servants, mahouts, and soldiers who had assembled to see them off. The women were wearing blue saris, edged with semiprecious stones, and their hair had been lacquered and teased into giant headdresses that rose above their faces like pagodas. The soldiers were clad in khaki, and everyone else was sporting shades of purple. It was all quite cheerful and colorful, and no doubt she would have found it encouraging except for one thing: they were all smiling frozen smiles of polite terror.

Behind the crowd, the royal palace glowed in the early morning sunlight: a vast, sprawling building of pearl and apricot-tinted marble, roofed in gold leaf, decorated with jeweled dragons, exploding lotus blossoms, and multiarmed gods dancing on the bodies of their enemies. If she could have understood all that symbolism, perhaps she might have known what to do next, but the message might as well have been written in Chinese.

"*Anga to vhula,*" the crowd murmured. The encouragement was taking on a desperate note.

"What are they saying?" Cassie asked. "Because whatever it is, it sounds eerie and weird, and I don't think I like it."

"I think they're saying that we better get on with it."

Lucy frowned at the red silk ladder that dangled down from the summit of the elephant. Ordinarily she would have scrambled up it, climbed into the howdah, pulled Cassie up after her, and maybe even reached out and given the beast a friendly slap on the rump to get it moving. Rock climbing was one of her hobbies, so she had no fear of heights, and she had been riding horses since she was seven, but a horse was one thing and an elephant was quite another. She decided Cassie was right: the encouragement from the crowd was unnerving, and she didn't like the look in the elephant's eye, but what choice did they have? A royal wedding was a strictly planned event, and you couldn't be late for it, especially not when the hour had been selected in advance by fourteen trained astrologers who had been paid off in diamonds.

Unfortunately, just as she had mustered the courage to try again, the elephant suddenly gave an irritable heave, knocking off three of the six bare-chested mahouts. As the mahouts scrambled to get hold of the ropes again, a cry of agitation went up from the ladies of the court who clutched at each other and drew the tail ends of their saris over their faces as if they couldn't bear to witness what was going to come next. Since the ladies, who had come to attend them, were not actually going to have to ride the elephant, their reaction was disturbing.

"Good Lord," Cassie exclaimed, dropping Lucy's hand and taking five or six quick steps backward, "why didn't Mila warn us that this was going to be so dangerous?" The wind whipped at her green-and-gold sari and blew at the hairdo the royal dressers had so carefully composed, picking out unruly curls and twisting them into snarls. Cassie looked as if she was unraveling, and Lucy could hardly blame her. She inspected her friend anxiously. It looked as if Cassie had changed her mind and was getting ready to turn and run for it.

"Don't panic," she pleaded.

"I'm not about to panic," Cassie snapped. She was upset that Lucy could have imagined for one moment that she was going to abandon her. She glared at the elephant and wished with all her heart that the beast had been de-tusked. Serving as Lucy's matron of honor—or whatever the Patanese equivalent was—was not turning out to be the exotic fling she had imagined.

The elephant reared back suddenly, lifted his trunk, and made a trumpeting sound. Lucy grabbed Cassie's hand again, and the two of them stood there, clutching at each other while the mahouts prodded the poor beast with hooked canes and yelled out commands in Patanese.

"You should have brought along your camera," Lucy said in as calm a voice as she could muster. "You could have caught all this on film, and then we could laugh over it later in the safety of the palace." She was glad to have Cassie's hand to hang on to, but she also knew that if she didn't at least *attempt* to make casual conversation, the two of them were going to need some third person to turn to for support, and almost everyone who spoke more than two sentences of English was either up at the temple or outside the gate waiting for the procession to commence.

"I thought it would look tacky," Cassie said as the elephant made another lunge, "snapping pictures of the royal wedding. I didn't want to mar the solemnity of the occasion by looking like an American tourist." She relaxed her grip on Lucy's hand and inspected the elephant with a more professional air. "Still, there are some great shadows, and the backlighting is terrific. If I shot up from this angle with a wide lens . . ."

She went on talking about the photographs she might have taken, and Lucy began to relax, soothed by the sound of her voice. When Cassie got on the subject of camera angles, she wasn't afraid of anything, not even raging elephants. Lucy had often told her that she should make a career out of taking pictures if she loved it so much, but Cassie, who was being pressured by her father to become a famous botanist, had herself convinced there was no future for her behind a camera.

Yielding at last to the commands of the mahouts, the elephant knelt and heaved a deep sigh. His trunk went limp, and at last he seemed to lapse into a more obedient frame of mind.

"He's calming down," Lucy said. "Come on, Cass, let's get this over with." Picking up the heavy skirts of her wedding sari, she strode resolutely toward the silk ladder, feeling about as nervous as a bride could feel but determined not to show it in front of the courtiers. She had wanted to get married in white, but both Mila and the king had been horrified when she suggested it. In Patan white was the color of mourning. So here she was decked out in flame red silk, with a flame red veil over her face and so many diamonds sewn into her skirts and draped around her neck that she could hardly stand up. The sari was a hundred years old and weighed forty pounds.

Assisted by the chief mahout, she grabbed the sides of the ladder and hauled herself into the howdah, silently cursing the heavy, gold-encrusted shoes that were also a mandatory part of the bridal outfit of Patanese princesses. Cassie labored up after her.

"If you didn't mean more to me than almost anyone in the world except maybe Andy, I wouldn't be risking my life for you on this thing, Lou."

"Come on, Cass. Don't give up. Here, let me give you a hand. Now look at this howdah. You love it; you know you do. It's incredibly exotic. Besides, how many people get to be matron of honor for what the press is calling the 'wedding of the century'?"

"Wedding of the century, that's a laugh." Cassie settled down on the comfortable red silk pillows and smiled weakly at Lucy as two of the mahouts quickly drew heavy veils around the howdah. "I don't mean to detract from the splendor of the occasion, but this 'wedding of the century' line is mostly something the newspapers have invented to increase their circulation. The truth is, Grace Kelly had the wedding of the century in Monaco."

"How true," Lucy agreed. She could tell that Cassie was trying to make her feel less nervous by making the whole ceremony seem less important. She felt a wave of gratitude.

"Who's Mila anyway? Crown prince of a country ninety miles wide and one hundred sixty-three miles long. Hang on to the guy, and you'll end up queen of something the size of Illinois."

"You're right." Lucy nodded.

"But—" She stopped in midsentence as the elephant rose to his feet, tilting them forward and then back. Cassie clutched at her and went white again, gasping "I should be on the ground; I'm not cut out for this."

"Neither am I, but the worst is over."

Cassie looked unconvinced.

Led through the main gate by four burly mahouts, the elephant strode forward delicately, bells jangling, rocking the young women softly from side to side as if they were in a small boat. Through the massive red and gold veils they could see the first of the crowds that had been waiting all night, lining the streets to catch a glimpse of the royal bride: women in bright cotton saris; men in long white shirts and loose cotton pants; children beautifully got up for the momentous occasion, their heads covered with brilliant red caps that made them look like bouquets of roses.

"*Falla inah, Qua leh!*" "Ten thousand years of life, beautiful Princess!" the crowd called up to Lucy in musical Patanese as they tossed garlands of flowers under the feet of her elephant.

"Health and joy, American bride of our God-Prince!"

"Much wealth! Many children!"

"Lean out and wave to them," Cassie suggested.

Lucy shook her head. "I'd love to but I can't; it's against the rules. The royal bride isn't supposed to be seen by the public until she gets off her elephant at the foot of the temple stairs."

Cassie shuddered. "Don't even mention getting off the elephant," she pleaded. "Getting on was bad enough."

The cheering continued, rising and swelling around them as the elephant strode through the narrow, twisting streets past shrines to the Buddha and Krishna, past freshly painted houses decorated with red and gold prayer flags, past gilded pagodas and stands of merchants selling souvenirs and sweetmeats. Sindhala, the capital of Patan, was a populous city but not a large one, and soon they were passing through the eastern gate, beyond the walls, into the countryside.

Through the veils Cassie could see the main valley of Patan stretching out toward the snow-capped Himalayas like a large green carpet. Purple and white rhododendron bushes bloomed along the borders of the terraced rice paddies; water buffalo grazed next to clusters of stone huts roofed with bright red tiles; dozens of small irrigation ditches ran toward the river, glittering in the sun like threads of quicksilver. It was better outside the city, fresher and less terrifying somehow. Gradually Cassie began to calm down and even to enjoy the rocking motion. The elephant obviously wasn't going to stampede, not for the moment at least. She inspected the rice paddies with a professional eye and tried to remember what genetic characteristics rice required to survive at this altitude. "I'm beginning to think I could get to like this kind of transportation," she informed Lucy. "The view's spectacular." Lucy was uncharacteristically silent. "Are you still feeling upset?"

"I'm fine."

"You don't sound all that fine to me. You aren't getting seasick, are you?"

Lucy smiled wanly. "No."

"What is it then? You look pale."

"I'm about to marry the Son of God and it's making me nervous." Nervous was hardly a strong enough word. Her whole body felt as if it were tied into a knot. Now that the crisis with the elephant was over, the full impact of what she was about to do was beginning to hit her.

"I thought Mila's father was the reincarnation of Vishnu."

"Same difference," Lucy muttered, too preoccupied to explain that according to the Patanese all gods were one god, and one god was all gods. She swallowed the knot in her throat and reached for Cassie's hand. "You know, Cass, without you I don't think I could survive this. We've been through so much together."

"Constable, if you keep this up, I'm going to bawl like a baby."

"I can't help it; I'm in a sentimental mood. This is my wedding day and I'm leaving everything behind that I've ever loved: my country, my language, my whole world. But there's one thing I'm not going to leave: that thing is you, Cass. I want you to know that even though we're going to be thousands of miles apart, I'm going to stay in touch with you, because nobody ever—and I mean *ever*—had a better friend."

"You damn well better stay in touch." Cassie reached up and surreptitiously wiped her eyes with the corner of her sari. "I expect a phone call every week and letters at least three times a month, and on my birthday I expect you to send me twenty pounds of fancy chocolates, and— Good grief! Will you look what's going on out there!" Cassie suddenly leaned over the side of the howdah and pushed her nose up against the veils to get a better view of the spectacle that was marching past down below. She was relieved to find an excuse to cry a little in private and what an excuse it was! The elephant had paused beside the road to let the front part of the wedding procession go by, and the noise was deafening. Cymbals crashed, drums boomed, horns blared. The clamor rose and rose, like water in a closed space, until it filled the whole howdah. Wiping the last of the tears out of her eyes, Cassie pulled her head out of the curtains and said something, but Lucy couldn't hear her. She could only see her lips forming the words *Get a load of this!*

Shaken out of her sentimental mood, Lucy looked too, and what she saw made her gasp. She and Cassie both had been given a detailed guide to the procession, but seeing it firsthand was something else. There was a momentary lull in the noise as the trumpeters caught their breath. "It looks like something straight out of a Cecil B. De Mille movie!" Cassie yelled.

Cassie wasn't exaggerating. The first group to pass the elephant consisted of Buddhist monks in red robes with shaved heads who were beating on drums, blowing on long brass horns, and chanting "*Om mani padme om*," which according to the program meant "The jewel is in the lotus," or more simply, "God is within you." The monks were followed by an equal number of Hindu priests, resplendent in bright orange, foreheads striped with white sandalwood paste, pulling behind them four great wooden carts piled with scarlet and gold camellias. On the first, which was at least as large as a small house, a plaster statue of

Ganesh, the elephant god, danced a wedding dance, his blue trunk smeared with clarified butter and red dye to symbolize fertility. Behind Ganesh rolled the second cart, dragged along by the straining barechested priests yelling out the seven hundred names of God. The god on this one was a local deity, lion-faced, grinning out at the crowds over a huge erection that stretched from his loins very nearly to his chin.

Behind the lion god came other carts: one of Kali, one of a dragon, and then troops of musicians, rows of small girls scattering flower petals, a contingent of snake charmers, members of the jugglers' union and the brass workers' guild, and a regiment of soldiers led by General Arjuna, a stern-looking man with ramrod-straight posture who wore a splendid sky-blue uniform covered with gold braid. After the general and his troops passed, there was a short break, as if the procession had taken a breath, and then sixteen Cadillacs appeared, moving in a stately line, each car jet black and shined to perfection, windows tinted, designed to carry the nobility of Patan and the most important wedding guests safely past the gazes of the vulgar crowd.

"Andy has all the luck," Cassie yelled.

Lucy nodded. Andy, Cassie's husband of less than two weeks, was in one of the Cadillacs, along with Lucy's only close relatives, Aunt Kate and Uncle Hank. Uncle Hank, Lucy's father's younger brother, was a well-known neurosurgeon and professor of clinical medicine at Stanford, and she had lived with him and his wife in Palo Alto for the better part of four summers after her father died. Today they were standing in for her mother and father, but she had to admit that they were poor substitutes. Not that they didn't try to be affectionate, but they were both reserved, rather unemotional people. Undoubtedly they loved her in their own way, but the only time they ever informed her of their feelings was when they sent her greeting cards at Christmas and on birthdays. On other occasions, Aunt Kate was pleasant, but distant; as for Uncle Hank, he worked an average of ten hours a day six days a week, and when he wasn't working he was slumped in front of the television, too exhausted by his insane schedule to do much more than hurl wisecracks at Walter Cronkite. Cassie felt much more like her family than they did; still, they were good people and she was glad they had come.

She gripped the side of the howdah and watched the cars stream by. They are all going to the temple, she thought, and the truth of it seized her suddenly, making her almost dizzy with anxiety. Her knuckles went white, her throat felt like sandpaper, and her stomach heaved. Soon the elephant would also be moving again, walking toward the temple step by step, carrying her toward the moment when it would be too late to turn back. She looked at Cassie's gold-and-green sari, and then at the veils that shut out the brilliant Himalayan sunlight, and a cold, nauseous feeling came over her that could only be described as dread. She hated closed spaces; they made her claustrophobic. She had been raised in the American West, where the sky was limitless and a person could ride for hours without seeing a house or even a fence. Even in Cambridge she had felt trapped, but here, shut up in this little box of a howdah like a caged animal, she could hardly breathe. The noise began to lessen as the drums and cymbals moved farther away.

Finally there was something approximating silence. Lucy sat staring at her hands; a few seconds passed. "I shouldn't be here," she said at last. Her own voice sounded strange to her; she tightened her fingers into a fist. Tears were stinging her eyes. She was scared, breathing fast like a runner near the end of the course, and she thought about hyperventilation and how she should probably be breathing into a paper bag to calm down, only she hadn't had the foresight to bring one along.

"Right. I agree," Cassie said absently. "Neither of us should be here. The Cadillacs would have been a *much* better choice."

"That's not what I mean, Cass. I mean, what am I doing riding an elephant in a forty-pound sari? I'm a modern woman; I've come here to help Mila bring Patan into the twentieth century, and"—she waved at the curtains—"is this any way to start out?" She started to get to her feet and immediately lost her balance.

"Hang on." Cassie exclaimed, catching her by the arm. She deposited Lucy back on the cushions. "Sit down and catch your breath. You're just having an attack of premarital jitters."

"No," Lucy protested, "it's worse than that; it's—"

"Three deep breaths," Cassie commanded. "Right now. Take them." Lucy took them. "There, that's better, right? No, don't try to talk. Just listen for a minute. I don't imagine that there's a bride in the world who doesn't think, at least for a second, that she's making a big mistake. But don't worry; it *will* work out. It's completely reasonable to begin your marriage by giving in a little to the customs of your adopted country, and besides, pomp and circumstance are part of your job. On other days you can be a modern woman, but today you're a royal bride. Just think what brides wear in America: flowing white dresses with long trains, veils that hide their faces. They even let their fathers lead them down the aisle. In my opinion it's not so important *how* you get married, but *who* you get married to, and Mila is a wonderful person, surely you don't doubt that."

Lucy leaned forward and stared at Cassie anxiously. The deep breaths had calmed her a little but not enough. "I love Mila," she said, "I know I love him."

"What are you going on about? Of course you love Mila. He's handsome, intelligent, and so good to you that three quarters of the girls in the dorm were sick with envy."

"But I can't get . . ." Lucy stopped in midsentence and snapped her lips shut.

Cassie did a double take. "Go on," she ordered. "Finish that sentence."

"Never mind."

"No, I mean it. Go on. Out with it. Who's the lucky man you can't get out of your mind . . . as if I didn't know. That is what you were going to say, wasn't it?"

Lucy bit her lower lip and stared at the floor of the howdah to avoid the look Cassie was giving her. She closed her eyes and saw a man's face, handsome and square-chinned, with curly black hair and gray eyes. It was not the face of the man she was about to marry; it was a face that she had promised herself she was going to forget. "I love Mila, but I think I'm still in love with David," she mumbled.

Cassie sat back and took a deep breath of her own. "I'm going to pretend I didn't hear you say that."

"There's no use pretending. I love David; I've never gotten over him." She shuddered. She was remembering things she had no business remembering: the touch of David's hands on her spine, the smell and weight of him. Even though she wasn't married yet, she felt as if she were committing adultery.

"You know what you need? A drink." Hiking up her sari, Cassie exposed a small silver flask taped to her leg. Removing the flask, she unscrewed the cap and poured a shot of clear liquid into it. "Drink," she ordered, offering it to Lucy. "I came prepared for this. I only intended to use it in dire circumstances, but I think this is dire enough."

"What is it?"

"Vodka. I bought it in the duty-free store when the plane stopped over in Athens."

Lucy waved the vodka away with a grimace. "How would it look for the future princess of Patan to show up drunk at the church or temple or whatever?"

"How would it look for her not to show up at all?" Cassie countered. She placed the cap in Lucy's hand and wound her fingers around it. "Now drink."

What Cassie was saying made sense. Lucy drank. The vodka burned on the way down, but she finished it and handed the empty cap back to Cassie. The effect was immediate and dramatic. Her ears burned and her urge to cry dissolved in a fit of coughing.

"Good." Cassie nodded, patting her on the back. "That's much better. Now let's approach this logically. Let's do a worst case scenario. Suppose you decide that since you can't stop loving David, you can't marry Mila, whom you also love? What do you think would happen if you leaned out of this jeweled cracker box and told the mahouts down there to turn this elephant around?"

Lucy stopped coughing and thought it over. The vodka had done something to her misgivings—not eliminated them entirely but made them subside enough to be manageable. "Nothing much would happen," she admitted at last, feeling a little foolish. "They couldn't behead me for treason or anything because I'm not princess of Patan yet. There'd be a terrible scandal of course—"

"The biggest single scandal since Wallis Simpson snagged Edward VIII."

"You're exaggerating, Cass."

"I'm glad to hear you say that. It shows you still have some perspective on all this. You're right; I am exaggerating. On a scale of one to ten it would be about a number seven scandal. The newspapers would have a field day, but let's suppose you could survive that."

"I'd survive," Lucy agreed.

"So you're a free agent, no one's forcing you into this marriage. Right?"

"Right." Cassie had a good point. No one was forcing her to do this.

David's face began to dissolve and a languid sensation crept over her. She stretched and readjusted the pillows behind her back. She had been too nervous to eat breakfast this morning, and now, thanks to the vodka, she was slightly drunk. The world was beginning to seem like a friendly place, the howdah felt larger, and the idea of marrying Mila no longer sent her into a panic of second thoughts.

"Good. That's step number one." Cassie poured another shot of vodka and watched Lucy as she downed it. "Now suppose, just for the record, you tell me what you think would happen if by some miracle you got back together with David."

"He'd probably leave me again; probably take off after a few weeks and not even write." Normally it would have upset her to make such an admission, but the words came easily. Thanks to the vodka, she felt detached from the pain of David's betrayals. She wondered if perhaps she had underrated the positive effects of alcohol.

"And if he didn't leave you? What kind of husband would he make? dependable, faithful?"

"David faithful? Don't make me laugh."

"He'd be sleeping with other women before you had a chance to celebrate your first anniversary. Right?"

"Probably."

"Not probably, Lou. Definitely. Face it: David Blake is bad news. He's so preoccupied with his immortal poetic gifts and his ongoing Jack Kerouac imitation that he doesn't have time to love any face other than the one he sees every morning in the mirror." She took Lucy's hand and squeezed it comfortingly. "I'm sorry if this sounds harsh, but I can't stand to hear you consider getting reinvolved with David."

Lucy was quiet for a long time. Cassie poured herself a shot of vodka and sipped it slowly, not wanting to rush her. A breeze blew in through the veils, ruffling her hair and making shadows dance across the skirt of her sari.

Lucy stared at the blowing curtains without seeing them. She was thinking of her so-called love for David. It had been an obsessive, destructive love that had left her hurt and drained. Her love for Mila was something entirely different: it was positive, nurturing. And yet— she had to admit it—loving Mila wasn't as dramatic or as exciting as loving David had been. With David there had been fights, rushes of adrenaline, grand tragedy on an almost daily basis. With Mila there was steadiness, goodness, peace. Still, a woman would have to be a fool not to know which of the two men she was better off marrying.

"I love Mila," she said at last, "I really do, Cass. Forget what I said about David. I don't know what I could have been thinking of. All these weird traditions are making me tense. I must have gone temporarily insane. Mila and I are going to do wonderful things for Patan."

"You and Mila are both reformers at heart." Cassie raised her vodka in a toast. "I'm sure you'll do a terrific job."

"Mila is a good man and I'm lucky to have found him."

"He's the best," Cassie agreed.

Onward the soft-footed elephant padded, carrying the young women to the steps of the Golden Temple where the rhesus monkeys gibbered and scampered over the ten thousand statues of the gods of compassion. Rocking to a stop, the animal knelt in two giant lurching motions. Lucy clung to Cassie, and the two young women steadied themselves against the frame of the howdah.

"Well," Cassie said cheerfully, "this is it, Constable. You're about to become the first member of the class of '66 to marry a prince." She looked at Lucy sharply. "You're going to put David out of your mind, right? Never think of him again."

"Of course."

"Promise me, Lou."

"I promise. Cross my heart." She gave Cassie a quick kiss on the cheek.

The two young women dismounted from the elephant looking thoughtful. The problem was, they knew each other too well. Cassie wasn't convinced that the issue of David Blake was resolved, and as for Lucy, she had lied or, if not lied, made a promise she wasn't strong enough to keep.

Fireworks exploded in blossoms of red and silver, cymbals crashed, drums thundered, temple bells rang. Up Lucy climbed, followed by Cassie, past the blue, yellow, and crimson statues of the ten thousand compassionate gods, passing under gigantic arches of tropical flowers on her way to the throne that awaited her, on her way to marry Mila whose golden robes glittered so handsomely in the bright Patanese sunlight.

BOOK ONE

Cambridge, Massachusetts
January 1964

• 1 •

*L*ucy Constable met David Blake her sophomore year at Radcliffe, four days before her nineteenth birthday. It was the day of the big ice storm: the day when the phones went out in the dorms, a tree fell across Garden Street blocking traffic, and students hurrying to the Radcliffe library to study for their final exams had to abandon their bicycles and walk. All the previous night it had rained quietly and steadily as the temperature dropped below freezing. By morning when Lucy emerged from Holmes Hall with her green canvas book bag slung over her shoulder, the whole of Cambridge was coated in a thin sheet of ice from the tips of the Harvard bell towers to the brick sidewalks. The small twigs on the privet hedges were frozen in neat little cases, stalactites dripped from the bicycle racks, and the sidewalks were so slippery that she had to skate her way toward Radcliffe Yard.

She had bundled herself up for the trek, putting on heavy, green knee socks, a pleated wool skirt, two sweaters, a muffler, boots, gloves, and a new green loden coat with stylish rope button loops, and it wasn't a long walk to the library—only fifteen minutes or so—but the ice gave her an eerie feeling that she didn't much like. Not only did it slow traffic and make walking difficult, it made her feel cut off from the physical world, as if she were living in a museum where everything had been sterilized and sealed off from any human contact. She was an English major, and she often thought of her life in terms of poetry, but there was nothing in the entire *Norton Anthology of English Literature* gloomy enough to fit Januarys in Cambridge.

She sometimes felt isolated at Harvard even when the ice wasn't glittering off its buildings. Since World War II, Radcliffe and Harvard students had gone to class together, taken the same examinations, even received the same diplomas, but when it came to important things like getting the best tutors and using the best undergraduate library,

'Cliffies were second-class citizens. By November of her freshman year she had learned there was nothing much she could do to remedy this situation except complain to the deans, which she had done several times without success. So, being a sensible person, she had reconciled herself to squeezing the best education she could out of whatever Harvard was willing to offer to women. But today, as she slipped her way toward the library, the ice revived her sense of being on the outside looking in.

I'm banished to the North Pole, she thought as she trudged down Garden Street, fighting the bitterly cold wind. In two months when the snow begins to melt, they'll find my body in some corner frozen solid. And then she remembered that Cassie would miss her even if no one else would, and the thought cheered her up enough to make it to the library where Radcliffe students were already lined up impatiently waiting their turns at the reserved books.

All morning trucks ran up and down the streets spewing out salt, and by noon the weather had changed and the ice had begun to melt. By evening, when Bill Bishop came to the dorm to pick her up for their regular Wednesday night date, she was in an infinitely better mood. Putting on a madras blouse, a gray wool jumper, and a pair of black wool tights, she insisted that they ride their bicycles the mile and a half to Dunster House.

"Don't be ridiculous," Bill protested. "It's still slippery; we'll break our necks."

"I can ride anywhere on any surface," Lucy told him. "In Colorado my dad and I once rode our horses through a blizzard; I have bicycle wheels attached to my legs. Have some sense of adventure for heaven's sake, Bill. Sometimes you act like you're older than Beowulf."

"It's so annoying of Blake to do his reading in Dunster," Bill grumbled. "It's all the way down by the river, and it's going to be absolutely hideous riding back uphill afterward." What Bill was really saying was that although Dunster had a literary magazine called *Fergus*, it was no place for a poet, especially not a successful one. The university never tired of insisting that house members were drawn on an equal basis from the entire freshman class, but everyone knew that all Harvard houses weren't equal. Poets and writers and preppies and the most elite of the elite lived in Adams House, which besides being the most beautiful of the houses was convenient to everything in Harvard

Square. Jews lived in Leverett Towers, jocks lived in Dunster, and so forth. The real losers lived in the co-ops and worked for a living, but they were so beyond the pale that Bill probably didn't even think about them when he went through the ratings.

Lucy strode stubbornly over to her bicycle and began unchaining it from the rack. Bill's snobbishness was his most annoying trait. As she fumbled with the frozen chain she tried to remind herself of his good qualities. He was generous, sophisticated, witty, and not bad-looking if you liked the underfed, Philadelphia-bred, hawk-nosed, blond preppy type, which presumably she did since she'd been dating him steadily for almost a year.

"Blake should be reading in Lamont, in the poetry room," Bill continued as he watched her struggle with her bike.

"In which case I wouldn't be allowed in to see him," Lucy reminded him. Women were absolutely forbidden to set foot in Lamont, the undergraduate library, on the theory that the Harvard men upon catching sight of them would throw down their books and run amok, committing sex crimes between the unabridged dictionaries. The fact that she couldn't go over to Lamont to check out books was a touchy subject, and Bill knew it. The poetry room in Lamont was an even more touchy subject. Lucy had spent the better part of the last two years looking longingly at announcements of special events that she was not allowed to attend. So far she had missed readings by Carl Sandburg and John Berryman, not to mention Robert Frost's last public performance.

"I'm sorry," Bill apologized, throwing his white silk muffler around his neck and taking his own bike down from the rack. "It completely slipped my mind you were banned from Lamont. Not that you're missing much. It's a hellhole most of the year, full of unshaved guys in sweaty socks cramming two thousand years of Western civilization into their overworked brains. Lamont's a madhouse, a cradle of insanity. It makes me shudder to think that the future leaders of America are being bred in such an environment. Sometimes I imagine that one of those wonks will become president and blow us all to kingdom come because he's haunted by memories of Lamont library and the smell of unwashed jockey shorts."

Lucy chuckled. Bill was doing his best to make her feel better about her second-class status, and she appreciated it. He could be very diplomatic when he put his mind to it, which was a good thing since he was planning to join the foreign service when he got out of graduate school.

They pedaled along in companionable silence down the dark, mostly deserted streets, across Harvard Square, past Holyoke Center and Adams House, heading for the river. In some ways Bill Bishop had everything a woman could want, Lucy thought, inspecting him out of the corner of her eye as they turned east on Mount Auburn. He was twenty-three, a good four years older and more sophisticated than she was; he was wealthy, not a major qualification in her book but certainly convenient. He had graduated from Harvard *summa cum laude* two years before with an honors thesis on political unrest in Italy that had been so good the State Department had virtually told him that anytime he wanted a posting to Rome he could have one. Rome, however, might be a few years in the future because at present Bill was a graduate student, working on his Ph.D. in government, a course of study that usually took at least six years to complete even if you were brilliant, which he obviously was. He was good-looking; he was chivalrous; he loved her as sincerely and as passionately as his nature permitted, and although he had failed so far to get her into his bed, it was only a matter of time.

She took a deep breath and tried to imagine what it would be like making love to Bill. Probably fairly exciting. He was the kind of man who researched everything; no doubt he had read up on every possible sexual technique and method of pleasing a woman from Ovid to the present. Plus she knew for a fact that he had had at least three previous lovers, one of whom had been an Italian model named Gina, six feet tall and ten years older than he was. Gina was going to be a hard act to follow.

She and Bill were undoubtedly going to end up sleeping together. He'd already asked her to marry him and she'd said she was too young even to consider it, but once she started spending from four to seven o'clock every afternoon in the sack with him, that excuse was going to crumble fast. Lucy grinned as she thought how parietal hours set the sexual clock for Harvard-Radcliffe students. The Radcliffe dorms admitted men upstairs only on Sundays, and the walls were too thin to make romantic trysts practical, not to mention the requirement that the door to each girl's room had to be kept open at least six inches at all times. The Harvard houses offered more privacy, but with limitations.

Women were allowed on the upper floors only in the late afternoon, so every day at 4:05 the parade of hormone-crazed couples began filing through the wrought-iron gates past the security guards who forced them to sign the guest book. Three hours later, the same couples emerged—exhausted and screwed to a frazzle—just in time to sign out again. By spring she'd no doubt be part of the procession, and then in 1966 when she graduated, she and Bill would get married in Memorial Church and spend their honeymoon driving around Italy, and she wouldn't have to figure out what to do with her life until 1996 when the last of the children left for college.

It was a pleasant life scenario, full of the kind of security she'd never had as a child, but it made her rather uneasy to think of it unfolding in front of her so relentlessly. She could introduce some variations, of course: juggle raising her children with having a career as so many of her classmates were planning to do, or follow in the footsteps of her Aunt Kate and volunteer for community services. It was easy for her to imagine herself at thirty, running the PTA or raising funds for a children's hospital. She'd always done some sort of volunteer work, and there would be no need to cut back once she married Bill. She might even go to graduate school herself, take an advanced degree in the social sciences or child psychology, because she enjoyed helping people, especially children. Perhaps she'd grit her teeth and enroll in law school, not to make money but to have some real power to argue for the rights of the powerless. Whatever she decided to do, Bill would support her decision. He would be the perfect husband, except for one minor detail: She didn't love him.

Still, love wasn't any guarantee of a successful marriage. As an English major, she constantly read about men and women who started out crazy for one another and ended up badly. Look at Romeo and Juliet, look at Abelard and Heloise. Better to end up with Bill than to commit suicide in the crypt of the Capulets. Besides, she had to marry someone sooner or later because she intended to have a lot of children. She hadn't had a real family since the summer she was six and her mother left, eloping with a rich lover who had killed her six weeks later by driving into a bridge abutment in a long drunken swerve that left two tire marks on the pavement that looked like giant black question marks. Not that her father hadn't tried to make a home for her, but the dear man hadn't had the slightest idea how to go about it. Her life had been an endless stream of bungled dinners, unwashed clothes, and incompetent housekeepers until she turned seven and went away to boarding school.

Lucy swerved her bicycle automatically to miss the protruding tail fins of a parked car and pedaled furiously down the hill, the wind whistling through her hair and numbing her ears. She felt elated by the speed of her descent. She wanted children, lots of them, four at least, and she wanted to make their lives a hundred times happier than hers had been. Bill would make a great father.

The truth was, she had never been in love, not even for a moment. She'd never had crushes on Ricky Nelson or Elvis when she was a teenager, never felt anything but friendship for men. She just wasn't a passionate woman by nature. So why not marry Bill Bishop? By all rules of logic, he was the perfect choice.

But I want to fall in love! some part of her cried silently. Lucy sped on through the darkness, trying to ignore the inner voice that told her she was missing the best part of life.

When they arrived at Dunster they found the common room crammed with Harvard students who stood in small knots, drinking sherry and eyeing one another speculatively. Lucy could see that all the usual literary cliques were already there: the *Advocate* people, the *Crimson* people, even a few stragglers from the *Lampoon* who were always hunting for material to parody. God knew they'd find plenty of it here tonight. There was nothing like a poetry reading to bring out the factions. She took a glass of sherry from a table beside the grand piano and sipped it, looking from face to face, trying to decide which of them was David Blake, the poet. Probably the tall guy in the corner, she decided, the one next to the grandfather clock who's wowing his little circle of admirers. The tall man's mouth seemed to be hanging from a hinge as it beat relentlessly up and down. She couldn't hear a word he was saying, so she couldn't tell if he was brilliant or not, but he looked like a bird champing on a worm. Over his head, perched on the top of the clock, a bare-chested Atlas grunted and strained, trying to hold up the world. This was a poor beginning. She was going to have to struggle to keep a straight face. She loved poetry but she hated pretension, and pretension was all too often the essence of these events. Even Bill treated readings as if they were religious services. The last time she had had a fit of barely suppressed giggles in the middle of a literary soiree, he had barely spoken to her for the better part of a week.

"Bishop, there you are. We've been looking for you. Blake's about to arrive and instigate his customary riot, and we were just discussing the best way to prevent bloodshed." Sandy Roberts loped across the room, nodded at Lucy, and rolled his eyes toward the ceiling in mock desperation. He was a bony, sharp-tongued, excessively pale history and lit major with an endless lust for power, both real and imaginary. For the past two years Sandy had virtually run the editorial board of the *Harvard Advocate*, deciding who was worthy of being published and who was to be consigned to oblivion. T. S. Eliot, Norman Mailer, John Dos Passos, and e. e. cummings had published in the *Advocate* when they were undergraduates, and Sandy never tired of telling anyone willing to listen that he had standards to maintain.

Bill drained his sherry glass and put it back on the tray. "What's Blake done?" he asked Sandy. "Climbed on the table and recited a parody of 'Interlocutions'?" "Interlocutions" was a thirty-page poem Sandy had published in the last issue of the *Advocate*. The poet, who had used the pen name Hyperion, was none other than Sandy himself. In Lucy's opinion "Interlocutions" was one of the stuffiest, most lifeless poems she had ever read, but so far she had refrained from telling Sandy that.

"No," Sandy shook his head, "but I think he's perfectly capable of any atrocity. When we dumped him off the board for his ridiculous diatribes against academic poetry, we should have put out a contract on him and had him disposed of once and for all. The man is totally irresponsible, and why he's been given this reading is beyond me." Sandy rolled his eyes again. "I suspect someone was paid off."

"Bill tells me Blake's new collection of poetry has won all sorts of awards," Lucy observed. "And how about that quote Frost gave him for the jacket?" She was always astounded that Sandy could have such passionate convictions about who was a real poet and who wasn't.

"Frost was in his dotage," Sandy sneered. "I consider it low of Blake to have written him for a quote when he knew the man was practically on his deathbed. As for awards, well, my dear, I personally wouldn't call winning the Walt Whitman Award an honor. I'd call it a blot on his reputation, not that he has a reputation. Look at the committee that gives out that award. They know so little about poetry that last year they gave it to Allen Ginsberg. I mean, really! Have you read Blake's *Living in the Volcano*? Have you actually sat down and let the poetry flow through you?" He made little waving motions with his hands, indicating the course of the tides.

"Not yet," Lucy admitted. "Copies are hard to get." Sandy would have killed to get the Walt Whitman Award. She decided that Blake's poetry must be good if it could incite such envy.

"I'm glad to hear that," Sandy tapped the tips of his fingers together, "because the so-called poetry in that book is *hideous*. It's hard to believe it was produced by a man in his senior year. It sounds more like it was written by an illiterate beatnik alcoholic with nothing better to do than rage against Harvard. Rank ingratitude, I call it."

"Actually," Bill said, "his name isn't really Blake. That's his nom de plume. His real name is Sullivan, *Patrick* David Sullivan."

"So he's shanty Irish." Sandy lifted his eyebrows and shot Bill a knowing look. "That explains a lot." He was about to say something more, but he stopped in midsentence, and an odd expression came over his face. "Hello," he exclaimed. "Here's the little Benedict Arnold himself in the flesh."

Lucy turned toward the door and saw a short, dark-haired man entering the room. His hair was curly and worn long, and he had a compact body, a square chin, and a broad forehead, but what she noticed most of all was what he was wearing, or rather what he wasn't wearing. Harvard men always wore coats and ties—in fact they had to, to get served their meals in the dining halls—but David Blake, who lived in Dunster and presumably had to eat in a coat and tie like everyone else, had changed into a white T-shirt, blue jeans, boots, and a dirty blue peacoat. He also wore a black beret.

"He's terribly affected," Sandy said, helping himself to the sherry. "Thinks he's Brando in *The Wild One*."

Lucy looked at the black beret and the five-o'clock shadow on the young poet's face and decided that for once Sandy was right: David Blake was a phony.

Forty-five minutes later she was clapping wildly, stunned and more than a little awed by what she had just heard. David Blake slapped his book closed and looked out over the audience defiantly, his gray eyes hard with excitement and triumph. He had not so much read his poetry as declaimed it, chanted it, crammed it down their throats and into their hearts, and he was inordinately pleased with the results. That would show those bastards on the *Advocate*. They had sat together in the back row, like vultures on a fence, waiting for him to screw up, pretending they'd heard it all before, smugly convinced that no Irish drunk's kid could write anything worth casting their patrician eyes on, and now they were being treated to the sight of the whole damn audience applauding him as if he were the reincarnation of Walt Whitman. He wished his mother and sisters could be here to see this, and even his father. Let the old man smell the stink of success and try to make sense of it. How many times had Mike Sullivan batted his only son across the room for reading Ginsberg and Ferlinghetti, bellowing at him that he should be out digging ditches or parking cars to earn more money so he, Mike, could drink it up?

Shoving *Living in the Volcano* under his arm, David headed into the crowd to hear those poor bloodless wimps tell him how great he was. Inside, he was still unable to believe that they had actually liked his poetry. In the deepest part of his soul, he had wanted their acceptance so much that it had almost made him sick, but he'd hidden that weakness so well none of them had ever guessed what pain it had caused him when Roberts and his clique threw him off the editorial board of the *Advocate*. Tonight was the same: no one in the Dunster common room guessed what David Blake was thinking as he made his way through his admirers. The way he shook hands and slugged down sherry he looked every inch a victor.

"He was great," Lucy said to Bill. "Admit it."

Bill shrugged. "Let's not get overly enthusiastic. The man has a sense of drama, I admit. He reads well, but how do you suppose those poems of his would look in print? Awkward, I'll bet, straggling, like a Sears, Roebuck catalogue. Why, without him gesticulating and yelling at the top of his lungs, you just have a half-baked imitation of Ginsberg, who in my book is a half-baked Whitman and so forth."

"I agree," Sandy nodded. "Blake should be on the stage of the Loeb Theater doing . . . what?"

"*Lear*," Bill suggested, "the mad scene." They both laughed. Lucy frowned, thinking that the two of them were being awfully snobbish. It was at times like this she was convinced that the main thing people learned at Harvard was how to put other people down. It was a brutal tradition, and it was infectious. Bill, for example, wasn't usually given to one-upmanship, but when he got near Sandy he started speaking the same language. She'd have to have a talk with him about exercising his wit at the expense of other people. Blake's performance had been superb. It had made the hairs on her arms stand on end. If that wasn't real poetry then nothing was.

"I disagree with both of you," she said, letting a sip of sherry slide down her throat.

Sandy lifted his eyebrows. "Well, well, Bishop," he said. "Looks like you have a bit of a rebellion on your hands."

"Lucy's entitled to her own opinions." Bill gave Sandy a look that said that there'd been enough sarcasm for the moment and that if there were any more, Lucy wasn't to be the object of it. She liked him for jumping to her defense that way.

"David Blake is one hell of a poet," she said to Sandy, "and if you people on the *Advocate* don't understand that, you might as well stop publishing."

"So," a voice behind her said, "someone around here isn't dead from the neck down."

Lucy turned and found herself facing David Blake. He was holding an empty sherry glass in his hand, and his face was slightly flushed. His eyes were intense and narrow, gray with blue tints like a cold ocean. He must be Black Irish, she thought, a Celt, which would account for both the poetry and the rebelliousness. He was staring at her almost rudely so she stared straight back, determined not to let him know how embarrassed she was that he'd overheard her last remark.

Sandy's face took on a stony expression. "Hello, Blake," he said. "It's been a while."

David ignored him. He was looking straight into the face of a beautiful woman who was looking back at him with open interest, and he didn't intend to be distracted by the likes of Sandy Roberts. She had honey-blond hair with red highlights; a delicate neck; pointed, small breasts; slender wrists and ankles; lush, round hips; and intelligent, frank eyes without a trace of the condescending buzz-off look that so many 'Cliffies gave you. "What's your name?" he asked.

"Miss Constable, Mr. Blake," Sandy said with a stiff wave of his hand.

"Let the lady talk for herself, Roberts." David smiled at her, smiled that warm, winning smile that made him look sweet and slightly vulnerable. It was a smile designed to confuse a woman, pique her curiosity, and throw her off base. "What's your name?" he repeated.

"Lucy Constable." She reached out and shook his hand, feeling amused and wary. One minute he was angrily reading his poetry, and the next minute he was doing his best to charm her. Beside her, Bill was bristling like a tomcat who'd been challenged on his own turf. She was surprised to realize that she rather enjoyed making Bill jealous.

Blake clasped her hand and held on to it. "Hello, Lucy Constable. How did you get into this room? Where are you from? Where are you going? Tell me about yourself from beginning to end, past to present to future."

Bill snorted with annoyance. "Come off it, fellow," he muttered.

Lucy was annoyed by Bill's attitude. "I'm not from anywhere in particular," she said pleasantly. She laughed. "I'm always riding off to points unknown."

"I'm glad to hear that," David said quickly, "because if you aren't going anywhere in particular, that means you can come to Elsie's with me for a cup of coffee and I can recite the poem I made up in your honor."

"She's going back to Radcliffe with me," Bill said irritably.

"Not so fast, Bill. This is just beginning to get interesting." Lucy turned back to David, put her sherry glass down on the table, and smiled one of those sweet, dangerous smiles that Cassie would have recognized as a sign that all hell was about to break loose. "What do you mean you made up a poem for me? We just met."

"Wrong," David said. He talked to her as if there were no one else in the room. "You're an English major, right?"

"Right." She wondered where all this was leading.

"And you're taking Shakespeare." Sooner or later all English majors took Shakespeare, usually in their sophomore or junior year.

Lucy paused for a moment and her smile broadened. "That's right. I'm taking Shakespeare from Levin."

"But," Bill objected. She nudged him into silence and stood waiting for David to make his next move.

"I came to the class one morning," David continued. "And I saw you, and it was like—" he gestured, "like an explosion happening in slow motion. There you were, sitting beside me, leaning over your notes with your chin in your hand, and there I was stunned, moved, paralyzed. I grabbed a piece of paper and I wrote a poem to you on the spot, but I was too embarrassed to show it to you."

"Bullshit," Bill said. "This is the most ridiculous crap I've ever heard."

"So you saw me in Harry Levin's Shakespeare class and you wrote a poem to me. What was it about?" Lucy's eyes narrowed in a way that Cassie would also have identified instantly, but David was too busy impressing her to notice.

"Sex and death." He paused as if waiting for the effect of his words to sink in. "I compared you to a fire that burns through everything, a rampage of destruction that leaves the forest in ashes." He leaned toward her, intense and deadly serious. "I called it 'Wildfire.'"

"Very impressive," Lucy said quietly. "There's only one problem."

"What's that?"

"I'm not taking Shakespeare until next fall."

Bill and Sandy broke into guffaws as David went pale. "Touché," Sandy said. "I guess she caught you red-handed, Blake."

"That was a bitchy thing to do," David said through clenched teeth.

"It wasn't very nice of you to pretend to have composed a poem about me. I'm not an idiot, you know. Would you care to apologize?"

"Go to hell," David snapped and walked quickly away from them. Their laughter followed him, stinging. On the table near the fireplace was an unopened bottle of sherry. Pulling out the cork with his teeth, he filled his glass and drank it all down in one gulp. If they thought he was a barbarian, why not act like one.

"Blake certainly met his match tonight," Bill observed as he and Lucy rode back toward Radcliffe. "You put him down, but good."

"I don't want to talk about it." Lucy lowered her head and fought her way up the hill, feeling guilty that she had let herself get sucked into the general put-down of David Blake.

"Why not?"

"Because I'm not particularly proud of myself. The poor guy was just trying to impress me, and I made a fool out of him."

"He deserved it. Sandy tells me he has a whole stable of 'spontaneously composed' poems that he trots out to wow pretty women. So you caught him in the middle of his act. So what?"

"I just feel sorry for him, that's all."

"You're too soft-hearted. That's always been one of your major problems, darling. You love to take in stray cats."

Lucy braked to a stop. "I am not too soft-hearted." She had meant to wait for a better time to tell Bill what she thought about the evening, but he seemed so completely unaware of how snobbish he had been that she couldn't keep quiet about it another second. "Blake is Irish, and all you WASP preppies treat the Irish like trash; he's from a poor family, he's an incredibly talented poet, and you guys treat him like dirt. Naturally he's insecure. Naturally he tries to impress people. Why shouldn't he? I'm just sorry I got drawn into ganging up on him."

"Lucy," Bill's voice was gentle but firm, "let's not fight. Blake isn't even worth discussing."

"No, Bill. I don't agree. He is worth discussing. And as for fighting, let's do it. Instead of just aiming nasty epigrams at each other, let's have a real brawl for once." She thought with another twinge of guilt of the hurt look on Blake's face when she had caught him in the middle of his little lie, and suddenly she was disgusted with everyone involved in baiting him, herself most of all. "We're so damned civilized it makes me sick. Let's put aside the fake good manners we learn here at Harvard. Let's come out in the open and yell at each other and throw snow and have a real, honest, undisguised row."

"Lucy, what's gotten into you? We'd catch pneumonia. I've never seen you act like this before."

"Oh, Bill," she pleaded. "Don't you understand? David Blake has something we don't have. He's real, he's alive, and I'm ashamed of the way we treated him."

"Lucy, you're not making any sense. We're both alive, and as for Blake, all I can say is that he's a mediocre poet and a rather bad liar. Now if it's all the same to you, I'd rather not discuss him any more."

"Fine." She suddenly felt very tired. Bill obviously didn't understand what she was trying to tell him. Getting back on her bicycle, she began to ride slowly up the hill. Her legs ached and she was chilled to the core and she wished she hadn't insisted on bicycles. They could have taken a cab and been back at the Quad by now. There was a long silence broken only by the sound of passing cars.

"Mad at me, sweetheart?" Bill asked as they reached the Square.

"No," Lucy said. "Of course not." Riding through the cold was clearing her head, and she was beginning to feel a little sheepish about having gotten so stirred up over David Blake. Bill was essentially a kind person who just got off the track every once in a while. If she hadn't felt so guilty about her own snobbishness, she never would have jumped at him that way.

She let him kiss her good night on the steps and then went inside still feeling out of sorts. Upstairs Cassie was sitting in the second-floor kitchenette with Ann Barrows, Roberta Cain, and Joyce Lindsay. All four had their hair done up in huge pink rollers, and they were deep in some kind of serious conference over the remains of a pan of brownies.

"Disaster has struck," Cassie called out dramatically when she caught sight of Lucy. "The Iguana found Watusi." The Iguana was Miss Irene Lolland, the dorm mother, and Watusi was Cassie's very illegal pet tomcat.

"What's the penalty?" Lucy settled down beside Cassie and helped herself to a brownie. The brownie was burned on the bottom, which was a sure sign that Cassie had baked it, but it had a half inch of chocolate frosting smeared on top, which compensated for its other defects rather nicely.

Ann Barrows sighed and drew her embroidered satin bathrobe around her matching set of pink satin pajamas. Her father owned the largest chain of department stores in the Midwest, and Ann, a small, foxlike young woman with a sharp nose and perfect teeth, possessed the most extensive collection of lingerie at Radcliffe. "They may put Cassie on disciplinary probation for a month," Ann said.

"On the other hand, they may not," Cassie observed optimistically. "The real problem is, where does Watusi go now that he's been bounced from the dorm? If we leave it up to the Iguana, the poor beast will probably end up at the pound."

For a half hour the five of them sat around worrying about what to do with Watusi. By the time they broke up the emergency caucus and went to bed, Lucy had forgotten all about David Blake.

* * *

It was a busy week. On Sunday Lucy celebrated her nineteenth birthday by spending almost the entire day in the library, studying for final exams in two of her favorite courses: Main Currents of French Literature and Major Victorian Writers. On Monday and Tuesday mornings she took the exams, and on Tuesday afternoon, still reeling from writing a fifteen-page essay on the novels of Charles Dickens, she boarded the MTA and rode over to Boston to do three hours of volunteer work at Mass General Hospital, passing out magazines and candy to patients and generally doing her best to spread good cheer. Then hurrying back to Holmes, she put on a pair of stockings, pinned up her hair, and went to a House meeting to listen to Cassie defend herself against charges of concealing Watusi from Miss Lolland.

Fortunately the meeting was packed with cat lovers. Cassie was put on only one week probation, and Watusi, who was by now quite famous, found a new home with one of the cooks.

On Wednesday, just as she was beginning to recover enough to begin studying for still another exam, Lucy ran into David Blake again, this time on her own turf. She was in the folk music library in the basement of Holmes checking out a record when she spotted him standing by the counter in his black beret. His blue peacoat looked shabbier than ever, but he seemed cheerful, even jaunty, as he stood with pursed lips, whistling silently as he read the program notes on a Folkways album entitled *Songs of the Rural South*. For a moment she considered leaving before he spotted her but decided that would be a cowardly thing to do.

"Hello," she said, striding up to him. "Written any more poems lately?" She could have bitten off her tongue. It was the worst possible thing she could have said.

He turned around, surprised, and his face hardened when he saw her. "Oh," he said rudely, "it's you. Back for another pound of flesh?"

She took a deep breath and controlled her impulse to reply with something equally scathing. He was certainly touchy. "I just wanted to tell you that I'm sorry about the way I acted toward you the other night." She expected some reaction, but he just stood there looking at her with those cold, gray-blue eyes of his, so she rambled on, feeling a little foolish. "It wasn't very nice of me to trap you like that and—"

"Wait a minute," he interrupted. "Are you actually apologizing to me?"

"Yes," she nodded, determined to carry this through to the end now that she'd started it. "I'm apologizing. I acted like a creep and I'm sorry."

His whole face softened and a fog seemed to lift off his eyes. Breaking into a grin he put the record jacket down on the counter. "Amazing. I wish I had a tape recorder. I don't think I've ever heard a 'Cliffie apologize before. You're a real human being."

"Thanks." She was a little bewildered by his reaction. It seemed to mean so much to him that she'd said she was sorry. She'd thought he was too tough to give a damn.

"Let me take you out for coffee." He picked up the record and stuffed it into his book bag. She caught a glimpse of fat manila envelopes, blue notebooks, and a metal harmonica case. "I've got something to say to you. Not a poem," he added hastily, "an apology of my own. Come on, hear me out. What have you got to lose? You've already seen through me. I'm harmless. I don't have fangs despite what Sandy Roberts told you."

An hour later they were sitting in Bartley's Burger Cottage sipping strong, milky coffee and nibbling fried onion rings. Bartley's, a noisy, barren sort of place located directly across the street from Widener Library, was favored by Harvard and Radcliffe students for its cheap food. The tables, which had Formica tops and sturdy metal legs, were always piled high with obscure tomes on biochemistry, medieval land tenure, and Sanskrit. In the winter, when storms blew in off the Atlantic and no one saw the sun for days at a time, Bartley's became a miasma of wet tweed and pipe smoke as students slouched on their leather elbow patches discussing their dissertations and trading the latest departmental gossip.

Bartley's was also famous for its exceptionally rude waitresses, rude even by Boston standards. At the moment one of them, a large, middle-aged woman named Ronda, was in fine form, because some simple soul—probably a visiting physicist from MIT, from the looks of him—had made the mistake of asking her to bring him some ketchup.

"Get your own!" Ronda bellowed, planting her meaty hands on her hips.

The physicist stared at her from behind his thick horn-rimmed glasses, amazed. "But . . ." he protested, "I only asked for ketchup."

"What do you think I am?" Ronda thundered. "Your servant? Get your own ketchup, mister."

David grinned at Lucy. "Think we should request some salt for the onion rings?"

"Don't even think of it," she advised. "Don't even let the idea cross your mind. The last person I saw ask her for salt nearly got disemboweled." They laughed and took sips of coffee, checking each other out. For the last twenty minutes they had been talking about nothing: about Ronda and the onion rings and the weather and even for a time about folk music, which it turned out they both liked. They had traded names—Leadbelly, Mississippi John Hurt, Jean Ritchie—and he had even told her that he played the blues harmonica and was learning the guitar, but under it all the real conversation was still lurking. Lucy wondered what it would be, but she didn't know how to get it started, so she bided her time.

David took another sip of coffee, picked up an onion ring and then put it down again. "Let's cut out the game," he said slapping the palm of his hand down on the table. "All this small talk is driving me crazy."

"Me too." Lucy leaned forward. "I keep wondering what you took me out to coffee to say, and why you aren't saying it." She smiled a pleasant, slightly teasing smile. "I've been imagining all sorts of weird revelations."

He smiled back at her, and his entire face relaxed. Grabbing two onion rings, he bolted them down, wiped his mouth on the back of his hand, and sat back looking satisfied and amused. "I thought you'd pretend you didn't know what I was talking about. Women usually do that. They make you jump through hoops and I'm not very good at jumping. I lack the social graces."

"That's true. You do. You're not suave at all, but I find that a relief."

He leaned toward her, put his elbows on the table, and gave her a long, searching look. "I want to get to know you, so I have a suggestion to make. Let's quit beating around the bush. Let's talk to each other like we're old friends. Let's be completely honest. No phoniness, no faking. We talk for the next twenty minutes and see where it gets us. If we find out we like each other, we move on to the next step. If we don't, neither of us is in for more than the price of a cup of coffee."

"That's an unusual proposition."

"I'm an unusual guy."

Lucy thought it over. It would be ridiculously stuffy to turn down his offer, especially since she was the one who was always talking about how important it was to be open and frank. She looked him up and down, taking the measure of him, wondering if he was going to turn out to be a third-rate Holden Caulfield obsessed with phoniness. It rather impressed her that he didn't flinch under examination. "Fine, we'll exchange confidences on one condition: you go first." She stirred some more sugar into her mug, stalling for time. "So what's the most important thing I should know about you?"

He frowned and took a swallow of his coffee. There was a short silence, interrupted only by the waitresses yelling out orders for burgers and fries. "I grew up in Somerville," he said at last.

"Why is that so important?"

"Because it means I've got no business being at Harvard. Somerville's a slum, a real hole, and my family is right on the bottom of the shit pile. The best job my dad ever had was pushing a broom around the Cambridge Latin School. He's a drunk and right now he's dying of cirrhosis. A meaner son of a bitch doesn't walk the face of the earth. He's punched out my mother so often that all she does is shuffle around the house like a whipped dog. My oldest sister, Theresa, walked out the night he came home drunk and tried to screw her, and we haven't seen her since." He took another swallow of coffee. "Am I overwhelming you?"

She was a little shocked by his confession, but at the same time she was moved. He'd had a difficult life, come a long way against great odds. "I think—" she paused, trying to find the right words, "I think you're very unusual." She wanted to tell him that she had heard the pain in his voice when he spoke of his family, but she wasn't sure how to go about it. He seemed too proud to accept sympathy. "I hope you won't wish you hadn't told me all this. I mean, we hardly know each other and—"

"I'm a poet," he proclaimed, toasting her with his coffee mug. "Poets lack restraint. It's part of the job description. Ever read Rimbaud? Baudelaire?"

"Yes, in French 20."

He seemed to find this amusing. "You read Baudelaire in French 20. Wonderful. Did they happen to tell you that he was virtually impotent, that he had a black mistress, and died of syphilis?"

"Syphilis and impotency, eh?" Lucy chuckled. "Sounds like the worst of both worlds."

He laughed and his eyes glittered wickedly. "You have a sense of humor. And you're no prude. How the hell did you get into Radcliffe?"

"I could ask you the same thing. How does a slum boy from Somerville get into Harvard?"

"Brains," he shrugged. "Want me to be more modest? Forget it. Where I come from, modesty is only for mama's boys. I won a full scholarship to our beloved alma mater, complete with all the frills. I got a perfect sixteen hundred on the SATs. Was that a lucky break or wasn't it? I'm still trying to decide. On one hand, I want success. I'm sick of being poor. I want to graduate from Harvard and get a piece of the action. I want to make so much money that I never have to take shit from anyone again. On the other hand, I want to be free: no job, no commitments, just me and my guitar and my poetry, like Kerouac, on the road, a rolling stone. At the present moment I'm in a working-within-the-system mood, but who knows. I go back and forth: wanting money one day, wanting freedom the next. Tomorrow I just may wake up and put on my traveling boots. Well, that's enough about me. Now it's your turn. What's the most important thing I should know about you?"

Lucy ate an onion ring and turned the question over in her mind. Now that it was her turn, she was beginning to regret that she'd agreed to exchange confidences, but it certainly wouldn't be fair to back out at this point. She decided to be what she'd promised to be: completely, ruthlessly honest. If he didn't like what she had to say, then too bad for him.

"I suppose the most important thing to know about me is how I feel about my mother." She took a deep breath and continued on staunchly, determined to lay all her cards on the table. "Actually, to be more accurate, I didn't have much of a relationship with her. She died in an automobile accident when I was six. She'd just left my father for another man. She was smart and very pretty and rather wild—part French; her family was originally from New Orleans—but her beauty and her intelligence didn't do her much good because, like your dad, she drank too much. When she was sober she would smother me with love, take me to the zoo, buy me candy, sew me pretty little dresses, all the things small girls adore, but when she drank she couldn't stand the sight of me. I think I reminded her of my father, and I don't think she loved him. She was a very restless woman; she wanted to live in a big city, but there she was, stuck with my father, who hated any town that had more than one stop light. I can remember hearing her downstairs, pacing back and forth across the kitchen linoleum in her high heels; she liked to wear heels and gloves and fancy hats and silk blouses. 'Elegance,' she'd tell me. 'Life, Lucy my dear, is nothing without elegance.' I think our neighbors often found her rather ridiculous; she knew that and scorned them for being hicks and fools. The point is, she didn't fit in. You always got the feeling that she was on her way to somewhere else, somewhere better and more exciting."

She fell silent for a moment, lost in the memory of the hot, cramped little house in Utah where the three of them—she, her mother, and her father—had lived during those last few months before her mother walked out of her life forever. Her father, who was a civil engineer, had been building a big dam of some sort. She remembered the dam because there had been a scale model of it on the dining room table, complete with trees and small doll-like people. Her mother had smashed that model the day before she left, slamming it down on the floor, and the doll people had scattered all over the yellow linoleum, mixed in with the fake trees like victims of a terrible flood. Her mother's hair had been wet; she had just gotten out of the shower, and her blue eyes were bloodshot from crying—or maybe drinking, Lucy thought in retrospect—but despite that she looked beautiful. She had on a sea green dress of very fine cotton with a full skirt that swirled out around her as she stomped back and forth across the kitchen floor, trampling on the doll people without noticing them. Lucy's father had noticed, of course, and he had knelt down without a word of protest and begun picking up the pieces. He looked crumpled and small compared to her: a gentle, ordinary man in a short-sleeved white shirt and old pair of jeans, balding slightly, perched unsteadily on the toes of his cowboy boots while she towered over him like some kind of Greek goddess of fury spurning an unworthy worshiper.

"I won't stand in your way, Janet," he'd said awkwardly as he gathered up the dolls and trees and bits of wood, "but I think . . . I think, it's . . . no good, you doing this. Matt's nothing more than a . . ." He'd groped for words. "He's not dependable. No, he's not. His grandfather made the money and Matt spends it, and . . ."

He'd gotten to his feet, red-faced and inarticulate, choking on his own emotions, because he was horrible at expressing himself, especially when he was upset. Even at the age of six Lucy had known this; she had seen his throat muscles going tight, and she had wished very hard for him to find the right words, but he had gone on floundering. "Matt won't treat you right. . . . He won't give you a decent life. And, and what about Lucy? Think of her. How will she get on without . . . a mother?"

"Go to hell," Lucy's mother had yelled. "Don't you care that I'm leaving *you*? Aren't you going to tell me that you love me? Of course you aren't. You never loved me, George. You don't know what love *is*."

The argument had gone on and on, and Lucy had stood in the doorway unnoticed, watching her mother yell at her father, watching her father's tongue freeze to the roof of his mouth, and she hadn't understood. She had been frightened and confused by the uproar, but her child's mind had not grasped that this was their final argument. She remembered hoping that some of the doll people would escape because they were small and perfect, and she longed to take them into her room and put them in her dollhouse, and she remembered wondering when they would stop so her mother could make dinner. George and Janet Constable. How neatly they had set the boundaries of her life for her: passion and cruelty on one side, security and kindness on the other, and no middle ground where the two could dwell together harmoniously.

She lifted her head and saw David waiting for her to continue. "I've tried to understand why my mother was the way she was." She sighed, ate another onion ring, and drank some coffee. "It must have been hard for her to live with my father because he wasn't anything like her. He wasn't good at small talk or socializing. He liked to go out to the construction sites and work side by side with his men, or sit in the kitchen and build models of the projects he was working on, or take off on horseback on week-long fishing trips. Later, after she died, I spent my winters in boarding school and my summers with him, and I began to understand what she must have gone through. He was a good, kind, gentle man, and I know he loved me, but he was never able to tell me so in so many words. We talked about his work, the weather, politics, horses—he loved horses—but we never had what you could call an intimate conversation. He always seemed to be embarrassed by his own emotions. I think that must have driven my mother crazy. She must have kept throwing herself against him, trying to make him say something passionate, something wonderful and unexpected that would make her life with him seem romantic and interesting, because she had no patience, none at all, and his silence must have bored her and frustrated her and made her angry."

She pursed her lips and frowned. "Obviously the two of them should have never gotten married. But even if she was unhappy with him, that's no excuse for the way she acted. She didn't have to drink so much; she didn't have to pick herself a lover who was so irresponsible that he drove her straight into a concrete bridge rail . . . on a dry road in broad daylight. She could have lived another fifty years. She could have gone out, gotten a job, done something useful and satisfying with her life. And she certainly didn't have to take out her frustrations on me. I was just a child; I wasn't the cause of her trouble. Cruelty to children is something I can't tolerate. They're so trusting; they expect grown-ups to be decent and loving, and when they aren't, when any adult, especially one of their parents, betrays them, it plunges them into a terrible, painful confusion. Believe me; I know. I've been there."

"So have I," David said.

"Yes," Lucy agreed, "yes, so then you'll understand how I've never forgiven her for abandoning me. The day my mother left us, something froze inside me." She shrugged. "Oh, I'm bright enough and pretty enough; I know all that. But I didn't come out of my childhood completely intact. I don't mean to sound self-pitying. My father did love me, and I think that his love saved me from being really screwed up. I'm fairly happy with myself, but the truth is, I've ended up a little— how shall I put it?—cut off from intimacy. Not as cut off as my father was. As you can see, I'm perfectly capable of talking about my emotions, but my ability to feel has been injured. I don't have the kind of emotions you have, at least the ones you write about in your poetry. I lead a fairly calm, eminently reasonable, guarded sort of life. Good enough, I suppose, but not very exciting. Still," she leaned back in her chair and delivered the final verdict on herself, "I'm more or less content."

"Bullshit," David said abruptly.

Lucy gasped, taken by surprise. She felt set up. "Where do you come off making a judgment like that?" She glared at him, so angry she could hardly speak. Picking up her purse, she exacted her wallet and placed seventy-five cents on the table.

"What's that?" David demanded.

"My half of the bill." Her face was hot, and she felt on the verge of tears. Damn him, she thought. Bill warned me; I should have listened.

"You're leaving?"

"Of course. What did you expect after the rotten way you reacted? I feel like you got me to pour out my soul to you so you could patronize me. I've got an exam on Milton to study for, and I can't see any reason to continue this conversation. Besides, I don't think I like you."

"Don't go yet," he pleaded. "I'm sorry if I shocked you. I told you I lack the social graces. It's just that I hate to hear you trying to convince yourself that you're content when you're obviously nothing of the sort." Somewhat appeased by his apology, she put her wallet back in her purse. They sat in total silence, confronting each other over the empty coffee cups.

David sighed and shook his head. "You know what's wrong with you? You're afraid of life."

"My turn to say 'bullshit.'" She was irritated by his ongoing attempt to analyze her on the basis of a three-minute revelation. "I plunge into life full speed ahead. Ask anyone who knows me. I do more things in a week than most people do in a month. Guess again."

"That's not what I mean." He leaned forward. "I mean that you're a passionate woman who gets herself trapped in relationships with men who bore her. Don't tell me you aren't passionate, because I can see it in your eyes. For some reason I can't quite figure out, you've decided to use your mother as an excuse to live in a safe, snug little prison of your own making. Am I right?"

"Perhaps." There was something in what he was saying.

"If I were to guess why you're living the way you're living, would you get up and leave, or would you sit here and hear me out? Never mind; don't answer that. I'm going to risk it." He put the tips of his fingers together and looked at her appraisingly. "My best guess is that like me you're torn between a desire for security on one hand and a desire for adventure on the other. You oscillate between those two poles like a compass that's out of whack, not because you lack courage, but because you're afraid of ending up like your mother."

She was startled by how quickly his mind worked and how acute his assessment of her was. It wasn't as if he were telling her anything she didn't already know, but she was impressed with how much he could deduce about her from the little she had told him. She stopped feeling angry and began to feel intrigued and even perversely grateful that he had understood her so easily and so well. Bill would never have been that astute after such a short acquaintance. This guy should be a psychiatrist, she thought. He could make a fortune.

David leaned closer. "I am right, aren't I?"

"Not completely, but in many ways, yes, you're right," she confessed. "Sometimes when I'm just sitting in class, I'm seized by an almost irresistible impulse to get up and do something crazy like throwing my shoes through the window or yelling at everyone that they're dead. And when I try to tell my boyfriend, he never understands; he wants to marry me, but he doesn't understand the most fundamental part of me." She shut her mouth, realizing that she had said far too much, but on the other side of the table David was looking at her sympathetically.

"I'll defrost you," he said. His voice was quiet but there was something wild in his face that both exhilarated her and frightened her, and she knew it was no idle promise, and that he meant it, and that she was getting in over her head.

"Thanks." She tried to laugh, but her laughter was nervous and unconvincing. "But if I want defrosting I'm perfectly capable of doing it for myself." His words excited her, and she realized again that he wasn't like any man she had ever encountered before. She saw now, with painful clarity, that Bill and his friends were cold, intellectual, dead at the center, that all their witty conversation was a kind of frost that nipped a woman in the bud. But David was intact: he had brains, but the animal inside him hadn't died the way it had died inside Bill.

Alarmed by the intensity of her reaction, she tried to reason with herself. He's dangerous, she told herself sternly, and probably not trustworthy. He's not the kind of man I should get involved with, and if I had an ounce of sense I would get up from this table and walk out of here and never think of him again.

"More coffee?" he asked.

"Yes," she said. She discovered that she was incapable of leaving.

Her feet felt nailed to the floor; logic seemed like a foreign language she no longer wanted to speak.

Two days later she was called down to the bell desk of Holmes Hall to find David waiting for her with a poem. This time there was no question that he had written it for her. Utah was in it, flat and barren, just the way she'd described it to him. She read about the salt flats, and the great dry inland sea, and the unbearable heat; about a mother who left her daughter, and a father two thousand miles to the east who was drinking himself to death in front of his small son, and she was moved and impressed and troubled and grateful, and she knew that all this was happening much too fast.

• 2 •

Ordinarily Cassie would have been aware of what was happening to Lucy. The two friends had been through various crises of the heart together in the three and a half years they had been roommates, first as juniors at Echo Valley Preparatory School in Colorado, then at Radcliffe. It was Cassie who had shepherded Lucy through her first fullblown adolescent crush on a lifeguard named Roger, counseled her to avoid the advances of the infamous Mr. Norman (known as the "Norman Conquest" partly because he taught Early British History and partly because his own conquests were legendary), and fixed her up with Bill Bishop. Lucy, in turn, had offered sympathetic advice on each of the three separate occasions that Cassie "lost her virginity": first to a tennis pro, next to a Negro jazz musician, and most recently to her section man in Biology 111 (Structure and Physiology of Trees). Had things been going along as usual, Cassie would have scented the David Blake passion with the same deadly accuracy she sniffed out corn being popped in the kitchenette, and would have demanded an explanation. She would have heard Lucy out and then implored her to use common sense; she would have given her excellent advice, including a detailed rerun of her theory that romantic love was a kind of infestation, rather like mealy bug or aphids, that needed quick doses of mental DDT to keep it from spreading. But by an unfortunate turn of events, February was the month that Cassie's father Lawrence Quinn, professor of botany at the University of Michigan, announced that he was about to make his yearly pilgrimage to Cambridge, and once Cassie heard that her father was coming, she had no time to pay attention to what was going on around her. Lucy could have dyed herself with woad and sacrificed chickens in the closet, and Cassie wouldn't have noticed. She was too preoccupied with her own survival.

Ann Barrows brought the bad news in the form of a telegram. Since it was Valentine's Day, Ann also brought a bouquet of spring flowers wrapped in pink tissue paper and tied with a red silk ribbon. Ann was wearing one of her most elaborate robes that morning: a romantic sweep of white lace that gave her an air of having just stepped out of a Hollywood movie. Her thin face was flushed, and she had parted her hair in the middle and combed it into an elaborate French twist. Not knowing the facts of the case, she was excited by the flowers, and she had obviously stopped off to dress for the occasion. "Look what you got, Quinn!" she yelled, bursting into Cassie and Lucy's room.

Their room was the kind of place that stopped most people in their tracks. Tucked into a corner of the second floor, it had originally been designed as a single. When the college had converted it into a double, they had provided a pair of ugly brown bunk beds, two narrow dressers, a pair of minuscule desks, and a closet designed to hold the wardrobes of two nuns sworn to a life of poverty. Lucy and Cassie had tried to cheer the place up by sticking French travel posters on the walls and hanging a pair of bright red curtains at the window, but there was not enough space to stow all their possessions out of sight. Taking one quick look at the obstacle course of books, clothes, and camera gear, Ann hiked up her robe and nimbly picked her way across the mess toward Cassie. "Wake up," she insisted. "Heave your body out of bed and look at this *fantastic* bouquet!"

Lucy, who was perched on the top bunk struggling with her boots, saw the flowers and gave a small moan of recognition. Cassie sat up in bed groggily, pulled the pink rollers out of her hair, and threw them into a corner. She was only neat by fits and starts, and today was definitely one of her let-it-all-pile-up-until-it-begins-to-rot days.

"Huh?" Cassie said. At eight in the morning before she'd had her coffee, "huh" was an extremely articulate remark. She didn't come alive until noon, her brain didn't start working until one, and she hadn't voluntarily gotten up before eight-thirty since she'd escaped the horrors of Echo Valley Prep's six o'clock reveille.

Ann waved the bouquet over her head and descended on Cassie with such naive enthusiasm that Lucy could only close her eyes and wait for the blow to fall. "Look. Aren't they fabulous! Come on, Quinn, get out of bed. It's Valentine's Day and you have an admirer, you lucky girl." She sniffed the bouquet, and her small, foxlike chin twitched ecstatically.

Cassie took in the flowers and her eyes narrowed ominously. "Did you say 'Valentine's Day'?"

Ann nodded cheerfully. "Aren't they spectacular? hyacinths, daffodils, baby's breath . . ."

Leaping out of bed, Cassie padded over to her, grabbed the flowers, glared at them for a moment and then thrust them back into her arms. "Here," she growled, "if you like these things so much, then take them." Snatching the telegram from Ann's hand, she wadded it into a ball and slammed it into the closet.

"Bit touchy this morning, isn't she?" Ann turned to Lucy. "What did your roommate do last night? Eat raw tiger liver?"

"The flowers are from her father." Lucy pulled on her other boot. "He sends them to her every Valentine's Day, and she always gives them away or throws them out."

"Damn right I do." Cassie grabbed her pea-green terry-cloth bathrobe, threw it on, and stood glaring at the flowers as if they were likely to attack at any moment. "My father gets flowers wholesale, and *he* doesn't send them to me. His *secretary* sends them to me. That's one of the advantages of having a research lab the size of a small kingdom. You don't have to do anything banal like personally sending flowers to your own daughter. You have well-paid slaves to do it for you." She paced across the room, slid between the desks, and threw open the window. "It's a fine, gray, gloomy day out, Ann. Thanks for helping get it off to such a great start."

Ann held the flowers awkwardly in both hands wondering if an apology was expected. "I take it Cass and her dad don't have the best of relationships," she said to Lucy.

"It's complicated," Lucy sighed.

Cassie slumped up against the wall in her lumpy green bathrobe looking like a giant, wilted plant. Behind her a line of black-and-white photographs climbed toward the ceiling: cats done in close-up, gravestones in the snow, bicycle wheels covered with ice, several large noses and thumbs that might have belonged to anyone, but no complete human faces because Cassie's photography had been in an artistic phase lately. "He's never sent me anything in his life," she grumbled. "He never even notices my existence unless, of course, I'm doing something brilliantly botanical. Even when I was fifteen and in the hospital having my appendix out, he had his secretary send me a get-well card, and she misspelled my name."

"I take it you hate him."

"She loves him," Lucy said, climbing down from the top bunk. "She adores the ground he walks on, right Cass?"

Cassie sighed and unhunched her shoulders. "Lucy's right. I worship the bastard. He's charming, brilliant, handsome, irresistible, and I'd give anything to be like him, and I'm ashamed to say that when he's anywhere near me I stand around like a fig tree waiting to be watered."

Lucy pointed toward the closet. "You better retrieve that telegram and see what he has to say."

"I don't care to know." Plopping down on her bed, she began to pick defiantly at her toenails.

"Ambivalent, isn't she?"

Lucy nodded. "We go through this every year. Every year she wads up his telegram, and every year I make her read it."

"Not this year," Cassie snarled, attacking the big toe of her left foot. "This year I'm declaring my independence. Professor Lawrence Quinn's homely daughter is pleased to announce that she no longer gives a damn what her genius father thinks of her."

Walking over to the closet, Lucy bent down and retrieved the telegram, which had lodged itself in a pair of bright pink pumps. Cassie had two kinds of clothes: outrageous ones in shades of purple, chartreuse, and shocking pink that she wore when she was in her rebellious moods, and drab, proper, earth-tone outfits from a mail-order house in Maine that she donned when repentant. Unfolding the telegram, Lucy smoothed out the wrinkles and presented it to Cassie.

"Open it," she suggested. "You're going to anyway. You know you are, so why prolong the agony?"

Snatching the telegram, Cassie ripped it open and read it, gnawing on her lower lip. Then she wadded it back into a ball and threw it out the window, or rather tried to throw it out the window. Unfortunately she missed, and it ricocheted back into her face, hitting her squarely between the eyes. "He's coming to Cambridge in *two weeks!*" she wailed, rubbing her forehead. Jumping to her feet, she began to pace around the room.

"Now the plans begin," Lucy told Ann. "Now she decides how she is going to shock him when he shows up; but the hell of it is, she never goes through with it. Last time, for example, she was all set to fail her Biology 115 final. If there's one thing her father can't tolerate, it's academic failure. She cut lectures, she didn't do most of the reading, she even failed to show up at lab, but at the last minute she chickened out and ended up at the top of the curve."

Seized by a wave of despair, Cassie suddenly sat down on the floor and stared glumly at the linoleum. The whole world seemed like a desert of brown vinyl littered with mismatched shoes and unread books. Lucy sat down beside her and put a sympathetic arm around her shoulder. "Hang on," she advised. "It's not the end of the world."

"He won't even notice me; he'll look right through me. To get his attention I'd have to dress like a chloroplast." She put her chin in her hands and looked down at her bare feet. There were four different shades of polish on her toenails, running the range from blood red to purple. "I'm going to have to take desperate measures."

"What are you going to do?" Ann squatted down beside Cassie and inspected her with poorly concealed curiosity. She wondered if she'd be as eccentric if her father were so emotionally remote. Fortunately her own father treated her like a princess. Cassie ignored Ann's question. She seemed lost in thought. Ann stood up. "What's she going to do?" she asked Lucy. "What's the usual scenario?"

"She's going to take another lover," Lucy said. "I can see it coming."

Ann attempted not to look surprised. Before she came to Harvard from Cincinnati, she had been perpetually amazed by most things, but in the last two years she had mastered the art of appearing blasé. "Ah," she said, as if she had fully expected something of the sort.

"I'm going to take another lover," Cassie agreed.

"Don't," Lucy begged. "As your best friend, I'm telling you it's a mistake."

"Why?" Cassie frowned and went back to picking at her toes.

"Because you've done it three times, and you never once had the courage to tell your father. Remember that tennis pro? He was perfect. You were only sixteen and Alex was at least thirty and he didn't have a brain in his head. Your father would have had the guy prosecuted for statutory rape if you'd only flaunted that little affair in front of him the way you swore to, but you kept it a secret."

"This time will be different."

Lucy groaned inwardly. Cassie suddenly looked optimistic, cheerful, and full of energy; Lucy knew from long experience that this wasn't a good sign. Up Cassie's roller coaster had gone again, all the way to the top of the hill, and what lay on the other side was anyone's guess. She stood up and brushed off her skirt. She probably should keep track of Cassie for the next few weeks and try to persuade her not to do anything crazy, but she felt stretched thin. Cassie wasn't a child, after all, and given the mess she was making of her own love life at present, what right did she have to give Cassie advice?

Ann left for class, and Cassie and Lucy finished dressing in silence. Each felt comforted by the presence of the other, but each was too preoccupied with her own problems to trade confidences. Cassie was thinking of a tall, good-looking, Jewish botanist named Andy Rabinowitz, who was her lab partner in Halliwell's Plants and Human Affairs course, and Lucy was thinking of David. She had had coffee with him at Bartley's several times over the past three weeks and eaten dinner with him twice. In all fairness she should tell Bill Bishop about these meetings, but Bill had been down in Washington doing research at the Library of Congress and he wasn't due back for another three weeks. She didn't want to discuss the matter with him on the phone, because she strongly suspected that Bill's reaction to the news wasn't going to be pleasant.

Pulling on her gloves, she said good-bye to Cassie and went out to unlock her bike from the rack so she could ride to her ten o'clock lecture. It was hard for her to figure out from one day to the next exactly what her relationship with David was. So far he hadn't so much as held her hand, but the looks he was giving her could have melted glass.

Four hours later, Cassie stood with her arms folded across her chest sizing up Andy Rabinowitz, who stood with his back to her trying to light a Bunsen burner. Of the seven Harvard students working in the lab this afternoon, he was the tallest, six feet at least, and he was good-looking: dark haired, a little thin but wiry and strong with broad shoulders and powerful wrists. She liked the way he stood, feet apart, as if no one could catch him unaware and knock him off balance, and she remembered that she liked his eyes, which she couldn't see from this angle. They were brown eyes, plain enough but intelligent, parked behind a pair of horn-rimmed glasses that she would enjoy removing. In short, he was definitely a possibility.

"There," he said with satisfaction as the gas caught with a small, gulping sound. The fire burned, lifting itself up toward the glass bottom of the beaker. Andy turned and consulted his lab manual, and Cassie quickly did the same, not wanting him to notice that she'd been staring at him. The diagrams on the page were a blur. To her left, she was conscious of Andy's arm stretched out on the wooden tabletop, fingers drumming impatiently. She scratched her nose and tried to concentrate on the manual. Around her the other students were brewing up various potions, and the air smelled of coffee and cigarette smoke and more exotic things.

Today they were doing the Masticatories, Fumitories, and Intoxicants section of Halliwell's course: chewing silver-coated betel nut from India that Professor Halliwell had stored in his freezer, sniffing intoxicating snuff used by the witch doctors of an obscure Indian tribe in the Amazon, cutting each other plugs of molasses-soaked chewing tobacco from Virginia, and generally making themselves thoroughly dizzy and thoroughly sick. There were rumors that at one time this part of the course had included the smoking of cannabis, but unlike Professor Leary, who had been fired a few years ago for experimenting on students, Halliwell was an extremely ethical sort, and once marijuana began to be popular he immediately dropped it from the labs. Still, even without the cannabis, there were fifteen separate substances to be sampled this afternoon.

Andy cleared his throat. "Coffee's next," he announced, pointing to paragraph six, subsection two. A coffee bean lay neatly diagrammed on the page next to a fuzzy black-and-white photograph of a group of Parisian students drinking café au lait somewhere on the Left Bank— talking about existentialism no doubt. Now there was a philosophy Cassie could get behind. Define your life by action. Full steam ahead and don't think about the consequences. Grabbing the jar of instant coffee, she unscrewed the lid and flashed Andy a bright, reckless smile. He smiled back, surprised.

"You like coffee?" he asked.

"I adore it," she told him. "Did you know that in the seventeenth century it was considered an aphrodisiac?"

He appeared slightly startled. "No, I didn't." He began to fumble with his manual. "Where does it say that?"

The coffee smelled wet and musty, and most of the grains were clotted together in the bottom of the jar. It looked, she thought, like something left over from the 1885 Harvard expedition to Brazil. Andy handed her a teaspoon, and she swiftly measured out two doses of the ooze and dumped them into the beaker of water that was now rolling and boiling and singing a little song composed of bubbles and steam. It seemed silly to make a cup of coffee—after all everyone knew what it did—but Halliwell insisted that nothing be neglected. When they did grains, he had had them popping popcorn; when they did roots, he had made them choke down instant mashed potatoes and chips.

"Is there any cream?" she asked. Pressing his lips together, Andy shook his head. A casual observer might have concluded that he was too absorbed in his work to make small talk, but actually his heart was going at a hundred beats a minute instead of the usual seventy—not just from the snuff but from her last remark, which had pushed him off balance. *Aphrodisiac*, she'd said. Did he look to her like a man who needed one? Or had it just been a fact, thrown out at random, from her brilliant encyclopedic 'Cliffie mind?

Tantalized, he picked up a glass rod and stirred the boiling coffee, trying not to get his hopes up. He knew she was Lawrence Quinn's daughter, and he was curious about her and at the same time a little awed, although he wasn't usually awed by women. At the age of eleven he had read Quinn's classic *Growth of Plants*, and the book had turned him into a botanist overnight, and now here he was, standing next to Quinn's only daughter three and a half hours a week, curious as hell about her but respectful, not wanting to intrude on her thoughts.

Cassie sighed and scratched her elbow. She was wearing a bright orange Mexican blouse embroidered with chartreuse flowers, a red Guatemalan skirt, and black boots, but Andy, whose mother favored ethnic clothes, didn't find the combination unusual. In fact he thought she looked great. He smiled at her again and that was his undoing. Cassie smiled back and yawned, and came to a decision. She was going to get him to ask her out. The yawn was purely theatrical. She was nervous, but after all what was the worst that could happen? Tact was going to be necessary. She didn't want to startle him. Close in slowly, Quinn, she told herself. Stalk the prey. She yawned again and her tongue was pink and catlike. "Is there any sugar?" she purred.

"Afraid not." The coffee was ready. Using a pair of tongs, he gingerly lifted the beaker off the Bunsen burner and set it on an asbestos pad. Pouring out two cups of the bitter liquid, he handed one to Cassie.

She took a sip and made a face. "Ugh," she said. "This is perfectly terrible."

"Instant coffee never amounts to much," he agreed.

They sat for a few moments in silence, drinking the coffee.

"You know," Cassie observed casually, "the Jolly Beaver serves much better coffee."

Andy knew a hint when he heard one. He felt a small thrill of pleasure mixed with triumph. So she did want to get to know him! He drank his coffee and took five or six deep breaths.

"Like to drop by there with me after the lab's over?" he asked casually.

"Sure," she said. *Clip, clap*, the first part of the trap was sprung. So far it had been easy.

The Jolly Beaver was furnished with about fifteen small round tables, surrounded by walls hung with fish nets, glass floats, and hunks of driftwood. In the center of each table was a round, red, glass candleholder encased in a red nylon web, and inside each candleholder lay one dim, flickering candle that put out about the same amount of light as a dying match. At five on a February afternoon it was as dark as a cave.

"Sandwich?" Andy took a seat and fumbled for the menu.

"No, thanks." Cassie rubbed her hands together to warm them and looked at him, wondering where to begin, wondering if this was the right time, wondering a vast number of things all of which made her feel slightly drunk and reckless. Pushing her hair out of her eyes, she leaned forward on her elbows. The table felt sticky, and she had a momentary failure of courage, but she shoved her fear aside. "Andy," she began, "I'm not the kind of girl who enjoys empty formalities, so I'll level with you." But she didn't level with him, she just sat there, balanced on her elbows frowning at the candle.

"Well, what is it?"

"I want—" Her mouth snapped shut.

"You want the soup maybe? I hear the soup is good." He knew perfectly well that it wasn't the soup she wanted, but he couldn't think of anything else to say. She was giving him a strange look.

"No." She began to chuckle and then laugh and then went into a coughing fit. "I don't want soup." She wiped the tears from her eyes with the corner of her napkin and shook her head. "Andy, do you have any idea how difficult it is for a woman to send out the right signals?"

"No, I don't suppose I do." Women, in his experience, often spoke in a code of their own, but if you just waited patiently, sooner or later you could figure it out.

She picked at the plastic web surrounding the candle, breaking it into neat shreds, and cleared her throat. "We have to hint, imply, be indirect, or else you poor fellows run scared. Ever think what a burden that is on us? We don't get to call you on the phone; we have to get you to call us." She sighed. "So here I sit, wanting something from you, but not having the slightest idea in hell how to get you to suggest it to me. It isn't fair; it isn't equal. It's the worst rotten part of the rotten double standard. What am I supposed to do? Hypnotize you?"

Andy wondered what she could possibly want from him. "Why don't you just tell me what you need?" he suggested.

"Because you won't like it; because you'll probably be very polite and then walk me back to the dorms and never speak to me again."

"Not a chance," Andy assured her. "I'm a red diaper baby. My parents met at a seminar on The Woman Question. Nothing you have to say can shock me. So out with it. What is it you want?"

"Okay, you asked for it." She took a deep breath and threw away the last shred of caution. "I want a friend."

"A friend, eh?" He was surprised and pleased. "That sounds fairly innocent."

"Not the kind of friend I want. You see this friend should be a very, very, very good friend. In fact, he should be the kind of friend who does things with you that are very pleasant—if you get my drift."

"A friend who does things with you?" He still didn't get the picture. "You mean like go for walks with you along the Charles or to Bogart movies at the Brattle? That sort of thing?"

"No, no, no." She shook her head vigorously. "I give up. I'm out of euphemisms. Sit back and hang on to your chair and I'll give it to you straight: I want a lover."

He was so startled that he almost knocked the candle off the table. "A lover," he managed to say. "A lover." He knew he was repeating himself but he couldn't stop.

"Right," Cassie nodded. "That's about the size of it. I'm in need of a lover."

"That's very interesting," Andy said mechanically. His mind was squirrel-caging and he couldn't think. "Who did you have in mind?"

"You."

"You're joking."

"Couldn't be more serious."

A thrill of excitement ran through him. He looked at her breasts, which were beautiful and large, and at her face, which was so intelligent, so much like Quinn's. In the twenty years he had inhabited this planet, no woman had ever offered herself to him so directly. He opened his mouth and closed it again like a fish gasping for air. He wanted to be witty and sophisticated, but he was dumbstruck. Shape up, he told himself. Chances like this don't come along every day.

"Well, don't keep me in suspense. Are you interested or have I completely repelled you?"

"I'm interested," he said quickly, "very interested, but why did you decide on me?"

She smiled and leaned toward him. "I thought that was obvious."

There didn't seem to be any answer to that. "Oh," he said. "I see what you mean." He didn't, of course, but this hardly seemed like the time to ask.

"Is that a yes, Andy?"

"Yes, sure." He laughed uncomfortably and picked at the net that surrounded the candleholder. The net was having a hard time this afternoon, but his hands seemed to have developed a will of their own. Melted wax spilled on his fingers, but he hardly felt it.

Her whole face relaxed. She smiled sweetly and touched him lightly on the hand. "How nice," she said. "How nice and simple. You have no idea what hell females go through trying to talk in code. It's so much easier this way, so much more honest and direct. Order me a ham on rye, will you, with an extra pickle." She grinned at him cheerfully. "I love pickles."

"But why—" he began.

She put one finger quickly over his lips, teasing and light. "No more questions," she commanded.

He instantly decided that he had better do whatever she wanted if he didn't want her to change her mind. In his wallet he had fifty dollars that he had been planning to spend on a new overcoat. Fifty dollars would more than pay for a hotel room. If she was really serious, he didn't want to take her back to Leverett. He didn't want three hours with her; he wanted as much time as he could get. And after that?

Still in shock, he ordered two sandwiches and two coffees. He was sure she was going to back out, but if she was reconsidering, she gave no sign of it. She ate her sandwich hungrily, swooping down on the crusts, demolishing the potato chips. He ate slowly, trying to regain his equilibrium. He kept wanting to tell her something about himself: how hard he had fallen for Linda, his high school girlfriend, for example, and how long it had taken him to get over her; or about Sam, his older brother, who had been killed in Korea in 1952. Sometimes he still had conversations with Sam. He knew perfectly well that these conversations were imaginary, but whenever he was in a tight spot he would find himself talking to his brother. It was a habit he had long tried to break without success. In fact, he was doing it right now. *Sam*, he thought, *this woman is eccentric and amazingly direct and she has fabulous tits.*

Cassie finished her sandwich and dabbed at her chin with her napkin. He was excited by her in every possible way, but also he felt worried and a little scared. He knew so little about her. What did she really want? Was she just out for a fling? He hoped not, because he really liked her. *Relax*, the Sam voice in his head advised. Andy drank his coffee and did his best to relax. When it came to women, nine times out of ten Sam was right.

Room 7A in the Charles River Hotel cost $24.95 and came complete with a walnut dresser, two glasses wrapped in paper, a heavy, brown plastic ashtray, and a Boston telephone directory. A mere sixteen hours after she had approached Andy, Cassie stood with her back to the dresser looking off into space as Andy tipped the bellhop who had insisted on carrying their suitcases up to the room. She was wearing a conservative blue suit, a white blouse with a frilly bow at the neck, low-heeled blue pumps, a small pillbox hat, and white gloves, but the disguise wasn't working. She suspected that the bellhop had figured out that she was only impersonating a respectable woman and that both suitcases were filled with books instead of clothes because he gave her a knowing grin as he bustled around opening drapes and pointing out soap and extra towels. On the other hand, maybe he thought she and Andy were newlyweds. Nine o'clock in the morning wasn't the most common time to be checking into a hotel. She hoped fervently that he hadn't figured out they weren't married. Fornication was still illegal in Massachusetts. She imagined the police bursting in, flash bulbs popping, herself behind bars doing time. RADCLIFFE STUDENT CAUGHT IN VICE RAID. Would Lucy agree to smuggle her a file buried in a fruitcake?

Gnawing on her lower lip, she looked uneasily at the double bed, which was covered with a sedate blue spread imprinted with sailboats. It looked as large as a hockey field. *Get a grip on yourself, Quinn,* she commanded. *The guy is a harmless, horny scientist and you're no virgin.* She reminded herself that her father would hate the idea of her sleeping with a botanist, and felt comforted. Daddy would loathe Andy. He would grind his teeth, seethe inwardly that his daughter had taken this bright, poor Jewish boy into her bed. Despite his liberal pose, Quinn was secretly both anti-Semitic and a snob; he breathed money and lived for success, not to mention that he was determined to be the only botanist in her life.

She relaxed a little. Taking off her gloves, she threw them on the dresser next to the phone book, taking care to flash the fake gold wedding ring that she was wearing on the third finger of her left hand. The bellhop departed at last, leaving a large silence behind him.

Andy cleared his throat. "Would you like a drink?" He loosened his tie, took off his jacket, and hung it up on the back of a chair. He was wearing shiny brown shoes, and his shirt looked as if he'd just picked it off a rack. Despite her nervousness, she was amused that he'd bought new clothes for this occasion.

"Sure, I'd love a drink." Going over to the bed, she kicked off her heels and sprawled defiantly on the spread. Come on, she thought. But Andy wasn't yet in a rutting mood. Opening his suitcase, he took out a bottle of wine, not just any wine, but a '61 Bordeaux. Cassie was surprised. She'd expected cheap Chianti at best. Producing a corkscrew and two glasses with fluted stems, he poured out the wine and handed it to her.

"Cheers," he said. He swirled a sip of wine around in his mouth, savored it, and then swallowed it carefully. Putting his glass back down on the night table, he went back to the suitcase and extracted two candles, a pair of glass candleholders, a white tablecloth, a round of imported cheese, a box of cream crackers, a tin of imported pâté, a bunch of grapes, and two apples.

Cassie drank her wine and decided it was excellent. She was astounded to see one delicacy after another emerging from his suitcase. She thought of her last lover, the section man in Biology 111 who had specialized in feeding her Franco-American spaghetti cooked over a hot plate. Who would have thought that Andy Rabinowitz would have come equipped with a romantic meal for two? She wondered if he fancied himself a great Don Juan. What else did he have in that suitcase? a silk smoking jacket? satin sheets? Anything seemed possible. "Where did you get all this stuff?" she asked, helping herself to a cracker.

"Here and there." Andy threw the tablecloth over the night table, pulled the drapes, and lighted the candles. Producing a can opener, he opened the pâté, put it on a small china plate, and added a sprig of parsley for garnish. Cutting the apples into quarters, he arranged them on another plate with the crackers.

"This is quite an amazing show." She finished off the cracker and took another sip of wine. "And this is a really tasty wine. How did you know what vintage to buy?"

Andy sat down beside her on the bed and cut the cheese into small wedges with the precision of a brain surgeon. "I asked the clerk at the liquor store to recommend something good." He grinned. "Actually I've never had a good wine before."

She found herself warming to his frankness. Drinking off her wine, she held out her glass and he refilled it. The room looked much better by candlelight she decided, much less puritan.

They ate and made small talk and she found herself beginning to relax. After the cheese had been reduced to rinds and there was nothing left of the grapes but the stems, Andy took her hand and laced his fingers through hers. His touch was warm and quiet. They sat for several minutes, holding hands, drinking the last of the wine, not saying much. Then suddenly he bent over and kissed her. It was a good, substantial kiss, firm and passionate. She relaxed into it, tasting the wine on his lips, the salt from the crackers, closing her eyes. *Go for it!* she ordered herself.

Once she had made up her mind to go through with it, she did it the way she did everything else: with total commitment. She had a way of getting lost in desire that let her turn off her mind as if it were a radio. She liked to turn off her mind; it was on too much as far as she was concerned.

She let herself go. Andy kissed her again, and her consciousness became a boat floating downstream with no one at the helm. It was a bubble in a vast ocean; it was nothing, only the beat of blood throbbing in her temples. She let him take off her clothes, helping him with her stockings, but all the while she wasn't really there. She was in her own private rainbow palace, a large glass room filled with light and green plants, and she was rolling in a bed of blue feathers and laughing to herself, and this was her private dream, and she had it over and over no matter what man she was with. The room was always full of light and it shone like a huge crystal and she lay naked at the center, caught in a web of prisms, sometimes floating in a pool, sometimes curled in a nest of silk pillows, and this was very exciting and outside of time and it made her feel free and immortal and the only problem with it was that there was never anybody in that room but her, and so there was always a small pang of loneliness at the end.

Andy made love to her and she stayed in her fantasy. Afterward, she lay in his arms feeling a little dissatisfied but content enough on the whole. He felt good, lean and warm, and she liked putting her head on his shoulder. The candlelight cast pale shapes on the ceiling, and through a slit in the curtains you could see the cold grayness of another Boston morning. She thought of many things, none of them very romantic: of a paper she had due soon, of a dentist appointment, of the sound of dripping water that was coming from the bathroom. She wondered how long she would have to wait before she could decently propose leaving.

"Cassie?"

She sat up on one elbow, rather surprised he had spoken. She had imagined he was asleep. "What is it?" she asked guiltily. She wondered if he had sensed how far away she had been.

He looked at her searchingly for such a long time that it made her uncomfortable. "You didn't come, did you?" he said at last.

"Sure I did." She sat up and stretched, wondering if he was going to prove difficult. Her nose itched and she scratched it vigorously. The afterwards was always the hardest part; men were so touchy. You'd have thought they were actors waiting for the reviews to come in. She grinned at the thought of herself as a sex critic. *Mr. Andy Rabinowitz turned in a vigorous and original performance yesterday morning at the Charles River Hotel, assisted by . . .*

"You don't show any of the signs." Andy persisted.

Her grin faded; she was mildly annoyed. "What are you talking about?"

"You're supposed to have a flush that spreads from there to there." He drew an imaginary line from the tip of her breast to the base of her throat. "And your lips are supposed to get fuller, and you're supposed to be relaxed afterward, but none of this is happening."

She was astounded. "How do you know so much about orgasms?"

He grinned sheepishly. "I researched it."

"You what?"

"I went to the Harvard medical school library last night and researched it."

"You're kidding."

"No, really. I've got the whole thing down on three-by-five cards if you want to see them."

She giggled. "On three-by-five cards? You've got to be the strangest guy I've ever met. Who are you trying to become, the next Kinsey?"

"No," he said, "just the best lover you've ever had."

Cassie sat back against the head of the bed and let this sink in. "Since you went to so much trouble to compile a bibliography," she said, "I'll confess something: I've always thought I had orgasms, but I've never been absolutely sure."

"If you'd ever had one you wouldn't have mistaken it for anything else. I got hold of this text in French, one of the only ones in the library on the subject. According to it, eighty percent of orgasmic women say that it feels like a giant sneeze. Of course they were French. Maybe American women are different."

They were both laughing now like naughty children.

"A sneeze?"

"A sneeze."

"I never sneezed that way before."

"Sure?"

"Positive."

"Then you've never had an orgasm."

That was depressing news. Cassie stopped laughing.

"But don't worry," Andy said quickly, "it's never too late to learn. In fact one of the books I found gave rather explicit instructions."

He leaned over and began to stroke her lightly with the tip of one finger. This wasn't at all what she had expected, but it was very pleasant. She closed her eyes and made a small noise of encouragement. The oddest thing about it was that, although she got excited, she didn't go off anywhere. A warm sensation spread slowly from her feet to her pelvis, and her breasts began to tingle.

"Mmmm," she said, "that's nice. Try moving your finger a little to the left." He immediately moved his finger as she had suggested, and the tingling sensation increased. It was a lovely feeling. She felt weightless and full of joy and a little intoxicated and she wanted him to go on touching her. "Kiss me," she said. He leaned over and kissed her, and she smelled his after-shave lotion and the scent of wine on his breath. He was warm and solid and he kept kissing her and she stayed with his kiss, feeling the joy flowing through her whole body, opening her mouth, clinging to him and swaying under his touch. There was no crystal palace, no bed of blue feathers, no fantasy. Just Andy.

Ten minutes later, she experienced her first full-fledged orgasm and found it the sweetest, most satisfying sexual experience she had ever had. As she curled up next to Andy for the second time, she realized that she wasn't going to be able to use him to irritate her father, but that thought didn't upset her the way it would have a half hour ago. On the contrary, she felt pleased and rather smug. She liked Andy; he was a great guy. As she lay beside him, relaxed to the tips of her toes, she wondered by what piece of good fortune she had managed to stumble on him.

* * *

Cassie's father, Professor Lawrence Quinn, always paid a visit to the Liberty Lobster House when he was in Boston. The Lobster House was a dark cubbyhole filled with brass, polished wood, and fishing gear, and a man sitting in it could imagine that he was in the hold of a ship, or at least that was what Cassie thought her father imagined when he kept choosing the place over brighter, more modern restaurants. On the last day of February at six o'clock in the evening, she went there to meet him for dinner, dressed in an outfit so demure that she might have passed for a Catholic schoolgirl. Her blue wool jumper was a good two inches too long, her blouse was gray with long sleeves, and she was wearing knee socks with penny loafers.

"Hello there, darling," Quinn called out, waving his napkin at her. He inspected her from top to toe as she came toward him, and she could feel his relief. The last time they had had dinner together, she had worn a yellow and purple polka dot ensemble just to annoy him.

"Hi, Daddy." She walked over to his table, feeling graceless as she always did in his presence, and gave him a tentative peck on the cheek. He looked spectacular, but then he always looked spectacular. He was fifty-seven, but there wasn't a gray hair on his head. The waitress, a tall, clumsy young woman who reminded Cassie all too much of herself, was beaming at him as if he were a movie star. Little did she know, Cassie thought, that the dashing man in front of her went through women as if they were disposable paper cups.

"How's Sarah?" she asked, settling down in the chair across from him. Sarah had been her father's graduate student for the past three years and his mistress for the last six months. Cassie, who had met her at Thanksgiving, liked her better than the two previous girlfriends, both of whom had waited on her father hand and foot as if he were some kind of oriental potentate. Sarah had a sharp mind and a quick tongue, and even though she was only five years older than Cassie, she was more of a match for Quinn than the others had been.

"Sarah's out of the picture." Her father smiled at her and handed her the menu. "It's Wendy now. Would you like the lobster au gratin or the whole boiled lobster? I recommend the boiled lobster with drawn butter and some of this Orvieto." He pointed to the bread basket. "Help yourself to the French bread. You have no idea how lucky you are to be able to get bread with a decent crust. I dream of this bread in Ann Arbor. Even the best restaurants serve soda crackers wrapped in cellophane."

How typical of her father to announce that he had broken up with Sarah and not even spare a word of regret for her. Cassie glared at the menu and decided that she would order the lobster au gratin. She'd liked Sarah, dammit. And who was Wendy anyway? Her father had begun one of his usual one-sided conversations: telling her about the grants he had applied for, the honorary degree he was getting from Yale, and the plans he had to expand his lab. Whenever she saw him, she always hoped that he'd ask her something about her personal life, but he never did. Correction: he always asked, but he never listened to the answer.

He paused in his monologue, took a sip of wine, and brushed a lock of hair out of his eyes. "And what have you been up to?"

Screwing, she wanted to tell him. Screwing nearly every day for the last two weeks, going at it so hard I can barely walk. His name is Andy, and I think I'm falling in love with him. But her tongue stuck to the roof of her mouth. She cared about Andy too much to hand him over to her father just for the shock effect. "I've been studying," she mumbled, grabbing her water glass and taking a long drink. The water was so cold that it made her teeth ache.

"Ah," her father said, "not too hard I hope." That last line meant that he hoped she would tell him that she'd been studying botany twelve hours a day, but, as usual, he didn't give her a chance to reply. "I spoke to Halliwell about you," he said.

Cassie put her water glass back down on the table so hard that some of the water sloshed over the edge. "Daddy, you didn't!" Her father knew every important botanist in the world on a first-name basis. "You promised not to interfere again!"

"Relax." Quinn sat back in his chair and loosened his tie. "I didn't try to get him to give you special treatment because you don't need it. Halliwell told me that the term paper you wrote on the economic botany of the Bedouins of the Rub' al Khali was one of the best he'd ever gotten from an undergraduate."

"Really?" Cassie was suddenly suffused with warmth from her toes to her fingertips. She had pleased her father, actually pleased him.

Her sense of triumph was short-lived. She was still in a good mood as she stood in the Park Street station waiting for the train to take her back to Harvard, humming bits of Bach to herself and swinging her purse in tune to the music, but by the time she got as far as Central Square an uncomfortable feeling had begun to settle over her. It wasn't anything specific or palpable, only a dull ache somewhere in the back of her head like the beginning of a hangover. The headache grew worse, and by the time she had emerged from the MTA station, unlocked her bicycle from the rack in front of the Harvard Coop, and pedaled back to Radcliffe, she felt so tense she could hardly refrain from snapping at Lucy, who was innocently sitting at her desk in her nightgown banging away on the typewriter. The sound of the clicking keys made Cassie want to jump out of her skin. Retreating to her bunk, she pulled the pillow over her head.

Lucy stopped typing and looked at Cassie, curled up in a knot under the covers. "Are you okay?" she asked. She had expected Cassie to go into a funk after seeing her father, but this one looked worse than usual.

"Mm," Cassie mumbled from the darkness under the pillow.

Lucy walked over to the bed and sat down near Cassie's feet. "Your dad give you a rough time again, Cass?"

Cassie pulled the pillow off her head and sat up. She looked rumpled and slightly dazed, as if she had taken a spill on her bicycle. "No," she muttered, "for once he didn't give me any trouble. In fact, he complimented me on a paper I wrote for Halliwell. It's my head; I think I've got a migraine or something. Maybe I'm coming down with a cold. Have you got any Bufferin?"

Lucy produced two aspirins and brought them to Cassie along with a glass of water. Then she packed up her typewriter and moved down to the kitchenette to finish the paper she was writing.

That night Cassie had two dreams. In the first, she was sitting next to her mother on a large leather couch looking through a photograph album. Like all dreams, this one seemed to take place in a strange time that had never really existed. Cassie was fourteen, which meant that it must be 1959, but her mother—who should have been sick with lung cancer—was young and healthy. Her face glowed with energy, her auburn hair was tied back with a paisley scarf, and she had on a warm-brown dress that matched her eyes.

"This is your great-grandmother," Cassie's mother said in the dream, pointing to a torn, sepia-toned print of a soft-faced woman wearing an old-fashioned black bathing suit. "Her name was Cassandra too. Cassandra Victoria."

"Really, Mom?" Cassie was surprised. She inspected the photograph, trying to see some resemblance between herself and her great-grandmother, but although Cassandra Victoria was tall, she was willowy instead of skinny, pretty instead of homely. Cassie felt a slight pang of jealousy. She wondered, not for the first time, why all the good looks in the family had gone to other people. The light in the photograph was unusual; it seemed to be moving, although that was impossible, of course, since this was a still picture. As she watched, the light gathered into long, semitransparent rays, all centering on Cassandra Victoria's face. The effect was beautiful but eerie and a little disconcerting.

"I loved your great-grandmother a great deal," Cassie's mother murmured, bending over the photograph. "Everyone did. I think I can say she was universally loved, without exception."

"What did she do?"

"Nothing."

"Come on, Mother. She must have done something really impressive if you loved her so much."

"No, Cass, I just loved her for existing. She could have sat in a chair for her whole life and never lifted a hand, and I still would have loved her."

"I don't understand."

"I know you don't, honey." Cassie's mother put an arm around her and drew her close. "But you have to try." She paused and lit a cigarette with her free hand. The smoke curled around her head, blue and thick like a picture frame. "I want you to understand something, darling. You can't buy love, not from me, not from your father, not from anyone."

"I don't know what you're talking about." Cassie cried, and as she said the words her mother began to grow thin and unsubstantial like a ghost. Cassie tried to cling to her, but she was slipping away. "Come back," she begged, "wait. We're not finished talking. I want to ask you—" She never finished the sentence because right in the middle of it she drifted up on the smoke, away from her mother, out of the first dream into the second. As she drifted, she felt her father's power take her over, and her mother's warning was erased, and she forgot and forgot until her mind was a great blank, waterless and dry as a desert.

"Hello," a familiar voice said. "It's time for you to dance for your supper." Looking down at her body, she saw that she was something not quite human—a bear or a parrot or a dog or a mixture of all three—and there was a chain around her neck, and a great dark thing was holding the other end, swinging it and making it rattle. "Dance!" it ordered. "Dance!" Terrified, she tried to dance, but she was too tall and too awkward, and she kept tripping over the chain, falling, and skinning her knees and elbows. The third time she fell, the chain fell beside her in a clinking pile, and the voice of the dark thing said, "I give up, Cassandra. You'll never do. You can't dance at all, can you?"

The dream split like a torn piece of black cotton, and she woke suddenly to find herself back in her own bunk. Above her, Lucy's body was pressing a soft, round form into the mattress and the room was flooded with the dull, gray light of another Cambridge morning. Cassie began to cry silently, feeling angry and humiliated. The dreams had left a sour taste in her mouth. Now she understood why she had felt sick after seeing her father.

"It was like I was having another orgasm," she raved to Andy later that same day. "I sat there and basked in his approval and even ordered the goddamn boiled lobster when I wanted lobster au gratin. I'm gutless, hopeless, and I didn't mention you at all."

Andy sat down on the bed beside her and put his arm around her. They were in his room at Leverett. On the wall were two posters: one of Karl Marx and one of Groucho. Andy had inherited radical political views from his parents, but he maintained a sense of humor about them. "Don't be so hard on yourself," he counseled. "The man is your father. Of course you want his approval; it's natural."

Cassie slammed her fists into the pillows. "I want him to love me, but he doesn't. He never has and he never will. He just wants me to perform for him like a trained seal."

Andy grabbed her by the wrists and pulled her close to him. "*I* love you," he said. He kissed her hard, wanting to take away the pain. "I really love you, Cass. I've been wanting to tell you for almost two weeks: you're the greatest. And I don't mean the greatest botanist. I'd love you if you couldn't tell a rose from a redwood tree."

"You would?" She began to cry, feeling so hurt by her father's coldness and so relieved that Andy loved her for herself alone.

"Of course I would."

"Say it again."

"I love you, Cassandra Quinn, and I'll keep on loving you if you never look at another plant. Drop out of school; do anything you want. Become a photographer or an aluminium-siding salesman: I'll still feel the same about you."

Cassie wiped her eyes on one of the pillowcases and smiled weakly at Andy. She felt much, much better. It was hard to lie around feeling sorry for herself when someone as nice as Andy kept saying he adored her. Snuggling up against him, she took a deep breath and let herself float in the luxury of feeling absolutely secure. She liked almost everything about Andy: the way he tasted, the way he smelled. She liked his mind too, but she liked his heart most of all. It was a good heart: kind and loyal. "You really do understand, don't you?" she whispered.

"Of course I do." Andy stroked her hair; his face grew thoughtful. "You're not the only one who's been pushed to perform. Harvard is full of people whose parents only loved them when they produced. The only people who make it into this joint have been conditioned like rats since about the age of five to put out or die."

"You sound like you're speaking from experience."

Andy nodded. "I am, Cass. Remember my older brother, Sam? the one who died in Korea?"

"Of course I remember. You said you still talk to him sometimes." She took Andy's hand, turned it over, and kissed his palm lightly. "You know, I was a little jealous when I heard that. All these silent conversations with Sam that I never get to participate in. It's like you have a whole secret life."

"In a way I do. The conversations with Sam are harmless, imaginary, and enjoyable, but there's another side of the story, one I don't talk about much because it's too painful. When I think about it, I get moody and depressed."

"You don't seem moody to me."

"I hide it well, but I don't want to hide anything from you, not anymore, especially not after what you've told me about your father." He paused for a moment and sat there, lacing his fingers into hers. Cassie had never seen him look so somber. "My parents adored my brother," he said at last. "I don't use the word 'adored' lightly. Their attitude toward him bordered on worship. When he was killed in Korea, they were devastated." He paused again, lost in some painful memory of his own. Cassie held his hand carefully, not wanting to disturb him. Finally he took a deep breath and continued.

"All through my childhood, Sam was held up to me as the model of what a son should be. Although my parents never actually said it out loud, it was clear that I was supposed to take his place and compensate them for what they'd lost. That was impossible, of course: I wasn't as handsome, or as charming, or as smart as Sam, but no one was willing to admit that, so I kept trying. I worked myself sick in school; I went out for basketball even though I hated it, just because Sam was once team captain. But no matter how much I did, I could feel my mom and dad looking at me, thinking that Sam would have done it better. They didn't mean to be that way, Cass, but they couldn't help it. In a lot of ways they were wonderful parents. They never badgered me the way your father did. If you'd looked at our family from the outside, you would have said that no two people could have been more supportive or affectionate, but I could always hear their voices in the back of my head saying, "Andy just isn't going to be the man his brother was."

"That sounds unbearable."

"It was. I didn't fail very often, but when I did, it felt like the end of the world. What I'm trying to tell you, Cass, is that I know the pain of trying to buy love; I know it from the inside. You'll never have to perform for me. Never. I swear it." Lifting her face to his, he gave her a long, sweet kiss.

They spent the rest of the afternoon making love, and by the time they finally climbed out of bed, put on their clothes, and went down to the Leverett dining hall for dinner, they both felt as if a bargain had been sealed between them.

· 3 ·

Sex seemed to be in the air that spring along with a lot of other things. It was a season of sudden upheavals: in early March, Steve Singleton and his friends started putting together plans for a Freedom Summer in Mississippi, and Ann Barrows underwent a transformation so extreme that none of her friends could figure out what had happened to her. Whenever Lucy looked back on the day she finally and inextricably involved herself with David, she always remembered that it had begun with a very upsetting conversation with Ann.

"Steve's founded a new organization called the Harvard Coalition," Ann announced one morning. Six young women, Lucy included, were sitting around one of the big tables in the Holmes Hall dining room having breakfast together, and the conversation up to that point had been about the weather, which was dreary as usual. "A whole group of us is going down to Mississippi this summer to work with the Student Nonviolent Coordinating Committee." Ann's announcement fell into their midst like a bombshell. Steve Singleton was her fiancé, known around Harvard for both his wealth (his family owned a rather large chunk of Manhattan) and his radical political views. In place of an engagement ring he had given Ann a civil rights button showing a strong black hand shaking a strong white hand in a symbol of racial harmony, but no one had expected Ann to take his politics so seriously.

Amazed silence spread in all directions. Ann, who seemed either unaware of the sensation she was causing or secretly pleased by it, ate a spoonful of oatmeal. "He's been inspired by the struggle of Doctor Martin Luther King for some time, you know," she continued, "and when Steve is inspired, then everyone else gets inspired too. We're going to register Negro voters, thousands of them. The South won't have seen anything like this since Reconstruction." She helped herself to the butter and spread it on her toast. She drank her milk in quick gulps, and her small green eyes sparkled with excitement.

The others stared at her in astonishment. Ann Barrows had never done anything political in her life as far as any of them knew. Her father was a New Deal Democrat who owned one of the largest chains of department stores in the Midwest, and Ann sometimes bragged that he had once gotten a personal Christmas card from the Kennedys thanking him for his support, but when people began debating the merits of Johnson versus Goldwater, or arguing over how to desegregate the Boston schools, she usually retreated into a book or remembered that she had some terribly important errand to run. Last summer when busloads of students cut their vacations short to march on Washington and hear Martin Luther King, she had been at Lake Michigan learning to water-ski. Of course that was before she met Steve.

"But, Ann," Kathy DeVelt objected, "how are the local people going to react?" Kathy was a lanky blond whose family had diamond mines in South Africa. Her voice was always calm and husky as if she were trying out for a role as Tallulah Bankhead.

"Don't you mean, how are the *white* southerners going to react, Kathy? Or don't you consider the Negroes 'local people'?"

"I don't think Kathy was making a racial remark," Joyce Lindsay said. Joyce, a talented violinist, was always trying to quell anything inharmonious. "It's just that there's been so much violence down there: police dogs, electric cattle prods, fire hoses, buses being burned, demonstrators getting thrown in jail under terrible conditions. Female civil rights workers have been raped. It's terribly dangerous."

"I know it's dangerous," Ann lowered her head and took another bite of toast, "but if you aren't willing to stand behind your ideals what good are they?"

That was a good question. Lucy ate some oatmeal and tried to think of a way to dissuade Ann, but the more she thought about it, the more she felt Ann was right. She wondered if there was anything in the world she would be willing to risk her life for. She found it disturbing that nothing leapt to mind.

"The next president of this country is going to have to take Negro voters into account," Ann said, "or there'll be a wave of civil disobedience like you've never seen before."

Kathy DeVelt poured some cream into her tea and stirred it. "Frankly, I find it odd that you of all people have become an advocate of passive resistance. Oh, it's all very pleasant in theory, darling, but don't tell me that you're actually asking us," she waved at the group around the breakfast table, "to believe that you're willing to lie down in front of a tank if necessary, because," she laughed lightly, "such suicidal pacifism just doesn't fit your personality. I've seen you snap at people who borrowed your nail polish. Turning the other cheek isn't—how shall I put it?—your forte."

Ann bristled. "If it would get Negroes their rights, I certainly would be willing to lie down in front of a tank, and I don't appreciate your snide—"

"It won't work," Kathy interrupted. "I hope you realize that. If you lie down in front of those ignorant southern sheriffs, they'll roll right over you. You're making a pitch to their consciences, but they don't have any. They think civil rights workers are scum."

"And what do you think they are?" Ann said in a low, hard voice.

"Fools," Kathy said, flipping her blond hair out of her eyes. "Or perhaps communists."

Ann rose to her feet, picked up a cup, and for a moment it looked as if she were about to hurl coffee into Kathy's face. But instead she slammed the cup down on the table, turned, and walked out of the dining room.

Kathy's face was pale. "Ann doesn't do a very good imitation of Gandhi," she said. She laughed and waited for everyone else to join her, but no one did. In two years of Radcliffe breakfasts, it was as nasty a moment as Lucy could remember.

The day did not improve after that. The weather got worse and so did the emotional climate. At eleven Lucy had a date to meet Bill at Elsie's for roast beef sandwiches and a confession. Bill, who had just returned from Washington, did not know that the confession was on the agenda, but she had been waiting to tell him about David for weeks, and it wasn't fair to wait any longer.

Elsie's was hardly larger than a closet, but it sold roast beef sandwiches that were legendary. The sandwiches, which contained enough beef for two meals, were served on large rolls with pickles and onions. You could also get pastrami if you wanted, but not much else. By noon Elsie's would be so crowded that the customers would be packed three deep around the counter, but at eleven it was nearly empty which was just the way Lucy had planned it.

She found Bill sitting on one of the stools near the door, attacking his roast beef with the air of a man who already suspected that something unpleasant was in store for him. An untouched cup of tea sat on the counter beside him. When he caught sight of her, he smiled gloomily.

"Hello," he said. "It's good to see you again." He kissed her on the cheek. "The shuttle flight from D.C. was horrible. Nothing but turbulence." There was a small, awkward silence.

"It seems like you've been away for months," Lucy said, thinking how fashionable and stiffly proper Bill looked in comparison to David.

He motioned for her to sit down beside him. "How was your Chaucer lecture this morning? You must have gotten halfway through *The Canterbury Tales* while I was away."

She put her book bag down on the floor, climbed up on the stool beside him, and ordered a Coke and a roast beef special with everything. "I didn't go," she said. "I was too upset." She described the argument between Ann and Kathy, trying to convey the nasty flavor of it, but even though Bill kept shaking his head and making sympathetic noises, she could tell his mind was somewhere else. Well, so was hers. Get on with it, Constable, she told herself. She took a deep breath and reminded herself that she wasn't engaged to Bill and had never agreed not to see other people. She didn't want to hurt his feelings, but it was important to be honest and direct with him.

"Bill," she began, "there's something I have to tell you."

Bill hunched his shoulders and looked at her sadly. "You don't need to tell me, Lou." He put his sandwich down on the wax paper. "I already know. Sandy Roberts saw you and Blake together at Bartley's last week. He asked Ronda about it, and she told him that you've been coming in for coffee together regularly. He met me at the airport with the news."

"Sandy spied on me!" Lucy was furious at the thought that Sandy had carried tales to Bill. She felt terrible that he had found out secondhand. "I ought to wring his neck."

"Don't bother." Bill picked up his tea and put it back down again without tasting it. "I told Sandy that if I ever caught him nosing into your business again, I'd make sure he had to take a medical leave of absence."

Dear Bill, gallant to the end. Lucy was touched. He always had defended her, and she was probably a fool to be giving him up. Only maybe she wasn't giving him up. Frankly she wasn't sure what seeing David meant. She told Bill that and he took it well.

"Let me know when this infatuation is over," he said. "Meanwhile, if you need a friend . . ." He let the words trail off, waiting for her to reassure him that she'd always be his friend too, which she did quickly and without hesitation. They finished their sandwiches and parted with a handshake. It was an awfully formal way to end a year-long relationship, but then Bill had always hated scenes. Lucy rode off to her next class feeling as if something that was supposed to have happened hadn't. What had she expected Bill to do? Break down in tears? She should be glad that he had taken the news like a gentleman.

By the time she got to Harvard Yard, she had decided that that was the problem with their whole relationship: Bill had always been a perfect gentleman, and darn it, that was boring; it was emotionally unsatisfying.

It was a long afternoon. At five, when her last class was over, she rode to Dunster to see David. On the way there she decided not to tell him about her conversation with Bill. It would seem too much like a declaration, and there was nothing to declare, at least not yet. She was fairly sure that she was going to end up being more than just a friend to David, but maybe not. Only one thing was certain: David was different from any man she had ever gone out with, and that, she decided, was exactly what made him interesting.

David met her in the courtyard, signed her in, and took her straight up to his room. Shortly thereafter she found herself keeping an eye on some potatoes that he had thrown into his fireplace. The plan was to have an early dinner together, that is if the wood held out. She hoped the potatoes cooked quickly because David had actually been known to burn furniture when he ran short. The first time she visited his room, he had dumped some books out of the orange crates that served as his bookcases, started a blaze, and tossed in a can of pork and beans. She had been terrified, expecting the beans to explode any minute, but they had turned out fine. David prided himself on his hobo skills; like his hero Jack Kerouac, he was always preparing to go on the road.

David, who was sitting in a battered red armchair playing his harmonica, paused in the middle of a moaning rendition of "Dust Bowl Refugee" and eyed the potatoes hungrily. "How're they doing?" he inquired.

She poked at the potatoes with the tip of a large machete that had the words *Souvenir of Mexico* engraved on the blade. "Not done yet."

"Rats." David went back to his playing.

She put down the machete and looked around David's room. It was an incredible mess, but she didn't mind. She'd been shocked the first time he brought her here, but over the past few weeks she had come to appreciate the fact that his sloppiness reflected the freedom of his spirit. Dirty clothes lay in heaps mixed with every small-press poetry publication to come out in the Boston area in the last four years. A pyramid of beer cans leaned up against one wall, a molding towel was draped across a curtain rod, and a mobile of chicken bones dangled from the ceiling. But the most striking things were the posters, nailed, taped, and stapled to every available inch of wall space. There were six posters of Bob Dylan alone, not to mention two of Joan Baez, three of James Dean, and one each of Brando, Bogart, W. C. Fields, Martin Luther King, Marx, Trotsky, Freud, Dylan Thomas, Robert Frost, Hart Crane, Jack Kerouac, Alan Watts, and Daffy Duck. Aubrey Beardsley was represented, as were van Gogh, Hieronymus Bosch, two anonymous Algerian terrorists, and an Indian god with forty-six arms (Lucy had recently counted them). Between the posters, taking up every remaining bit of space, were poems, about three quarters of them by David himself, the others by Baudelaire, Verlaine, Rimbaud, and other French poets that David had translated, including a long strip that ran from the fireplace to the bathroom entirely devoted to the ballads of François Villon.

Lucy contemplated the poster of Martin Luther King and sighed. "I'm worried about Ann Barrows," she said. She told him about the conversation at breakfast. "I think she may be going off this summer to Mississippi to get herself killed."

"Sounds like fun." David turned his harmonica upside down and knocked out the spit. "Maybe I'll join her."

Lucy took another jab at the potatoes. "Be serious," she commanded. "I know it's hard to believe that Ann could be interested in anything but clothes, but Steve Singleton seems to have hypnotized her. She's all excited about the good they can do down there working for the rights of

Negroes. Of course in a lot of ways she's right; someone should go to Mississippi and register those voters, but the way they've got it organized it sounds like the Children's Crusade."

"Ever meet Steve?" David pocketed his harmonica.

"Once or twice. He's so busy he doesn't have much time to socialize. I think he runs every political organization at Harvard that's more than two degrees left of center."

"We were in a section of Western Civ together freshman year." David yawned and stretched. "Steve's charismatic; he used to keep everyone talking for hours about his vision of the future. He was gung ho for Kennedy in those days, spoke of the man so that you were sure the Second Coming was at hand, but after the Cuban missile crisis, he declared himself disillusioned with big government, said he was going back to grass roots. In short—" he paused and frowned, "he's a perfect example of a rich-kid radical."

"He's got Ann completely spellbound."

"At least he's got her doing something interesting with her life. At least she's not sitting around agonizing over which of her five leather coats to wear." He got up. "The only problem is, his motives are completely screwed." He waved at the poster of Freud. "Ever wonder why all the real political extremists like Steve have rich fathers? It's easy to explain, especially when you sit on the outside looking in like I do. In the first place," he tapped the chicken bone mobile and watched it twirl, "they feel guilty about their unearned wealth, and in the second place," he tapped the mobile again, "they're convinced that they're born to rule. And in the third place," he grabbed the mobile and stopped it in midair, "they know that if they get in trouble, Daddy will bail them out."

Lucy thought it over and decided he was right. Steve's radicalism was another version of Harvard's perpetual game of one-upmanship. She liked the way David's mind worked. Conversations with him were never dull. In fact nothing about him was dull. She looked at him standing there, and a small thrill ran through her. He was a very sexy guy, much more sexy than Bill. Something is happening to me, she thought. I seem to be thawing.

David released the mobile and walked over to his desk. The desk, which had been issued by Harvard along with the room, was a sturdy wooden affair with massive drawers and a top large enough to carve up a Christmas turkey. Opening one of the drawers, he pulled out a small tin box that had once contained imported peppermints.

Sitting down beside Lucy, he opened the box and took out a pack of cigarette papers and a small quantity of marijuana. "Want some?" He rolled the cigarette deftly, pinching off the ends to keep the marijuana from spilling out. The stuff was expensive, and David always smoked every bit of it, even eating the leftover butts and popping the seeds in butter.

Lucy shook her head. "No thanks," she said automatically. This was the third time he had offered to share his marijuana with her and the third time she'd refused. The thawing continued. She looked at the marijuana and then at David. He had such wonderful eyes. She wondered what they would look like if she smoked some of this stuff. It was supposed to change the way you saw the world. She imagined kaleidoscopes, hawk eyes, blue-gray glass marbles rolling around in his head. The effect might be scary, but it certainly wouldn't be dull. On the other hand . . . She moved restlessly. Picking up the machete, she gave the potatoes another turn. They were getting black on the outside, but they still weren't done. Half-baked, she thought, rather like me.

David grinned and shook his head. "Still worried you're going to turn into a werewolf?"

"No, that's not it." She had made a promise to herself the day she learned that her mother had been killed in a drunken accident. The promise had been simple and childish: *I won't be like her.* Over the years it had turned into a promise never to be intoxicated with anything, not alcohol, not drugs. Not even with love, a voice said inside her head. She tried to still the voice, but it persisted. She looked at David, who was committing a felony and seemed so relaxed. You're torn between security on one hand and a desire for adventure on the other, he had told her only a few weeks ago, and he'd been absolutely right. Right now she had a growing urge to plunge off into the unknown, and at the same time she could feel something restraining her. Why did her life always have to be so neat and safe? Wasn't it time to put her mother's death in perspective? She wanted to be more like Cassie or even Ann. Ann might be naïve, but at least she was plunging into life with never a backward glance.

David licked the cigarette to make it burn more slowly. "This clears your head and loosens you up. It's a lower-class pleasure, you know, or at least it used to be. Recently it's gotten trendy." He lit the cigarette and inhaled, holding his breath. Exhaling, he relaxed and sat back. "Ah," he said. He looked over at her and began to laugh. "You know what you remind me of? You remind me of a kid outside a bakery store looking in at the cakes."

A few weeks ago, she would have been offended; in fact, she might have gotten up and left. But the two of them had talked for hours during those weeks, establishing a friendship that wasn't easily shaken. Lucy knew David wasn't laughing at her but at that part of her she wanted to get rid of, that rigid, good-girl part that made all of life seem like the inside of a refrigerator. Maybe this is the day, she thought. Maybe when I said good-bye to Bill, I said good-bye to the sensible, boring part of my life.

"Here." David leaned forward and stuck the end of the cigarette between her lips. Instinctively, she backed away, but he persisted. The paper was damp and the marijuana tasted like burned leaves. "Give it a try," he pleaded. "Come on. Just once. It won't kill you."

"It doesn't taste anything like tobacco," she observed, "and it burns going down." She looked around the room. "Nothing's happening. I don't think it's working." She was disappointed. Finally she'd taken the plunge, and the water had turned out to be three inches deep. So much for grand adventure.

"Give it time," he told her, offering her another toke.

Determined to experience something—anything—she inhaled as much of the smoke as she could and held it in her lungs for a good thirty seconds before she exhaled. It rasped her throat, and it tasted like dead leaves, but she didn't care. Thaw me, she commanded the stuff.

"Way to go," David said. "Have another."

A half hour later she was so stoned she could hardly stand up, but that didn't matter because she was standing with her back to the wall, naked, pressed up against a poster of Brando, and David was holding her and kissing her very slowly. She felt the warmth of his lips against hers, the pressure of his thighs, the rough scrape of his jeans against her bare flesh. It was very exciting, and it all seemed to be taking place in slow motion so that she got to appreciate every bit of it: the smell of the marijuana on his breath, the faint prickle of his beard, even the beat of his heart pulsing next to hers.

Gathering her in his arms, he picked her up and cradled her and then lay her down on the mattress in front of the fireplace. She watched him take off his clothes without feeling the slightest embarrassment. He looked golden in the firelight: a strong, handsome man; lean; his chest covered with black, curly hair; his legs and arms well muscled.

Then he was beside her and on top of her and holding her so close that she could hardly breathe. He drew her to him and she came, willingly, not thinking any more, letting herself go as the firelight danced over their bodies. There was a moment of pain when he entered her, but she pulled him closer; he pressed her against the mattress until her shoulders burned and he rocked her and she moaned his name, and suddenly it didn't hurt anymore. Swept away by passion, she stopped being herself and became a thing of pure pleasure that cried out and wept and laughed and begged him not to stop.

That was the day she discovered sex, something so fierce and elemental that it cured her forever of any fear that she was cold. It also very nearly stripped her of her place in the class of '66 because David, she soon learned, liked to take chances, not just small chances like asking her to stay the night in his room, but crazy risks that could easily have gotten both of them expelled. They made love under insane conditions: in Mount Auburn Cemetery in broad daylight, in other people's parked cars—everywhere and anywhere, the more insecure the better. Sometimes as they sat at dinner in Dunster, he would slip his hand under the table and run it up under her skirt while she struggled to keep up polite conversation.

"I never thought I'd enjoy sex so much," she told him one afternoon as they lay on the mattress in front of the fire. "I feel like I'm flying, like I've finally broken out of my old cocoon. I'm happy, I really am, but"—she paused and frowned, "except for my volunteer work at the hospital, everything in my life is going to hell. I haven't been studying; I haven't been seeing my friends. I have midterms coming up, and—"

"Don't tell me," he said, closing her mouth with a kiss. "I want to imagine that the only life you have is the one you live when you're with me."

"But David, that's not reasonable." She sat up, and he pulled her back down beside him.

"I've come to erase the word *reason* from your vocabulary," he proclaimed. He kissed her neck and her shoulders and held her very close and it was sweet and wild and she felt as if she were swimming through him, as if his skin was a great warm bottomless lake. What's reason anyway? she thought. A heap of old obligations, a junkyard of boring duties. It's time to let go of reason. The idea of letting go of reason thrilled her. She had never been irresponsible before; she had never let herself be swept away by anything or anyone until now.

Every day she fell more in love with him, until that love filled her every waking moment, until she could think of nothing else. She knew that by her old standards this wasn't a healthy state of affairs, but the old standards didn't apply any more. That entire spring she was elated and a little drunk because thanks to David her life had finally thawed out, and she was feeling everything with an intensity she hadn't experienced since she was six years old: she felt the grass turning green, and the weather changing, and the pressure the crocuses exerted when they exploded along the sidewalks on Garden Street, and she felt David's skin next to hers even when she was alone in her own bed.

"Slow down," Cassie begged. "Blake has a horrible reputation as far as women go. If you insist on getting so involved with him, I hope you're at least having the sense to use condoms. Andy and I always do. Listen, if you're too shy to buy them, you can have some of mine. I'm serious about this, Lou. Your life looks completely out of control."

"You're going to fail the entire semester if you don't concentrate on your work," her tutor warned. "What's come over you, Miss Constable?"

Dean Baker even called her in to have a little chat. The dean was a rosy, determined middle-aged woman with a large bunch of violets pinned to her suit. Her office in Fay House was light and airy, full of modern paintings and furniture made out of metal tubes, but her attitude was old-fashioned and rather motherly. "Miss Constable," she said, "your midterm grades were well below your usual standards, and we were wondering, my dear. Is something wrong?"

"I heard Joan Baez sing 'We Shall Overcome' last night," Lucy said defiantly. "She was playing for a huge rally to raise money for voter registration in the South. And last week I went to a coffeehouse to hear Allen Ginsberg recite his latest poems. He chanted them so loud that his voice made chills run up and down my spine." She pressed her lips together stubbornly. "I feel that I'm finally getting an education." And

I'm finally getting a taste of passion, she thought, but she didn't say that because she doubted the dean would understand.

The dean gave her a worried look. "Going to hear famous people is all very well and good, my dear, and I'm sure that on many levels it's quite educational, but your midterm grade in Chaucer is a C minus."

Lucy shrugged. "I'm sorry. I know my grades are horrible. My academic life seems to be falling apart, but I just can't seem to care." She knew it was the dean's duty to warn her to pay attention to her work, but the warning seemed musty and Victorian. If you only knew what was really happening, she thought, you'd envy me, Dean Baker. Something had broken inside her, and, as Cassie had said, she was being swept along out of control. And she didn't regret that, not for a moment. She liked riding the peak of the wave; she liked watching her old life smash up. It had been a boring life, a life unworthy of a woman of spirit.

The night after she talked to the dean, she and David made love in the little garden behind Lamont library. It was a secluded place, totally deserted after the library closed, and it was filled with flowers. For the rest of her life, whenever she chanced upon the word *romance*, she thought of that garden: the warm soft grass, the moonlight, the passionate kisses they gave each other. Years later, she could close her eyes and see David bending over her, his face silvered and almost unearthly; she could smell the flowers and hear the noise of the traffic passing by on the other side of the wall. They loved each other so perfectly that night that afterward they lay speechless in each other's arms. Then David rose and began to pick daffodils for her.

"Don't do that," she protested. "It's against the rules." Hearing what she had just said, she began to laugh. "Oh my God," she said, rolling over on her stomach and retrieving her shoes from under a bush, "listen to me. 'Picking flowers is against the rules.' As if what we were just doing wasn't."

David piled the daffodils in her arms and then began to make a chain of them to hang around her neck. The stems were too hard to knot, so he made little slits in them and slipped in the flowers head to head. "Sweets for the sweet," he said, "and flowers for the fair. The real crime isn't ours." He pointed to Lamont. "It's theirs. It's a crime that you can't go into Lamont and see the poetry room, Lou."

Lucy looked at the library, looming up dark and unfriendly. "I'll go in

there some day," she vowed. She was moved by David's understanding. It gave her strength.
"You bet you will," David promised, draping the chain of daffodils around her neck, "and when you do, I'll be right beside you."

When it was raining or they'd tired temporarily of taking risks, they adjourned to his room, built a fire, and lay in front of it until the seven o'clock curfew. They often emerged so dizzy and giddy from their passionate entanglements that neither could utter a coherent sentence. On calmer days, they talked endlessly afterward. Harvard, they agreed, was changing. Things were different from the way they had been only a few months before.
"It's Yeats's beast slouching toward Bethlehem to be born," David told her one afternoon in late April. "Look around you. America's falling apart. There's a crisis of confidence in any institution you care to name, starting with the presidency and working down. Look at the Civil Rights movement: right on the edge of turning violent. Look at poetry: coming out of the universities and walking the streets. Look at middle-class morals: no one, including us, gives a damn about them any more. Look at our industry gearing up for war in Southeast Asia. Look at Johnson and Goldwater: do you want either of those guys with their finger on the nuclear button? We could be vaporized overnight and everyone knows that and no one wants to look at it. America is hiding out in the suburbs with its head stuck up the exhaust pipe of a lawn mower, and the world is coming apart at the seams."
"I agree that things are changing," Lucy insisted, "but I don't think the Apocalypse is at hand. Civilizations take a long time to break up. The Roman empire was falling for about five hundred years before it finally came down. The things you are talking about may just be currents of unrest that will ebb and flow and disappear like all the others." She almost could hear their minds getting sharper as they honed them on each other. Arguing with David was almost as good as making love with him, and she reveled in it. "Twenty years from now, the United States will still be intact, and people will be talking about this era as the good old days, just like they talk about the Depression and World War Two."
He shook his head. "You don't see it because you're cloistered. You're

an intelligent woman, but you're being given an education designed for a bunch of nineteenth-century upper-class British do-nothings who died in the trenches in World War One. Harvard is a dinosaur thrashing around, too dumb to know it's dead."

"You're exaggerating."

"Come out of your ivory tower and look around."

"Where am I supposed to look, David, under the bed?"

"Try across the river."

"'Across the River'? That sounds like the title of a spiritual."

"Oh, it's a real enough river, all right: full of dirty water and old tires, but it's the dividing line."

"The dividing line between what and what?"

"Between Cambridge and the real world."

That Saturday they crossed the Charles River and walked into Boston to a large apartment not too far from the Common. The apartment was inhabited by ten people, none of whom seemed related to one another. Crystals hung from the ceiling on invisible threads of fishline, and one room was covered entirely in aluminium foil. In the kitchen the shelves were lined with exotic spices, and the ceiling had been painted with a giant rainbow decorated with gold stars. On the back porch a tall man sat in a battered rocking chair playing a metal Jew's harp to an audience of a half dozen children of so many different colors and races that they reminded Lucy of a UNICEF Christmas card. She stood in the doorway looking at the children, thinking that perhaps David was right. Perhaps some new era really was about to be born. She had never seen so much color and exoticism, such an attempt to change the basic stuff that life was made of.

"Meet Lloyd," David said pointing to the man in the rocking chair, "Harvard class of '63, former student of Professor Timothy Leary, now spiritual guru of five of the best unemployed rock musicians on the East Coast." Lloyd put aside his Jew's harp and got to his feet. He had blond hair that hung down to his shoulders and wore a pair of gold wire-rimmed glasses that Lucy had always associated with former Peace Corps volunteers. Lucy, who had never seen such long hair on a man, found it all very daring. She noticed that he had a string of beads around his neck. If the Cambridge townies ever caught sight of that necklace, they'd beat him to a pulp. She wondered how he dared go out on the street. New rules, she thought. New genders. Everything here is up for grabs.

"Hi," Lloyd said. He shook her hand with a cordial grip and led her to a large room full of musical instruments where four young men were making an amazing racket on drums and electric guitars. A fifth man stood in front of a portable microphone, singing at the top of his lungs. His voice had a warm, gravellike quality that Lucy instantly recognized as a rather good imitation of Bob Dylan.

> *Lucy, Lucy*
> *Sweet fire in your thighs*
> *Come sail with me*
> *To the Land of Surprise*
> *Where the sun is purple silk*
> *And I'll drink you up like milk*
> *And there'll be jewels in your eyes* . . .

She stood transfixed, stunned to hear her own name coming out of the man's mouth.

"Blake writes incredible lyrics," Lloyd said, taking a joint out of his shirt pocket and lighting it. He inhaled slowly and smiled at her.

Lucy turned to David, who was tapping his foot in time to the music. "You wrote that?"

"I plead guilty." David's eyes were bright and his face was slightly flushed. Lloyd had handed him the joint, and he was taking deep drags. Between drags he waved the joint at the band like a conductor's baton.

The music built toward a climax, drums and guitars urging each other toward the finale. The rhythm of the song was driving. Lucy began to tap her foot, half dancing beside David, and everything in the room seemed to vibrate: the walls, the ceiling, Lloyd's hair, David's body. The vibration enveloped her and she felt stoned even though she wasn't sharing the joint. *Lucy, Lucy*, the singer repeated.

"This is about me, isn't it." She turned to David, touched that he had done this in secret and given it to her as a surprise.

"Who else would I write about?" David laughed. "My God, you should see your face. You're glowing. You look like you stuck your toe in an electrical socket."

The spring Lucy fell in love with David was also the spring of the comet. It was a large comet, and even while she was at Lloyd's listening to the song David had written in her honor, the comet was hanging in the sky overhead, growing more and more brilliant, or at least that was what the newspapers reported. For people living in the Boston area, it might as well have stayed in the remote regions of outer space because clouds and smoke made it invisible.

There was great interest in the comet at Harvard: literature professors paused in the middle of their lectures to remind their students that in the Middle Ages such events were thought to be forerunners of disasters; in Dunster House the astronomy majors temporarily took over the dining hall, put up a huge chart, and marked off the comet's daily path with rows of colored pins. Even the Harvard Outing Club got into the act. An expedition to the nearest mountain was organized, so that students could actually see the comet.

The comet outing was scheduled for the following weekend, and Lucy decided to go despite the fact that she should have been living in the library, reading Chaucer night and day. David was going to be busy that weekend, madly editing the spring edition of *Fergus*, the Dunster literary magazine, and she was in no frame of mind to study. The comet, she told herself, was a once-in-a-lifetime event, and she hadn't been out in the country for months, so she bought herself a box of chocolate doughnuts, made a thermos of coffee, and obtained permission from Miss Lolland to leave at three in the morning to join ten other hardy souls bound for the comet watch.

They drove for several hours through the darkness, climbed the mountain, and sat down to wait. The comet was scheduled to appear at sunrise, but no one was sure if the sky would be clear enough to see it. As it turned out, they were in luck. Dawn came, beautiful and purple gray with only a few low, floating clouds. Just before the sun rose, the last of the clouds cleared, and the comet suddenly appeared above the horizon.

As Lucy sat with the Outing Club members, munching on her breakfast and looking at the graceful, scarflike tail of this visitor to the earth's atmosphere, she thought of many things: of how good it felt to be out of the city, of how much Cassie would have enjoyed the sight, of how large the universe was and what rare things it contained. But most of all, as was usual these days, she thought about David. There was no doubt in her mind that she loved him, and although he had never come out and said it, she was sure he loved her. This morning, away from him for the first time in weeks, she felt particularly close to him. She took another bite of her doughnut, thinking that it was a good thing that none of the other students could read her mind. She loved David so much that it was almost embarrassing. If I don't watch out, she thought, I'll start talking like one of those mushy popular love poets David's always putting down, but I don't care. I'm happier than I can ever remember being, and if it's at all possible I want to spend the rest of my life with him.

She tried to imagine herself married to David, but it was hard going. No matter what kind of life she tried to envision for the two of them, she couldn't see David settling into it. In fact, she couldn't see David settling into anything. Still, they'd work it out somehow. Maybe they'd go to Paris and live like bohemians, or maybe they'd spend the rest of their lives wandering around the world. They were close and getting closer all the time, and in the end that was all that mattered.

She looked at the comet and thought of how long it had wandered by itself through the cold darkness between the planets. People shouldn't have to live like that, she thought.

The crimson domes of Dunster sparkled in the warm May sunlight, and a fresh spring breeze blew up from the river, shaking the maple trees and sending winged seeds whirling down to the red-brick sidewalks. At nine o'clock that same morning, David sat at his desk in front of an open window looking out at the tulips that were blooming against the wrought-iron fence that ran along the far side of the courtyard. It was an absolutely beautiful day, and he was in an absolutely terrible mood.

Picking up an envelope, he ripped it open, read what was inside, crushed it in his fist, and gave a snort of disgust. The final issue of *Fergus* was going to be a disaster if he didn't get some better submissions. For some reason everyone writing poetry this term seemed to feel obliged to rave on and on about the assassination of Kennedy. The poem he had just reduced to a wadded lump was by a premed student named Kevin Taylor, who had entitled it "Burn On, Burn On, Eternal Flame."

Jesus, David thought, give me a break. He tried to comfort himself with the thought of the famous writers who had sat in Dunster looking out at the same tulips. Norman Mailer had lived in the room just above his, and Thornton Wilder had camped out down the hall. Not that either of them had been satisfied with dear old Dunster. Mailer had hated looking out at the river, which constantly reminded him that he had failed to make the Harvard crew, and Wilder had complained that his room was the size of a broom closet.

Shoving six unopened envelopes into a desk drawer that was already stuffed with unread submissions, he picked up his pen, opened his blue notebook, and tried to begin a poem of his own, but his mind was as blank as the page. Something was gnawing away inside of him, destroying his creativity, turning him into a fifth-rate poet who could only grind out song lyrics. He fumbled for his Muse, but she had flown out the window and was standing on the ledge jeering at him.

What the hell is wrong with me? he thought. I'm falling apart. He forced his pen to glide across the page but all he got was garbage. The tulips festered and wrapped themselves around the iron fence, and the river turned into something so trite that it made him want to shred his notebook and set it on fire.

Getting to his feet, he began to pace around the room. He felt trapped. He felt as if his life were going nowhere. The walls were closing in. This room was a prison, and his cell mate was a big, mean, tattooed case of writer's block. What was eating at him? What was sucking his life force out his ears and leaving his brain a pile of mush?

Suddenly he froze in midstep, and an odd expression came over his face. His tutor, who idolized James Joyce, would have probably called the moment an "epiphany," but David thought of it in Somerville terms. Everything that had been hidden was suddenly revealed to him: he finally knew what the fuck was the matter.

When Lucy got back to Cambridge, she gave David a call, but he was out. That was a little unusual, but since she was tired, she went to bed early and thought no more about it. They had a date on Monday at four-thirty as usual. But she got out of class early, and it was closer to three forty-five when she got on her bicycle and made the fifteen-minute trek to Dunster. Signing herself in, she went up to his room, humming happily as she climbed the five flights of stairs. David's door was the last one on the left. Without bothering to knock, she opened it and stopped dead in her tracks.

David, who was supposed to be putting together *Fergus*, was doing nothing of the sort. Instead he was standing beside his bed, cramming books into a duffel bag. There were no posters on his walls anymore, only tape and staple marks and rows of nail holes. The pyramid of beer cans had been knocked over, and the mobile of chicken bones lay in a heap in the wastebasket. Her first thought was that he had been expelled.

"What's going on?" She took off her sweater and surveyed the devastation, trying to make some sense out of it. The room looked ten times as dirty as she'd ever seen it. In fact the only island of order was David's guitar, which lay packed in its case. "Are you okay?"

"I'm leaving." David picked up a shirt and stuffed it into the canvas bag without looking up.

"You're what?" She was sure she had misunderstood him. The word *leaving* floated around the room, and she caught at it and tried to make it hold still so she could translate it. He must have meant "going to visit my mother for a few days" or . . .

"I'm leaving," David repeated, and there was no mistaking his meaning this time. "I'm going south with Steve Singleton."

When had he made this decision? The last time she'd seen him he hadn't given her the slightest hint he was planning a trip. A burst of anxiety hit her in the pit of the stomach. Calm down, she told herself. He's just going away for a week or so, although why he'd go anywhere with Steve is beyond me since he thinks Steve is a rich kid radical. She swallowed and forced herself to be reasonable. He was an adult after all and he had a right to go on trips whenever he wanted and she certainly didn't intend to nag him. Only . . . he was taking so much stuff. Her mouth went dry, and she felt her hands begin to tingle. "You didn't forget that we were going into Boston tomorrow to hear the band, did you?" She folded her arms across her chest, holding in her anxiety. Everything would be okay. He'd explain why he'd decided to empty out his room. "I don't understand what's going on here, David, and I'd really appreciate it if you'd quit packing for a minute and tell me when you're leaving."

David went on packing without looking up. "We're leaving at six."

But that was only *two* hours from now! Lucy's confusion turned to anger. What the hell was going on here? She didn't like the way he was avoiding her eyes and she didn't like the tone of his voice. "You're leaving in two hours, and you just got around to telling me?" She took a deep breath and controlled her temper. "That's not very considerate. If I'd been planning to go somewhere, I'd have let you know weeks in advance. What would have happened if I hadn't come over here earlier than we'd planned? Would I have walked into your room and found a note?" Instead of answering, he picked up another pile of books and began to sort through them, throwing some into the wastebasket and some onto his bed. He *had* planned to be gone before she arrived. She could see it in the way he was standing, defensive and close with his shoulders hunched slightly. It was a "get off my back" way of standing and it made her . . . furious. Striding over to his side of the room, she confronted him. "Look at me, David. Put those books down and tell me what's going on."

"I don't want a scene, Lucy." Finishing with the books, he picked up a pair of shoes and started to put them in the bag, but she jerked them out of his hand.

"What do you mean you don't want a scene? What are you doing? Why won't you look at me? You've cleaned out your room and it looks like you're moving out. Are you just taking a trip or are you leaving for good? If I'm being left, the least you can do is tell me in so many words." She didn't know what to do with the shoes. She felt silly holding them and silly dropping them on the floor and she didn't want to give them back to him because if she did he would only go on packing.

David took a deep breath. "Shit," he said. "I knew this was going to be unpleasant." He reached for the shoes and took them out of her hand. "I'm splitting. I'm hitting the road and not coming back. Is that clear enough? I didn't want to tell you this way, but you insisted."

"Oh, no," she moaned. She wanted to shake him and make him take it back. "Why are you going? I thought we—" She was going to say *I thought we were in love*, but it was too humiliating.

"I'm going down to Mississippi to register Negro voters." David's eyes were hooded and distant. He wrapped a belt around his hand, secured it with a rubber band and added it to the pile.

She felt panic and incredulity. He was leaving her, just as her mother had left her without a word of warning. "But you're a *senior* and you've got final exams in less than two weeks." Her voice shook, but she managed to keep on talking. "You'll lose your scholarship and you won't graduate, and I don't see how you can leave for Mississippi, not now, not right at the end of the semester."

"Screw my exams, my scholarship, and my Harvard diploma." David grabbed his gray sweatshirt and crammed it into the bag. "I'm a poet not a stockbroker. Besides, one of the great things about this hallowed institution is that it's almost impossible to flunk out. I've arranged myself a 'leave of absence for psychological reasons.' Has a nice ring, doesn't it? If I change my mind and decide that what I really want to do is make a million bucks, I can come back and get my priceless degree from America's number one certifier of the ruling class. But I doubt I'll want to come back."

This was pure self-destruction. He'd spent four years fighting to be accepted at Harvard, and now he was throwing it all away. How could he do this to himself and to her? Didn't he know how much it would hurt? Didn't he care? She bit her lower lip, clenched her fists, and willed herself to be rational, but the wall of logic inside her head wasn't holding. "It's dangerous down in Mississippi." She paced across the room. "Don't you read the papers? Civil Rights workers are getting arrested and imprisoned."

David shrugged, picked up his only tie, and threw it into the wastebasket. "I don't give a damn. In fact I like the idea of danger. Danger's interesting; it keeps the adrenaline flowing. It's what I'm going down there for." He smiled a weird, ironic smile that gave her chills. "I like to think of myself as the Lone Ranger, riding into Mississippi to clean things up."

This was too much! The wall of logic crumbled, and she was suddenly very angry and very hurt. "You're living in a fantasy world," she yelled. "Can't you see that by going away like this you're wrecking both our lives? If you had any real convictions I'd understand, but the thought of you Lone Rangering it into Mississippi and getting your head blown off by some racist redneck makes me sick. You're not making sense."

"You still don't get it, do you?" he yelled, picking up a book and slamming it down on the floor.

"No, I don't. All your reasons stink! I want to know why you're leaving; why you tried to sneak out without seeing me. I want to know what's going on."

"Okay, you asked for it." He pointed at her. "There's your reason: it's you, Lou. I'm leaving *you*. *You're* the reason I'm going to Mississippi." He began to pace around the room waving his arms in a way that frightened her, but she held her ground. "I'm not a fanatic about Civil Rights. I could go to a lot of places: Denver, Mexico, even Europe. But Mississippi is where it's happening at present." He pointed at her again. "I need something to wash you out of my mind. You, Lou. *You*. Danger might just do it, and Mississippi is about the most dangerous place in the country at present. If I still lived in Somerville I'd probably join the Marine Corps, but that's a five-year hitch, and I never knew a woman I couldn't get over in six months."

"Stop," she commanded. "Be quiet. I don't understand why you're attacking me like this. Why are you deliberately insulting me? It's cowardly and immature. Why do you need to 'wash me out of your mind'?" Her voice broke and she began to cry. She'd never loved anyone so strongly and he was leaving her behind like she was the trash in his wastebasket or the tape on his walls. "I've thought of you as my best friend, and now you're just walking out. Why? What have I done? Why are you doing this?"

"Because it's too much," he mumbled.

"Don't talk in riddles." She wiped her eyes and coughed, trying to calm down because the more she got upset, the more angry and distant he became. He'd pulled the ultimate trick of one-upmanship: he'd withdrawn and left her to do all the feeling. "What do you mean it's too much?"

His eyes were hard. He stopped in front of her and put his face close to hers. "You're pushing me over the edge. Keep this up and I'm going to tell you."

"Tell me then," she demanded, scared but determined. He couldn't intimidate her, and he owed her an explanation.

"Fine, you win. I'll tell you." His eyes narrowed, and he jabbed his finger at her. "It's you. *You're* too much. I started out planning to have a hot little fling with you, but that's not the way it worked out. Somewhere along the way, as we were screwing our brains out, it turned serious, deadly marriage-bound serious. I feel like I'm losing my balls and my self-respect. One more week—maybe one more day—of making love to you and talking to you and I'm going to end up working the rest of my life to make payments on a house in the suburbs."

"That's crazy. I never once tried to get you to marry me. What house in the suburbs? What are you talking about?"

"Don't give me that shit. Let's at least be honest with each other if we can't be anything else. Oh, sure you want wild sex and adventure in your life, and I've given you plenty of that, but you want children too."

She hadn't expected this line of attack. For a second she was speechless. "Is that so terrible?"

"Yes." He put on his peacoat and began to button it. "Yes, it is."

"You always knew I wanted children. I told you that the first time we had coffee at Bartley's." He was taking everything she had confided and using it against her, and it wasn't fair. The hell of it was that she suddenly felt as if she was the one in the wrong. "Is wanting children such a crime?"

"With me, yes."

"Did I ever say I wanted to have kids with you? I knew you didn't want them, but I loved you anyway. I won't try to tell you that I didn't hope you'd change but—" She stopped and looked at his face, at the set of his mouth and the wary expression in his eyes. "This isn't about children, is it? It's about something else. What is it? Have you found somebody else you like better, is that it?"

"I wish to hell I had." He went back to the bed. Grabbing his shaving kit, he began to throw things into it: a razor, soap, a brush, a tube of toothpaste. "Every time we make love I can feel your baby-making machinery gearing up." He crammed his toothbrush into the kit. "Yesterday morning it struck me: if I keep on seeing you, I'm going to end up giving you what you want and giving up everything that ever meant anything to me: my freedom, my poetry, my whole rebellious, unpleasant, bohemian, irresponsible attitude toward life." He slammed the shaving kit in on top of his shoes, drew the strings of the duffel and tied them in one quick motion.

So it was his freedom; so that was it. Lucy sat down on the bed and put her hands over her face. She couldn't say that he hadn't warned her. *I go back and forth: wanting money one day, wanting freedom the next.*

Tomorrow I just may wake up and put on my traveling boots. He'd said that the first time they'd had coffee together, but she hadn't listened, hadn't wanted to understand. Some instinct told her that she had perhaps one more chance to talk to him before he left. She forced herself to stop crying. When she looked up he was still there waiting for her to say something. "David," she spoke slowly, choosing her words with care, "I'll be honest with you. I admit I've fantasized about us having . . . children together. I think that whenever women are in love they do that. I think that perhaps it's instinctive, that it's part of our passion. But I've always been rational enough to see that it wasn't what you wanted. I swear I'd never trick you into marriage. I have too much pride to do that, and too much sense to think that it would work. I don't want to limit your freedom, and I don't want anything from you that you don't want to give me."

"Lucy, that's just the problem." He started to touch her, and backed off, as if she were too hot. His hand hovered in the air for a moment; then he dropped it to his side. His face was gray and there were small beads of sweat on his upper lip as if at last he were feeling something. "I do want to give it to you. The house, the kids, everything." That was the last thing in the world that she had expected him to say.

"Oh." It was more like a cry than an exclamation. "I don't understand you. I don't understand you at all."

"Let me make it simple for you." He swallowed hard and his eyes seemed to tighten. "I love you. I wish to hell I didn't, but I do, and that's why I'm getting the hell away from you before I do something I'll regret for the rest of my life."

He had never said he loved her before. She stared at him, caught between delight and the crushing realization that this was his exit line. "You say you're leaving me because you *love* me?"

"I didn't expect you to understand. Women aren't constituted so that they can grasp things like this."

He was as confused as she was; he had to be. He wasn't making sense and he was hurting himself and her and this wasn't necessary because together they could solve it or turn it aside. This was a waste of love and life, and he might even get himself killed. Getting to her feet, she stood and put her hand on his shoulder, and her fingers trembled. "David," she said quietly, "you're right. I don't understand. But there are two things I do understand: I understand that I want you to stay; I understand that I want us to go on loving each other."

"I can't do it." He shrugged. "Sorry." He blinked, pressed his lips together, bent down and kissed her lightly on the cheek. "Good-bye. Take care of yourself." Then he turned, threw his duffel bag over his shoulder, picked up his guitar, and walked out the door.

It was as quick as that. In the blink of an eye he was gone. The room was empty. She stood for a moment as if someone had knocked the breath out of her body. She heard the sound of his feet on the stairs, the sound of the door closing after him. A stereo was playing somewhere in the distance and the shouts of a ball game filtered up from the banks of the river. I will not run after him, she thought. I will not throw open the window and call his name. If he wants to leave me, then let him go, damn him.

Walking over to the phone, she lifted the receiver. She was going to call Cassie and tell her the news, but she never got beyond the first three numbers because she started to cry again. Rushing back to the bed, she picked up the corner of the sheet and stuffed it into her mouth so the four Harvard students in the suite next door wouldn't hear her. David was gone; he had left her, and he was never coming back. She hated him for leaving her, she wanted him back, she cursed him and blessed him and pleaded with him and told him off.

A half hour later, exhausted and dry-eyed, she walked out of Dunster, got on her bicycle, and rode back to Radcliffe.

• 4 •

The hills of Palo Alto, California, were golden brown under the hot summer sun, and the air was hazed with heat and smog, but the architects who had built Dr. Henry Constable's office had taken summer into account. Inside the brown stucco building on Camellia Avenue, the air conditioner hummed away quietly, making the air semi-arctic. Lucy, who sat behind a gray metal desk updating patients' files, wore a yellow sweater over her white cotton dress and kept a pair of socks in the bottom drawer to pull on over her nylons when she turned blue from the cold.

She had been working for her uncle in one capacity or another every summer for four years, starting in 1960 when her father had died of a heart attack. It was lonely work because the regular secretary always took her vacation while Lucy was in town, and Uncle Hank spent most of his time at his lab doing research or at the hospital directing an experimental neurosurgery unit, so the office itself often seemed rather deserted. On the other hand, she had plenty of time to think.

For the most part she enjoyed spending her summers in California, but sometimes, on days like today, when the air conditioner was cranked up full blast and the walls of the office seemed to be closing in on her, she thought wistfully of the sweeping horizons of Wyoming and Utah. Every year her father had rented a place in the country to celebrate her return from boarding school, and from June through August the two of them had spent their weekends hiking, riding, and even on several memorable occasions trying to herd cattle. They had climbed mountains, camped out under the stars, eaten cold beans from cans, swapped stories around campfires, and enjoyed a sense of freedom that Lucy had never found anywhere else, not in Palo Alto and certainly not in Cambridge.

This morning, as she sat conscientiously putting her uncle's records in order, she found herself thinking about those summers and about her father. She had been missing her dad a lot lately, remembering small things about him: the way he talked to the horses when he put them away in the barn, the tuneless songs he whistled to himself when he was caught up in some important project, the look of surprise and pride he always gave her when she got off the train or the plane, ready to spend another summer with him, as if he couldn't quite believe that she had changed since the last time he'd seen her.

"You've grown a mile," he'd say, as he reached for her suitcase, and she'd nod, embarrassed the first few times because it seemed to her that a grown-up should know that children didn't stay the same, and then as she got older and began to think of herself as a young lady, she would be a little annoyed with him because, for heaven's sake, of course she was maturing.

In the winters, when she was at boarding school, he had written to her once a month, drawing pictures in the corners of his letters: a sketch of a new dam he was building, horses grazing by a campfire, a stand of aspens . . .

His last letter had been postmarked April 28, 1960. A week later, she had been called out of Latin class to find Uncle Hank and Aunt Kate standing in the hallway next to the head mistress, everyone looking pale and grim. She hardly knew her uncle, having only seen him on four occasions, each time for less than a week, but she knew at once why he was there, and she was crying before he told her the news, feeling her father slipping out of her life and a great coldness rushing in. *Oh, oh, oh,* she had cried, in inarticulate grief. Uncle Hank and Aunt Kate had stood there awkwardly, waiting for her to get over the first shock, and when she finally stopped making a scene they had both looked relieved. They immediately invited her to come and live with them in the summers, and having no alternative she had accepted.

They meant well, no doubt, but she had needed something more, something neither of them was capable of giving her. They were polite, generous, well-meaning people, but they were childless and reserved; it would have been hard to get close to them even if she had had the energy to try. That first summer in Palo Alto, she was numb with grief. She helped out her uncle in a daze, moving mechanically, glad for any distraction. She had kept her father's picture on her bureau all that summer with a vase of fresh flowers in front of it: roses mostly from Aunt Kate's garden; some wild poppies, until she found out that it was against the law to pick them; surprise lilies in August, blue and round and . . . It had been a sentimental thing to do, perhaps, but she was only fifteen.

She shook her head, trying to stop the river of nostalgia, but it kept rolling along, carrying her with it. Ever since David had walked out on her six weeks ago, she had felt very alone in the world, and although remembering her father made her feel a little less lonely, it was a dangerous indulgence, because attached to every good memory of him was the memory of his death. *Stop this right now,* she ordered herself.

What she really needed was not old memories, but someone to talk to, but Cassie, who had shepherded her through the first weeks of the split-up, was spending the summer at Harvard with Andy, working in Halliwell's lab, and as for Uncle Hank and Aunt Kate, as usual they meant well, but subsequent summers at their house had made her no closer to them, and they weren't the kind of people she felt comfortable confiding her pain to, especially not the kind of pain she had been feeling about David. It was a gnawing pain, one that turned the whole world slightly gray, and although she was doing her very best to shake it, it persisted. Nights were the worst. Sometimes she lay awake, going over that last conversation, trying to figure out if there was anything she could have said that would have made things turn out differently. Worse yet, she dreamed about him. Either way, it was a dead loss.

Taking a sip from the Coke that was perched on the desk beside her, she looked at the two postcards from Ann Barrows that she had tacked to the bulletin board. The cards, postmarked Matoon, Mississippi, both depicted the same large, red-brick courthouse surrounded by blooming magnolia trees. Quite a beautiful scene until you noticed that next to one of the quaint iron park benches was a drinking fountain labeled Whites Only.

The entire back of the first card was covered with Ann's feathery scrawl.

Dear Lucy,
 You can't believe what it's like down here. I'm teaching in a Freedom School. Most of the Negro children in Matoon can't read or even write their names, but they're smart and making tremendous progress. We had two bomb threats last week and someone slashed Steve's tires, but we're learning techniques of passive resistance, singing to keep up our spirits, and have even started a voter registration training center. Mississippi may be dangerous, but it's the most exciting place I've ever been in my life.

The second card, which was unsigned, bore the cryptic announcement "Steve and I got married. What do you think of that?" Lucy finished her Coke and looked out at the palm fronds swaying in the wind. The magnolia trees of Matoon seemed ten thousand miles away from Palo Alto. She thought of Ann getting married to Steve, and she thought of the Freedom School, which was probably being conducted this very minute in some unpainted tar-paper shack, and she thought of David, who had not written or called for six weeks, and she felt lonely and bereaved and sad, but that was nothing new.

Putting the empty Coke bottle on the floor next to her purse, she went back to filling in medical records. By cramming fourteen hours a day for two solid weeks, she had managed to pass her final exams with a C average, so she was going back to Harvard next fall. Meanwhile she was trapped on this air-conditioned desert island doing work so routine that a monkey could have taken her place.

Now that was a dreary thought, absolutely crammed with self-pity. Things could have been much worse. Eight more weeks in Palo Alto, and she could go back to Cambridge. Meanwhile the beach was only a half hour away, and the Stanford library was full of enough interesting books to keep her supplied with something new to think about every day for the rest of her life. Cassie called at least once a week from Cambridge; one of Uncle Hank's grad students, a bearded, pipe-smoking fellow named Dan Moore, had asked her to go sailing with him on Sunday, and she had the best tan since the summer of 1953 when she and her father had spent three months living by a mountain lake in northern Utah; not only that, she had survived the breakup with David without becoming hysterical, going into a permanent slump, or doing anything melodramatic or self-destructive.

She picked up the next file, opened it, and sat for a moment staring at the first entry. There was only one catch: Ever since David walked out, she only had felt half-alive. Existence in Palo Alto was about as exciting as the summer reruns on Uncle Hank and Aunt Kate's new color TV. She was just thinking that she absolutely had to do something to shake herself out of this growing numbness when the phone rang.

"Hello, Lou," a familiar voice said. "It's me, Cassie."

"Hi, Cass." Lucy was surprised. Cassie never called in the middle of the day. She always waited until the rates went down. "What's up?"

There was an uncharacteristic silence on the other end of the line. "I've got horrible news for you," Cassie said finally.

Lucy sat up so quickly that she knocked a pile of records off the desk. "What sort of horrible news?" She gripped the receiver imagining car accidents, plane crashes, Andy taking up with another woman. "Are you okay?"

"I'm okay, but have you been listening to the radio?"

"No. Why?"

"Walter Cronkite was just on CBS talking about Matoon." Cassie paused, and in the brief silence between sentences a hard knot of anxiety formed in Lucy's throat. She could hear fear in Cassie's voice. Something very bad indeed must have happened down in Mississippi. It's David, she thought. David's dead and there's no way she can bring herself to tell me the news. She picked up a pen and gripped it so tightly her knuckles went white. Say it, Cass, she thought. Just go ahead and say it.

On the other end of the line Cassie took a deep breath. "Four members of the Harvard Coalition are missing. Cronkite said that it looks like a repeat of Goodman, Schwerner, and Chaney."

The names sent a chill up her spine. She grabbed the pen tighter. Her mind turned in circles, and everywhere it turned there was something worse to imagine. Schwerner, Goodman, and Chaney: their names had been on the front page of every newspaper in the country. Three missing students, and what had happened to them God only knew—God and the Ku Klux Klan. President Johnson had sent two hundred unarmed sailors into Mississippi to search for the three civil rights workers, but so far not a trace had been found, dead or alive. The South was a trap, and David had gone down there of his own free will. He was a reckless fool, and she was angry with him and afraid for him and for herself because the horror of it was slowly creeping over her. I have to ask Cassie who's missing, she thought. I have to ask her now. "Who's missing?" she said. She was amazed how calm she sounded. She let go of the pen. It fell back on the desk and rolled to one side.

"Three Negro students: Allen Randall, Rick Hill, and Mark Johnson, all from Mississippi." Cassie came to a full stop and took a deep breath that was clearly audible over the three thousand miles that separated them. "Oh, hell, I hate to tell you this, Lucy, but you're going to hear it on the radio anyway. The fourth missing student is David."

"Oh my God." Lucy was so frightened that she could hardly speak. She looked at the postcards of Matoon, the magnolia trees, the courthouse, the water fountain with its threatening sign. Missing was only one step from dead.

"Calm down, Lou. Try to hear me out. There's more. The governor of Mississippi is claiming that the four of them are just hiding out to get publicity."

"What!" Lucy rose to her feet, thinking of the governor sitting safely in his mansion while David and the three Negro students lay in some shack being terrorized and threatened. "That's outrageous!"

"Right," Cassie said. "My reaction exactly. The hell with him and the FBI too. They can't find anyone."

"What are we going to do? What, for God's sake? I can't stand here and listen to you tell me that David is missing and not do something!" She walked out the length of the phone cord, over to the window where the palm fronds were still rustling in the wind and the sun was still shining as if nothing had happened. "I suppose I should hate him, Cass. I suppose I should. He left me flat, and I suppose I shouldn't care what happens to him, but—" But I still love him, she was going to say, only there was no need to say that because Cassie knew.

"Lucy, calm down and listen to me. I got through to Ann Barrows on the phone, and she says that every civil rights worker in the state is combing the swamps and forests looking for them. She says more people may get shot and that it's a war zone down there and that we can't possibly comprehend what's going on and she's begging us to come down and help out any way we can."

"We'll go." Lucy spun around and walked back to the desk. "Of course we'll go."

"Of course."

Lucy relaxed her grip on the receiver and began to breathe more normally. The decision was something she could grab on to. Cassie was with her. Not only with her, but ahead of her. Plans had been made, Cassie explained. Andy had already gassed up his car and checked the oil, and the two of them had packed and were leaving Cambridge that night. The trip would take about twenty-four hours, thirty on the outside. Lucy should fly to New Orleans to meet them, not Jackson. "People coming to work with the Coalition have been trailed from the Jackson airport and had the shit beaten out of them," she warned Lucy. "Ann says the hostility in Mississippi is unbelievable."

Lucy felt sick at the thought of David being trailed and beaten. Reaching out with her free hand, she ripped the evil-looking postcards off the bulletin board, wadded them into a ball, and threw them in the wastebasket. She would hate brick courthouses and magnolias for the rest of her life.

"We'll meet you Wednesday morning," Cassie concluded.

"Wednesday," Lucy agreed, "in New Orleans." After she hung up the phone, she put her hands over her face and sat for a moment, appalled by the strength of her obsession with David. God help me, she thought. If he's dead I'm going to mourn him as if I was his widow, but I'm not. Sure he said he loved me, but he ran away from that love. He went to Mississippi to get me out of his system, and if he's still alive, all he wants is to forget he ever met me. He doesn't want me; he wants his freedom. Why can't I get that through my head? Why doesn't it make any difference to me?

At seven on Wednesday morning, Andy and Cassie met her at the New Orleans airport looking completely exhausted from the long drive. Cassie was wearing a wrinkled denim skirt, sandals, and a bright orange blouse, and Andy had on a Harvard T-shirt and jeans. Lucy, who had done her best to dress anonymously, frowned anxiously when she caught sight of them, and then decided that it didn't really make any difference. In a town as small as Matoon, there was no way they were going to cut a low profile, especially not in a VW Bug with Massachusetts plates.

The traffic going into New Orleans was heavy at that hour of the morning, so they stopped in the French Quarter to wait it out and have some breakfast before heading east toward Matoon. Over an exotic meal of grillades, grits, and chicory-flavored coffee, they tried desperately to reassure one another that there was nothing to worry about.

"David will be okay," Cassie proclaimed. "I can feel it in my bones."

"Right," Andy agreed. He pushed his glasses up on his nose nervously, reached for the sugar, dumped two heaping spoonfuls on his grits, tasted the results, and grimaced. "By the time we get to Matoon, chances are the four of them will have shown up with some cock-and-bull story that will make David come off sounding like James Bond."

"Maybe they got stoned, or lost, or their car broke down where there's no phone," Lucy speculated. But she convinced no one, not even herself. Ever since she had stepped off the plane, a cold fear had begun to envelop her. No one in New Orleans had done David any harm, but the accents all around her were southern, and when she spoke people looked at her strangely. She felt as if she had entered enemy territory, and if she felt this way here, how was she going to feel in Matoon?

Conversation faltered. They ate the rest of their breakfast in silence, staring at the lacy balconies and the flowers in Jackson Square, afraid to meet each other's eyes.

Once they left Louisiana and crossed into Mississippi, the road deteriorated into a strip of worn asphalt full of potholes. They drove on steadily through cloying humidity without stopping again for anything but gas and sandwiches. It was pretty country, lush, filled with birds and flowering vines and small family groceries that advertised Moon Pies, RC Colas, and exotic things like frozen chitlins. From time to time they passed large houses surrounded by groves of oaks bearded with Spanish moss, but more often they drove by tumbledown shacks with refrigerators abandoned on the front porches and dismantled cars rusting next to wooden outhouses. When they turned north, away from the gulf, the cane fields disappeared and pine forests began to replace the stands of bald-headed cypress. Mile by mile, the earth took on a rich red hue that reminded Lucy of blood.

At noon, just as they were coming into a little town named Tullo, Cassie turned on the radio to catch the news, and they learned that the bodies of two of the missing members of the Harvard Coalition had been found in a pine forest about a hundred miles west of Matoon. The announcer spoke of outside agitators and said the names of dead students were not going to be released until their next of kin were notified.

Lucy's face went white. She clutched the back of the seat and tried to breathe. She felt as if a heavy weight were pressing against her chest, pushing all the air out of her lungs. "Cass, they've killed David; I know they have."

Cassie's face was grim. "Don't say that," she begged. "Don't even think it. They didn't give any names. David could be alive."

"Where is he then?" But there was no answer to that question, nothing except the frightened look on Cassie's face that was like an echo of her own. Hunching herself into a ball, Lucy crawled into the far corner of the backseat and forced herself to shut up. She could feel the terror rising around her. It came off the asphalt in waves, like the heat; it was in the smell of the honeysuckle and the faces of the children who played beside the road. Andy pulled a Nehi from the ice chest and gave it to Cassie, who opened it and handed it to her, but the terror was in the drink too. The smell of the cold orange liquid made her sick. She was so scared for David, for herself, for all of them.

The day grew hotter and hotter until they felt as if they were breathing warm syrup. Around one-thirty they spotted a tall white water tower with the word MATOON emblazoned on it, and ten minutes later they were driving down Main Street past the red-brick antebellum courthouse whose picture had hung for so many weeks on Lucy's bulletin board. The magnolia trees weren't in bloom, but the fountain was still there, and the Whites Only sign sported a new coat of paint. To their left a row of small shops dozed under a long wooden roof that covered the main sidewalk. Through the open doors of Mirabeau's Hardware Store they could see rakes, axes, and bins full of nails. In Stark's Drugs and Sundries, wrought-iron chairs and tables rested in the semidarkness under revolving fans. Three or four mud-splattered trucks and cars were parked in front of the combination grocery store and post office, and next to the gas station a mule stood patiently hitched to an iron-wheeled wagon. The benches in front of the courthouse were occupied by old men in overalls who were passing their time talking and playing checkers.

Lucy looked at the stores and the men and the cars moving lazily down the dusty street, and shuddered. She could feel the town closing in around them. From time to time, she checked the rearview mirror, just in case, but nobody was following them. Not yet.

"What century are these people in?" Cassie exclaimed as they halted for Matoon's only stop light. She gestured in the direction of the mule. "It looks like nothing's changed around here since before the Civil War."

"Think again," Andy said grimly. The old men on the benches had abandoned their checkers and were looking at the Massachusetts plates on Andy's VW Bug with unconcealed hostility. Andy put the car into low gear and crawled cautiously away from the stop light, and Lucy could feel the hatred following them all the way down the street.

* * *

The Coalition had its headquarters in a house on the far edge of town. It took them a long time to find the place because they didn't dare ask directions, so it was well past two-thirty before they pulled up in front of the overgrown yard. The house, which rested on brick piers, sagged alarmingly. Painted five or six different faded colors, it seemed to have been cobbled out of a half dozen abandoned shacks. The front steps were made of cinder blocks, the porch pieced together from torn, mismatched screens. A tire hung from an oak tree, wash fluttered from a makeshift clothesline, and two scrawny cats lay on the porch swing. In the driveway Steve's new Plymouth sat with its windshield broken and its tires slashed.

"Good grief." Cassie leaned forward and clutched at the dashboard. "Will you look at that. What a welcome mat."

Lucy looked at the disabled car and felt another wave of paranoia. Throwing open the door of Andy's VW, she climbed out of the backseat and ran up the front steps. The porch creaked under her feet and the cats scattered. Lifting her fist, she pounded on the front door repeatedly, but no one answered. "Ann," she yelled, "Steve, where are you? It's us. Answer the door. It's us."

A tattered lace curtain moved at the front window, and two women's faces appeared, one black and one white. With a start Lucy realized that one of the faces belonged to Ann. The last time she had seen Ann, her skin had been soft and pampered, adorned with expensive makeup; now Ann was sunburned almost beyond recognition. The two women stared at Lucy warily, then Ann let out a cry of welcome.

"Lou!" The door opened and Ann catapulted herself out onto the porch, threw herself into Lucy's arms, and hugged her as if she never meant to let go. Lucy hugged back, trying to get used to Ann's altered appearance. Gone were the fancy skirts, the expensive silk blouses, the cashmere sweaters. Ann wore rough, unfamiliar clothes: muddy boots, faded jeans, a man's work shirt. A torn red bandana was wrapped tightly around her head, and her nails were bitten to the quick. Cassie and Andy came up the front steps, and Ann hugged each of them in turn and began to cry.

"Hold on," Cassie murmured, "we're here now. Calm down, Annie. You're okay."

"I'm sorry." Ann wiped her eyes roughly on the sleeve of her shirt.

She grabbed the hand of the small, fierce-looking Negro woman who was standing beside her. "I want you to meet my friend Mavis Jeffers; she teaches with me in the Freedom School; I don't know how I would have survived the last few days without Mavis."

"How do you do," Mavis said, shaking hands all around. She wore a crisp blue cotton blouse, but her face was worn and discouraged. "Welcome to Matoon; I wouldn't wish a trip to this place on my worst enemy, but welcome because we sure as hell need all the support we can get."

"I'm a mess and I just can't seem to stop crying," Ann took another dab at her eyes, "but we only got the call a few hours ago and I still can't believe it. Did you hear? They're dead: two of the best people in the world. They were so good, so brave; I get crazy thinking about them. They went out to try to persuade the sharecroppers on Lyle Stark's place to register to vote and, oh Jesus, somebody drove them clear to the Homochitto National Forest and shot them point-blank through their foreheads."

"Who was shot?" Lucy demanded. She clenched her fists and dug her nails into her palms. Her head felt jammed, as if it might explode. "Who?"

Ann looked at her as if she didn't understand the question. "You didn't hear the news?"

Lucy shook her head, too upset to speak.

Cassie took one look at her face and knew that it was going to be up to her to explain things to Ann. "The radio didn't give any names. All the announcer said was that two bodies had been found." She shot Lucy a look of compassion. That look said so much about their friendship. I can read your mind, it said. I can ask the question you can't bear to ask. "Is David dead?"

"Oh my God." Ann reached out and clutched Mavis's hand again. "I had no idea they were withholding the names. No, no, David isn't dead. It's Mark and Allen." Her voice broke and she swallowed hard. "Their bodies were found this morning over in the Homochitto. We know Stark and his gang killed them, but try to tell that to the cops. Stark is one of the biggest planters in the county. He has maybe a thousand acres that he works with sharecroppers."

Mavis's face hardened. "Stark's brother-in-law is the sheriff," she said. "His cousin is the circuit court judge; his nephew is the mayor.

The Stark family runs everything. Hell, you can't even buy a tube of toothpaste around here without dealing with a Stark. We'll never be able to convict him of anything, not in this county. But at least David's alive. Not in the best shape, but alive. He's in jail, up in the courthouse in the White's Only Section, charged with drunk driving and grand theft auto, and Sheriff Lorman isn't letting any of us see him on the theory that we'll try to bust him out, which wouldn't be such a bad idea if we could get away with it."

Cassie and Mavis went on talking, but Lucy no longer heard them. David was alive. Neither of the bodies had been his. Sitting down in the porch swing, she grabbed the rusted iron chain and hung on to it as the front yard swam in front of her. David was alive, and she was having heatstroke. She wanted a glass of cold lemonade and ice packs on her wrists, and she wanted to hear that the two Negro students weren't dead after all. She thought of their grisly end, and she was filled with a pity and anger so great that once again she could hardly breathe. She gritted her teeth and watched the ground buckle and the house tremble. She would not faint. David was alive. Thank God.

"Steve and a couple of the other men are in Natchez now identifying the bodies," Ann was telling Cassie and Andy, "but there's no question who it is because, oh my God, they were Negro and that's why the bastards lynched them and shot them and—" She stopped dead. "I can't even say it," she said grimly. "I can't even think about it. Come inside. Have a cold soda. Steve will be back soon. He has some kind of plan to get David out of jail, but he hasn't told us what it is yet. Meanwhile Mavis and I are keeping a vigil, waiting for news of Rick."

David lay on a narrow metal bunk in a cell on the second floor of the Matoon County courthouse looking up at a dirty gray plaster ceiling stained with huge yellow splotches. It was Thursday, maybe Friday. He'd lost track. A cockroach was making its way from splotch to splotch like a small brown boat sailing between islands. He tried to concentrate on the roach, not because he liked them—they were filthy and gave him the creeps and he'd hated them ever since he was a little kid and his father made him go down in the basement to change the fuses—but because if he didn't concentrate on something outside his own body, he would feel the full force of the pain and maybe pass out again giving the bastards downstairs a perfect chance to beat him to death.

The problem was that pretty soon he was going to have to stop watching the roach and go to the can, or rather to the bucket in the corner that served as a toilet, and every time he moved it hurt like hell. He tentatively lifted one arm and fell back with a groan as hot needles of pain ran from his shoulder to his hand. His mind shifted and lurched out of gear, and he tried desperately to hang on to it because he was scared—hell, more than scared, he was terrified—and he knew that the more helpless he got the more he put himself at Lorman's mercy. He told himself for maybe the hundredth time that the sheriff wouldn't hit him as long as he was conscious.

He thought of Lorman sitting downstairs drinking a cold one with Bo Dramer, his cracker deputy. Lorman wasn't your regulation fat-bellied southern cop from the movies but a scrawny little cowardly shit who wore his star like he'd gotten it as a premium in a box of Wheaties: *Sheriff* Lorman, Lyle Stark's brother-in-law, related to half of the Klan members in Matoon County, old buck-toothed Lorman with his rat face, who was so cowardly that he'd only hit a man who was too hurt to hit back. Not all that different from his own father when you thought about it.

Thinking how much Lorman was like his old man gave David a burst of energy that he didn't know he had, and he managed to crawl out of bed and use the bucket. His urine was still tinted with blood, and he had to hold on to the wall with his good arm because he kept having waves of black and red like when he smoked too much Acapulco Gold, only he was in pain now and not high and he'd give anything for a joint or even a couple of aspirin to dull the pain. At the very least he figured he had a sprained arm, maybe a concussion, and from the looks of it kidney damage from where Stark and his pals had kicked him with their goddamn boots.

He felt a little crazy standing up at all because it hurt so damn much, and he wondered if he'd ever heal up again and if the pain in his balls would ever go away, and he imagined how he must look, every inch of him bruised, cuts all over his face, a tooth missing, and for some reason the thought of himself looking so bad made him start to laugh, but then he thought of Mark and Allen and Rick, and the laughter crumpled in his throat because he was almost sure they were dead, and he'd liked them a lot, and what had happened to them could happen to him any time.

Staggering back to the bunk, he sat down and began to run over the events of the last few months, trying to keep them in sequence because someday if he survived this he would tell the story to the world in a series of poems: poems that would make the revolutionary poetry of Guatemala look tame, poems that would send Stark's gang to prison for the murdering bastards they were. He promised himself that he'd yell those poems from the rooftops if he had to, or better yet write them into song lyrics and get someone real heavy like Bob Dylan to sing them.

He spread his fingers and began to count. Fact number one: he'd come to Matoon two months ago with Steve and half a dozen other members of the Coalition and they'd spent the first six weeks setting up the Freedom School and the voter registration drive. It had been hard going, but everyone had been full of big plans, like registering so many Negroes that they'd carry the county in November, and it had been a blast at first, swaggering around town staring down rednecks. Oh, sure, he'd felt the danger, but he'd liked the smell of it, and when the local Negroes warned them that they were in for trouble, that had just made it all the more exciting. He'd enjoyed telling them that the time for being afraid was over, that he and his friends had come to help them to a new future. God, the arrogance of it. He was ashamed now of the lectures he'd delivered, because those people had been right. They'd known the score. While he was prancing around like the Lone Ranger, they'd been trying to warn *him*, and had he listened? Shit no. Instead he had driven out to Stark's plantation every couple of days or so with Mark, Rick, and Allen to try to convince Stark's sharecroppers to register to vote.

Fact number two: on Monday night they were halfway to Possum Slough when they were ambushed by armed men with pillowcases over their heads, not that David had the slightest doubt who the men were. The men—there'd been seven of them—had taken Allen and Mark and Rick away at gunpoint, and when David had tried to stop them, they'd beaten him senseless with the butt ends of their shotguns. Fact number three, and this was the hardest part to remember: he had come to at the wheel of a stolen car, smelling of moonshine. The car had been smashed into a tree, there was a gun on the seat beside him, and Sheriff Lorman was standing at the window, pistol drawn, grinning like a weasel. It was all so obviously a frame-up that for a minute he couldn't believe they actually expected him to take the charade seriously, but when Lorman jerked him out of the car and handcuffed him, he knew it was for real and that they had him.

The sound of footsteps echoing down the corridor of the jail jerked David back to the present. He struggled to his feet and backed up against the wall and waited, wondering if Stark and his buddies had come back to finish him off while Lorman looked the other direction, but to his astonishment he saw Bo Dramer, Lorman's deputy, entering his cell with a tray of food.

" 'Evening, asshole," Dramer said, putting the tray down on the end of the bunk. "Here's your supper." David stared at the food in amazement. There was half a roast chicken, sweet potatoes, green beans, corn bread, and coffee. Shit, what kind of trick was this? In the four days he had been in this hole they'd only given him water and grits and meat so rotten it had made him sick to look at it. A prickle of fear climbed his backbone. Maybe Lorman had decided to shoot him and this was his last meal. No, not likely. Lorman wasn't the kind to mess with last meals. If he'd wanted to get rid of him, he'd just as soon shoot him and say he was trying to escape. So what was the food for? He eyed it suspiciously and his mouth watered. Chicken, and a lot of it too, but what kind of sucker would he be if he reached for it? You didn't grow up in Somerville without learning about taking candy from strangers. What did you do, you shithead, he thought as he glared at Dramer. Poison the stuff?

Dramer slouched up against the wall, extracted a pouch of tobacco from his pocket, and proceeded to roll himself a cigarette. Lighting a match on his butt, he took a long drag, looked David over, and chuckled. "Hell, you look like something the cat dragged in. Eat it before it gets cold, boy. It won't kill you."

Keeping one eye on Dramer, David reached for a piece of chicken, gobbled it down, and then reached for another. Every movement hurt, but he was so hungry that he didn't give a damn. Dramer stared up at the ceiling and began to whistle tunelessly as if waiting for something.

Five minutes later, after David had finished off the chicken, beans, and sweet potatoes, he found out what that something was. Under the cornbread was a small square of yellow notebook paper. Pouncing on the note, he unfolded it and read:

> David—don't give up. Money talks in Matoon. We've bought you this meal and we're going to buy your way out of jail. The "Good Old Boys" are demanding a stiff price, but Steve's selling his car and we're going to raise the money, so hang in there. We all love you.

He had to bite his tongue to keep from letting out a whoop of joy. His friends were going to save him! He wasn't going to die in this hole! Please, God, let it be true because he wanted out so badly. He didn't have the makings of a hero or a martyr. He read the note again, overwhelmed with gratitude. He knew it was authentic because it was in Ann's handwriting; he recognized the little circles over the *i*'s that she always made and the slanted crosses on the *t*'s, so it must be for real. They must have bribed Dramer to bring it in on his supper tray, which meant maybe that they really could buy his way out.

He tried to fold the note back up, but his hands were shaking and he could feel himself coming apart. When Stark and his thugs beat the shit out of him, he had cursed and yelled at them the way he'd yelled at his old man, but this hope was more than he could take. Letting the note drop to the floor, he put his hands over his face and began to cry with relief.

Dramer picked up the note and stuffed it into his shirt pocket. "You Harvard boys are real pansies," he said contemptuously. "Lord, I don't know why your mamas ever let you come down here to Matoon to make so much trouble."

· 5 ·

The day David was released from jail the air was thick and damp, filled with small biting flies and a musty sunlight that lay in the streets of Matoon like stale water. Lucy, Cassie, and Andy stood on the curb in front of the courthouse for over an hour, swatting at the flies and making nervous conversation as the local people walked by giving them hostile glances. Everything felt explosive and dangerous. The minutes crawled by. Finally, around two-thirty, the courthouse door opened, and Sheriff Lorman came out leading David. When Lorman saw the three of them waiting, he smiled and spit a wad of tobacco juice onto the ornamental hedge.

"Y'all can have him," he said, giving David a shove.

The shove didn't look like much, but David nearly fell. He seemed dazed and unsteady. Catching at the cement banister, he limped down the courthouse steps, blinking at the hot sunlight. His face was swollen and bruised almost beyond recognition.

"Look at him!" Lucy cried. She was shocked by the sight of his face; it made her furious and a little crazy. "What did you do?" she yelled at the sheriff. "Did you torture him like you tortured—"

"Cool it," Cassie whispered, grabbing her arm. "David is alive and that's all that counts. Shut up, or we'll have to buy you out too, and we don't have the cash."

She was right: they didn't have the cash. It had taken over $2,000 to bribe Lorman and Dramer to let David out of jail and drop the charges against him. Steve had even bought a new set of tires for his Plymouth, driven it down to New Orleans, and sold it, but for a moment Lucy didn't care about being safe or reasonable or even about surviving.

"I can't stand it," she cried, trying to jerk her arm loose. "I can't stand to keep quiet when they've—"

"You have to stand it," Cassie commanded. "Now shut up, for God's sake." Lucy finally came to her senses and gave up trying to fight Cass, who had a grip of iron. She was right: protest would be suicidal.

David shuffled closer and stopped in front of her. "Hi, Lou," he said in a shaky voice. One of his front teeth was missing and there was a cut over his left eye. He reached out and put his arms around her, and they hugged each other silently. Lucy's eyes filled with tears; she held on to him, pressing her cheek into his shoulder. She loved him with a fierce, protective love that filled her whole body. He was so weak, so thin; the bastards must not have fed him.

David released her and stepped back. "Let's get out of here," he whispered. He looked as if he might collapse, and even his voice shook. Lucy nodded, not trusting herself to speak. Draping one of his arms around her shoulder, she helped him the rest of the way to the car. He was heavy and she staggered under his weight, but when Andy tried to help, she waved him away. David was hers.

They walked slowly, past the water fountain and beds of obscenely bright flowers. All the way down the sidewalk Lucy could feel Lorman standing behind her fingering his gun, looking for an excuse to arrest all of them. "Just a little farther," she whispered. She propelled David toward the car without looking back. He stumbled and she caught him, and she saw gratitude in his eyes. Andy opened the door, and the three of them helped him into the car. They had blankets and pillows and bandages and food and even a cold six pack of beer waiting for him, and she realized that it had been crazy to put together so much stuff, but she didn't care because this way David could see how much they cared about him. Sliding in beside him, she took his hand in hers.

"I still love you," she whispered. "I never stopped." It was a confession that she had never intended to make, but the words flowed out of her spontaneously.

David gripped her fingers weakly like a small child. "I don't deserve your love, Lou."

"Don't say that. Who cares who deserves what."

"I need you." He clasped her fingers more tightly. "I never should have left you. I was a stupid, selfish fool." His voice trembled. "Forgive me, please."

"Of course I forgive you." She kissed him on the cheek, gently so as not to hurt him any more than he was already hurt. His suffering moved her. He had been cruel and foolish, but he had paid for it. She thought of the pain he had caused her when he walked out, the weeks of loneliness. It had been a rotten summer, a summer to be forgotten as quickly as possible. They'd put it behind them, start fresh.

Andy shifted the car into first gear, pulled away from the curb, turned left, and the courthouse disappeared from sight. Opening one of the beers, Cassie offered it to David, but when he tried to drink it he couldn't. He complained that the coldness hurt the stump of his tooth.

When they got back to the Coalition House, a debate began that lasted most of the afternoon. Everyone, including Lucy, wanted David to leave town right away, but he refused to go anywhere until Rick was found. For hours they pleaded with him, but for someone in such bad physical shape he was amazingly stubborn. From three until six, he sat in the porch swing with his arms folded over his chest, not saying much except no, and "I owe it to Rick to wait." Finally they gave up, held a house meeting, and reassigned the bedrooms. Steve and Ann agreed to move out of their room in the back of the house and throw their sleeping bags down on the side porch, which had some tattered screens that might keep the mosquitoes out. The living room was already being occupied at night by six of the men, and the two minuscule upstairs bedrooms were filled to capacity by the women.

That afternoon Ann and Steve moved out—not much of a job since all they had were two suitcases—and David and Lucy moved in. The room was spartan, furnished with a cheap white iron bedstead, two broken chairs, and a tall, battered dresser with three cavernous drawers that either stuck fast or pulled out so quickly that you fell over backward trying to get to your underwear. The walls were fly specked, the light unshaded, and the screens had holes large enough to let in possums, not to mention mosquitoes and flies.

After apologizing for being too weak to help, David stretched out on the bed with his shirt off, drank bourbon, and watched Lucy unpack. On a chair beside him sat a bowl of beef broth that he didn't touch, but she could hardly blame him for drinking whiskey instead of eating because he was still in pain from the beating they'd given him.

She wrestled with the dresser drawers and scrounged up coat hangers. They talked about nothing in particular, and she was happy to hear his voice and surprised how content she was just to be in his presence. When she was finished, she walked over to the window, pulled aside the curtains, and stared out at the heavy, black Mississippi darkness. Crickets dinned softly in the tall grass, and from time to time a bird gave out a long, unfamiliar cry. The night was so smooth that it reminded her of a huge pond of still water.

"The moon looks like a sliver of bone," she said.

"That's a nice way to put it." David took a sip of bourbon. "Maybe you should be the one writing the poems."

"I remember when I was a little girl, my mother used to look at the moon and say that it didn't matter where on earth you lived, the moon was the same everywhere." For once the memory of her mother came to her without causing pain. She felt deeply peaceful and happy. She ran her finger lazily along the ledge of the window and watched the moon.

David put down his glass. "Come over to my side of the bed." She walked over to his side of the bed and sat down carefully so as not to jar his arm, and he examined her for a moment with a peculiar expression on his face. Picking up his glass, he drank the last of the whiskey. "How about taking off your blouse. I'd do it myself only I can't manage the buttons with one hand."

She was surprised. "Is this an invitation?"

"You bet it is." Reaching out with his good arm, he caressed her shoulder, running his fingers in small circles over her skin. She pulled away, feeling anxious and ambivalent. She wanted him, and yet he was so fragile-looking she was afraid if they made love it might hurt him. "I thought you were too sick for this kind of thing." She tried to keep her voice light and casual, but she was trembling with excitement.

"Don't tease me," he commanded, "kiss me."

She held back for an instant more, trying to resist him, but she didn't have the strength to do it, not even for his sake. Leaning forward, she kissed him, softly at first, then passionately. His lips sought hers, and she felt his breath quicken. "Mmmm, that was first-rate," he murmured. "Do it again."

She did it again, and then again, and it was like launching herself into sweet, dark water. That night they came together again as if they had never been apart. All the old scars were healed. Afterward, falling asleep in David's arms, Lucy felt as if she had finally come home.

Cassie had been known to observe on occasion that life was like photography: every stage had a cosmic negative filed away somewhere waiting to be developed. So it came as no surprise to her that while Lucy and David were putting their relationship back together, things in the Coalition House were going to hell. A week passed with no word of Rick, and the atmosphere grew more and more tense. You could almost hear the Coalition crumbling, little pieces of it dropping away hour by hour. No one knew what to do. Should they keep searching the swamps around Matoon? continue the voter registration drive? organize a demonstration? write their congressmen? or just face facts, give up, and go home?

On the twelfth of July things came to a head. The day started out pleasantly enough. That morning around eight, Lucy and Andy pulled out of the driveway, with David comfortably folded into the backseat. They were on their way to New Orleans to get David's arm X-rayed. It had taken much persuading before David would agree to see a doctor, and Cassie was relieved that he didn't change his mind at the last minute. She saw them off and then went over to help out at the Freedom School, which was still limping along with five children and a half dozen out-of-date textbooks. After class, she spent a good two hours in the swamp photographing unusual plants. It was a fruitful expedition, and she even managed to snap a shot of a huge snapping turtle sunning itself on a log, so she came back to the house in a particularly good mood, washed up, and went in to dinner whistling under her breath, only to find the entire Coalition sitting around the table like mourners at a wake. Her first thought was that Rick's body had been found, but five seconds of listening to Steve and she knew what was the matter.

When she came into the dining room, Steve was standing at the head of the table making a speech. All the white Coalition workers—Meg, Tim, Ann, Loreen, Carl, Frank, Jeff, and Candy—were hanging on his words like a line of cobras swaying to the snake charmer's flute, but Mavis, Francis, and Oden—the three remaining Negro students—seemed unimpressed, if not openly hostile, especially Mavis, who was a veteran of the Birmingham freedom rides.

Steve was a handsome man, broad-shouldered with a square chin, a long, aristocratic nose, and curly brown hair, and Cassie had noticed on previous occasions that when he spoke people acted as if they were hearing marching music or listening to an angel handing out the truth, but tonight his charm wasn't working. A heavy silence hung over everything, and his words were falling into it, breaking up and disappearing. Cassie could feel him fighting for control, but the magic was gone.

"The South was founded on the blood of slaves," he proclaimed, waving his arms. "It was conceived in violence, born in violence, and it is violent today."

"Right," Ann murmured. The day David was let out of jail, she had taken a T-shirt and silk-screened two fists on it, one black and one white.

"The violence is institutional, the violence is governmental, the violence is federal and local, the violence is . . ."

Cassie sighed, sat down, and helped herself to some fried potatoes. She wished he would stop speaking in slogans, but he never did. Even when he was right, she had trouble agreeing with him. Tonight, she had to admit he was in top form, but it was clear that only half the people at the table were listening. The other half was glaring at him over glasses of melting iced tea, stabbing at slabs of fried ham, muttering as they helped themselves to sliced tomatoes, string beans, and slaw.

Steve's eyes were filled with a passionate intensity that sent a chill down Cassie's spine. If she hadn't known better, she would have been convinced that he was on the verge of crying or running wild. "Because Rick is black, the FBI is going to call off the search and send the federal marshals home." Steve leaned forward, hands planted flat on the table, trailing a cloud of light and excitement behind him. You could feel the level of discontent and anger rising in his wake. The white members of the Coalition shifted and murmured, and something scary began to fill the room, making it seem close and small and airless. "Are we going to let them get away with this?" Steve demanded. "Well, are we?"

"No!" Ann exclaimed. She raised her fist to match the fists on her shirt and her eyes sparkled and she opened her mouth, as if she were excited or being kissed, as if this were the great pleasure of being Steve's bride, the pleasure of cheering him on.

"So what are we going to do?" Steve demanded.

"March," Tim Moore yelled, throwing down his fork and getting to his feet.

"No, we aren't," Steve said, wheeling on Tim, "because marching is for suckers. All a march does is give Lorman and his deputy a chance to turn their dogs loose on us. Don't you people get it? The days of nonviolent protest and civil disobedience are *over.*"

"Hold it right there," a voice called from the far end of the table. Mavis was on her feet, standing stubbornly with her hands on her hips and her chin thrust forward. "I can't listen to this shit for another second."

"Sister Mavis," Steve's voice was smooth and placating, "I can understand your frustration—"

"I'm no sister of yours, Steve." Mavis stared at the white students, one by one, and then she turned back to Steve. "I hear gun talk coming up," she said, "and I won't have it. You understand what I mean, *brother* Singleton?" She leaned forward, past the bread and the salt and pepper shakers, slapping her own hands down on the table so hard that the iced tea glasses jumped. "The Civil Rights movement was built on nonviolence. That's what the Reverend King preaches and that's what we believe in."

Steve shook his head. "I pity you, Mavis. We all know you're dedicated, but you've always been a minister's daughter and you always will be. Face facts. If you turn the other cheek in Matoon County, you get it shot off. How many more Civil Rights workers are going to have to be murdered before you realize that it's time for us to defend ourselves?"

"Bullshit!" Mavis yelled. "I'm tired of your violent fantasies. You start carrying guns and you'll be like the Klan: just another mob of white vigilantes taking the law into their own hands. And who'll get shot?" She pointed to the black Coalition members. "Us, that's who."

"How about Rick? How do you feel knowing that he's out there somewhere with swamp water in his mouth?"

"Even if Rick's dead, guns won't bring him back to us." Mavis glared at Steve. "You know what I been thinking lately? I been thinking you white kids should go back North and leave the South to us. Go home, Steve, and clean up your own mess. You come down here making fool plans to arm yourselves, getting people hurt. And another thing: you don't even recognize your own prejudice."

"Who are you calling prejudiced?" Steve yelled. "I gave up everything to come down here, dropped out of Harvard, cashed in half my stocks, risked my life."

"*You*, fool! That's who I'm calling prejudiced." Mavis's eyes snapped, and she clenched her fists angrily. "You act like God or something, coming in here, telling us how to run our own liberation."

"I'm not going to honor that kind of provocation with a reply," Steve yelled. "I'm not trying to run anyone's life, white or black. I'm just pointing out that if we have guns, those crackers will think twice before they try to ambush us again."

Cassie looked down at her plate and tried to blot out the sound of Mavis and Steve's shouting match. Lately all the meetings and most meals had deteriorated into fights between the Negro and white members of the Coalition, and this one evidently wasn't going to be any different. She was very upset by the turn the Civil Rights movement was taking. She wished Lucy and Andy were here, but they weren't due back until tomorrow.

Steve was still haranguing Mavis about how they had to carry weapons to defend themselves. The scary thing was, the more you listened to him, the more convincing he sounded. She was just thinking that maybe she could slip out the back door unnoticed, when the phone rang.

"Somebody answer that," Steve ordered. He hated to be interrupted when he was in the middle of a fight. Eager to escape, Cassie got up from the table, walked into the kitchen, and picked up the phone.

"Hello," an unfamiliar voice said, "is this the Harvard Coalition House?"

"Yes."

"This is Dan Carson, Mississippi station chief for the FBI." There was a long pause and a rustling of paper. "I'm sorry to tell you that our men found Richard Hill's body about half an hour ago near Natchez." Cassie stared at the phone, too stunned to reply. "Hold on a moment, please. We're connecting up to Washington. The president's aide would like to speak to you."

Rick's death briefly reunited the Coalition for the last time. Despite their strong internal disagreements, no one could let Rick's death pass without protest, so phone calls were made, reporters contacted, signs constructed, banners sewn. A week after Rick's body was found, on a warm Saturday afternoon, the Coalition staged its final mass demonstration. For forty-eight hours beforehand, Civil Rights workers from all over the South poured into Matoon to march on the courthouse. By Friday they were over two thousand strong, and by Saturday morning there were either four or five thousand of them depending on who was doing the counting. Along with the demonstrators came reporters, film crews, half the Mississippi Highway Patrol, a heavily armed unit of the National Guard, and a specially trained team of German shepherds.

As the demonstrators marched down Main Street eight abreast, arms linked, singing "We Shall Overcome" and "Keep Your Eyes on the Prize," Bob Mirabeau and Lyle Stark stood at the entrance to the hardware store handing out ax handles and baseball bats, but although there was violence in the air, it never materialized. The tear gas grenades were never launched, the water hoses remained coiled in the fire trucks, and not a single shotgun was fired. Rick Hill's mother walked the six blocks to the courthouse and presented a petition to the mayor demanding that her son's murderers be brought to justice, and the mayor, to everyone's astonishment, accepted it from her and even made a brief speech reassuring her that everything possible was being done.

After that things more or less fizzled out. Since there were no riots or confrontations to film, the television crews packed up their cameras and left. The demonstration broke up into groups of tired, hungry people; the National Guard and the Highway Patrol departed, and the ax handles went back into the barrel at Mirabeau's Hardware. By seven o'clock, except for some paper cups in the gutters and a few stragglers sitting on the curb in front of Stark's Drugs and Sundries, Matoon was back to business as usual.

The morning after the demonstration, David was sitting on the porch swing in a bad mood, full of self doubts and second thoughts. It seemed the more he recovered his health, the worse he felt about everything. Back in Cambridge the danger in Mississippi had seemed exciting, and he'd headed for it like a fool, with a head full of old cowboy movies and half-digested fantasies, but the deaths of Mark, Allen, and Rick had purged the romance out of violence for him forever, and now, hour by hour, he felt more disillusioned and more cynical. He had gone from believing in everything to believing in nothing, and his head sometimes felt as if it were slowly filling up with a cold fog. So, to distract himself he had been trying to learn to whittle, which you would have thought was easy enough the way the locals picked up a block of wood and turned out birds and flowers and whistles and so forth, but all he'd managed to do so far was to sharpen the end of a stick to a point, cutting himself twice in the process.

The screen door slammed and he looked up to see Steve and Ann emerging from the house loaded down with suitcases and rolls of bedding. "Hi," Steve announced. "We're leaving."

David put down his block of wood and folded up his knife. He wasn't the least surprised somehow that Ann and Steve were getting out, and even less surprised that they hadn't told anyone in advance. The two of them had been separating themselves from the group for weeks, forming a little movement of their own based on Steve's cockeyed theories of armed revolution. All of which were completely screwed up and ridiculous because David would bet that Steve didn't know which end of a gun to put the bullets into. They're just armchair revolutionaries with trust funds, he thought, looking them up and down. He felt a little disgusted, and he thought of his uncle back in Somerville, an ex-marine who could have pinned Steve to the wall with one finger. "Where are you going?" he asked.

Ann shifted a pillow from one arm to the other and got a better grip on her suitcase. "We don't have any idea," she smiled, "but we want you to come along with us."

"That's an appealing invitation." David's voice was heavy with sarcasm but Ann didn't notice. He gave the porch swing a push. "I like the idea of going off to nowhere land, but the problem is I don't think we'd travel all that well together." He could see Ann standing there, waiting for him to mention Lucy, but he didn't. She probably thought she knew why, but she was wrong.

Ann smiled again. "I wouldn't say that. I'd say given recent past experience, we'd all get along wonderfully."

Steve put down his suitcase and took a deep breath, and David knew by the way his eyes went bright around the edges that he was about to become irresistibly convincing. "The thing is," Steve pushed his hair off his forehead, "the thing is that, like it or not, it's time to break up the Coalition. As I said a few nights ago at that dinner you missed, nonviolent protest just doesn't work anymore. Take yesterday's demonstration for example: we put every bit of our resources into it, and it didn't make more than thirty seconds on the national news. If one demonstrator had gotten clubbed or a snarling dog had charged Rick's mother, we'd have gotten international coverage. I don't think it was pure luck that things went so peacefully. I think someone has been giving Lorman and his boys advice about not making any more martyrs."

David pushed the swing back and forth a few more times and thought this over. "So you're for drawing blood to get a longer spot on the six o'clock news?"

"Not necessarily, but if it takes violence to attract the attention of the press to the justice of our cause," Steve shrugged, "we may not have many other options." He leaned forward as if confiding some great secret. "We're going to have racial equality in this country, even if we have to impose it by force."

"I don't see how I fit into this." David gave the porch swing another push, thinking that Steve was one of the most power-hungry people he had ever encountered. That was what happened when you were born filthy rich. You got the message that you could run the world any way you wanted to. Screw 'em, David thought. "I'm a coward at heart," he told Steve. "Guns make me nervous, Singleton. I couldn't shoot one if I had to."

"Don't be ridiculous," Ann said briskly. "You're no coward. You're hurt and disillusioned, anyone could tell that. For the last two weeks, ever since you got out of jail, you've been moping around here looking like you didn't know what to do with yourself. Well, we've got something for you to do."

David looked them over: Ann with her overstuffed two-hundred-dollar leather suitcase; Steve with his L. L. Bean sleeping bag and his Italian knapsack. He wondered what would happen if they ever had to work for a living instead of sapping off their parents, and he wondered how long they'd survive once their trust funds were cut off and Daddy stopped answering the polite letters requesting non-interest-bearing loans. They were about as practical as two tropical parrots about to migrate to the Yukon. A fine pair of underground commandos they'd make. Ann would probably have a breakdown and turn herself in to the cops as soon as she ran out of toothpaste.

Ann came over to the swing, sat down beside him, and looked at him coquettishly. "So are you coming with us or not?"

"Afraid not, Annie." Her face fell, and for a second he felt almost sorry for her. He imagined her waking up every morning with only Steve to talk to. Living with him would be like being forced to listen to records of the great speeches of Winston Churchill twenty-four hours a day. No, going with them was out of the question. His Somerville survival instincts told him that Ann and Steve were heading straight for big trouble. On the other hand, the more he thought about leaving Matoon, the better the idea sounded.

Lunch that afternoon was a gloomy event. The demonstration seemed to have left everyone in the Coalition with a hangover, and

Steve and Ann's sudden, unannounced departure had created a void that no amount of conversation could fill. David ate silently, not looking at anyone, gulping down his ice tea and swallowing his sandwich automatically. Lucy could tell that something was on his mind, but she didn't know what. Finally he wadded up his paper napkin and threw it onto the table.

"How about a walk?" he suggested. He paused and looked away from her, out the door at the heat rising up off the front lawn. Picking up his glass, he took a last swig of tea. "We have to talk."

She knew at once that whatever he had to say wasn't going to be pleasant to hear, but she had come a long way from the naïve girl who had let him walk out at the beginning of the summer, so she put on a hat to keep the sun out of her eyes, laced up her tennis shoes, stuffed her anxiety back into the farthest corner of her mind, and suggested they stroll down to the creek.

The creek was one of her favorite spots. Green and clear, it flowed into shallow pools that reflected the pine trees; the bank was cool, and she always found it soothing. On the walk down the hill, they talked about superficial things: the weather mostly and how it always seemed to be about to rain. But once they got to the creek, David fell silent. Taking off his shoes and socks, he sat down on a rock and put his bare feet in the water. He let the current swirl around his ankles for several minutes as he gazed into the shadows under the rocks. A stranger looking at his face would have assumed that he was checking the creek out for fish, but Lucy knew better. She waited for him to say something, but he just sat there with his lips pressed together and his chin set. Everything about him was pale, even the scar on his forehead.

"Lou," he said after much too long a silence. "I hate reruns, but that's what we've got here."

She felt a twinge of panic. Picking up a stick, she began to scratch in the mud with it so that she would have something to do with her hands. "What do you mean?" she said, making her voice calm and even, making it like the water.

Another long silence. He took a deep breath. "The Coalition is breaking up. In a few days, a few weeks at the most, everyone will be gone. I hate wakes. I can't stand them. I—" He cleared his throat and looked at her angrily as if he were feeling guilty and it was her fault.

"Hell, let's stop beating around the bush. I'm getting out while the getting is good, and I'm not asking you to come with me."

His words hit her like a physical blow. Surely he wasn't walking out on her a second time, not after he'd opened her up and gotten her to love him again! The pain of this second betrayal was worse than the first, but she clung to her pride and sat dry-eyed, determined to play it differently this time. She resolved not to panic or get upset or plead, because pleading had gotten her nowhere. "I didn't think you were the quitting kind," she said in a low, even voice. She drew a circle in the mud, enclosed it in a square, and then added another circle. "I thought you were the Lone Ranger."

Her sense of humor surprised him, and he flashed her a weak smile. "Oh, I am, under usual circumstances."

"Mind if I ask what made you decide to turn in your black mask and your stash of silver bullets?" She drew furiously in the mud, her hand trembling: circles, squares, triangles—a whole labyrinth with the two of them at the center. It seemed to her that she had spent her whole life being abandoned, first by her mother and now by him. She felt overwhelmed by the loneliness of having tried once again to love someone who was willing to walk out on her.

David was silent for a moment. "In the aftermath of getting the shit beaten out of me by Stark and his buddies," he said, "I had a mystical experience: it was revealed to me that I don't give a damn about politics." He cleared his throat again and looked away from her, down at the water and his bare feet and the dark, sliding shadows of the creek. "Somewhere between Possum Slough and the Matoon jail, I realized that I'd gotten involved with the Civil Rights movement for all the wrong reasons. Back in Cambridge it all seemed so simple: I'd go down to Mississippi and clean the place up, but it hasn't been a heroic experience at all. There haven't been any silver bullets or faithful Indian guides. The whole mess has been stupid and cruel and tragic." He turned toward her, his face white, lips tight, and she thought that she had never heard him sound so bitter. "Let other fools risk their asses for high ideals; if Steve is right and American society is too corrupt to be reformed by peaceful methods, then I don't want any part of it." He picked up a stone and flung it into the water. "I'm like that stone, detached from the continent, seceding, as of now. In the future you can think of me as David Blake, a rebel republic of one. I'm dropping out, not halfway out this time but all the way, and I'm heading for California to do what I should have been doing all along—write poetry."

Lucy took one more look at the labyrinth and made a decision. She wasn't six years old anymore; she didn't have to sit around like a victim waiting for the front door to close and the sound of her mother's footsteps to fade out forever. Tossing the stick into the water, she brushed the mud off her hands. "Fine." She turned to face him. "When do we leave?" She heard the bravado and denial in her voice, but a current of stubbornness rose up in her and flowed through her, sweeping her along with it. This time she wouldn't let him get away with leaving her, and that was all there was to it.

"What do you mean 'we'?"

"I'm going with you, of course."

"Oh, Jesus, didn't you hear me tell you that I wasn't asking you to come with me? Don't tell me you thought for even a minute that it was possible." He seemed sincerely surprised.

"Of course it's possible. You don't think I'm going to let you walk out on me again, do you, not knowing what I know."

"What is it that you know?"

"That you love me."

"What does love have to do with anything?" he yelled in exasperation.

"How can you say that! Love is what gives life meaning. It's rare and delicate, and you can't go kicking it around every time you get an urge to take a vacation!"

He pulled his feet out of the water and began to put on his socks, muttering something about the impossibility of making women understand simple things. "We have different priorities, Lou. We're from two different planets talking two different languages. Love may be the center of your life, but it isn't the center of mine."

"I don't believe that."

"Fine," he snapped. "Then I'll make it brutally clear: I *don't* love you and I never have. I'm incapable of it."

"I don't believe that either! I know you meant it when you said you loved me. You may have left me, but you meant what you said. Now you're denying it to drive me off. But it won't work, David. I won't buy it."

He put on his shoes, tied them with angry, rapid motions, and glared at her. "Let's get one thing straight: you aren't coming with me."

"Try to stop me," she yelled. "Buses are public; trains are public; if you hitchhike, I'll be there beside you with my thumb in the air; take a shrimp boat to Panama, and I'll book the same passage."

He stood up. "You know what? You're driving me stark, raving mad. You're the most unreasonable, fanatical, stubborn woman I've ever met. Sometimes when I'm around you, I feel like you've jabbed a fishhook into my jaw."

She leapt to her feet and stood in front of him, not giving an inch. "I'll take that as a compliment. It's true except I'm not reeling; you're swimming toward me with every ounce of strength you have. I'm your salvation, David. I keep you from falling into that nasty little black pit at the center of your being, the one you're always running away from in your poems." She picked up her hat and sat it firmly on her head. "Let's go back to the house. I know you're in shock over Rick's death and the whole mess down here, but after a while you'll recover, and when you come to your senses, you're going to be glad to have me for a companion."

That afternoon, Cassie was stomping through the swamp outside of Matoon with her camera slung around her neck, dressed in a straw hat, a pair of heavy denim coveralls, and a long-sleeved shirt to keep off the clouds of mosquitoes that rose in swarms from the muddy water. A swamp was a rich visual environment, and she usually enjoyed her afternoons walking around in the mud more than most people would have enjoyed dinner at a fancy restaurant, but this particular afternoon she was so preoccupied with her own thoughts that she never once took a photograph.

Three things were bothering her: in the first place, the discovery of Rick's body and the departure of Steve and Ann had everyone in the Coalition House so on edge that it was like living in a zoo; in the second place, Andy had driven back to Cambridge to get some things in order before the term started, and she was lonely without him; and in the third place, well, in the third place, she had some more bad news for Lucy, and frankly she was getting sick and tired of being stuck in the role of evil messenger.

Thinking that she should have left with Andy instead of staying behind to give Lucy moral support, she sat down on a log, took a peanut butter and jelly sandwich out of her pocket, and munched on it while she considered her alternatives: Should Lucy be told what David had been up to, or should she be allowed to go off with him and find out for herself? Leave well enough alone, Quinn, she thought. Don't be such a busybody. Take Andy's advice and let Lucy and David work it out without sticking your nose in where it doesn't belong. The peanut butter was dry and the bread was stale, and it made her feel about a hundred years old to be so sensible. Throwing the remains of the sandwich into the swamp, she watched it sink into the ooze.

The hell with reason and logic, she thought. This is a matter of friendship.

"Lucy," Cassie ordered, "sit down. There's something I think you should know, and I don't think you're going to want to be standing up when you hear it."

Lucy sat down in the only comfortable chair in the living room: a big, brown, overstuffed recliner from Sears that Steve had bought on his father's credit card. She was wearing a white blouse, white shorts, and white tennis shoes, all white like a sacrificial lamb, Cassie thought, and a beautiful one at that. Damn David for not appreciating her.

Folding her arms across her chest, Lucy looked at Cassie speculatively. "Well, what is it, Cass?" she demanded. "Are you about to try to persuade me not to go off with David, because if you are, save your breath. My mind's made up."

Cassie ran her fingers through her hair, fluffing it up into even more of a mess than it was already. "I'm not trying to persuade you of anything. I just think you should know the facts." She sat down on the footstool so their faces were level, nose to nose like two cats about to get into a fight. "Nobody is going to tell you this but me, and I'm only telling you because you're my best friend. It's David. He's been—well hell, I don't know how to put it without being my usual crude self—but he's been screwing around." She saw the shock and hurt fill Lucy's face, but she went on, determined that if she had to be cruel she'd do it all at once. "For example, he's been sleeping with Meg off and on all summer, and that didn't stop when you showed up."

Lucy gasped. She hadn't been prepared for this, hadn't even suspected it. It was like a punch to the stomach.

"Not that he was miserly with his attentions," Cassie continued. "He's also been sleeping with Candy for sure and probably with Loreen, although Loreen's not talking on the subject. Believe me, all of them were pretty pissed when they found out he'd been making the rounds. Only Mavis seems to have had the sense to turn him down. She told me she didn't want to belong to his collection."

"I don't believe any of this." Lucy hunched down in the chair and glared at Cassie, who was being cruel and irresponsible and who wouldn't shut up. The thought of David sleeping with other women made her sick. Her mind reeled back and forth, and her thoughts came in fragments: what if? . . . no, never . . . but maybe . . . no, impossible. She would have known. "Be quiet," she hissed at Cassie. "Stop this. You never did like him, and now you're trying to make me turn against him, only it won't work!"

"Fine." Cassie sat back. "I didn't think you would let yourself hear me, but I thought it was my duty to tell you anyway because you're making a complete fool of yourself insisting on going away with him." She leaned forward. "Everyone in the Coalition knows about David's love life except you. You're an object of pity. How does that sit?"

Lucy glared at her even more fiercely. "Not very well, to be frank. In fact I could easily hate you for telling me this." She clenched her fist, making her body into a wall, shutting out everything Cassie had told her, but somewhere deep inside her, the pain of being betrayed was already boiling up, scalding and terrible. What if it was true?

"Hate me then." Cassie waved her arms. "Loathe me, spit when you say my name. Only do me a favor: stop tagging along after David, stop making yourself into a laughingstock. You're talking brave, but I can see that you're completely desperate, and as your best friend, I'm begging you: take care of yourself."

David was in the kitchen making himself a sandwich with the last of the cheese and half of a dried-up red onion. On the counter beside him stood a jelly glass half full of whiskey; from the expression on his face, the other half of the glass was already inside him. Lucy stood in the doorway for a long time trying to pull herself together. She felt upset at the sight of him, but she was so quiet that he didn't notice her.

"David," she said, and then like a fool she started to cry. "Is it true? Is it?"

"Is what true?" He grabbed two slices of white bread and slapped mayonnaise on them, still not looking at her.

"Cassie tells me you've been sleeping with Candy and Meg." The names burned her tongue and she felt humiliated reciting them.

"Cassie should keep her damn mouth shut." Cheese on the bread, pickles, onions, lettuce; he grabbed the sandwich, slammed it together, and cut it in half.

"Please," she begged, "just tell me it's not true and then we can forget it. I have to know." She wiped her tears away and tried to smile as if maybe this were all a joke, but there was a shadow on his face that froze her, and she suddenly knew that there was not going to be any easy denial.

He took a bite of his sandwich and a swig of whiskey. "Yes, it's true." Another swig of whiskey. "I've been sleeping with them. So what?" He felt defiant. All day she'd been giving him trouble, and his patience was at an end. Also, he was slightly looped, which made him reckless. He wasn't going to lie. She should be grateful for that because how many other men would give it to her straight? But he knew she wouldn't be. "Why shouldn't I sleep with two, three, or even four women at the same time?" He took another sip of whiskey, wiped his lips, and scowled, annoyed that he'd let her corner him. "Give me one good reason why I shouldn't; they're both great girls, and if you have to know the truth, I write better when I'm on the make."

With a cry of pain, she walked across the room, grabbed the glass of whiskey out of his hand and slammed it down on the counter. "I can think of plenty of good reasons: you lied to me; you betrayed me; you made me into a fool." She was crying openly now, hurt and ashamed and angry. "I know we aren't engaged, but I thought we had an agreement—"

"Well, you thought wrong." He retrieved the glass and took another sip of whiskey, thinking that she had no right to force him to defend himself. "I made a mistake being faithful to you for as long as I did." Since she'd brought this up, she'd just have to hear the truth, and if it hurt her, well, that was too bad. He'd be damned if he'd make false excuses. "I don't believe in monogamy." He took another sip of whiskey and flourished the glass. "I believe in freedom. Lovers shouldn't try to own each other; they shouldn't treat each other's bodies like private property."

"What is this, David? Karl Marx goes a-wenching?" The more hurt she was, the more sarcastic she became, but it was a sarcasm born of desperation. She was holding her own, but inside she felt as angry and hopeless as that six-year-old child who had stood in another kitchen and watched her mother walk out the door forever. She thought of the good times she and David had had together, of the intimate conversations, the passionate lovemaking. Hadn't that meant anything? Was she just a convenience? Was she just part of his collection?

David finished off his whiskey and threw the ice cubes into the sink. "Nice comeback," he said quietly, "very witty, and not all that far from the truth. I have to hand it to you, Lucy, you've got a way with words. And you're right; the bourgeois family *is* a training ground for capitalist oppression—a fact that you'd be able to see if you weren't already so enmeshed in it."

She couldn't look at him anymore. Walking across the room she stared out the window at the backyard: piles of rusty tin cans, a tangle of blackberry briars and kudzu vines. She felt strangled by anger and pain. She put her forehead against the screen and the threads bit into her flesh. Stop crying she commanded herself. Stop. But she couldn't. The tears flowed down her cheeks, bitter and salty. She thought of her mother again, of long, hot summer afternoons like this one when she had sat by herself in the backyard, a lonely, frightened child, wishing the world would change, but the world never had. "I just don't understand. I just don't see how you could seem to care so much for me when we're in bed, and so little when we've got both feet on the floor."

"Let me make it easy for you." David poured himself another glass of whiskey and took a long chug. It was the best moonshine in Matoon County, and he knew if he drank enough of it, the expression of betrayal on her face would cease to bother him, fade out slowly and pleasantly like a sunset. The whiskey lay warm in his belly, and he felt himself becoming more tolerant. "I do care about you in my own idiosyncratic way." Now that was a generous remark and he hoped she appreciated it. "But like I told you two months ago, I don't believe in marriage or commitment or in anything that ties a man down. We never should have gotten back together, but I was sick and vulnerable when I got out of jail, and I was stupid enough to let you take care of me when I should have been taking care of myself." He chugged more of the whiskey, realizing he was drinking the stuff much too fast but not giving a damn. "But nothing has changed," he continued. "I started sleeping with Meg to get you out of my system, and when that didn't work, I tried Candy. I don't want to love you, and if I have to put twenty women in your place to quit being hung up on you, then that's what I'm going to do. I'm sorry if that sounds cruel, but that's just the way it is."

"It is cruel!" she cried, turning toward him. "Incredibly cruel! Why couldn't you at least have told me about Meg and Candy? Everyone knew and I didn't. My God, I was such a fool." Her face burned with the shame of it. "Why?" she said. "Just tell me that."

"Odd as it may sound, I didn't tell you because I didn't want to hurt your feelings." He smiled, feeling generous. The dirty yellow walls of the kitchen looked like fresh butter, and even Lucy's face seemed to soften. He had the impression that he had just said something good and noble, but evidently she didn't agree.

"Oh, you're the soul of consideration." She hated herself for sounding so sarcastic and bitter, and she felt for the second time that summer as if all love and all hope were dying inside her. "But at least you're getting what you want." Walking over to the counter, she picked up the whiskey bottle and refilled his glass. Her hand trembled and whiskey spilled out onto the floor. Circles within circles and the world never changed. Not when you were six, not ever. "Here," she said, "drink up and celebrate your freedom. Leave whenever you please. I won't be coming with you."

• 6 •

Lucy opened her notebook, wrote *October 10, 1965*, at the top of the page, and settled back to listen to Professor Henry Jordan. Jordan was a short, balding man who looked as if he should be selling used cars, but he was one of the world's leading experts on child psychology, and his Monday-morning lectures were always packed.

"So far we have discovered only two things that children are instinctively afraid of," Professor Jordan told the assembled students of Social Relations 150, "loud noises and falling. Things that might distress an adult—like snakes or fire—are of no interest to an infant. As far as we can tell, a healthy baby will cheerfully pet a tiger or curl up next to a cobra without a second thought."

Lucy put all this down in her notes, underlining the words *loud noises and falling* with a red pencil and drawing a star in the margin. Jordan's thrice-weekly lecture was one of the reasons why she was glad she'd changed her major from English to psychology. Around her, some two hundred Harvard and Radcliffe students scribbled away furiously. Leaning back, she gnawed on the end of her pen and thought about the limits of human innocence. If fear was something you learned, then maybe evil was also an acquired trait. And if evil was learned, then maybe it could be unlearned. She thought about the three children she was tutoring twice a week—two girls and a boy, ten, nine, and twelve, none of them more than barely literate. Their lives, from what she could tell, were full of the most uneventful, grinding poverty: parents always out of work, never enough money for new shoes or decent clothes, educated up to this point in their lives—if you could call it being educated—by overworked teachers who had used such advanced pedagogical techniques as breaking rulers over their hands and throwing erasers at their heads to get them to shut up. Was it possible for her to make a difference in their lives? By working with them for four hours a week could she unteach failure, give them confidence, restore them to that innocent state where all they had to fear was loud noises and falling? She certainly hoped so.

Jordan continued his lecture with charts and statistics, but she had stopped listening. Instead of taking notes, she began to write a fantasy letter to David.

Dear David,
    If you could see me now, you'd be sorry you left. I'm in great shape, look wonderful, and am doing useful things with my life. I spent last year dating so many guys it made my head swim, and even now when

I've tried to cut back a bit to get my academic act together, they keep calling. My grade point average has gone from C to A−; I survived Statistics and Animal Behavior, and am about to write an honors thesis on learning problems among children of welfare recipients. Cassie and I have moved to one of the off-campus houses on Garden Street, so I can pretty much come and go as I please. I'm happy, I'm successful, I'm . . .

. . . still missing you like a lost leg or an amputated arm, still mooning over you, dammit. Ripping the fantasy letter into fantasy shreds, Lucy threw it out without a backward glance. She was getting better at nipping these attacks in the bud. For the first nine months after he left, she had written him real letters, addressed to his home in Somerville, but at least she'd had enough pride not to mail them. Now all that remained were the fantasies, and if she kept her wits about her, not many of those. Picking up her pen, she began to take notes again in a neat, well-organized hand. Bill Bishop, who was still laboring away on his doctoral dissertation, had resurfaced in her life recently to ask her to a performance of *Winnie the Pooh* in Adams House. Mr. Resnick, one of the house tutors, was playing Pooh and was reputed to be very funny. Impulsively, she decided to accept Bill's invitation. One thing you could say for Bill: he might be boring but he was reliable, and he gave new meaning to the word "persistent." What other guy would keep asking you out after you'd turned him down five dozen times in the past year and a half? She thought of that afternoon at Elsie's when she had told Bill about David, and he had offered to wait until her "infatuation" was over. Bill hadn't exactly been a monk while he waited; she knew for a fact that he'd had at least two affairs, both brief, both with other grad students, but he had phoned her regularly at least once a month, sent her Christmas cards, and never forgot a birthday.

Thinking about Bill's devotion was a good antidote for thinking about David's lack of it. She grabbed a curl of hair and twisted it around her finger thoughtfully as she reread her notes. Dimming the overhead lights, Professor Jordan began to show slides of young children poised on the edge of steep drop-offs. The drop-offs were covered with glass, but the children had no way of knowing that. Lucy was fascinated by the way the children clung instinctively to the side of the cliff. Too young to talk, they seemed to sense the danger of making false moves better than most adults. For the rest of the hour she didn't think of David once.

At that very moment, out in San Francisco, David was having a mystical-psychedelic-musical experience that was scattering his brains like confetti all around the Mayfair Auditorium. A few months ago the Mayfair had been an abandoned ice skating rink with chewing gum plastered to the walls and cockroaches nesting in the rafters. Now it was competing nightly with the Filmore for the stoned and the high, the lovely and the hip, for all the young groovy people who came to San Francisco to gyrate to the new bands that were springing up like magic mushrooms everywhere in the Haight.

David stood in front of a green plastic garbage can dipping out strawberry Kool-Aid with a paper cup as the beat of the electric guitars sliced through his skin, making the hairs on his arms stand up, making him feel like his legs were strung on wires that were being pulled up toward the ceiling and down toward the floor, making his body feel charged with atomic energy. The Kool-Aid was laced with Owsley's best LSD, and David had already had one cup of it earlier in the evening. Now he was so high that he hardly knew who he was because when he went into the bathroom and looked into the spotted mirror, his face kept melting into all the faces he had ever known in his life: his sister's face, his father's face, even the face of that bastard Sandy Roberts who had thrown him off the *Advocate* back at Harvard three hundred centuries ago, but the face melting didn't freak him out or even particularly bother him because he'd taken enough acid by this time to know that it was a normal effect of the stuff.

Besides, he was too happy to be frightened because the woman on stage was singing his song, the one he'd written for her last week. Her name was . . . what? He searched what was left of his memory and came up with the name Trina, which sounded about right. What he knew for sure was that she lived upstairs from him on Clayton Street with six guys who had hair down to their asses. The seven of them comprised a band called Nickel Lid, and maybe they weren't The Doors, or Jefferson Airplane, or Big Brother and the Holding Company, or even Moby

Grape, but they were pretty good, and David was glad to have Trina up there in her Indian bedspread halter top and fringed miniskirt wailing out his words:

> *Just ask van Gogh!*
> *Just ask Rimbaud!*
> *The two of them knew the way to go!*
> *Open up the doors of perception*
> *Get beyond all deception*
> *Your brain's a jet plane*
> *Taking off for space*
> *Embrace! embrace!*
> *Erase! erase!*

    David sipped the Kool-Aid and watched the light show playing on the wall above Trina's head. There were about ten things going at once: an overhead projector with vast, amoebic splotches of red and purple oil leaping to the music; an old Laurel and Hardy film running half speed so that Oliver floated down a long flight of stairs like a fat angel; a strobe that made Trina's whole body seem to twitch in and out of consciousness; black and white moiré patterns doing a hurricane behind the drummer. If he hadn't been stoned, it would have all seemed like chaos and craziness. But on acid everything took so long to happen that even the strobe seemed stately, and the splotches of oil took forever, like great waves of ice getting ready to crash along a frozen beach.
    Trina finished the song, stopped for a minute, looked out over the audience, and waited for the applause to die down. Then putting the microphone back on its stand, she walked off the stage and came straight toward David. From his perspective she was like a sailboat, getting bigger and bigger instead of closer and closer, her large breasts swelling up and her face expanding as if someone were pumping her full of helium.
    "Well, what did you think?" She tossed her long mane of straight black hair out of her face with a shake of her head and smiled, and he saw that one of her teeth was inlaid with a small skull and crossbones, only maybe that was a hallucination because he couldn't ever remember seeing it before.

"Great," he managed to say. He handed her the Kool-Aid, and she drank it down in one gulp, then handed him the empty paper cup. Nickel Lid was playing a slow tune, and before he realized what was happening, the two of them were dancing together and she was rubbing up against him.

"You write great lyrics," she yelled because the music was loud enough to make your eardrums bleed. Her eyes glowed like two coals, and he was getting very excited dancing with her, only it was a strange, suspended excitement that seemed to be coming right out of the walls. Taking him by the arm, Trina swam him off the dance floor and guided him behind the stage over coils of electrical wires, which looked too snaky for David's taste, and through a door, down a long, dark hall into her dressing room. There was a pile of cushions in the corner. She fell on them and pulled him down after her. He could still feel the music throbbing in his ears, and the dressing room seemed barren and concrete, like a cell, and for a moment, remembering the jail in Matoon, he almost panicked, but then she grabbed his hand and shoved it up under her halter and he felt her nipples growing hard.

"If I ball you, will you write me more songs?" she murmured running her tongue around the inside of his ear. "Man, you write absolutely fantastic, out-of-sight songs, and I could go straight to the top with them."

"Yeah," he said, "sure, Trina. I'll write you all the songs you want." And then some time had passed and he didn't know how, but he had her halter off and her skirt off and they were naked together and rolling around on the cushions and it was great and he got the feeling that their desire was a liquid and they were swimming in it, doing the breaststroke and the sidestroke in an ocean of skin. Only then he made a mistake: he started to get really excited and suddenly the whole thing turned into a cheap lunch stand at Woolworth's, and he remembered too late that this wasn't what he had wanted to do with his life. He had wanted to write poems—important, serious poems about the deaths of Mark and Allen and Rick—only he hadn't been able to. So he'd been writing Trina songs instead, and he didn't want to waste himself on crap like that but his talent had dissolved somewhere in the acid and the dope and the screwing of strangers, and he couldn't seem to call it back.

He closed his eyes, but that only made the bummer worse.

"What's wrong?" Trina asked. She sat up and reached for her halter.

He opened his mouth, but no sound came out and all of a sudden she seemed very far away at the end of a long, dark tunnel that he didn't want to go down, and he was depressed and scared, and for a minute he wanted to talk to Lucy of all people because Lucy would have understood what it was like when the real poems wouldn't come, but instead there was only Trina sitting there half naked looking at him in a disappointed way as if he'd stood her up. A great iron-cold cell of loneliness closed in on him, and it scared him to think he might never write another serious poem, only cheap dope-and-sex song lyrics that Trina or someone like her would sing, and he wasn't sure he could live with being such a sellout.

"I have some news, ladies," Bill Bishop announced as he sat down at the dinner table in Holmes Hall and helped himself to the platter of London broil. He looked, Lucy thought, rather like an English lord slumming it. His suit was a sporty brown Irish tweed that spoke of stomping across the fields at dawn with packs of purebred dogs; his tie, a furl of delicate brown and red silk that she knew for a fact cost as much as the books for Soc. Rel. 150 because she had seen it for sale in one of the expensive men's stores in Harvard Square. He was perfect in every way: blond, handsome, charming—making every woman at the dinner table prickle with desire every time he flashed his blue eyes and launched forth with another witty epigram, every woman, that is, except Lucy, who couldn't help seeing him as good old predictable Bill. She picked at her peas and mashed potatoes, wondering if it had been a mistake to invite him to Sunday dinner. The food at Radcliffe was famously terrible, but he'd taken her to Durgin Park twice this month, and it was unfair to let him go on feeding her without offering something in return, especially since she wasn't providing him with any other entertainment outside of an occasional, unenthusiastic goodnight kiss.

"What kind of news?" Kathy Develt purred. She toyed gracefully with her water glass and looked up at Bill as if she were taking him apart and putting the pieces away for future use.

"I'm getting a roommate." Bill smiled at Lucy and carved himself a piece of London broil. He buttered his potatoes, covered them with pepper, and sat back satisfied and baronial to assess the effect of his announcement. There was a short silence as the four women at the table took in the news.

"Why in heaven's name would you want to do a thing like that?" Joyce Lindsay asked, helping herself to the gravy.

Why indeed? Lucy thought. Harvard graduate students didn't ordinarily have roommates, and Bill had been living by himself since the second semester of his sophomore year when he convinced one of the deans that his mind was too finely tuned to tolerate sharing a bathroom with lesser mortals.

"This isn't just an ordinary roommate," Bill explained. He paused dramatically. "This is the ultimate, *sine qua non* of roommates."

"Don't tell me," Cassie said, shoveling mashed potatoes into her mouth, "let me guess. You've persuaded Norman Mailer to come back and help you edit the *Advocate*."

"Close," Bill nodded, "very close. The man may not be a famous novelist, but he is a prince."

"Oh, come off it," Cassie moaned.

"No, seriously. I'm not speaking in hyperbolic metaphors. He's a prince, plain and simple."

"A real prince?" Kathy DeVelt leaned so far forward that she nearly knocked over the water pitcher.

Bill nodded. "As real as they come. His name is Milarepa Tsayi Koron, and he's the heir apparent to the throne of Patan."

Kathy frowned. "Patan? What kind of country is that? I've never heard of it. Good Lord, I wish someone had made me take geography in my youth. I've only recently been able to find Vietnam on the map, and now you bring up Patan. I know I should be impressed, but Patan sounds like something a girl in a short skirt and white boots should twirl over her head at a high school football game."

"Not *baton*, *Patan*." Bill looked annoyed. "For a girl who's been around the world on her daddy's yacht three times—"

"Four," Kathy corrected.

"Four times, ten, what does it matter? You might as well be living on the moon. Don't you ever read the papers? Patan may be small, but it's as strategically important to the United States as . . ." he sputtered to a stop.

"Rhode Island?" Cassie offered through a mouthful of mashed potatoes.

Bill glared at her. "Very funny, Cass. I can't tell you how much I adore being the target of 'Cliffie wit. For your information Patan is a small kingdom in the Himalayas, between China and India. In the Middle Ages it was on the Silk Road. You can find it mentioned in Marco Polo's *Travels*. It's been closed to foreigners until recently, but now the royal family is hell-bent on modernization."

"I, a humble student of photosynthesis, bow to your greater knowledge." Cassie brandished her fork dramatically. "Forgive me my ignorance. I am but a hunk of blue-green algae floating on a sea of scientific provincialism. Patan sounds great."

"Like Nepal or Bhutan," Joyce observed.

Bill smiled and relaxed, pleased to have finally made his point. "Patan's infinitely richer than any other kingdom in the region," he said, helping himself to the bread. "It has a variety of climates: tropical lowlands along the Indian border that produce silk and rare hardwoods; a middle plateau that's a veritable rice bowl; and mountains that contain at least three fabulously productive gold mines, not to mention diamonds as big as hen's eggs."

At the mention of diamonds, Kathy's face took on an expression of professional interest. "Ah," she said, "then it was probably a good idea to get this prince what's-his-name for a roommate."

"A good idea! Surely you jest, my dear." Bill took a bite of his bread and washed it down with a drink of milk. His lean face glowed with triumph. "It was the coup of the decade, took weeks of the most delicate, diplomatic negotiations. Throwing all modesty to the winds, I can safely say that if I weren't a *summa* in government and Professor K's fair-haired protégé, I never could have brought it off. According to the extensive biography that the Patanese government sent in lieu of an admittance application, the prince has had six royal companions who've been with him from birth and he wanted to stash all six of them in Adams House, can you imagine? We'd have had an oriental court on our hands, not to mention that King Marpa is convinced that his son is going to be assassinated by some crazy group called the Patanese Liberation Front if he isn't surrounded by armed guards night and day. I told the king—or rather the king's representative, because one doesn't address Marpa the Magnificent personally—that it would be hellishly inconvenient to have fellows with machine guns or spears or whatever following the prince to the library. 'His Highness Prince Mila is the son of God,' the lord high nabob of Patan informed me in all seriousness. 'Well,' I told him with a perfectly straight face, 'then he'll be in good company because here at Harvard we have the sons of all sorts of famous men.'"

Lucy laughed along with the others. This was Bill at his best: outrageously snobbish without a shred of mercy. "When does this marvel arrive?" she asked.

"Next Monday." Bill finished off his bread and started in on his peas. "And don't point out to me that it's the middle of the semester, because everyone is quite aware of that. It seems the prince has had the kind of education that makes stepping into Harvard in midstream a piece of cake. According to the biography, he had three wet nurses, one of whom spoke English, one of whom spoke Patanese, and one of whom spoke Mandarin. He's been trained for twenty years in some strange form of tantric Buddhism. He's a math wiz and a chess master, plays the thrum, which is some kind of native harp, to perfection, has read everything ever written in the fields of economics, government, applied physics, astronomy—"

"Stop!" Lucy begged, "you're giving me a headache. He sounds like a living library. Surely he can't be human."

"Oh, he's human enough, all right. Did I mention that the prince also plays world-class polo? Seems that the Patanese invented the sport using the decapitated heads of their enemies, but rumor has it that recently hard rubber balls have come into fashion."

Kathy DeVelt picked up her knife and began to draw small circles in the spilled salt. "What does he look like?" she asked casually.

Bill lifted his eyebrows. "Why, Miss DeVelt, for the first time in years I hear sincere interest in your voice. Are you by any chance calculating the odds of snagging yourself a crown?"

Kathy grinned and put down her knife. "Maybe yes, maybe no." She shrugged. "My parents didn't send me to Radcliffe just to learn about transcendentalism. According to Jane Austen, a single man in the possession of a good fortune is always in want of a wife, and I can think of worse fates than becoming a princess."

"Forget it. The prince is out of your class. In fact he's out of my class." Bill grinned wickedly. "I admire your unconcealed greed—greed, after all is what made this country great—but Prince Mila isn't going to be exactly easy to entrap into matrimony, despite your many obvious charms. The heirs to the throne of Patan are trained from earliest childhood in techniques of lovemaking we mere Harvardian mortals can barely imagine. Traditionally they're given their first concubines at the age of ten."

"Ten!" everyone gasped.

"Bit better than receiving a Lionel train for Christmas, wouldn't you say?" Bill smiled, delighted to have shocked them. Reaching out, he patted Kathy's hand in a patronizing fashion. "Cancel your subscription to *Bride's* magazine and don't even waste your time in fantasy. The only marriage he'll ever make is a marriage of state. His father the king married the raja of Landpor's eldest daughter when he was twenty-eight and she was five. Face it, Kathy, even with all the DeVelt diamonds in your pocket, you're a pauper in comparison, not to mention well over the hill when it comes to age."

"Rats," Kathy grumbled, "just my luck." Cutting herself a large hunk of London broil, she chewed on it thoughtfully.

After dinner Bill and Lucy sat in the common room of Holmes Hall drinking coffee from tiny china demitasse cups the size of thimbles. The demitasse cups were part of Radcliffe's official policy of "gracious living," a program designed by the wealthy alumnae to transform female barbarians from the West and Midwest into ladies of culture. As a female barbarian, Lucy often resented the tiny cups, which made her feel like a clumsy peasant, but the coffee was good and hot and free, and you could have as much of it as you were willing to ask for.

Bill put his feet up on the sofa and looked at her with all the eagerness of a large dog. Gone was the jaded, snobbish facade he'd cultivated so carefully during dinner. "As soon as the prince gets unpacked, you'll have to come over and meet him. How does that strike you?"

"That would be nice." She tried to sound enthusiastic, but it wasn't easy. Bill got at least two thirds of his identity from other people, a fact that made her feel a little sorry for him. Also, to tell the truth, his announcement at dinner had annoyed her. It was obvious that he'd wangled himself a famous roommate to further his own career, but why should she care to meet him? From Bill's description, Milarepa Tsayi Koron sounded like a pedantic, spoiled pain in the ass. She could just imagine him strutting around demanding homage. Well, he wasn't going to get it from her. She valued qualities in people other than wealth and prestige. In her eyes the prince of Patan wasn't any better than the poorest Negro child in Matoon.

"You don't sound very eager," Bill observed.

"I'm not," she admitted. She imagined Yul Brynner in *The King and I* stomping about with his hands on his hips yelling at his subjects. The prince would probably be bald and have a foul, dictatorial temper, and Bill would undoubtedly regret the day he ever agreed to share a room with him.

Bill sighed. "Ah," he said. "I see."

"See what?"

There was a short silence. Bill sighed again and toyed with the end of his tie. "Frankly, I think you're being a snob."

"Me!" Lucy was so surprised she nearly spilled her coffee all over the couch. "How can you say such a thing? Why, I'm the least snobbish person you'll ever meet, Bill Bishop!"

"Not a regular snob," Bill said gently. "I fill that category to capacity, as I'm all too aware. You're a reverse snob. Forgive me if it hurts to hear that, but for your own good I think you should know."

She slammed her demitasse cup down on the end table. "Just what do you mean 'a reverse snob'?"

"Just because the man's a prince, you hold it against him. If he were poor, preferably disabled, with some kind of protein deficiency and a third-grade education, you'd be over there in a flash to shake his hand and welcome him to Cambridge."

Despite herself, Lucy was amused by the description. "Am I as bad as all that?"

Bill nodded. "You're ruthlessly judgmental when it comes to wealth."

She grinned and relaxed. "You know," she said, "you're absolutely right: I am unfair to the rich."

"The rich have their problems like anyone else."

"Sure, like where to park their elephants; which gold plate to eat lunch off of; will the peasants storm the palace today or tomorrow; is caviar fattening?"

"A prince is a person."

She shrugged. "My heart bleeds for him; I may not be able to sleep tonight worrying about his welfare."

"Come over and meet the poor fellow." Bill got to his feet, picked up his tweed coat, and slung it over his shoulder. "Give him a chance. He's never been to the United States before, and he's bound to be lonely, and personally I think the two of us should show him around a bit."

"I'll think the invitation over," she said, kissing him lightly on the cheek, "but I'm not making any promises."

The royal Patanese jet circled Boston lazily, the double gold crowns on its side gleaming in the sunset. Mila, who had ordered this aerial tour, gazed out the window at his new home and was pleased. True, the red-brick buildings looked a bit dirty and worn compared to the clean snowcapped mountains and green rice paddies of the Sindhala Valley, but having been to London several times he was accustomed to the soot and disorder of Western civilization. He liked the signs of industry: the smoke from the factories, the great ships in the harbor. The curve of the Charles River had a pleasing, serpentine grace, and he was fairly sure that the spires and domes clinging to its northern bank belonged to his new alma mater, Harvard. Now if he could only spot the Old North Church, his happiness would be complete.

"Shall I tell the pilot to take another turn, Your Highness?" the steward asked deferentially in lilting Patanese.

"Yes, if it's not too much trouble," Mila said. He was always polite with inferiors, not that he thought of them in those terms. Thanks to nearly twenty years' training in Buddhism, he saw other people as suffering, sentient beings trapped temporarily in mortal bodies. Of course, when he was in a more Western, scientific mood, he was fairly sure that reincarnation didn't exist, which made it all the more important to establish good relations in the here and now. Actually he would have been perfectly happy to do without servants altogether; he secretly longed to wash his own clothes and clean his own toilet, as his beloved Mahatma Gandhi had, and sometimes on hunting trips into the wilds of Patan he had almost reached this marvelous state of simplicity. But unfortunately servants were thrust upon him by tradition. If he refused their services, they'd have no jobs and their children would go hungry. Which was why it was a relief to be going to Harvard where for an entire year he would be an ordinary student without middle-aged men in gold-brocaded jackets bowing to him and offering him slabs of cold pheasant breasts cooked in the five traditional spices.

The plane circled again, and Mila picked out the Boston Common and an ancient sailing vessel that he was fairly sure had to be the *Old Ironsides* of Oliver Wendell Holmes's poem by the same name. Ten minutes later, when the royal jet landed smoothly on the private runway at Logan Airport, there was no crowd of reporters to greet it, no mayor bearing the key to the city, no political candidate exercising his rhetorical skills, no brass band, no red carpet—nothing but a few efficient men in mechanics' overalls wearing orange plastic ear muffs and holding illuminated batons. The reason for this lack of a reception was simple: the plane was exactly twenty-four hours and fifty-six minutes early.

"Please see to my luggage and get me a cab," Mila commanded the startled steward.

"A cab, Your Highness?"

"Yes, please, a taxicab." Mila smiled, picked up the plain Western-style black sweater that lay on the seat beside him, and prepared to disembark. He had no intention of beginning his life as a private person by riding the royal limousine into Cambridge even though his father had insisted that he drag it all the way from Patan in the cargo hold of the plane. Had he been able to work out the complexities of the public transportation system, he would have insisted on taking the MTA, but, alas, all he knew about the Boston subway was contained on a record by an American singing group called the Kingston Trio. Still, he was a patient man; there would be ample time for such adventures.

"I'm sorry," the monitor in the Adams House dining room said to the short, dark-haired foreigner, "but you can't come in here without a tie."

"I beg your pardon?" Mila stopped in midstride. "I don't think I understand."

"A tie, man. You have to wear a tie. Where have you been? You can't even eat breakfast without a tie around your neck. Now, do you want to go back up to your room and put one on, or do you want to wear one of the extras?"

"Please," Mila said politely, "one of the extras would be very appreciated since I brought no ties believing American student dress to be casual in the extreme and not knowing the rules."

"Okay." The monitor tossed a strip of gray material at him. "The extra it is. Here you are, and don't catch typhoid."

Mila looked at this thing that was supposed to be a tie. Surely there was some mistake. The frayed gray wool was splattered with ketchup, and encrusted with other unsavory-looking substances. Gingerly he tied it around his neck.

"Smashing," the monitor said. "You look like a prince. Now pick up your baby tray and head for the scrod."

"Scrod?"

"You're new here, right?"

"Yes," Mila admitted. "This is my first meal in Adams House."

"Well then, let me fill you in on the basics: *scrod* is the past tense of *screw*, and you'll get used to it because we have it about three times a week. Of course, since some rich alum laid an ice-cream endowment on fair Harvard, we have that stuff every single goddam night . . . vanilla, usually."

"Thank you," Mila said. "I appreciate you taking the time to initiate me into the system."

"Don't mention it," the monitor said, waving him down the line. "I'm a Soc. Rel. major, and I can use all the practice I can get. Next."

"Baby trays" turned out to be large disks of cream-colored plastic neatly divided into three separate compartments. The trays served as plates, thus reducing the time and expense needed to wash them. From his architectural training, Mila could see that they were not only efficient, but substantial and particularly well balanced. Sitting alone at one of the far tables, he ate a dinner of overcooked fish and mushy brussels sprouts and tried to calculate the velocity at which one would have to throw the tray to achieve the aerodynamic lift implicit in its structure. American life already appeared to be full of an endless array of practical inventions that he might some day take back to Patan to improve the life of his people.

Humming happily to himself, he measured the plate by spanning his hand across it, pulled out a pen, and made a few calculations on his napkin. Bill Bishop had been wrong. The prince wasn't the least bit lonely.

· 7 ·

On the day Bill Bishop finally persuaded Lucy to meet Mila, it looked like rain. Low clouds hovered in a bruise-colored sky bordered with black thunderheads; the Charles River was a sheet of gun metal winding between brown sooty strips of hibernating grass, but the dozen or so foreign students who were playing a makeshift game of soccer near the Weeks Footbridge seemed oblivious to the fact that all hell was threatening to break loose. Laughing and yelling in five or six different exotic languages, they kicked a black-and-white soccer ball back and forth with the most amazing dexterity Lucy had ever seen. Bill stopped and stood for a moment contemplating the soccer game with an ambiguous smile that Lucy couldn't quite read. "Pick out the prince," he suggested.

She frowned and studied the soccer players romping on the riverbank. Three of them were obviously black African students, and two were blond—German, perhaps, or Danish—which left some seven possibilities, but as soon as she thought about it she knew that only one of the seven could be the prince: a short, burly, mean-looking fellow who was slamming the ball around with the aggressive force of a pile driver.

"That one," she exclaimed, pointing triumphantly, "the testosterone case in the crimson sweatshirt."

"I'm disappointed in you, my dear; I thought your instincts were better than that. The beast in crimson is José Sapota, son of Martin Sapota, the dictator of Argentina. He's majoring in history, and as I recall his field of specialization is the Spanish Inquisition, which should come in handy when he takes over from his *padrecito*. The prince of Patan is that fellow over there, the one in white."

Lucy followed his finger and found herself looking at the most graceful man she had ever seen. Dark-haired, golden-skinned, and slender with a compact body that seemed to be made out of India rubber, he moved with the ease of a gazelle, bounding in and out of the game, stealing the ball from Sapota, and guiding it toward the cardboard box that marked the goal. "Why, he's amazing." She was awed. "He moves like a dancer."

"Bit effeminate for my taste," Bill observed, stuffing his hands into the pockets of his overcoat. She was surprised to hear a sharp edge in his voice and was about to quiz him about it when a cheer went up as the prince kicked the soccer ball into the box, ending the game. The players on his team spent a few minutes clapping him on the back and shaking his hand enthusiastically before they wandered off the field. "Look at that," Bill said, shoving his hands still deeper into his pockets. "Would you believe the fellow has been in Cambridge less than a week? He's already made more friends than most of us make in four years. I swear, our suite in Adams has been like some sort of oasis on the Silk Road. Every Asian, African, and Latin American student at Harvard must have marched through our living room in the past five days, and not just because he's a prince and they're curious to see what princes look like close up. My new roommate seems to have a positive predilection for students from underdeveloped countries; he embraces them, takes them to his heart, and treats them like bosom buddies."

"Sounds pleasant," Lucy murmured, her eyes fixed on the prince who was now carting the remains of the goal box off to a trash can like any other mortal.

Bill lifted his eyebrows ironically. "I suppose it is pleasant if one likes running a restaurant. You can't imagine how those foreign fellows eat. Pizza mostly. Seems they find anchovies and pepperoni vastly exotic. And there's no way one can study in the din."

"Doesn't the prince study? I thought he was some kind of super-intellect."

"Oh, he studies all right. Gets up at five, meditates to some kind of droning chant, and then spends the morning reading economics and government in three or four languages. I don't know when he sleeps, or if he sleeps, but his stamina is inhuman."

"Sounds like you're already regretting your choice of a roommate."

"Certainly not, certainly not." Bill pressed his lips together and adjusted his angora muffler. "I'm absolutely overjoyed. Living with him is a wonderful experience for a future diplomat. It may sound a bit immodest of me to mention the fact, but I'm already becoming known as the 'prince's roommate,' which twenty years from now is going to be a hell of a lot better for my career than having been on the editorial board of the *Advocate*." And he might have said more, only at that moment, having disposed of the box, the prince himself came running toward them with a warm smile on his face. Lucy was amazed by the warmth and by his teeth, which were so even and white that for an instant she wondered if they were false.

"Hello, roommate," the prince called out waving cheerfully at Bill. "How goes your day, and who is this lovely person who accompanies you?" On closer view he looked rather like an American Indian. His forehead was broad, his nose long, his cheekbones high and delicate, his hair straight, jet black, and thick. But it was his eyes that were his most striking feature. Dark brown, large, and bright, they flashed with good humor and lively intelligence. She decided on the spot that she had to persuade Cassie to meet him. Cassie wasn't going to believe how good-looking this guy was. Not that Cassie was in the market for a new boyfriend—she and Andy were still going as strong as ever—but Cassie had a particular fondness for dark, handsome types.

The prince skidded to a halt in front of Bill and stood there expectantly, panting and covered with sweat. He was only wearing a T-shirt and shorts, but he seemed to be warm enough to roast chestnuts on, which in itself, Lucy thought, was fairly amazing.

"Lucy," Bill said casually, "this is Mila, my new roommate. Mila, meet my friend Lucy Constable." No ceremony, no titles; Bill was in top form. He treated the prince with the perfect mixture of friendliness and nonchalance. You could almost see him twenty years from now having a comfortable little chat with the prime minister of England about trade deficits.

"Enchanted." Mila seized Lucy's hand and gave it a vigorous shake. "Is that the proper salutation one should use with American ladies?"

"Yes." Lucy smiled, thinking that he was delightful and nothing at all as she had imagined. She wondered if he was always this egalitarian. Back in Patan, people probably threw themselves at his feet and kissed his shoes. She was amused by the thought. His Keds were as grubby as any she'd ever seen. No way she'd ever get near them.

Mila smiled back and looked at her, wondering what to say next. He'd had a fair amount of experience with Western women, including a memorable affair with an American movie actress one summer in New

Delhi, but this one fell into a completely new category. She was dressed rather plainly in a gray wool jumper and those horrible black tights that the female students at Harvard seemed to favor, with a wide white collar that made her look like a French nun, but her hair was long and gold-colored and she was very pretty. He wondered if she was Bill Bishop's woman. Doubtful, he thought. She doesn't look at him or stand next to him as if they belonged together. There was a small, slightly awkward silence.

"You play a great game of soccer," Lucy volunteered. It wasn't easy to start a conversation with a prince, but in her experience men were always willing to talk about sports. Even Bill occasionally waxed eloquent on the merits of the Harvard crew. She didn't know much about soccer except that the players didn't wear any padding, but from the performance she had just witnessed, Mila had to be good. He'd run circles around the other players and even dodged the steamroller advances of Señor Sapota.

Mila was relieved; if she cared to discuss soccer, he'd be more than happy to oblige her. "That's one of the best things the British left behind when their empire collapsed," he said enthusiastically. "Patan was never a British colony, of course, but I consider that they gave us soccer and we gave them polo. Of course I have some unfair advantages over the other fellows." He shrugged modestly as if to say that his skill meant nothing. "Sindhala, the capital of my country, is at six thousand feet above sea level, so at present I have a bit of extra lung capacity, and then too I've been doing *tummo* yoga since I was six, so I can run around in half the clothes the others need, even when it's below freezing."

"*Tummo* yoga? What's that?" She felt easy with him; there was none of the formality or stiffness she had expected. He might be a prince, but as far as she could tell he was less snobbish than Bill.

Mila was delighted that she had asked. "*Tummo* is a traditional way of activating body heat," he explained, rocking forward slightly onto his toes as if he were about to make a dunk shot. "You spend a few years reciting various prayers and practicing all sorts of visualization techniques, and then for your final exam the lamas—that is, the teachers—take you up into the high mountains and sit you on a glacier and put wet sheets over you and you have to dry them out with the heat of your body. Seven dry sheets and you pass."

"Really? How interesting. You mean to tell me you can raise your temperature just by *thinking* about it?"

"It's quite a handy trick," Mila laughed. "Saves a fortune in mufflers and mittens."

"I should learn it then. My toes don't usually warm up until mid-August, and I love to ski."

Bill opened his mouth to say something and then closed it without speaking as Lucy plunged ahead enthusiastically, leaving him no room. He frowned and tapped the tips of his fingers together, but neither she nor Mila noticed.

"You like outdoor sports?" Mila asked her.

"Sure, especially skiing, hiking, and rock climbing. I went to high school in Colorado, and I still miss the mountains."

"So do I." Mila looked wistful. "In Patan, you see, we are not so developed in a technical sense, and nature is still everywhere. From my window I could always see the mountains and the snow, and here already I feel a bit confined. Where, I ask myself, are the wild birds and the primeval forests, and the Great Lakes that I have read about in your author James Fenimore Cooper? Where is Niagara Falls?"

Lucy pointed west. "Well, Lake Ontario is over three hundred miles in that direction and Niagara Falls is another hundred and fifty or so farther, and there haven't been any primeval forests around here for about three hundred years. But if you want to get out into nature, I suggest you check into the Harvard Outing Club. In fact, my roommate, Cassie, and I were planning on going rock climbing with them this weekend if you'd like to come along." She was suddenly embarrassed. Imagine asking a prince to go rock climbing with you five minutes after you'd met him, but it was too late to take back the invitation.

"Thank you," he said quickly. "I'd be delighted. I've climbed in the Himalayas, and I love it." He spread his arms. "On top of a high peak looking out over the vast stretches of untouched snow, you feel like an eagle."

"This isn't Mount Everest. It's only a rock quarry, and maybe you'd find it dull."

"Oh, no." He shook his head and smiled. Either he was sincerely pleased by her invitation or he was a consummate actor. "I assure you I won't find it dull in the least. What time are you departing on this expedition, please?"

"Seven in the morning on Saturday."

"Well, look at you two," Bill interrupted, "chatting away like old friends." Lucy saw the hurt in his face and realized with a sudden pang of guilt that she and the prince had been ignoring him.

"You'll come along too, won't you?" she said awkwardly.

"Ah, please do," Mila begged. "How can I climb my first American mountain without the companionship of my good roommate?" He seemed completely sincere, and Bill softened slightly.

"Certainly, I'll come." He looked at Mila and then at Lucy, and a strange expression crossed his face. "We'll make it into an expedition. Lucy and Cassie can pack us a picnic lunch, and I'll bring the wine." He paused and smiled what was probably supposed to be one of his witty, sarcastic smiles, only in Lucy's opinion it came off as a bit lonely. She felt ashamed to have gotten so caught up in talking to the prince. She hadn't meant to neglect Bill. Maybe I am a snob after all, she thought. I don't usually react to strangers this way. But Mila is such a wonderful combination of the ordinary and the exotic, you can't help being fascinated.

The rock quarry favored by the Harvard Outing Club was a jumble of sheer walls and rubble, ringed by maples and birches. Overhead, the sky curved in a glossy blue dome, so perfect that when she first saw it, Lucy felt as if she were encapsulated in a vast crystal paperweight. The quarry was, in short, a memorably beautiful bit of wilderness, but it quickly became even more memorable when shortly before noon, Bill Bishop froze on a narrow ledge and refused to move.

"This is total folly!" Bill yelled. He was at the midpoint in a ninety-foot climb when he looked down and panicked, and there was no way anyone could get to him from the top or the bottom of the quarry, so there he was, stuck with only the birds for company.

Phil Klein, who had seen this sort of thing happen before, groaned. "Come on," he yelled impatiently. "It's not dangerous. Get your ass up there, Bishop, and quit screwing around!" Phil was the president of the Outing Club and hence responsible for bringing them all back in one piece. Harvard disliked accidents, which had a nasty way of turning into lawsuits, so they had all signed releases. Should they be crushed, broken, smashed, mangled, drowned, or paralyzed, the university was not going to cough up one cent of consolation.

"It's my fault." Lucy slumped down on a rock beside Cassie, who was amusing herself by taking pictures of the fiasco. Loosening her muffler, Lucy kicked at a piece of gravel. "I knew he was afraid of heights, but I asked him along anyway." The gravel rolled down the slope, starting a small landslide. She kicked another piece after it. Poor Bill, he was obviously scared to death, and she really did feel sorry for him; his pride was going to be smarting for weeks because he liked to think of himself as a combination of Hemingway and Mailer.

Mila walked over to where Phil was standing. His black hair was sleek like the winter coat of a bear, and his skin glowed with warmth even though it was well below freezing. "I'll go up after him," he told Phil.

"Forget it," Phil snapped. "I was lying when I told Bishop that it wasn't dangerous. If you come in from above, you'll break your neck."

"I think not," Mila said firmly, "because the cliff face is quite solid, and although streaked with snow it is free of ice."

Phil was surprised by the prince's reply. The little foreigner seemed to know something about rock climbing. "That ledge is pretty small," he objected. "If it weren't so damn narrow and crumbling, I'd have been up there myself."

"I shan't be using the ledge," Mila said. "A rope will suffice. Of course, I'd like someone to be on belay in case I slip." He smiled thoughtfully. "I have no plans to slip, of course, but it is always best to anticipate every eventuality. Gravity, like all the great forces of nature, is just but unforgiving."

Phil knit his eyebrows together and made some private calculations. "Maybe I'll let you give it a try," he said at last. "How much expertise do you have with ropes? I don't relish the idea of scraping your remains off the floor of the quarry when Bill panics and makes a grab for you."

"I've done a bit of climbing."

"He's scaled Mount Everest," Cassie interposed, "only he's too humble to admit it."

"Everest?" Phil's eyebrows shot up.

"Cassie is paying me the most unfair compliments; I only climbed a little way up the great mountain when visiting some relatives in Nepal."

"That settles it," Phil ordered. "Grab a rope, get your ass to the top of the quarry, and show us what you can do. I'm getting tired of Bill's craziness. I'll be on belay for you."

What Mila could do proved to be impressive. Climbing to the top of the quarry, he threw a rope over the edge. Then, with Phil on belay, he tied himself into a second rope and rappeled down until he was even with Bill. By some sleight of hand that Lucy couldn't quite make out, he secured part of the free-hanging rope under Bill's arms, wove the rest of it into a sling, and persuaded Bill to sit in it. A few seconds later, Bill was back on solid ground.

Bill stamped his feet to restore the circulation and stared at all of them defiantly. "I am never, and I mean *never* coming on another Outing Club expedition," he announced. He looked grimly at the group, dressed in their parkas, boots, and wool caps. "You people are suicidal." He waved at the cliff. "You all have a death wish."

"That cuts me up," Phil snapped. "God knows we'll miss you, Bishop. It won't be the same next Saturday without some asshole to rescue."

Ignoring the insult, Bill turned to Mila. "Thanks," he said, clapping the prince on the back. "You're a real pal and a hell of a roommate, and if you ever get stuck anywhere where I can help you out—like in a rare book library or a fine restaurant—just give me a call."

"Ah," Mila shrugged, "it was nothing. A small climb, a bit of encouragement, nothing at all."

"Oh, yes it was," Bill persisted. "If you hadn't come for me, I'd still be up on that cliff being battered by gale-force winds while this pack of morons tried to find a tree to tie their ropes to. I'm in your debt and I'm grateful and I intend to keep thanking you until it registers, because frankly, Mila, you're overly modest."

Lucy probably liked Bill more at that moment than she had in all the years she had known him, and as for the prince, he was a never-ending source of surprises. As the five of them sat on the floor of the quarry with the other members of the Outing Club, eating sandwiches and drinking hot coffee from Cassie's thermos, she looked at Mila with increased respect, thinking that there seemed to be very little he couldn't do.

On the Monday after the quarry fiasco Cassie's father, Professor Lawrence Quinn, sat in the Liberty Lobster House contemplating one of the red, succulent crustaceans from which the establishment took its name. The lobster, which was gigantic, not only covered his plate, but the front claws hung over it onto the tablecloth. Beside the monster was a tiny aluminum vat of drawn butter, a bottle of Orvieto, and a generous serving of tough-crusted French bread.

Quinn drummed his fingers impatiently on the table, eyed his dinner, and then cast another restless glance at the door. Cassie and Andy had promised to arrive at the Lobster House at seven-thirty, but they were late as usual. Still, this particular evening he wasn't as annoyed as he might have been because he had something else on his mind, a piece of great good fortune which wasn't as good as winning the Nobel Prize of course—what ever could be?—but which was good enough in itself to rate a first-class celebration in the form of a giant lobster and a bottle of expensive wine. The trip from Ann Arbor to Boston had certainly been worth the price of the plane ticket; it had indeed.

At last he spotted Andy and Cassie coming through the door of the restaurant. "Hello there," he called out.

"Hi, Daddy." Cassie strolled up to him and gave him a tentative peck on the cheek.

"Hello, sir," Andy said, shaking Quinn's hand nervously. The boy's awe both pleased and annoyed Quinn. He waved away the "sir" with a gesture that spoke of an equality that didn't, and never would, exist. "How many times do I have to invite you to call me Larry?" he protested, beaming at Andy.

"Hi, Larry," Andy said with awkward delight. His suit was blue and wrinkled, and from the looks of it, it had probably belonged to his father, but Quinn didn't hold that against him because from what he'd seen of the boy's work he was a talented researcher—very talented indeed—and most scientists of any talent tended to look rumpled and unkempt, except Quinn and a few others like Watson, of Watson-Crick DNA fame, who was also a dapper dresser.

"Daddy," Cassie was saying. He realized with a start that she had been talking to him.

"What, darling?" He beamed at her, too, as she settled into her chair, but she didn't beam back, which always annoyed him because she was almost the only woman on the planet who didn't. Her mother had sometimes been the same way, and that wasn't a pleasant memory. Quinn put the late and not very lamented Mrs. Quinn out of his mind as thoroughly as if she had been a picked-over lobster.

"I said," Cassie grumbled, "that Andy and I have a surprise for you." Talking to her father was like talking to someone who was in another room: every once in a while he would stick his head around the door frame and notice that she was still there. Tonight she felt especially hurt by his indifference, but if there was a way to hold his attention for more than a few minutes at a time, she hadn't found it.

Quinn pounced on the word *surprise* with the alacrity of a tiger. "And I have a surprise for you too," he announced. Cassie fell silent, but he didn't notice. Summoning the waitress, he ordered two more lobsters, drank off his glass of wine with radiant good cheer, and looked hospitably at the two of them calculating how best to break the spectacular news.

"If you don't mind," Cassie said pettishly, stuffing her mouth with bread, "how about letting me tell my surprise first." She was close to tears. Reaching under the table, she grabbed Andy's hand and squeezed it. Andy squeezed back as if to say, *Hang in there, honey.*

Quinn was magnanimous. He saw that somehow he'd hurt her feelings again. A pity she was so touchy. "Go right ahead." He poured wine into their glasses and then into his own. Raising a daughter was not the easiest thing a man could do, but he liked to think of himself as an attentive father, the sort who could be confided in. "I'm all ears."

Cassie took a deep breath and looked at Andy. "We're engaged," she announced. Suddenly she felt happy and light as if a great weight had been lifted off her. Andy smiled at her lovingly, put his arm around her, and looked at Quinn with surprising firmness.

"Cassie and I are getting married in June, sir."

"June?" Quinn felt an odd sensation in his chest. He put down his wineglass and stared at them. "Isn't that rather soon?"

"We've been going together for nearly two years," Cassie said, "remember?"

"Two years?" Quinn felt as if he were choking. Picking up his water glass, he emptied it. The first thought that crossed his mind was that they were absolutely crazy to get married before they finished graduate school. Doing research and writing a dissertation was hard enough without domestic complications. He liked Andy, but he certainly hoped Cassie didn't intend to spend the rest of her life pregnant. What a waste that would be. He'd trained her to be a first-rate botanist, and she had his genes. The thought that she might fritter her talent away washing dishes and herding around a pack of children annoyed him excessively. "Are you sure you know what you're doing?"

"Is that all you can say?" Cassie snapped. She should have expected this reaction. Her father had a fantastic talent for ruining the special moments of life.

"Cassie," Andy protested, "give your dad a break. This is probably a shock for him."

Quinn, sensing that there was no use trying to reason with her, recovered with the dexterity of a juggler. Suddenly he was all smiles. Leaping to his feet, he seized Cassie and gave her a huge, fatherly bear hug. "Congratulations, darling. How wonderful." He tried to think of something more affectionate to say. "I wish your mother was alive to hear this. She'd have been thrilled." Cassie was stiff in his arms, but at the mention of her mother, she softened.

"Thanks, Daddy," she said meekly.

Quinn pumped Andy's hand. "Welcome into the family, Andy. This couldn't have happened at a better time. You're going on for your doctorates, of course, and now I'll be able to welcome you into my lab." Cassie started to protest, but he was too fast for her. Heading off her objections, he deftly herded her toward Ann Arbor where he could keep an eye on her. That was the secret of getting what you wanted in life—lightning reflexes and the guts to play your hunches. Andy might look mild-mannered, but Quinn could smell ambition a mile away: Andy wanted to get his own Nobel Prize, and what better place to do it than in the lab of his father-in-law, the famous Lawrence Quinn? And where Andy went, Cassie would follow.

"No," he lifted his hand, "don't thank me. I won't have to pull any strings. The University of Michigan would admit the two of you and give you fellowships even if I didn't exist. You're talented scientists, both of you. My golden kids." That was the truth: they were both talented botanists, and their research should be both original and reliable, and he could already think of a half dozen useful tasks to put them to. "But it so happens that I do exist, and not only that, my lab more than exists." He paused grandly. "I just got a three-*million*-dollar grant from the government to do more research on plant hormones. Three million. Biggest grant ever awarded to anyone outside of Jonas Salk." He laughed genially. "If it weren't so carefully administered, I might be tempted to flee to Brazil and lie on the beach for the rest of my life." He picked up a lobster claw, cracked it, sucked out the meat. The two of them were staring at him, too stunned to speak. "Surprise," he said, helping himself to the melted butter. "You can get married in June and come to Ann Arbor to work on your dissertations in my new laboratory under my supervision, and I'll see that you go straight to the top. Why, ten years from now, I wouldn't be surprised if both of you were *teaching* at Harvard."

"That's a wonderful offer," Andy said weakly. He looked elated and dazed and rather awestruck by his good fortune, which was just the effect Quinn had been trying for. Cassie, on the other hand, didn't look pleased at all. She was glaring daggers at her father, and Quinn wondered, not for the first time, what in the world the girl wanted and why it was so impossible to satisfy her.

Cassie consoled herself for her father's visit by spending most of the following month in bed with Andy, which meant that she wasn't around the off-campus house at 24 Garden Street very much. Lucy missed her, but her life was fairly busy with course work, three term papers, a tutor who worked her mercilessly, and a growing friendship that began to take up a great deal of her time. The friendship was something she would have enjoyed sharing with Cassie because it was with a very unusual person: Mila.

Just how unusual Mila was became obvious fairly quickly. The two of them ran into each other by accident in Widener Library the Wednesday after the trip to the quarry and spent a pleasant half hour standing in front of the card catalog talking about—of all things—the Patanese welfare system, or rather the lack of same. The card catalogue room was an odd place for such a conversation. It was filled with racks and racks of wooden boxes with small metal handles and forbidding labels that promised everything from Aardvarks to Zymurgy. Only a few hundred yards away two giant murals towered over a flight of marble stairs, and a Gutenberg Bible lay encased in glass, but here everything was grim, utilitarian, and dusty. Mila, however, didn't seem to notice.

"I have grand plans," he informed her, waving at the rows of drawers. "I may look like a coddled princeling, but at heart I'm a wild radical, at least that's what my uncles keep telling my father." He scribbled furiously in his notebook, underlining things, reaching out to flip through the cards for more references. "This is a wonderful library. So many resources. How I love it."

"It's one of the best in the world," Lucy agreed. She hesitated, not wanting to pry but terribly curious about those plans of his. Mila continued to turn the cards over like a squirrel digging for nuts. Every time he found a good book, he made a small noise of pleasure. It was amusing to watch him. She'd never seen anyone scramble after knowledge with such enthusiasm, at least not anyone who was also able to rappel down a sheer cliff face. Most scholars, in her experience, were about as vibrant as mildew. The heck with it, she thought. So what if he thought she was prying. How many times did you get a chance to quiz a prince? "What are these great plans of yours?" she asked.

Mila closed the drawer and came up for air. "I plan to reform Patan entirely from the bottom up." He waved his arms. "At present we have only one hospital, and that is for the rich. I plan to start by establishing rural clinics staffed by what the Chinese have called 'barefoot doctors.' This is a term perhaps which you have not heard since I think it exists only in Chinese. It means people trained in basic first aid and emergency medical skills." The librarian at the desk glared at him and put a warning finger over her lips.

"I am talking too loud." He apologized, lowering his voice. "I always become overly excited when I discuss this. I shall attempt to contain my enthusiasm. Perhaps we should speak a bit more of your work with the children of Boston. I have a special interest in the welfare of children. In Patan, you see, we have a terribly high infant mortality rate. Of every ten born, only four survive to adulthood."

"That's the worst statistic I've ever heard!" Lucy was horrified. "Why don't you do something about it right now!"

Mila sighed. "You're so very American, expecting problems of a thousand years to be fixed overnight. I admire that trait in your people, but it won't do for me. I may have to wait until my father dies to build my first rural clinic. I am sure that must sound like a very hardhearted thing to say, but I assure you I love my father. However, the blunt truth is that while he approves of roads and industrial development, he stands in the way of certain basic social reforms. If I were to try to build my clinics without his consent, it would be seen as an act of open rebellion."

"So meanwhile the children continue to die?"

"They do."

"I don't like that, not at all. In fact, it's intolerable. Can't you convince him to listen to you?"

"Unfortunately, no. I've tried repeatedly with no success. He's a good man, but he's divided. Half of him wants to westernize Patan, and the other half wants to preserve our traditional way of life. He grew up in another world, you see, one in which western ideas were seen as the enemy."

"You shouldn't stop trying, not with all those children's lives at stake. You should drag him out on the streets if necessary and make him see the misery around him."

"I wish it were that simple," Mila sighed. "But there is a powerful general named Arjuna, who heads up an ultraconservative faction that opposes any reforms, not to mention that my eldest uncle, who is third in line for the throne, is seriously ill, which means that . . ." He went on to describe a mixture of politics, power, tradition, and intrigue that Lucy could barely follow. Realizing that she was getting in over her head, she decided to move the conversation onto safer ground.

"Listen, if you're so interested in children, you should be auditing Soc. Rel. 150." She briefly described Jordan's course to him, and told him when it met and where, not expecting him to listen to her, but to her surprise he came to the next lecture and to every subsequent one for the rest of the semester.

"Hello there, Princess," Kathy DeVelt said, ambushing her one morning on the stairs. Kathy had also recently moved to 24 Garden Street; in fact she seemed to have taken up permanent occupancy of the one bathroom that served all twelve occupants.

"Forget it," Lucy snapped. "It's not like that at all."

Kathy made a crown out of her fingers and smiled knowingly. "Sure," she said. "And I'm a duck-billed platypus. I hear Bill Bishop is quaffing sherry in his club and complaining that you haven't given him a date in over a month. What are you doing in the prince's room from four to seven every afternoon? playing tiddlywinks?"

Lucy was attracted to Mila; in fact she found him quite sexy, but that was none of Kathy's business. Besides, he didn't seem at all interested in her. "We sit, we drink tea, we discuss his plans to reform Patan," she informed Kathy.

"And then fall into bed and screw like crazed weasels."

"For your information Mila doesn't have a bed. All he has is a mat on the floor. He likes simplicity—something you probably can't even imagine. He admires Gandhi, and he's had so much luxury in his life that he finds it exciting not to own anything but books. In addition, I think he's celibate. Buddhists often are, you know."

"Don't count on the celibacy." Kathy removed one of the pink rollers from her hair and nibbled on the end of it archly. "He's probably just biding his time. You're so damn gorgeous that you'll undoubtedly snag him. And if you think I'm jealous, you're right."

"There is nothing—I repeat *nothing*—going on between us. Good grief, can't you ever think of anything but sex?"

"Not when there's a crown and three working gold mines involved." Kathy looked Lucy over from head to toe and then moved out of the way so she could squeeze by.

Well at least I've nipped that rumor in the bud, Lucy thought as she tossed her book bag into the basket of her bicycle and prepared to ride to her eight o'clock class, but if she had noticed the foreign-looking man in the gray topcoat watching her from the far side of Garden Street, she might not have been so confident.

· 8 ·

The inner workings of the Patanese embassy in New York were slow by American standards but quite efficient. Hence it was the second week in February, well after semester break, when Mila opened the door to find his uncle Rechungpa standing in the hallway.

"Good day, Nephew," Uncle Rechungpa said, striding grandly into the room. He was a short man with the sort of immense protruding belly that in Patan signified power, authority, and wealth. As the King's eldest sister's husband, he had all of these as well as an appointment as ambassador to the United States, and Mila knew from the moment he saw him that the visit was going to be neither casual nor pleasant. Sitting down in one of Bill Bishop's shabby overstuffed chairs, Uncle Rechungpa eyed Mila critically. "What," he sighed, "are we going to do with you, my boy?"

"I beg your pardon?" Mila said politely. His uncle was often cryptic beyond belief; in fact he delighted in labyrinths, so it wasn't unusual not to understand him for some time after he arrived. He usually had to be plied with tea and cakes for at least forty-five minutes before he came to the point. This morning, however, he proved unusually direct.

"I have been informed through the usual channels that you are seeing a great deal of a young unmarried American woman named Miss Lucy Constable."

"Yes," Mila admitted, "I am. But what does that signify? Here at Harvard University, as is the American custom in general, the sexes are educated together, so naturally there is much contact."

"It signifies," his uncle said sharply, "that your father is very displeased by the news. It signifies, as you know very well, that you are creating trouble for us again by consorting with foreign women: first that actress in New Delhi, then the French anthropologist, and now Miss Constable." He pointed one of his large, ring-encrusted fingers at Mila. "You must terminate this relationship immediately." He stopped and glared at Mila, expecting him to protest in some unseemly and unfilial fashion, but the boy only smiled quietly like Buddha under the bodhi tree, which as far as Rechungpa was concerned was one of his nephew's most annoying traits.

Mila actually was doing his best to keep his temper. Uncle Rechungpa never gave the slightest indication that he remembered he was talking to the heir apparent to the throne of Patan; he always treated his nephew as if he were a rebellious child who was refusing to eat his vegetables. Mila had often wondered what would happen when he became king. Would Uncle Rechungpa still stride into the palace and take him to task for some imagined violation of propriety? At times he rather hoped he would, but today the reprimand was annoying, especially since it was so ridiculously unnecessary. "Ah," he replied calmly, "I understand. There has been a mistake. Someone has informed you that this relationship with Miss Constable is sexual in nature."

"Do you deny this?" his uncle growled. "You who are filled with all the lecheries of the Kama Sutra?"

"Of course I deny it." Mila ignored the insult, which, coming from his uncle, was ridiculous. Uncle Rechungpa loved the Kama Sutra and often made references to it. In fact he had a rather famous collection of erotic manuscripts, which hardly put him in a position to lecture other people on their failings. "Miss Constable and I are merely friends."

Rechungpa gave a snort of disbelief. "There is no such thing as a woman friend," he proclaimed with a wave of his meaty right hand. "When a man and a woman are together—especially a young man and a young woman—there are only two possible results: sexual misconduct and the procreation of children, both of which would be of great distress to your father in this particular instance. This Miss Constable is not some concubine in whom you can freely take pleasure. This is a young American woman of good family who is attending one of the most prestigious universities in her country. Our investigations show that Dr. Henry Constable, her paternal uncle, is a famous neurophysiologist at Stanford University. How will this uncle react if you bring shame on his niece?" He pointed his finger at the ceiling and shook it dramatically as if summoning the gods to witness. "This so-called friendship must stop at once, do you understand? It is your father's belief—and I may add it is also mine—that your rash and immoral relationship with Miss Constable could have international repercussions."

Mila had become very pale. What was going on inside him was extremely unpleasant, and he did not intend to speak to his uncle until he could control his tongue. It seemed to him that the Eastern and Western parts of his personality had suddenly been pitted against each other like enemies on a battlefield. On one side stood his duty to his father, his respect for his uncle, his loyalty to the Patanese belief that family came before self. From his earliest childhood, he had been taught that it was his duty to obey his elders, yet at the same time he was overwhelmed with an urge to tell his uncle in no uncertain terms to mind his own business. Living in Adams House these past few months had made him feel independent; he loved his newfound privacy—no servants listening at doors, no anxious relatives and courtiers concocting intrigues every time he sneezed. What was it to his uncle—or to his father for that matter—whom he saw or what he did? He was twenty-two years old, which in America made him a completely emancipated human being, and he *was* the prince of Patan. Yet he was being treated like a traitor, spied on by the Patanese Secret Service, investigated, his friends evaluated, his sex life made a matter of public scrutiny. These accusations were insulting, not only to him but to Lucy. He sat silently for a moment trying to control his temper while the battle raged. "Things are different in America," he said at last. "Surely after twenty years in this country, uncle, you must know that customs are different. Even if I were sexually involved with Miss Constable, there would be no public protest from her family, and furthermore—"

"So!" his uncle pounced. "You admit it! It is the New Delhi actress all over again. You wicked boy. Have you forgotten the Eightfold Path entirely? Are you so corrupted by the West that you allow the customs of this decadent society to become your own?"

"I admit nothing," Mila snapped, "and I will not be lectured at like a thirteen-year-old. I requested from my father one year at Harvard to live like an ordinary person, and I will not be cheated out of that year by your unfounded suspicions." Angry words poured out of his mouth, and he realized with surprise that the Western side of him had won. "There is no sexual relationship between Miss Constable and me, and I have no intention of giving up her friendship. She is an excellent person, beautiful in both mind and soul. I have never met a woman so much my intellectual equal."

"Listen to yourself!" Rechungpa thundered growing red in the face. "Do you sound like a man who is merely engaged in a 'friendship'?"

Mila pressed his lips together and looked at his uncle defiantly. "I have nothing more to say except that I shall not stop seeing her."

"So, I come to you with a message from your father and I receive insolence and disrespect. Well, what could I have expected? It was against my advice that you were allowed to come here in the first place. Of all spots on the earth, the United States is the most corrupt."

"Hong Kong is more corrupt," Mila observed stubbornly, "as is Thailand. Paris is equally corrupt and Cairo is unspeakable. As for Harvard, it is not, I think, a particularly lascivious place. The students here study too hard; they have little time to spend in those infinitely varied seductions that so stimulate your imagination."

"Don't banter with me, you rude and immoral boy!" Rechungpa

yelled, banging his fist on the arm of the chair. His face turned red, and he seemed about to have a stroke or a heart attack. Mila realized that he had gone too far.

"I apologize if I seem rude, Uncle," he said quickly, "but you provoke me by these unfounded suspicions about Miss Constable."

"I do not accept your apology. It was a black day, the day I agreed to come try to talk some sense to you." Rechungpa leaned forward, his face still swollen with agitation and displeasure. "Let us understand one thing clearly: if you continue this liaison, your father will recall you to Sindhala."

"And if I refused to return?" Mila said quietly. "Then what?"

Rechungpa's mouth dropped open in amazement. "You cannot be serious. Do you realize the scandal such an act would generate? Do you have any idea of the shame this would bring to your people?" He rose to his feet. "Oh, this is worse than I could ever have imagined. Only one thing could provoke you to such insanity: You must be planning to marry the girl."

Mila was so dumbfounded by the accusation that for a moment he was speechless. His uncle paced across the room, reached the far side, and wheeled back. "If you are planning such a thing, there is only one alternative open to those who still care for the good name of this family: I will personally visit Miss Constable and inform her of a fact that will make this marriage impossible under American law."

Mila was suddenly more angry than he had ever been in his life. Leaping to his feet, he confronted his uncle. "If you speak one word to Miss Constable, I will—" He stumbled to a halt, unable to think of a strong enough penalty.

"You will what?" his uncle demanded. "Just what will you do? You know that if she is informed of the truth of your situation, Miss Constable will sever all ties with you of her own accord. And what will you do then? Refuse to return to your own country? Break your father's heart; bring shame and dishonor on your people? Abdicate your right to the throne as did Edward the Eighth? Enough. I see that you have no answer."

Mila realized he could not do all those things, and yet how could he give in? He would no longer be a man in his father's eyes, he would be a child. And what about Lucy? How would he explain that he had been ordered never to speak to her again? The foolish irony of all this was that he had never until this moment realized how much he valued her friendship. Was it just pride that made him resist his father's order so fiercely? Maybe he did love her. He had never considered the possibility until his uncle brought it up, but maybe he did. In Patan romantic love hardly existed; marriages were arranged. But he wasn't Patanese anymore, not completely. Part of his soul had broken off from the community soul and become his alone. If he did indeed love Lucy with that part of his soul, how could he throw that love away as if it had no meaning? There was only one thing to do if their friendship were not to be destroyed before he had a chance to see if it was more than a friendship: he was going to have to appear obedient and stall for time. "Please, Uncle," he pleaded, "don't go to Miss Constable. I implore you. There is no reason whatsoever to do so. I have never thought of marrying her until you, yourself, mentioned it."

"And do you think of it now?"

"No, of course not." Even as he denied it, he considered it seriously for the first time. Marry Lucy? Putting prejudices and politics aside, she was the perfect woman for him: beautiful, well educated, independent, compassionate, interested in the same social reforms he was interested in. Are you out of your mind? the Eastern part of him said. She's not even Patanese, and besides—

"So," Rechungpa interrupted, "you begin to show some sense." He was visibly mollified. "Perhaps we can at last come to an agreement. I," he pointed to his chest, "will not visit Miss Constable and neither will you. Well? Do you accept this bargain?"

"I don't know," Mila said through clenched teeth. "I need some time to think about it." All of this was very confusing in the extreme.

"And just how much time do you need?"

"A month."

"Much too long."

"Two weeks then. Surely two weeks is not too much time to ask to meditate on such an important decision?"

"The decision would be trivial were you not so stubborn," his uncle growled, "but take your two weeks. You have always kept your promises in the past. You are a rash boy, yes, but not a dishonest one. Nor, I think, are you so foolish as to risk your whole life over something so insignificant as a woman."

* * *

After such an argument, an ordinary Harvard student would have taken a long walk, played a hard game of squash, or gotten thoroughly and memorably drunk, but Mila did none of these things. Instead, after his uncle left, he went into his room, lit three sticks of incense, sat down on the floor, arranged his legs in a full lotus, and began to meditate. At first his mind was only a jumble of angry thoughts. He would defy his father, tell his uncle to go to hell, do what he damn well pleased. Slowly the thoughts turned into long waves of colored light, and he began to breathe deeply and unconsciously, caught somewhere between waking and sleeping.

Time passed without his being conscious of it. Three hours later he came back to awareness of his surroundings with the realization that his uncle had been right: the order from his father was indeed unfair, but the price of resisting it was much too high. As for love, meditation had also put that in perspective. He could see now that his feelings for Lucy were shadows without substance. Hadn't the greatest teachers written that love was only another trick of the senses designed to trap the human soul in suffering?

Placing the palms of his hands together over his heart, he bowed to the painting of Tara, the Buddhist goddess of love and compassion, that hung on the wall over his sleeping mat. He would obey his father, he promised the goddess, not of his own free will and not happily or with contentment, but he would obey him nevertheless. He was no Western prince like Edward VIII, willing to throw away his throne for a private passion; he was an Eastern prince who had a duty to his father, his family, and his country in that order.

Ending his meditation, Mila rose to his feet and walked resolutely into the living room to call Lucy and explain as diplomatically as possible that, due to circumstances beyond his control, he could no longer see her, but before he could dial the number, he changed his mind. He remembered suddenly that tomorrow she had promised to bring the three children she tutored into Cambridge to meet him. It would be a shame to break the date and disappoint the children. Surely under the circumstances not even Uncle Rechungpa could object to one last meeting. He would explain everything tomorrow in person.

Returning to his room, Mila sat down on the floor and took a half dozen deep breaths. With eyes closed, he inhaled the streams of sandalwood incense and again gave himself over to the peace of non-thought.

At two o'clock sharp, Lucy stood in Harvard Yard with the three children, waiting for Mila to come through Johnston Gate. They made an interesting group: a short blond 'Cliffie in a red ski parka, a black child in a bright purple sweater, a twelve-year-old girl in heels so high that she seemed in imminent danger of pitching forward on her face, and a tough little boy in a ragged denim jacket who slouched against John Harvard's statue like a miniature Marlon Brando.

"Is Mila a *real* prince?" Sally Gerner asked, jumping up and down and tugging at Lucy's skirt. Sally was a pretty ten-year-old with long braids, coffee-colored skin, and a smile that never seemed to fade even when she was cold and hungry, which was most of the time. She wiped her nose on the frayed sleeve of her ugly sweater. "Is he a prince like in the fairy tales?"

"Mila is as real as they come," Lucy assured her.

"I still don't see why some dumb old prince would want to meet us," Roy Sheehan objected. "Are we supposed to bow down to this guy? Well, I'm not up for it, no way." Roy spit through his front teeth and contemplated the results. "I bet he has a nice list of nosey questions for us like all the other social workers: Do you wet your bed, kid? Does your old man knock you around? How come you're so poor and so dumb?"

"Well, I think it's very romaaantic," Shirley said. "And it's so nice of Miss Constable to take us to Haaavad." Shirley, whose last name was O'Shaughnessy, strung out her *a*'s like a line of freight trains. With an accent like that she'd never be able to get a job that paid more than minimum wage; worse yet, she'd recently started missing her tutoring sessions. Lucy wondered what Shirley was up to, but she didn't dare ask. She was only twelve, but in lipstick and high heels and a new gold leather jacket, she looked much older—sixteen at least. Lucy hoped fervently that the jacket had been a present from Leon, Shirley's stepfather.

For the next twenty minutes the four of them stood in front of University Hall as Lucy pointed out the historical sites and the children bombarded her with questions. Why did all the Harvard students wear coats and ties and walk so fast? What was the food like? Was it true everyone in sight was the son of a millionaire? Mila was a few minutes late, and when he showed up they were visibly disappointed.

"I thought you'd have on a turban," Shirley said.

"Or maybe ride an elephant," Sally suggested.

"How do you do, how do you do," Mila replied, shaking hands all around. "Would you children all like to go to Brighams for some ice cream?" He shot Lucy a rather strange look, which she took to mean that he was asking her permission to feed the children sweets. Of course, she nodded back, by all means. The strange look remained on his face, and she wondered fleetingly what had him so preoccupied.

"Whadda you think we are," Roy objected, "dorks or something?" He looked Mila up and down and grinned. "I figure it this way, Prince: if you're going to take our time, you should pay us for it."

"Roy!" Lucy exclaimed. "What a thing to say!"

Roy stared at Mila unabashed. "Ten bucks apiece," he demanded. "Take it or leave it."

Mila smiled. "So you're hiring yourself out as an experimental subject? A very sensible attitude, very American. Capitalism at its most primal. How old are you, if I may ask, young sir?"

"Nine," Roy said sheepishly.

"In my country," Mila said, "ten dollars is a great deal of money. Grown men rarely make that in a week. I feel that in this instance something in the range of a dollar would be more appropriate. Would a dollar and fifty cents be acceptable?"

"You bet it would!" Sally yelled, jumping up and down and clapping her hands.

"Well, sure, yeah." Roy appeared amazed that he'd gotten anywhere with his outrageous demand.

"Oh, I just couldn't take money," Shirley kept protesting. "Naah, I just couldn't." But when Mila offered it to her she grabbed it and stuffed it into her purse. The afternoon went beautifully after that, and by the time they took the children back to Boston on the MTA, the three of them were calling Mila by his first name and treating him like an old friend.

"I'm sorry they hit you up for money," Lucy said apologetically as she and Mila rode back toward Harvard Square. "Roy's very difficult sometimes. The problem is he's very smart and he's in a terrible school. When he cuts up in class, he gets sent to the assistant principal for a beating; then when he gets home his father beats him for getting beaten in school. These children's lives are so bleak that sometimes I wonder if there's any hope."

"Roy had a good point," Mila said, "and as for the money, I didn't mind his request, I assure you. The boy was right: why *should* the children of the poor always offer themselves up as free subjects for our curiosity?"

For the rest of the trip he was uncharacteristically silent. After a few unsuccessful attempts to make conversation, Lucy gave up. Something was obviously on his mind, and she supposed that he would tell her what it was when he was good and ready. At Harvard Square he shook her hand, thanked her for the afternoon with the children, and left abruptly. Well, that's odd, she thought. We usually have coffee together. Did I offend him?

Riding back to Radcliffe, she had dinner at Holmes Hall and then pedaled over to 24 Garden Street, climbed into her favorite flannel nightgown, and spent the rest of the evening reading. She went to bed early and fell asleep almost at once, only to be awakened several hours later by the sound of gravel hitting the window. Thinking that Cassie had returned a day early from her trip to New York and had managed to get herself locked out, she stumbled over to the window, opened it, and looked down. There, standing in the side yard by the bicycle rack, was Mila. It was snowing like crazy, and all the garbage cans and bushes and bicycles were covered with at least two inches. The snow whirled around Mila, piling up in his hair, and she saw that, as usual, he didn't even have on a pair of gloves.

"What in the world are you doing down there?" she said softly, not wanting to wake up the whole house.

"I'm sorry to wake you," he whispered, "but I need to talk to you as soon as possible."

It was two in the morning according to Cassie's alarm clock, and all that she could imagine was that something terrible had happened. "Hang on," she told him, "I'll be right down." Five minutes later, dressed in her warmest clothes, she tiptoed downstairs, signed out in the big book that no one ever checked (there were some privileges associated with being a senior), and cautiously opened the front door so as not to wake Kathy, who had a room just off the front hall. Mila was waiting for her on the porch, pacing back and forth, making footprints in the freshly fallen snow. His face lit up when he saw her.

"You came."

"Of course I came." She waited for him to announce the bad news, but he didn't. He just stood there looking at her. The snow fell between them, dancing across the porch light and settling on the banisters. Lucy shifted from one foot to the other to keep warm and waited for him to get on with whatever he had come to talk to her about.

"Would you please take a walk with me?" he asked at last.

"A walk? Where to?" She stared at the blowing snow and then at Mila, who was looking at her hopefully. If she hadn't known that he never touched alcohol, she would have thought he was drunk, but he was sober and clear-eyed as usual. He's certainly a good-looking man, she thought, but a little weird. If an American fellow turned up on my doorstep at this hour, I'd think he was romantically attracted to me. Now that's an interesting possibility. Could it be? She scrutinized Mila's face, but his expression told her nothing. Forget it, she told herself. The two of you have been alone together for hours, and he's never so much as tried to hold your hand. Maybe in Patan it's customary to stroll around in blizzards.

"I thought we might head in the direction of Fresh Pond," Mila suggested.

The idea of walking to Fresh Pond at two in the morning in the middle of a snowstorm seemed bizarre to say the least. It was a good mile away, maybe more. She reverted to her original theory that something was seriously wrong. "What's happened, Mila? Are you okay?"

He gave her an odd look and smiled sadly. "If you don't mind, I'd rather discuss it as we walk." But they didn't discuss it, whatever it was. They walked for blocks in silence. The snow fell harder, piling up in doorways, covering cars, filling in their footprints almost as fast as they made them. Mila trudged along, not looking at Lucy but intensely conscious that she was next to him. Soon he was going to have to end their friendship, and he felt himself wanting to delay that moment as long as possible. Why are you waiting? the Eastern half of him kept urging. This afternoon you showed a shameful lack of courage. Now you've wakened her, and still you put it off.

"The snow looks pretty," Lucy observed. She could feel the tension growing between them. It definitely felt sexual, but she couldn't be sure. This was all pretty confusing. She was no virgin, but Buddhist princes were out of her realm of experience. She wondered if he was going to try to kiss her, and if he did what it would feel like. It would feel good, she decided. It hadn't escaped her notice that he was a very sexy man, but until tonight he'd been so polite. She looked at his dark, silky hair and tried to imagine how it would feel in her hands. She imagined him pulling her toward him and— Just listen to her! What was she dithering on about? He was probably thinking about something else entirely.

"The snow is very pretty," Mila said through tight lips. She realized that he was agreeing with what she had said several minutes ago. At this rate, whatever conversation they had was going to take until dawn.

After about twenty minutes, they came to a deserted playground ringed with a tall wire fence. By day it was probably a cheerful place, but at this time of night it appeared lonely and abandoned. The seats of the swings were covered with snow, and the slide seemed forlorn and in need of repair. Mila looked at Lucy and then at the open gate. Do your duty to your father, the Eastern side of him urged. Do it now.

Get off my back, the Western side of him snarled. But the Eastern side was bigger and more powerful and it was obviously useless to put off this unpleasantness any longer. Leading Lucy into the playground, he brushed off one of the swings and settled her on it.

"Lucy, my friend," he began, "I have something very sad to tell you."

"What's that, Mila?" She was so beautiful sitting there on the swing with the snow frosting her eyelashes that it was unbearable. He thought of what a fine person she was and how she loved the children she taught and what a great unkindness he was about to commit, and suddenly everything in him rebelled. He knew that he couldn't give her up because she was his anchor to the West, and it would break his heart never to hear her voice again. The sacrifice they were demanding of him was stupid and unnecessary. Placing his hands on her shoulders he lifted her to her feet, leaned forward impulsively, and before he could stop himself, he had kissed her full on the lips. They were warm and sweet, and he thought with regret of all the weeks he had wasted not kissing them.

Lucy was shocked, not by the kiss, which she had fully expected, but by how exceptionally good it felt. "Mila," she protested, "what are you doing?" Instead of answering, he kissed her again, and she responded passionately. A tremor of sensuality stirred in her, and she felt heat rising up from the soles of her feet, filling her whole body.

Mila chuckled, and then he laughed a full, free laugh that made him feel as if he were floating up to catch the falling snow. "You look so surprised," he said, "so startled."

"I am surprised," Lucy admitted. She decided that this was hardly the time to tell him that he was one of the best kissers she had ever encountered. If that was the way he kissed, then how did he make love? She remembered Bill saying that Mila had been given his first concubine when he was ten. She was amused. Evidently he's been putting the time to good use, she thought.

Mila kissed her again, and this time she let herself go completely. For a few seconds the rest of the world ceased to exist. Ah, she thought coming up for air. This has real potential.

"Oh, this is wonderful, wonderful," Mila said, stroking her hair. "I always wondered what it would be like to kiss a respectable American girl, but I've never done so before, although I must admit some kissing of unrespectable ones. Do you know that in Patan, if I kissed you and my relatives did not appear at your parents' house tomorrow morning with an offer of marriage, your father and your brothers would be obliged to hunt me down and slice off my head with a large, sharp knife?" He made a cutting motion across his throat and smiled happily at her. "But fortunately I believe you have no father or brothers, so my head is safe, yes?"

Lucy laughed, feeling dizzy and intoxicated. Around her the snow danced off the swings and scattered down the slide like a group of children playing in the schoolyard, and everything was white and swirling and warm at the center. Sober up, she commanded herself. Kissing him was one thing, but going to bed with him was next on the agenda and that presented problems. He's a prince, she reminded herself. Spelled p-r-i-n-c-e. She giggled, thinking helplessly of the frog prince in the fairy tale, but Mila gave no signs of turning amphibian. My God, she was punch-drunk. With considerable effort she forced herself to be logical. She'd never wanted a crown, but that surely was what people would think if she got involved with Mila. Kathy DeVelt would have a field day; the rumor mill at Harvard would grind away at top speed; and their affair might even make the newspapers, all of which would be embarrassing in the extreme. On the other hand, it was hardly fair to hold the fact that Mila was a prince against him. Hadn't she always proclaimed that she believed in treating all human beings equally? Suppose that he was an ordinary student with no throne to complicate matters. What would she do under those circumstances? Wouldn't she give him a chance? She was lonely and she liked him and that had been a very hot kiss. "Mila . . ." she began.

"Oh, lovely sound!" Mila exclaimed, opening his arms to embrace her. "Let me kiss my name off your sweet lips!"

"Hold it." She caught his wrists, thinking that if he went on talking like that, she was probably going to do something mid-Victorian like swoon at his feet. "Not so fast; we're going to have to take this very, very slowly." That is, she added to herself, if I can manage to keep myself from falling into bed with you the first chance I get.

He raised his hands and stepped back a few steps. "I'll move like a glacier," he promised. "I haven't frightened you, have I, my dear Lucy? I have no wish to make you feel like a female tiger surrounded by a pack of hounds. You are my respected friend and companion, and I will kiss you only as you wish to be kissed and no more. I do not crave your pelt in front of my fireplace."

Lucy grinned and shook her head, trying to shake some sense into herself, but the snow kept falling, turning the wire fence into lace, making prisms around the streetlights. "I'm glad to hear you're not about to turn me over to a taxidermist," she said. She pushed the swing and went up in the air, scattering a trail of snow behind her. When she came down Mila was there, catching the swing, bringing her to a stop and into his arms again.

"My snow queen," he whispered between kisses, "has there ever been a woman like you?"

"Cassie's like me," Lucy murmured, "but she's taken."

"Then what great good fortune I have," Mila said gallantly, kissing the snow from her lips and eyelids. "What fortune to have encountered, because you, I think, are not taken, my dear friend, and I am surprised at that, I must admit. I was not aware before I came to Harvard that American men could be so blind to the treasures that lay in their path."

Dear Uncle [Mila wrote the next morning], I have decided that I cannot agree to stop seeing Miss Constable. As for your threat to visit her and reveal what should never be revealed, let me say with all due respect that such a move would be most unwise, since you would risk provoking the very scandal that you yourself ordered me to avoid. In short, my esteemed relative, I have realized that you were bluffing. It was a very convincing bluff and you carried it off, as you do all things, with great skill and diplomacy. I remain, your admiring nephew, Mila.

"Oh, damnable boy!" Uncle Rechungpa thundered when he read the letter, and he sent off a message at once advising that Mila be recalled immediately to Sindhala. But to his surprise and intense annoyance, the king refused.

Let the little mouse play elephant [the king wrote]. This infatuation will come to nothing. And he was right, you know, Rechungpa: we were bluffing.

THINK OF THE SCANDAL [Rechungpa screamed via diplomatic pouch]! WE ARE SETTING A FEAST FOR OUR ENEMIES!

My dear brother-in-law, the king replied sternly, there will be no scandal unless you yourself provoke it. Leave the boy alone.

• 9 •

The bathroom door at 24 Garden Street was bolted from the inside.

"What the hell are you doing in there, Constable?" Kathy DeVelt yelled, pounding on it and rattling the lock. "I have to put on my face. My date's coming in less than half an hour!"

"Try going out without all that paint on for once in your life," Lucy suggested. "Surprise the poor sucker with the real you." She settled back comfortably in the warm bubble bath and contemplated the pile of wet stockings she had pulled off the shower and flung into the corner— fourteen pairs all belonging to Kathy. Around the room, on every level surface, windowsill, and shelf, lay Kathy's basic necessities: eyeliners, lipsticks, bottles of French perfume, eyelash curlers, rollers, boxes of dusting powder, astringents, moisturizing creams. If Kathy ever left two square inches available for anyone else to store a box of bobby pins, it was by accident.

"What the hell are you doing!" Kathy called through the closed door. Sentence variety, Lucy reflected, was not her strong point.

"Thinking."

"Thinking about what, for chrissake?"

"Thinking about how some people—who shall remain nameless—think they own the bathroom."

"Very funny." Grumbling audibly, Kathy gave up on the door and sulked back to her room where she had enough makeup stashed to stock a small department store. Alone at last, Lucy floated among the bubbles trying to relax, but it wasn't easy. Dipping a sponge in the water, she squeezed the scent of soapy lilacs over her shoulders and then took a couple of swipes at the glittering mounds that surrounded her. Killing innocent bubbles—look what sexual frustration was reducing her to. She should be taking a cold shower, running laps, rolling in the snow. For the last three and a half weeks things with Mila had continued to develop kiss by kiss and stroke by stroke, button by button, so slowly that she was about to go out of her mind.

She slapped impatiently at the bubbles, popping them by the thousands. Why didn't he just get on with it? Listen to her—she who had proclaimed that she wanted to take things slowly so that there would be no misunderstandings. Well, he'd certainly taken her at her word. He was seducing her by the inch. Not that it wasn't exciting. Good grief, if she got any more turned on she'd start clawing the walls. Dropping the sponge, she watched it float to the other end of the tub like a small brown island that had been cut loose from the continent. What was she going to do? Just exactly how did you tell a prince that it was time to shift into high gear?

Several possibilities presented themselves, all completely unsatisfactory. She sat in the tub for a few more minutes taking deep breaths and contemplating her bare toes. Finally, she gave up. Leaning forward, she fumbled around for the rubber stopper. Hot water and bubbles were obviously not going to relax her. She might as well surrender the bathroom to Kathy.

* * *

A week passed and then another. The snow melted, buds began to appear on the trees, and then one afternoon Bill Bishop came back to Adams to find a very unpleasant surprise waiting for him: the door to Mila's room was closed and a gray wool tie was draped over the knob. Bill looked at the door and then at the tie, which he recognized as Mila's. Uttering a low moan, he strode over to the cabinet, poured himself a stiff shot of Scotch, and drank it off in one gulp. The tie on the doorknob was a Harvard tradition, and Bill himself had used it on several memorable occasions. *Sex taking place* that tie warned. *Do not disturb*. The tie glared at Bill like an evil eye. No, like a snake. What did it matter? Metaphors were useless and poetry sucked.

Grief overwhelmed him. Pouring himself another shot of Scotch, Bill thought gloomily of the great disasters of life: earthquakes, plagues, airplanes that crashed into mountains spewing passengers all over the landscape. He was still in love with Lucy and had no doubt she was the one Mila had bedded. Ah, the irony of it all. He had pulled every string he could to get the prince as a roommate. He had forced Lucy to meet the son of a bitch. Lifting his glass in an ironic toast, he threw back his head and drank the whiskey so quickly that it stung his throat, but he didn't give a damn. He was Fortune's fool; he was a man without luck of any sort.

In Mila's room Tara, goddess of love and compassion, was getting an eyeful. On the floor in front of her portrait, wrapped in a tangle, the lovers lay head to foot, sweetly exhausted. Lucy was snoring softly through slightly parted lips while Mila lay awake, dreamily contemplating her ankles. They were the most beautiful ankles he had ever beheld: slender, delicate, with the grace of bamboo and the whiteness of glacial snow, and he wanted to write poems to them on watered silk and immortalize them in stone and take pictures of them with his new Pentax, but he was not a poet or an artist, and he knew that anything he could possibly write or create would be inferior to the beauty that lay in front of him.

Below her ankles, like two flowers on graceful stems, were her feet, rosy, arched, teasing, and he could imagine them dancing even now when they lay so still. *Khus feet*, a great Patanese poet had called them, but no, he would not call them that, not even to himself because the sweet-smelling Khus root was an Eastern image, and there was nothing Eastern in him anymore except the most remote and inaccessible memories. He had been reincarnated without benefit of dying, and now he was 100 percent Western, a simple twenty-two-year-old college student in love, without rituals to trip and strangle him, without relatives hovering around him like jailers, and he loved this new life fiercely and was never going to give it up, not for his uncle or his father or even for Tara, who hung on the wall looking at him so disapprovingly.

Tonight, after Lucy left, he would take that portrait down and put it in his closet because although the East had many things—a culture thousands of years old, a great spiritual tradition, a sensitivity to natural beauty that made Westerners seem barbaric—it had one great flaw: it had never valued romantic love. Duty, yes. Companionship, yes. But not love. And love, Mila saw now, was the greatest teacher.

He had thought before that he had experienced love, but he hadn't. The other women in his life—and there had been many—had been kind and often beautiful, but there had always been something missing. In retrospect he could see that they had all been like fine china, too delicate to withstand him. But Lucy was no vase. She not only had beautiful ankles, she had force and fire and intelligence. She inspired him to passion and tenderness and she stood up to him and was his equal in every way and he admired her so much that he wanted to throw open the window and yell, "I have found the perfect woman!"

Love was only possible between equals. What a simple truth. Why hadn't he known it years ago? Leaning forward, he gently kissed Lucy's feet. In Patan this would have meant *I bow to you; I who am your inferior*, but here it meant *Friend, I salute you; lover, I cherish you.*

Lucy stirred, throwing off the blanket. Sitting up, he moved to the top of the mat and rearranged the covers so that her bare shoulders were protected from the cold. Tomorrow he would buy a decent bed and an electric heater. Yoga pads and brisk drafts were fine for a monk, but not for the lucky man who had found a mate.

"So what's he like?" Cassie asked. She settled back on the couch, kicked off her pink fuzzy slippers, and wiggled her toes in Lucy's general direction. "Is he great? Is he nothing to write home about? Would you rather be conjugating irregular French verbs? Or does he make you feel like Lady Chatterley?"

Lucy grinned and helped herself to the aluminum bowl of buttered popcorn that lay between them. "I haven't the slightest idea what you mean," she said.

"Oh, come on," Cassie persisted, "don't play dumb with me. I've lived with you for—what is it now?—over five years, and I've never seen you in this state. You walk around like there's a string quartet playing somewhere in the background. You haven't groused at me for throwing my dirty laundry on the floor for weeks. To be blunt, you act like a woman who's getting it."

Lucy arched her eyebrows and went on eating her popcorn. "My lips are sealed."

"Good grief," Cassie moaned. "Here my best friend is making it with a real live prince who has had concubines since he was old enough to walk, and she won't share any of the details with me. What have I done to deserve this? Didn't I give you a blow-by-blow account of my first time with Andy right down to the vintage of the wine?"

"You sure did," Lucy agreed. "I tried to stop you, but it was impossible. For weeks I could hardly look Andy in the face without thinking that he wore Fruit of the Loom jockey shorts."

Cassie giggled. "You're right. I'm a shameless hussy with the discretion of an orangutan in heat." She helped herself to the popcorn and chewed it thoroughly, spitting the unpopped hulls into the palm of her hand. "Come on," she insisted. "I can't stand it. I know you're the soul of discretion, but surely you can tell me *something*."

Lucy sighed. "You aren't going to give up on this, are you?"

Cassie shook her head vigorously. "No. I could say that I realize it's none of my business, but the truth is I'm probably going to pester you until you come clean." She tossed the unpopped kernels back into the bowl. "So how about it? What's he like?"

"I surrender," Lucy said. "I'll describe the general situation, but I am not—and I repeat *not*—going into detail."

"Rats," Cassie sighed, "that's not what I'd hoped for, but I'll take what I can get." She crossed her legs and made herself comfortable. "I'm all ears."

There was a short silence. "Well, in the first place," Lucy said at last, "Mila is much more sensual than you'd think just by looking at him."

"I knew it!" Cassie exclaimed. "I said to Andy just the other day that—"

"Please," Lucy protested, "take five deep breaths and try not to tell me what you've been telling Andy because I'd like to be able to see him without wondering if he knows what size underwear *I* wear. As a matter of fact," she looked at Cassie sternly, "if you don't swear never to breathe a word of this to anyone, I'll stop right now."

"I promise," Cassie said, "I swear. This is girl talk between best friends and I'll hold it sacred. Wild horses won't drag it out of me. Should Ann Barrows Singleton appear out of the mists and offer me her brown antelope skin coat which I coveted for two solid years, I will refuse to divulge your secrets."

"In that case," Lucy said as she leaned back on the pillows, "I'll continue. Mila, as I was saying, is a very sensual person. It seems he was trained in making love the way you and I were trained in penmanship, and the results are definitely in the A-plus range."

"He excites you? He satisfies you?"

Lucy smiled and helped herself to another handful of popcorn. "Let's put it this way. He makes me feel like my thighs are attached to my pelvis with ball bearings."

Cassie was elated. She leaned forward, almost knocking the bowl of popcorn to the floor. "That's great news. I'm happy for you." She grabbed wildly at the popcorn bowl, saving it in the nick of time. "How serious is it? Do you love him?"

Lucy frowned. "I think so, but I'm not completely sure. All I can tell you is that I rarely think about David anymore, and I'm happier than I've been in a long time." She came to a full stop and looked at Cassie questioningly. "What do you think I felt for David anyway? Was it really love, or just some form of mental illness?"

"A little of both, I'd say."

"That's what I think. The affair with David took over my whole life. My feelings for Mila don't do that. I'm fond of him; we have absolutely fantastic sex; we're friends on the deepest level; we get along great in bed and out, but there's not as much . . ."

"Zing," Cassie suggested.

"Right," Lucy agreed, "not as much zing, which is absolutely crazy because frankly Mila is an infinitely nicer person than David, a far more considerate lover, and what could be more romantic than a living, breathing prince?"

"If you ask me," Cassie said grimly, "the day David Blake walked out on you was the luckiest day of your life."

"I know," Lucy agreed. "That's what I keep telling myself. Mila is a thousand times better for me."

"Wrong. He's two thousand times better."

"So do I really love him or don't I?"

"Who can tell?" Cassie shrugged. "Maybe yes, maybe no, maybe time will tell, but my advice to you is to go for it. I haven't heard you wax so enthusiastic over a man in years. And meanwhile, should you experience the slightest urge to contact David, let me know so I can kidnap you and hold you captive in some suitably dank place until you come to your senses."

It was April, and outside Adams House the chestnut trees were in bloom. Inside, Lucy and Mila sat naked on Mila's new bed, their arms wrapped around one another, listening to sitar music. The music flowed up and down invisible hills, tracing a distant geography that seemed both remote and wonderful. Mila's body, too, was a path into mysterious places. Lucy rested against his shoulder, feeling warm and safe and more or less at peace with the universe. Mila was an amazing man: he knew more about loving than she had ever imagined a man could know, and yet, at the same time he was her companion and her friend and she grew closer to him every day.

The music stopped, leaving resonances in the air; the candle sputtered and flickered; when the silence was perfect again, Mila rose to his feet, crossed the room, and opened the closet door. Bending forward, he became part of the shadows; the muscles in his back rippled like the muscles of a dancer. He straightened up, turned, and walked back toward Lucy holding a small white box. The box was ivory, inlaid with gold. On the sides and lid, Patanese court ladies from another century sat beside a pool filled with swans and lotus blossoms.

"For you," he said, placing the box in her hands.

She examined it in wonder. Every detail was perfect, right down to the tiny feet of the ladies and the sharp beaks of the swans. She'd never seen anything so finely made. She turned the box over and discovered the small red seal of the artist stamped on the bottom: two fish swimming under a quarter moon. "Thank you," she said softly, awed by its perfection. "I don't know what to say. It's absolutely beautiful."

Mila sat down beside her and ran his finger over the lid of the box. "I'm glad you like it." He smiled. "It belonged to my mother."

"Are you sure you want to part with it?"

"Open it," he suggested.

She lifted the lid and there, lying on a pillow of blue satin, was a diamond necklace. Matched perfectly, the strands of diamonds sparkled like a chain of fire. "My God," she gasped, "you can't be serious. I couldn't possibly accept a present like this."

Mila picked up the necklace, held it for a moment in the palm of his hand, and then fastened it around her neck. The diamonds were cold on her bare skin, and she shivered as they touched the base of her throat.

"Marry me," he said. He put one finger over her lips. "No, don't tell me you can't because I'm a prince and you're a commoner. That sort of prejudice is ridiculous; it belongs to another world, one that died centuries ago. I am not going to let my family select a wife for me. I have learned here in America that love is completely democratic; love doesn't care about money or social class or what other people will say. I'm speaking from my heart, and I'd say the same thing if I was the poorest peasant: I love you, Lucy. Marry me, and I'll do my best to make you happy."

She stared at the fire in his eyes and the pleading in his face, and she thought a hundred thoughts, none of them coherent. For the first time in her life she had the sense of being on the edge of some kind of destiny greater than herself, and it frightened her. She loved him, she didn't doubt that any longer, but when she tried to imagine herself leaving her own country to live in Patan, she felt a chill of alienation. She couldn't see herself as a princess. The idea of wearing a crown seemed almost laughable, like something out of a child's storybook. And there was something else, something she hated to admit even to herself: she still loved David. She didn't want to, but she did; David was buried in her flesh like a fish hook, snarled around her soul, and she kept trying to struggle free and never quite succeeding. It wouldn't be fair to Mila if she married him and only give him part of herself. She felt a long pang of regret; she loved Mila in so many ways, but not enough . . . "I'm sorry," she stuttered. She reached up to take off the necklace, but the clasp seemed stuck and her fingers didn't work right. "I can't marry you. It's not possible."

"Why not?" Mila's face changed suddenly as if a cloud had passed across it.

"Because," she paused, looking for words to soften the blow, "because even though I love you, I don't love you . . . enough to marry you."

"Is that the only reason?"

"Yes," she whispered. "I'm so terribly sorry."

To her surprise he looked relieved. "But you like me, yes?"

"Of course I like you, Mila. You and Cassie are my best friends in the world." She felt terrible. Her eyes burned with tears.

He took her hand in his and held it for a moment and there was a long silence. "In my country," he said at last, "we believe that liking is what is important. Love for us isn't the same as it is for you. Here, in America, you sing of it as an uncontrollable passion that sweeps the lovers out of their ordinary lives and transforms them, but love for us is more like the music of the sitar: it doesn't rush toward a climax but grows slowly and almost invisibly like a great tree. For us love most often comes after marriage." He smiled ironically. "It's strange I should be saying all this to you because, you see, I love you in the Western way. Yet I am asking you to love me in the Eastern way—to marry me and trust that your heart will follow."

"And if it doesn't?"

"It will, I promise you."

She looked down at the box in her hands, at the ladies sitting beside the pool listening to distant music, and she knew that she had to tell him the ugly, plain, unadorned truth. "I was completely in love once, with someone else—a poet."

Mila's face tightened and he let go of her hand. "Oh," he said, "I didn't know. What was he like, this poet?"

"Unkind, crazy, not very dependable."

"You suffered?"

"Yes, I suffered."

He seized her hand again. "I hate this man who made you suffer; the thought of anyone causing you pain is unbearable to me. I would like to take him and strip him and tie him to a thorn tree and let the wild tigers feast on his intestines."

The thought of David stark naked waiting for the tigers had an undeniable appeal. Lucy smiled despite herself. "Thanks, but that's probably not going to be necessary. The last I heard he was out in San Francisco destroying himself with drugs, and no tiger could do a better job."

"Good," Mila said grimly. "I'm glad to hear that, because you're going to be my wife. I will defend you against all suffering, and any man who causes you the smallest pain in the future will regret it a thousand times over."

She started to protest again, but he wouldn't let her. "I don't care what your past is or how many wicked poets you once loved. I only want you now, in the present, and I warn you, I'm a very determined person who has been terribly spoiled. I'm used to getting what I want, and I want you, Lucy, my dear friend. I'll win that heart of yours."

"I wish that were true." She suddenly felt sad and lost and a bit ridiculous, and she wished—not for the first time—that she had never met David Blake. Taking off the diamonds, she put them back in the box, closed the lid, and sat for a moment looking at the ladies and the swans. How innocent they seemed; how she longed for that kind of peace. "I'm not sure I have a heart left."

"You wonderful woman!" Mila cried, embracing her. "Of course you have a heart! You don't believe me? Then I'll prove it to you." He kissed her hands and her neck and her bare chest. "Here it is, right here. I can feel it beating. I know that heart of yours; I know your goodness and your noble nature. And if you are really convinced that you can't love anyone completely ever again, then I know how to cure that. I know where the love in you is hiding, and I know how to make you feel it."

"Mila, don't; it's just no use."

"You think I'm making wild promises that I can't keep. But you're wrong. I can keep them."

Lucy gave up. It was useless trying to reason with him. She wished he could do everything he promised, but he obviously had no idea what he was up against.

Leon Milner, Shirley O'Shaughnessy's stepfather, looked out the front window and saw Shirley sitting on the stoop in her gold-leather jacket chewing a wad of pink bubble gum and reading a book that her tutor, Miss Constable, had given her for her twelfth birthday. He was relieved to see that there were no lizards in sight. "Lizards" were what Leon called the packs of adolescent boys who hung around Shirley trying to get into her pants. He ran them off whenever he could, but they seemed to go off into alleys, multiply like cockroaches, and come back hornier than ever. They were as sorry a pack of losers as Leon had ever seen, and he worried about Shirley getting knocked up by one of them, but there wasn't a damn thing he could do except shuffle out on the porch and growl at them when they got too thick. If he hadn't been out of work, he would have moved Shirley and her mother out of this crummy neighborhood, but he couldn't afford even the first and last months' rent on a new place, so they were stuck.

Settling back into his recliner, Leon opened his first beer of the day and began to watch a game show not because he liked the damn things, but because he had nothing better to do. He was wearing a flannel shirt and carpet slippers, his usual uniform since that memorable day six months ago when he had been laid off from the cardboard box factory. About halfway through the part of the show where all the contestants began to tell intimate secrets about their husbands and wives, the phone rang. Probably a wrong number. Leon drank his beer and waited for it to stop, but it went on ringing like a crying baby until he couldn't ignore it any longer. Stomping across the room, he picked up the receiver.

"Hello," he snarled.

"Leon Milner?"

"Yeah." The game show was blaring so loudly that he had to put a finger in his other ear to hear the voice on the receiver.

"This is Frank Silva."

Leon was speechless. Mr. Silva, who owned Containers Unlimited, was not in the habit of calling ex-employees.

"Leon, are you there?"

"Yes, sir," Leon said. "I'm here."

"I don't believe in beating around the bush, Leon, so I'll get straight to the point: I want you back at the factory tomorrow morning at eight."

Leon was so stunned he almost dropped the phone. "You mean you're giving me my old job back?"

"No," Mr. Silva said, "not exactly."

"I knew it was too good to be true." Leon sighed. "For over six months I've been looking for work. A man gets discouraged, Mr. Silva, not that I blame Containers Unlimited for laying me off but—"

"I'm offering you a promotion to foreman, Leon. How does that strike you?"

"Foreman! Holy Jesus."

"It pays about twice what you were making, and there's a company house thrown in—a little place out in the suburbs where your stepdaughter, Shirley, could grow up with some green grass around her."

Leon Milner had never heard of a foreman's job that paid double and included a house, and he had no idea how Mr. Silva knew he had a stepdaughter named Shirley, but he wasn't about to question his luck. He jumped at the chance to work again.

Roy, Joe, and Danny were throwing their knives into a telephone pole when the third-floor window slammed open and Mrs. Sheehan, Roy's mother, stuck her head out.

"Roy," Mrs. Sheehan yelled, "get yourself up here this minute!"

"Your old lady sounds mad as hell," Joe said. Like Roy he sported a dragon on the back of his jacket. "Betcha gonna get a licking."

"So what," Roy said, retrieving his knife from the pole. "I got lickings before, and she don't hit very hard anyway."

"What did ya do? Eat all the fucking lunch meat and cop one of your dad's beers again?"

"Hell if I know," Roy said. "It's always something."

Upstairs his mother was waiting for him with a pleased, rather stunned look on her face that Roy had never seen before. "Some man just called."

"Oh yeah." Roy went to the refrigerator and helped himself to a carton of milk.

"Said he was the 'headmaster' of some school called Winchester. Ever hear of it?"

"Nah," Roy said, "why?"

"They want you to come there to school. He said they'd pay all your expenses."

"What's the catch?"

"That's the strangest part. There ain't any catch."

Roy put down the milk carton. "Real funny, Ma," he said. "Great joke."

Marie Gerner was feeding Pablum to baby Brian when the phone rang. "Sally," she called, shovelling Pablum deftly into Brian's mouth, "get that, will you?"

"Yes, Mama." Sliding across the tattered linoleum like a figure skater, Sally grabbed for the phone. "Hiya," she said cheerfully, wiping her nose on the frayed sleeve of her purple sweater.

"Is this the Gerner residence?" the man on the other end of the line asked. He had a slightly foreign accent that reminded Sally of that prince Miss Constable had introduced them to, only he was older and fatter sounding and you could hear him breathing hard.

"Yes," she said, "it is." She wondered if this was going to be a breather call and if the man was going to say something dirty, in which case she would yell into the phone as loud as she could and slam down the receiver.

The man cleared his throat. "I'm happy to tell you that the Gerner family has won the Sindhala lottery."

"Won what, mister?"

"The Sindhala lottery, my dear child."

Marie Gerner looked up from the baby to find Sally staring at the phone like she'd never seen one before. "What's wrong, honey?" she asked, parking Brian's spoon on the edge of his high chair.

"Man on the phone say we just won ten thousand dollars and a house."

Marie Gerner sighed, picked up the baby's spoon, and began to send cooked carrots after the Pablum. Sally was a good girl, but she had too much imagination.

Lucy ran into Mila's room and threw her arms around him so hard that she almost knocked him off his feet. "You saved my children!" She pulled away from him and strode from the door to the window, eyes bright, hair flying out behind her, and he thought that he had never seen her look so beautiful. "You're generous and kind and thoughtful and it's most amazing and I hardly know what to say except thank you and thank you again."

"Don't thank me." He laughed. Placing his hands around her waist, he lifted her off her feet so she could dance on the air itself like Shiva dancing the world into being. "It was a purely selfish act."

"Selfish! Don't be ridiculous. It was grand and fine of you."

"Ah no, it was sneaky and sly. I knew saving the children was the one temptation you couldn't resist."

"I don't care what your motives were. Sally and her family are eating regularly; Roy is away from his drunken father; Shirley's stepfather is working again."

"And you're happy?"

Lucy came back to earth, flushed and breathless. "Very happy. For months I tried to help those kids and got nowhere; it was terribly frustrating. I thought they were trapped in the slums forever."

Mila shrugged and sat down on the edge of his bed. "It was nothing. It only took a few phone calls."

She sat down beside him and folded her arms around her knees, and she felt her heart overflowing with love for him. It was complex love, a mix of gratitude and respect and passion, and she sat there letting the emotion sweep through her. I could marry him, she thought. I actually could.

Mila began to stroke her hair lightly with the palm of his hand. "We have a saying in my country that the bridge to love is compassion. We say that if you want to feel love, you need to offer it to others." He paused, and she felt his hand moving across her head, caressing her. "If you marry me, we can save thousands of children; we can save an entire nation. We can do it together, you and I."

His touch was almost hypnotic, and so was the vision he presented to her. He spoke quietly for a long time, describing his plans for the future of his country, and she began to see that future as he saw it: clean, well-run clinics built in remote mountain villages; healthy children playing in front of cinder block homes equipped with electricity and running water; schools staffed with teachers using the latest books; wells free from typhoid; paved roads so farmers could get their goods to market; stores overflowing with rice and vegetables.

"I've already told you that my father opposes these reforms," he concluded, "but I think I can persuade him to let us carry some of them out, perhaps not every single one, but many." He paused. "I tried before without success to convince him that the time was right for change, but I didn't try hard enough, I can see that now. Married to you, I would have ten times the motivation. I would persist and persist, and I think I would ultimately win. He loves me, after all. He's my father, and I can't imagine that he wouldn't come around. We would have to be patient, of course, but ultimately we would win him over." He smiled at her. "No man could resist you for long, not even him."

Lucy sat there bathed in his love, looking at a future full of possibility and promise. If she married Mila, the course of her whole life would be changed. She thought of how lonely she had been since her father's death; she thought of the power she would have as Mila's wife and how much good she could do with it; she thought of how much she loved Mila, and still she hesitated. There was no way to be rational about a thing like this, no way to check off the positives and negatives and arrive at a sensible conclusion. Either you felt in the pit of your stomach you should marry a man or you didn't.

Mila took her hand in his and kissed it. "What are you thinking?" he asked.

"I'm thinking that I need more time to think this over."

"Take all the time you need," he said. "I can wait as long as it takes for you to be absolutely sure."

In the end, it was his patience that convinced her she was making the right decision. It took another week for her to puzzle things out, and not once during that time did he pressure her for an answer. Finally on a rainy Tuesday, having walked the length of Cambridge from Harvard Square to Fresh Pond and back again, she stopped at the Coop, put a dime in one of the pay phones, and dialed his number.

"I'll do it," she told him. "I'll marry you." It was such a relief to have finally come to a decision that she began to cry right there in front of the rows of Harvard mugs and racks of crimson sweatshirts, but people often cried in the Coop because of low grades or lovers' spats or just general depression brought on by the gloomy spring weather, so no one looked twice at her, and it was a private moment after all with Mila whispering in her ear that he loved her while all the books on the shelves blurred into a bank of pastels.

But the privacy didn't last long. That night she and Mila called Uncle Hank and Aunt Kate and told them the news. They had planned to keep their engagement a secret from everyone else until Mila received formal permission from his father, but Cassie came in in the middle of the conversation and she called Andy, who brought over a bottle of peach brandy and some chocolate cookies so they could celebrate in style. While they were drinking the brandy, Joyce Lindsay and her roommate Laura happened by and joined in, Kathy poked her head in to see what all the laughing was about, and the race to spread the news was off and running. By Friday there was probably no one at Harvard who didn't know that the prince of Patan was marrying a 'Cliffie.

In Bolinas, California, Trina put down her hash pipe and gave a sigh of envy. "Oh, wow," she exclaimed, blowing out perfectly good hash smoke as if it were tobacco. "Some American chick is marrying a prince." She folded the newspaper neatly in half and waved it in David's face. "Page one, big headline. Come back to planet earth and have a look."

"Big deal." David put his boots up on the coffee table and began to roll himself a cigarette using Zig Zag papers. He had just kicked Redwood and Creek out of Nickel Bag, taken over the band, appointed himself lead singer, negotiated a record contract with Columbia, and it looked like "Ask van Gogh" was going to go gold, so what the hell did he care? In a couple of months he was going to have enough cash to buy and sell princes like they were used cars.

"Her name is Lucy Constable," Trina read slowly, dragging out each syllable the way she always did when she was stoned. "Say, isn't that the name of that chick from Harvard you're always talking about?"

David rose to his feet, grabbed the paper out of her hand, and read the story. "Oh, shit," he exclaimed. "I don't believe this!"

"What are you getting so bent out of shape about?" Trina said languidly. She rooted around in the pills that filled the brass bowl on the coffee table and came up with a small green one marked with an X. "Drop this and mellow out," she suggested.

"Shut up," David snapped. "Jesus, you don't have a brain in your head, do you?" But he took the pill from her and put it on his tongue and when he swallowed it, it went down with a bitter taste.

BOOK TWO

The Kingdom of Patan
October 1966

• 1 •

Wrapped in *Mila's arms*, Lucy slept a dreamless sleep between red silk sheets in a golden bed shaped like a giant lotus. Caught up in the turmoil of Vietnam, the United States was highballing toward 1967 like a freight train out of control, but she had disembarked. Only five months had passed since she became a princess, but already she had drifted into a rhythm of life that had not changed in a thousand years.

Overlooking the city of Sindhala, the royal palace rose out of the earth like a vast guardian spirit, four stories high, built of pearl-tinted marble from the ancient quarries of Sashmir. Mirrored in four lakes, one for each point of the compass, it floated in perfect detachment as if commenting on the futility of the material world. Night in the valley was as thick as velvet. The stars were so brilliant that the wood carriers walking toward the city along the royal highway could see their shadows sliding over the cobblestones. Not a single machine chattered away in the darkness to disturb her sleep. When she woke, long after daybreak, Mila was gone, and the room was suffused with sunlight that looked like gold lacquer.

"Madam, your tea with *garam masala*."
"Madam, your *sambar*."
"Madam, your devoted servant offers you a fresh honeycomb from the valley of Taklan."

Three young Patanese women dressed in scarlet saris stood around Lucy as she ate breakfast, catering to her every wish. Their names were Asana, Kala, and Radha, and although like most Patanese women they had not been educated beyond the most elementary level, they were intelligent, articulate, interesting people who probably would have made good friends, but although they spoke English and were willing to entertain her endlessly, real contact had proved difficult. They jumped when she spoke, bowed when she entered the room, never brought up a subject she hadn't introduced first, and what their true opinions were on things like equality, arranged marriages, and lifetimes of endless childbearing was anyone's guess, because they spoke only of inconsequential pleasant things: fashions, the weather, festivals, and religious duties. By custom they should have been on their knees in her presence, but she wouldn't have that. When she first arrived, she tried to order them to sit or to leave her alone and go off and do whatever it was they did in the mornings, explaining patiently that she could feed herself and hadn't needed help since she was in a high chair. But the women had protested and wept and said that unless they served her they were nothing and had no place in life. They begged her not to deny them this honor, so she had finally given in and said that they could attend her, only they were never to *praniyam*. When people praniyamed in Patan, they fell to their knees, put their hands over their breasts, and beat their heads against the floor, which she found highly upsetting to say the least, even if she herself had learned to do it in the presence of her father-in-law on state occasions.

"More tea with *garam masala*, madam?" Radha, a plump nineteen-year-old, held out the teapot and waited respectfully. Her hands were adorned with dozens of jeweled rings, and her eyes were bright and mischievous like the eyes of a small, intelligent bird. But whatever mischief she did, she did it privately, out of Lucy's sight, which was a pity.

"More *sambar*?" Asana was thin and yellow and a little clumsy, and Lucy always had to keep an eye on her to make sure the things she offered didn't end up on the floor. An awkward woman in a land where almost everyone else was as graceful as a dancer, she seemed to bear her homeliness with a good humor that often made her seem like a Patanese version of Cassie. Kala, on the other hand, was always sad-looking, which was ironic since she was one of the most beautiful women Lucy had ever seen: doelike and honey-colored, with thick shining black hair long enough to sit on and feet and hands so small that they might have belonged to a child.

Lucy looked at Asana and felt a small burst of optimism. For once she hadn't said "madam." In fact all three of the ladies seemed a little less formal than usual this morning; perhaps she was finally breaking down their reserve. In time she was sure she could make friends of them. It was going to take patience, of course, and a lot of prodding, but since they had been assigned to her for the next fifty years or so, there was no rush. She imagined the four of them in the year 2016, toothless and gray, sitting around on cushions gumming jellied sweets and chattering away a mile a minute in Patanese. Of course she was going to have to learn Patanese first—a task which was proving difficult since it was a tonal language and she'd never had an ear for music. Still, she was taking lessons three afternoons a week and making some progress. Yesterday, for example, she had learned to say, "Please pour me a cup of tea."

Feeling encouraged, she tried the phrase out on Radha and was delighted when the white, milky tea laced with *garam masala* fell steaming into her cup. *Garam masala* was a spice mixture imported from India that had half a dozen different flavors Lucy could never identify. Mixed with tea and heavy cream, it was a meal in itself. The *sambar* was a lentil soup, also heavily spiced, with turmeric, cardamom, asafetida, and hot peppers—a combination that had an electrifying effect on the human body that was difficult to describe. Lucy drank the tea, spooned up the sambar, and sucked at the honeycomb, wishing there were toast to go with it. She could have had a Western breakfast complete with eggs and bacon and even Wheaties if she'd wanted. Mila usually did and so did his aunts. You could get any kind of food you wanted in the palace at any time of day, no matter how exotic. The king was especially fond of English bangers and kippers, and there were stories of visitors who had requested things like seviche and Tab, but she had decided that to get to know a country you had to eat its food, so garam masala tea and sambar for breakfast it was, and *dalbat*, a mixture of spiced lentils and rice eaten bare-fingered from the dish, and even (when she could stand it) rancid yak butter, which was, unfortunately, a traditional Patanese delicacy.

She was just licking the last of the honey off of her fingers when the phone rang. It was an ordinary phone, not gold, not ivory, not embossed with dragons or crowns, but black sturdy plastic forged in the phone factories of Ma Bell, and before Kala could carry it to her on a silk pillow or present it to her under glass like a pheasant, she leapt on it because it was Monday morning and she had a standing call in to Cassie on Mondays.

"Hello," she yelled into the receiver.

"Hello," Cassie yelled back, "hello, hello, are you there, Lucy? This thing is making so much racket that I can barely hear you." The phone crackled and chanted like the monks in the main temple of Sindhala, and the thousands of miles between Ann Arbor and Patan vibrated in Lucy's ear.

"Don't hang up," she yelled. There were no direct phone lines between Sindhala and the outside world, only ship-to-shore-type radio communications beamed to northern India, and thence to God knew where, to cables maybe under the Pacific or maybe to Europe—she should ask Mila some time to explain the route. But however Cassie's voice reached her, it always seemed to pass through hurricanes and typhoons, ending up garbled and almost chipmunklike, fading out at inconvenient times, and on more than one occasion vanishing altogether. Dismissing Asana, Radha, and Kala, she sat back and waited for the static to settle down.

"Cassie?"

"Yes?"

"Can you hear me now?"

"Yes. That's a lot better. What did you do? Execute your operator and get a new one?"

"I don't execute anyone, remember. This is a benevolent monarchy."

"Too bad." Cassie chuckled. "I prefer the idea of heads on pikes. Decapitation has a nice, Elizabethan touch to it, don't you think?"

"Ixnay on the okesjay." Pig Latin wasn't a very sophisticated code, but Lucy hoped the Patanese operator wouldn't understand. There was no privacy on the line, something Cassie never managed to remember. Perhaps the king would be amused at the suggestion that she went about beheading incompetent phone operators, and perhaps he wouldn't, but why find out.

"Sorry," Cassie apologized. She yawned audibly. "It's one A.M. here in Ann Arbor and I'm beat to a frazzle. Andy hasn't come in yet from the lab, and I can't go to sleep without him because it's too cold. Men, as far as I can tell, were designed to heat up beds for women. How's Mila? Still putting out the BTUs?"

"Better than ever." Lucy smiled, thinking of last night and how sweet the lovemaking had been. So far one of the major advantages of being a princess had been endless amounts of time.

"Glad to hear it," Cassie said. "Who would have believed that we'd both end up happily married old ladies. Now if I could just quit having this fantasy of feeding my father steak with a side order of poison mushrooms, life would be sweet indeed. I think he's working Andy too hard, and you should see the new Quinn Institute—six stories of cement and glass. It looks like a goddam ice tray." She yawned again. "So how's the princess biz?"

"Not bad." Lucy propped her feet up on the table and wiggled her bare toes lazily. "Ninety percent of it seems to consist of planting trees, cutting ribbons, and making speeches. This afternoon, for instance, I'm going out to officiate at a ground-breaking ceremony for a new grade school. The king is very interested in the *trappings* of Western development." She hoped that the word "trappings" was not in the operator's vocabulary and that Cassie would get the ironic emphasis. King Marpa was indeed interested in westernization, but as far as she could tell his interest was only superficial. He ordered his ties and cars from London and loved nothing better than staging events designed to impress visiting foreigners with how progressive his kingdom was, but it was mostly window dressing. Take the new grade school, for example. It was going to have an elaborate lunchroom, a cricket field, and a small film library, and no doubt the children who went there—all of whom were from rich families—would get a superb education. Meanwhile 94 percent of the population was illiterate. None of this could be explained on the phone, however. Nor could she tell Cassie something else even more important, something that she was absolutely dying to tell her.

"Other than that," she continued, "not much is happening. Last Saturday there was a memorial ceremony for Mila's uncle, the one who died in May. It featured the usual chanting and public procession, but since I never had a chance to meet the man, I felt rather on the outside of the whole thing."

"Well, I have some real gossip for you."

"What's that?"

"David Blake has a hit record."

Lucy sat up so fast that she nearly knocked the remains of the sambar into her lap. "David has a hit record? You've got to be kidding."

"Couldn't be more serious. It's called 'Ask van Gogh,' and right now it's at the top of the charts. You can't go anywhere without hearing it. And that's not all."

"What more could there be?"

"Big time, fast lane. A new Porsche, a house in Bel-Air, Janis Joplin over for quiet little dinner parties, bales of Acapulco gold flown in from Mexico by some weirdo named Snowman, a whole fishbowl full of Colombian cocaine on the cut-glass coffee table, tanks of laughing gas in the kitchen, and a party that never stops."

"How do you happen to know all this?" Lucy did her best to keep her voice casual, but the mention of David's name had its usual effect. Suddenly the sunlight in the room wasn't as golden, and the clear air of Sindhala seemed murky and tropical and hard to breathe. "Did one of his numerous girlfriends spill her guts to the press?"

"No, weirder than that." Cassie paused and cleared her throat. "He called me last week."

"Why?"

"To ask about you, of course."

Lucy felt a small, irrational surge of pain. "Oh," she said, "you don't say. Well, what did you tell him about me?"

"I told him you were deliriously happy with Mila and that if he made any attempt to contact you, the Patanese secret police would castrate him and stake him out for the vultures."

"You didn't!"

"Well, not in so many words, but I think he got the point. It was a very interesting conversation. Seems he ran into Steve and Ann Singleton a few weeks ago on some kind of rural commune in Vermont when he was on tour with his band." There was another pause, longer this time, and Lucy could hear the static rising into the silence like a thousand humming crickets. "Guess what our old friends are up to."

"I haven't a clue."

"Target practice."

"What?"

"You know," Cassie said cryptically, "bang, bang."

Lucy suddenly realized what Cassie was trying to say: Ann and Steve were living on some kind of radical commune learning how to shoot guns. She was so stunned that for a moment she just looked at the phone trying to imagine Ann with a pistol in her hand, but the Ann in Lucy's memory was still the Ann of midnight brownies and pink curlers and freshman year in Holmes Hall. "But why in the world would they be doing something like that?"

"Can't say on the onephay."

"Dammit." Lucy tapped her fingers on the inlaid table wishing she could interrogate Cassie further but knowing it was out of the question. "I leave home and everything falls apart."

"You said it. Things are changing here. You can't imagine how fast. There've been big demonstrations, riots, everyone seems to be going crazy."

"But I've only been gone five months!"

"Well, it might as well be five years." Cassie laughed a mirthless, worried laugh. "But never fear, your personal clipping service is still functioning. I'm sending you some articles on a big demonstration in Washington against the war. The papers reported that there were only about two thousand people there, but they were really off the wall. There must have been at least ten."

" 'Off the wall'? What does that mean?"

"It means they were wrong, deceptive, not playing by the rules. You know, like when you heave something at a wall and it bounces back in your face."

"I'm getting worried." Lucy frowned at the black receiver full of holes that was her only link to the life she'd left behind. "I'm gone five months and you're using expressions I've never heard before. At this rate after I've been in Patan five years, we'll have to talk through an interpreter."

"Don't worry," Cassie said. "I'm sending you a list of the new slang so you can keep up, and, oh yeah, I'm also sending you David's new hit record. It's full of sound and fury, signifying nothing, which is as good a summary of Blake's character as anyone could ask for, right?"

They talked for nearly an hour, and Lucy could easily have gone on for another hour, but it was two o'clock in Ann Arbor by that time, and Cassie began to fade out into some sleepy, dark nighttime space that she couldn't share. After Lucy hung up, she put on a light blue and white silk sari and went out to take a walk in one of the gardens until Mila got back from seeing to his polo ponies. Saris were comfortable and cool, but they took getting used to. Nothing held them on except a series of ingenious tucks and folds, and she always had the feeling that she was wandering around in a large bath towel. As she walked toward the garden, she reminded herself not to clutch at her clothing. It didn't do for a princess to look as if she were afraid of stepping out of her dress.

Actually there were sixteen gardens in the palace (or maybe it was seventeen—she had more or less lost track—not counting the small one behind her apartment). Each of them was built around some special theme. There was an English garden with a white gazebo, a French garden with clipped hedges and classical statuary, a Hindu garden with a huge statue of Vishnu floating in a pond full of lilies and exotic spotted carp, and so on. She enjoyed all of them, but this morning, feeling upset by the strange news from home, she was drawn to the kitchen garden. Although she only visited it once or twice a month, it soothed her in a way the other gardens could never match. She loved the familiar sight of cucumbers and green beans and onions, which reminded her of her childhood and the small, struggling kitchen gardens her mother had planted, gardens that had always somehow managed to survive the desert heat.

The only problem was that when she was in the garden the kitchen servants wouldn't come out and pick the vegetables. She didn't even like to think about the time she had gone inside to urge them to carry on as usual. My God, she had very nearly given the chef a heart attack. He had fallen to his knees with a soup ladle in his hand and praniyamed himself almost to death, and the whole staff had flattened out on the tiles as if she'd knocked them flat by stepping through the door, and she had been terribly embarrassed. So now she only gave herself an hour among the vegetables.

Sitting down on a wooden bench, she adjusted her sari, watched the bees pollinating the pea plants, and tried to put David and the Singletons out of her mind, but they buzzed in the back of her head like a bad phone connection. Patan seemed to have strange seasons that didn't correspond in any way to the ones back home. The monsoon rains that had thundered down on the Sindhala Valley during July and August had suddenly stopped and she had awakened one morning to discover that white-capped mountains had burst out of the fog. Now it was October, but it felt like spring instead of fall.

Looking up at the mountains, she thought of the day ahead of her. At noon, Mila would return from the stables, and they would have a private lunch together. Then she was scheduled to plant a tree on the site of the new school and afterward attend a big Western-style reception, where her job would consist mainly of nibbling curried hors d'oeuvres and being gracious. What was left of the afternoon would be spent with her secretary planning the following day's activities. If she was lucky, she might have time for a short nap, which she would need because tonight after dinner there was going to be another film showing in the royal theater, and they always ran well past midnight. The king was crazy about foreign films—especially westerns—and what he watched, they all watched. You would have thought that a sophisticated monarch with a first in philosophy from Oxford would have preferred Bergman to John Wayne, but she had sat through *The Alamo* six times already, and she had a sneaking suspicion that tonight it was going to be *Rio Bravo* again.

Gradually her anxiety dissolved in the peace and quiet of the tomato plants and rows of spinach. At exactly twelve o'clock, she got up and went back to her rooms to meet Mila. As she strolled through the long, cool corridors, she thought about how much living in the palace was like living in a large dorm. It was a huge building, so monstrously complex that she probably hadn't seen half of it yet, but no matter where she went, she was never really alone. Mila's aunts and uncles and cousins lived in one wing; members of the highest orders of the nobility occupied another; the king and his companions took up enough space for a small village.

Lucy gave a small sigh of exasperation as she noticed that, as usual, she was being watched from all angles by devoted servants ready to hop forward with whatever she might require. When she'd fought Kathy DeVelt for the bathroom at 24 Garden Street she'd had more privacy. Still, she really shouldn't complain. Mila had been great about helping her adjust to this fishbowl. She knew for a fact that the king had not been happy about the marriage, but he had given Mila formal permission within a month, which was evidently something of a record. As far as she could tell, Marpa bore her no particular ill will for capturing Mila's affections. He was distant but very cordial, and following his lead, everyone down to the most minor of minor cousins had done his best to make her feel at home. She was lucky; they could have resented her for being a foreigner or even hated her for marrying Mila, but so far the Patanese were the most polite people she had ever met, and if she was a little lonely and homesick and sometimes longed for Cassie and her old friends, well, that was to be expected. Soon she and Mila would receive permission to begin setting up the rural health clinics, and then all her time would be taken, and she'd spend no more leisurely mornings waiting for him to get back from seeing to his ponies. Meanwhile, she was still on her honeymoon in one of the most romantic places in the world. Mila was still her best friend, and making love with him was better than ever.

She stopped for a moment in front of a large blue Chinese vase adorned with flying cranes. Touching her belly lightly with the tips of her fingers, she smiled a smile that no servant, no matter how astute, could have penetrated. Life in the palace might be like living on "Candid Camera," but she did have one real secret: her period was a week late. She was thrilled by the thought that she might be pregnant.

King Marpa's throne room was partially a replica of the Hall of Mirrors of Versailles and partially a reconstruction of the Royal Reception Hall of the sixteenth-century Patanese ruler Vandu the Great. Running the full length of the palace, it had been designed to awe, intimidate, and cower anyone who had the temerity to walk through the forty-foot-high wooden doors. Frowning demons and snarling tigers rampaged across a ceiling adorned with enough gold leaf to fund a good-sized Swiss bank. The floor, paved with priceless antique Chinese tiles, was perfect for groveling, and the massive ebony throne that dominated the far end of the hall was encrusted with so many jeweled dragons, exploding lotus blossoms, copulating gods, and golden lightning bolts that it took the full-time attention of three servants just to keep it dusted.

Unfortunately, however, for all its grandeur the throne room was a cold, gloomy, rather depressing place to sit, so Marpa never used it except to receive foreign ambassadors, vastly preferring the small, cozy chamber behind the throne which he kept furnished in nineteenth-century Victorian antiques that reminded him of those happy days at Oxford when he had nothing to do for months on end but box, play cricket, and read Spinoza.

On this particular Monday, having finished the work of the morning, he was just watering the three Japanese bonsai trees that sat on his desk—a job he entrusted to no one—when there was a discreet knock at the door.

"Yes?" Marpa said, not looking up from the trees.

The door opened and the lord chamberlain entered and praniyamed, tapping his head on the thick Belgian carpet. Marpa had had the carpet installed because, although he approved of the practice of praniyaming to the king, the chamberlain was an old man who had served his father, and he had no desire to watch him end each day with a bruised forehead. He liked to think of himself as a progressive monarch, within reasonable limits, of course.

"Well, what is it?" Marpa said impatiently. No one could speak to him until he spoke, which was probably a good custom since it instilled respect for kingship, but it was often rather inconvenient.

The lord chamberlain struggled to his feet, looking relieved to have been recognized so rapidly. The king intimidated everyone, even his oldest servants. Standing behind his desk with the silver water pitcher in his hand, he looked like an old lion: gray-haired, stocky, buddha-bellied, with a stubborn chin, and arms that still displayed the muscles of a man who in his youth had been a champion bantam weight boxer. As a prince he had been famously handsome, and some of the old charm still clung to him, but five years ago he had had a mild heart attack. Although he had recovered remarkably, his blood pressure was still dangerously high and his after-dinner rages, although rare, were the stuff of legends. Fortunately this morning he seemed to be in a good temper; breathing a sigh of relief, the lord chamberlain bowed again, this time in the Western manner, and delivered his message quickly and precisely, because if there was one thing the king couldn't stand it was formality and circumlocution. "Radha, second lady of the princess's chamber, requests an audience with Your Majesty."

"She does, eh?" Marpa put down the pitcher. "Well, what are you waiting for? Send her in." A minute later the second lady of the princess's chamber was praniyaming on his carpet, her red sari spread out around her like one of those trumpet flowers the hummingbirds loved so much. "You have news of the princess, madam?" Marpa asked, wiping off the water pitcher with a clean linen handkerchief and replacing it in his desk drawer next to the great seal of Patan.

"Yes, O Divine One."

"Well, out with it, woman." She was pretty and plump, but her sensuous beauty left Marpa more or less cold. He had wasted far too much time on women in his youth.

The second lady of the chamber cleared her throat and, as custom dictated, carefully avoided looking him in the face. "The princess's period is six days late, O Divine One, and it is thought among her ladies that she may be with child."

Well, Marpa thought, that was good news. He'd been against this foreign marriage from the moment Mila had announced his engagement, but the boy had been stubborn and determined, two traits Marpa rather admired since they reminded him of himself. To have resisted his whim might well have driven him to do something even more foolish, so Marpa had given in and blessed the match with as much good grace as he could muster, hiding his annoyance. But if this Western wife was going to prove fertile, then perhaps it was for the best, after all. For some reason the kings of Patan had always had trouble begetting heirs.

"Does the princess know that her ladies have been keeping track of her menses?"

"No, Divine One."

"Make sure she has no suspicion," he ordered. "Her customs are different from ours, and to realize that she is being watched would undoubtedly cause her great anxiety. Should she get her period, I wish, of course, to be informed at once." Marpa kept his face stern and kingly, but his voice was warmer than usual. He was pleased by this fortunate turn of events. If the princess bore a male child, then the succession would be ensured, a particularly important issue now that his brother was no longer alive. He could go gracefully into his old age without worrying that his line would die out; on the other hand, if she bore only girls, Mila could always take another wife. He himself had had several wives, all now dead or living in retirement on various country estates. And when one tired of wives, there were always concubines to take care of a man's needs. It was a convenient, sensible system. Marpa often wondered why Westerners insisted on marrying only one woman, but his years at Oxford had convinced him that there was no use trying to reason with them.

* * *

The news of Lucy's pregnancy spread rapidly. General Arjuna was getting a massage when he heard about it, lying naked on a softly padded table while his bodyguard gently worked the pain out of his left shoulder. The bodyguard, who also served as an aide to the general, was a burly giant who often conducted private interrogations at Arjuna's country estate, but he was also capable of touching the human body with incomparable grace and delicacy. The general, in contrast, was a short, bowlegged man who seemed to be made out of strings of raw leather.

"You say the princess may be pregnant?" Arjuna frowned, sat up on one elbow, and motioned to his bodyguard to stop massaging him for a moment so he could concentrate on the bad news that his informer had just brought to him.

"Yes, my general." The informer was a pretty, childlike woman with silky black hair whom Lucy would instantly have recognized as Kala, her lady-in-waiting.

"Most unfortunate." The general growled, reaching for a towel. He turned to his bodyguard. "If this foreign wife bears a male child, it would be a disaster. Go get me Dr. Sukra at once." The bodyguard bowed, wiped the oil from his hands, and left the room immediately. He was a man of few words, a trait Arjuna prized. Securing the towel around his waist, Arjuna threw his bandy legs over the edge of the table, leapt down to the floor, and strode over to the wall safe. Inside were a dozen small envelopes containing fixed amounts of money, from ten to a thousand Patanese rupees, all prepared in advance because the general had many informers. Pausing for a moment, Arjuna scratched his chest and calculated what the information was worth. A hundred now, a hundred later, he thought. Selecting a hundred-rupee packet, he handed it to Kala.

"Come back tomorrow morning," he ordered.

Kala did an abbreviated praniyam, even though praniyams were supposedly reserved for gods and the royal family, because the general was powerful and he paid well and it never hurt to flatter him as much as possible. "Yes, my general."

"You will, of course, make sure no one knows you have been here." His voice was soft, but there was enough of a threat in it to make Kala pale. The general was famous for his revenges on the informers who betrayed him. There was a whispered story that he had once sacrificed a clumsy spy to Kali.

"I will make sure," she promised, too frightened to meet his eyes.

"Good." Arjuna dismissed her with a wave of his hand, went over to the concealed liquor cabinet, and poured himself a shot of the finest French cognac money could buy. As a Hindu he was not supposed to touch alcohol, but he considered that rule did not apply to him. The superior man didn't follow the morality of the herd; he created his own. Even in the Hindu tradition itself, the enlightened being could perform acts forbidden to those still lost in ignorance.

Sitting down on a large cushion, the general folded his legs into a half-lotus and considered the implications of the news that the pretty little informer had brought him. The king was ill, his son a westernized, idealistic fool who ignored traditional values and was soft on the kind of socialist nonsense that might bring about a communist revolution like the one in Vietnam. Arjuna saw himself as the keeper of the traditional Patanese way of life, guardian of an ancient system in which all the social classes knew their place. As the king's third cousin, head of the Patanese Secret Service, and one of the wealthiest and most powerful men in Patan, it was not out of the question that he, Arjuna, might someday succeed to the throne, especially if he had an army behind him. For the past year in the remote southern jungles, he and his two younger brothers had been training and equipping their own private forces. In another year, two at the most, they would be ready to stage a coup, but if the princess had a son and heir, the child would become immensely popular with the lower classes who would hail the boy as a new god and fight to defend him. In Arjuna's mind there was only one solution to this dilemma: the princess must never have a child, now or at any time in the future.

Dr. Sukra, head of the Royal Hospital, was the obvious choice. His politics were conservative, he owed Arjuna many favors, and best of all he was something of a coward. There should be no trouble getting some sort of medicine from him that would end this pregnancy before it really began. And after that, then what? The general drank his cognac thoughtfully. Birth control pills, perhaps. No, it would be too hard to slip them in her food every morning without getting caught, and besides, from what he'd read, there were often noticeable side effects.

Perhaps Sukra could suggest something that would render her permanently sterile.

    Dear Cass [Lucy wrote a week later], Do you remember that old joke we used to tell when we were in high school, the one about the typewriter that skipped a period? Well, I think that maybe—just maybe—I've become the punch line. Don't tell anyone: not Andy, not even your new cat. This is optay ecretsay. I haven't even told Mila yet for reasons you can probably figure out, because what if I'm mistaken? I'd feel like that idiot character in "Who's Afraid of Virginia Woolf," the one who bloated up with a false alarm—what was her name? Honey, I think.

    My God, Cass, just the hint of it would bring the world down on me: astrologers casting the Potential's chart; official announcements to three hundred of the closest relatives; *pujas* chanted at all the main temples. I'm gearing myself up to survive all that, but for now, just for now, I want to keep the good news to myself until I'm absolutely sure. The prospect is exciting, but a little scary, too, like getting onto a bobsled and wooshing down a tunnel of ice. Ever since I turned fourteen, I've had the same body, and over the years it's grown as comfortable and predictable as an old pair of shoes. Now it's developed a mind of its own. I feel like an adolescent again. Oh, Cass, I'm so happy. Keep your fingers crossed for me, and pray to whatever god you're observing now—the great Earth Mother or the Jolly Green Giant or the Immaculate Lady of Cross Pollination—that this isn't a false alarm.

    It took over a week for the letter to reach Ann Arbor and make its way into the mail slot of Cassie and Andy's apartment in the University of Michigan Married Students Housing Complex. It arrived about ten o'clock in the morning, as Cassie was sitting in the bathtub eating a late bowl of oatmeal and reading a copy of Halliwell's *Ecology of Tropical Bromeliads*. As soon as she heard the postman, she put her book down, crawled out of the hot water, grabbed a towel, and padded toward the front door, leaving small puddles on the ugly green linoleum that the university provided to all its married graduate students for the modest sum of $125 per month plus utilities. Lucy's letter, which had fallen into the small Mexican basket by the door, was unmistakable. The Patanese made a tidy profit on their stamps, which were beautiful; this one was bright red and featured a large elephant.

Shades of Lucy's wedding day, Cassie thought, pouncing on the letter and tearing it open. Andy, who slit his letters neatly at the end, was always trying to get her to penetrate the mail with more grace, but she liked to eviscerate it, rip the envelope to shreds, and tear out the contents. Unfolding Lucy's letter, Cassie read it quickly, growing more excited with every word. So Lucy was pregnant! She'd have to call her up, congratulate her, wish her health and . . . She was halfway across the living room and already reaching for the phone, before she realized that calling was out of the question.

Rats, she thought. This is supposed to be Optay Ecretsay, and those Patanese operators have ears like bats; they can hear gossip into the high frequency range, and if they get wind of this, Lucy's never going to forgive you. You're her confidante, so cool it, Quinn. And then, recalling that she was now a Rabinowitz, legally and in her heart, she rephrased that order to herself: Cool it, Rabinowitz. Only as much as she loved Andy, her new last name still sounded foreign and awkward, as if she were using an alias.

Running her fingers through her hair, she reread Lucy's letter several times, then folded it up and took it into the bedroom with the vague intention of hiding it somewhere well out of sight since Lucy had commanded that Andy, too, be kept in the dark, at least for the moment. Now where should she put the thing? She looked around the room. On one wall her best photographs were displayed, neatly framed in pieces of tropical wood that she and Andy had brought back from Costa Rica. The other walls sported brightly colored Guatemalan blankets that they had bought during a stop-over in Quezaltenango. What a bus ride that had been: twenty-four hours to Guatemala City and then eighty-eight hours from Guatemala City to Ann Arbor! By the time they finally arrived at the university, she and Andy were hallucinating from fatigue, which, when she thought about it, was probably not all that bad a way to end a honeymoon.

Walking over to the dresser, she pulled open the top drawer and stuck Lucy's letter under her spare socks. What a brilliant hiding place; some spy she would make. But of course Andy would never pry. He was a very ethical person, very. She hadn't appreciated how ethical when she married him. Andy wouldn't even read a postcard if you left it out in the open.

All the rest of the morning, she went around feeling excited. Lucy's secret burned inside her during her Botany 425 lecture, so that she could barely concentrate on the slides of Amazonian flora that Professor Patterson was tossing up on the screen. "A tropical forest is much like the ocean," Patterson informed the class. "Most of the light is concentrated in the upper canopy," but Cassie's notes consisted of doodles, all of them round and pregnant.

At one-thirty, she met Andy for lunch in the Student Union, one of the few times during the day that they got to see each other since he had started taking classes in biochemistry. She found him sitting at a table with a pile of computer punch cards at his elbow, making some calculations in a small black notebook. His shirt was wrinkled, and he looked bleary-eyed and tired, which wasn't surprising since he had been up all night trying to get a computer program to run.

"What's with you?" Andy said the second he saw her. "You look strange."

"Strange?" Cassie ducked her head and consulted the menu. "I don't know what you mean."

"You look guilty, honey. What's up? Did Watusi, Junior, climb up on the kitchen counter and eat our supper again?"

"Umph." Cassie shook her head and pretended to be lost in a decision between a hamburger and a grilled cheese.

Andy reached across the table, took her hands, and kissed them. "Cass," he said, "give up. I always can tell when you have a secret. What is it? Are you failing phytogeography? Having an affair with Patterson? I'd ask you if you'd dented the fender of our car, only we don't have a car, so what is it?"

Lucy's pregnant! Cassie thought, *that's what!* and she was so tempted to say the words out loud that she had to excuse herself abruptly, take herself off to the ladies' room, and splash cold water on her face. Fortunately, when she got back Andy was looking at his computer cards and shaking his head, too distracted by the discovery that he'd punched some of them wrong to go on with the interrogation.

Lucy's orders had been clear and specific. *Tell no one, not even your new cat,* but Watusi, Jr., was a dear, dumb beast, and that night sitting around in her slippers and bathrobe waiting for Andy to come back from the computer center, Cassie transgressed and told Watusi, Jr., whispering it into one furry ear while she scratched her on the stomach. "Wat, old girl," she said, "my best friend is about to have a baby. What do you have to say about that?" But although Watusi, Jr., looked sympathetic, she had no comment beyond a quick lick at Cassie's wrist.

Picking up a pen, Cassie found a piece of paper and tried to write Lucy a discreet note of congratulations, only the more cryptic she tried to be, the more obvious it all seemed, as if she were writing *baby* in red letters on every inch of the paper.

Frustrated, she stuck the pen back in the cracked coffee cup that held her favorite writing implements and temporarily gave up. The problem wasn't just that she had to write Lucy in some kind of code that would pass the censors; the problem was her own life. She was happy for Lucy, excited, even thrilled. But also, for the first time she could remember, she was a little jealous of her, too, not because Lucy was pregnant, although that did give her a bit of a twinge, but because Lucy was so obviously happy with Mila, riding smoothly on the crest of what seemed to be a perfect marriage, while she, Cassie, was confused and even a little worried about what seemed to be happening between her and Andy; correction: of what *didn't* seem to be happening.

She sat for a moment, looking down at her white bedroom slippers, and then at her robe which was sexy enough, blue and quilted and edged with lace, bought for their honeymoon and never used for it because they had gone to the hot lowlands of Costa Rica, thanks to Halliwell, who had gotten them a grant from the National Science Foundation. I don't look bad, she thought, so why doesn't Andy come home early enough to make love to me while we both still have the energy? And then she thought how unfair she was being and how hard Andy was working and how much they loved each other, and she felt a bit petty and like one of those nagging wives you saw in cartoons: Andy's old lady, his ball and chain. Only the difference was that she hadn't said a word to Andy yet about how she hated being alone so many nights in a row, except for trying to warn him about her father and how Larry Quinn pushed and pushed and how he was pushing Andy without Andy realizing it.

The apartment was very quiet. She could hear the clock ticking in the bedroom because the walls were paper thin. Enough of this, she thought. I can't expect Andy to want to make love every single night like he did when we were on our honeymoon. When he's here, he's wonderful and attentive and passionate. How many wives are that lucky? Giving herself a brisk shake, she got to her feet, went over to the minuscule stove in the combination living room/kitchen/dining room, and put on a kettle of hot water with the intention of making herself some tea. After the water boiled, she got out a bag of Lipton's, dunked it a few times, and took the result over to the kitchen table where she sat sipping it, trying to talk herself into a more reasonable frame of mind, but it was hard going.

She found herself thinking nostalgically of how happy she and Andy had been when they first got married. There had been the adventure of going to Patan to attend Lucy's wedding, and then their long honeymoon on the remote Peninsula de Osa in Costa Rica. They had lived in a wooden house on stilts, making love on two army cots lashed together with vines that Andy had macheted down from the rain forest. The forest itself had been tall and cool and green, filled with parrots and fabulous plants, and it had been surprisingly temperate, like a great cathedral of shade. In the mornings they had gone out early while it was still cool to collect specimens of various tropical plants for a monograph Halliwell was writing, and by noon they had been finished for the day, free to swim in the stream or lie around lazily on their cots, drinking rum mixed with warm Coke.

It had been an idyllic life, very laid back, and except for a few bouts with mosquitoes and one memorable confrontation with a large snake, very peaceful. And then one morning, quite by accident, Andy had made a discovery and their life began to change. The discovery had seemed trivial at first, nothing more than a few unusually large plants growing around the edge of a leaf cutter ant nest. The plants were something the locals called *Bruja Mala*, members of the family *Umbelliferae*, which made them distant relatives of the carrot, and all of them seemed to be infected with a white fungus.

Intrigued by the possibility that there might be some connection between the fungus and the size of the plants, Andy had collected a few specimens, brought them back to Ann Arbor, and let them sit in a cardboard box for several weeks while he and Cassie unpacked, enrolled in the university, and tried to get their lives in order. Then sometime in early September, he had stumbled on them, and out of curiosity taken them to Quinn.

Now, sitting here alone drinking her tea, Cassie could see with the wisdom of hindsight that that had been a mistake. Her father had pounced on the specimens, examined them, and informed Andy in no uncertain terms that he might be "on the track of a new natural gibberellin"—which, translated into plain English, meant that Andy might have accidentally discovered a substance that would make plants grow faster. Clearing out a place in the huge greenhouse that was attached to his new laboratory, he had commanded Andy to grow the plants, complete with fungus. "You've got your doctoral dissertation, son," he'd said, patting Andy on the back in a way that had made Cassie practically gag, and then he'd ordered Andy to take more courses than any human being could be expected to survive: Advanced Biochemistry, Molecular Genetics, Ecology of Forest Fungi, Morphology and Evolution of Vascular Plants, a Plant Physiology lab, not to mention Computer Science, which was a whole semester of torturous work in itself. So for nearly two months now, Andy had been working himself sick, getting maybe four hours of sleep a night, eating irregularly when he ate at all, coming home at crazy hours. Cassie had pleaded with him not to exhaust himself; she'd begged him to slow down, take fewer courses, not let her father push him so hard, but Andy had been high on the prospect of making an important discovery; he was off somewhere in the ozone of ambition, not meaning to neglect her, sweet and loving when he was home, but home so little.

In some ways, the worst part of all this was how excited he was. She had to hand it to her father: he had a genius for motivating his students. It was as if he had intuited Andy's whole history, as if he'd known, without being told, that Andy had always been compared to his older brother, that he was driven by a sense of being second-rate, that he'd do anything to succeed because failure felt like the end of the world.

Cassie took a sip of tea, looked at her watch, and wondered how late Andy would be tonight. Then she tried once again to tell herself that she was worrying unnecessarily, that this was just a transition period. Andy wouldn't work this hard for the next four years. In January they were both planning to take their Preliminary Examinations and request admission to Candidacy. After that, surely things would slow down.

Picking up her pen, she began once again to compose a letter to

Lucy. This time, by some fortunate quirk of fate, she was inspired. "Dear Lucy," she wrote, "Congratulations and Happy Birthday!" Lucy would get the message; it was nowhere near her birthday, which didn't come around for another two months. Grinning, Cassie proceeded to write a letter full of wonderful, cryptic nonsense. By the time she finished, she was in a much better mood.

• 2 •

"Move aside."

"Prepare for the passing of Her Majesty, the princess."

"Pick up those baskets of vegetables, old woman."

All Monday morning the royal army moved through Sindhala along the route that Lucy would take in the afternoon, herding cripples and beggars out of sight, replacing ragged children with neatly dressed students from Sindhala Preparatory School. The soldiers needed no guns to accomplish this cleansing of the route. The poor moved obediently out of the way where their unsightly suffering would not offend the royal eye. None of them offered the slightest resistance. Things had always been this way. For over a thousand years when the princesses of Patan moved through the city, they had seen it at its best.

"Sindhala isn't at all like you described it," Lucy told Mila that night as they lay together in the lotus bed listening to one of his favorite Modern Jazz Quartet records.

"In what way, my love?" Mila stroked her wonderful golden hair, and kissed the curve of her neck. In the background Milt Jackson launched into a vibraphone solo that filled the air with notes so clear they seemed like broken crystal.

Lucy frowned, sat up, and reached for the pitcher of cold lemonade that sat on the night table. Pouring herself a glass, she drank it off and then poured herself another. "I'd thought from what you told me back in Cambridge that things were in a terrible mess, but frankly the people look like something out of *National Geographic.*" She drank more lemonade, licked her lips with a quick sweep of her tongue, and tossed her hair out of her eyes. "Oh, there's poverty, that's plain enough. Some of those older houses near the market look as if a dozen families are crowded into places built for half that number, and the blacksmiths' shops around Kalpa Square are little pits from hell, but today on my way to dedicate the new school site I rode all the way across the city and didn't see a single beggar. And the children looked as well fed as any I've ever seen." She put down the glass and folded her arms around her knees. "In fact they looked too well fed. Is it just my imagination or are things being cleaned up for my benefit?"

"It is not your imagination." Mila found to his surprise that he was embarrassed by her question. He had always taken the cleansing of the streets for granted, but now he saw it through her eyes and was ashamed. It was just the sort of thing an underdeveloped country would do—herd beggars into alleys where they wouldn't mess up the scenery; he couldn't imagine why he had let it go on for so long without protest. "It is an ancient custom to clear the streets for the passage of the royal family," he admitted, "not that that makes it any better."

"Aha! I thought so." She leaned forward, her face flushed and eager as if she had just solved a difficult puzzle. "It's just like Potemkin and Catherine the Great."

"Pardon?" He was puzzled by the reference, but then he was often puzzled by how much this lovely wife of his knew. She seemed to have a whole library of odd facts stored in her brain.

"Potemkin was Catherine the Great's prime minister, her lover, too, so they say. He had some crazy plan to colonize the Ukrainian steppes, but he underestimated the cost, so when Catherine came to inspect his progress he erected fake villages along the riverbanks. The villages were filled with 'peasants' who danced and sang and waved flags, rather like those chubby schoolchildren I went past this afternoon. Where do they get them, the children I mean? Fly them in from Hollywood?"

"They come from Sindhala Preparatory School."

Lucy giggled. "Well, that's a relief. I was afraid they were professional midget actors." She stretched and yawned. "When do I get to see the real children? The ones not on the royal payroll?"

"Soon," Mila promised. But he knew even as he said the words that it wasn't going to be that easy. His father would have to approve any visits to the real poor of Sindhala, and so far he had been uncooperative to say the least, not that Mila hadn't tried to reason with him, but it had been like trying to talk to a wall. He was tempted to admit to Lucy that his father was being a stubborn fool, but that meant he would also have to admit that he wasn't yet able to keep the promise he had made to her when she agreed to be his wife, and what would she think of him then? It was perfectly understandable that a man trying to persuade a woman to marry him might be overly optimistic about what he could accomplish, but Lucy might not see it that way. She might feel deceived. He dreaded losing her respect; he adored her, and if she looked at him for even one second with contempt, it would be more than he could bear. Her beauty dazzled him even now, and he gazed longingly at her bare shoulders, honey-colored in the candlelight, thinking that she was a source of endless energy: *Om Mani Padma Om*, the jewel in the lotus.

Stretching out beside him again, Lucy put her bare feet against his legs and rested her head on his shoulder. "You know," she said, "despite all these school openings and ground breakings and my Patanese lessons, I feel positively unemployed," and then she laughed to take the sting out of the complaint, because the truth was she was very happy with Mila and didn't want him to think she was ungrateful.

He kissed her, promising himself that tomorrow he would go to his father and again insist that he let Lucy set up at least one rural clinic. She kissed him back, and they lay quietly for a long time, mouth to mouth, as the candle burned and flickered into a blue-gray shadow. After a while, Lucy sighed softly and moved even closer. Lifting one leg, she slid it around his side and stroked him with the velvety inside of her thigh. Mila felt a ripple of pleasure run through his body. *Make love to me*, her leg was saying. Spreading her hair out on the pillow, he hid his face in it, inhaling the oranges and musk and roses of her skin, rolling her in his arms, feeling her hands tremble on his back, listening to her cries of pleasure, answering her body with his own.

The next morning, immediately after breakfast, Mila went straight to his father's study. "Lucy and I are still waiting for your approval to set up the rural clinics," he said, as if his father hadn't refused him twenty times before and the approval were merely a formality.

"Impossible!" Marpa snapped. "How often must I tell you that setting up rural clinics is too radical a project?" He was having an attack of liver and was in no mood to deal with his son's whims.

"I think you're wrong." Mila was determined not to give in this time. "As I have pointed out on several occasions, those clinics would improve the life of the peasants immensely."

"Certainly." Marpa flicked at an invisible speck of dust and placed one of his pens at a right angle to the blotter on his desk, reminding himself that his son was young and addled with love. "Not to mention lead to a revolution. You should read the reports General Arjuna has been submitting." He thumped a stack of large black folders marked with the crest of the Secret Service. "The communists are doing their best to organize the peasants and arm them. This week alone, Arjuna's men have had to deal with the infiltration of seven village councils."

Mila frowned, knowing only too well what "deal with" meant when it involved Arjuna's death squads. He disliked Arjuna intensely and had long tried to convince his father to dismiss him, but Marpa was terrified of a communist revolution, and Arjuna was adept at playing on that fear.

"The Patanese Liberation Front would like nothing better than an excuse to tell the peasants that the clinics were part of a plot to poison them and make them sterile," Marpa continued. He saw the disappointment on Mila's face and softened a little. "I know this means a lot to your wife, but there are other things she can do."

"Like what?"

"Dedicate more schools; get to work on the new operating room. Build some kind of cultural center."

"But what she wants to do is set up the clinics."

The whites of Marpa's eyes were yellow with fatigue and his stomach churned; Mila's stubbornness enraged him because it was a mirror of his own. "When you inherit the throne you can do as you like," he said. He tensed his boxer's shoulders and leaned forward like an old, irritable lion about to spring. "But as long as I am king, I am not going to risk a military coup d'état on the one hand and a peasant revolution on the other." He pointed to a pile of communiqués on his desk. "I have other worries: China is sitting on our northern border waiting for the slightest excuse to roll into the Sindhala valley; India has reinforced the southern perimeter with two more battalions. And you want me to spend my time helping your wife hand out Band-Aids!"

"That's not fair, Father!"

"Running a country isn't based on fairness. It's based on hard, cold realities. When you're my age, you'll realize that."

Mila rose to his feet. He was too stubborn to give up entirely, especially when Lucy's happiness was at stake, but it was obvious that today he would get nowhere. "I'll come back when you're in a better mood. I can see there's no reasoning with you."

"Not if what you call reason consists of sentimental, ill-thought-out plans pressed on you by your foreign wife. It seems she has you under her thumb, as the English say, or to put it more crudely . . ."

Mila didn't wait to hear his father put it more crudely. Turning his back on Marpa, he walked out of the office into the great throne room with its marble pillars and copulating gods and millions of dollars of gold and jewels—obscene wealth wrested from the soil of Patan by generations of peasants. He paused in the center of the room, breathless and angry. How was he going to tell Lucy that the peasants were going to have to continue going without medical care because of political considerations? How was he going to admit that he couldn't yet give her what he'd promised? She was so American, so bursting with the impulse to do something immediately.

By the time he got back to his apartments, he had come up with half a dozen good rationalizations for being patient: he was still convinced that his father would relent; perhaps the political situation would improve; perhaps in a few months, when Lucy was more accustomed to life in Patan, he could try to explain the crazy web of intrigues and political considerations that surrounded every move she made. Meanwhile, it would be kinder simply to put her off and give her other projects as his father had suggested.

So Lucy's life went on, pleasantly and smoothly without any incident to break the chain of love and happiness that she and Mila were forging. When her pregnancy was confirmed, Mila was overjoyed, the king offered his warm congratulations, and although the news was not yet official, Lucy suddenly found herself surrounded by smiling, approving faces. Dr. Sukra, head of the royal hospital, pronounced her in perfect health, prescribed vitamins, and told her to keep busy and get moderate exercise, so she went ahead with her winter schedule, dedicating another school site and involving herself in plans for the new operating room.

When she grew restless she was taken on excursions to the country, flown to Hong Kong in the royal jet to buy the latest fashions. Parties were arranged for her, books ordered by the crate, concerts staged, films premiered for her pleasure. Her uncle and aunt wrote faithfully, and each Monday she called Cassie and talked as long as she wanted. What spare time she had was mostly occupied with ceremony: an hour of formal meditation three mornings a week in the company of Mila's six aunts; prayers for the dead conducted once a month in the palace temple; the nightly dinner with the king, attended by the entire court.

On Wednesdays, Fridays, and Sundays, she had her Patanese lessons. Her teacher, Miss Udana, was a retired member of the faculty of the Sindhala Preparatory School. A small, bright-eyed woman of about seventy, she drilled Lucy patiently, correcting her with formal politeness.

"Gracious Princess," Miss Udana would say, "may I please remind you that the word *tiu* is pronounced in the ascending form when it signifies *bread*. Your Highness has just pronounced it in the descending form, whereupon it takes on a different meaning altogether."

"What does it mean in the descending form, Miss Udana?" Lucy would then have to ask. She often tried to get Miss Udana to loosen up, but it proved impossible. She would never tell Lucy exactly what she had done wrong unless Lucy demanded to know, and every sentence she uttered automatically seemed to contain at least one honorary title, sometimes two.

"*Bat*, Gracious Princess."

"In other words I just said, 'The bat is on the table'?"

"Yes, Gracious Princess." Miss Udana would nod soberly.

Lucy would then sigh and try again. "*Tiuuu*," she would say, drawing out the final vowel and sending it upscale as if it were a question. If she was anywhere near the mark, Miss Udana would reward her by covering her mouth with her hand and smiling behind it, another polite custom Lucy could never get used to. "That was perfect, Your Highness."

"Perfect" was probably an exaggeration but still, more often than not, Lucy felt encouraged. Each day she felt a little less isolated by her inability to speak fluent Patanese, and as time passed—except for an ongoing battle with ascending and descending forms—she was more or less able to make herself understood. Instead of sitting on the sidelines, she could join in the endless gossip, fortune-telling, and card playing that the palace women loved, and although such pursuits seemed rather silly, they made her feel like less of a stranger.

Sometimes, of course, she grew bored and restive, but for the most part, except for a few bouts of homesickness, she was content. Life in the palace was surprisingly sophisticated and westernized, but beneath all the modern amenities something much older and more seductive was weaving a spell around her. Every gesture of court life whispered of centuries of peace and privilege, and although she never gave up her good intentions or ceased to ask Mila when they were going to get permission to build the rural clinics, her pregnancy made her more patient. As the first weeks passed, she fell into a dreamy, satisfied state where time seemed infinite. Besides, she saw so little real misery in the streets of Sindhala that she began to forget about it the way you could forget about hunger when you yourself were well fed. And then, quite suddenly and without the slightest warning, the illusion that everything was perfect began to fall apart, and all because of a yellow dress.

She had over six hundred dresses, four hundred for day wear and two hundred for evening, including twenty priceless antique gold-encrusted saris dating from the nineteenth century, but this dress was particularly pretty: simple, scoop-necked, loose, and long-sleeved, embroidered with small yellow flowers. Although yellow wasn't really her color, she had bought it in Hong Kong mostly for the fine handiwork along the hem and bodice and because it would fit her during her pregnancy, but partly too because it had reminded her of a dress her mother had once worn to some long-ago party. Packing it up in tissue paper, she promptly forgot about it, until one night, unreasonably bored with the excessive luxury of almost everything she owned, she plunged into the huge temperature-controlled room that contained her clothes, and found the yellow dress hanging behind a plastic rain poncho that she had used on a trek months ago. Why her maids had hung it in such an obscure spot was a mystery, and so she paused to take it out and look at it, and decided that it was the very thing to wear to dinner that evening.

The only problem was that once she'd put it on, she could find no jewels to go with it. Her collection was extensive and rather fabulous, including rubies from Ceylon, sapphires from India, strands of precious black pearls from Japan, diamonds given to her by sultans, emirs, and rajas, but she really had nothing that suited her own rather simple taste, and certainly nothing to go with a modest yellow silk dress.

Finally, after rummaging through the royal jewels, she came upon a small gold locket that must have been a keepsake. Inside was one of those amazing Patanese miniatures of Krishna playing his flute while his gopis danced around him. Allowing a silent, frowning Asana to fasten it around her neck, Lucy looked in the mirror and breathed a sigh of relief: the locket would do. Rushing toward the royal dining hall, she arrived exactly twenty-five minutes late, which by Patanese standards wasn't particularly excessive, but as soon as she walked through the door she realized that something was terribly wrong.

Conversation stopped dead as all eyes turned in her direction. Along the great, linen-covered table, forks hovered above plates of curried shrimp, as cousins, aunts, and courtiers stared at her in openmouthed horror. The sitar and tabla players fell out of rhythm and crashed to a halt. Servants gasped, and a rustle of panic ran through the room.

"What's wrong?" Lucy asked, walking toward Mila to take her seat at the table. "Am I so terribly late as all that?" She laughed awkwardly, trying to make amends for whatever she had done, but no one laughed with her. Instead Lakshmi, Mila's eldest aunt, rose to her feet and gave a piercing cry of grief. Covering her head with her shawl, she rushed from the dining hall followed by her ladies-in-waiting.

"Is your aunt sick, Mila? Is something wrong?" Mila was on his feet, stretching out his arms to her with a look of sympathy on his face, but why did she need his sympathy? What was going on? Confused, she let him seat her, which he did gently, as if she were made out of eggs, after which he glared defiantly down the table as if daring someone to say a word.

"What's wrong?" she whispered.

"Nothing, darling," he said firmly. "You've done nothing wrong; just ignore these fools." The silence grew and grew until it became unbearable.

"Enough!" the king thundered, slamming down his knife. "Resume the music!" Instantly the sitar sprung back to life and the tabla player began drumming. Someone coughed and conversation resumed, all of it in Patanese, low and angry like the humming of wasps.

Mila took a plate of lamb kebabs in cumin sauce from one of the servants and offered it to Lucy. "You look lovely in yellow," he said loudly, "like a ray of sunshine."

"You seem to be the only one who thinks so. Everyone else is looking at me like I just invited the Chinese communists to drive their tanks across the border."

"They're primitive, superstitious idiots," Mila said. "I'm ashamed to be related to them. Just relax and eat your dinner, and I'll explain later when we're back in our rooms." He flashed her a warm, encouraging smile and began to talk loudly to her about unimportant things. Lucy tried to eat, but the food stuck in her throat. As one course followed another, no one except Mila said a single word to her. His aunts looked through her; his cousins found the salt shakers in front of them amazingly interesting; his uncles locked themselves in discussions of tiger hunts and horse breeding. Too proud to cry in front of all of Mila's relatives, Lucy made a brave show of talking to him about a cardiac monitoring machine for the new operating room as she choked down the lamb and rice and a honey cake, but the only thing she tasted was humiliation. The meal seemed to drag on forever.

"What was *that* about?" she asked Mila when they were back in their rooms. "What the hell did I do? Walk on someone's grave?"

"You did nothing." Mila took off his coat and threw it on the couch, loosened his tie, and rolled up his shirt sleeves. "My relatives are fools, and I'm deeply ashamed of them. I apologize for their uncivilized behavior. You must think you've married into a family of barbarians." He paced across the room. "How could you possibly have known that you weren't supposed to wear yellow in my father's presence?"

"Yellow?"

Mila pointed to her dress. "They took one look at you in that yellow frock and regressed to the time of Vandu the Great. How do they ever expect to become citizens of a modern country with attitudes like that? You wore yellow in the presence of the king, and it's an open secret that you're pregnant. Did you know that those facts put together would cause a scandal? Of course not. Someone should have told you; I should have told you. In fact I blame myself for not giving you a list of the stupidities of Patanese court life, but I kept telling myself that there was no need because they'd all reformed. But now I can see that they'll never reform. Their progressive Western attitudes are merely a veneer. Underneath, I'm ashamed to say, my relatives are still as superstitious as savages."

Lucy sat down in a chair and fingered her locket trying to puzzle it all out, but there seemed to be a piece missing. "I still don't understand, Mila: What did my wearing a yellow dress have to do with what happened at dinner?"

"I hate to tell you," Mila moaned, "it's so stupid. I hate to burden you with it."

"Tell me anyway."

Mila shook his head. "You're not going to believe this, but wearing that pretty dress was a grave breach of etiquette." He took out a silk handkerchief and mopped his forehead. "Laugh if you want to; I certainly wouldn't blame you for finding the custom ridiculous, but no one ever wears yellow in the presence of the king . . . or in my presence for that matter. It's the color of death. Also, in your case, it's the color of death for the baby you're carrying—that is, if it's a boy."

"You're joking."

"I wish I were."

Lucy got to her feet and paced across the room. "I thought white was the color of death." She whirled on him, relieved it was something so trivial, not knowing whether to be angry or amused. "Remember when I wanted to wear white to our wedding, and your head priest told me it was a death color. Just how many death colors do you people have anyway?"

"Only two," Mila said sheepishly, "but of the two, yellow is the worst. It's specifically the color of a royal death. When my father dies the whole court will be wearing yellow, but until that time the color not only isn't worn, it isn't even mentioned, at least not anywhere where he's likely to overhear it."

"You have to be kidding. What do your father's servants call the color of his egg yolks? Blue?"

"It's an insane custom, and as you could see, my father doesn't support it. By tradition, he's supposed to banish anyone who wears yellow in his presence, but you saw the way he commanded the music to go on and the way he stared down my uncles. I was proud of the old man." Rising to his feet he walked over to her and took her hand. "I'm sorry, darling," he said gently. "I'll make it up to you somehow. If you like, I'll see to it that you get an apology from everyone involved in tonight's fiasco."

"Oh, no." Lucy was horrified at the thought. "Don't do that. They'd all resent me in addition to thinking that I'm bad luck." A smile suddenly trembled at the corner of her mouth. "Yellow! Yellow of all things! How could I have possibly guessed? Well, I certainly made a memorable faux pas, didn't I? I'm really sorry. I feel like a blundering fool, but I guess there's no real harm done, is there?"

"No," he told her, "no harm done at all." He was relieved that she was taking it so well. He was proud to be married to such a rational, well-educated woman. She had a good heart and a good sense of humor, and although she got angry, her anger passed quickly like a summer thunderstorm in the high mountains.

A few days after the yellow-dress incident, Mila and Lucy took an entire day off from their official duties and rode together to the shrine of Tzbaga, the goddess of fertility and happy motherhood. There were no roads to the shrine, which lay on the Bagdak River about seven miles outside of Sindhala, but foot paths converged on it from all directions because it was a pilgrimage spot for pregnant women who came from as far away as India and Nepal to kneel beside the muddy, fertile waters and send banana leaves filled with flowers and lighted candles down the river. Kneeling among them, Lucy sent her own leaf full of flowers and hopes into Tzbaga's keeping.

Thank you, Tzbaga, she prayed, for getting me with child. I've dreamed so long of being pregnant and I'm so happy that it's happened, and if you're in any way responsible for it, thank you and thank you again. May the baby be as strong as your river and as pretty as these flowers, and may its life be as full of light as these candles. It was a little odd to pray to a blue-haired, six-armed goddess, but Lucy was so grateful that she could have happily prayed to anything. As she rose to her feet, she thought with amusement of what Aunt Kate and Uncle Henry would think if they could see her. Aunt Kate, who was a Methodist, would probably find it all rather pagan.

Afterward she and Mila rode out into the country and ate a lunch of cold curry and smoked fish under a large tree that was covered with white blossoms the size of tea roses. For dessert they had honey cakes that Kala had made for them with her own hands. The cakes had a faintly bitter taste, as if the bees had been feeding on pine needles, but it had been thoughtful of Kala to provide them and Lucy finished two.

The weather was cold and clear, and she felt especially happy. The ride reminded her of the happy summers she had spent with her father, and if she closed her eyes and inhaled the scent of the horses grazing nearby, the tiny prickle of homesickness that was always with her dissolved. She could almost imagine that she was back in Utah or Colorado.

It had been a long time since she and Mila had been alone together like this, off on an expedition like two students in love, with nothing to do but roam the countryside. For over an hour they sat silently looking at the wall of blue mountains, and then they rode back to Sindhala hand in hand. That night they fell exhausted into bed and went to sleep almost at once.

Several hours later Lucy woke in terrible pain. Every muscle in her abdomen was cramping and her lips felt numb. Half blinded by the agony, she moaned and curled herself into a ball. Biting her lip, she tried to find the strength to reach out and wake Mila, but the pain kept coming in waves, turning her inside out, making her dizzy and nauseous. She dug her nails into her palms and tried to fight back, but the cramping was nothing that could be fought; it took her over completely.

"Help me!" she cried.

Mila was awake in an instant. "What's wrong?"

"I don't know," she moaned.

He sprang to his feet and turned on the lights and saw to his horror that the sheets around her were covered with blood. "You're miscarrying." He grabbed her in his arms as she began to cry and protest.

"No, I can't be!" Clenching her fists, she pounded on the bed, raging against her own body, feeling betrayed by it, but the cramps kept coming closer and closer together.

"I'm going to call for Dr. Sukra," Mila said.

Her body jerked, and she screamed in pain as another series of cramps seized her. Giving up the fight, she lay back, panting and terrified. "Yes," she begged, "do, I can't stand it anymore."

* * *

"How could you have let her on a horse!" King Marpa yelled at Mila when Lucy was out of danger. "Have I a complete fool for a son!"

Mila threw himself into a chair, too upset and exhausted from the long vigil to yell back. He looked wearily at the bonsai trees on his father's desk, clipped and controlled and stunted. His father expected him to do the same to Lucy, but Lucy had spirit and courage. He'd never confine her to the palace the way his father had confined all his wives. "She's an independent Western woman. I can't keep her imprisoned in her quarters as if she were in *purdah*."

"You don't treat her like a woman at all. You treat her like a man."

"I treat her as she wishes to be treated."

"You let her ride fourteen miles on a horse when she was pregnant. Why not simply order her to have an abortion?"

Mila lowered his head stubbornly, refusing to fight because there was no way either of them could win. He reminded himself that his father had high blood pressure and a history of heart problems. "There's no harm done," he said quietly. "Dr. Sukra says she can have other children."

"Meanwhile this one, a son, is dead."

"It was a fetus of three months, father, not a son."

"It was a male fetus that would have been my grandson! If you don't care about my feelings, you might at least consider the future of your country. Your uncle is dead, and unless you want your idiot cousin to end up on the throne, you need to produce an heir. Don't you feel any guilt at all?"

"I feel great guilt," Mila said through tight lips. He was enraged at his father's reaction to Lucy's miscarriage, but yelling back was worse than useless. Things would only escalate. "I feel tremendous guilt, but not toward you and not toward some future generations of Patanese. I feel guilty that I married Lucy and that I brought her here to be a stranger surrounded by strangers who don't understand her and never will. I want her to be my equal, but I can't keep her out of the cage we Patanese design for our women. So I feel guilty; I feel I have failed her."

Marpa looked at the pained expression in his son's eyes, and his rage suddenly subsided as quickly as it had come. "Go back to her," he said softly. "Comfort her; make the best of it. Get her pregnant again as soon as you can. And try to see that her life is tranquil and amusing. I'm sorry that I yelled at you, but I, too, am grieved. I am not in the best of health, and I want to see my grandson before I die."

When Cassie called two days later, Lucy told her the bad news as calmly as she could. There was no use mourning what couldn't be helped.

There was a shocked silence on the other end of the line. "I'm sorry. God, I'm sorry, Lucy. That's terrible. You must feel awful."

"I'm okay."

"The hell you are. Don't give me that stiff upper lip stuff. This is Cassie, remember? Do you want me to take the next flight to Sindhala?" Lucy thought of the miles that separated her from her best friend. She wanted Cassie's arm around her, but all she had of Cassie was a distant, sympathetic voice drowned in static.

"No," she said bravely, "it's all over. These things just happen."

"I suppose they do, but it was a hell of a piece of bad luck considering how much you wanted that baby. Honestly, how do you feel?"

"Fine, physically. I'm already back on my feet, and the doctor says I can try to get pregnant again in about three months."

"And mentally?"

"Fine."

"You don't sound fine."

"I'm perfectly healthy," Lucy said brightly. "Dr. Sukra says there's no reason why I can't have a dozen kids, so there's no use brooding about this, only . . ."

"Only what?"

"Only, I know this is crazy, but I feel like someone died." And then she broke down and sobbed, while ten thousand miles away Cassie sat with the telephone receiver in her hand trying in vain to comfort her.

· 3 ·

Lucy's miscarriage marked the start of a bad winter, a winter that seemed to go on and on until Cassie was so sick of rain and sleet and hard work that she was sometimes tempted to pack up and head for Florida or California or any place where depression didn't seem to be settling over everything like soot. Usually she took life in stride, but as the new year grew closer and the weather grew more foul, she felt herself slipping out of harmony with the universe. She worried about Lucy, about Andy, about herself, about almost everything from the war in Vietnam to Watusi, Jr.'s ear mites. At night she found herself dreaming of sandy beaches, sunshine, brisk hikes down mountain trails, but even if she and Andy had had time to get outside, Ann Arbor was a Siberia of bad weather that turned a simple walk around the block into a fight against glare ice and driving winds. The two of them were not even free to wander around under the lowering gray sky getting chilled to the bone. Instead, they studied every day from the first bleak light of dawn until far into the night. Preliminary Examinations were only a month away, and there was more to learn than they could ever hope to master.

"Sometimes," Cassie grumbled as she made a fresh pot of coffee, "I'm tempted to ditch it all and do something else with my life, like teach high school. I didn't realize that getting a Ph.D. was going to be like joining a fraternity. I feel as if we're going through Hell Week." She wiped her hands on her skirt and looked at her reflection in the coffeepot. Her face was distorted: size ten nose above a size two chin. "I think the system stinks."

"It's not so bad," Andy mumbled without looking up from his book.

"Not so bad! How can you say that?" Cassie waved her arms at the stove and sink as if they were the examining committee. "Look what they're throwing at you: an exam in enzymology and energetics; an exam in metabolic regulation and cellular compartmentalization; another exam in molecular genetics. That's three *three*-hour examinations, nine hours total, all on new material. And God knows what they'll ask, especially with my father on the committee that designs the damn things." She grabbed two mugs, filled them with coffee, and slapped them down on the kitchen table so hard that some slopped over the sides.

Andy, who was used to such disasters, grabbed a napkin and built a dam around his books. "Don't get so upset, Cass," he pleaded. He was used to her bursts of rebellion, but they always had an odd effect on him. When she began to wave her arms, he started feeling tender and protective, which was probably a good thing because if he had started waving his arms, too, there wouldn't have been a piece of unbroken china left in the house. "You always want to pin the blame on your dad, and maybe half the time you're right, but this time it's my own fault. After all, I'm the one who decided to switch my emphasis from botany to biochemistry. Otherwise I'd be sitting here next to you reviewing the phytogeography notes we took at Harvard."

"We have my father to thank for that too. I don't know why I ever agreed to come to Ann Arbor. I should have my head examined. I'm used to how he pushes people, but you aren't. You let him talk you into taking—"

"Cass, please, let's not go into that again."

"Why not? I don't want to interfere with your research, but the man's riding you, and I'm worried. Look at yourself: you're not just studying for your prelims; you're down at the greenhouse five nights a week babying your experimental plot like it was a sick cat. That's just the kind of inhuman schedule my father encourages his graduate students to follow. He doesn't care that you've lost weight, that you're grinding your teeth in your sleep." She felt so much love and apprehension for him that she could have cried. *You've lost interest in everything but that damn fungus!* she wanted to say. But she bit her tongue instead and stood looking at him, wishing she could convince him to stop driving himself so hard and get some sleep before he fell apart.

Andy sighed and wished for a fleeting instant that he had spent this evening in the library instead of sitting at his own kitchen table. What she was saying was probably true from her perspective, but there were some things she never seemed to understand. Sure Quinn was pushing him, but the research was exciting and he loved it. Not more than her, of course. He didn't love anything more than her. But he loved his research right next to her. It gave him hope and made him feel important in the world, as if he were crawling up a narrow, dark tunnel that was getting wider and lighter all the time. He was going to discover how to synthesize a new growth regulator, he knew it. It was only a matter of working hard and not getting discouraged. "We don't have time to argue about your father," he said soothingly. He wished that she wouldn't worry about him so much. "Let's postpone this discussion until after the exams are over. If you still feel the same way about your father in the spring, maybe we'll talk about transferring to some other graduate school. But we can't do anything now, not in the middle of the year." Not, he added silently, until I have some definite results.

Cassie took a deep breath, sat down beside him, and picked up a book on plant systematics. The print danced in front of her, and again she felt as if she might cry. "I'm sorry," she said. "I don't mean to make things harder than they are already. You're right. I'm not being helpful; I'm being a complete bitch."

Andy reached over and patted her hand. "I wouldn't say that, Cass. I'd say that you're more like a fine, proud, spirited horse that refuses to be broken. But that's what graduate school's all about: breaking and taming. So we might as well accept it."

"You're right." Cassie swallowed hard and stared at her coffee cup until it, too, danced in front of her. "I don't know what got into me."

"You're just freaked out by the prospect of sitting for nine hours filling up blue books. It's perfectly understandable. But don't worry. You'll pass. You're smart, Cass, and you've been studying this stuff since you were old enough to walk."

But will *you* pass? Cassie thought, but she couldn't say that to him, so she went back to her book and tried not to worry, but it didn't work. Her mind went on piling up anxieties as if they were satanic Christmas presents.

It turned out that her worries were well founded. On January 15, they sat for their examinations, and on February 14, Valentine's Day, they got the results. Cassie came home from class that afternoon around five-thirty. It was already pitch dark. Lugging a large bag of groceries from the bus stop to the front door, she fumbled with her key. As she was trying to get it into the lock, she leaned a little too far forward, and the bottle of Chianti that she had bought for Andy's Valentine's Day dinner fell out and broke all over the concrete stoop.

The wine splashed up, spotting her boots and skirt. Cursing, she kicked the straw holder and pieces of broken glass into a pile next to her bicycle where it could stay until spring for all she cared.

Pushing open the door with her elbow, she stumbled inside. The apartment was dark but warm, which was odd because she and Andy always turned down the heat before they left in the morning. Flipping on the light, she was startled to see Andy sitting on the couch looking out the window. Actually he wasn't looking out the window because he had neglected to open the curtains, but he was staring fixedly in that direction. A small bouquet of flowers lay on the rug beside him next to a large red cardboard heart.

"Hello," she said. "What are you doing sitting around in the dark?"

"Nothing," he said, still staring at the curtains. His face was haggard, and he spoke in a flat tone of voice that she had never heard him use before.

"What do you mean 'nothing'? Are you sick? You've still got your coat on and it must be at least seventy-five in here. You aren't running a fever, are you?"

"No."

She walked over and put her hand on his forehead. It was cool. As she touched him, he closed his eyes. There was pain in his head and his mouth and his arms, pain in his whole body, but it wasn't the pain of being sick. Her touch rippled through him, down through all the layers of sadness to a dark core. At the center of his being he was nothing, a perfect vacuum. The vacuum was the only thing about him that was perfect, and when she took her hand away, he felt himself being sucked into it in slow motion, like a man drowning in a small, tight pocket of quicksand.

"Andy?"

He could hear her voice coming from very far away.

"Andy, talk to me for God's sake. Don't just sit there like a statue." Cassie was beginning to get frightened. She had never seen him act like this before. She took his hand, but it was limp and unresponsive. "Andy," she begged, "what is it? What's going on?"

"I screwed up," he mumbled. His tongue felt heavy, like a piece of lead. It was an effort to form the words. He wanted her to turn out the light and leave him alone again, but he didn't want to hurt her feelings by suggesting it. He looked at the cardboard heart on the floor and the two envelopes lying beside it like white voodoo bones, and he knew he should pick them up and hand them to her only he felt too tired to bend over and pick them up. "I screwed up," he repeated.

"Screwed up what? What are you talking about? I can hardly understand you." Only that wasn't the truth; she did understand. She had followed his glance and seen the envelopes. Suddenly she had known what must have happened to make him so depressed, only she didn't want to admit it to herself. She just sat there, holding his hand, closing off the truth the way you close off a disaster when you hear it on the radio: flip the knob to music, pretend that you didn't hear about the assassination or the airplane crash or the declaration of war.

"We got some mail today, Cass." His voice jarred her back to reality, back to the truth that there was no escaping. Slowly, with great effort, he bent over, picked up the two letters and held them for a moment. One was open, the other still sealed. The envelopes felt expensive and heavy: cool and white as if they had come from some unimaginable heaven of bureaucracy where the quick and the dead were judged and disposed of. One was addressed to Mr. Andrew Rabinowitz, one to Mrs. He held the Mrs. out to her. Too upset to speak, she took it and tore it open.

Dear Mrs. Rabinowitz [the letter began],
   The Dissertation Committee of the Department of Biological Sciences is pleased to inform you that you have passed your preliminary examinations with a score of eight out of a possible nine. Within the next two weeks, we will recommend to the Divisional Graduate Affairs Committee that you be admitted to Candidacy. . . .

Cassie stopped reading and sat for a moment, feeling a sense of relief so great that it made her dizzy. The letter dropped out of her hands. Admitted to candidacy. Home free. And then she felt a paralyzing wave of guilt. She had passed her prelims, but what about Andy? Would he have been sitting in the dark if he'd gotten the same news? She tried to convince herself that he had passed too, but one look at his face removed any hope. "You failed?" she said.

Andy nodded. "Five out of nine."

"Oh, no," she cried, "you couldn't have failed five out of nine! Two maybe, three tops; but not five. That's impossible. It's ridiculous. There must be some mistake. You studied so hard. You—" She wanted to take him in her arms and kiss him and fold him away from all the pain of failure, but he was so stiff. "I love you," she said fiercely, as if that would fix it.

"I thought," he murmured, "I really thought . . . that I did okay."

"Well, of course you did. Look, Andy, they must have mixed your score up with someone else's."

"No, Cass. I don't think so. Look." He held the remaining envelope out to her, and she took it, pulled out the letter, and read:

Dear Mr. Rabinowitz,
   The Dissertation Committee of the Department of Biological Sciences regrets to inform you that you failed to pass your preliminary examinations. You may arrange to retake your examinations in January of 1968. According to departmental regulations, graduate students in the biological sciences are allowed only two attempts to complete the preliminary requirements. Attached is an evaluation of your responses to assist you in preparing yourself more thoroughly in those areas in which you have displayed deficiencies.

Sure enough, there were two single-spaced typewritten sheets of criticism so merciless that Cassie could barely read through it. No wonder Andy had gone into a tailspin. This was enough to plunge anyone into a depression.

Student shows a lack of understanding of some of the basic principles of molecular genetics. . . . Student deficient in . . . inadequate in . . . not fully prepared in . . .

She stopped reading and sat there feeling sick for him. Poor Andy. To fail after all that work. Leaning over, she brushed the hair off his forehead and kissed him gently. The mother lion will kill to protect her young, she thought, which was crazy because he wasn't her young.

"This isn't the end of the world," she said. "We can get the—" She was going to say "get the hell out of here," but she stopped in midsentence, remembering that they couldn't go to another graduate school now, not with this on Andy's record. They were trapped in Ann Arbor until he passed his prelims. She swallowed her words and shifted abruptly. "We can get through this. I'll—" she groped for some way she could help him, "I'll do all the housework so you'll have more time to study." She forced herself to smile. "I'll even do the cooking if you think you can survive it." She took his hand again and squeezed it. "Next year you'll pass those exams with a perfect score."

Andy shook his head very slowly. "I don't think I can face . . . taking them again. I'm such a complete . . . failure. I can't cut it, Cass. I'm not smart enough. I thought I was, but I was wrong. I'm just . . . average." And then to her surprise, he started to cry. The sight of him in tears made her feel as if her own heart were breaking. She held on to him, letting him sob, rocking him, muttering soothing things: telling him that he was intelligent, no not just intelligent, brilliant, and that if the university didn't appreciate that, it was a pack of fools, and that she, Cassie, should know he was brilliant because she talked to him every day, didn't she? "I love you," she kept saying. "I love you, Andy." But she wasn't sure if he heard her or if her encouragement did any good.

At last he stopped crying and grew still in her arms. Sitting up, he wiped his eyes. "I'm sorry," he muttered.

"Whatever for?"

"For falling apart like that. For being so weak."

"I don't think you're weak." She put her hands on his shoulders and kissed him again, on the nose this time, a quick, affectionate peck. "It takes a strong man to fall apart."

He seemed a little better after that. They talked for another half hour, going back and forth over the exam, conducting a postmortem. Finally, after there was nothing more to be said, Cassie made him a hot buttered rum and watched while he drank it; then she took off his shoes, brought him his pajamas, and tucked him into bed.

"Sit with me," he said. So she sat with him, holding his hand. It was strange to see him so docile and childlike, strange and a little frightening. For the first time she felt that marriage was a strange thing, full of unexpected twists and turns, laden with secrets that no one on the outside could ever understand.

At last Andy fell asleep. When she was sure that he was not going to wake up again, she carefully detached her hand from his, went out to the kitchen, sat down at the table, and read the letters over again. The final paragraph of Andy's evaluation caught her eye: "It is suggested that the student take the following courses to remedy the above lacunae: Medical Biology, Regulation of Cellular Metabolism, Hormones and Plant Development . . ." The list went on and on, suggesting so many courses that not even Watson and Crick could have gotten through them in less than two years.

Now who on the examining committee would use a word like *lacunae* when the word *gaps* would have done just as nicely? Who would tell a student to take twelve advanced courses? To put it bluntly: Who was responsible for this fiasco? As far as Cassie could see, there was only one likely candidate.

Going over to the refrigerator, she pulled out the bottle of vodka she and Andy had bought for New Year's Eve. Pouring herself a stiff shot, she drank it straight off without even coughing. Larry Quinn, she thought, this is one time too many.

The next morning, after she had made Andy breakfast, fed him two cups of industrial-strength coffee, and told him again that he would certainly pass his exams next time, she took the bus to the central campus and went straight to her father's office. The office was at the very top of the new laboratory building, positioned in the south corner where it caught whatever sun there was to be caught. To give her father credit, it was modestly furnished: a modern steel desk, a well-padded swivel chair, wooden bookcases, some hanging plants. Modestly furnished, that is, if you ignored the letter from the Nobel Prize Committee that hung on the wall; modest if you discounted the Wang computer, the snapshots of Quinn with every former president since Truman, the plaques, the testimonials, the honorary degrees. Sometimes when Cassie came into his office, she felt as if she were walking into the Lawrence Quinn Museum of Distinguished Accomplishments, but today she didn't feel much of anything: she was too mad.

She found her father sitting in the swivel chair eating a dish of yogurt. Other professors smoked pipes or puffed away on cigarettes, but not him. He was going to live forever. When he saw her, he put down his yogurt and smiled.

"Hello, there," he said.

"Hello there yourself," Cassie snapped and then immediately regretted it because she had imagined this scene taking place in an aura of detached sarcasm. She had planned to deliver withering, cold remarks, but as usual, as soon as she saw him, the emotional roller coaster took off, dragging her up hills of ambivalence. She managed to control her urge to pick up the piece of fossil amber on his desk and throw it through one of the large plate-glass windows. "Did you know that Andy failed his prelims?" she asked him through tight lips, keeping her eye on him because there was never any telling what he might do next.

"Of course," Quinn nodded. "I was the one who failed him."

He said it so matter-of-factly that she thought for a moment she had heard him wrong. "You what?" she cried. She strode over to his desk and grabbed on to it as if she were about to try out for the role of Superwoman. "You did what?"

"Calm down," Quinn advised. "There's no use getting so emotional about it. Andy needs more background to carry out his research." He shrugged. "What better way to keep his nose to the grindstone than by letting him know that he has to retake his exams next year? It's standard operating procedure, Cassie, and I think you, of all people, should be able to see that it's for the best." He smiled his most charming smile, the smile that always made Cassie want to puke.

"He studied himself sick," she said, "*sick.*"

"Well, I'm sorry about that," Quinn said, "but it can't be helped. Graduate school is the place for studying. Of course Andy is probably overdoing it. He's an ambitious young man, but that isn't a bad thing. Ambition is one of the marks of a high-powered scientist. It's the fuel that feeds the obsession. Frankly," he looked at her and shook his head, "you could do with a bit more ambition yourself."

Cassie flinched, and her face turned white. Quinn, who had had no intention of insulting her, was surprised. She was so damn touchy, he thought. Just like her mother. He tried to think of something to make up for the comment, but nothing sprang to mind.

"You don't seem to get it," Cassie said in a voice so pale and low he could barely hear her. "Andy is depressed, so depressed that it scares me. Last night I came home and found him sitting in the dark. This morning, he didn't want to get out of bed. He just lay there looking at the ceiling, and he wouldn't even talk. I wouldn't call this keeping his nose to the grindstone. I think I'd call it sadism, what do you say?"

Quinn was beginning to get annoyed with her. Sadism, indeed. If she didn't have such a need to dramatize things, her life would go much more smoothly. It would be logical and clear like his own. But he had learned from long experience that that was too much to expect. "I'm sorry to hear that Andy is taking it so hard, but if you ask me he needs to get some perspective on the whole process. A significant percentage of graduate students fail their prelims the first time through. If it will help, you can tell him from me that next time he'll probably pass."

"It won't help."

Quinn lifted his eyebrows. "And why not?"

"Because he won't believe me, because he's suffering right now, because his depression is real and he's not going to be comforted by the assurance that twelve months from now he'll *probably* pass."

"I don't understand," Quinn said, and he honestly meant it, because what did a bright young man have to worry about when it was obvious to anyone that he would merely have to delay his admission to candidacy for a year?

"I know you don't," Cassie said. "You don't understand the human cost of anything. You're like someone who had his ability to empathize amputated at birth. I shouldn't even be talking to you about this. I should be talking to Andy. I should be trying to convince him to leave this place or at least to work under another professor, but I've tried that already and he won't listen. As usual, you've convinced him that you're God. He's going to keep on working under you; he's going to let you push him and push him until he either comes up with some wonderful, fabulous, earth-shaking results or falls apart completely, and I can't do a damn thing about it except refuse to watch."

Quinn was shocked. He sat up straight, and his face got very sober. "What do you mean you're going to refuse to watch? Are you planning to leave him, because if you are, I think I should tell you that there are very few men like Andy in this world. He tolerates your emotionality in ways that—"

"Save your advice," she interrupted. "I'd never leave Andy; it's you, I'm leaving."

"Me?"

"You, Daddy. I'm going to ask Patterson to be my major professor."

"Patterson," Quinn stuttered, "Patterson, that has-been, that dud? You're walking out of my lab to work with *Patterson*?"

"You bet," Cassie nodded. "That's just what I'm doing."

"But why?" Quinn pleaded. "It's senseless; it's professional suicide. Patterson of all people. Why Patterson?"

Cassie let go of his desk and backed away from him. With every step she felt more sure that she was doing the right thing. "Why Patterson?" she said. "I think I'll let you figure it out. You aren't stupid, Daddy. You won a Nobel Prize, remember? It's up there on the wall."

In Patan Lucy followed the whole progress of Cassie's terrible winter by letters and phone calls, but she was helpless to do anything more than sympathize with her. Fortunately, her own life was taking an upward course that season, so much so that sometimes she imagined that she and Cassie were on the opposite ends of a giant balance, one of them going up while the other went down.

Unlike India, Patan had two wet seasons. From early December through late February, snow piled up on the high mountains creeping down toward the rice terraces like a sheet of blank paper slowly unfolding one section at a time. Then, as quickly as it had come, winter stopped. As the days grew longer, the snow began to melt and retreat and become a tame thing again, and the whole valley suddenly blossomed with a million small red flowers that flickered among the new rice like tongues of flame.

On the fourth of May, the new royal operating room at the hospital was inaugurated in a gala ceremony that involved ribbon cutting, speeches, twenty orange-robed monks from the main temple, and so many garlands of flowers that the gleaming modern machinery was temporarily transformed into a garden. As usual the event was a typical Patanese mixture of East and West. Dr. Sukra, who had been trained at Johns Hopkins University, officially thanked the prince and princess for equipping the hospital with what was undoubtedly the most advanced surgical facility north of New Delhi. Then, to Lucy's amusement, the cardiac monitoring unit was dedicated with a formal puja, and the whole room was soberly fumigated with incense to drive out evil spirits. She always remembered that morning as the high point of her life in Patan. She had recovered from the miscarriage and regained her health and good spirits. The operating room was perfect in every respect, and she had the satisfaction of knowing that she and Mila had made it happen. She thought of it as the first in a long series of projects that would modernize Patanese life, and there was nothing in the moment to disillusion her or suggest that this was the end of something and not the beginning. Standing beside Mila, she placed her hand on his and cut the ribbons that had been stretched across the green, tiled doorway. Afterward, proud and happy, she went to the reception where suddenly, without warning, the invisible avalanche that had been hovering over her since the day she married came thundering down.

The messenger of grief looked harmless enough at first glance. She was about sixty, heavyset, dressed in a plain brown sari of the kind favored by peasant women. Her gray hair was done up in a tight bun, there wasn't a ring on her finger or a single strand of gold around her neck, and she was wearing rubber-soled sandals of the coarsest kind. In that room of jeweled, silk-clad, sophisticated courtiers, she stood out like a sober brown turkey in a flock of preening pheasants. Intrigued, Lucy waited for the woman to be presented to her along with the other guests, but when the reception line formed, she stood to one side, watching the bowing and handshaking with an ironic expression on her face.

Well, Lucy thought, if she won't come to me then I'll go to her, and etiquette be damned; so when the formal part of the reception was over, she walked to the far side of the room. "How do you do," she said in halting Patanese to the woman in the brown sari. "Welcome to the hospital."

The woman inclined her head in the faintest of praniyams. "You do me great honor, Princess," she replied in flawless English, but there was something about her tone of voice that suggested that it was a mixed honor and one she didn't particularly care for. There was a long, awkward silence while Lucy waited for the woman to introduce herself, but the woman didn't oblige her. She just stood there, cool and simple in her coarse sari, smiling a self-contained smile that made Lucy feel like an awkward child.

"I don't believe I've met you before."

"No, you haven't. I spent the last five years in India."

Lucy was amused. She had longed to meet someone who would treat her as an ordinary person, but she hadn't quite imagined it would be so surprising to run up against indifference. Being a princess was obviously spoiling her. "May I ask your name?" she said.

"I'm Mrs. Arjuna."

"Any relation to General Arjuna?"

"His mother."

"Of course. Forgive me, Mrs. Arjuna. I should have remembered that you were on the guest list."

"I'm not."

"I beg your pardon?"

"I'm not on the guest list, Princess."

"I don't understand."

"I was not invited to this reception. I am considered *persona non grata*. A troublemaker."

Lucy laughed. "You hardly look like someone who would make trouble. You look more like Mother Teresa."

"I worked with her in Calcutta."

"How fascinating. I've always admired her immensely. What's she like?"

"A plain woman of great complexity."

"You must be very proud of your association with her."

"Pride isn't something she encourages."

"I'm puzzled, Mrs. Arjuna. Why would someone who has worked with Mother Teresa want to crash a reception where the most interesting object is a solid ice elephant filled with curried yogurt dip?"

Mrs. Arjuna smiled and shook her head. "You underestimate your own importance, Princess. I didn't come to look at the ice elephant; I came to talk to you. I would have preferred a more private interview, of course, but my son has made it impossible for me to apply for an audience through the official channels. I wasn't expecting to be permitted within twenty feet, but I thought it was worth a try, and here you have saved me the trouble. I'd heard that you were unconventional, and now I have proof of it." Lucy smiled. "I'd also heard," Mrs. Arjuna continued, "that you're young and idealistic and that you don't have the slightest idea what's really going on in this country."

Lucy stopped smiling. "What do you mean?"

"I'll be frank, Princess: To put it bluntly, you're a burden."

"To whom?" Lucy was startled.

"To the people of Patan. They work to keep you and the rest of the royal family in palaces and fine cars and trips abroad; they send you their rice in taxes when they can't afford to feed their own families. Look at yourself: you think you're helping the poor by dedicating that useless operating room, yet all the while you're wearing enough jewels to feed a peasant village for twenty years. Wake up; stop acting like a blind woman. They say you went to Radcliffe, so you must have some brains. Look around you. Everyone knows that the king is never going to let you make any real changes. All you're doing is throwing a sop to the people to keep them quiet when what this country really needs is land reform. Patan is controlled by fifty families who own eighty percent of the arable land, the average peasant eats under one thousand calories a day, and conditions in the gold mines are unspeakable."

"I know that," Lucy snapped. "I'm perfectly aware that this country has serious problems, and I'm doing my best—"

Mrs. Arjuna shook her head impatiently. "You don't understand. It doesn't matter what you do. You're hemmed in by plots and intrigues. You're a pretty butterfly caught in a spider web that you can't even see. And some day the spider is going to come home for lunch and," she snapped her fingers, "suck the pretty butterfly dry."

"That sounds like a threat."

Mrs. Arjuna laughed. "A threat? Not from me. I'm an old woman. I don't threaten anyone anymore." She pulled the loose end of her sari over her head. "I'm going now, before your guards throw me out, but remember what I said. In a kingdom of six million people, I'm the only one who had the courage to warn you." Turning her back on Lucy, she hurried out of the room, passing through the chattering crowd like a brown ghost.

Lucy stood with her punch glass clutched in her hand, too angry to move. A few moments passed, and then she felt Mila's hand on her shoulder.

"I'm sorry that happened," he said. "The guards wanted to expel her, but I stopped them. She's too old to be treated with such disrespect. She's not well, and in my opinion she's harmless. What did she say to you?"

"A lot of nonsense. The conversation began normally enough, but then it got weirder and weirder. Who is she, anyway?"

"Mrs. Arjuna, General Arjuna's mother, one of the richest women in Patan."

"She told me that, but it was hard to believe her. She didn't look rich."

"She is, believe me. Her husband died in a hunting accident about ten years ago and left her something in the range of five million dollars, but she always dresses as if she'd just spent the morning sweeping the streets. From what I've heard, she despises show and thinks that wearing a decent sari or a complete pair of shoes when people are starving is a sin. I sympathize with her attitude—I'd like to live more simply myself sometimes—but she takes it to a fanatical degree." He shrugged. "I'm afraid the rest of us don't stack up too well in Mrs. Arjuna's book."

"She told me that I was a burden to the people of Patan."

Mila sighed. "I'm not surprised. She's a sad case. She's an intelligent woman, but her husband's death unhinged her. She kept insisting he was murdered, although no one could ever turn up a scrap of evidence to support the accusation. Then a few years ago she lost a lawsuit against her oldest son, and it made her bitter. She wanted to give all her money to the poor—not in any sane, organized way—just hand it over to them in baskets in the middle of Kalpa Square, but since she's a widow she needed the general's approval, and he, of course, wouldn't give it. He got the court to commit her to a mental hospital in Hardwar for a few years, and since she's come back from India he's had the Patanese Secret Service keeping track of her. It doesn't seem to bother him in the slightest that he's spying on his own mother. I can't tell you how many hours I've spent trying to persuade my father that having her followed is a waste of time and money."

"She said I was surrounded by plots."

Mila's eyes narrowed. "Did she say who was doing the plotting?"

"No, just that I was surrounded by them."

"We can't just dismiss a warning like that. I'll have it checked out."

Lucy spent the rest of the reception trying to put the incident out of her mind, but Mrs. Arjuna's accusation that she was a burden struck a chord in her, and as she chattered graciously with the guests, she found herself thinking that some of what she had said had made sense. She and Mila had been waiting for months for the king's permission to start establishing the rural clinics. As she stood at the door shaking hands with the departing guests, she reassured herself that she was not naïve or powerless; there was a great deal she could do without consulting anyone.

The day after the reception, General Arjuna paid a visit to his mother, who lived in an apartment on a small side street just off Kalpa

Square. The apartment, which consisted of one tiny room and a minuscule closet, was part of a large building let mostly to blacksmiths and their families, so one often had to yell to be heard above the din of the hammers. Filled with charcoal smoke, dry rot, rats, and cockroaches, it was the kind of barren, desperate place that bred thieves and communists, but his mother loved it, of course. Not only did she get self-righteous pleasure from living among the poorest of the poor, she revelled in the shame she was bringing on her son, or at least that was how Arjuna saw it.

He found her sitting up ramrod straight in a Western-style chair writing a letter. The only other furniture in the room was a table and the straw mattress that served as both her couch and bed. On the wall hung a large picture of Mother Teresa, Mrs. Arjuna's rusty black umbrella, and a small string of onions. She cooked on a charcoal fire out on the balcony like everyone else, carrying her water up five flights in a plastic bucket.

"Good morning, Mother," Arjuna said.

Mrs. Arjuna looked up from her letter. "Good morning, Ajiti," she said. "What brings you here?"

"I've come to pay my respects."

Mrs. Arjuna put down her pen. "Why?" she said. "Why now after so many months?"

Arjuna took off his hat and fanned himself with it. The room was close and smelled of onions and rancid cooking oil. Flies buzzed near a paper strip that dangled from a nail in the ceiling, and roaches scuttled along the window frames. The clang of hammers from below was deafening, but as far as Arjuna was concerned that was a distinct advantage.

"I think it's time we were reconciled, Mother," he said.

"What? I can't hear you."

He raised his voice. "I said that I think it's time we were reconciled."

All the hammers stopped suddenly as if on cue. The noise of the market filled the room. Fish vendors called out their wares; children laughed. Somewhere, far away, a horn honked.

"So," Mrs. Arjuna said quietly, "you have come to ask my forgiveness."

Arjuna nodded. "Yes, Mother."

"You were always a vile boy, Ajiti," she sighed, "and now you have grown into a vile, treacherous man. I hear that you torture children in front of their parents to extract confessions; I hear that you force your recruits to return to their own villages and commit atrocities all in the name of anti-communism. Here in the market they call you 'the butcher,' but only in secret since it is well known that your spies are everywhere."

"Those are only rumors, Mother, planted by my enemies."

"Are they? Ah well, of course, you never would admit it. Even as a child you always lied instinctively. Even so, I loved you. A mother always seems to love her sons no matter what their character, but you were wicked from the very start." She shrugged. "I suppose if you want to be reconciled, I must agree to it. You always get what you want."

"You didn't always feel that way about me, Mother," Arjuna protested. "Remember how when I was a boy I used to sit with you and rub your neck when you were tired, and we would laugh and tell stories."

"I remember." Mrs. Arjuna nodded. "That was so long ago. I was a young, silly wife, and you were just a boy."

"You look tired, Mother. Let me rub your neck again, for old times' sake. Going out socially must be tiring at your age."

Mrs. Arjuna's eyes narrowed. "You found out that I was at the reception, didn't you?"

"Yes."

"I thought so."

"What did you tell the princess, Mother?"

"I told her there were plots against her."

"Why do you always work against me! What demon drives you to seek my destruction? Do you want to get me executed for treason? Would that please you?" Mrs. Arjuna said nothing. "I think you've gone completely mad again, Mother. I think you need professional help."

"In India, I suppose."

"Yes, in India. Another stay at the Hardwar Refuge for the Mentally Disturbed might calm your mind. No one would blame me for committing you again, not after what you did yesterday."

Mrs. Arjuna shook her head. "What a disgusting boy you are, and so completely predictable. The problem is, you've always lacked imagination, even as a child."

"I'm serious, Mother. If you don't stop spreading poisonous rumors about me, then I'm going to have no choice."

"Your threats don't affect me in the slightest, Ajiti. I'm an old woman who's seen too much suffering." She folded the letter she had been writing in three parts, slipped it into an envelope, and turned to him defiantly. "Come rub my neck," she commanded, "and try for once to be gentle. I always have the feeling that you long to snap it."

"I do not understand, Lord Chamberlain, why it is so hard to arrange a trip to Dakmati." Lucy tapped her fingers impatiently on the inlaid table, a sign that she was particularly frustrated, but it was evidently the lord chamberlain's job to frustrate her because he, as usual, gave no sign of hearing her. Sometimes she wondered if the old man was deaf. If she hadn't known for a fact that he spoke fluent English, she would have blamed herself for not addressing him in Patanese. Probably it wouldn't have mattered if she'd tried to communicate with him in Urdu. He seemed determined to wait at least a full minute before replying to the simplest question.

"Gracious Princess, the time is not right. The town is in the midst of celebrating the great Kali festival, and its resources are strained to the limits." He waited humbly for her anger to subside, and suddenly she was embarrassed to realize that once again she was playing the game of the princess berating a faithful servant, but she held on stubbornly, determined for once to get to the bottom of why all her plans to see the poorer villages of the countryside never seemed to materialize.

"Dakmati is one of the poorest villages in Patan. How does a town so poor manage to celebrate the Kali festival so lavishly? Have the people stumbled on a gold mine?"

The chamberlain bobbed up and down again, and for a moment she was afraid he was going to fall to the floor and do a full praniyam. "Is the gracious princess not aware that the Divine One has designated Dakmati one of the towns to be modernized?"

Lucy was so stunned that she stopped tapping her nails on the table. "What? The king is modernizing Dakmati? Why in the world didn't you tell me this weeks ago! You know I wanted to go there because I thought the people there were poor, and now you're telling me that my father-in-law is pouring money into the place?"

"That is correct, madam." The lord chamberlain smiled a silken, conciliatory smile. This, Lucy thought, was ridiculous. For over three months she had been trying to arrange to go to Dakmati, and no one had told her it was the wrong place. She sat back feeling more foolish than she had in some time. Well, that was what she got for trying to keep the trip a secret from Mila. She'd wanted to surprise him by doing a preliminary search for clinic sites, and instead she had been thrashing about issuing orders that were totally inappropriate. Thanks no doubt to the Patanese concern with saving face, no one had dared tell her she was making a fool of herself.

Dismissing the chamberlain, she spent what was left of the morning drinking tea with garam masala and brooding. She was never going to understand the way these people thought, not if she lived among them for the rest of her life. Every day, instead of seeming more familiar, Patan seemed more foreign. What would they have done if she'd said she wanted to go to the moon? Probably politely built her a rocket ship out of neatly soldered tin cans. In Sindhala soldered tin cans were made into everything from lamps to dishes. That at least was something she could understand.

"Radha, Asana," Lucy announced, "I have news for you this morning."

"What news, Lucy?" Radha asked timidly. How hard Lucy had worked to get them to use her first name and how much it pleased her when one of them did. She smiled at Radha whose plump, glistening forehead bore streaks of sandalwood paste and a red third eye, neat as a dot. Being a good Hindu, Radha painted on the signs of her second sight each morning as conscientiously as Kathy DeVelt had put on her eye liner.

"Kala has suggested we explore the palace." Lucy sat down on the bed, folded her bare legs under her, and waited for them to react. She did not add that she had temporarily given up on her plans to travel to the countryside, because she hated to admit even to herself that once again she was going to have to ask Mila to intercede for her. The royal bureaucracy was more baroque than anything she had ever imagined, and it had been incredibly frustrating to find out that she had been wrong about Dakmati. She'd decided to take a vacation from red tape for a few weeks. She was bored and exhausted and needed something new to take her mind off of having made a fool of herself, so why not start with the thing closest at hand: the palace itself. She should have explored it months ago, but something more interesting had always come up.

She smiled at Kala, who stood shyly in the corner, and then she inspected Radha and Asana for signs of interest, but they just stood there in their red saris, blank and graceful like two butterflies that had just landed on the same flower. Getting no response, she elaborated. "As Kala pointed out, I've lived here for over a year, and I've only seen the main parts: the throne room, the king's study, the central gardens, the dining hall, Mila's aunts' quarters, of course, and the apartments of some of the cousins, but I don't have any real idea of how it's all laid out or how big it is, except that it seems to be endless. So I thought we'd spend the next week or two poking around. How does that strike you?"

Radha looked at Asana and opened her mouth, but no sound came out. "Whatever madam wishes," Asana said quickly.

"Oh, come on," Lucy objected. "That doesn't sound very enthusiastic. Kala has made a great suggestion, and the two of you look like I've just ordered you to go on a forty-day fast." A suspicion suddenly crossed her mind. "There isn't any reason why I shouldn't see the palace, is there?"

"No, madam," Kala said quickly. Radha and Asana looked at her in astonishment.

"What's going on here? Why don't I believe you? What is it that tells me I'm running up against another one of those little hidden traps that you people scatter around for clumsy foreign princesses to tumble into? If I'm about to violate some big taboo, tell me for heaven's sake" She thought about the yellow dress fiasco and more minor things, like the time she had held an incense stick in her left hand (bad luck) or openly admired a baby (more bad luck). The catalogue of Patanese superstitions was hefty. She never knew when she was about to stumble over some new prohibition. She stood there for a moment, feeling homesick for her own country where at least she knew the rules: green meant go, red meant stop, and you never put your elbows on the table in polite company. Come on, she thought, out with it. Don't make me plead.

"There is no taboo, madam," Radha said softly.

"So we're back to 'madam,' are we?" Lucy was annoyed at the way Radha and Asana had suddenly turned back into ladies-in-waiting. Well, the heck with them. If they wouldn't tell her what she was about to do wrong, she'd find out the hard way. She'd just blunder around with Kala until she discovered the torture chambers or whatever it was they were hiding from her.

At lunch she asked Mila if any part of the palace was off limits.

"Of course not," he said. "You should have yourself announced before you enter any private apartments, but other than that . . ." She realized later that she had asked him the wrong question. What she should have said was, "I'm about to explore this place room by room. Is there anything you don't want me to see?"

The next morning, pilfering a compass from Mila's desk, she and Kala began to explore the palace unaccompanied by Radha and Asana, who were obviously reluctant to go along. It turned out to be fun. The palace covered acres, and inspecting it was rather like rambling through a large museum. By midweek they were spending a good part of every morning hiking down remote hallways to discover small gardens, rooms full of Chinese antiques, and on one memorable occasion a small chamber full of rare Tibetan tanka paintings and brass ceremonial horns that must have been at least six feet long. They visited the apartments of obscure cousins who almost fainted with delight at the honor of being called on by the princess; they entered the servants' quarters where Lucy dandled babies on her lap, thus endearing herself permanently to every scullery maid and gardener in the palace; they scouted out storerooms filled with enough beds to stock at least half a dozen clinics; and they generally had a wonderful time. And then, just when Lucy thought she had seen everything, she stumbled on Sala.

That morning Kala had led her to the far northwest wing of the palace, down a labyrinth of halls that was beginning to look vaguely familiar, but as they strolled through the Indonesian garden Kala had suddenly stopped, thrown herself on a wooden bench, and put her face in her hands.

"What's wrong?" Lucy asked sitting down beside her. "Are you sick?"

"It's my head," Kala moaned. "It feels like it's in two pieces."

"Perhaps we'd better go back."

"No," Kala insisted, "you go on. I don't want to spoil your morning, Lucy."

Lucy spent a few more minutes trying to reason with her, and then gave up and let her go back by herself. Not having Kala along took some of the pleasure out of wandering down the halls, but soon she became absorbed in new sights: a pretty shrine to Tzbaga, a room full of small ivory statues, a case of butterflies collected over a hundred years ago by some long dead lepidopterist, all neatly dusted and labelled. She was just about to turn back when she came to a large, plain door. The door was heavy and seemed to be stuck. Tugging on it, she raised a cloud of loose mortar that sent her into a sneezing fit. This was definitely the outer limit of the palace; perhaps it was even a door to the street. She gave the door another good, hard push, it swung open, and she found herself in a tiled hall like dozens of others. Oh, well, she thought, why not check this out? Who knows, it might lead somewhere.

The hall led as usual to the sort of open courtyard that usually marked a cluster of family apartments, only in this particular instance the fountain in the center was more elaborate, the flowers around it more lush, the tiles more like those in her own part of the palace. Sitting down beside the fountain, Lucy dipped the end of her sari into the water and slapped a little on her forehead. She wondered why this pretty fountain was hidden in such a remote part of the palace, who it had been built for, and if there was some romantic story connected with it. It was incredibly hot, and she was just about to take off her slippers and splash her feet in among the goldfish when a voice spoke, so close to her elbow that she jumped.

"You look like the pictures of the royal princess. Are you the princess?"

Lucy turned around to find a young girl staring at her with unconcealed curiosity. She was a thin, rather fragile girl with a sad face and thin arms, and Lucy's first thought was that she had never seen a more lonely looking child.

"Yes," she said, "I am." She hoped the child wasn't going to praniyam. She didn't mind it so much from the adults anymore, but it bothered her to see children tapping their heads against the floor in her honor. But the girl evidently had no such thing in mind, quite the contrary.

"I'm a princess too," she said, sitting down beside Lucy.

"Oh, you are, are you?" Lucy was amused. She noticed that the child was wearing a beautiful embroidered sari and a small necklace of rubies. Pretty diamond earrings dangled from her ears, and her small hands were heavy with gold rings. Obviously she was the daughter of one of the noble families who lived in the palace, and she had fantasies of being a princess. Well, why not? When Lucy was her age, she, too, had played at being a princess, only in her case the game had turned real. "And what are you princess of?"

"Of Patan," the little girl said with a perfectly straight face. "At least I should be, but I'm not recognized, you see."

"And why is that?"

"Because mamaji fell sick and lost her beauty and died and daddyji took another wife." She gave Lucy a shy look and toyed uneasily with her necklace. "Now Daddyji still comes to see me often, but I miss my mama."

Lucy was moved by this sad little story, which in so many ways was like her own. No wonder the child dreamed that she was a princess, poor thing. The thought crossed her mind that if the girl's father were neglecting her in any way, then perhaps she might be about to do something about it. "Who is your father?" she asked gently.

It was instantly obvious she had made a mistake, because the girl suddenly looked frightened. "I can't say." She got to her feet. "I have to leave now."

"Wait a minute, please, not so fast. I'd like to know who your father is."

"I promised not to tell," the child said through white lips. "My ayah made me promise on the statue of Kali that my bones would rot and my heart would stop if I ever told a living soul."

Nice vow, Lucy thought, quite the equivalent of a first-rate nightmare. No wonder the little girl was reluctant to give out information. Kali, the goddess of creation and destruction, was usually represented dancing on corpses with a chain of human skulls around her neck, and what eight-year-old was going to break a promise to a horror like that? Could Kali be outranked? Could she as princess of Patan release the child from this terrible vow that her ignorant nursemaid should never have made her take in the first place? It was at least worth a try. "Suppose I command you to tell me," she said. She smiled at the girl to encourage her. "After all, I am the princess and you're supposed to obey me, right?"

"Yes, madam," the girl said in a shaky voice. She rocked back and forth on the line of tiles closest to the door. "If you order me to tell, then I must tell."

"Fine." Lucy got to her feet and went toward the girl, afraid that she might bolt before she could convince her to talk. "I hereby relieve you of your promise to Kali and command you to tell me who your father is." To her horror the child threw herself to the floor in a full praniyam and began to beat her head against the tiles.

"My father is your husband!" the child cried. "My father is your own honorable husband, the prince of Patan!" Running to her, Lucy swept her up in her arms, and the child bowed her head and clung to her sari sobbing.

When Mila returned for lunch, she was waiting for him with Sala beside her. Mila stopped in the doorway and his face went white.

"Daddyji!" Sala exclaimed, running forward to embrace him. He caught the child, lifted her, and gave her a hug. "Hello, little flower. What a surprise to find you here." His voice trembled, and he put the child down carefully and turned to face Lucy. "How did she get here?"

"The usual way," Lucy said calmly. "She walked." She had no intention of helping him out. She had been betrayed twice before by people she loved: first by her mother and then by David, but she had never expected to be betrayed by Mila. She had recovered from her first shock, and now she was angry. How could he have had a child and not told her, especially when he knew how much she wanted children? How could he have kept such a secret? She felt hot and cold simultaneously. Picking up a carved fan, she began to fan herself in short, sharp bursts, thinking that he had better have a good explanation.

"I mean," Mila stammered, "what are we going to do about her?"

"Feed her lunch of course." She cut off each word with a beat of the fan. She was very upset, almost on the verge of tears, and there were hundreds of things she could have said to him, but she wanted to make him sweat a little first. Maybe that was an ignoble attitude, but she couldn't help it.

"Lunch?"

"The child is hungry, Mila. So we're going to feed her. What could be more simple." Lucy put down the fan and pressed the small bell beside her, and Radha and Kala appeared carrying trays of hot food. Avoiding Mila's eyes, they bowed, sat the food down on the table, and hurried out of the room.

Lucy settled down at the table and motioned for Sala to take the chair beside her. "Do you like curried chicken and apples?" she said pleasantly. She had no intention of fighting with Mila in front of the child, who was obviously not to blame for any of this.

"Yes," Sala said, "very much."

Lucy opened one of the silver dishes and spooned curried chicken and apples onto Sala's plate. She poured her a glass of fruit juice, unfolded her napkin and placed it in her lap. "Well," she said to Mila, "aren't you going to join us?"

Stunned, Mila sat down at the far side of the table. He tried to pour himself a glass of water, but spilled half of it instead. He was sweating, and his throat felt as if he had swallowed sawdust.

Lucy's hands were shaking but she managed to eat without spilling anything. No one looking at her would have realized how hurt and upset she was, but underneath she was having an attack of what she and Cassie would have called the Medeas—that old-fashioned female urge to rise up, snake-haired and vengeful, and cut a swath of devastation in all directions. On the other side of the table Mila was going through the motions of eating as if the food on his plate were raw worms.

Let him squirm, she thought; let him wonder what I'm going to say when the two of us are alone. She put down her fork and took a sip of tea. "Sala tells me she has a pet bird," she said.

"I do," Sala said. "Ayah bought it for me in the market. A real parrot named Doti, big and blue and red with yellow feet." She smiled shyly at Mila. "It talks, Daddyji. It says, 'Sala, Sala, Sala.'"

Mila opened his mouth, but no sound came out.

"Your daughter is telling you about her new bird," Lucy said mercilessly. "What do you think of it?"

"It sounds like a nice pet," Mila gasped.

For the next half hour Lucy engaged Sala in conversation, while Mila sat paralyzed with anxiety. All in all, it was the worst half hour of his life, and Lucy did nothing to make it any better. In fact, she enjoyed every minute of it. When Sala finally spooned the last bit of mango sherbet into her mouth, Lucy called Radha back into the room.

"I think the princess Sala is tired and needs to rest," she said. "Take her into our room and put her in our bed."

"I'm too old for a nap," Sala objected. "I want to play or read a book."

"Take her out in the garden then," Lucy ordered Radha, "and give her something amusing to read." She bent over and kissed Sala on the cheek. "Daddyji and I will come out and join you in a little while." Radha took Sala's hand and led her out the door. There was a long silence. They sat face to face, staring at each other across the picked chicken bones and dirty dishes.

"Why didn't you tell me you had a daughter?" Lucy said. Mila reached out to take her hand, but she pulled away from him. "No, don't touch me yet. First I need to find out what's going on."

"Lucy, please. I can explain."

"You can? Good, great, I'd like an explanation. I'm walking around the palace, minding my own business, and I stumble on an eight-year-old child who tells me that my husband is her father. It was a shock, Mila. It was like something out of a Gothic novel—like Jane Eyre finding Rochester's mad wife in the attic. Speaking of mad wives, I don't suppose you have one hidden around here, do you?"

"No," Mila said. His lips trembled slightly. "Sala's mother is dead."

"Well, that's a relief." Lucy threw down her napkin and got to her feet. "I don't know what to do, Mila. I don't know whether to yell at you for playing me for a fool or cry my eyes out or try to be understanding, but I do know one thing: if you can't explain why you didn't tell me you had a daughter, I may have to go back to the States for a while to think things over. I'm not saying that I'm going to leave you for good or ask for a divorce or even stop loving you, but how can I keep living here," she waved at the room, "when for all I know you've got sixteen children and twenty concubines and a trained dog stashed away waiting for me to trip over them?" He sat silently, letting her anger flow over him. "Dammit," she yelled, "say something! Don't just sit there! I hate it when you retreat into your damn Buddhist silence!" She threw herself onto the couch and broke into tears. "I'm not letting you talk," she sobbed. "I'm doing all the talking, aren't I? But I can't help it. I'm so upset."

She felt Mila sit down beside her and put his arm around her, and this time she didn't draw away. Turning to him, she buried her head in his shoulder and let him stroke her hair. "Explain," she begged, "please explain. I don't understand what's going on. Who was Sala's mother? What did she die of? I need to know."

"Her name was Tulasi," Mila said softly, "and she died of a lung inflammation complicated by a high fever. She insisted on being treated by a traditional herb doctor who fed her teas and powdered roots, and dangled pendulums over her. When Dr. Sukra tried to convince her to take penicillin, she wept and refused it, claiming that he was trying to murder her. No one could persuade her to try Western medicines until the very end, and by that time it was too late."

"Did you grieve for her?"

"Yes, but we had been separated for a number of years, so mostly I was sad for Sala's sake."

"Did you love her?"

"No. Not really." He paused, thinking about the past and Tulasi and how she had loved all the things he had never cared for: jewels and silks and sweet foods and religious festivals. She had loved palace gossip and hated books, liked melodramatic movies imported from India with fat mustachioed men swearing eternal love and ladies with madeup faces fainting and making secret trysts. When he had made love to Tulasi she had turned off the lights and buried her face in the pillows and clenched her fists as if his touch brought her pain. She had been a good woman, but not a companion like Lucy. "There were too many differences between the two of us for love to exist," he explained. "It was an arranged marriage. I never saw her until our wedding day. She gave me a toy bank shaped like an elephant for a wedding present, and I think I gave her a ruby brooch. She was twenty-four you see, and I was only six."

"Six!" Lucy was so shocked that she stopped crying. "You mean to tell me you got married when you were *six* years old?"

"Child marriages used to be common in Patan." Mila picked up the loose end of her sari and began to wipe the tears out of her eyes. "I'm sorry, my love. Truly sorry. I should have told you sooner, but I hadn't lived with Tulasi for so long by the time I met you that I had trouble thinking of her as my wife. Our marriage was consummated when I turned fourteen and it lasted a grand total of two weeks before I realized that it was all wrong."

"Two weeks?" Lucy was so relieved that she didn't know whether to laugh or cry. He'd been married for two weeks. It sounded farcical; it should be in the *Guinness Book of World Records* under Shortest Royal Marriage on Record. "What did you do? Get a divorce?"

"No," Mila shook his head, "divorce is forbidden to members of the royal family. I just—" He halted, ashamed at how this was going to sound to her, yet not really sorry for what he had done because even Tulasi had been happier for it. "I just told her that our marriage was over and that I never wanted to see her again."

"That sounds cruel."

"It was, but remember I was only fourteen, a spoiled little oriental prince puffed up with his own importance. It's not a part of my life I'm proud of. Still, I don't think Tulasi was unhappy. Our two weeks together produced Sala, whom we both loved, and Tulasi had many friends right up until the end."

Lucy was moved by the story of his sad, loveless marriage. She placed her hand gently on his. "Why didn't you tell me this when we first met? Did you think I'd care that you'd been married before? Did you think I'd reject Sala? You know how much I want children." She was suddenly overwhelmed by the memory of her miscarriage and her voice broke. "I'd have understood," she said.

"No, you wouldn't have," Mila said quietly, "because it isn't that simple. You see, when we got married, Tulasi was still alive."

"What!" Lucy let go of his hand and stared at him in amazement. "You can't be serious."

"I'm afraid I am."

"You were married to both of us at the same time!"

"Don't get so upset," he pleaded, "please."

"Don't get so upset!" She felt as if all the blood in her body were rushing to her head. "Where I come from that's called bigamy."

"Not in Patan."

"How many wives can a man have in this country?"

"As many as he can support. It's perfectly legal."

"I don't care if it's legal! It's immoral; it's degrading to women. How would you feel if I had three husbands?"

"The marriage to Tulasi was only a technicality," Mila pleaded. "It meant nothing."

"Nothing!" Lucy moaned. "Maybe not to you, but it does to me. Child marriages, polygamy, what next? I knew I was coming to a foreign country, but this is foreign beyond my wildest dreams. Why didn't you tell me I was going to be the *second* Mrs. . . . Jesus, Mila, you don't even have a reasonable last name!"

"Calm down," he begged. "I know this is hard for you, but please try to understand. I had no relationship with Tulasi when I met you; I hadn't for years. I know I should have told you the truth, but what was the truth—a legal fiction, a burden thrust on me in my childhood. I was on the verge of confessing my situation to you a hundred times, but one thought always stopped me: Lucy will never marry me if she knows I have a living wife. For the first time in my life I was in love and I was terrified of losing you. I wanted you. I wanted to spend the rest of my life with you. Anything else was an inconceivable nightmare. How could I have told you about Tulasi? How could I have lost you just when I'd finally found you?" He slid to the floor to his knees. "I worship you. You're my Tara, my goddess." He seized her hands and began to cover them with kisses. "Forgive me, Lucy. My life would be nothing without you."

"Mila," she commanded, "don't do this, get up; this doesn't solve anything." It embarrassed her to see him on his knees, and yet the sight of his begging her for forgiveness moved her. She thought of David and how he had never once apologized for anything. Mila was a different kind of man. He might not be perfect; he might have hurt her and even deceived her, but he was fundamentally decent. He knew when he'd done something wrong, and he was man enough to admit it.

"Forgive me," he insisted. He apologized; he explained everything over again in more detail; he reassured her that he loved her and only her. She didn't give in easily, but at last she began to soften. Gradually her anger evaporated, leaving her puzzled and sad. She still didn't understand completely why he had done what he had done, but she saw that there was no use fighting over it any longer. She realized with a pang of regret that they might never really be able to understand each other. He moved through this world with ease; she stumbled into hidden traps. She thought in English; he thought in Patanese. He was East and she was West, and yet she loved him, she had no doubt of that. "I'll forgive you," she said at last, "on one condition."

"Anything!" he said passionately. "I'll do anything."

"Never lie to me again, Mila. I'll take Sala and treat her like my own daughter, and I'll learn to live with the idea that you were married to Tulasi, but never lie to me again. Tell me the whole truth whatever the consequences."

"I promise," he said. He rose and kissed her on the forehead and sat down beside her. "I swear by Kali that—"

"Don't swear by Kali. Swear by God or Buddha or by your own

conscience, but don't swear by Kali." The mention of Kali made her feel cold all over. She thought of the black goddess with her necklace of skulls and her terrible dance of destruction, a dance that she didn't want to join, not now, not ever. She shuddered, and Mila reached out and took her in his arms.

"I'll never deceive you again," he said, and she knew that he meant it.

• 4 •

That evening, true to his promise, Mila told Lucy the whole truth about their life in the palace, and when she heard what he had to say she understood why he had tried to spare her. After Sala had been put to bed under Asana's care, he led her out into the small garden behind their apartments.

"Let us sit here so we can speak privately," he whispered, pointing to the bench that was the farthest from the door. He paused for a moment and looked around, but there was no one else in sight, only the rose and rhododendron bushes. The sun was setting, casting a brilliant pink glow against the white stucco walls. A net of shadows overlay the light, twigs and leaves, and the serpentine curve of the grape arbor. He wasn't sure how to begin, and he didn't want to frighten her unnecessarily. "Do you see those shadows," he whispered, pointing to the tangle in front of them.

"Yes," Lucy nodded. She was a little puzzled by the question. He looked so serious and grave. She reached out and plucked a leaf from one of the grape vines, and as she did so the shadows trembled and rearranged themselves, forming a new pattern on the wall.

"The court," Mila said, "is like those shadows." He put his hand out and the pattern of the twigs was repeated on his flesh, and he sat there as if holding it for a moment, looking at her, choosing his words carefully. "On the surface life looks peaceful, boring, solid enough to grasp, but in reality," he dropped his hand, "that is an illusion. No matter how hard we try, neither you nor I will ever be able to know exactly what is going on around us, any more than we can pick up the image of these twigs and put them elsewhere. Life in this palace is a fantastically complicated net of plots and intrigues, of power struggles that never surface. Because you and I are who we are, we are always being watched. Do you understand what I'm saying? Even now, we're probably being spied on." He took her hand in his and held it tightly and searched her face, trying to calculate what impact his words had had on her. She had gone pale and her lips were set. "I didn't tell you this before, because I didn't want you to feel insecure here, but this is a fact of court life. I've lived with this knowledge ever since I was a child, and now, I'm afraid, you must live with it too."

Lucy had felt every muscle in her body go tense at the words "spied upon." She looked at Mila and then at the shadows that were fading even as they spoke, and she tried to assimilate what he had told her. She remembered Mrs. Arjuna's warning, and the look on Kala's face when she suggested that Lucy explore the palace, and so many things, small in themselves: coming into her room to find a letter she had been writing moved from one side of her desk to the other; the feeling that unseen eyes were watching her when she sat in the Vishnu garden. "Who is spying on us?" she demanded. She looked at the rose bushes, growing so calmly in the dusk, their large yellow blossoms motionless; she looked at the far wall, at the dark corners of the garden, and then she looked back at the door to their apartment. The door was a dark shadow. Beyond it there was nothing but an indistinct shape that she recognized as one of the living-room couches. "Who are they," she repeated, "and why can't we get rid of them?"

Mila shook his head. "I wish I could answer that question, but no one can tell us who the spies are. All we can be sure of is that at least some of them are the people closest to us."

"Does that include Asana, Radha, and Kala?"

Mila nodded, and Lucy suddenly felt real fear. She had thought of Patan as something between an exotic travelogue and her own private Peace Corps assignment, but from what Mila was saying, it was clear that it was something quite different, something much more sinister. The walls of the garden felt oppressive; she felt trapped inside them like a fly in a glass bottle. Her mouth went dry with anxiety and claustrophobia.

Mila's confession was long, painful, and hard to listen to. There was more, but it all added up to the same thing: they were surrounded by intrigue. "I suspect, for example, that someone is standing in the way of the clinics. I don't know who or why or what they hope to gain, but my father won't hear me out on the subject. It's as if—" he paused, "as if someone has gotten to him, whispered in his ear that it will be the end of him if he gives in." He described how he had argued with Marpa time and time again, and how Marpa had rejected his ideas one after another on the grounds that they would encourage the communists.

Some of Lucy's fear vanished in the face of this new revelation. She sat somberly, feeling sad and weighted down as she took in this news which was the worst of all. So there might not be any clinics as long as Marpa lived? She tried to imagine herself waiting patiently for years, but she couldn't. This is a stupid, senseless situation, she thought, and she felt angry at the waste of it, at Marpa's stubbornness, at the invisible plots that boiled up around them, tainting everything. "But social reforms are the one thing that might save this country *from* the communists," she objected. "Surely your father must see that."

"He doesn't," Mila said. "He flies into a rage when I try to reason with him, which is why I suspect that something is going on that I don't know about. But I'm not giving up; I swear to you. I'll keep going back. I'll keep fighting him." He let go of her hand, and his voice took on a tone she had never heard him use before. "If only I had some real power, but I don't, not yet. Until he dies, I'm only a figurehead, but how can I hope that my own father will die in time for me to save my country? It's an impossible situation."

Lucy thought that it did indeed sound impossible. She was proud of Mila for fighting his father, but she wished he had won. She could tell that for all his promises never to give up, he was discouraged. Reaching out, she put her arm around him. "We'll see this through together," she said. She swallowed hard, feeling upset for him and for herself. "I have to admit that I'm disappointed, though. I had such hopes." She didn't rail at him or remind him of the promises he had made to her when he proposed, because what would be the use? He had been trying as hard as he could. She could see that in his eyes and in the way he was sitting, and she knew that the disappointment was as bitter for him as it was for her.

"I had hopes too," Mila said. He put his arms around her, and they hugged each other for a long time.

The next few weeks were difficult. The routine of the court, the meditations and temple visits and card games, all seemed hollow to Lucy. Sometimes when she looked at Mila's aunts, sitting around a large silver tray eating sweets and gossiping, she felt so restless and bored that she had to excuse herself until she was calm enough to return to her place at the table and join in the conversation. At night, in the privacy of the garden, she and Mila talked the situation over from every angle, but they got nowhere.

Lucy would have fallen into despair during those weeks if it had not been for Sala. The child's presence was a great consolation, and she was sometimes able to put the failure of their plans out of her mind for a few hours as she played with her new stepdaughter, talking to her and gradually winning her trust. Dismissing the old ayah who had terrified the child with tales of Kali and other demons, she hired a healthy young girl named Lali. Lali, who had been educated in a small school run by Catholic nuns, spoke fluent English as well as Patanese, and soon it became common to see the princess, her stepdaughter, and her stepdaughter's nurse sitting in one of the gardens talking in a mixture of both languages.

Still, the disappointment was bitter. At the back of her mind, she was never reconciled to the idea that Marpa had the right to stand in the way of reform. It didn't seem fair or just or even possible that one man should have such power, especially not when people like herself and Mila were willing to make the necessary changes. Instead of growing resigned, she grew more restive and rebellious with each passing day. In the afternoons she would often sit in the Vishnu garden, feeling trapped and frustrated.

September passed, the rains lessened, and the clouds that capped the mountains began to dissolve, exposing the implacable white ice of the high peaks. On the twenty-eighth, several members of the Nepalese royal family arrived in Sindhala to make a pilgrimage to the famous Goloka monastery, and Mila, as custom and courtesy demanded, offered to accompany them. Since they were scheduled to take part in a special religious retreat for men only, Lucy was not invited on the expedition. "You won't be missing anything," Mila reassured her. "Once we get to the monastery, we'll be spending ten hours a day chanting and meditating in an unheated hall. The last time I took visitors up there, the monks set us to work digging out the monastery sewer system. They're great believers in teaching the rich and powerful humility."

For over a week, the palace buzzed with frantic activity as the great trek was organized. The pilgrimage had to be made on foot, so porters had to be found to carry the food and equipment: not a minor undertaking, for although the journey might end with digging out the monastery sewers, the route there and back was to be one long party.

As the gargantuan project neared completion, Lucy wandered through the stores, appalled at what it was going to take to sustain four nobles and their servants for three and a half weeks. To ensure that the royal guests never suffered a moment of boredom while on the trail, the porters were to carry a portable movie projector and a small electrical generator. There were radios, record players, volleyball nets, and, most incredibly, a full-sized rowing machine. She thought of the peasants who lived from one harvest to the next with never quite enough food to feed their children. No wonder Marpa worried about a revolution. In the end it took 160 porters to carry everything.

After Mila left, Lucy wandered around aimlessly, missing him. She still had her official duties to perform, but the king, who was rumored to be suffering from a bad cold, temporarily suspended the formal dinners, so she was able to eat alone in her own quarters. In her free time she read, but mostly she sat in the garden and thought. For the first time since her marriage, she had an opportunity to concentrate exclusively on herself with no distractions, and listening to her own inner voice she found that she had the beginnings of a solution: she might not know how to change Marpa's mind and erase his prejudices, but she knew what *she* needed to be happy in Patan. Her solution was not sweeping or grandiose; it was small and personal and perhaps it would be ineffectual, but it was hers and hers alone, and if it brought down Marpa's wrath, Mila wouldn't be implicated.

"I'm going to start acting like a normal person again," she informed Cassie the following Monday. "To hell with protocol and tradition. I'm going to be myself, Lucy Constable, an ordinary middle-class American girl who wears blue jeans, drinks Cokes, listens to the Beatles, and does what she damn well pleases. I'm surrounded by such walls of hypocrisy and prejudice that I don't know any other way to break out."

Cassie chuckled. "You never were ordinary, Lou. Not by anyone's standards."

"Well, stand back. I'm about to be so ordinary that Patan may never recover from the shock. For example, I just dug my old clothes out of storage, and I'm sitting here in a Harvard sweatshirt and cutoffs, barefoot, drinking real coffee and not garam masala. I intend to go where I please when I please without a pack of ladies-in-waiting and bodyguards trailing after me." She wished that she could tell Cassie about the intrigues that surrounded her and how trapped they made her feel, but that was unwise. She had no hard evidence that her calls were being monitored, but there was no way to be sure that they weren't. She hoped Cassie would understand that if she was rejecting the rules and customs that hemmed her in, there must be some very serious reason.

"Can you get away with that?"

"Why not? Who's to stop me? I just sent one of the gardeners out to buy me a bicycle, a nice rusty one like the one I used to ride at Radcliffe, complete with a dented basket and a bell, and tomorrow I intend to stroll out of the palace unaccompanied, climb on my bike, and take a tour of the city."

"Won't Mila be upset?"

"No." She realized that she was going to have to offer some explanation. "He's off on a trek, and besides considering what happened with Sala, I hardly think he's in a position to object. He knows I'm dying to get out of the palace." She looked impatiently at the gold bed, the Chinese screens, the antique rugs, silk curtains, and all the rest of the sumptuous paraphernalia of her bedroom, thinking again of all the things she wanted to tell Cassie but couldn't. It was frustrating to communicate this way, but it was better than nothing. "I've been living in this fancy cage for over a year now, and it's time I saw the real world." She chose her words carefully. "I'm tired of spending my nights in the royal theater watching *Rio Bravo* and *The Alamo*. I'm sick of not being able to take a step without worrying if it will offend the king. I want to get dirt under my fingernails again; I want to do something useful."

"Like what?"

"Who knows, but whatever it is, it won't include cutting ribbons, planting trees, and eating hors d'oeuvres." Actually she knew exactly what she was going to do, but if her phone was being tapped, she didn't intend to give Marpa any advance warning. It was definitely time to change the subject. "Enough about me. How's your life? Is Andy still down in the dumps?"

"Aha," Cassie said. "I was wondering when you were going to ask that." The static crackled behind her voice like a drumbeat. "As a matter of fact, he's on the upswing. I hardly recognize the man: he smiles, he eats three helpings of dinner, he . . . well, let us draw a curtain of good taste over what else he's doing again, but suffice it to say it's putting a smile on my face too. He hasn't shown me his data yet, but just between you and me I think he's on the verge of a breakthrough. Remember how hard he slaved all summer to isolate the compound that was making those wild carrots of his grow like crazy?"

"Do I ever." Lucy shifted the phone to her other ear and poured herself a fresh cup of coffee with her free hand. "And I also remember how disappointed he was when he put the stuff on some bean plants and they keeled over dead."

"Well, he's finally figured out what went wrong. At least he thinks he has. It turns out that he was probably using the compound in too strong a concentration. So a few days ago he started using it in a highly diluted form, and guess what? The plants are still alive and they look hardy, very hardy indeed, big and sassy. It's too early to tell if their growth has been accelerated, but at least we aren't holding a wake for them. I haven't seen Andy in such a hopeful mood since before he failed his prelims. In fact I think he's finally stopped worrying about having to retake them in January, which is perfectly logical because if he gets good results with his experiments there's no way they're going to throw him out of this joint. On the contrary, the department will probably see that he gets a scholarship. I'm already having all sorts of greedy visions: steak, new tires for our bicycles, not to mention that reconditioned Pentax I've been lusting after."

"Well, congratulations. It's about time." Lucy toasted Cassie with her coffee cup, thinking that it was too bad she couldn't have her there in the flesh.

"You can say that again. Personally I'm so happy to see Andy smiling again that I'm afraid my brain is going soft. I find myself doing feminine, wifely things like scraping the calcified carrots off the kitchen floor and doing some of the wash that has been piling up since last January, and I've even—get this—gone back to working in my dad's lab."

"No, I don't believe it. You who swore that you'd never cross the threshold again?"

"Me. The prodigal daughter."

"How did this great reconciliation come about? Did Mother Teresa handle the negotiations, or has your father started smoking dope, declared himself a hippie, and begged your forgiveness?"

Cassie sighed. "Would that it were so, but I'm afraid the truth is much more prosaic. Patterson didn't have enough room for my bromeliad collection, so I was looking around for some suitable space when—surprise!—Larry Quinn calls me up and invites me back on his turf, which as you may recall contains a greenhouse roughly the size of Detroit. As far as I can tell, this is his way of apologizing to me for failing Andy, not that he'd ever admit that, but all the signs are there. Also, to be frank, I think *he* thinks that Andy is going to come up with something pretty interesting. I know how his mind works: he doesn't want to risk the possibility that I may persuade Andy to leave Ann Arbor, so I'm being coddled and courted."

"So your dad has a human side after all."

Cassie chuckled. "I wouldn't go so far as to call it *human*. Let's just say that for the moment he's doing a good imitation of a decent—ouch!" Cassie ended the sentence with a scream.

Lucy was so startled she nearly dropped the receiver. "What's going on? Are you okay?" Through the static she heard Cassie giggling wildly.

"It's okay," Cassie gasped. "No need to panic; it was the cat; she just jumped me and tried to take my big toe off. You should see how smug she looks. She lies in wait for me, Lou. Conceals her wicked little self behind the couch until I forget she's there, and then, when I least expect it, she strikes. How am I ever going to train her to differentiate between my toe and a mouse? It's hopeless."

Lucy was relieved. She settled back and picked up her coffee cup again. "If I were you, Cass, I'd think seriously about dogs. Dogs rarely pounce."

"Humph," Cassie snorted. "No way. I adore this fur psychotic. She goes everywhere with me. We're inseparable. I even take her to the lab. Besides, it isn't entirely her fault that she's in a wild mood. Frankly, I think she's about to go into heat again. All the signs are there: she's been giving the tomcat next door amorous glances, and yesterday," Cassie chuckled again, "she bit my father."

"Oh, no," Lucy said, "she didn't; she couldn't have."

"Oh, yes, she did. His Highness, Lord of the Lab, came in to inspect the slaving peons, and she went for his finger: the little one with the gold signet ring on it that Candy or Wendy or whatever her name was gave him. Then, being a cat of extraordinary sense, she leapt out of his way, upsetting an entire beaker of Andy's compound all over both of them in the process. He bellowed, she meowed; both of them stank to high heaven. It was quite a scene."

Lucy knew she should feel some sympathy for Quinn, but she didn't. The image of him being successfully routed by a ten-pound cat was too much for her. She broke into a peal of laughter. That was the wonderful thing about talking to Cassie. No matter how serious their lives got, they almost always managed to laugh at least once during every conversation.

Although Lucy had boasted to Cassie that she intended to stroll out the front gates of the palace, she realized, soon after hanging up the phone, that the pleasure of shocking the court wasn't worth the price of letting them know what she was up to. Once her ladies saw her leaving, custom would require them to follow her; with the ladies would come guards, more attendants, and so forth, and in no time at all she would find herself in the ridiculous position of leading a parade through the streets of Sindhala. So the next morning after breakfast, she dispatched Radha, Kala, and Asana on long, complicated errands. When she was sure they were safely out of the way, she hurried to the kitchen garden where her bicycle was waiting for her as ordered: behind a bush, tires filled, chain freshly greased. As she wheeled it toward a small side gate she found herself humming happily. Ah freedom, she thought as she swung herself onto the seat and felt the old, familiar pressure of the handlebars dig into her palms.

The city of Sindhala was not a normal destination for tourists, since it had no Western-style hotels, no nightlife of any kind, and no regular commercial air connections with foreign countries, but fortunately for Lucy's plans, there were other Westerners in town. Most of these in the fall of 1967 were French and German hippies who had driven from

Europe by way of Afghanistan, Pakistan, and Nepal over roads so tortuous that only the truly intrepid made it. The first wave had arrived in gaudily painted VW vans, looking for paradise, closely followed by a second wave, even poorer than the first, who had hitchhiked. Now they sat on street corners or clustered at small tea stalls in the market, stoned on hashish, discussing Herman Hesse and the Maharishi, complaining about the dirt and the lack of cold beer, and making plans to smuggle dope back to Paris or Berlin by hiding it in hollow heels in their shoes or taping it to their legs. A piece of hashish the size of a baseball, which cost about the equivalent of twelve francs in Sindhala, could be chopped up into small pieces and sold for nearly five thousand francs in the Latin Quarter, and there were many plans being made to realize a fortune.

Since the French and German hippies rarely did anything but smoke and talk, and since they broke no important laws, the police ignored them as did almost everyone else except small children who found their tie-dyed clothes and beads fascinating, which was convenient because it meant that when Lucy rode away from the palace wearing her jeans, she got only a few curious stares. Blond women were no longer rare or exotic in Sindhala, especially not ones who rode rusty bicycles, and as for anyone recognizing her as the princess, it was simply inconceivable.

As she started down the hill, the mountaintops that ringed the valley were clearly visible, and every flower in the city seemed to be in bloom. Pink and white blossoms the size of powder puffs hung from the trees that bordered the main highway, and monkeys swung from branch to branch like teams of acrobats, chattering wildly. At first she was so drunk with freedom that she hardly noticed the city itself. Gracefully she dodged traffic as she had done a thousand times before on the streets of Cambridge, skimming around the edge of bullock carts, avoiding other bicyclists, skidding to a stop to avoid colliding with a line of women carrying baskets of onions on their heads. Cars were still a rarity, and only once did she have to come to a halt to let a large, shiny Cadillac pass. Inside, sitting in air-conditioned comfort, was a middle-aged woman whom Lucy recognized as one of Mila's fifth cousins, a minor but wealthy member of the nobility. Beside the woman was an expensive portable radio, blaring out a song by Engelbert Humperdinck. The woman cast a bored glance at Lucy and turned back to the romance magazine she was reading. The magazine featured Lucy's face and the headline A DAY IN THE LIFE OF THE PRINCESS OF PARADISE. Lucy smiled, amused at the woman's failure to recognize her. She was also relieved.

Climbing back on her bicycle, she rode toward the market, threading her way through crowds of people on foot who seemed to be carrying every item invented by nature or human ingenuity. Ranging in age from five to perhaps sixty, they all had one thing in common: a braided band of yak hair strapped around their foreheads from which dangled a huge, cone-shaped basket. In the baskets were piles of red tomatoes, tiny hot peppers, blocks of salt, pieces of freshly slaughtered meat, charcoal, wood, cumin, ginger root, tin cups, braids of garlic, patties of cow dung, boxes of matches, tins of cooking oil, even—on several occasions—spare parts for automobiles. Sometimes small babies perched on top of the loads, dressed in brightly embroidered wool caps, clinging to their mothers' heads and looking around calmly as if riding in this style was the most natural thing in the world. It would have all been very picturesque except that the closer Lucy looked the more she saw the signs of hunger and desperate poverty. The arms that clasped the headstraps were skeleton thin; the eyes of at least half of the people were glazed and dull, filled with hopelessness. Old women and young children struggled past her, bent double under burdens that seemed to be crushing them. When she examined the babies in their embroidered caps more carefully, she saw sores on their lips, inflamed eyes, little bellies protruding from malnutrition.

She had seen the streets of Patan before, but never from such a close perspective. When she had passed by in royal splendor, she had been confined to the main thoroughfares, and the curbs had been lined with schoolchildren waving flags. The shops had been closed, and she had not been able to see what was going on inside them. Now she rode slowly, fascinated and upset by the scene that was unfolding all around her. Painted the same Oz-like shade of blue, the shops that lined the narrow, twisting streets were little more than dank, unventilated closets, littered with filth of every description, yet inside each dark hole there were rarely less than a dozen people busily at work. In some, Tibetan refugee women spun huge piles of wool into yarn, using wooden spinning wheels no larger than dinner plates. In others whole families of herbalists packaged and pounded roots and flowers into pills and potions guaranteed to restore potency, attract lovers, and cure everything from pneumonia to cancer. China menders sat cross-legged painstakingly rejoining the fragments of broken cups and bowls; shoemakers stitched sandals, pulling the leather threads through the soles with their teeth; fullers dipped cloth in smoking vats of blue and red dye; sari merchants hawked their wares, leaning out of their shops to offer her lengths of gaudily embroidered cotton. She noticed there were no printed signs over the shops, only large cartoonlike pictures: a huge tooth over the booth of a dentist, a pair of gigantic spectacles indicating that eyeglasses were sold within. Slowing down, she studied the picture signs, and it struck her that they must be there because almost no one could read.

The streets grew narrower as she approached the market, and the murmur of the crowd increased to a clamor. A stench rose from the gutters that made her almost dizzy, and she was surprised to see adults squatting down in the street to relieve themselves. Itinerant monks in saffron-colored robes began to appear, crouched in doorways, nearly naked, with sandalwood stripes painted on their foreheads and begging bowls in their hands. Their arms were thin and infected with sores, and some of them seemed drunk or stoned. Beside the monks sat cripples and beggars: women without legs or arms, men who seemed to have been burned in some kind of terrible accident, mothers holding more listless, sick-looking infants with crusted eyes and running noses. This sort of misery was exactly what she had expected to see in Sindhala; still, it made her feel sick.

She pedaled faster, but things only got worse. Rounding a corner, she suddenly came on an entire row of lepers dressed in foul rags. There must have been two dozen at least, each with an empty coconut shell in front of him ready to receive scraps or alms. Beside the lepers sat a small, thin man making change so that charitable people could give a rupee to each.

"Alms, lady," the lepers cried.

"Food, money, for the love of God."

As she stopped to avoid colliding with a cart full of rice stalks, one of the lepers—an old man without a nose—came stumbling toward her and tugged at her shirt sleeve. His eyes were yellow and rheumy, and his fingers had worn away horribly until only the last joints were left. "Rupees," he lisped, "money, please lady." Lucy reached into her pocket and pulled out a fifty-rupee note and handed it to him. The old man looked at it as if he had never seen one.

"Rupees," he insisted.

"That is rupees. Many rupees." Lucy started to back away from him, and then gritting her teeth she stopped and held her ground. If she was going to deal with the sick, then she was going to have to learn how to take these things in stride. Could you get leprosy from being touched, or was that just superstition? Wasn't leprosy called something else these days? Hansen's disease, that was it. And it wasn't incurable. There were medicines to treat it, inexpensive medicines like Diasone, which meant that all this suffering was unnecessary. She gripped the handlebars of her bicycle and forced herself to look at the ruined faces that surrounded her. If she had been king, she would have set up treatment programs for these people long ago.

She rode on, through the filth and the noise, through puddles of sewage and piles of rotten fruit, past stalls where the meat was black with flies. The market swelled around her, alive and chaotic and overwhelming. Hoping to escape it, she turned into a side street and headed toward the river, which she had seen so many times from her window in the palace. From a distance it had looked like a band of silver running through the green rice paddies, bordered by quaint temples and thatched huts. For a moment she was alone again, able to breathe. The street twisted and turned back on itself, ran down a steep hill, and suddenly she was at the edge of the river looking at a line of women washing themselves in the water. The women were fully clothed, and they were dumping brass pots full of river water on their hair, talking and laughing happily. It was a relief to see them.

Parking her bicycle, Lucy wandered along the riverbank toward Sindhala's only bridge, a lacy span of steel that had been given by Queen Victoria to Mila's great-great-grandfather. She had crossed the bridge dozens of times, and each time she had noticed that there were fires burning downriver, cooking fires, she had assumed, lit by pilgrims who had come to visit the temple. Now as she approached the temple, she saw that she had been mistaken. What she had thought were cooking fires were fires from the Hindu cremation *ghats*. The smell was horrible, sweet and cloying like roast pork.

Climbing on her bicycle, she headed back toward the palace, skirting the market. But the morning wasn't over yet. As she stopped near a public fountain to splash water on her face, a group of children ran up to her. The children were thin and ragged, and the youngest of them was barely old enough to walk.

"Rupees, lady," they begged. The older ones held up the little ones. "We're starving," they cried. "We're dying." They stretched out their hands to her, pleading in a chorus. "Feed us; feed us." Reaching into her pockets, Lucy gave them every bit of money she had left, a pitiful handful of coins that they received with smiles and blessings. Then sitting down beside the fountain, she put her face in her hands. She'd learned more about Patan in the last hour than she'd learned in more than a year of living in the palace, and what she'd seen made her feel depressed, frustrated, and impatient with Marpa and his idiotic refusal to do anything for his people. She had known there was poverty, even suspected it was extreme, but to actually witness it firsthand was a completely different experience. This wasn't the same city she had gazed at from her window every morning. It looked more like pictures she had seen of Calcutta. There was no end to the misery, and if it was this bad here, what must it be like in the country where she knew for a fact that there were no doctors or schools?

Returning to the palace, she threw off her clothes and took a hot shower. The smell of the city seemed to cling to her hair and to linger under her nails. Even when she was sitting in her own drawing room again, dressed in a clean sari, the suffering she had witnessed surrounded her like invisible smoke. She ate very little for the rest of the day, spoke very little, and was impatient with everyone, even Sala. Brooding, she drank cold tea and thought guiltily of how much time she had wasted living in a world of wealth and privilege.

General Arjuna was also thinking about wealth and privilege that afternoon, but entirely without guilt and from a very different perspective. Sitting in a comfortable chair beside a pool full of pink lotus blossoms, the general was reading the *New York Times* and sipping an ice-cold martini. Dressed in a silk suit made by one of the finest tailors in London, he looked healthy and prosperous, as indeed he was. The world, Arjuna was pleased to note, was in a terrible state and getting worse all the time. Thanks to the Six-Day War between Israel and the Arabs, Europe's oil supply was in danger. The United States seemed bogged down in Vietnam, as blacks rioted in Detroit and students marched on Washington. Inflation was spiraling, there had been riots in Hong Kong, and the British chancery in Peking had been looted and burned. Arjuna turned the page and took another sip of his martini. With all this economic insecurity, investors would be falling all over each other to buy gold, and he owned a gold mine. What could be more satisfactory?

He was interrupted in his revery by a discreet clearing of the throat. Looking up he saw his bodyguard standing in the archway.

"Yes?" Arjuna said.

"Message from the lady Kala," the bodyguard said laconically. "The princess went out this morning."

Arjuna put down his *Times* and considered the implications of this. "Where did she go?" he asked, eating the olive out of his martini.

"To the market," the bodyguard said, "on a bicycle."

Arjuna was pleased. He'd expected something like this from the moment the prince brought this foreign wife to Patan. Going out to the market on a bicycle, oh, this was rich, it was wonderful, it was too good to have hoped for. "Did she go alone or with her ladies?" he asked. He knew the answer, of course, but he prided himself on being a methodical man who never overlooked details.

"Alone, my general."

"Did she meet a lover there?"

"The lady Kala couldn't say, but she thinks not."

Arjuna was slightly disappointed. Ever since Dr. Sukra had convinced him that it would be impractical to try to sterilize her, Arjuna had been hoping that the princess would do something wild and shameful that would get her banished to some remote country estate. A lover would have been perfect, preferably one of those French hippies who hung around the tea shops in Kalpa Square, but still, handled right, this escapade had promise. The king would not be happy to hear that the princess had been wandering around Sindhala unescorted. "Tell the lady Kala that if the princess goes out again, she is to arrange to have her followed," he ordered his bodyguard.

"Yes, my general." Bowing, the bodyguard left the courtyard as unobtrusively as he had entered it. Arjuna finished off the last of his martini, picked up his *New York Times*, and turned to the financial section.

The morning after her ride through Sindhala, Lucy went to the royal library and looked up everything she could find on the common diseases of Central Asia. Most of the books were far too technical for her to understand, and the others were too elementary. The first-aid pamphlets issued by the World Health Organization were the most helpful, but they all seemed to presume that a well-stocked Western-style hospital was just a phone call away, and that all one had to do was stop the bleeding or keep the patient breathing until a doctor arrived to take over. She was just about to give up when she came across a typewritten manuscript bound in black leather with the royal crest stamped on the cover. The manuscript proved to be a Patanese translation of a Chinese manual entitled *Barefoot Doctors*. Remembering that Mila had once praised the Chinese rural health system, she plunged into it with the aid of a dictionary and was elated to discover that one section of the manual dealt with common diseases of the Himalayas.

For nearly a week she spent every waking hour laboriously translating the Patanese into English, and by the time she reached the final page she had a working knowledge of what she might encounter. Treatment, however, was another matter. The manual emphasized that there were some diseases, leprosy and cancer for example, that were beyond the scope of anyone who lacked extensive medical training. But there were others, scores of others, that even an amateur like herself might cure if she had the right supplies.

She spent a long time wrestling with her conscience. She knew so little compared to a real doctor. What if she did more harm than good? Even the most common drugs had side effects. How would she feel if she killed someone in the course of trying to cure them? It seemed like an awesome responsibility, but at last she decided that even if her knowledge of medicine wasn't perfect, it was far better than nothing.

That night she sat up until two o'clock making a list, and early the next morning, without announcing her impending visit, she asked to be driven to the royal hospital. She found Dr. Sukra in his new office with his gold spectacles perched on his forehead, reading the most recent issue of the *Lancet*. Sukra was a round, pale man who always dressed in a Western-style suit, and he had an annoying habit of never looking her directly in the eye.

"Good morning, Doctor," she said. "I hope I'm not disturbing you."

Dr. Sukra jumped to his feet and groped for his glasses. He was obviously startled to see her since he always called on her at the palace, but he managed to regain his composure. "Not at all, Princess," he said. "This is indeed a surprise and an honor. Please sit down."

Lucy sat down and immediately got to the point. "I need medical supplies," she said.

"Medical supplies?" Dr. Sukra blinked several times and adjusted his glasses.

"Simple ones," she said briskly. "Kaopectate, Lomotil, paregoric, antibiotic creams, tetracycline, bandages, iodine." She pulled the list out of her purse and consulted it to make sure she'd left nothing out. "Disinfectant, water-purification tablets, tongs, gauze, and some kind of vermifuge—I'm not sure what—gentian violet, perhaps. Also some large bottles of Kwell if you have it."

Dr. Sukra rubbed his hands together and again adjusted his glasses. "May I ask what the princess wishes to do with these things?"

"No," Lucy said firmly, "you may not. Nor may you mention this to anyone. Is that clear?" If she was forced by circumstances to be a princess and live in the palace while the rest of Patan suffered and died around her, then she would be a princess to the hilt. She didn't have much power, but what little she had, she intended to use. Reform in Patan was going to start with her. Perhaps it was quixotic of her to think that she could make the slightest difference, but she would try. If she failed, no one would be any worse off than they had been before, and she would at least have the satisfaction of knowing that she had not sat idly by while people who might have been helped sickened and died.

"When would the princess like these supplies?" Dr. Sukra said humbly. He was terrified of crossing her. When she had first walked into his office he was sure she had found out about the Swedish medicine he had given to General Arjuna; he thought she had come to tell him that he was going to be tried for high treason and executed in Kalpa Square like a dog. When he found it was only tetracycline she was after, he was so relieved that he would have given her every drug in the hospital if she had asked for it.

"I'd like them at once," Lucy said. "Without delay."

"Yes, Gracious Princess," Sukra nodded, "of course, at once."

Half an hour later, Lucy left the royal hospital with two large bags filled with medical supplies.

The next step was obvious. She divided the supplies into four compact bundles, put one of them in the basket of her bicycle, tossed in her translation of the *Barefoot Doctor*, and rode back out into the streets of Sindhala. She continued to have doubts about her own competence, but she tried not to let them overwhelm her. Her reading had reassured her that leprosy wasn't particularly contagious, and as for most other diseases, you didn't need four years of medical school to see what needed to be done. The people who lived in the filth around the market didn't need heart-monitoring machines or brain surgery: they needed paregoric and tetracycline to cure their diarrhea, clean water to drink, antibiotic ointment to rub into their eyes so they wouldn't go blind. They needed to have sores dressed and cleaned with disinfectant, the worms purged from their bodies with gentian violet, and the lice washed out of their hair with Kwell.

But it was easier to know this than to put it into action, and by the time she got to the outskirts of Kalpa Square, she was still having second thoughts. How did you approach people and tell them that they needed medical attention? Wasn't that a typically arrogant American, do-good sort of way to act? What kind of barefoot doctor was she in her forty-dollar hand-tooled sandals? Maybe she should have ordered Dr. Sukra to come along with her. She had gotten herself into such a state of apprehension by the time she reached the stalls of vegetables that she was on the verge of turning her bike around and going back to the palace. Instead, she forced herself to dismount. The crowd flowed around her, separating and then rejoining in an endless human stream. To the left was a small shrine, built on a low stone platform. Inside was the laughing figure of Ganesh, the elephant god. Ganesh's trunk had been smeared with red ointment, and there were pop bottles full of fresh flowers lined up in front of him along with minuscule bowls of rice.

The sight of the offerings in front of Ganesh lifted her spirits. People wanted help; they were praying for it. So what if they thought she was an eccentric hippie. At least there was almost no chance that anyone would recognize her dressed as she was dressed. If they rejected her attempts to do something, it was only her pride that was going to be hurt, and what did that matter? "Move over," she said to Ganesh. Climbing up onto the cement platform of the shrine, she untied her bundle of medicine and waited.

Her first patient was an old, toothless woman, bent nearly double under a basket of radishes. The woman limped along, moaning to herself, came to the edge of the shrine, sat down beside Lucy, pulled a bunch of radishes out of her basket, and started fanning herself with the leaves.

"Oh," she moaned, "ah, oh, ah. Poor me."

"What's wrong?" Lucy asked politely in her best Patanese.

The old woman gave her a startled look. Evidently she was not accustomed to hearing a blond woman in blue jeans speak her language.

"My stomach hurts," she moaned. "The demons from the Hell Realms have nested in it, and when I eat, the food turns to water in my bowels, but what does the pretty lady want to hear the cares of an old woman for."

"How long has this been going on?" Lucy asked.

"Forever," the old woman muttered.

Lucy consulted her translation of the *Barefoot Doctor* and found four pages on diarrhea and dysentery. Among the possible causes were amoebas, bacterial infection, and Bilharziasis, not to mention yellow fever and food poisoning. The old woman watched her curiously as she poured through the book.

"The lady is very educated."

Lucy refrained from disillusioning her. She reread her notes and decided that, from the woman's description of her symptoms, she most likely had either a bacterial infection or worms. If her dysentery had been caused by amoebas, it would have been more severe. "I think I can help you," she offered.

The woman stopped fanning herself and looked at Lucy with astonishment. "What does the lady mean?"

"I mean," Lucy said, picking up a bottle of paregoric and spilling a few tetracycline tablets into the palm of her hand, "that I can stop your pain at once and perhaps fix things so it won't come back again. That is, if you'd like me to."

The old woman shook her head. "I'm a poor woman. I can't pay you for a cure. Better to leave it to Ganesh."

"I don't want money; the medicine is free."

"Free, eh?" The old woman's face brightened.

"Free," Lucy assured her politely.

The old woman smiled a toothless smile. "Well then," she nodded, "I'll take it."

The paregoric, which was a solution of opium in alcohol, worked immediately as Lucy had known it would, and after the old woman was out of pain she gave her enough tetracycline to kill any bacteria lingering in her gut. In some ways it was a dubious cure. No doubt the drinking water was so polluted in Sindhala that she would be reinfected in no time, but it gave Lucy a great deal of personal satisfaction, and from that moment on she didn't lack for patients. Within minutes word had spread through the market that a lady was handing out free medicine, and from that moment on Lucy never had time to question whether or not what she was doing was appropriate.

For almost two hours, until she ran out of supplies, she swabbed and cleaned and doled out pills, until she was so exhausted that she could barely stand up. Often she had to stop to consult her notes, but none of her patients seemed surprised that their doctor was reading up on their disease in their presence. They waited patiently, many of them so ill that in the end she had to turn them away. She sent the most desperate cases to the hospital, giving them what money she could; others she treated cautiously, doing her best not to make any serious mistakes. She knew that it was only a drop in the bucket, but it was her drop. No bureaucracy came between her and the people she helped, and all in all it was one of the most satisfying afternoons she had had in years.

Unfortunately, it was not an afternoon that was to be repeated. The palace was like a small village, and nothing went unreported for long, especially when it involved the princess. By that evening the king had heard of her escapade from five different sources, and he was not pleased. Servants were summoned, orders issued, and by nine o'clock the next morning everyone from the lord chamberlain to the youngest scullery maid knew that the princess was about to be summoned into the royal presence for a stiff dressing down.

The only person who wasn't warned ahead of time was Lucy. She had used a side gate in the kitchen garden to leave the palace, and the next morning when she arrived to pick up her bicycle, she found it gone. In its place, standing under a lemon tree, was the lord chamberlain.

"Good morning, Gracious Princess," he said, praniyaming deeply.

"Good morning," Lucy said. She looked around for her bicycle, but the garden contained only the usual rows of vegetables and herbs. She knew instantly that it had been taken. Tucking her bundle of medicines firmly under her arm, she turned to the lord chamberlain, who was eyeing her uneasily. "Have you seen my bike, Lord Chamberlain?"

"No, Gracious Princess."

"Let me know if it rematerializes. Meanwhile, I'll be in Kalpa Square if you want me." She started for the gate.

"The king, the divine one," the lord chamberlain said as he moved around in front of her, panicked, "wants to see you in his study."

"How kind of him. Tell him that I'll come as soon as I get back from the market, say around three o'clock." She tried her best to sound polite; there was no use antagonizing Marpa unnecessarily.

"But he wants to see you at once."

"Well, please go back to him and say that I can't come right now. I have sick people waiting for me, and I can't disappoint them."

"You're refusing to obey the divine one's summons?" The lord chamberlain looked so startled and horrified that it was all that Lucy could do to keep from laughing.

"Yes," she said. "I'm afraid I am." She had no desire to make Marpa more angry than he already was, but she had promised herself when she began all this that the sick would come first. She planned to keep handing out medicines no matter how strongly the king objected. It was not only a matter of conscience, it was the only humane thing to do. Stepping around the lord chamberlain, she walked through the garden gate without a backward glance. When she got to the market, a crowd of sick people was already waiting for her at the Ganesh shrine, and for the next few hours she cleaned infected legs, fed crying babies Kaopectate, rubbed antibiotic ointment into swollen eyes, and passed out tetracycline tablets, working in the hot sun until her hair hung down in strings around her face and her body was covered with grime and sweat. She no longer minded the smells and dirt of the streets, and the suffering around her seemed less horrible now that she was doing something about it. As she consoled worried mothers and soothed frightened children, she thought uneasily of what was waiting for her back at the palace.

Shortly before noon, she ran out of medicine, which was just as well because she was exhausted. With regret, she turned away the rest of the crowd, promising to return tomorrow. Walking over to one of the tea shops, she ordered herself a bowl of hot noodles in chicken broth and sat eating it, looking out at the market. In three days it had become a familiar place. Already she was starting to recognize some of the vendors and most of the hippies who hung out by the central fountain. Ordering another pot of hot tea, she sipped it slowly and thought about what life would have been like if she hadn't married Mila but joined the Peace Corps instead. She might very well have been assigned to a country like Patan. Finishing her tea, Lucy dumped out the leaves on the table and sat for a moment, wishing she knew how to read them. What kind of future did she have in front of her? It was, she decided, an unanswerable question. Getting up, she threw a half-rupee tip down on the table, nodded to the waiter, and walked back to the palace, changed into a court sari, and went off to face the king.

Marpa was furious. He sat behind his desk as if it were a barricade, glaring at Lucy with unmitigated disapproval. He understood adolescent rebellion in men; he'd been something of a maverick himself in his youth. Young men needed to try their strength and defy authority, and he had given Mila a great deal of leeway based on this premise. But young women were a different matter. They should be soft-spoken and pliant and obedient. Even in England he had disliked the brash, masculine, hail-fellow-well-met air of so many of the females, and Americans were worse by far. They had a hard, unyielding edge, and they strode about as if they expected men to get out of their way. This one looked sweet enough, blond and angelic, but that was only an illusion. She was far too intelligent for a woman, which was no surprise since she had gone to Harvard, which should never, in Marpa's opinion, have admitted women in the first place. Give women a superior education, and they make their own lives and the lives of everyone else around them miserable.

"You didn't come when I summoned you this morning," he said. He kept his voice low and even because she was married to his son and was a royal princess, a position he still respected even if she didn't. "Why? Were you ill?"

"No, I wasn't." She looked at him uneasily, as well she should. "I was busy."

"Busy?"

"I was in the market, handing out medicines." Her eyes brightened and her face became flushed with enthusiasm. "You should have seen the people lining up for help; the response was amazing."

"I'm sure it was," Marpa said through tight lips. So she had gone out on her own, without his permission, in express defiance of his wishes, to make a public spectacle of herself, and now she had the gall to speak of her disobedience as if she had done something commendable. He was so enraged by her impertinence that it was several seconds before he trusted himself to speak. When he did resume the conversation, his voice had an icy, contemptuous edge to it that was not lost on Lucy. "If you were not my son's wife and princess of Patan we would not be having this conversation. You would be under house arrest."

"Why, Your Highness? What have I done wrong?" She knew full well what she had done, and she hadn't expected him to be happy about it, but she was shocked, nevertheless, by the word *arrest*. Arresting her was within his power, of course. Anything was. But she couldn't imagine him carrying out such a threat. She decided that he was bluffing. At least she hoped that was what he was doing. All sorts of angry replies rose to her lips, but she held them back and tried to look as nonbelligerent as possible. It would do no good to provoke him, and despite what Mila had said about his father's stubbornness, there was always a possibility that she might be able to bring him around to seeing things her way, not much of a possibility, perhaps, but she had to try.

"You have degraded the crown," Marpa informed her, "and exposed the royal family to public ridicule."

"I still don't understand. How does tending to the sick degrade the crown? I would have thought it would have just the opposite effect." Be patient, she commanded herself, but her patience was wasted.

Rising to his feet, Marpa exploded. "In this country, respectable married women don't go wandering through the streets unaccompanied! Only peasants and whores do such things. Don't you have any respect for anything?"

"Yes, I respect the truth." She forced herself to speak calmly. He had all the power and she had virtually none. She tried a softer approach. "I'm sorry if I seem to lack respect, Father." The word *father* stuck in her throat, but she said it anyway, hoping to soften him a little. He looked so fierce and offended, and his face was so red that she was afraid he might have a stroke. "I'm only trying to talk to you as if you were a normal person instead of a king. Perhaps that's not such a good idea, but I don't know how else to do it, and I have a lot to tell you. Do you realize that out there in the city there are babies needlessly dying at this very minute from simple diarrhea? Do you know that your people are going blind because they lack two cents' worth of antibiotic ointment? Are you aware that there are several hundred lepers in Sindhala alone?"

"I'm quite aware of the social problems of Patan. And I don't need *you* to lecture me on them."

"If you're aware of them, why don't you do something? Please. I beg you. You stall and you stall, and the people keep suffering and dying like flies, and when I go out to help them, you act as though I'm committing a crime. What sense does that make? This country is in terrible trouble. Reform has to start somewhere. Let it start with me. I'm hardly doing anything; let me go on doing that little bit. Your people need help and I need to help them. I can't sit by idly. I'm not that kind of person. What I really want, what I'm begging you to do, is to commit yourself to major social reforms, but if you won't do that, at least don't stop me from—"

"Sit down," Marpa yelled. Shocked, Lucy sat down. Marpa took a deep breath and looked at her, reminding himself that she was his son's wife and a foreigner. "Let us try to conduct this conversation in a more civilized manner. It's clear that you have no idea of the political implications of what you have been doing, so I'd like to tell you what they are. Putting aside the fact that I do indeed consider it degrading for the princess of Patan to mix with thieves and beggars and prostitutes, there is your safety to be considered. I don't wish to terrify you, but there are fanatics loose in the streets who would be delighted to assassinate you should they discover your identity." He sat down and let her take this in. "Perhaps you are unaware that Patan has been on the verge of a revolution since the Chinese communists took over Tibet in 1951, and that the Patanese Liberation Front has made two attempts to kill me in the past ten years. You could easily be their next target." She was a long time in answering. Good, Marpa thought. He'd succeeded in terrifying her. Now perhaps she'd act as a woman should.

But he was wrong. She wasn't terrified. Intimidated, yes, and even frightened, but not paralyzed with fear the way he had expected her to be. She was thinking that perhaps he was lying to her. "It's hard to believe that someone would want to kill me for helping sick people, but even if it is true, I can't see any alternative that I could live with. You can't imagine what it's like for me to sit in my apartment knowing what is going on out there in the streets. If you're so worried about me, why not assign me some bodyguards. I wouldn't want them to be obvious, because they would frighten people, but I'd be willing to have some in plain clothes. Maybe they could even help."

"Bodyguards," Marpa snorted contemptuously. "Do you think they could protect you for one minute in a crowd like that?" He was extremely annoyed. He had expected her to run back to her rooms and thank whatever god she worshiped that he was looking after her safety, and instead she was reacting like a man. "In any event there's no need for you to martyr yourself. If you will just be reasonable, this whole matter can be resolved. Do you insist on practicing medicine without a license? Very well, then I'll make arrangements for you to work two days a week in the royal hospital under the supervision of Dr. Sukra. Surely that should satisfy your need to imitate Florence Nightingale without exposing you to danger."

"No," Lucy shook her head, "I'm sorry, but that won't do. It's not the people in the hospital that I want to help; it's the people in the streets, the ones who are too poor to afford a visit to a doctor."

"You're impossibly stubborn!"

"I'm sorry you see it that way."

"You give me no choice but to forbid you to go out of the palace."

Lucy stood up. "I've been very patient," she said. "I've tried to explain what I was doing and why I was doing it, and all you've done is yell at me. So I guess you give me no choice but to tell you that I'll continue to conduct my clinic. There are a lot of sick people who are depending on me to show up tomorrow morning."

"One last time: You're in Asia, not the United States. As princess of Patan you have a duty to the state."

"To you, you mean."

"Yes, to me. To your king."

Lucy finally lost her temper. It was not a wise or a diplomatic thing to do, but he had insulted her and condescended to her, and now he was demanding she obey him like a slave, and she was too American, too full of phrases like "freedom of speech" and "created equal" to hold her tongue. "You're not my king. I don't have a king." Leaning forward, she confronted the old man. He was as full of power and pride as a puffed-up frog, and she felt a twinge of contempt for him, sitting there giving orders, and expecting the world to kowtow. "You may have a degree from Oxford, but you're acting like a petty tyrant. Your idea of westernization is laughable: banks, private schools, modern operating rooms. What about basic health care? What about the hungry? If you ignore your own people for much longer they *are* going to rise up and overthrow you. Read some history. Every country that's ever had a revolution has had a king like you. From what I've heard the Patanese Liberation Front is about as bloody and violent a group of fanatics as you could ask for, and you're handing this country over to them."

"Be silent! You're talking treason!"

"No, I won't be silent. The first time you yelled at me, I was frightened, but I'm getting accustomed to your attempts to intimidate me. Frankly you're starting to remind me of a psychology professor I had at Harvard who got his kicks yelling down anyone who disagreed with him. So go ahead and yell." She shook her head. "It won't make any difference. Tomorrow morning I'll be back in Kalpa Square handing out tetracycline tablets."

"Marpa is a pompous, blind fool," she told Cassie when she called on Monday, "and Patan is so backward you wouldn't believe it. Sometimes when I walk down the streets, I feel like I'm back in the Middle Ages. It's not 1967 here; it's 1348."

"Should you be saying all this on the onephay?"

"Probably not, but I'm reaching some kind of breaking point. Forget what I said; it just slipped out. Patan is Paradise; Sindhala is Eden. The king is as wise as Solomon."

"And you're going to stay in the palace like a good girl?"

"Right, of course." Lucy poured herself another glass of Coke and tossed the bottle in the wastebasket. Her rooms were finally starting to look lived in: a skirt on the back of a chair, a pair of shoes sitting next to the door. She'd ordered her maids not to clean the apartment. She didn't want to be spied on any more than necessary.

Cassie chuckled. "You sound like you're in fine form."

"The best," Lucy assured her.

They talked for only another ten minutes, because Cassie had to get back to the lab to check on an experiment she was running. "Suppose I call you again on Wednesday," Lucy suggested as they were saying good-bye.

"Great," Cassie agreed, "Wednesday it is. Good luck and keep me posted."

A half hour later Marpa was reading a transcript of this conversation, and by noon General Arjuna had received his copy. The king was outraged that she had described him as "a pompous, blind fool," but Arjuna was pleased. The princess was doing exactly what he'd expected her to do. Locking the transcript in his safe, the general went to his private gymnasium and did one hundred and fifty sit-ups, lifted weights, and took a long, hot shower. Soon he would summon his bodyguard and give him the appropriate orders, but there was no hurry.

On Tuesday morning Lucy arrived at the kitchen gate to find it padlocked. Annoyed, she went to the front entrance. When the soldiers in the guard box saw her, they snapped to attention. They were all strangers: young Patanese boys, none over eighteen, fresh from the country by the look of them. The older guards, whom she knew by name, had evidently been dismissed, and as soon as she saw this new group, standing stiffly in their freshly starched uniforms, she knew there was going to be trouble.

"Good morning," she said. "Please open the gate."

One of the soldiers detached himself from the rest and threw himself at her feet in a full praniyam. "Gracious Princess," he said, "wife of the son of the son of God, it is my unpleasant duty to tell you that the gate cannot be opened for you."

"By whose orders?"

"By the order of the divine one, king of heaven."

"Wonderful, just what I needed to hear. I'm a prisoner." She looked at the wrought-iron gate, embossed with double crowns, tigers, and lightning bolts. It was about thirteen feet tall and had nasty ornamental spikes all along the top, rather like the spikes that topped the fence that enclosed Dunster House only sharper. Twice in the heyday of her affair with David she had been forced to climb the fence to get out of Dunster without being caught and put on academic probation, a fairly easy feat because she was agile and the House security guard was old, feeble, and so nearsighted that Harvard students had been known to smuggle their dates past him by dressing them in men's clothing. This gate, however, was a different matter. Climbing it was obviously out of the question. Not only was it twice as high, it was guarded by six fanatically loyal teenagers armed with submachine guns. She looked down at the guard who remained at her feet, his head bowed respectfully. "What would happen if I waited until you opened the gate for someone else and then made a run for it?" she asked. "Would you shoot me?"

"Oh, no, Gracious Princess." He seemed sincerely horrified at the thought. "But please, Gracious Princess, do not, I beg you."

"Why not? What's to stop me?"

"If Her Serene Highness were to leave the palace, we would be held responsible." There was a stirring among the other guards. Their faces had paled, and they looked terrified.

"What would happen to you?" Lucy persisted. "Would you be court-martialed?"

"No, Gracious Princess," the soldier pounded his forehead in the dust three more times, "we would be shot."

Storming back into the palace, Lucy tried to place a call to Cassie.

"I'm sorry, Your Highness," the Patanese operator said, "but that call can't go through."

"Then give me Doctor Henry Constable in Palo Alto, California," Lucy ordered, "and ring until his secretary picks up the phone."

"I'm sorry, Your Highness," the operator said, "but that call can't go through either."

"Am I to understand that I can no longer make long distance calls?"
"Yes, Your Highness."
"I don't believe this!" Lucy yelled into the receiver. "There's got to be a mistake! Put me through to Palo Alto at once!"
"I'm terribly sorry, Gracious Princess," the operator said in a quavering voice, "but the divine one has ordered that—"
Lucy didn't wait to hear what the "divine one" had ordered. Slamming down the phone, she headed for Marpa's study to tell him what she thought of his plan to cut her off from the world.

• 5 •

Ordinarily the lord chamberlain would have intercepted her, but one look at Lucy's face and he let her pass without a word. The door to Marpa's study was closed, and she paused for a moment, debating whether or not to go in unannounced. According to court etiquette, only Mila was permitted to walk in on his father without first securing an appointment, but if she made such a request there was a good chance Marpa might put her off or even refuse to see her. Then she would have to disobey him openly, and that, she decided, would be much worse than simply paying him an unscheduled visit. Taking a deep breath, she opened the door.

At the sound of her entrance, Marpa looked up. He was holding a small pair of scissors in one hand and a bunch of leaves in the other, pruning his bonsai trees, forcing them to grow the way he wanted, just as he forced people to bend to his will. Beside him, dressed in a military uniform, was General Arjuna. She had seen Arjuna on numerous occasions but never really had a conversation with him, and he had always struck her as a sinister sort of person. He was thin with a scrawny turkeylike neck, and he often wore the kind of high black boots that she associated with Nazi commandants. This morning, in addition to the boots, Arjuna was decked out in a half dozen heavy gold chains and a pair of mirrored sunglasses that hid most of his face. When he saw

Lucy, he did a sort of abbreviated praniyam, bowing his head and pressing the palms of his hands together.

Lucy acknowledged the praniyam with a nod of her head, and turned to Marpa. "I want to know what's going on," she began. She did her best to sound reasonable, even though he had pushed her beyond all reasonable limits. "Why have you ordered the guards not to let me out of the palace? Why are you blocking my private phone calls? Why—"

"Sit down," Marpa ordered. He didn't yell at her this time, but he might as well have. His voice had a sharp edge to it; it was the voice of power and unlimited authority, the voice of an irritable old man who had decided that he had no more time to coddle foolish young women.

"I'm sorry, but I cannot sit down or do anything else until you tell me why you are holding me prisoner in the palace against my will."

"Suit yourself." Marpa put down his scissors. Cupping the leaves in his hand, he deposited them neatly in the silver wastebasket beside his desk. He looked at Arjuna and lifted his eyebrows. The general shook his head slightly as if to say, *What can you expect?*

Lucy took a deep breath again and did her very best not to lose her temper. "I told you I was going back out on the streets to dispense medicines," she said, "but I hardly expected you to call up an armed guard to stop me." She paused and tried to see what effect her words were having, but Marpa was looking at his bonsai trees as if deciding whether or not to prune off more leaves. She felt insulted that he was ignoring her; obviously that was the way he meant her to feel. "Surely you can see that you've overreacted. Do you honestly think you need six soldiers to stop a one-hundred-and-five-pound woman from passing out tetracycline? You're acting as if I'm a dangerous criminal."

Marpa placed the scissors in a small gray calfskin folder and put them in his desk. Sitting down, he folded his hands and looked at her coldly. His huge ruby ring caught the light; the stone was square-cut and sharp and brutal. "Are you quite finished?" he asked.

"No, I'm not." Lucy pressed her lips together and folded her arms across her chest, holding in her anger. "I think it's unfair of you to confine me like this while Mila is away. What's he going to say when he comes home? How is he going to react to the fact that his father has imprisoned his wife?"

"The royal palace is hardly a prison."

"As far as I'm concerned, any place I can't walk out of whenever I wish is a prison."

Marpa shook his head and looked at her wearily. "You cause an inordinate amount of trouble," he said, "but I suppose that's the way of Western women. Did it ever occur to you that I might have made this decision for your own good? I love my son, and for that reason, although I disapprove of your conduct in every possible way, I would not have interfered in your ill-advised missionary work except under the most extreme provocation."

"I don't understand how what I've been doing can be called a provocation. I ride my bicycle into the market—at least I used to ride it before you had it confiscated; I tend to several dozen of your sickest subjects, and then I come back to the palace in time to help Sala's ayah give her her bath and put her to bed. I'm not—"

Marpa held up his hand. "Enough. This is getting tiresome." He turned to Arjuna. "I think it's time you explained the princess's position to her, General."

Arjuna bowed a formal, Prussian sort of bow and clicked the heels of his boots together. "Yes, Your Majesty." His voice didn't match his body; it was low and precise and emotionless without the slightest trace of animation, as if he'd learned his English from a machine. He smiled at Lucy, but the smile didn't go beyond his lips. He stood on the balls of his feet with his knees slightly bent, like a Doberman about to spring.

"As you know," Marpa said, "General Arjuna is the head of the Patanese Secret Service, and he has received some very disturbing information about you."

Lucy was taken completely by surprise. What information was he talking about? She stared at Arjuna, but all she could see was her own face reflected in the lenses of his sunglasses.

The general bowed and clicked his heels for a second time and then, just for good measure, pressed his palms together. "It is an exceptional honor to see you again, Princess. We have never had the pleasure of a real conversation, but I believe that you once had a long and charming discussion with my mother." He took off his sunglasses, folded them, and put them in his shirt pocket.

Lucy looked at the rings of white skin around his eyes, the small blue veins that crisscrossed his lids. "Yes," she said, "I remember her well." The conversation with his mother could have hardly been called "charming," but she had no desire to discuss it with Arjuna. His eyes were tight and cruel, and there was something about the appraising way he was looking at her that made her feel as if he were fitting her into some invisible system of his own contriving.

The general sighed and caressed his gold chains. His hands were small and delicate, the nails neatly manicured. On his fingers were several large diamonds and a signet ring embossed with a dragon. "I am afraid that perhaps the conversation was not enjoyable after all. Let me apologize. I fear my mother can be rather difficult on occasion."

"Tell her what happened to your mother," Marpa ordered. "Let her see what she might be risking."

Arjuna bowed to Lucy again and smiled, most inappropriately considering what he said next. "My mother has had another nervous breakdown, and I've had to send her to India to recover. She is, as you no doubt noticed, very eccentric. She insisted on living in a tenement just off Kalpa Square in a terrible neighborhood infested with the dregs of society. Last week she was attacked—I think you Americans say 'mugged'—by two men who tried to rob her of the pittance she kept in her purse. One of the men struck her, and although she suffered little physical damage, the consequences for her mental health have been—how shall I put it?—most unfortunate."

Lucy was horrified. For the first time she felt sympathy for Arjuna. She thought of his mother beaten, knocked down in the street; she was an old woman, physically fragile. What an ugly story. "That's awful!" she exclaimed.

"Yes, it is," Marpa snapped, "but when a woman wanders around Sindhala unaccompanied, it is to be expected." He waved his hand in the direction of the window. "I do not count the Western hippie women, of course. They move about as they wish since everyone is aware that they have no money and are whores as well, but when a respectable woman ventures out alone . . ." He paused and let the threat hang in the air. "Now do you see why I have been trying to prevent you from going out on the streets?"

Lucy said nothing. She was upset by his dismissal of the hippie women as whores. It was clear from Marpa's tone of voice that he wanted to frighten her. She began to wonder if he was telling her the truth.

Marpa turned to Arjuna. "Tell her the rest," he ordered.

The general cleared his throat. "It is also possible that my mother was not attacked by thieves but by members of the Patanese Liberation Front posing as thieves." He cleared his throat again and again caressed his gold chains. He glanced at Lucy as if waiting for her to react, and when she did, a subtle expression of satisfaction passed over his face. "Several things point to this," he continued, "including the fact that everyone knew she kept almost no money in her purse. She was involved with various charitable projects, and the PLF doesn't like it when the ruling class starts showing a social conscience. They say it saps the so-called revolutionary fervor of the people." He sighed. "So even if she hadn't fallen apart afterward, I would have had to send her to India for her own safety."

Lucy knew he was lying, but she didn't know why. His words were clearly enunciated and precise as if he were filling in a police report, and although his face was properly somber, she had the distinct impression that he was not all that upset by his mother's breakdown. *Life in this palace is a fantastically complicated net of plots and intrigues*, Mila had warned her. She wondered if Arjuna was weaving some kind of plot. Had he made all this up, including the attack on his mother?

"It's shocking to hear that Mrs. Arjuna was attacked by anyone under any circumstances," she said cautiously. She felt cornered. Marpa was nodding, satisfied with what she was saying, and there was a look of triumph on Arjuna's face that he was trying his best to conceal. "It's completely shocking. I had no idea Sindhala was so dangerous. It seems like such a calm city." How convenient for Arjuna this nasty story was. It had allowed him to commit his mother to a mental hospital, no questions asked.

The general bowed and clicked his heels. "Thank you for your expression of sympathy, Princess."

She turned to Marpa. "I see now why you've been so concerned about me riding into town." She tried to keep the suspicion out of her voice. Am I being completely paranoid? she wondered. She felt cold and strange, and she wanted to walk out of the room, away from all this deception, only what if it wasn't deception after all?

"Well," Marpa exclaimed, "at last you're demonstrating some sense!"

"On the other hand," Lucy swallowed her fear and decided to take the risk, "while I appreciate your concern for my safety, I don't intend to let what happened to Mrs. Arjuna prevent me from going out in public." There, she'd said it. She could see the shock and disappointment in both their faces because they thought they had won, and she'd pulled their victory back from them at the last minute. "We have plenty of violence in the United States. If I'd let every story of a woman being attacked make me afraid, I'd have spent my whole life hiding in my room, but I've always preferred to take my chances. I used to walk back to the dorms from Radcliffe library alone at eleven o'clock at night. So if it's all the same to both of you, I'll decide what risks I want to take."

Marpa stood up. For a moment they were balanced on opposite sides of his desk like two boxers looking for an opening. "Your problem," Marpa said, "is that you think you've married into the British royal family or you're that Swedish princess—what was her name? the one that went to your beloved Radcliffe?"

"Princess Christina," Lucy supplied. "She waited tables and sat at the bell desk like a perfectly normal person, and she went wherever she wanted."

"Princess Christina lived in the West," Marpa scowled. "And you live in the East, in Asia to be specific. There are times when I feel you should be presented with a large map of the world with Patan circled in red ink." He turned back to Arjuna. "Tell her the rest, General."

Arjuna bowed. "Gracious Princess, I regret to inform you that the Patanese Secret Service has determined that you may be the target of a similar PLF plot." He picked up an expensive black leather briefcase, opened it, took out a black file folder stamped Top Secret, and offered it to Lucy. "You'll find the details set forth here, but in brief, we recently arrested two known PLF cadre. One was a thirty-three-year-old woman from the Sindhala valley named Sakti Gunas; the other a blacksmith named Manu Buchari, age twenty-five. Buchari, by the way, is suspected of being one of the leaders of the local executive committee of the communist party. Both of them confessed during interrogation that you are targeted for death."

For the first time, Lucy was really afraid. She had never heard of either of these people, and the idea that total strangers would plot to kill her was chilling. Perhaps Arjuna had been telling the truth all along. How was she ever going to be able to tell which dangers were real and which were being fabricated? She looked at the mirror hanging on the wall behind Arjuna, gold-framed and massive, positioned so it reflected another smaller mirror on the other side of the room. In the large mirror Arjuna's image appeared over and over again in infinite regression, as if he were offering her an infinite number of different realities.

"Tell her how she is supposed to die," Marpa ordered.

General Arjuna shrugged. "I'm afraid that, as usual, your death would be very brutal. Ever since we prevented the assassination of His Majesty ten years ago, the PLF has gone to extreme lengths to ensure success. You are to be followed and your habits determined. Then you are to be blown to bits with several pounds of dynamite. It is a crude but effective technique. I regret to say that five years ago when the minister of agriculture was assassinated, six innocent bystanders were also killed, and we could not recover enough of the individual bodies for a decent burial."

"So," Marpa said, "now do you finally understand why I have confined you to the palace?"

Lucy imagined the shock of the explosion carrying her up and up in the air into one of the infinite realities of the world of mirrors. She looked at Arjuna and again saw satisfaction on his face. She could feel him offering fear to her as if it were a box of poisoned candy. If she accepted his version of reality, she would have to stay in the palace. The thought of being confined made her feel as if she were suffocating. I won't buy this, she thought. The price is too high. She spread her hands, as if to push out the walls that were closing in on her. I won't imprison myself voluntarily, whatever the danger. I couldn't stand it. I'd go crazy. "I understand," she said.

"Good," Marpa said, misinterpreting her reply.

"But I'm afraid that I still have no intention of obeying your orders." Her mouth was dry, and she felt her hands trembling. Illusion versus reality, the old theme of a hundred Harvard essay questions: discuss the themes of illusion and reality in *Oedipus Rex*, in *Great Expectations*, in . . . in the life of Lucy Constable, who needs to tell them apart for her own survival. Dynamite and her body flung through the air: illusion or reality? Suppose reality? Even so, how could she waste the rest of her life gossiping with her ladies and cutting ribbons at school sites? Even with Sala to take care of, there wasn't enough to do inside the palace to keep her sane. She needed fresh air and open horizons, and the sick of Sindhala needed her attention. In Kalpa Square she had a use; inside the palace she was useless. And suppose that all this talk of assassination *was* a lie. Wasn't that equally as likely, perhaps even more likely when you looked at Arjuna's face and saw the shadows and the cunning in it? She swallowed and stood up straighter, frightened and defiant, feeling trapped in a situation where there were no reasonable solutions because reason had been thrown out the window. "I'll disguise myself," she told Marpa, "if that will make you feel any better." She turned to Arjuna. "Why hasn't my husband been told all this? If I'm in such serious danger, if my life is at stake, why didn't you inform him immediately?"

"Gracious Princess," Arjuna's voice was smooth, but he touched his gold chains again the way someone else might have bit his nails or gone for a cigarette, "we only recently received this intelligence and . . ." He began to explain why Mila couldn't have possibly been told, but Marpa didn't let him finish.

"Disguise yourself!" Marpa interrupted, scowling at Lucy as if she were a mad woman. "You fool! With that blond hair of yours and those foreign blue eyes, you might as well wear a target on your chest." He leaned forward, his eyes yellow and cold. "This foolish idea of disguise is like your equally foolish idea to go out in the streets with bodyguards. It's a child's fantasy." He blinked and his pupils contracted so that they looked like tiny, hard stones. "I see that you will never listen to reason, so I am going to stop reasoning with you and tell you what I expect of you from this day forward. You are the princess of Patan and I expect you to act like a princess and not like a spoiled American engaged in adolescent rebellion. If Mila cannot govern you—and it is obvious that he cannot—then I will. The Western world may be going mad with its 'counter culture' and its 'generation gap,' but here we will have peace and order and dignity. From this moment on you will live like a traditional Patanese woman: in the palace where you belong."

"And I tell you," she said through gritted teeth, "that I won't." There was nothing more she could say after that. Turning her back on the king, she walked out of his study. Out in the throne room, she stopped and put her forehead against the wall, feeling the coldness of the marble. What have you gotten yourself into, Constable? she thought. Defying Mila's father; deciding that the general is lying to you? Where's the accommodating little 'Cliffie who used to believe everyone meant well? She told herself that she'd done the right thing, that Marpa had given her no choice, that Mila would have approved. But what was she going to do now? Obviously Marpa had the power to keep her in the palace. Who could she turn to for help?

Fifteen minutes later, still shaken, she was back at her apartment and on the phone to the American ambassador, relieved to discover that they were still letting her make local calls. Mila would return in four days. Meanwhile, she would ask the ambassador for help. She had always liked Willis Elderby, a bald, jolly man who seemed to like his patriotism mixed with liberal amounts of rich food and good whiskey, and she expected him to sympathize with her predicament. Perhaps he could help her separate illusion from reality, or at the very least perhaps he could offer her a version of reality she could live with.

But to her dismay he did no such thing. Arriving at ten o'clock the next morning, Elderby listened respectfully to her complaints and then shook his head. "I'm sorry," he said, "but I don't think we can do much for you. As you know, when you married the prince you gave up your United States citizenship, so as far as the U.S. government is concerned you're a foreign national and as such you're subject to the laws of Patan."

Lucy was shocked. "But surely the United States has an ongoing interest in my welfare." She'd expected the ambassador to fly to her aid; after all, wasn't that what ambassadors were for? "Can't you at least lodge a protest of some sort?" she pleaded. "I'm not even being allowed to call my aunt and uncle."

Elderby shook his head. "That's just not possible at present, I'm afraid. This problem you are having with your father-in-law has come at a particularly bad time. Our relationship with the royal family is rather delicate as it is." He paused and cleared his throat. "You may remember that incident with the girl from Pennsylvania, the senator's daughter who was sentenced to twenty years in prison for hashish trafficking? It seems that her partner in crime was one of the king's cousins, nephews, or something of the sort—I never can keep the Patanese genealogy straight. In any event, it took all the resources of the embassy to get her extradited to the States, and I hardly think we're in a position to try to pull strings again so soon after that. Then too, there's always the risk that we could have a Vietnam-type situation on our hands here if the PLF ever got a real foothold. King Marpa is one of our strongest allies in this region of the world. He stands between Chinese communism on one hand and Indian supernationalism on the other, and we can't afford to offend him in any way."

"In other words I'm expendable?" Lucy looked at Elderby sitting so calmly across from her, at the white linen of his shirt, and the fashionable cut of his suit, and she thought of the marines who protected him, and the layers of diplomatic immunity that separated him from Marpa. She felt angry that he was being so unsympathetic.

"I'd try not to look at it that way if I were you." Elderby cleared his throat again and leaned forward. "The truth is you've made your bed, and you're going to have to lie in it. I know that must be hard for you to hear and I don't particularly enjoy saying it to you, but we must face facts in these situations. All in all, I'd say you should consider yourself pretty lucky that things are no worse. My last posting was in the sultanate of Al Akla on the Persian Gulf and the problems American women had there were a nightmare compared to this. Those who had married Arabs often found themselves literally shut up in harems, and when they tried to leave they were beaten and their children were taken from them. One was very nearly stoned to death for adultery before the embassy could intervene, another underwent some barbaric version of female circumcision. The horrors were endless. If I were you, I'd count myself fortunate to be in Patan."

Lucy shuddered at the thought that there were American women worse off than she was. "Is that the best advice you can offer me, Mr. Elderby: that I should count myself fortunate not to have been stoned to death?"

Elderby sighed and spread his hands as if letting go of all responsibility for her. "I wish I could be more helpful, Princess. I think I can speak for the entire embassy staff when I say we would like your life here to be as happy as possible, but you must understand that our hands are tied. The political implications of your situation are enormous. When it comes to the internal relations of the royal family, our policy has always been strict noninterference."

"Mr. Elderby," she begged, "I realize that my personal problems don't warrant changing United States foreign policy, but surely there's *something* you could do to help me get word out that I'm being held here against my will. Perhaps you could let me send a letter to my uncle in the diplomatic pouch."

Elderby pursed his lips and frowned as if thinking this over. "Well, yes," he said, "that might be possible."

She was elated. "Thank you. I'm so grateful that—"

"But not at present," he continued. "Some time in the future, yes. If things calm down and the political situation changes, I'd say a message via diplomatic pouch might be just the thing, but at present," he shook his head, "it's just not feasible."

She was bitterly disappointed. Elderby went on explaining his position, and with each word the possibility of getting a message out of Patan seemed more remote: "If the press had the slightest hint that you were being confined in the palace against your will," he concluded, "it would cause an immense scandal, and I don't think the king would look favorably on the United States government's role in such an exposé." He got to his feet and stood for a moment looking at Lucy as if trying to figure out how best to placate her. She could see him thinking that although she might be in trouble at the moment, some day she was going to be queen of Patan. "If I were you, I'd try to relax and ride this out. The king can't keep you isolated from the world. Sooner or later he's bound to give you more freedom, and then if you want to call your uncle you'll only have to pick up the phone. And if you decide that you want to leave Patan—a course of action I'm by no means suggesting, mind you—then we can process your application for American citizenship. You're a rather romantic figure back home, you know, 'Princess of Paradise' and all that, and I'm sure there would be several cosmetic firms who would fight to sponsor you if you'd agree to hawk their wares. In any event, I can almost promise you that you wouldn't have to come in under the ordinary rules for Asian immigrants, which is a good thing because the waiting list stretches from here to Jakarta." He extended his hand, and Lucy, defeated, shook it. "I'm afraid," he said, "that for the moment you're just going to have to make the best of things. A palace isn't such a bad place to be confined." He paused. "Officially, you know, you're on a religious retreat." He must have seen the surprise in her face, but he went on smoothly, as if telling her something she already knew. "I'm sure you're aware that the palace released a statement this morning saying that you were about to leave for the Nokalu monastery to undergo a six-month course of instruction in the advanced practices of Tantric Buddhism. So your relatives won't be worrying about you for quite a while."

Dropping her hand, he gave her a polite nod that was not quite a bow. The nod said that, although he sympathized with her plight, this piece of news was all she was going to get from him.

For the next three days she barely ate or slept. Closeting herself in her apartment, she paced back and forth waiting for Mila. The lord chamberlain sent word that the formal evening dinners with the king were being resumed, but she refused to attend. It was too humiliating to sit at the table and see the knowledge of her confinement written on every face. The luxury of her rooms oppressed her, and she began to hate the Chinese screens and silk sheets and brocaded furniture. In her worst moods, she imagined the whole palace burning. She would pick up Sala and carry her out the gate and find Mila, and the three of them would leave Patan forever. They'd go back to the United States and do something useful with their lives; perhaps she'd go to graduate school. They'd live in married students housing the way Cassie and Andy did, and Patan would become a dim memory. Consoled by this fantasy, she went out on the morning of the second day to walk in the gardens, but everywhere she went, sooner or later, she came to the wall that ran around the palace. That night she dreamed she was trapped in a tight, windowless box, so small that she couldn't sit up or lie down. She woke up covered with sweat and gasping for breath. Hurrying out into the garden, she stood in her night robe under the open sky gulping in fresh air, but even the sky seemed tight and low.

On the morning of the third day, Mila returned among much pomp and chanting. Sending word that she was ill, Lucy refused to attend the welcoming ceremony. Not only would she have to suffer two hours of being with Mila without being able to say a word to him, she would also have to face Marpa again, and she wasn't sure she could trust herself not to do something outrageous and shocking that would make the present situation even worse. What would happen to her if she stood up in the middle of the ceremony and delivered a speech on the rights of women? It was a tempting thought, but her common sense told her that it was better not to find out.

Sending away her ladies, she sat in the living room waiting. She could hear the noise of horns being blown and fireworks exploding. The throne room would be full of monks in saffron-colored robes, and Marpa would no doubt have on his god-hat—the twenty-pound triple crown that he always wore on state occasions. The crown had a diamond in it the size of a golf ball. She hoped it gave him a headache.

Some time around noon there was a twenty-one-gun salute that shook the palace. Then the chanting stopped, and she could hear the noise of people returning from the ceremony. Her nerves stretched to the breaking point. She sat looking at her watch, counting the minutes until Mila arrived. She grew a little light-headed thinking about how he was going to help her out of this mess. He'd be outraged when he heard how his father had been treating her. After Mila was done with Marpa, Marpa would never dare to confine her in any way. She'd be free to come and go as she pleased.

At twelve-thirty Mila walked through the door, still wearing his ceremonial robes. He looked competent and strong; elated, she ran across the room and threw herself into his arms. "Thank God you're back!" she cried. They kissed, and she knew that things would soon be set right again. "Have you heard?" she asked. "While you were at the monastery, your father and I collided, we blew each other apart; it's a disaster, a battlefield. I can't go out of the palace. It would be funny if it weren't so insulting and serious and crazy and—" To her surprise she began to cry. She felt so relieved to see him and at last have someone she could talk to. She buried her head in his shoulder and sobbed, and Mila held her, stroking her hair.

"My poor darling," he whispered. "There, there. Calm down. It's going to be all right. I heard the whole story." He hugged her tightly. "I heard about the shrine of Ganesh, the medicines you were giving out. No one has been talking about anything else since I stepped through the front gate. I'm sorry. I never should have left you alone. You were brave and compassionate and the work you did was pure charity. I'm proud of you and ashamed of my father. Marpa is a . . . ," and then he said something harsh in Patanese. It wasn't a word Lucy had ever heard before, but she had no doubt what it meant.

She felt the warmth of his body, the power in his arms. No one can come between us, she thought fiercely, not even Marpa. She was so relieved by Mila's reaction that she felt shaken and light as if a half ton of rock had been lifted off her chest. They stood for a long time, holding each other, and gradually she stopped crying. Her hands trembled and her mind buzzed with quick, irrational thoughts that came like telegraph messages, too quick to catch. Beauty and the Beast, the Princess in the Tower, the myths of female confinement that were not myths to her anymore. "I feel like Sleeping Beauty trapped in the Castle of Briars," she said. She tried to laugh at the comparison, but she started coughing instead. "I need my prince to rescue me." She stopped, too overcome to go on. Sitting down on the couch, she swallowed the last of her tears. Only then could she speak like a rational woman. "I can't live like this." She folded her hands in her lap and twisted her wedding ring, which was gold and simple the way she had wanted her life with Mila to be. "I've started snapping at Sala and making Radha, Kala, and Asana's lives hell. I'm getting claustrophobia." She described her dream to him, the tight windowless box. "Your father doesn't know what a monster he's creating by shutting me up."

"We'll go see him right now," Mila said, "and get this straightened out." His lips were white with anger, an anger that matched her own, the anger of an ally. "As soon as I can get out of this ridiculous ceremonial robe, we'll go straight to his study." He unsnapped his heavy gold collar and threw it on the couch. He dropped his ruby rings into a glass bowl as if they were nuts, and kicked off his shoes. The shoes had curled toes like the ones in the *Arabian Nights*. He stood before her, barefoot and glowering, and his anger was electric.

He's completely on my side, Lucy thought, and she felt her world expanding and the walls moving out again. She kicked off her own shoes, tucked her bare legs under her, and watched him undress. Unbuttoning his diamond-studded coat, he tossed it aside. His movements were all hard and quick, and she could feel his impatience. He actually wanted to take Marpa on. He wasn't the least bit ambivalent or afraid. I admire this man, she thought. He has courage. "You know what I miss the most?" she said.

"Tell me and I'll see that you get it."

"Cassie's phone calls. I thought I'd miss helping people, and I do, but I must not be as much of a saint as I thought, because it's Cassie's voice that I long to hear. She's all that I have left of home, and I didn't realize how much I'd come to depend on her."

"An hour from now," he promised, "you'll be talking to Cassie." He unbuttoned his ceremonial robe, wadded it into a ball, and shot it neatly toward the bedroom. The robe fell into a heap like an old dead cat, stiff with rigor mortis, glittering with pillage. "Help me find something else to wear. I don't want to go to him dressed like a Hindu idol."

Marpa was sitting at his desk eating a peach when they burst in on him. He had a linen napkin spread out in front of him and a small silver knife in his hand, and the peach was already neatly sectioned. Lucy hadn't known what to expect. She had imagined that the king might leap to his feet and order them to get out as soon as he caught sight of them, but he did no such thing. Instead, Marpa looked at them with old, cynical eyes that seemed half dead and full of cunning.

"Good afternoon, Son," he said to Mila. He nodded at Lucy. "Good afternoon, Daughter-in-Law. I see you have recovered from your illness." He picked up a section of the peach, dark yellow and glistening with sweetness, and ate it slowly, bite by bite, never taking his eyes off them. "What brings you here?"

Mila lowered his head stubbornly and put his arm around Lucy's shoulder. "Father," he said, "it seems that while I was away, you decided to mistreat my wife."

Marpa raised his eyebrows and picked up another slice of peach. "Ah yes," he said, "your wife." He looked at Lucy coldly. "Well, my advice to you, Son, is to take another wife. This one," he pointed the tip of his knife at Lucy, "is entirely too much trouble."

"What did you just say!" Lucy exclaimed.

Mila had gone absolutely white. He pulled Lucy closer. "Father," he said in a low, furious voice, "this woman is part of me, body and soul, and I would rather spend my next twenty reincarnations in the Hell Realms as a Hungry Ghost than part from her."

"Then die and be damned," Marpa said.

At that point the two of them broke into a violent argument in Patanese. Lucy tried to follow what they were saying, but she could only catch random words. It was frightening to hear them yelling at each other. Mila pounded his fists on the desk, and Marpa waved his knife, and it looked as if they were going to come to blows. The yelling went on for a long time, and then suddenly, Marpa reached into his desk, pulled out a black folder, and slapped it down in front of Mila. Mila grabbed it, opened it, read something, and his face went from white to red. There was another heated exchange between him and his father. Throwing the folder back down on Marpa's desk, he seized Lucy by the wrist and dragged her out of the study.

Trembling with anger, he guided her through the throne room, muttering to himself in Patanese. She half expected Marpa to send his guards after them, but the door to his study remained closed.

"What happened?" she asked, pulling Mila to a stop. "What was he saying to you?"

Mila turned and took her in his arms and hugged her. "Damn him. Stupid old man. Brain eaten by demons. He was saying you were a spy." He added something incomprehensible in Patanese.

"Speak English, please," she begged. "What's this about me being a spy?" She was totally confused.

"That folder, the one he threw at me, was a report from that son of a dog Arjuna. It seems his secret service not only suspects you of being the target of a PLF assassination attempt, they also suspect you of being a PLF agent."

"Me? A PLF agent?" She felt logic slipping again, felt the infinite mirrors of Arjuna's reality sliding out in a long line in front of her like a snake. It was a sickening sensation, like trying to stand up on a roller coaster. "That's crazy."

"Of course it is. I defended your integrity. I told him he was *insane* to make such an accusation. And I told him a few other things that maybe I shouldn't have, only, *gods!* how the man provoked me. He was deaf and stubborn and proud and abusive. He kept yelling that Arjuna—curse his name—had signed confessions from two PLF cadres who were arrested last May. They claim you had been supplying the Communist Party with inside information on the king's movements. As if that were not insane enough, the general has set forth the ludicrous theory that your social work was only a cover for your Marxist sympathies. It seems someone has discovered that you once belonged to some peace group at Harvard called Tocsin. That, combined with the confessions, has convinced my father that you are not to be trusted outside the palace or anywhere else for that matter, at least not until all this can be cleared up."

Lucy was stunned. "My God, this is the most paranoid fantasy anyone has ever thought up." She looked into the dark shadows of the throne room, feeling violated and spied on and grossly misjudged. "Tocsin was a group of very dedicated Harvard students who wanted nuclear disarmament. They were pacifists, not communists, at least not to my knowledge, but since I only went to two meetings my freshman year, I hardly qualify as a former member. Why didn't your father confront me with that file when I came to him to complain about being confined to the palace? I had no idea he held these suspicions. I could have explained."

"Arjuna only gave him this information yesterday."

"Yesterday? I don't understand. You said those people who accused me of being a member of the PLF were arrested in *May*. Where are they? I'd like a chance to confront them and ask them why they lied about me."

"They are dead." Mila put his arm around her again, and she could feel his heart beating fast and angrily.

"Both of them?"

He nodded. "The story is that they were shot trying to escape from prison. That is a lie, of course. This is all a lie. Arjuna undoubtedly tortured them into signing those confessions and then had them murdered."

The word *murder* hit Lucy's mind and echoed there, growing like a great, senseless noise, blotting out all reason. She felt frightened and angry and lost, and even Mila's arms no longer seemed to offer her protection. "Mila, this is a nightmare. I thought I was marrying you; instead I seem to have married into a world of conspiracies and spies and secret accusations. Now you say someone was tortured and murdered to discredit me." She looked back at the door to Marpa's study, dark and shadowed, and then at the throne room itself with its snarling tigers, golden lightning bolts, and grinning, copulating gods. No place had ever seemed more foreign to her. She felt as if she didn't understand anything about Patan. "What the hell is going on here? Do you know? If you do, for God's sake tell me before I go crazy. I don't care how bad it is; I have to know."

Fifteen minutes later they were sitting in their own garden again, and he was whispering to her, his voice buzzing in her ear, so low and so soft that it was like a breath of wind.

"Not sure . . . but have a theory," he was saying. "A conspiracy to discredit you . . . Arjuna . . . engineering the whole thing. . . . The trek . . . my Nepalese cousins . . . secret intelligence reports. . . .

Arjuna . . . an army in the southern jungles . . . Arjuna keeps my father terrified . . . communist threat. . . ."

The web of intrigue was too complicated. As Mila spoke, Lucy tried in vain to make sense of what he was saying. If she had heard him correctly, he had received intelligence reports from his Nepalese cousins indicating that General Arjuna was secretly training an army in the southern jungles. For some reason it was to Arjuna's advantage to keep Marpa terrified of the communists. Also, Mila suspected that Arjuna was conducting a conspiracy to discredit her.

"But why?" she begged. "I don't understand what I have to do with all this?"

Mila leaned closer, and his words took on individual shapes. "Does the name Nada-Bindu mean anything to you?" he asked.

"Isn't that your cousin, the one who's—"

Mila nodded. "Yes, the one who is retarded, the one who is next in line for the throne if I die without a son." He put the palm of his hand against her belly. "That is why Arjuna is trying to discredit you." And then he said more words, among them *assassination* and *revolution*, and at last Lucy understood the dark forces that surrounded her. If the intelligence reports were correct, Arjuna was planning to launch a right-wing coup d'état with the aim of putting himself on the throne. But first, he would have to eliminate any opposition. The most efficient way to do this would be to assassinate Marpa and Mila, and install poor Nada-Bindu as a puppet king, but that was messy and complicated and might lead to resistance. Mila suspected that Arjuna had come up with a two-fold plan: first, he would increase his power over Marpa by terrifying him with stories of communist infiltration; second, he would make sure Mila never had a legitimate heir. Part of his plan seemed to be to get Lucy into such disfavor with the king that she would be exiled permanently to one of the country estates. Mila would be forbidden access to her and . . .

Lucy felt every muscle in her body go tight. The garden seemed to shake and dissolve in front of her, and the heat became terrible, as if the sun were beating down through the leaves of the grape arbor and pounding out molten patterns on the stone path. Mila was explaining that there might be a plot to imprison her *forever*. She remembered her dream of the tiny box. No matter how much she loved Mila, she couldn't stay in Patan if it meant being caged like an animal. She wanted release. She wanted to walk in the open: in a forest, on a beach, in a field, far away from this garden and this palace where she had lost her personal freedom and her dignity and— Her mind twisted, not completing the thought because something else struck her. It was a grief that she had repressed for months. "The baby," she whispered. "You said Arjuna doesn't want you to have a son. Did he make me . . . ?" She couldn't say the word *miscarry*. It stuck in her throat, and it was too horrible to contemplate.

"If I believed that," Mila said, grabbing her hands and holding them so tightly that her wedding ring cut into her fingers, "I would kill him as if he were a mad dog." He lifted her hands to his lips and kissed them, and she saw that there were tears in his eyes. "My love, my darling," he said fiercely, "I promise I will take you away from here until the danger has passed." And then they both wept together, very quietly, holding each other.

But Mila couldn't take her out of the country. That soon became clear. Or rather he could, but not at a price that she was willing to let him pay. Four times he went back to argue with Marpa, warning him about Arjuna, begging him to let Lucy go abroad, and four times father and son fought loudly and bitterly.

"I would rather see your communist wife dead than in America speaking to the press and bringing shame on the throne, on you, and on your people," Marpa yelled.

"You're Arjuna's puppet!" Mila yelled back. "He is driving a wedge between you and me, using Lucy as the bait. He is raising an army against you, he is—"

"Silence! These are rumors and lies whispered in your ear by your cursed wife. Arjuna hunts down the communists, so of course she is against him."

"I will not be silent! I will talk to you and reason with you and tell you the truth until you hear me. Remember reading the play *Oedipus Rex* at Oxford? Remember how he refused all advice? Listen to me, Father. I love you, and because I love you, I tell you that you are full of pride, and if you keep up this way, you will fall as Oedipus fell."

"You are poisoned with Western thoughts." Marpa spit in his left hand, raised it, and pointed two fingers at Mila. "Your wife is a white-faced Western demon, and if you come here to plead for her again, I will curse you with a father's curse, and not all the monks in Patan will be able to remove it from your soul."

"A curse!" Mila stormed. "A curse! This from a man who has studied at Oxford!" He paced across the living room, past the couches and screens, his face mottled with anger and frustration. "He has reverted to the Middle Ages, and nothing—*nothing*—moves him to reason." He closed his eyes for a moment and stood silently, and she could see the suffering and fatigue in his face, and she wondered how much longer he could go on like this. "The worst of it," he said at last, "is that even though I know he is wrong, it pains me terribly to lose his love and respect. It pains me to see that he does not know you or love you as he should; and it pains me to see my father"—his voice trembled—"manipulated by a scoundrel." He opened his eyes and sat down on the couch. "He is not a well man. He had a heart attack five years ago, and may have another. Each time I go to see him, I feel that I am shortening his life." Lucy sat down beside him and tried to think of something comforting to say that she hadn't already said. She couldn't ask Mila to stop demanding her freedom, and yet it was horrible to watch him fight his father endlessly with no results.
"There is one thing I could do," Mila whispered.
"What's that?" She bent forward to catch his words. Their voices were scarcely louder than their breaths.
"I could pay someone to kill Arjuna." She could feel the tension in his body, and his breath quickened against her cheek. "Princes have done such things before."
"Could you live with yourself afterward?"
He shook his head, and his face was a pale oval in the darkness of the room. "No," he said. "It would violate everything I believe in."
"I couldn't live with it either," she whispered. They never mentioned such measures again.

The fifth time Mila went to see Marpa, he was refused an audience. The chamber was blocked by armed guards who declined to move aside at his order. That was the afternoon he gave up trying to get his father's permission to let Lucy leave Patan.

"I will take you out myself without his consent," he told her.

But she had thought of that alternative before he offered and she knew that it wouldn't do. She had come a long way since Mila had first described the power struggles and conspiracies to her, and she was starting to think like a courtier, taking the most complicated, darkest view of things possible. "But if you take me abroad without your father's consent, he may disinherit you. Even if he doesn't, his health isn't good, and the stress may make him sicker. If he falls ill or dies while you're gone, won't that give Arjuna just the opportunity he's been looking for?"

Mila stood up and paced across the garden, and she could see by the tension in his shoulders and the quickness of his steps that she was right, that he couldn't afford to go abroad even for a week. His absence would be an open invitation to Arjuna to kill Marpa and put Nada on the throne.

Mila came back and sat down beside her. "I am trapped," he whispered. He slammed his fist into the palm of his hand, and it was the loudest sound heard in the garden for days. "In some ways I am more of a prisoner than you are. I am imprisoned by duty and by my responsibility to my people. You are right. If I take you abroad, there may be . . ." He said the words *assassination* and *revolution* again, and this time he added another word that made Lucy shudder. The word was *bloodbath*.

Lucy felt a chill run up her spine as Mila described how Arjuna would eliminate all opposition. "I can't let you risk it," she told him. "It's out of the question. God knows I want to get out of here, but I can't let you take me out when there is a chance that hundreds of your people would be slaughtered." He started to protest, but she put her finger over his lips. "No," she ordered. "We'll talk about this no longer."

The next possibility was that he could help her escape without actually going with her, but that, too, presented problems.

It was two, perhaps three, days later when he took her out in the garden to tell her that he had arranged for a plane to smuggle her into India. They were both weary of holding all their conversations among

the roses by now, and Lucy was so excited by the prospect of leaving that he had to remind her to whisper.
"Two weeks from today," he said. "I'm sorry we have to wait so long, but right now the moon is full, and the pilot is afraid the plane will be spotted and intercepted as it crosses the Indian border. I'll take you to a small airfield about two kilometers outside of Sindhala." He went on to describe how he would have a fake passport made up for her, how he would establish a secret account for her in a Swiss bank, how he would join her as soon as the political situation improved.
Lucy held his hand and tried to think of some way to go away without leaving him behind, but they had exhausted every other possibility. "I'll miss you terribly," she whispered. She bit her lip and looked away from him, at the roses and the garden, and the wall that surrounded everything. "But this is only a temporary arrangement. We'll see each other soon."
"Of course we will," Mila agreed, but he didn't look at her either. Both of them knew there was no guarantee that the separation would be short or easy to bear. They sat for a few moments, hand in hand, and she felt a painful loneliness descend on her, as if a cloud had drifted across the sun. Be reasonable, she commanded herself. There is nothing else we can do, *nothing*.
She forced herself to concentrate on practical matters. She asked him if he thought the plan to smuggle her out of Patan would succeed, and he reassured her. The pilot was trustworthy; they had an alternative date set if the weather was bad; getting her a passport would be no problem. As he explained away each obstacle, she began to get excited again, and for the first time in days she allowed herself to believe that things were going to work out. Then, just as she was about to agree that it really was the only possible thing for them to do, a question occurred to her: "What's going to happen to you when your father finds out you helped me escape?" she whispered.
"Nothing," Mila said. His reply was a shade too quick, and he didn't meet her eyes. She knew that something serious was wrong, and he wasn't telling her what it was. Studying his face, she realized that the expression on it was familiar. She had seen that same expression before—six times to be precise—on the faces of the six soldiers who guarded the gate of the palace. She took his hand in hers. "Why don't I believe you?" she said softly.

Mila was silent for a long time. "Because I'm not a very good liar," he finally admitted.

"Would you be shot?"

He shook his head. "No, nothing like that. I'd probably just be exiled to one of the country estates for a while."

She didn't like the word *exiled.* "For how long?"

"It's hard to say. My grandfather exiled one of his sons for thirteen years for refusing to marry an Indian princess. I imagine that, under the circumstances, I would be permitted to return to Sindhala in half that time."

"You'd spend seven years in exile for me?"

"Yes," Mila said simply. "I would. It would be a small price to pay for your liberty."

From that moment on, Lucy knew that if she was going to escape from the palace she was going to have to do it herself; not just do it, but do it in a way that would make it clear to everyone that Mila hadn't lifted a hand to help her.

Yet for almost a week, she did nothing. The price was so high—the loss of Mila, the loss of Sala. the word *loss* haunted her, tumbling through her mind as she walked in the Vishnu garden, or bathed Sala, or ate breakfast with Mila. Not *separation* but *loss.* How could she go on deluding herself that they would all be reunited someday? If she left Patan on her own, fled without implicating Mila in her escape, then she could never return, at least not as long as Marpa was alive. Perhaps that wasn't entirely true. Perhaps there was some small chance that the king would have a change of heart, but it was a chance so slight that when she tried to hold on to it, it shrank to nothing. No, the blunt, ugly truth was that Marpa could live for a long time, and as long as he lived and listened to Arjuna's lies, Mila would have to stay in Patan. Five years could pass, ten, twenty. If the separation were long enough, she and Mila would grow apart; they would get on with their lives. Perhaps his father would even force him to remarry.

In her worst moments she thought: I'm about to do to Sala what my mother did to me: walk out on her. I'm about to do to Mila what my mother did to my father: run away from him. Those thoughts were the cruelest of all. They made her feel half sick with guilt and grief, and so she vacillated, put off her departure, made plans, and never carried them out. Then, on the day that would have been Thanksgiving back in the United States, she received a piece of news from the outside world that made her realize she could wait no longer.

Mila brought the news to her as she was having her breakfast. She knew as soon as he entered the room that something bad had happened. He walked softly as if he were approaching an invalid, and his face was even more drawn and haggard than usual. Her first thought was that he had had another fight with his father, but then she saw the telegram in his hand. It was printed on blue paper, of course, because yellow in Patan was the color of death, but it didn't matter because the message was the same in any color.

> DEAR LUCY I HAVE BEEN TRYING AND TRYING TO CALL YOU WITH NO SUCCESS. I KNOW YOU ARE ON RELIGIOUS RETREAT BUT THOUGHT YOU SHOULD KNOW THE BAD NEWS AT ONCE. REGRET TO TELL YOU THAT HANK DIED LAST NIGHT OF A MASSIVE STROKE. WE WILL NOT SET DATE FOR FUNERAL UNTIL WE HEAR FROM YOU SINCE WE KNOW YOU WILL WANT TO ATTEND. WE HAD NO WARNING HANK WAS ILL. LIFE IS TERRIBLY SHORT ISN'T IT? COME HOME IF YOU CAN. LOVE AUNT KATE.

Lucy stared at the words, stunned. Uncle Hank, her only relative, was dead. She remembered the kindnesses he'd shown her when her father died. He had taken her into his home and cared for her, put her through Radcliffe without once objecting to the expense. She remembered the smell of his pipe and the way he used to wisecrack at Walter Cronkite as he watched the evening news, and the madras Bermuda shorts he played golf in. She had never been close to him the way she had been close to her father, but she would miss him. One of the last links that tied her to home had been severed forever. She was alone in a foreign country, and Uncle Hank, who might have come to her aid, had gone to a country even more foreign, one he'd never come back from.

Dropping the telegram into her lap, she put her hands over her face and began to cry. When she looked up again, Mila was standing at her side holding a glass of water. She took it from him and drank it, grateful for the numbing coldness of the ice.

"Is your father going to let me go back to the States to the funeral?" she asked.

"No," Mila said. "He isn't. I tried to talk to him one last time, but the guards . . ." He shrugged and pressed his lips together. There was no use asking him what had happened. It was clear that he had tried to get past the guards and that he had been unsuccessful. What that meant for him and for his future, she didn't know. She only knew that Mila had risked enough for her.

Taking his hand, she sat for a long time holding it, not saying a word because there was nothing left to say.

· 6 ·

Lucy and Mila lay in their golden lotus bed. The red silk sheets were smooth and cool and smelled faintly of sandalwood; the room was softly lit with candles burning in brass sconces. If anyone could have seen them stretched out so peacefully side by side he would have assumed that they were both sound asleep, but Lucy, who lay so quietly with her eyes closed, was not sleeping; she was waiting.

Time passed. Outside, the moon rose briefly and then set. The night was cold and the stars obscured by clouds. Gradually Mila's breath grew deep and regular. When she was absolutely sure that he was asleep, she opened her eyes. For a moment she lay perfectly still, afraid to move. Above her the ceiling danced in the candlelight as painted flowers and glass lamps moved back and forth in a slow, solemn pavane. To her left, the great golden wardrobe that held Mila's ceremonial robes seemed to lean over for one last look.

Carefully, without the slightest sound, she slipped sideways out of bed and landed catlike on the balls of her feet. Mila's breathing changed, and she froze for a long, worried moment until he settled down again. His face was calm, and he slept with his arms thrown out to one side; his eyes moved quickly under his eyelids so she supposed that he was dreaming. She wondered where he was now. Usually they told each other their dreams at breakfast, but tomorrow morning when he woke, she would be far away, and perhaps she would never again get to hear him tell her what adventures he had had.

She didn't want to leave him. A hundred ties of love and affection bound her. She remembered the first time she had ever seen him: he had been playing soccer on the banks of the Charles River, and she had been awed by his grace and quickness. She had been headed toward another life, and then she had met Mila and a whole future that she had never even imagined had come rushing toward her. Now she was about to turn her world upside down again, and who knew where she would end up this time? She was tempted to climb back in bed, wrap her arms around him, and forget the whole thing. The candles burned lower, sputtered, and went out, and Mila's face faded into the darkness until all she could see was the shadow of his profile. Dangerous amounts of time passed.

At last she shook her head and quietly slid back, away from the bed. Walking carefully across the thick oriental carpet, she made her way out of the bedroom, careful not to make the slightest sound. Ever since the death of her uncle, two soldiers had been assigned to "guard" the apartment. At this hour of the night they were no doubt drowsy, but there was no use taking chances. The living room was cold and dark except for a single gold lamp that put out no more than a finger's width of light. Still it was enough to see by. Sitting at her writing desk, she took out a sheet of stationery embossed with the royal crest and wrote a note that would clear Mila of all blame. It was a cruel note, and every word in it was a lie, but as she struggled to find precisely the right tone of stubborn defiance, she hoped he would understand that she meant none of it.

By the time you get this note, I'll be long gone. Our marriage is over. I don't love you anymore. I want to be free. I asked you to help me escape, but you refused, and I'll never forgive you for that. Forget me and get a new wife—one who's willing to obey your father. I'm not willing and never will be. Lucy.

The note was awkward and mean and blunt, but that was how she meant it to be. With a little luck, it would spare Mila seven years of exile. Feeling sad at the thought of him opening it, she sealed it in a heavy white envelope and left it prominently displayed on the writing desk. She wanted to write him another note, a long, passionate, personal one telling him that she loved him and that she would always hope to see him again, but there was nowhere she could leave it. She thought of slipping it into one of his shoes or taping it inside his closet, but a maid or a guard could find it first. No, she decided, there could be no last letter. In Patan everything was poisoned with intrigue, even saying good-bye to the man you loved.

Her eyes burned with tears; wiping them away roughly with the back of her hand, she forced herself to stand up and turn her back on the writing desk. On the other side of the room the couch lay waiting for her, heavy and dim in the lamplight. She crossed to it and sat down feeling the brocade pillows give under her weight. Her situation was certainly ironic. For nearly two years the press had been calling her the "Princess of Paradise," but the paradise had proved rotten to the core, and now she was a prisoner in her own home, about to flee into the night like a refugee. Her uncle was dead and her closest friend was ten thousand miles away. Even Mila, who loved her and would do anything for her, couldn't help her. She was more alone than the poorest rag seller in the market, a fugitive without even a country to call her own.

Self-pity was a dangerous trap. Later there would be time for regrets; now she had a job to do. Lifting the cushion next to her, she fumbled for the things she had hidden yesterday afternoon. The first was a bottle of brown shoe polish, a wonderfully lucky discovery. She had come on it in her wardrobe room, stuffed into the lower back corner of one of the closets by a careless maid. Pulling out the bottle of polish, she reached into the lining of the couch and took out the next item: a pale pink sari bordered with gold trim. White would have been better for her purposes, but white, of course, was one of the colors of death, so she owned nothing white, not even a pillowcase. Under the sari was a small velvet purse containing her driver's license, a compass, six hundred rupees, and the diamond necklace Mila had given her as an engagement present. The driver's license, issued in Massachusetts, had expired a year ago, but it was the only identification she had. She hadn't needed a passport to come to Patan. She'd been the pampered bride of the prince, welcomed with flowers and chanting monks. Whoever would have imagined less than two years later she would be trying to sneak across an international border? The purse, which dangled from a strong leather thong, was designed to be worn around the neck to thwart thieves. Cassie had given it to her as a joke on the day she left Cambridge. The final items hidden in the couch were the rubber-soled sandals she sometimes wore as shower clogs and her sewing scissors.

Seizing the scissors, she quickly cut the gold trim off the sari and stuffed it into the cloth bag that had contained the bottle of shoe polish. Then, without a sound, she slipped out into the garden, and set to work perfecting her disguise. First she took the pretty sari and rubbed it into the dirt until it was covered with grime. Next she ripped it in a few places, and rolled it in the dirt again just for good measure. Satisfied, she turned to her next task. Picking up the scissors, she cut off most of her hair and buried it in the soft earth beside a flowering rose bush. After unscrewing the lid on the shoe polish, she applied it liberally to her face, hands, neck, arms, shoulders, feet, and what was left of her hair. When she was done a little polish was left, so she dripped it onto the sari and rolled everything in the dirt for a third and final time. Stripping off her nightdress, she put on the damp sari, winding it around her waist and drawing it over her head peasant-style. Tying the purse around her neck, she positioned it so it couldn't be seen. Then she knelt and buried her nightdress beside her hair. Sooner or later, of course, the Patanese Secret Service would find both, but by that time she hoped to be far beyond pursuit.

Strapping on her sandals, she kicked dry earth over the holes she had made and blotted out her footprints so that the gardeners wouldn't wonder who had been digging in the rose bed. She inspected her hands and feet, trying to see if she had covered all her skin with the polish, but it was hard to tell. She hoped that she now looked like a young widow, one of the poorest of the poor, but she had no way of knowing if her disguise was complete. She needed a mirror, but the nearest mirror was in the bathroom next to where Mila was sleeping, and she didn't want to risk going back. Once again she was tempted to give it all up. Perhaps there was some way she could stay and learn to tolerate this life for Mila's sake, but she could think of nothing new, and besides it was too late. If she came back and lay down beside Mila, stained with shoe polish, her hair cut off, then at best her ladies would think she had gone mad and at worst they would know exactly what she had been up to. She would be watched and imprisoned and perhaps separated from Mila, and she might never have another chance to escape. It was now or never.

Squaring her shoulders, she walked down the gravel path toward the back wall of the garden. The sandals pinched her feet and she winced, but she told herself that they would toughen in time. She had two hundred pairs of shoes in her closet, most of them much more comfortable, but they were too well made and expensive to go with her disguise. Until she escaped from Patan, she would have to dress like a peasant.

The garden wall proved ridiculously easy to climb. Low and sealed with rough plaster, it offered plenty of hand holds in the form of trellises and vines. Phil Klein, the former president of the Harvard Outing Club, would probably have given it an amateur rating. Scrambling over it, she dropped softly into the next garden, and found to her surprise that she was standing in a three-foot-deep fish pond. Putting her hand over her mouth to stifle a yell of surprise, she waded to the far edge and pulled herself dripping wet up onto the ornamental tile sidewalk. Her first thought was for the shoe polish, but fortunately, as far as she could tell, it hadn't washed off.

The pool she had landed in was none other than the one that held the floating Vishnu. In the dim light she could see him smiling at her from his lotus pad, his six arms spread out in welcome. This meant that her calculations had been correct: She was in the Hindu Garden, and on the other side of the wall directly in front of her was freedom.

There was only one catch. Ever since the PLF had tried to make a midnight raid some ten years ago, the entire palace complex had been guarded by armed soldiers with machine guns. On ordinary occasions, especially during the day or when foreign visitors were present, they were discreet, keeping out of sight except for the ones posted at the front gate. But at night they patrolled in pairs, watching for anything suspicious. She had determined that there were six such patrols. But they worked on a random schedule so there was no way to predict when they were likely to pass by this particular bit of wall; hence she couldn't simply bolt over it and make a break for the city. She was going to have to climb slowly, up thirteen feet of almost sheer concrete-faced stone and, once at the top, cling on long enough to make sure she wasn't about to fall right into their arms.

Tucking up her sari, she walked through the fresh-smelling flowers, past lingams smeared with sandalwood and benches carved with the dismembered parts of Shiva's consort, Sati. Sati, according to myth, had been sliced up by Vishnu into fifty-one parts, which, when they fell to earth, became the sacred pilgrimage centers of the Tantric tradition. It didn't seem like a particularly good omen. Grabbing an outcropping on the wall, she began to climb. She had gone about three feet when her hand slipped, throwing her off balance. Clawing at the cement, she fell, scraping the skin off her right elbow and both knees. For a moment she lay still, trying to catch her breath, afraid someone might have heard her, but the only sound was the bubbling of Vishnu's fountain. Getting up, she wiped the blood off her elbow with the end of her sari and started climbing again. As she inched up the slippery face of the wall, she decided that Phil would have rated it about 5.6. Too bad she couldn't have managed to smuggle some pitons and rope out of Mila's trekking supplies, but they were stored in another wing. Still she was strong, and her rock-climbing experience served her well.

Inch by inch, she pushed her way toward the top. Twice more she fell, and twice more she picked herself up. By now she was a mass of bruises and her sari was torn in several more places, but except for the fact that the scrapes stung, that was probably for the best. The worse she looked, the less likely anyone would recognize her. Finally, on the fourth try, she managed to reach the top of the wall. Clinging to the ornamental spikes, she held her breath and waited, listening for the guards, but there was nothing below her but darkness and beyond that the dim outline of the street.

Now she was faced with another problem. Climbing up had been hard enough, but climbing down would be even harder. Fortunately, she was prepared. Unwrapping her sari, she swiftly looped it over one of the ornamental spires and used it to lower herself in an awkward rappel. The material strained in her hands and made ripping sounds, but it held. She thought of Bill Bishop and how terrified he would have been swinging down through the darkness toward an unseen goal. Bill, the last she heard, had been given a posting in Italy. He was probably sitting in a café in Rome at this very moment drinking red wine.

At last her feet touched the cobblestones. Exhausted, she stood for a moment in the street, too winded to move. Then, pulling at the hem of the dangling sari, she unlooped it and caught it in her arms as it fell. Putting it back on, she tied it clumsily around her waist, pulled the loose end over her head to conceal her eyes, and ran as fast as she could toward the nearest side street and freedom.

The hardest part of her journey still lay ahead. Like all the major cities of Patan, Sindhala was walled, served by four narrow gates at the north, south, east, and west. At night the gates were closed and carefully guarded; at first light they were opened to let in peasants who came from the countryside to sell vegetables and firewood in the central market.

Her only chance was to be at the south gate at dawn and slip through before anyone at the palace noticed that she was missing.

Unfortunately Patan had no buses or trains, only one paved road that ran straight from the Indian border to the Chinese border, a road that by tomorrow afternoon would be swarming with soldiers all bent on finding her and dragging her back to the palace. She had considered going to one of the foreign embassies in Sindhala and begging for political asylum, but she had read too many accounts of refugees like Hungary's Cardinal Mindszenty, who had lived for decades in embassy compounds. There was no use trading one prison for another. She would have to avoid the main highway, stick to the footpaths that crisscrossed the countryside, and work her way south toward the Indian border. There would be no road signs, of course, but she had a compass, and the stars should be plainly visible at this time of year.

Fortunately the border wasn't very far away—nothing was in Patan. In the ornately illustrated atlas she had consulted last night, it looked as if she were going to have to walk about forty miles. Unfortunately the atlas was not topographical, and she had not dared go to the palace library and request a more elaborate set of maps, but she knew that the terrain sloped downward from the Himalayas, merging with the jungle lowlands not far from the border. Surely she could manage to walk downhill for forty miles.

The border itself presented more difficulty. Because the jungle was so dense, there were only three possible crossings: one at Harabar on the main highway, one at Pashnath near the Nepalese border, and one at Pritvhi where the Chanpat River flowed into India. After puzzling over the map and taking detailed notes, she had decided to try to cross at Pritvhi. Pritvhi would be easy to find: she would only have to follow the Chanpat River downstream. It was less heavily guarded than the other border crossings; in fact it had a reputation for being something of a smugglers' paradise because large numbers of Indian pilgrims passed back and forth each day to worship at the famous shrine of Sati. It would probably take her three days to get there, four at the outside. When she arrived, she would wait until dusk, join a group of pilgrims returning to India, and slip across the border unnoticed. Meanwhile, she still had to find somewhere to spend the rest of the night.

Hurrying away from the palace down the dark, narrow streets, she came upon whole families sleeping in the gutters: babies resting next to their mothers, children huddled together without a blanket to cover them. Sometimes as she passed, someone stirred, rose to one elbow and looked at her with blank desperation, but she was only another ragged shadow in a world of ragged shadows. As she approached the market, the sleepers became more numerous, and she had to walk carefully to keep from treading on arms and legs. By the time she reached Kalpa Square there was hardly a patch of unoccupied pavement. For a moment she stood in awe, looking at Marpa's subjects, these wretchedly poor people whose very lives he owned. They lay sprawled on the cobblestones by the hundreds like corpses, as if a great catastrophe had passed over them. Shuddering, she drew her sari closer and hurried on, thinking that Sindhala was a city of the dead.

She spent most of the rest of the night in a storm sewer by the river, just within sight of the south gate. The sewer was dark and smelled foul, but it hid her well and she was glad for it. She had not meant to doze, but she was exhausted and must have fallen asleep because suddenly she awoke with a start as something small and furry ran across her arm. All around her the sewer pipe had come alive with scurrying sounds as thousands of small feet scraped across the tiles, disappearing into the darkness. Outside, the sky was pale gray; the rats of Sindhala were returning from their night's foraging.

Biting her lips to keep from screaming out in horror, she fled from the pipe.

"Gone?" Marpa slammed the silver watering can down on his desk and looked at Mila through narrowed lids, prepared for another confrontation. When he had heard the insane rumor that the princess was no longer in the palace, he let the prince past the guards. Now he eyed him suspiciously, wondering if this were just a trick to gain an audience. "Explain immediately. Where has your wife gone?"

"I don't know." Mila was frantic. "I just woke up and she wasn't there, so I assumed that she'd gone for a walk in one of the gardens, but then I found this note." He thrust the envelope in Marpa's hand, thinking, Read it, old man. See what disasters your cursed pride and arrogance have brought on us. But he kept the rage out of his voice because now there was nothing to be gained by fighting with his father. "I'm afraid she's been kidnapped." By Arjuna, he wanted to add, the same murderous Arjuna whom you trust to save you from the communists.

"Don't be ridiculous." Marpa read the letter, and a look of contempt passed over his face. "The note speaks for itself. She's run off, or at least she claims that she has. Frankly I doubt that she can get out of the palace. The walls are nearly three times as tall as she is, and we have ten patrols on duty day and night. As for her being kidnapped, there were two guards posted outside your door who, according to you, saw and heard nothing. Besides, if she had been taken by force, the kidnappers would have left a ransom note, not this ill-natured commentary on the state of your marriage."

"Where is she then?" Mila demanded, forcing himself to ignore his father's condescending tone. He was thinking that if Lucy had not been kidnapped, then she must have fled to save him from being exiled, but he could hardly tell Marpa this. If she had only waited another week, he could have had her flown to India, but she had loved him too much. He should have realized that she was planning to escape without his help, and he was angry with her for not telling him, and worried about her, and the loss of her was almost more than he could bear. He knew he might never see her again, but he still couldn't accept it. He wanted to find her and hold her and make love to her. He wanted to protect her; he wanted to call up the army to look for her before Arjuna got to her first, but only his father had the power to do that, so he must listen to him and play the dutiful son again when inside he was seething with impatience.

"She must be somewhere in the palace," Marpa said in a kinder tone of voice. It was clear from the expression on his face that the boy had done nothing to help his wife commit this mad act of defiance. Why Mila should want this woman back was beyond him. Except for the scandal, Marpa would be happy to see her disappear forever. She had come between father and son, sown dissension where none had existed, been a political liability and possibly even a spy, but there was no reasoning with love. It was an insanity that unmanned even the strongest. He himself had had a dose of it back in Oxford: a married woman, the wife of another student, French, not English. Odd that he couldn't even remember her name, because she was the reason he had sworn off entanglements with women.

"But where in the palace?"

Marpa shrugged. "Who knows. Women sulk and hide. We've had

this kind of thing happen a dozen times. Only last year Marut, one of your eldest aunt's ladies, spent almost three days in a tool shed near the English garden after her husband told her he was taking another wife. Everyone, your aunt included, was sure she'd committed suicide, but instead she crawled out, shamefaced and hungry, to help prepare the wedding feast." Marpa spoke confidently, but he was growing more worried by the minute. The princess was quite capable of committing any sort of idiocy in the name of independence. Suppose she had managed to get over the wall and elude the patrols? That meant that at the present moment she was wandering around unaccompanied, asking for trouble. If she were attacked or kidnapped or assassinated, or even if she merely managed to slip across the border, there was going to be a scandal greater than Patan had seen since the sixteenth century when Queen Purusha eloped with the king's youngest brother. "I'll have the palace searched at once."

"Good, thank you." It was hard to thank his father after all the violent arguments they had had, but Mila meant it. He wanted the palace searched and the city searched and the whole country searched if necessary because he was afraid for Lucy. Arjuna would be after her. He tried not to think about the general because when he did he felt a burst of hatred so strong that it made him feel like his head was on fire. In a sane world, he could have told his father all this, but bringing up the topic of Arjuna might be fatal right now, so he swallowed his anger and held his tongue.

Marpa saw that he was going through some kind of struggle and decided that the boy must be half-crazed with anxiety. He was too sensitive to be a king, Marpa thought. He didn't know how to manage power, not even the power a husband had over a wife. The next wife he married the boy to would have to be docile to the point of idiocy, like Tulasi. There was a princess in Nepal who would be perfect, a healthy virgin with the personality of a cow. She'd produce sons like a prize heifer, and they'd have no more nonsense about the rights of women. Love was too powerful an emotion to be allowed to exist between a prince and a princess, and the sooner Mila realized that, the happier he would be.

That morning on Marpa's orders, the palace was thoroughly searched, but no trace was found of Lucy. Over Mila's protests, the Patanese Secret Service was called in, and by the next morning General Arjuna's agents had found the princess's hair and her nightdress buried by a rose bush in the garden outside her apartment. The nightdress was covered with brown stains that were at first mistaken for human blood. On closer examination, however, they proved to be brown shoe polish. From that moment on, it was assumed that the princess had not met with foul play but had indeed fled the palace in disguise.

Marpa immediately placed the army, police, and secret service on alert. In an attempt to avoid scandal as much as possible, a cover story was invented: a blue-eyed Western woman—five feet two, a hundred and five pounds—was trying to flee the country. The woman, who was probably disguised as Patanese, was a dangerous drug dealer and possibly a PLF spy. She was to be stopped, arrested, and brought back to Sindhala for questioning. Under no circumstances was she to be shot; under no circumstances was she to be interrogated by anyone but officials at the highest level. A reward of ten thousand rupees was offered to the man who apprehended her.

By the next morning the biggest missing-person hunt in Patanese history was underway. The airport was watched, roadblocks were set up on the royal highway, security forces at the borders were doubled, and soldiers began to pass through the streets of Sindhala, pulling the saris away from women's faces to check the color of their eyes. In any Western country such a massive operation would have made the front page of the newspapers, but in Patan the press was silent. The hunt for the princess was conducted in the strictest secrecy. Although everyone in the palace believed that she had run away, no one wanted the story to leak to the outside world. For once the nobility united and closed ranks. If the princess could be apprehended before she crossed into India or China, then she could be quietly brought back to Sindhala. If, on the other hand, she managed to escape, Patan would be shamed before the rest of the world for decades to come.

But as Mila had known from the start, there were some people who were not at all anxious to have Lucy returned alive. On the second day after her disappearance, General Arjuna met with a man who had worked for him on several previous occasions. The man's face was unremarkable, but his body was tattooed with initiation scars from a Taiwanese prison gang. He was large, strong, and dressed in clothes exceptionally well designed not to attract attention. Once he had had a real name, but he lost it long ago. Now he called himself Tamas after the Hindu force of destruction. Half Chinese, half Patanese, he had been trained in his art in a dozen prisons all over Asia. His most peculiar trait was his tender loyalty to his mother and six brothers and sisters back in Taiwan, whom he supported with hair-raising crimes that rarely made the newspapers.

Arjuna was brief and to the point. "The princess has run away and is probably heading toward the Indian border. I don't want her to resurface and I don't want to know what has happened to her. Is that clear?"

"How much are you paying?" Tamas asked. He liked cash deals in American dollars whenever possible, but Arjuna was a regular customer so he was willing to give him a bit of leeway.

"More than all the other times put together," Arjuna told him. "Half a million Patanese rupees."

"Make it seven hundred thousand," Tamas suggested.

Arjuna nodded in agreement. Getting to his feet, Tamas slipped out of Arjuna's house like a silent shadow to begin the hunt.

Lucy opened her eyes and moaned. She was lying in a ditch near a rice paddy, covered with mud, almost lame, and so hungry that all she had been able to think about all day was the tea with garam masala and the sambar Asana used to bring her for breakfast. Ever since she saw the soldiers going from house to house in the valley, she had been afraid to knock on peasants' doors to buy food. Her stomach growled, but she ignored it. Taking a handful of green rice stalks, she chewed on them slowly, trying to absorb energy from the raw plants. The stalks pricked her mouth and made her tongue bleed, but she went on chewing them anyway. If she hadn't been in such bad physical shape, and been missing Mila so badly, she might have enjoyed the scenery. The sun was just setting, turning the sky a violent red-orange. Above her, almond-shaped clouds blew south toward India and freedom. In front of her were the last traces of the mountains of Patan, a ridge of low green hills already showing signs of jungle. Down there, at least, she wouldn't be cold at night.

Stumbling to her feet, she stood trying to gather her strength. How long had she been traveling now? five days? six? She had lost count. The forty miles downhill had turned into a nightmare of rugged mountains, swollen streams that had to be forded, paths that disappeared into bogs filled with mud and mosquitoes. The sky had been overcast at night, hiding the stars. The compass was little help. All it could do was guide her straight south: off the edge of cliffs, down more dead-end paths, or into villages where she would be captured. She had been lost dozens of times. The Chanpat River had to be nearby, but so far she hadn't been able to find it.

Now she was beginning to feel feverish, and that worried her. She couldn't afford to get sick, not now with only fifteen miles or less to go. She needed to buy a hot meal and a dry place to sleep, but so far the money in her purse had been virtually useless. She had had to stay away from villages, and many of the peasants had nothing to sell in the way of food except a few raw radishes and a handful of rice. She comforted herself with the thought that her hunger was part of the price she was paying for anonymity. So far her disguise had worked perfectly. No one she had met on the footpaths had given the young widow in the dirty sari a second look. Evidently to be female and poor was to be invisible.

She waited a few minutes longer, until the sun set and darkness began to fall. It came quickly, tropical and sudden, descending like a dark cover over the rice paddies. In the distance two water buffalo shimmered for a moment in the twilight and then were erased as if the artist who had created them had decided to try again. Feeling confident that she couldn't be seen from the village, she began to walk through the wet mud toward the path that led south. It was a narrow path, not much more than three feet wide, and she hoped that she wouldn't miss it. Last night, she had spent an hour looking for it, testing the ground with her bare feet until it hardened under her. She wished fervently that she could travel by day, but that, of course, was out of the question.

Her throat was burning with thirst and it was torture to walk through the water knowing that it was polluted. Last night she had found a log filled with rainwater and had drunk to her heart's content, but all day today she had had nothing but rice juice. All she had to do was bend down and scoop up a handful of water, but who knew what lived in it: parasites, worms, microbes, things that would make her instantly and desperately ill. She remembered how many people in Sindhala had been suffering from chronic diarrhea. Why hadn't she thought to bring paregoric, Kaopectate, and tetracycline for herself?

At last the thirst became too much for her and she gave in, bending down to fill her hands with the invisible water. It was warm and smelled like mud, but when she put her mouth to it, it had a sweet, pleasant taste. She drank and drank and felt much better. Shortly afterward, she came upon the path and began her nightly trek south in good spirits. In India, she told herself, she would have a hotel room, a bed to sleep in, air conditioning, hot meals, clean clothes.

By midnight she was descending the hills into the jungle through a gorge. Far below her at last was the Chanpat River, or at least what she took to be the river, although all she could hear in the darkness was the sound of water thundering over rapids. The air took on a warm, sticky quality. Strange birds called to one another, and once a large fruit bat flew so close to her face that she screamed involuntarily. But the bat had no interest in her. Lumbering on, it disappeared into the tall trees that blotted out the night sky. She couldn't see the trees, only their white, skeletal trunks, but she could feel them hanging over her. They gave weight to the night, and she felt protected by them. Once she heard a roaring sound so close that it made her hair stand on end. Breaking into a run, she tripped over a large root and landed facedown in the mud. But the roaring wasn't a tiger after all. It broke into a trill and became the song of a bird or perhaps a large frog, and she lay there for a moment, amused by her own panic, thinking that at least the mud didn't matter, for how could she be any more muddy than she was already? When she began walking again, she felt cheerful and almost invulnerable. She'd been afraid of the jungle, dreaded the hours she would have to spend crossing it, but now that she was finally here it didn't seem half as bad as the rice paddies where she had constantly been in danger of discovery.

She walked on through the darkness, feeling lighter with every step. Inside her the beginnings of a serious illness were producing a temporary state of drunkenness. Her temperature was 101 and rising, but instead of feeling sick, she suddenly felt better. She was traveling through one of the most beautiful places on earth, and if she walked well and hard, by this time tomorrow she would be out of Patan forever.

Although Lucy didn't know it, she was walking into a trap. Several miles ahead, only a few minutes' walk from the border crossing of Pritvhi, four men were impatiently awaiting her arrival. One was a man with tattoos on his arms and chest, and the others were Kang. The Kang was a local tribe that specialized in smuggling drugs and guns over the Indian border. For the right price they would also perform other services including murder. Tamas had hired them because he needed reliable assistants who wouldn't blink at the idea of killing an unarmed woman.

He had conceived a brilliant plan. Actually it was not a particularly original plan; it was the classic plan to catch a tiger. As soon as Arjuna had told him that the princess had fled, he had known that the chances of finding her in the unmapped countryside were slim. She was, from all accounts, a highly intelligent woman and thus would no doubt avoid the villages. To hunt this she-tiger, Tamas decided, it was necessary to predict where she would take cover and when she would try to run.

To make sure that he would get her wherever she surfaced, he had stationed paid assassins along the roads that led to the main border crossings at Harabar and Pashnath, and even put three men at the entry point into communist China. But he was betting that she would attempt to cross into India at Pritvhi. She would have enough sense to know that the crossings at Harabar on the main highway and at Pashnath near Nepal would be under heavy surveillance. Unless she wanted to leave the paths altogether and head out into the jungle—where she would most certainly die—the only other reasonable crossing was at Pritvhi where the constant stream of pilgrims returning from the shrine of Sati would offer her a chance to slip across unnoticed.

Tamas knew the region well, having done some free-lance gunrunning there in 1964. Five miles before the princess reached Pritvhi itself, she would be traveling through the Chanpat River gorge on a narrow trail with a sheer cliff to her right and a steep drop-off to her left. As far as he knew, the gorge was not on any map. Border areas were purposely left vague to frustrate invading armies, so there was every chance that the princess would walk into it unaware. In short, the gorge was the perfect tiger trap. There he would take her.

After placing his men at all the other border crossings, Tamas had left immediately for Pritvhi. There, in the no-man's land between India and Patan, he had had a stroke of luck. Three Kang were on their way back to their village after having done a job that none of them cared to describe. He found them in the miserable little town of Hoshgawila, sitting in the square taking shots at a bullock cart whose frightened driver had taken refuge beneath a load of manure. Tamas had hired them on the spot.

He explained that they were going after an American drug dealer who had burned him on a large hashish sale. She was heading for the Indian border and would be traveling in disguise, so to catch her they would have to work in pairs. He and one of the Kangs would set up an ambush point halfway down the gorge; the remaining two would keep watch at the southern end. The Kangs' orders were simple: they were to stop all travelers, male or female, and look into their eyes. If the eyes were blue, they were to bring her—for it would be her—to Tamas, who would deal with her in a professional manner. On the night Lucy entered the gorge, they had already been waiting for her for almost a week.

She was sick, terribly sick. Drinking the water out of the rice paddy had been a big mistake. She staggered along the narrow trail, wracked by cramps and nausea. The moon had risen, which made walking a little easier, but her head felt as if it were full of hot coals, and for the past two hours she had been seeing things that weren't there. She knew that they weren't there because when she looked straight at them they disappeared, but each time they materialized in front of her again, she felt as if she might die with fear. Some of them were beasts from the jungle: giant cats who leapt out of the underbrush, birds with soft wings that brushed her cheeks, but the people were the worst. She had seen David and Cassie and Mila and even her mother beckoning to her from the shadows, and the sight of them made her feel as if she were going mad. Mostly, however, there were just swirling colors and lights where no lights were shining. In a brief moment of lucidity, she realized that her fever must be incredible, yet she kept on walking, putting one foot in front of the other, no longer feeling the stones in the path or the sharp points of broken sticks. She had to get to the border. Sometimes she couldn't even remember why this was true, but she knew that if she stopped and lay down she would never get up again.

She could hear the river roaring below her, swelling as it raced down toward the plains of India. Once she had seen it through a break in the trees, churning and white in the moonlight. It looked fast: full of rocks and logs, thick with mud, and its banks were probably infested with mosquitoes and perhaps snakes, but she no longer feared anything except being too sick to keep on going. She had lost all track of time, but she had to be almost to the border by now. It seemed as if she had been walking through the gorge for days. Stumbling over a rock, she sent it crashing down the embankment.

One of the Kang rose quietly to his feet and stood in the darkness listening. A few feet to his left, Tamas lay asleep in a hammock, invisible under a canopy of camouflaged mosquito netting. The frogs had stopped calling to one another, and the night birds had fallen silent. Someone or something was coming down the trail. Pulling out his gun, the Kang moved into position without disturbing so much as a twig, but he needn't have bothered to be so careful. Lucy was too sick to hear him. He saw her coming a long way ahead, a dim shadow stumbling wearily down the path, and his first thought was that she was another peasant woman returning to Pritvhi. He was tempted to let her pass. He had stopped a lot of peasants in the last week, and he was getting tired of it; they always thought he was going to rob them, and usually they screamed and tried to run, which meant he had to chase them down.

Then she stepped out of the trees, and the moonlight shone on her, and he saw a flash of white flesh under the edge of her sari. Drawing back into the brush, he waited, listening as she came closer and closer. She was mumbling something incoherent and half-delirious, singing it under her breath as if it were all that was keeping her going. It wasn't a song the Kang recognized, but that wasn't surprising. The song, which was in fake Latin, was something every Harvard freshman learned by heart. Roughly translated it meant, "Don't let the bastards grind you down."

He waited, letting her draw so near that he could smell the sour sickness of her flesh. When he knew that there was no possibility she could escape, he stepped out behind her and seized her suddenly, clapping his hand over her mouth. To his surprise, she struggled and tried to bite him, but he knew how to stop that. Grabbing her by the shoulders, he shook her so hard that he nearly snapped her neck. When he felt her grow limp, he let her fall to the ground where she sat, panting and terrified. She was a ragged bundle of filth and she didn't look anything like a Western woman. The Kang was disappointed.

"Your name," he demanded. She made gestures to indicate that she was a deaf mute and he slapped her across the face so quickly that she didn't even have time to flinch. "I said what is your name?" Shuddering with fear, she wrapped her hands around her knees and lowered her head as if expecting another blow, but she remained stubbornly silent. Wearying of the game of terrorizing her, he grabbed her by the hair, jerked back her head, and held her for a moment while he lit a match on the sole of his boot, but once again she frustrated him by closing her eyes. Swearing in Kang, he jabbed his thumb under her left eyelid and lifted it. The eye that gazed out at him was a bloodshot blue-gray.

Putting the barrel of his gun against her head, he marched her back into the small clearing where Tamas, wakened from his sleep, was sitting on a tree trunk wearing nothing but a pair of khaki boxer shorts. In his hand he held an unlighted cigarette. Tamas looked at Lucy, who still had not said anything. "Blue eyes?" he asked the Kang.

"Yes." The Kang nodded.

Tamas shone his flashlight on Lucy, who shrank from the beam, putting her hands over her face. "You made a mistake. You've brought me another peasant." Instead of answering, the Kang reached out and pulled Lucy's sari down around her waist. Her breasts were exposed, white and vulnerable; rings of shoe polish surrounded her neck and arms. Tamas looked at her nakedness without feeling the slightest twinge of sexual arousal. "You're right," he said with satisfaction. "It is her." Striking a match against a stone, he lit a cigarette, the first he had had in a week. Smoke was too easy to smell in the jungle, and he never indulged his habit until the hunt was over. He inhaled and examined Lucy with a professional eye. She was at the breaking point, and if he had wanted her to confess anything, now would have been the time to push her, but there was nothing that he wanted her to confess except her own identity, which was obvious enough. Her whole body was shaking, but Tamas wasn't impressed. He knew that no matter how sick she was, she wasn't to be underestimated. He could tell that there was a stubborn streak in her that meant she was perfectly capable of trying to escape even under the most impossible conditions. If she had been a man, he might even have admired her, but in a woman it seemed a perversion of nature. He reached for his gun and remembered that he had left it in his hammock.

"Kill her," he ordered the Kang.

The word *kill* jerked Lucy back to lucidity. Suddenly realizing what was about to happen, she gave a yell of surprise and terror, and tried to bolt, but the Kang pulled her back, twisting her arm. She struggled fiercely, moving in close so that it was hard to get a good shot at her. "Don't kill me," she begged. The Kang slapped her; he was getting tired of slapping her.

"Be quiet and hold still," he ordered, but she went on struggling and pleading and fumbling at the purse at her throat. He was just about to pull the trigger, when she thrust a wad of dirty rupee notes in his face. "Do you want money?" she cried. "Here. Look. There's a lot. I'm giving it to you." The Kang gave a grunt of interest, lowered his gun and took the money from her. It was a big wad, stained with sweat; on the top bill King Marpa looked sternly off into space, weighted and potent under his triple god crown.

The barrel of the Kang's gun shone dully in the moonlight. In a moment he would quit examining the money and shoot her, and she had to think of something to stop him because she wanted to go on living. The seconds ticked by, and she could feel death coming closer and closer. Her hand closed around the diamond necklace. Pulling it out of the purse, she dangled it in front of him. The diamonds caught the moonlight, sparkling and brilliant. "Let me live," she pleaded. Pressing the diamonds into the Kang's free hand, she gestured at Tamas with a cunning born of desperation. "I can pay you more than he can." Holding her breath, she prayed that it would be enough to tempt him. If it wasn't, she was dead; she had nothing left to bargain with.

The Kang fondled the diamonds, dazzled by their weight and fire. He had never seen anything so obviously valuable. They were like stars, and he could sell them for millions of rupees in Pritvhi. "Good," he muttered.

"Not bad," Tamas said casually, "but nothing special." He was lying; he could barely contain his excitement, and his fingers twitched with the desire to hold the necklace in his own hands. He had a good eye for gems, having fenced quite a few in his time. Even in moonlight the diamonds had superb color and radiance; there wasn't a stone on that necklace under a carat. He did some quick calculations and decided that the matched strand would bring at least $10,000 in any of the shops in Hong Kong that specialized in jewelry of undisclosed origins. He wondered what else the princess had in her purse. As soon as the Kang killed her, he would kill the Kang and take the necklace. It was a highly satisfactory arrangement, one that got the job done and left no witnesses.

"Well, what are you waiting for?" he said. His voice was too rough and greedy and he stopped at once, annoyed with himself. "Go ahead and shoot her." He was wheedling now, conciliatory and honey-toned, and he shrugged at the Kang in his best, most comradelike way. "You've done a good job and you can keep the diamonds, but we need to kill her and get back to Pritvhi before the girls at Loang's get too tired to help us celebrate." Loang's was the best whorehouse in southern Patan; it had real carpets on the floor, which the Kang would never see because in five minutes he was going to be dead and out of the way.

The Kang examined the diamonds and then looked at Tamas. His eyes narrowed and he licked his lower lip hungrily. His face sloped to a triangle from a wide forehead to a small sharp chin, and his two front teeth protruded slightly. Dressed in camouflage with his hair slicked back with water buffalo fat, he looked snakelike and cunningly stupid. "She says she can pay me more than you can."

"Well, she's lying." Tamas exhaled a curl of blue smoke and smiled at the Kang, thinking that he never should have hired him. The Kang were good killers but greedy bastards; this one obviously thought he could do better by selling out to the highest bidder. He imagined with satisfaction what the Kang would look like dead. "Can't you tell that she's setting you up? She wants the two of us to get into a fight over her little strand of rocks, but of course we aren't going to do that, are we? Not two smart men like us. Shoot her and we'll go back to Loang's and share a couple of bottles of Zu."

Lucy could see that the Kang was faltering and that he might shoot her after all. Touching the necklace, she sent the diamonds swinging in front of the Kang's face, filtering the moonlight through hundreds of prisms so it came out blue and green and red. There was blood in them and money, and the Kang watched them, half hypnotized. "I'm the princess of Patan," she cried. "Take me hostage, hold me for ransom, and you'll be a rich man." Her mind was moving at a dizzy rate now, spinning out plans like spokes on a wheel. "Alive, I'm worth a fortune to you; dead, I'm worth nothing."

The Kang fingered the diamonds. "So you're the princess, are you?"

"Yes," Lucy nodded.

"Prove it."

Tamas could see that the Kang was going to bargain with her; he was going to stand there and sell him out like he was a dumb whore who had forgotten to ask for her money in advance. Tamas snapped. He was tired of this shit. He wanted her dead, now, without further delay. Instinctively he reached for his gun, and again he remembered that he had left it in his hammock. The oversight infuriated him; he was getting sloppy. "Kill her, you stupid bastard," he yelled. "What the hell are you waiting for?"

The Kang frowned. Caressing the diamonds he dropped them into his pocket. "You're the stupid bastard," he said. "She's making me a good offer."

"I'm the one who's paying you."

"Not anymore."

"Cross me and I'll cut your heart out," Tamas raged. "I'll hang you up by your balls and let the vultures pick you over, and then I'll—"

"Shut up," the Kang said, waving the gun in his direction.

"You son of a bitch," Tamas's face went white with fury. The gun didn't frighten him. He had taken men with guns before, kicked their skulls in before they could pull the trigger. Lunging at the Kang he grabbed his wrist and twisted it so fast that the Kang didn't have time to scream before the gun flew out of his hand. Both men fell on it, the Kang howling with pain, Tamas cursing.

They crawled forward through the dirt, pulling each other back, locked in a deadly embrace, snarling and biting and gouging at each other. The last thing Lucy saw before she bolted out onto the trail was Tamas's face twisted into a grimace of triumph as he dived toward the gun.

A shot rang out, and then there was silence broken only by the rumbling of the river and the sound of frogs calling to one another. In the shadows along the trail, a man sat up and automatically smoothed back his hair. It was the Kang; Tamas lay beside him, dead, shot in the heart. How it had happened even the Kang couldn't have said, but karma was a strange thing and death was common and he didn't waste a moment trying to figure it out. Rolling Tamas over, he inspected him to make sure he was dead. He saw at once that there was no doubt. The whites of Tamas's eyes shone in the moonlight, and his mouth gaped open in surprise, as if he had been about to say something before death interrupted him.

Giving a hiss of satisfaction, the Kang got to his feet. The girl couldn't get far; he'd go after her in a minute, but first he had some business to attend to. Walking over to Tamas's hammock, he tore open the mosquito net, threw Tamas's clothes on the ground, squatted beside them, and began to go through the pockets. He found what he was looking for hidden inside a roll of socks: 12,000 Patanese rupees secured by a rubber band. Only after he had counted the money and stashed it safely in his boot did he return to the problem of the girl. She had taken advantage of the fight to escape, but that was no problem since there was nowhere to run to. If she went up the trail, he could easily follow her; and if she went south, his two fellow Kang would get her before she exited from the gorge. The Kang decided to go after her. He wasn't sure he believed her story about being the princess; she might have burned Tamas in a hashish deal and gotten the diamonds that way, but there was no telling what else of value she had in her bag.

Crouching in the path, he examined it for a few seconds and nodded, satisfied with what he saw. Her footprints were clearly visible, heading downhill. He moved silently, and soon he heard her, running along the trail like a terrified deer. Breaking into a smooth, practiced lope, he closed in on her thinking of diamonds and more rolls of rupees and how much the whores of Loang's loved money. "Stop," he yelled. He was happy, half-ecstatic with the prospect of being rich forever, and she was only a woman. Of course she would stop, so he was surprised when she didn't. Annoyed, he halted, steadied his gun with both hands, and prepared to fire a warning shot over her head. His wrist still hurt and he didn't want to miss and wound her in some vital place. If she was the princess, killing her would be a waste since he could demand a fat ransom for her, but she could be scared or even lamed, winged in the back of the leg and made cooperative. "Stop," he yelled again, not nearly so happily this time, and he fired.

At the sound of the gun, Lucy panicked. Bolting over the side of the trail, she began to scramble down the slope through the brush, tearing her hands on thorns, scraping the skin off her legs, falling and tumbling and catching herself on roots. Hanging from one bush, she dropped to another, wrenching her ankle so badly that the pain made her moan. The roar of the river grew terrifying, but what was above her was more terrifying still. She had no plan; she hardly thought. Her hands grasped without her guiding them, and her feet struck out for minuscule ledges that crumbled under her. Nothing bore her weight, but everything broke her fall. Screaming with terror, she grabbed for the last bush, missed and plunged into the river.

The Kang heard her scream and the splash of her body as it hit the water. Her head appeared for a moment, a dark spot on the churning froth, getting farther every second as tons of water crashed over her, hurling her downstream as if she were no more than a twig. As he watched, her head disappeared suddenly, sucked under by the current. He put his gun back in its holster. He couldn't have hit her from this distance even if he had wanted to. Better that her body wash up on the bank without a hole in it. He was sorry that he hadn't cut the bag off her neck when he had the chance, but at least he had the diamonds. There was no need to try to finish her off. The Chanpat River was a fierce god; it would do the killing for him.

The river rolled Lucy from side to side, sucked her down until her lungs burst, cast her up, battered her against rocks. She fought at it, trying to breathe, trying to keep afloat. You shouldn't fight a current; you should let it carry you and swim at an angle to it, but how could she swim? She was sick with fever and drowning and she was going to die. The roar of the water was deafening. It pounded on her eardrums. The crazy man who was trying to kill her was nothing in comparison to the river. It sucked her down and down into its blackest, coldest depths, and she knew just before she lost consciousness that she had escaped one death only to find another.

· 7 ·

Indira Gandhi, the new prime minister of India, had a problem. The princess of Patan had been found half-drowned and unconscious on the bank of the Chanpat River just inside the Indian border. At least that was what the Americans were claiming. There had been no word out of

Patan that the princess was missing, so the girl who had been found by the border guards might very well be an impostor.

Folding her arms across her chest, Gandhi contemplated John Christopher, the American ambassador to India who was waiting respectfully for her to say something about the report he had just handed her. Fifty years old and a veteran of India's struggle for independence, she was an imposing spectacle even though she was just over five feet tall. A single wide band of white ran through her black hair like a warning sign. Her eyes were dark and heavy-lidded, her brows thick, her nose almost Roman. Her resemblance to her legendary father, Jawaharlal Nehru, was uncanny. Rumor had it that at her birth one of the household servants had mistakenly congratulated Nehru for having produced a son.

Christopher pressed his fingers together and wished fervently that she would get on with the discussion at hand. Gandhi was famous for her long silences during which petitioners were left to squirm and wonder what she was thinking. He could feel his smile freezing on his face, and he had an overwhelming urge to scratch his elbow, but he restrained himself and maintained a look of respectful attention.

Gandhi noted his discomfort with satisfaction. Christopher probably once had been one of those robust, red-faced Americans with endless physical energy who bounded through their round of official duties like large dogs, but years of enduring the hot suns of the subcontinent had given him a bleached-out, weary look. At the moment he was looking particularly worried, which wasn't surprising since this was undoubtedly the most delicate situation he had faced since the India-Pakistan War of two years ago. On that occasion everyone had expected the United States to rush to India's defense as it had during the Chinese invasion in October of 1962, but instead President Johnson had cut off all military and economic aid and left the Indian people to fight Pakistan alone. In Gandhi's mind this had been an unforgivable betrayal. Making Christopher uncomfortable might be a minor act of retaliation, but it was the only one she could afford to take at the moment since India was dependent on the United States for the ten million metric tons of grain that stood between her people and starvation.

She let the silence grow until the ambassador began to show distinct signs of despair. "Are you sure, Mr. Christopher, that the young woman in question *is* the princess?" she asked at last.

Ambassador Christopher breathed a sigh of relief and nodded vigorously. "Yes, madam, I'm afraid so. I've just received an FBI report on her fingerprints, and they match those of the princess so perfectly that I'm afraid there can be no mistake." There was another long silence. Gandhi looked thoughtfully at something just behind Christopher's head, and it was all he could do not to turn around to see what it was.

"Just out of curiosity," she inquired, "how did you happen to have her fingerprints in the first place?"

Christopher cleared his throat. "I'm not sure, madam. That isn't my area." He had security clearance at the highest levels and had seen a CIA report on the princess that was several inches thick, but he did not indicate that fact by so much as the blink of an eyelid.

Gandhi frowned and stared at the bronze statue of Ganesh just behind Christopher's head. Ganesh, the elephant-headed son of Shiva, removed all obstacles, which was why she had placed him where she could see him and her visitors couldn't. She suspected the fingerprints had come to Christopher courtesy of the CIA, and she wondered if they had her fingerprints on file too. No doubt they did. It was annoying the way the Americans went around keeping track of the rest of the world as if they had been delegated to run the entire planet. At the moment, however, it was proving convenient.

"Could we run over the facts of the case one more time, Mr. Ambassador?" she asked briskly, returning her attention to Christopher. She had made him squirm long enough, and it was time to get down to business.

"Certainly, madam." Christopher opened the copy of the file that he had been holding ever since the commencement of the interview, and cleared his throat. "According to this report, your border guards spotted a young Western woman unconscious on the east bank of the Chanpat River yesterday morning at approximately six-thirty. They realized that she was a foreigner because she was unclothed, which was fortunate for her since otherwise—given that she had dyed her arms and face—she might have gone unnoticed."

Mrs. Gandhi frowned. "Not unnoticed. The dead are always noticed; but no doubt she would have gone unattended. You understand that we do not always have the resources?"

"Yes," Christopher said quickly, "of course. That's what I meant to say. In any event, the guards took a closer look and saw that she was wearing a bag of some sort around her neck. When they opened the bag they found that it contained a driver's license issued in the state of Massachusetts to a Lucy Constable, born January 22, 1945, height five feet two, weight a hundred and five pounds. Assuming she was an American tourist who had somehow met with foul play, they gave this information to their superiors who immediately forwarded it to our embassy in New Delhi. We recognized the name at once and were, to be frank, horrified at the possibility that it might be *the* Lucy Constable. Subsequent inquiries have only confirmed this."

"What do you suggest we do, Mr. Ambassador?" Gandhi sighed and pointed to the report that lay in front of her at neat right angles to the edges of her desk. "I can think of half a dozen good reasons why she might have fled Patan. It's a backward country, and even if it weren't, the position of a daughter-in-law is often intolerable for a woman, especially one of spirit and intelligence." She smiled wryly, and the corners of her mouth twitched in a way that suddenly made her look almost girlish. "As you can see, even I had to find another hobby to amuse myself." There was some truth in what she had just said: the burdens of family life had been heavy, and if she had not been widowed at the age of forty-three, she would not now be prime minister.

Christopher laughed dutifully at her little joke, thinking that this was all a hell of a mess. "Madam Prime Minister, I'd like to speak off the record here. In late October we received a communication from Willis Elderby, our ambassador in Sindhala, reporting that the princess was very unhappy in Patan. Her reasons were more or less as you surmised. Elderby warned that, in his opinion, she might take desperate measures to extract herself. Apparently, she has done just that. How she managed to get out of Patan, or even out of the royal palace, which I understand is walled like a prison, is as much a mystery to the United States government as it is to your own. The fact that her absence has not been made public adds yet another dimension to the problem."

Christopher paused to let this sink in. Patan was a bog of intrigue, and he pitied Elderby his posting there the way he would have pitied a man assigned to trek through a mangrove swamp. It seemed almost a rule of thumb that the smaller the country, the more trouble it was likely to cause. "Technically, of course," he continued, "Lucy Constable is no longer a United States citizen, and we have no responsibility for her except to report her presence in India to the proper authorities.

But the delicate nature of this situation and its potential impact on international relations have prompted discussion of the matter at the highest levels." He paused to emphasize the words *highest levels*. "I have been charged to convey to you that, in the opinion of my government, she should be sent back to Patan under the tightest security measures possible. Officially, of course, as I said, this isn't the United States's problem, but we're willing to work with you in whatever way we can. We want this kept under wraps as much as you do. The scandal will be incredible if the press gets wind of it."

"There will be no scandal in India," Gandhi said. "That I can assure you." She clenched her fist as if emphasizing that her control of the press was near absolute, although she knew that it was not so much the scandal that the United States was afraid of but its effect on the stability of Marpa's regime. Marpa was their man in the Himalayas. President Johnson had been advised on more than one occasion that if Patan fell to the PLF, then Nepal, Bhutan, and Sikkim would tumble into the Red fold like dominoes. Gandhi saw it more like a game of chess: With Marpa out of Patan and the PLF in, the whole region would be in checkmate. The PLF was Soviet-backed, not Maoist, so it would act as a buffer between India and China. Pakistan would be distracted by a new communist regime so close to its eastern border, thus postponing the day when it could launch another attack on India. Personally she had never liked Marpa, and she could see many advantages in having him out of the picture, but one could hardly admit that to the American ambassador.

There was another awkward pause. "Of course," Christopher said, "the problem may resolve itself."

Gandhi raised her eyebrows. "I'm not sure that I follow you, Mr. Ambassador. How?"

Christopher paused, trying to assess the impact of what he was going to say next. It was, as Mrs. Gandhi would instantly realize, the real purpose of his visit, but opinions about how she would react had been divided. "I understand that the young woman in question has been taken to a hospital in Lucknow, and that she is not expected to live. Should that happen, the United States government would respect the privacy of the Indian government: we would not expect to be informed about what steps you choose to take regarding the matter nor, to speak frankly, would we wish to know. Should the subject of the princess's whereabouts ever become an issue between India and Patan, our official position would be one of complete ignorance."

Not a muscle in Gandhi's face moved to betray what she was thinking. The silence this time was so long that Christopher began to think she was never going to speak. Finally, she leaned toward him; her dark eyes glittered with something that might have been anger or interest: Christopher couldn't tell which. "Are you suggesting that we put the princess back on the riverbank and pretend we never found her?"

"Of course not," Christopher protested. "I only meant to suggest that—"

"Thank you, Mr. Ambassador." Gandhi rose to her feet, dismissing him. "This has been a very helpful conversation." After he left she stood for a moment, lost in thought. Gradually her face softened, so much so that if Christopher had returned, he would have been rendered speechless by the contrast. Although the Americans thought of her as a cold fish and a ruthless power broker, Gandhi had a reputation for compassion among her own people. Her heart had always gone out to anyone who suffered from oppression and injustice, and as she thought of Lucy Constable lying near death in a Lucknow hospital, she wondered what horrors could have prompted the girl to flee Patan in disguise at the risk of her own life.

Picking up the report, Gandhi skimmed it for a few seconds, trying to read between the lines, but whatever had driven the princess out of Patan wasn't contained in Ambassador Christopher's account. As usual, the Americans were keeping the specific details to themselves. Well, that could be remedied by a proper investigation by *her* agents. Closing the file with an impatient shrug, she placed it in a wooden tray marked Top Priority. There were still a number of unanswered questions, but given that they could be satisfactorily resolved, she had come to a decision: she would offer Lucy Constable political asylum. If the girl refused and went back to Marpa's medieval little dictatorship, then when she was queen of Patan she would remember the kindness of the Indian people. If, on the other hand, she accepted asylum, Marpa's regime might be destabilized by the scandal.

Gandhi chuckled and tapped the report with her fingernail, thinking how horrified Ambassador Christopher would be when he learned of her decision.

Lucy was delirious with fever. In her dream she was walking through her own brain, pulling out file drawers, and in each drawer was a piece of her life. David was there, curled up tight in a fetal position around his guitar; her mother was there, putting on her lipstick in front of a mirror that reflected her face an infinite number of times; Ann and Steve Singleton were there, linked at the waist like Siamese twins, shooting guns at targets of Lyndon Johnson. Mila slept in his ceremonial robes in one drawer and lay naked in another. There were friends and strangers and people she had seen only in her dreams. She ran from drawer to drawer, faster and faster, pulling them out, exposing them to the light, begging them to talk to her and tell her what was happening, but none of them would. They just went on with their lives as though she were invisible. In the last drawer she found Cassie. *What's wrong with me?* she demanded. *Tell me, Cassie. I don't understand. What's going on? Where am I?*

Cassie sat up and rubbed her eyes the way she always did when someone woke her too early in the morning. *You're dying*, she said. *You're in India and you have typhoid fever and you're dying, but don't be afraid because I'll stay with you until it's over.*

Is this my life passing in front of my eyes?

Afraid so, Lou. How do you like it?

Not much. It seems like it was all such a waste.

Pain descended on her like a waterfall, pounding her back into consciousness. Opening her eyes she found herself caught in a web of plastic tubes. She tried to pull at them, and strange hands caught her arms, restraining her. The air smelled bitter and medicinal, and she choked on it.

"That's her," a woman's voice said. She looked up and saw a gray-haired elderly man in a high-collared white jacket gazing down at her.

"Is she conscious, Doctor?" the man asked, addressing someone out of sight to her left.

"No; as far as we can tell, she can't hear or see."

"Will she live?"

"We think not."

"That's a pity. The prime minister had hoped she would. If there is any change in her condition, either for better or for worse, the prime minister wants to be informed at once."

"Of course, Mr. Kapur."

Lucy closed her eyes and sank down to the bottom of the river where she spent an infinity drowning all over again.

The next time she woke a woman in a green sari was standing over her. The woman had a stethoscope around her neck and a small gold ring in her nose. On her forehead was a red dot indicating that she was Hindu.

"Lucy?" the woman said.

"Yes." Lucy heard her own voice coming from far away. Her tongue felt heavy and awkward.

"I'm Doctor Chatterjay. How do you feel?"

"Bad," Lucy managed to say. She didn't know where she was or how she had gotten there, and she half expected the woman to dissolve into another fevered dream, but the woman was solid. Behind her, bright sunlight streamed through the open window, making gold puddles on the green tiled floor. Two white curtains blew in alternating puffs, starched and clean, trailing the scents of jasmine and hibiscus mingled with disinfectant. Overhead was a rack that contained glass bottles filled with clear liquid. One of the bottles was attached to her left arm by a long plastic tube. The fluid in the bottle bubbled slowly, dripping into her. Behind it, on the far wall, was a framed print of a man in a toga giving a small child something to drink from an earthenware pitcher. The print was entitled *The History of Medicine*. She realized that she must be in a hospital room.

Her first thought was that she had been caught and taken back to Sindhala. She felt like weeping with frustration because that meant everything had been in vain. She'd been trapped and thrown back into the same pen. Clutching the hem of the sheet, she stared at this strange doctor, irrationally convinced that any minute she would leave, and Dr. Sukra would walk in to tell her that she was well enough to be imprisoned somewhere where she would never see Mila again. Before that happened, she had to get up and get her clothes on. She struggled to sit up, but there was no force in her arms or legs. Her ankle was swollen and painful, and her whole body felt like jelly.

Dr. Chatterjay put a restraining hand on her and gently pushed her back down on the bed. "You shouldn't try to sit up yet. You've been very sick."

"Wass wrong?" She had never been so weak before; she wondered if she had had some kind of brain fever. She felt paralyzed, frightened, stupefied with illness. If Marpa came in, he would be able to do what he wanted with her because she didn't have the strength to fight him. Even lifting her head was difficult.

"You've had typhoid fever. You nearly died." The doctor was speaking in English, not in Patanese. Her accent was Indian. Maybe, Lucy thought, just maybe I made it out after all.

"Innia or Patan?" she begged. The word *India* blurred on her tongue; she tried to straighten it out, but she couldn't.

"You're in India. You're quite safe. You have nothing to worry about."

"Innia!" It was the sweetest word she had ever heard. She rolled it around on her tongue like a gumdrop. She couldn't even say it properly, but that didn't matter. She was out of Patan. She had made it. Relieved, she lay back on the cool sheets. Her whole body was trembling, and the room seemed to move in slow circles as if it were dancing around her. Shiva, she thought, Lord of the Dance. Whose hair is the stars. Who brought me out of bondage. Everything was all mixed up. She wanted to thank some god for her deliverance, but she couldn't keep them straight.

She was consumed with curiosity; she struggled to ask more questions, but the sentences kept turning incoherent, tripping over one another and blending together until she couldn't remember where they started and where they ended. Her brain didn't seem to be working the way it usually did. Pressing her lips together, she found they were parched and painfully blistered. "Thirssy," she murmured.

Dr. Chatterjay picked up a glass from the bedside table, filled it with water, lifted her head, and let her drink. In her daily report to Mrs. Gandhi's assistant, Mr. Kapur, she would record that the patient was able to take fluids orally and had responded to the name "Lucy." Hanging at the foot of the bed was a chart made out in the name of Jane Murphy. Why the patient was being treated under a pseudonym was something that Dr. Chatterjay was too discreet to inquire.

The feeling of the cool liquid going down her throat was the most exquisite sensation Lucy had ever experienced. She decided that she would never again take the act of drinking water for granted. Closing her eyes, she drifted back into unconsciousness.

Slowly, day by day, she recovered her strength. At first the line between sleeping and waking was blurred and uncertain. There seemed to be many nurses, and often when she opened her eyes she found Dr. Chatterjay standing beside her bed, reading her chart. Once she saw the gray-haired man wearing a different colored high-collared jacket. He was looking at her with satisfaction, nodding his head.

As she lay on her back watching the play of shadows on the white plaster ceiling, bits of the recent past began to come back to her: the two men on the path, her suicidal plunge into the Chanpat River. I survived, she thought. For the first time, she understood what a close call she had had, and overwhelmed with gratitude and relief, she began to sob uncontrollably. I miss Mila, she thought. I made it; I'm alive, but I may never see him again. She imagined Mila's face looking at her with love, and that only made her cry harder.

"Are you feeling worse, miss?" A worried nurse immediately appeared beside her bed.

"No," Lucy shook her head. "I'm feeling better." She laughed and then began crying again and was embarrassed because she was too weak to control her emotions, but the nurse appeared to take her mood swings as perfectly normal. "Where am I?"

"You're in Lucknow, miss, in Krishna Hospital. You were having typhoid."

"Who brought me here?"

"I can't say, miss."

Lucy looked at the nurse, trying to decide if she should ask her any more questions. Dr. Chatterjay had called her Lucy, so they must know who she was. Probably they'd gotten her name off her driver's license. Now that she was thinking more clearly, she realized that she may have rejoiced too soon. Being out of Patan was one thing; staying out was another. Did the small, brown-eyed nurse standing in front of her know that she was a runaway princess, or did she just think her patient was a Western tourist who had had a piece of bad luck?

The nurse began to change the sheets on the bed, lifting Lucy gently up, turning her over, tucking the fresh-smelling linen under her. Her hands were cool and graceful as the hands of all Indian women seemed to be, but instead of being comforted, Lucy grew more anxious by the second. Her muscles ached, and her stomach felt as if she had swallowed lead. Was the nurse always this attentive to her patients? And the room—the more she looked at it the more expensive it seemed. Would an ordinary tourist, picked up on a riverbank, be given a private bath, curtains at the window, framed pictures on the wall? She doubted it. More likely she would be taken to a charity ward where hundreds of women lay on pallets.

This was first-class treatment, which must mean that they knew who she was. Or did they? They must have found her driver's license, but there could be more than one Lucy Constable in the world. Suppose they only suspected she was the princess but had no real proof? What should she do if they questioned her? Deny everything and claim she was just a college student who had come over to India to study at a yoga ashram?

She rolled the story around in her mind, but it didn't seem convincing. There were too many holes in it: the lack of a passport application from another Lucy Constable, the fact that her birth date was public knowledge. Well, one thing was certain: she'd never let them send her back to Sindhala. She'd fight them every step of the way. Meanwhile the best thing to do was to try to get herself reoriented as quickly as possible.

"What's the date?" she asked the nurse.

"January 2, 1968."

"1968?"

"Of course."

"Good God." Lucy gasped and stared at the nurse in amazement. "I've been sick almost three weeks!" She broke into laughter and then began crying again. In fact, it seemed as if she did nothing but alternate between laughing and crying for the next twenty-four hours. Although she was feeling better physically, she was afraid. Every bit of unusual attention she got only convinced her that they were going to send her back to Patan, and yet she didn't dare ask. If they hadn't already figured out who she was, then it would be crazy for her to tell them.

Fortunately for her pride, she did most of this emoting unobserved, because as soon as it was clear that she was well enough to begin asking questions, the English-speaking nurses were immediately replaced by two nurses with darker skin who spoke only Hindi.

Mrs. Gandhi looked at the latest report on Lucy Constable's condition and pursed her lips. Good, very good. The girl had completely regained consciousness and was recovering her strength rapidly. All her vital signs were strong, and there seemed to be little chance of a relapse. Closing the report, she sat silently for a moment and then addressed the elderly man who was standing respectfully in front of her.

"I think, Mr. Kapur, that it is time you had a talk with her."

The man nodded. "Yes, Madam Prime Minister."

Gandhi was pleased. If the preliminary investigation went as she expected it would, Lucy Constable would soon find herself receiving a formal offer of political asylum. Gandhi contemplated the bronze head of Ganesh, thinking that obstacles were being overcome more rapidly than she had anticipated.

The next morning after breakfast, one of the Hindu nurses wheeled Lucy out onto the hospital veranda, placed a light blanket over her legs, and hurried away. It was the first time Lucy had been outside since her illness, and she felt better at once. There were no other patients on the veranda, which was large and cool, but a few hundred yards away, a garden wallah was cutting the grass with a short-handled scythe. Bees buzzed in the white trumpet flowers, and the sky was an almost white-blue, like an Easter egg that had been dyed and left out to fade. She was just thinking that if it hadn't been for the mango trees and garden wallah's turban, she might have imagined herself in California, when she saw a stranger walking across the lawn holding a black umbrella under one arm, and a large ledger under the other. He was elderly, gray-haired, wore a high-collared gray jacket, and as he drew closer she realized that she had seen him before, leaning over her bed when she was sick.

"Good morning, Your Highness," he said in the perfectly clipped, musical tones of upper-class Indian English. "My name is Mr. Kapur. I am the prime minister's special assistant, and I have been sent from Delhi to talk to you about your presence in India."

At the sound of her title, the last vestige of hope disappeared. Sick at heart, Lucy motioned for him to come up on the veranda. "Good morning," she said. The whole idea of trying to bluff her way out suddenly seemed ridiculous and pathetic. This Mr. Kapur obviously knew everything about her that there was to know. She saw her fate imprinted on his face: she would plead, he would refuse, and soon she would be on her way back to Sindhala to spend the rest of her life imprisoned in the palace or somewhere even worse.

Mr. Kapur stood respectfully in front of her, his head slightly bowed. "Please sit down," she said. At least she was to be spared praniyams.

"Thank you." He sat down, parked his umbrella neatly against one of the pillars, removed a white handkerchief from somewhere, and wiped the perspiration off his forehead. "The car broke down on the way from the airport," he said apologetically, "and the driver had no idea how to fix it. I had quite a bit of trouble hiring a taxi because there are so many pilgrims in Lucknow this time of year, and in the end I had to take a *panga*."

Lucy had no idea what a *panga* was. She supposed it was some kind of horse-drawn carriage. She waited for him to quit uttering meaningless pleasantries and get on with the dirty business at hand. Mr. Kapur opened his ledger, took off his glasses, polished them with his handkerchief, which he then folded and replaced in his pocket. He adjusted his glasses on his nose and then readjusted them. If she hadn't known that he was the prime minister's special assistant, she would have taken him for an accountant.

"I hope Your Highness is feeling better."

Lucy nodded. "Much better," she said through tight lips. She wished he would stop stalling.

"As you probably realize, Your Highness's appearance in India, incognito as it were, places the government in a delicate position. In order to facilitate things, I'm afraid that I am going to need to ask you a few questions. Would that be acceptable?"

She nodded, resigned. Of course there would be questions. Formalities would be observed. It would all be very civilized.

"Please take your time replying. I know that you have been unwell; there is no hurry." Lowering his glasses, he looked over the tops of his frames. Lucy didn't flinch under his scrutiny even though she felt invaded by it. Inspecting the goods, she thought, making sure they aren't damaged. Mr. Kapur cleared his throat. "Before we begin, let me assure you that whatever you say, you will suffer no adverse consequences."

"I beg your pardon?" she started. This was not what she had expected.

"Your status won't change, or rather your freedom to determine it won't change."

Confused, she stared at him trying to figure out what he was talking about. She knew she should understand, but she didn't. Maybe the fever had boiled her brains after all. "Meaning what?"

"Meaning that if you decide to stay on in India—"

Seized by hope, she interrupted him. "Did I hear you say I might be allowed to *stay* in India?"

"Yes, that's what I've been sent to tell you. The offer of political asylum is not yet official but—"

"That's wonderful news! I hadn't thought, that is, I'd imagined you were going to say . . ." She was nearly incoherent with delight. "You see, I thought you'd come here to tell me you were sending me back to Patan."

"Oh, no." Mr. Kapur shook his head. "That is most unlikely, not unless you wish to return. I assume you left of your own free will?"

Lucy was seized by an urge to laugh. She wanted to hug the funny little man and shout with joy. "I escaped," she said. "I ran away." She was elated by her incredible good fortune. "I'll never go back of my own free will as long as Marpa is king. Patan was a nightmare, Mr. Kapur."

"Ah yes," Mr. Kapur said, "we rather thought you were disliking it." He smiled back at her. "What we have here is a need to establish your identity, so we can move on to the next step. After seeing you, I personally am convinced that I sit in the presence of the princess of Patan, but the Indian government also must be convinced beyond any reasonable doubt."

"Ask me anything you want."

"It's all very elementary. First," he consulted his ledger, "I would be most grateful if you would state your full name."

"Lucy Corot Constable."

"Constable is your maiden name, correct?"

"Yes, that's correct."

"You also have a married name?"

"Yes."

"Ah," Mr. Kapur said, and wrote something in his ledger. "And now what is your married surname?"

Lucy frowned. "That's a good question. I don't really know, or rather I have a choice of so many strange ones that I've never been able to decide. I think according to traditional usage I might call myself Lucy of Patan, although I'm not an expert in these matters. My husband usually goes by the names Milarepa Tsayi Koron, but none of those are transferrable to a wife upon marriage. Nor are his nine other surnames, which roughly translated mean Tiger of the Himalayas, Son of Vishnu, Elephant of Wisdom, and so forth."

"In other words, you are the princess of Patan?" Mr. Kapur was taking notes in a rapid, clean hand.

"Yes." Lucy nodded. "I am."

"Please give me the date and place of your birth."

"I was born January 22, 1945, at Tinker Field, Oklahoma, in the United States of America. My father, George Trantor Constable, was in the Army Corps of Engineers at the time."

"What was your mother's maiden name?"

"Janet Marie Leveau. She was part French."

"And your maternal grandmother?"

"Josephine Corot—like the painter. She died when I was two. That's where I got my middle name, Corot."

After asking her a half dozen more questions in a similar vein, Mr. Kapur closed his ledger, took off his glasses, and replaced them in the pocket of his jacket. "It seems you are indeed the same Lucy Constable who married the prince of Patan." He looked as if he were about to shake her hand, but restraining himself he smiled warmly instead. "Welcome to India, Your Highness."

"Thank you. If it's not rushing things, where do we go from here?"

Mr. Kapur cleared his throat. "Well, first I must ask you once again if you wish to return to Patan."

"No, absolutely not."

"Is Your Highness certain of this?"

"Absolutely. I nearly killed myself trying to escape. There was a conspiracy to discredit me engineered by a general named Arjuna, who convinced King Marpa that I was a communist sympathizer and a spy. Arjuna is interested in securing the throne for himself at any cost. The king, who is terrified of a communist revolution, confined me to the palace, and when my husband tried to secure my freedom, he—"

"There's no need to go into detail at the moment," Mr. Kapur interrupted hastily, "but I have been instructed to inform you that your plight has provoked sympathy and curiosity at the very highest levels. The prime minister herself has taken a personal interest in your situation, and has asked that I report the results of this interview to her no later than tomorrow morning."

Mr. Kapur picked up his umbrella and tucked it under his arm. "Your Highness has been most gracious and cooperative." He rose to his feet. "Now if you will excuse me, I will leave immediately for Delhi. If things go according to schedule, I will return—" he paused, and she could see him neatly adding up the hours, "let us say the day after tomorrow. At that time I will bring you a response from Mrs. Gandhi."

Lucy felt a thrill of excitement. She had always admired Indira Gandhi, and the prospect of receiving a personal message from her was heady. "Thank you, Mr. Kapur," she said. "Thank you so much. Please express my gratitude to the prime minister." After he left, she realized that she was shaking with happiness and relief, but she was feeling much stronger today and there were no tears.

That night she dreamed of making love to Mila. Putting his hand under her head, he lifted her face to his and kissed her. His tongue was warm and sweet, and she felt like crying with relief because she had been sure that she would never kiss him again. Her bones dissolved under his touch, and when they made love it was like dancing across a floor that kept moving under her, whirling her around until she was giddy. The sex was slow and lovely and it took centuries. Around her, giant flowers bloomed and dropped their petals; trees grew and died and new trees sprang from their roots. Mountains rose up where valleys had been; whole oceans were born, and still Mila caressed her.

In her dream, they were reincarnated a thousand times: sometimes she was male and sometimes he was female, but they were always together. At the end, just before she woke, they finally stopped making love and simply lay together beside a pool filled with golden swans. The swans moved gracefully across water as white as ivory. Everything was white and gold: the trees, the grass, even the pupils of Mila's eyes.

The dream was so clear it seemed like a message or a prophecy. When Lucy woke from it, she knew exactly what she was going to tell Mr. Kapur when he returned with the message from Mrs. Gandhi.

The second interview took place two days later, just as Mr. Kapur had promised. They met on the hospital veranda again, but this time an English-style tea had been provided on a small, linen-covered table. A silver teapot lay snugly covered by an embroidered tea cosy, banked by a plate of scones, cakes, biscuits, and Indian sweets. Lucy's first thought upon seeing the food was that she couldn't possibly eat anything so rich, but by the time Mr. Kapur appeared with his umbrella tucked under his arm, she had already finished a large scone covered with jam and whipped cream.

"Good morning, Your Highness," Mr. Kapur said, bowing slightly.

"Good morning, Mr. Kapur." Lucy waved him into the empty chair. She would have poured him a cup of tea, but only one cup had been provided, on purpose she supposed. Princesses, even those living incognito, were evidently not expected to eat with lesser mortals. "Do you have a message for me from Mrs. Gandhi?" Her throat felt tight when she asked the question, and she had to fold her hands together to keep them from shaking. So much depended on what he said next. Would she be offered political asylum, or had Gandhi decided to hand her over to Marpa after all? The look on Mr. Kapur's face was not encouraging.

"I regret to inform you," he said, "that the situation has changed. We have just received some very disturbing intelligence from Patan." He paused and looked around, but the veranda once again had been cleared of all other patients, and not even the garden wallah was in evidence. "The prime minister has asked me to tell you in strictest confidence that General Arjuna has put a price on your head."

Lucy turned pale. Putting down her teacup, she sat for a moment trying to accept this news, which was as bad as anything she could have imagined. First she felt afraid, and then she felt angry. Arjuna again, she thought, always Arjuna. She felt him throwing his web of intrigue around her like a huge, ugly spider, never leaving her in safety or peace. So there was a price on her head? Did that mean that the men who had tried to kill her had been hired by Arjuna? She remembered the smell of the jungle; the sound of a gun being fired; the long, terrifying fall into the river. Closing her eyes, she tried to convince herself that here at least she was safe. When she opened them, Mr. Kapur was looking at her with a worried expression on his face.

"Are you feeling unwell, Your Highness?"

"No," she said, "go on." She picked up her teacup and took a sip of tea, willing her hand to remain steady. "Please tell me whatever else you know."

Mr. Kapur looked around again, as if making absolutely sure that there was no one listening. "According to reliable sources, it appears the general feels you know too much about his plans to seize the throne. He also seems to suspect that you know a great many other things, although we have not been able to determine exactly what those things might be. Also, there is a matter of a more delicate nature."

"And what might that be?"

"Excuse me, Your Highness, but I am an old man and not used to discussing such things with ladies." Mr. Kapur extracted his handkerchief from his pocket, wiped his forehead, and looked at Lucy uncomfortably. "Mrs. Gandhi asked me to tell you quite specifically that General Arjuna also seemed to fear that you might be with child. That child, of course, would be heir to the throne of Patan, and—" He came to a full stop and averted his eyes as if inspecting the bougainvillea.

I wish to God I were pregnant with Mila's child, Lucy thought, but I'm not. I certainly can't go into the details with Mr. Kapur because it's obvious that he's terribly uncomfortable even discussing the matter, so I'll have to euphemize. She sat silently for a moment, thinking of the best way to phrase a response. "Please assure Mrs. Gandhi," she said, "that there is no possibility of the last-mentioned event taking place."

Mr. Kapur seemed greatly relieved. "That," he said, "will make what I must tell you next much easier for all concerned." He refolded his handkerchief in precise quarters and put it back in his pocket. "The prime minister has considered your situation from all possible angles and has charged me to tell you that under the circumstances, she regrets that she cannot offer you political asylum in India." He hurried on, not giving her a chance to protest. "So far we have managed to conceal your presence, but to maintain your anonymity much longer would be difficult, if not impossible. Your face is too familiar, and as a Westerner, you will always stand out. The Americans know you are here and so, we suspect, do the British, since the two nations often exchange intelligence. Sooner or later, General Arjuna will also learn where you are. Mrs. Gandhi has asked me to tell you that since we cannot guarantee your safety, we cannot run the risk that you will be assassinated on Indian soil."

Lucy felt as if she were choking. She tried to breathe normally, but the air was hot and thick and she felt sick, as if she were having a relapse of typhoid. "And so," she said, "you are sending me back to Patan after all, Mr. Kapur." She leaned toward him, pleading. "Don't do it. I beg you. Let me go home instead. Let me go back to the United States." Tears filled her eyes. "I never should have left."

Mr. Kapur was visibly moved. "Your Highness," he said, "Mrs. Gandhi has considered this possibility also, but the obstacles are formidable. I do not wish to be the bearer of unwelcome tidings, but she told me that in the event you made this request, I should ask you how you planned to return. You have no money and no resources, and you would have to travel under a false passport unless you wished to expose yourself to the threat of assassination. Obviously, the Indian government cannot risk assisting you to enter the United States illegally any more than it can risk offering you political asylum."

"Please, Mr. Kapur, give me a moment to think." Lucy closed her eyes. Let me be lucid, she thought. Let me be cold and logical. Let me figure out how to convince them not to send me back to Sindhala. None of the plans she had considered earlier would work now that she knew Arjuna had put a price on her head. They had all been based on the idea that she would return openly to the United States, but now she would have to hide for an indefinite period of time. Where could she get money and a passport? Suddenly she knew. Feeling more hopeful, she opened her eyes.

"Mr. Kapur," she said, "I would appreciate it if you would tell Mrs. Gandhi that the Indian government need have no involvement in my return to the United States, beyond simply letting me exit from India." She paused. "Actually, that is not quite accurate. I do need your government to do one thing for me, but it can be done quite discreetly: I need the Indian ambassador in Sindhala to request a private audience with Prince Mila. Such an audience is not an uncommon event and should provoke no comment. The ambassador need never mention my name. All he needs to do is to tell Mila that a Patanese citizen is in trouble in India and needs financial help. Mila will guess immediately that I am the citizen in question, but to establish my identity beyond any doubt, the ambassador should say: 'She is fond of carved boxes with swans on them.'"

Mr. Kapur was silent for a long time as if thinking this plan over. "So you think your husband will help you?" he said at last.

"I'm sure of it."

"What if he does not, madam? What if he tells your father-in-law that you are in India, and the king presents the Indian government with a formal request for your return?"

"Mila would never do a thing like that. He was going to help me escape by flying me out of Patan, but I couldn't let him take the risk and—" She stopped because Mr. Kapur was shaking his head slowly from side to side.

"No, Your Highness," he said. "I regret to say that this will not do. If the Indian ambassador were to request an interview with Prince Mila and your presence here were to become known to King Marpa, that act alone would place our government in an untenable position."

Lucy looked down at her hands, feeling almost sick with disappointment. "But you will carry my idea to Mrs. Gandhi, won't you, Mr. Kapur? You will let her make the final decision?"

"With all respect, Your Highness, I do not think that there would be the slightest hope that the prime minister would approve such a request. However, if I may make a suggestion . . ."

Something in his voice made Lucy look up. She was surprised to see that he was regarding her in a sympathetic, almost fatherly fashion.

"Should the Indian ambassador receive an anonymous plea from a Patanese citizen trapped in India, he might well be moved by humanitarian feelings to take this anonymous plea to Prince Mila without commenting on it in any way."

He was trying to help her. He cared about her. Lucy was so grateful that it was all she could do not to leap to her feet and give him a hug. "Will you ask Mrs. Gandhi—" she began.

"Mrs. Gandhi could not possibly know about such an anonymous plea being sent to her ambassador in Patan," Mr. Kapur said stiffly, but his eyes danced with encouragement.

"Should I write—" Lucy said, but again he interrupted her.

"If Your Highness will excuse me," he said, rising to his feet. "I must go attend to some pressing business. I will return"—he consulted his watch—"in about an hour. Should you have any letters that you would care to have posted . . ." He let the end of the sentence hang in the air, bowed slightly, and tucked his umbrella under his arm. "My eyes," he said, "are failing. I have neglected to bring my glasses with me this morning. I do not imagine that I could read anything as small as an address on an envelope."

"Thank you," Lucy said, "thank you. I'll never forget what you're doing for me."

"Your Highness is too kind." Mr. Kapur bowed again. "I'm afraid this has been a very disappointing interview for you. Shall I summon your nurse before I depart?"

"Yes," Lucy said, "please." There was obviously to be no break in the charade.

An hour later, Mr. Kapur returned, and she gave him an anonymous letter addressed to . . . but then Mr. Kapur could have no idea who it was addressed to because Mr. Kapur had forgotten his glasses.

Evidently her letter was never mailed but was taken directly to the Indian ambassador in Sindhala, perhaps in a diplomatic pouch. Lucy never knew for sure. She only knew that a mere four days later Mr. Kapur reappeared at the hospital with a small package under his arm. The package, which was wrapped in coarse brown paper, was bound with a strand of hemp. It was obvious that it had been opened and inspected. "Your Highness may wish to look at this in private," Mr. Kapur suggested.

Thanking him, Lucy ran to her room and tore off the brown paper. Under it was a cardboard box, and inside that box was another box made of ivory and gold. On the sides and lid Patanese court ladies sat beside a pool filled with swans and lotus blossoms. Lucy wept, kissed the box, pressed it to her chest, and then opened it. Inside were two passports, one for an Australian citizen named Katherine White, and one for a United States citizen named Louise Crest. Under the passports were a roll of bills and a triple strand of diamonds so brilliant that she gasped when she saw them. On the bottom was a letter in Mila's handwriting.

>   Dear Patanese citizen,
>   I have not been told your name, only that you are in trouble, but your plea has made me sure that you are more precious than any gift I could offer you. Australia is a good place for an English-speaking person to vacation for six months or so without being noticed, especially if she is being looked for elsewhere. To speak more plainly, you are in grave danger. The enemy, whose name I will not mention, has agents in many countries, but there are not many of them, I think, not enough to find someone who wishes to remain anonymous.
>   The money and the diamonds are to help you in your new life. I would have sent my heart too, but it wouldn't fit in the box.
>   Every day when I sit down to meditate, I bless the fact that you are alive and well. I miss you and love you and long to see you, but I understand your decision to leave. I wanted to give you a kingdom, but for now at least, it seems all I can offer you is your freedom; so go, and be free, and prosper. I will always love you with all my heart. M.

Lucy's eyes filled with tears, and she felt something great and dark rushing toward her. She longed to talk to Mila, to touch him, to look at him even from a distance. It might be years before she saw him again.

• 8 •

February was high summer in Australia. South of Sydney the public beaches smoldered in the sun while sharks patrolled just outside the safety nets. At Bondi, a large pink and brown stucco pavilion lay sprawled on the sand a hundred yards from the edge of the surf. Inside, Lucy sat at a small aluminium table eating lunch while all around her mobs of cheerful Aussies put away wedges of lemon meringue pie, hamburgers topped with pickled beets, and mounds of fried fish doused in malt vinegar. Taking a bite of beef pie, Lucy brushed away the flies with her free hand and watched the show. She had been in Australia for only three weeks, but already the desperate poverty of Patan and India felt like a bad dream.

She was glad Patan seemed so far away. She wanted to forget it. She looked around the pavilion, reassuring herself that no one was watching her, especially no dark, Patanese-looking foreigners. To her right two teenage boys were devouring baskets of french fries while two girls in string bikinis rubbed suntan lotion onto their shoulders and giggled. To her left an older couple was having a spat, glaring at each other as they took irritated licks from large chocolate ice-cream cones. She relaxed. I'm safe, she thought. She ate some more of her beef pie, thinking that curry would have improved it. The potatoes were a little underdone and the gravy tasted of flour.

Still, eating out in public was a treat. When she first arrived, she had been so afraid of being trailed by Arjuna's agents that she had barely ventured out of her hotel room, but in the past week she had gained more confidence. She had left India dressed in a cheap blue skirt and brown blouse, with sensible low-heeled shoes on her feet and no lipstick, looking like a missionary. It was an outfit designed to make her inconspicuous, but it was depressing to wear. Last Monday she had gotten up, put on the brown blouse, looked in the mirror, and decided that she couldn't take it another minute. An hour later, she was in a department store in downtown Sydney buying herself some decent clothes: crisp white shorts, Hawaiian-style blouses, a blue two-piece swimming suit made of shiny nylon, sandals with fat wedge-shaped heels, tennis shoes; a black silk dress for evening, a silk scarf, bell-bottom jeans, a pair of gold earrings. Money was no problem. Mr. Kapur had arranged for her to sell her diamonds before she left India and had helped her set up an account with a bank in Hong Kong that would wire her funds anywhere in the world and was not inclined to ask questions, so she bought to her heart's content. She felt a hundred times better dressed in clothes that had color and style, and no one looked twice at her. Well, that wasn't exactly true. After she got rid of the missionary outfit, the Australian men did look at her. They sized her up and whistled sometimes, but it was all harmless and cheerful and even slightly flattering. Not that she had any interest in them.

The truth was, the more the Aussie men looked at her, the more she missed Mila. Taking another bite of beef pie, she wondered what he was doing at this very minute. She liked to imagine that he was thinking of her, but he was probably asleep since it was early morning in Sindhala. Still, to comfort herself she imagined him sitting in the garden behind their apartment, but no matter how hard she tried to imagine him smiling, his face stayed pale and worried. If he had been real, she could have taken him in her arms and told him that she loved him, and then surely he would have smiled at her, but he was out of reach; he was only an image, a memory. And the worst of it was, he had faded a little, too, over the past few weeks, dulled around the edges so that the details of his face were no longer perfectly distinct. His eyes, for example: she could have sworn that she would never forget them, but now when she tried to conjure them up they weren't quite right. It made her sad to think that she might forget anything about Mila.

Enough of this. It wasn't healthy. She was here, in Australia, in a pavilion by the beach. Get a grip on yourself, Constable, she thought. You can't live in dreams and memories, and don't forget that most of those dreams—Mila excepted—are nightmares, anyway. It's time to get on with your life.

Pushing back her plate, she abandoned her half-eaten pie, got to her feet, and made her way to the nearest public phone. Reaching into the pocket of her jeans, she brought out a handful of coins and stacked them on the shelf beside her. Australian currency sported odd animals: wombats, kangaroos, emus, spiny anteaters. Dropping a shilling into the slot, she began the task of placing a long distance call to Cassie. She had waited three long weeks for this moment, and common sense dictated that she wait longer, but last night she had cracked, walked to a store, and persuaded a clerk to give her several pounds' worth of change. All night she had debated the wisdom of calling; even now as she dialed she was still debating it, but the temptation to hear Cassie's gasp of astonishment was irresistible. "Where the hell are you, Lou?" Cassie would yell, and Lucy would tell her, in guarded terms, not being too specific.

The call took a long time to put through, and she had to keep feeding shillings into the slot, but she didn't mind because in a moment Cassie or Andy would answer. She imagined the phone ringing in Ann Arbor, waking them up, Cassie cursing and fumbling for it and dropping it on the floor. "It's me," she would say, "me," no name, and Cassie would be speechless for a minute and then say, "Well, it's about time you called! Andy and I had nearly given up on you."

The ringing stopped suddenly and Lucy prepared herself to say hello to Cassie, but instead the Australian operator came back on the line. "I'm sorry," the operator said, "but the number has been disconnected."

Disconnected? Hadn't Cassie been paying her phone bill? She asked if there were any forwarding number.

"No, love," the operator said cheerfully, "no forwarding number."

Lucy felt anxious. She hadn't expected Cassie to be hard to get hold of. Where had she gone? Had she and Andy split up? Had they moved to a bigger apartment? Maybe Cassie had been in an accident or . . . She told herself that she was worrying unnecessarily. There was probably some perfectly good explanation. Maybe Cassie had decided phones were bourgeois. She wouldn't put that past her. Cassie had always said Ma Bell needed to be taken down a notch or two. "Could you please ask the American operator if there are any listings in Ann Arbor, Michigan, for an Andrew or Cassandra Rabinowitz?"

There was a short silence while the operators consulted. The teenage boys finished their french fries and ordered seconds. The couple that had been fighting got to their feet and strolled out of the pavilion with their arms around each other. Just as they reached the door, the Australian operator came back on the line. "Sorry, love, no such listing."

"Please," Lucy pleaded, "isn't there any way you can find out where they might have moved to?" There was another longer silence.

"Afraid we're up a gum tree here," the operator said, "the Yank operator says that information isn't available."

Lucy thanked her and hung up the phone. Emus, wombats, and kangaroos spewed out of the coin return, and she picked them up feeling puzzled and disappointed. She wondered if she could risk calling Quinn's lab and asking for Cassie's phone number. Here in Australia the idea that she had a price on her head seemed ridiculous, but Mr. Kapur had warned her that she was in danger, and Mila had confirmed it, and even though she had seen no signs of anyone following her, she had to take the threat seriously. Suppose Quinn himself answered the phone? She didn't much like Cassie's father, but maybe he wouldn't recognize her voice, and if he did, surely she could make up some sort of explanation short of telling him all the details. She weighed the pros and cons and decided to take the chance that Quinn could keep a secret.

She had to wait an hour until it was nine in the morning in Ann Arbor, and she spent most of that time drinking one cold soda after another and fretting about Cassie. Twice she almost decided that it would be folly to talk to Quinn, but when the time came, she gritted her teeth, jammed the coins in the phone, and waited while the operator again went through the routine of making an international connection. She might as well have saved herself the worry because Quinn not only did not answer his own phones, his secretary informed her that the professor was on sabbatical and not due to return until late October.

"Professor Quinn is in Europe," she said, "then he's going to the Soviet Union, Africa, Indonesia, Japan . . ." Lucy let Quinn's travelogue roll past. When the secretary paused, she asked the obvious question.

"Do you have his daughter's phone number, by any chance? I'm an old friend of Cassie's and I'm trying to get in touch with her."

There was a long silence on the other end of the line. When the secretary finally spoke, all the cheerfulness seemed to have been drained out of her voice. "I'm sorry," she said, "but I don't believe Cassie has a phone; at least if she has, she hasn't given us her new number."

"When she comes to the lab, perhaps you could ask her—"

"Cassie no longer works here."

"She doesn't?" Lucy was disappointed but not too surprised. Cassie must have had another fight with her father and moved out of his lab again. "What about Andy, surely you could get their home number from him." This time there was such a long silence on the other side of the line that she thought she had been disconnected. "Hello," she said, "hello, are you still there?"

"I'm sorry," the secretary said, "this really isn't something I feel comfortable discussing. I'm afraid that you're going to have to talk to Professor Quinn personally if you want any information about his daughter."

"But you just told me that he's on sabbatical until *October*." She tried for a few more minutes to get an explanation out of Quinn's secretary, but the more she persisted the less communicative the woman became. Finally she gave up.

The conversation left her with an eerie feeling. Something had to be seriously wrong. There were too many mysteries and unanswered questions. She tried to convince herself that Cassie and her father had had another fight, one so bad that neither she nor Andy was on speaking terms with him any longer. Perhaps Quinn had failed Andy a second time, and Andy and Cassie had left Ann Arbor altogether. Still, things had been going so well for Andy the last time she spoke to Cass on the phone. And even if he had failed his prelims, that didn't explain why the secretary was so reluctant to talk. Maybe the secretary was Quinn's lover and she was jealous of Cassie. Quinn seemed to cut quite a swath through his graduate students, so why not his office staff? But in that case, wouldn't the secretary have been in Europe with Quinn? None of this made any sense. It was all very upsetting.

She weighed the change in her hand and wondered if it would do any good to try Information in Cambridge and New York. Andy's family lived either in Brooklyn or in the Bronx—she couldn't remember which—and she had no idea what his father's first name was. She wondered how many Rabinowitzes lived in the greater New York area.

Fifteen minutes and many coins later, she learned from New York City Information that there were over 250. Discouraged, she hung up the phone. It was crazy to think of calling all of them from Australia on the off chance that she might hit the right one. She tried to think of some other way to contact Cassie, but nothing sprang to mind. She would just have to wait.

Time passed slowly after that. February seemed like a long month, crammed with endless, empty weeks of glittering blue sky and rising temperatures that left her feeling as if the normal progression of seasons had been turned upside down. The days crawled by with nothing to mark them off from one another; at night strange stars appeared: the Magellanic Clouds, Achernar, the Southern Cross pointing toward Antarctica. Deciding that she had to get her bearings, she went to a large bookstore on Pitt Street and bought guides to Australia, but that only served to make her feel more like a stranger. How could a person born in a temperate climate ever hope to feel at home in a country where tigers were marsupial, picnickers were eaten by crocodiles, and one of the biggest annual sporting events was a camel race?

By the time March finally arrived, she was thoroughly sick of sitting alone in her hotel room reading. Taking on a new identity had been exciting at first, but as the days continued their slow crawl Katherine White began to feel like an ill-fitting mask that rubbed in all the wrong places. Katherine was a cipher, a woman without a past who couldn't run the risk of making friends or taking a job, and Lucy longed to be rid of her. At night she dreamed lonely dreams: she would find herself struggling across a vast, featureless plain toward an uncertain destination; sometimes she was deaf or mute; and often she was under water, swimming through a thick, green silence, trying to catch up with groups of nameless people who had sailed off and left her behind.

On the tenth of March she woke up before dawn, feeling jittery and restless. Grabbing one of the guidebooks, she began to leaf through it, hoping to read herself back to sleep. Instead she read (for perhaps the sixth time) a glowing description of the outback. Why am I here? she asked herself, tossing the book back down on the night table. Doesn't it stand to reason that it would be even harder for Arjuna's men to find me if I were moving around? Wondering why she had taken so long to arrive at such an elementary realization, she leapt out of bed and began to pack.

Five hours later she was on a plane to Adelaide, and shortly thereafter she was sitting in the observation car of the Old Ghan Railroad, heading toward Alice Springs. For the next two and a half days the train carried her into the heart of the outback, over thousands of miles of blood-red earth covered by spinifex bushes. It was a land so breathtakingly empty that it made her feel as if she were being transported back to the moment when the first humans set foot on the continent. Defeated by the sheer immensity of it all, she retreated to the club car and spent the last twenty hours of the sixty-hour journey drinking tepid soda water, reading dog-eared magazines, and trying not to look out the window. The final leg of the trip was excruciatingly hot, and the flies were intolerable.

Still, she was less lonely traveling than staying in one place, so from that day on she moved from one part of Australia to another with a relentlessness born of desperation. She couldn't have said exactly what she was running from: from Arjuna's men, certainly, but from other things too. Perhaps she was trying to outdistance her own past or erase the unfamiliar name in her passport. Or perhaps on some deep, almost unconscious level she was imitating her mother, repeating that primal flight, running for the sheer hell of it, slamming the kitchen door, walking out on life. Whatever the reason, she kept to herself and made no friends. The cities blended into one unmemorable megapolis—Darwin-Cairns-Townsville-Melbourne-Perth—surrounded by flat horizons, herds of stringy cattle. Sometimes she imagined that she was being followed. When that happened she changed hotels quickly or left town ahead of schedule. Those incidents frightened her, but she could never be sure if they were real.

Gradually she beat the edge off her restlessness, and it became less compulsive. She found herself sleeping later, spending longer at each stopping point. In mid-April she decided to head north again to a place called Green Island to try her hand at snorkeling. Green Island was on the Great Barrier Reef, and she was looking forward to a few weeks of soaking up the sun and looking at exotic fish through her new mask, but less than three days after she arrived the morning paper hit her breakfast table like an explosion, blowing her newfound sense of complacency apart.

Cairns Post
Cairns, Australia
April 14, 1968
    PRINCESS OF PATAN DEAD. The former Lucy Constable, Princess of Patan, died after a brief illness while on a religious retreat at the Nokalu monastery in northeastern Patan. Often called the Princess of Paradise, Miss Constable married Milarepa Tsayi Koron, Crown Prince of Patan, in 1966 shortly after her graduation from Radcliffe College . . .

Lucy spread out the front page of the newspaper and reread the story, feeling chilled and frightened although it was already a good ninety degrees in the shade. According to the *Cairns Post* she had died on April thirteenth. The article continued for three full columns complete with a photograph of her in her wedding sari. King Marpa had issued an official statement of grief on behalf of the royal family and declared a month of mourning. The monks of the Nokalu monastery had cremated her body so that it could be transported down the steep trails to Sindhala. The funeral was to take place on Wednesday.

She stopped reading and looked at the breakfast table, at ordinary things like the salt and pepper shakers and the napkins. Her heart was beating so fast it made her dizzy, and her mouth felt dry. Who had made up this story? Was it a parting gift from Mila, who was trying to give her a chance to start all over again without fear of pursuit? Was it some piece of labyrinthine intrigue cooked up by Arjuna to warn her that if she ever tried to surface as Lucy Constable she would be instantly eliminated? Had Marpa concocted this lie to save face? Had a real body been found and misidentified as her own?

She thought of a hundred questions, but none of them had answers. She was dead—officially, publicly dead. It was upsetting to read your own obituary; it was like swallowing cubes of ice or letting someone put shovels of dirt over your eyes. It froze you up, blocked you off from the world. And yet . . . suppose that headline had read PRINCESS OF PATAN MISSING, wouldn't that have been worse? I'm safer this way, she thought, I really am. I should be relieved. But she wasn't relieved. She tried to pull her own death over her and find comfort in it, but it felt bad. It didn't fit, and it scared her.

Now, more than ever, she wished that she could call Cassie. Cassie was going to flip out when she heard the news. She might even fly to Patan for the funeral. If she knew Cassie, Cassie wasn't going to be pleased when she found out that on the day after her "death" Lucy had been sitting in an Australian beach resort reading her own obituary and drinking fresh mango juice.

Lucy tore out the obituary notice, folded it in half, and stuffed it in her beach bag next to her sunglasses. She was tempted to fly straight to the States, track Cassie down, and break the news to her before she wasted money on a plane ticket to Sindhala, but it was still too soon to resurface, even as Louise Crest. *Six months,* Mila had suggested. *Grave danger.* She imagined Arjuna, gold chains around his neck, mirrored sunglasses. Pulling the article out of her beach bag, she unfolded it and read it again, trying to convince herself that Arjuna's men had stopped looking for her, but the more she read, the more she was convinced that he was behind the whole thing.

Infinite regressions, she thought, mirrors within mirrors. She could put a stop to all this; she could go to the phone and call the press and tell them that she was alive. She could erase that headline and replace it with a bigger one. PRINCESS OF PATAN ALIVE.

Don't do it, part of her warned.

Why not? It's my life and I don't intend to die until I'm good and ready.

Because you could get yourself shot, Constable. That's why.

I'll demand protection from Interpol, from the FBI, from . . .

No one will protect you; you aren't a citizen of anywhere anymore. You have no country. And even if you hired bodyguards, Arjuna's men might get past them.

The dialogue went on in her mind, spinning out circle after circle. She felt trapped, as if once again Arjuna had thrown his web over her, and that made her angry.

I will not spend the rest of my life in hiding! she thought defiantly.

But for now, the voice of reason pleaded, *you won't do anything rash, because the consequences could be terrible. Cool down. Let time pass.*

In the end, the voice of reason won. Giving a sigh of exasperation, she got to her feet and headed back to her room to pack. No more fresh mango juice, no more skin diving on the Great Barrier Reef: she had just realized that if she wanted to preserve her anonymity she was going to have to return to Sydney or Adelaide or some other large city. With her face plastered all over the newspapers, there was too good a chance someone on Green Island would recognize her.

April passed, May passed, June passed. Time slowed to a crawl again, and except for the weather, which was growing gradually colder, all of Australia seemed to be preserved in a giant globe of amber like an insect from some prehistoric era. Meanwhile, across the Pacific, the United States was whirling through enormous transformations that left Lucy breathless when she read about them in the newspapers. The summer of 1968 was proving to be one of the worst anyone could remember. Martin Luther King was dead; Robert Kennedy was dead. Chicago had exploded as police clashed with students in a bloody riot. The black ghettos were burning; the Russians had invaded Czechoslovakia; French students had immobilized Paris; the war in Vietnam was getting bloodier and bloodier. All summer the newspapers arrived in Sydney every morning like Old Testament prophets crying that the end of the world was at hand. Lucy couldn't bear to read them anymore. She no longer understood what was happening in the States. Had the whole country gone crazy? Was there going to be a revolution?

On August first, she decided that she had hidden in Australia long enough. She had spent her six months in limbo; it was time to go home while there was still a home left to go home to. Tearing Katherine White into shreds, she flushed her down the toilet and became Louise Crest. The next morning she boarded a nonstop flight to Oahu.

It was quite a homecoming. She flew straight from Oahu to Detroit, passing through customs in Los Angeles without getting a second glance from the immigration officers. Her first impression was that nothing much had changed, but when she got to Detroit, exhausted and suffering from jet lag, she discovered that while she had been in Patan, the future had arrived in Michigan.

Her first hint that things were different came from a strange-looking newspaper called the *Argus* that she bought to read in the limo from the airport to Ann Arbor. The paper sported headlines drawn in psychedelic letters. According to a front-page story, a recent mass protest against ROTC recruitment had led to the police using something called "tear gas tanks" to quell the crowd. Windows had been broken; students had been clubbed to the ground and arrested. In the middle of it all a couple had evidently thrown off their clothes and engaged in sexual intercourse while an audience of several thousand sympathizers cheered them on, singing "Why Don't We Do It in the Road?" According to the *Argus*, sex in public was part of a plan to "destroy the war machine," although how the two were connected was more than she could fathom. She had read about the changes in American society so she wasn't taken completely by surprise, but seeing the photos on the front page of the *Argus* was another matter. A particularly memorable one featured a long-haired, bearded student in a gas mask heaving a tear gas canister back at the police.

The next day, after sleeping for ten solid hours, she got up and went out to confront this new world. As she walked from her rented room to the University of Michigan campus, everything seemed harder, slicker, and faster, as if the whole country had stepped onto a giant merry-go-round. Despite the war, there were signs of prosperity everywhere. Shops were crammed with goods: small appliances, television sets, expensive clothes. A whole new industry seemed to have grown up. Between downtown Ann Arbor and the university she counted six boutiques that featured things like giant plastic "surrealistic" pillows, expensive boxes of tarot cards, Day-Glo face paint, intricately decorated clips for holding on to the butts of marijuana cigarettes, tiny pipes for hashish, and—rather ironically from her perspective—rack after rack of expensive dresses made from the same Indian cottons that clad the poor of Patan.

On telephone poles psychedelic posters advertised rock concerts and community events. A band called the MC FIVE was going to give a benefit performance for the legalization of marijuana. Another band called Ozone was giving a free concert in the park on Saturday. There was going to be a pig roast, and the police were invited. Afterward a group called Students for Violent Non-Action were sponsoring an Eat-the-Rich Dance and were inviting people to come dressed as their "favorite peace fantasy."

Lucy strolled along, deciphering the Art Nouveau lettering on the posters and growing more and more disoriented. It was all too much to deal with on an empty stomach. Retreating into a quiet-looking coffeehouse on the edge of campus, she ordered a bowl of homemade tomato soup and a glass of milk. The soup was wonderful, full of sweet carrots and ripe tomatoes and fresh spices, and it came with a large wedge of fresh whole wheat bread. After months of eating lamb and overcooked vegetables, it seemed like ambrosia. She finished one portion, ordered herself another, and consumed it slowly, feeling more relaxed with each spoonful.

Today she would begin looking for Cassie in earnest. A quick survey of the Ann Arbor and Detroit telephone directories that morning had turned up nothing, nor had a call to university Information. She had Cassie and Andy's last address, so she might drop by and see if they were still there or if the new residents knew where they had moved to. As a last resort she could always try another call to Quinn's lab, although she didn't relish the idea of taking on his secretary again. Maybe if she showed up in person, she could get one of Quinn's graduate students to tell her what had happened to Cassie and Andy, but she was reluctant to chance it. Quinn was a magnet for high-powered botany types. It would be just her luck to run into someone from Harvard. She wasn't ready to be recognized, not yet. When the princess of Patan was resurrected, she would pick her own time and place.

She was just pushing the empty soup bowl away from her when she heard loud guitar music followed by a voice that sent a chill up her spine. The voice, loud and gravelly, wasn't the natural voice of the singer. It was more of a commercial product: a cross between Bob Dylan and Woody Guthrie remodeled into a moan of rebellion, but she recognized it at once.

> *The streets are full of fighting kids*
> *Stoned on love and peace.*
>
> *Get out of our way!*
> *We're the future and you know it.*
> *Get out of our way*
> *Before you blow it.*
> *Get out of our way!*
> *Hey, Hey*
> *We're the future*
> *And you know it.*

It was David. She sat for a moment, flooded by memories, as his voice blared through the coffeehouse. She saw him in his room in Dunster sitting on the floor playing his guitar and harmonica. She wondered if he still had his old peacoat, the one with the ripped pockets she'd sewn up for him on a winter evening a million years ago. She wondered if he was still writing poetry. She wondered if he ever thought about her and if he'd felt anything when he heard that she was dead.

A couple at the adjoining table began tapping their feet to the music, and the man, who had blond hair down to his shoulders, smiled at the pale young woman across from him and murmured: "Right on; that's great. We're the future."

"Excuse me," Lucy said, "but is that a very popular song?"

Both of them looked at her and laughed pleasantly, the way you might laugh at someone who was drunk and harmless. "You must be kidding," the man said. "That's 'Get Out of Our Way.' It's been at the top of the charts for weeks. I probably hear it five times a day minimum; the only thing you hear more often is 'Hey Jude.' "

"Did you just get back from the Peace Corps or something?" the young woman asked, toying with a strand of beads around her neck. She was wearing a semitransparent cotton blouse and had half a dozen pretty silk ribbons twisted into her hair as if she were going to a costume party.

Lucy nodded, thinking that was an excellent way to explain why she had no idea what was going on: she'd been in the Peace Corps. "I was in Guatemala," she said. She had once written a fifty-page paper on Guatemala, and perhaps she could still remember enough about it to pass for a returned volunteer. "I was in Quezaltenango."

The young woman smiled eagerly. "Wow, Guatemala! Was it far out?"

"Very." The expression "far out" was new to her, and she filed it away for future reference.

"Jake and I are going to get out of this country ourselves pretty soon," she said, as she toyed with one of her ribbons. "We're tired of struggling in the belly of the beast. After we graduate, Jake loses his two-S, so instead of going to Canada to avoid the draft, he and I are going to Patan. We hear it's a far out place."

The mention of Patan unnerved Lucy so much that she knocked over a bottle of ketchup. She went after it but found Jake ahead of her. Gallantly he retrieved the bottle and presented it to her, his face red and rather delighted as if chasing ketchup bottles in coffeehouses were a new sport.

"Judy and I are going to get enlightened in Patan," he said. "We hear they have some pretty heavy lamas there."

Wishing them luck, Lucy paid her bill and fled to the street with the sound of David's voice following her.

We're the future and you know it.
Get out of our way
Before you blow it.

The last address she had for Cassie and Andy was on a street named Cram Circle. For over a quarter of an hour she poured over a detailed map of Ann Arbor trying in vain to locate it, stumbling on it at last among a maze of small dead-end roads in the North Campus Married

Students Housing Complex. There was a free bus from the university to North Campus that ran every fifteen minutes, so she decided not to bother renting a car.

Boarding the bus, she sat back and watched Ann Arbor flow by. She was relieved to see that despite all the changes, it was still a small, very American-looking town. Except for Quinn's new lab—a huge upended rectangle of pink cement and glass that towered over the old copper-roofed buildings of the campus—there were few modern structures. The streets were broad and tree lined, the houses wooden or brick, with green lawns and gravel driveways. Only the fraternity houses were imposing; large and lavishly constructed, they sprawled at the edge of campus behind gigantic Greek letters and signs declaring that trespassing cars would be disassembled.

The married students housing complex was a warren of identical stucco cubes, perched on parklike plots among a litter of tricycles, old cars, and rusting deck chairs. Number 6 Cram Circle looked just like number 7 and number 5. Lucy was disappointed, but not particularly surprised, to see that the name on the mailbox wasn't Rabinowitz but Mbata. When she rang the bell, a black woman in a flowered robe opened the door. She was wearing a pair of yellow rubber gloves and had obviously been interrupted in the middle of doing the dishes.

"Good afternoon," the woman said politely, peeling off her gloves.

"Good afternoon," Lucy said. "I wonder if you could help me. Two friends of mine used to live here. Their names are Cassie and Andy Rabinowitz. Do you by any chance know where they've moved to?"

The woman shook her head. "I'm sorry. I recognize the name because sometimes we get their mail by mistake, but all I know is that this apartment suddenly became vacant in the middle of last semester and Baraca and I moved in."

Lucy thanked her, feeling discouraged. Where the heck had Cassie and Andy disappeared to? She was halfway down the sidewalk when she heard the woman calling after her.

"Wait please," the woman said. "I forgot; I have a letter."

Lucy hurried back up the sidewalk, and the woman shyly thrust an envelope into her hand. "It's for Mrs. Rabinowitz," she said. "Maybe at the return address they will know where your friends moved."

Lucy inspected the envelope and saw a return address for a life insurance company in Connecticut. Thanking the woman again, she stowed the letter in her purse and went back to the bus stop. On the ride to the main campus, she inspected the envelope again and decided that there was no reason why she shouldn't open it. Cassie had never been all that big on privacy, and it might contain some clue to her whereabouts. Slitting the end of the envelope with her fingernail, she pulled out the letter. It was from an organization called Browning Life Insurance, Inc.

Dear Mrs. Rabinowitz,
We are in receipt of your letter of June 10 asking us to reconsider your claim for compensation for the death of your husband, Andrew Martin Rabinowitz. We regret to say that after having submitted the matter to our adjusters, we must once again deny your claim on the grounds that Mr. Rabinowitz's death was self-inflicted. As you know, suicide on the part of the client voids the policy; hence we are not in a position to . . .

Lucy dropped the letter into her lap with a moan of anguish that brought curious stares from the people seated on either side of her. Andy was dead. Evidently he had taken his own life. No wonder she couldn't find any trace of Cassie.

The last time she had seen Andy had been at her wedding. He had asked Mila if he could kiss the bride, and then he planted a good, rousing kiss on her cheek, saying that if he got anywhere near her lips Cassie would kill him. The four of them had laughed, embraced, and everyone had seemed so happy and in love, as if life were a fine game with prizes along the way. Mila and Lucy, Cassie and Andy: they would stay married, they would be friends forever, they would grow old and trade pictures of their children and grandchildren and have wonderful reunions. Now, only two years later, she and Mila had been forced to part, and Andy—a kind, decent man, so gentle that he was reluctant to swat a fly—had turned on himself with unspeakable violence. How could he have done such a thing? What had possessed him? Sick with grief, she reread the letter, hoping there was some mistake, but the message stayed the same: suicide voided all compensation.

She was seized by a frantic urge to find Cassie. She decided that instead of getting off the bus, she would take it straight back to the married students housing complex and start knocking on doors. Surely the neighbors could tell her where Cassie had gone.

She had expected quick results, but for an hour she climbed stairs, threaded her way around rusting barbecue grills and bicycles, and knocked on doors without success. Married students at the University of Michigan apparently moved in and out faster than the occupants of a migrant labor camp. Finally, just when she was about to give up and risk a visit to Quinn's lab, she came across Frannie Stein.

Frannie, who immediately informed Lucy that she was writing a doctoral thesis on Jane Austen, appeared at the door wearing rubber thongs, a tan shirt, and baggy, Pablum-stained pants. Twin girls clung to her, eyeing Lucy shyly.

"Sure I remember Cassie," Frannie said. "She used to baby-sit for me, and wouldn't take a penny for it. I tried to pay her, but she said she didn't need the money and she liked my girls and besides she liked to have growing things around her that didn't contain chlorophyll. That was Cassie, always joking."

"Do you know where she moved to?"

"To one of the Dove People's houses." Frannie patted both her daughters soothingly. "Do you know where they are?"

Lucy shook her head.

"They're over on Arbor Street. There are three of them; I don't know which one she moved into, but they're all communal. You can't miss them. They have a giant dove painted on front." She paused and frowned. "I suppose you heard about her husband?"

"Yes." Lucy was suddenly seized by an urge to cry on this friendly woman's shoulder. "I heard."

Frannie sighed and shook her head. "It was terrible; no one could quite believe it. She was the one who found him, you know. At first she seemed to take it really well; I think she was in shock. Then when it really hit her, she started disassembling her life. She said she was disillusioned with the academic world; she dropped out of the university, and when the housing people told her she couldn't keep living in a married student's apartment any longer now that she wasn't married or a student, she moved almost overnight. I thought it was pretty cold of them to chuck her out like that, but she didn't seem to care. She came over to say good-bye carrying all her pots and pans and her toaster, and she gave them to me. She told me she was giving away almost everything she owned and moving into the Dove People's commune to work for peace."

"Why do you think he did it?"

Frannie shrugged, and the corners of her mouth tilted down. She drew her girls closer. "That's what we all wanted to know. Why? Andy seemed like such a nice guy, and you could tell they loved each other. So why? I don't know. No one knows except maybe Cassie."

The big lot on Arbor Street contained three houses connected by a multicolored dove of peace painted so that it spanned from the front porch of the first to the third story of the last and then flew off to lose itself in the sky. Lucy took off her sweater and tied it around her waist. She hadn't felt heat and humidity like this since she left India. The sun was getting hotter by the minute, pulling up moisture from the lawns and spreading in a pall over the rooftops. For a moment she stood looking at the door bell of the first house, wondering whether this was going to be another wild-goose chase. Be here, Cassie, she thought. Reaching out, she pressed the button. The door bell played the Doxology: that had to be left over from a former tenant. No one answered, so she rang again.

"Hold on a sec," a friendly voice called. There was the sound of someone running, and then the door opened. She found herself confronted by a short, tubby young man in a tie-dyed T-shirt and wire-rimmed glasses. Pinned to his shirt was a large yellow button that said Children Are Just Younger People. "Hi," the man said, "what can I do for you?"

"I'm looking for Cassie Rabinowitz."

The man's face froze suddenly. "Oh, you are, huh. Why?"

"I'm a friend of hers."

"What sort of friend?"

"We were roommates in college. I just got back from the Peace Corps—I've been in Guatemala—and I thought I'd look her up, but I've been having trouble finding her. A former neighbor of hers out on North Campus told me she'd moved here."

The man relaxed. "Oh," he said. "You're dressed so straight that I thought maybe you were the FBI. They've been keeping the place under surveillance ever since Ozone played a fund raiser to bail out the White Panthers." He extended his hand. "My name's Rusty."

"Hi, Rusty, my name is Lu—" She stopped in midsentence. "Louise," she said hastily, "Louise Crest." At the mention of the FBI she had panicked, but then she remembered that she was dead and that no one would be looking for her. Rusty was trying to give her some kind of strange handshake, but she fumbled it so he gave up and just stood there smiling. "Could I come in?"

"Sure, but I should warn you that a member of the family is in the process of giving birth."

Lucy was slightly horrified by the thought that one of the female commune members might be lying in the living room on the couch having a baby without benefit of anesthetic or medical attention. "Maybe I should come back later," she offered. "I wouldn't want to barge in at a time like this."

"Oh, it's just Miss Meow," Rusty reassured her as he ushered her into the hallway, "Paz's cat. Meow's produced three kittens so far, and it looks like at least two more are on the way. We thought she was too young to get pregnant; in fact we were going to have her spayed, but she beat us to it."

The hallway was full of shoes and boots and a rack of coats that seemed to indicate that quite a number of people were living in the house. The living room was decorated in what Kathy DeVelt used to call Grad Student Baroque. A battered couch slumped in one corner flanked by two large, shabby easy chairs. Several mattresses covered with Indian bedspreads lay on the floor along with piles of pillows, some balls of yarn, a stack of pamphlets, a half dozen back issues of the *Argus*, and one large rather moth-eaten-looking teddy bear. Board and brick bookcases lined the walls, and most of the windows were covered with squares of colored tissue paper, providing a stained-glass effect. Over the fireplace, someone had nailed a huge orange-and-green batiked banner that proclaimed Peace Now! To the left, the hall opened on a large dining room, empty except for a long table made out of sawhorses and unfinished doors, and a loom that occupied most of the rest of the available space.

"Make yourself comfortable," Rusty said. "I've got to go have a look at Miss Meow, and then I'll go find Paz."

"Is Cassie home?"

Rusty shook his head. "She used to live here, but she doesn't anymore. She moved a couple of months ago. Paz was her roommate. She can fill you in. It's a long story."

Disappointed, Lucy sat down in one of the easy chairs and waited for Paz—whoever that was—to appear and tell her what had become of Cassie. The books in the bookcase were an interesting assortment, everything from high school American history texts to advanced physics. There was a whole section on pacifism, including works by Tolstoy, Thoreau, and Kropotkin. She was just taking a look at *Civil Disobedience* when a tall, dark woman in a blue terry-cloth bathrobe wandered into the room. Her toenails were covered with chipped red paint, and she looked exhausted.

"Hi," the woman said, "I'm Paz. Are you Louise?"

"Yes." Lucy got to her feet, but Paz had other ideas. Falling wearily to the floor she sat cross-legged on the nearest mattress.

"I work the night shift," she said. "That's why I'm home now when almost everyone else is out. Pizza Bob's . . . open twenty-four hours . . . best pizza in town. Ever hear of it?" Paz didn't wait for an answer. "Not to mention that I'm enrolled in law school, running the rent strike, and doing most of the dishes around here. But that's life in the Movement. Miss Meow just had her fourth. Where did you tell Rusty you'd been for the last two years?"

"Guatemala." Lucy was finding Paz's rapid leaps from one topic to another rather hard to follow. "I was in the Peace Corps in Quezaltenango."

"Ever meet Cheryl?"

"No. Cheryl who?"

"Cheryl was in Guatemala. In Huchuetenango. She was in the Peace Corps too. I'm surprised the two of you never met." She looked at Lucy thoughtfully. "I hear you're looking for Cassie?"

"Yes, I am. I'm an old friend of hers."

"Look," Paz said, "I'll level with you. Before I tell you where Cassie is, I have to ask you a few questions to make sure you're not looking for her for the wrong reasons. I know it sounds paranoid, but we think the Dove houses have been singled out for some kind of federal harassment because of our peace work. Our phones are definitely tapped. Our mail isn't getting to us. Cars park across the street with guys in them and they don't move for hours. Why the feds would bother to watch us is more than I can figure out because we're absolutely dedicated to nonviolent means of protest. It's a waste of the taxpayers' money, but people in these houses have been getting pretty freaked out, so I really can't tell you anything until I make sure you really are Cassie's friend."

Lucy wasn't particularly happy at the thought of being interrogated, but she didn't seem to have much choice if she wanted to find out where Cassie was. She thought about how her own phone had been tapped, and that made her feel more sympathetic. "Ask me anything about her you want," she told Paz. "I've known Cassie since we were both sixteen. We went to high school together."

Paz bit her lower lip and thought for a moment. Her hair hung down around her face in damp strings. Evidently Lucy had gotten her out of the shower. "What's Cassie's favorite snack?" she asked.

"That's easy: Hershey's chocolate syrup on cottage cheese."

Paz smiled, obviously relieved that Lucy had come up with the right answer. "Her favorite color?"

"Orange when she feels like annoying her father; gray when she's in her dutiful daughter mood." Why did she always end up in conversations where she had to prove her identity? She thought of Mr. Kapur and his notebook. At least Paz wasn't writing this all down.

"Her favorite form of exercise?"

"She doesn't have one. Cassie hates all forms of exercise unless you count wandering around swamps photographing plants. Oh, I forgot, she once took judo; she claimed she liked banging people down on the mat, but that only lasted a month or two."

"Good," Paz nodded, "you do know her. I apologize for putting you through this, but these are weird times."

"So now can you tell me where she is?"

"She's in Boston."

"Why did she leave Ann Arbor?"

"Like Rusty probably told you, it's a long story. I suppose you know her husband swallowed a cup of coffee laced with cyanide."

Lucy winced. "I knew Andy had committed suicide, but I didn't know any of the details. Poor Cass, how horrible for her."

Paz nodded again, and her wet hair flapped softly against her cheeks. Her expression was sympathetic. "Cass was really broken up. When she moved in here, she talked about nothing else. She claimed her father pushed Andy into it—not on purpose, she never went that far—but she blamed him for what happened."

"Cassie never got along with her father," Lucy observed.

"No, I don't suppose anyone really does." Paz leaned back against the side of the couch, stretched out her legs, and crossed her bare ankles. "Quinn's a hard man to like, but he's a genius and his students hang around him hoping it will rub off." Paz shrugged and sighed softly. "In Andy's case the hanging around seemed to have worked. Cassie told me that Andy was doing research on plant growth hormones when he stumbled on something really wonderful: he found a substance that made plants develop much faster than normal." Her pale face colored and she waved her arms dramatically, letting the sleeves of her robe tumble to her elbows. "Just imagine: once you got the whole thing worked out, you might be able to have two crops a summer instead of one, feed the hungry of the world. According to Cassie, Andy was ecstatic. He went to Quinn and told him that life on this planet was about to improve in a big way. Andy, according to all reports, was an idealist."

"Yes," Lucy nodded, "he was. The last time I talked to Cassie, she told me he was on the verge of a breakthrough, but I didn't know he'd succeeded."

Paz frowned. "It would have been better for everyone concerned if his experiments had failed. Quinn had no interest in feeding the hungry. Everybody has known for years that he gets a lot of his funding from the Department of Defense. When he heard of Andy's discovery, he immediately saw other possibilities that neither Cassie nor Andy had ever thought of. I don't quite understand the technical details, but Quinn evidently realized almost at once that if you dumped enough of this stuff on plants they'd grow so fast that all their leaves would fall off and you'd end up with a super defoliant that would make Agent Orange look tame. So he called the DOD and told them the good news."

"Is that why Andy . . . killed himself?" She still had trouble saying the word.

Paz shook her head. "No, Cassie said Andy was upset, but not completely surprised. That was only the start. Things got worse."

"How could they?"

"Easy. Partly, according to Cassie, it was her own fault. When she found out what her father had done, she jumped on Andy's case. She has a temper, but on this occasion her anger was, in my opinion, righteous. She insisted that the two of them confront her father and do everything they could to stop him from helping the DOD develop the stuff into something that could be dumped on the jungles of Vietnam, but—surprise—Andy refused."

"Why?"

Paz shrugged. "He claimed that he was being patriotic, although if you ask me, he was badly mistaken. Evidently he'd lost a brother in Korea and thought that if you could save one American life by stripping Vietnam bare, then maybe you should do it. Also he was ambitious; he couldn't bear to throw his career away, not when he'd just made a discovery that was going to catapult him to the top. Meanwhile Quinn kept whispering in his ear that everything was okay, that science was apolitical, that just because you discovered something you weren't responsible for how it was used. From Cassie's point of view, Andy went over to the other side. She told me that he kept insisting he was doing 'pure research.'"

"It must have made her sick to hear him talk like that."

Paz nodded and said that sick hadn't been the word for it. Cassie had felt completely betrayed. She had stormed into her father's office and confronted him and told him she was ashamed to be his daughter, and then Quinn had called Andy in and dressed him down good for not controlling his wife. Andy had apologized—actually apologized—and said he'd keep Cassie in line in the future. Paz rolled her eyes. "When Cassie heard that, she really hit the ceiling. She and Andy had the fight to end all fights. According to her, he screamed that she was trying to sabotage his career, and she screamed that he was a coward and a rotten little sellout, and then they both broke down and confessed how much they still loved each other. The fighting was killing them, you understand. Neither of them could bear it any longer, so they negotiated a peace treaty: Cassie packed up her cameras and went to spend the Christmas holidays in the Everglades photographing plants, and Andy stayed in Ann Arbor. They were going to think over their relationship while they were apart and figure out how to keep from hurting each other, only they never had a chance because when she came back, he was dead." Paz paused, looked at Lucy and then at the banner over the fireplace.

"Why," Lucy asked, "did he do it? I still don't get it."

Paz got to her feet. "Come see Miss Meow's kittens." She started walking toward the door.

"What?"

"The kittens," Paz said, "the ones in the kitchen. Come have a look at them."

"But this is no time to look at kittens." She couldn't believe that Paz was actually about to walk out of the room. "You were telling me about Andy, about why he killed himself. I can look at the kittens later, but now I want to know what happened. Tell me the rest of the story."

"Come see Miss Meow's kittens," Paz insisted. "They explain everything."

In the kitchen Rusty was kneeling beside a cardboard box. Inside was a small yellow-and-orange cat with languid green eyes and a huge, fluffy tail.

"Meet Miss Meow," Paz said. "She's the daughter of Cassie's cat, Watusi, Junior. When Cassie left she couldn't take Watusi and her kittens with her, so she gave them away. Meow is the only member of the family left on the premises because I'm partial to orange cats and I adopted her." She turned to Rusty. "How many of the kittens are screwed up?" she asked.

"Two," Rusty said, "at least I think so. One definitely isn't right, and I'm not sure about the other one. It doesn't move much."

"I wish to God we'd had her spayed earlier." Paz frowned. "But all the books said she was too young." She waved Lucy toward the box. "Have a look," she said. "Watusi, Junior, Meow's mother, went everywhere with Cassie, especially to the lab. One day she knocked over a beaker and got soaked with a couple of quarts of XL-40 . . . stunk to high heaven. Everyone remembered the incident because it was so hard to clean the stuff off her fur. Before she got doused, Watusi had had a litter of perfectly normal kittens. When Cassie left for the holidays, she was expecting again. She gave birth to Meow and her littermates a few days after Christmas. That was what first clued Andy in that something was way out of line."

Lucy went over to the box and peered inside. Snuggled under Miss Meow, nursing happily, were five newborn kittens. Three of the nursing kittens looked healthy, but two seemed strange. Lucy looked closer and saw that one had a deformed back leg. "Oh my God!" she gasped. "Andy's compound . . ."

Paz nodded grimly. "The rate of defects is probably thirty to fifty percent; when you put rats in contact with the stuff the results are even worse." She touched the sick kitten gently with the tip of her finger. "We really screwed up by not getting Miss Meow spayed in time."

Lucy sat in the dining room across the table from Paz, drinking a cup of strong tea from a chipped mug that bore the motto Pizza Bob's. She hadn't completely recovered from the sight of the kittens. It wasn't that they were particularly horrible to look at—she'd seen far worse on the streets of Sindhala—but she couldn't help feeling sick at the idea of Andy realizing what his wonderful discovery had led to.

"When Andy went to Quinn with his suspicion that XL-40 caused birth defects," Paz said wearily, "Quinn did just what you'd expect him to do: he rationalized the whole thing, or at least he tried to, but by that time Andy wasn't buying any more rationalizations."

"So what happened?"

"They had a fight, a big, loud brawl that everyone in the lab heard. That's how Cassie found out about it later. According to all reports, Andy yelled at Quinn that the compound was going to mess up Vietnamese babies and American soldiers, while Quinn yelled back that he was being unprofessional, that he didn't have any data to support his fears."

"Sounds like a standoff."

"At first it was. The yelling went on and on. Andy screamed at Quinn that he'd tried the compound on fruit flies and that the rate of mutation was way off the charts, and Quinn ordered him to keep his mouth shut until he'd run the experiment on mammals. Finally, when Andy realized that Quinn was never going to give in, he threatened to go to the DOD himself and warn them before they started using the stuff on human beings. At that point, according to witnesses, Quinn lost it completely. He called Andy a hysterical liberal, told him to start acting like a scientist, said that if he so much as made a phone call to the DOD he'd personally see to it that Andy ended up driving a taxi for a living. 'Who is the DOD going to believe,' he kept yelling, 'me, a Nobel Prize winner, or you, a graduate student?' And then he dropped the second shoe: He told Andy that he had already sent the stuff to some field sites in California for testing. They grow a lot of cotton in that state, you see, and they have to defoliate it so they can pick it by machine. Since no one eats cotton, no one much cares what goes onto it, only the catch is that people work in the cotton fields and live around them, and some of those people are women."

"Oh, no," Lucy protested. "They couldn't have been testing it in the field, not that fast."

Paz hunched over her mug and took a long, slow drink of tea. "Maybe Quinn was lying, maybe he wasn't. Maybe he just wanted to scare Andy into thinking that he better not object because he was already in too deep. But Andy evidently thought he was telling the truth. He walked out of Quinn's lab, went straight to the Nat Sci building and told a friend of his—an entomologist named Calvin Roberts—that he needed to borrow some cyanide to make a killing jar for insects. Entomologists always have cyanide around, and Calvin gave it to him without a second thought. A few hours later, Andy was dead."

"That's crazy. Why didn't he try to fight Quinn? Why didn't he tell him to go to hell and call the DOD and tell them what he'd discovered? Why did he *kill* himself?"

"Who knows why people crack? I can't tell you what was in his mind. Cassie said he couldn't stand failure, that he always got seriously depressed when things weren't going well. Maybe he thought that he'd invented a monster that was out of control; maybe he couldn't face the idea that his career was falling apart; maybe he was angry, and instead of turning his anger on Quinn he turned it on himself. He did it, that's all any of us knows."

There was a long silence. Lucy looked down at her tea, frozen by grief and pity, appalled by what a terrible waste Andy's death had been. She felt sad and mystified. "Did he leave a note?" she asked.

Paz nodded. "Yes, he did. He wrote Cassie a one-sentence letter. All it said was 'You were right.' No signature, nothing. Just 'You were right'—the great you-told-me-so of all time. Then he drank his coffee and checked out on her permanently."

"That was a cowardly thing to do." Lucy leaned forward, her pity changing to anger. "I don't care how guilty he felt; he shouldn't have killed himself. What good did it do? He must have been temporarily insane."

Paz shrugged. "Maybe, but you have to see it from his point of view.

He probably thought of himself as a murderer. There was a good chance that unborn children were going to be maimed or killed because of him. On top of that he'd exposed both himself and Cassie over and over again. How could he face her and tell her that thanks to him they ran a thirty to fifty percent risk of having deformed children?"

"Still, he shouldn't have killed himself. What a waste. His death makes me so angry I can't even put it into words."

"That's what Cassie kept saying. She was furious at him too. She said he'd condemned and executed himself without a proper trial. She said he'd cut out on her and left her holding the bag. She said that she'd never forgive him for abandoning her."

"So after his death she came here?"

"Yes." Paz nodded and ran her finger around the rim of her cup. "But she didn't stay long. We were too tame for her. She did some draft counseling for us, but pretty soon she started complaining that only rich white guys were getting exemptions or making it to Canada. She said the war was still being fought by the poor blacks from Detroit. We could all tell that she was getting restless. She became more and more convinced that nothing she was doing here was making any difference. We all feel that way sometimes, but it was worse for Cassie. She isn't what you would call a patient person. I guess it got to be too much for her because a couple of months ago two old friends of hers came through town, and when they left she went with them. They were headed for Boston. I suppose they promised her some kind of action we couldn't give her." Paz frowned. "I've got their address upstairs, and I'll go get it for you in a minute, but if I think for a second I can remember her friends' names. You might know them. Let me see, the guy was named Steve and the woman was named—what was her name anyway?—Amy? Andrea? . . ."

"Was it Ann?"

Paz snapped her fingers. "That's right. That was it. Steve and Ann Singleton. Cassie went to Boston with them." She rose to her feet, retied her bathrobe, and started for the door. "I'll run upstairs and get her address for you." In the doorway she paused. "I gathered that Cassie was planning to join their political collective—Storm, I think they called it." She shrugged. "Doesn't sound much like Dove does it?"

· 9 ·

Lucy flew to Boston the next evening and checked into the Copley Plaza. At eight-thirty the following morning, she was standing on the corner of Marlborough and Exeter, first looking down at the piece of paper in her hand and then up at the tall, formal building that posed gracefully behind a low wrought-iron fence like a Victorian lady waiting to board a streetcar. The address Paz had given her had to be wrong. This house was three, perhaps four stories, gracious and demure, built of that rosy shade of brick that needed a good hundred years of Boston winters to look properly aged. It was much too fancy for Cassie. On the other hand, if it was Cassie's place, she had another problem: if Cassie was inside, then so were the Singletons.

Stuffing the address back into the pocket of her sweater, she cased the house one last time, looking for some sign of life, but the windows shone in the early morning sun like eyeglasses with no eyes behind them. Perhaps it was just as well that no one seemed to be up and about. If Steve and Ann saw her, they would recognize her instantly, and Ann never had been able to keep a secret. The only safe thing to do was to withdraw to some place where she couldn't be spotted, wait, and see if Cassie came out on her own.

Fortunately there was a small café across the street. Going inside she took a table by the window, ordered breakfast, and did her best to be patient. The eggs came soggy and undercooked, the toast was slightly limp, and the coffee was full of milk, Boston style. She'd forgotten that they always put milk in coffee in Boston unless you specifically asked for it black. Sipping it reluctantly, she plunged into the eggs, picking out the uncooked parts. She was just polishing off the last edible bits when the front door of the house opened and a man and a woman came down the steps. The man wore an expensive gray suit, polished black shoes, and a striped tie; he was carrying a brown briefcase and a furled black umbrella. The woman had on high heels, a green skirt, and a silk blouse. They were turned toward one another engaged in conversation, so she couldn't see their faces, but she knew at once that this couple couldn't be Ann and Steve. The last time she had seen the Singletons they had been wearing work shirts, dirty jeans, and steel-toed boots in solidarity with the working class. This pair looked like F. Scott Fitzgerald and Zelda out for a morning stroll. So much for Paz's directions.

Dumping a teaspoon of sugar into the tepid mug of milk that passed for coffee, she stirred it slowly, wondering how she was going to locate Cassie. Her disappointment was severe. Once again she had thought she was going to find her only to have the possibility evaporate.

The couple had paused at the foot of the steps. Concluding their conversation, they turned and began to walk in Lucy's direction. Dropping her teaspoon, she stared at their faces. She'd been wrong. Arm in arm, Steve and Ann Singleton passed by the window of the café: Steve, handsome and aristocratic as ever, Ann looking at him adoringly, her small, foxlike chin twitching slightly as she nodded in agreement to whatever he was saying. Lucy watched them until they turned the corner, then leapt to her feet, paid her bill, and headed for the house across the street. There was a large brass knocker on the front door. Lifting it, she banged loudly several times. Her heart was beating fast and she felt excited, because this time she was sure she had found Cassie. Cassie, she thought, be home, please.

There was a moment of silence, followed by the sound of someone coming down the stairs, humming "L'Amour" from Bizet's opera *Carmen*. She knew even before she saw her that it was Cassie. No one else plunged down the stairs that way, three at a time, and no one else ever tried to hum the high notes.

The door swung open, and Cassie stood on the threshold dressed in a suede jacket trimmed with fringe and a pair of faded bell-bottom jeans, altered by Cassie herself from the look of them since one of the inserted panels was orange and the other a violent shade of green. Oversized Mexican earrings dangled from her ears, and her hair, which had always been curly and difficult to manage, had grown into a fuzzy black crown that thrust itself out from her skull like a gigantic clump of steel wool. She looked homely and tired and wonderfully familiar, and Lucy felt like yelling with joy at the sight of her, but Cassie was the one who did the yelling. Suddenly realizing who was standing on the front step, she let out a scream of surprise and slammed the door in Lucy's face so hard that the brass knocker did a jig.

"Cassie," Lucy pleaded, grabbing the knocker and pounding it against the brass plate, "open up. It's me."

"Go away!"

"It's me, Lucy."

"Lucy's dead."

"I'm not dead."

"You are too."

"I should know if I'm dead or not. Now open the damn door."

The door cracked open an inch, and Cassie's large brown eyeball surveyed Lucy suspiciously. "Is it really you?"

"Yes, it's really me."

Throwing open the door, Cassie stood with her hands on her hips. Indignation steamed off her. "Well this is a fine thing to do to your best friend! pretending to be dead!"

Lucy was awed. She'd forgotten how big Cassie could seem when she was angry. "I knew you were going to feel this way, Cass, but I can explain. I had to . . ."

"Explain?" Cassie thundered. "You'd better explain, Lucy Corot Constable. I cried my eyes out. I actually sent flowers to your funeral, and you know how I hate sending flowers—fifty-five bucks' worth of forget-me-nots and a long letter to Mila and—" Her voice broke. Suddenly it was tender and friendly again. "Oh, Lou, you're alive, you really are." She enfolded Lucy in a bear hug. "You little rat," she cried, "I missed you so much." Tears welled up in her eyes.

"I missed you too," Lucy gasped, trying to wiggle out of her grip. Giving up the struggle, she gave in and hugged back. Cassie whooped with pleasure, lifted her up off her feet, twirled her around a few times, and set her back down in the front hall.

"Where the hell have you been?" she demanded.

"India, Australia, Ann Arbor . . ."

"Why didn't you let me know you were alive? Why didn't you call?" She pulled a Kleenex out of her pocket and blew her nose. "I've been devastated."

"I couldn't call you."

"Why not?" Cassie dabbed at her eyes, wadded the Kleenex into a ball, and stuffed it back into her pocket.

"I tried your old number in Ann Arbor, but your phone had been disconnected, and even when I got this address there was no listing under your name or under Singleton. Speaking of the Singletons, when are Steve and Ann coming back?"

"Who knows. Soon, probably."

"Then could we go somewhere else? I don't want to run into them."

"Why not?"

"It's a long story. Look, there's a café across the street; I had breakfast there and—"

"Perfect," Cassie interrupted. "They make the worst coffee in Boston. Under the circumstances I think I should take you back there and make you drink another cup by way of penance. On the other hand, if you really are sorry, I may permit you to order tea. They make it from bags, so it's possible to get it down without gagging."

As they walked to the café, Lucy tried to think of some way to ask Cassie about Andy. She could feel his death looming over every word they said, and the longer they went without mentioning it, the more awkward the unspoken topic became. We're going to have to talk about him soon, she thought, and she looked for an opening, but Cassie wasn't giving her one. She walked quickly, talking about all sorts of inconsequential things that had happened since they last spoke on the phone: she'd gone down to New York to see a show of Ansel Adams's work; she'd sold photographs to an underground newspaper; Kathy DeVelt had married the heir to an aluminum fortune; Joyce Lindsay was playing with the Boston symphony.

She's stalling, Lucy thought. She obviously isn't ready to talk about Andy yet. I've never known her to avoid painful topics. His death must have hurt her terribly. I'll have to be patient.

They found a seat by the window, and over two cups of strong tea Lucy gave Cassie an abbreviated version of the events of the past year. As she talked, Cassie's cheeks colored with excitement. "Go on," she kept saying, "you don't mean it! Marpa locked you up in the palace? I never did like Marpa. There was a plot to discredit you? Arjuna? Yes, I think I remember him from your wedding. A horrible little man in a blue uniform and high black boots, was that the one? So Mila fought for you, did he? Good for him! And you climbed over the wall to save him from going into exile! Good for you! How sad, how romantic. You must miss him awfully." She listened, fascinated, pleading with Lucy to tell her more, encouraging her to go on when she faltered, clasping her hands, and moaning with amazement in all the right places. Lucy had forgotten how satisfactory it was to tell Cassie a good story.

"So," Cassie said when she finished, "the long and the short of it is that you flew the coop, 'died,' and got yourself resurrected as Louise Crest, and right now Arjuna's men might or might not still be looking for you, so you have to lie low for a while. Do I have all this straight, Lou? Because I have to tell you that it's the most amazing story I've heard in a long time. It's frightening of course to think someone might be trying to assassinate you, and very sad that you had to leave Mila behind, but God it's exciting!"

"It's the kind of excitement I could do without," Lucy told her, "especially the hiding out part. You have no idea how lonely I got in Australia, and even now I still have to be careful that no one recognizes me. I'm in this country illegally on a forged passport. I don't really think the U.S. government would deport me to Patan if they found out I was here, but I can't be sure of that. The only good thing about being Louise Crest is that I get to live like a private person again."

Cassie sighed, picked up a stale doughnut, took a bite of it, and washed it down with a sip of tea. "You know," she said, "no offense, but I never did think you were cut out for the princess biz." She smiled warmly at Lucy, reached out across the table and squeezed her hand. "Seriously, I can't tell you how happy I am to see you. But tell me the truth, do you miss it at all? You were so rich. You were living out every woman's fantasy."

Lucy shook her head. "I never want to hear the word *Patan* again." She paused, remembering the gold lotus-shaped bed, the curve of Mila's body next to hers, the way he had told her his dreams when he woke each morning. "There's nothing I want to remember about the place except Mila." She bit her lower lip, fighting off a wave of grief. "I miss him terribly; sometimes I don't know how I'm going to make it through the day for missing him. I thought it would get better, but it doesn't. I don't see how we're ever going to get together, at least not as long as his father is alive, but I think part of me is always going to be waiting to see him again."

"Of course you miss him," Cassie agreed. "Mila was one in a million." She paused. "Like Andy."

At the mention of Andy's name a pall fell over them. Cassie dropped

Lucy's hand, and for a moment they sat in silence, staring at one another. She's finally ready to talk about it, Lucy thought, and she felt relieved and then very sad because Andy had been a good friend, and it was hard to hear his name without wanting to cry. The color had drained from Cassie's face, and she suddenly looked years older. "I suppose you heard," she continued, "about Andy, I mean." Her voice was steady, but the look in her eyes was almost unbearable.

Lucy struggled to keep from crying because if Cassie could be brave about Andy's death, then so could she. "I heard, Cass. I'm so sorry." Andy and Mila: both of them gone, but Andy gone the farthest; Andy gone forever. Who could have imagined this two years ago? Her tea suddenly tasted bitter. She swallowed hard and pushed it aside, thinking that life was much too short.

"I'm still angry at him." Cassie twisted the fringe on her jacket into a knot and looked down at the table stained with spilt tea and crumbs. Her shoulders were hunched and tense. "I've tried to forgive him, but I can't." She glanced up at Lucy, and her eyes flashed with barely suppressed rage. "First he sold out and then he abandoned me. Oh, suicide's a lovely solution; it destroys the lives of everyone you leave behind. Except the lives of people who don't give a damn about anyone, like my father." She clenched her fist into a ball and leaned forward. "Damn Larry Quinn!" she said. "He's always screwed up my life." She laughed a low, bitter laugh. "Know what the bastard's been doing? Sending me checks. I rip them into bits and send them back to him. I never want to see him again and I . . . I hate botany too. I'll hate it forever!" And then suddenly she was weeping with her hands over her face. "I loved Andy, I really did. I loved him so much. I keep thinking that if maybe I'd been more supportive and reasonable, if I hadn't flown off the handle, if—"

"Cass," Lucy begged, "don't torture yourself like this."

"Maybe I could have worked him through it," Cassie sobbed, "but I'm so much like my damned father, so self-righteous and, oh, Lou, I feel so guilty. I miss him so much. Every morning I wake up and expect him to be there beside me, only he never is. The pain's so bad. Every morning it hits me again: I loved him and I let him die. How does a person live with a thing like that? How do you get up and face yourself in the mirror and admit that you let someone you love take his own life?"

"When someone makes up his mind to die, there's nothing anyone can do to stop him."

"I feel like it's my fault, like I murdered him."

"But you didn't, Cass."

"Are you sure?"

"Yes, dear, I'm sure."

Cassie wept for a while, then stopped and dried her eyes on the sleeve of her jacket. When she looked up, she was smiling a sad, crooked smile that nearly broke Lucy's heart. "Thanks for the comfort," she said. "I've really been making a scene, haven't I? Good old Cassie Quinn; nice girl, but you can't take her out in public." She grasped Lucy's hand and held onto it. "At least you're back. Promise you won't die on me again."

"I promise."

"If you do, I'll never speak to you again." She began to laugh at her own joke. The joke was bad and her laugh was slightly hysterical, but it seemed to bring her comfort. Her face grew red and her eyes watered, so it wasn't clear if she were laughing or crying, but whatever she was doing it worked because presently she grew calm again. Catching her breath, she sat back. "Order us more tea," she commanded. Lucy was relieved to see the color coming back into her face. Cassie's sense of humor always saved her; it was a source of tremendous courage and sanity; as long as Cassie could laugh, she could survive anything.

She ordered them two more cups of tea, and they sat for five or ten minutes talking about nothing in particular while Cassie collected herself. Outside the sun was shining off the individual bricks in the pavement, making the trees glitter and the houses look freshly scrubbed. It was a warm, beautiful morning, and the two of them were together again. Cassie felt close to Lucy and Lucy felt close to Cassie and they floated for a while in that closeness, savoring their reunion as they sipped the mediocre tea and watched Bostonians hurrying past on their way to catch the MTA.

After a while they began to talk about Ann Arbor and the time after Andy's death when Cassie had decided to give all her things away. The toaster had only been the beginning. By the end of Cassie's anti-materialism phase, all she had left were her cameras, her negatives, a couple of changes of clothes, and her old green book bag from Radcliffe. She had moved into Dove House, become frustrated at the flakiness of the place, then Steve and Ann had come along and offered her something better.

Lucy asked her how she liked Storm, and Cassie was enthusiastic. She admitted that there were a lot of rules but insisted that when six people lived in the same house someone needed to impose some sort of order. She liked living collectively. It felt good; people supported and nurtured one another.

"We're doing all sorts of important things," she told Lucy. "Three days a week we staff a draft counseling center; we have a small photo-offset press set up in the basement, and we print pamphlets and posters. I'm in charge of that and I also do free-lance photography for the underground newspapers. Bryan and Sally make antiwar presentations with the slides I provide, mostly to community groups, high schools, local colleges, and the like. Charlie works outside the bars and strip joints handing out leaflets to sailors on shore leave and anyone else in uniform he can persuade to take one. Ann and Steve . . . well, what they do is a little difficult to describe, but I guess you'd call it liaison work. They conduct a voluminous correspondence, raise funds for us and for half a dozen other peace organizations, and manage to know practically everyone there is to know in the antiwar movement."

"Good grief," Lucy exclaimed, "when do you ever have time to sleep?"

"Sleep?" Cassie grinned. "Charlie's coffee takes care of that. It's as thick as mud and as black as coal tar; two or three cups, and you can stay awake indefinitely. Which brings me to the best part of this whole arrangement: housework. We all take turns, men and women alike, dishes, dusting, bathrooms, the whole bit. I've never lived in such a clean place." She chuckled. "There's nothing sweeter than the sight of a grown man up to his elbows in soapy dish water. Now that's my idea of liberation."

Lucy smiled politely as she listened to Cassie extol the virtues of collective living and even tried to show enthusiasm because she knew that Cassie would be hurt if she didn't, but she wasn't completely convinced that Cassie was telling her the whole truth. It was hard for her to imagine life with Ann and Steve Singleton being so utopian, not to mention that the more Cassie talked the more it became clear that there were rules for everything, most of them made up by Steve: personal possessions were strictly limited; everyone had to attend biweekly house meetings; personal phone calls could last no longer than four minutes; breakfast was served promptly at seven-fifteen, lunch at twelve-thirty, dinner at six; unless they had previously been excused, those who missed communal meals had to explain their absence in writing.

"I know it's none of my business," she said finally, "but don't you sometimes feel as if you've joined the Marine Corps?"

Cassie shook her head. Her hair curled around her face, electric with enthusiasm, and her eyes were bright. "No, I like the structure. It was a little hard to get used to at first, but I needed more order in my life. That's why I came to Boston in the first place. Like I said, Dove House was complete chaos. Storm isn't like that, thanks to Steve. I can't say I adore him; to tell the truth, for all his charisma he's something of a cold fish. But he's a wonderful organizer."

Lucy drummed her fingers on the table and pursed her lips. There was a question that she longed to ask Cassie, but she wasn't sure if this was the right time or the place. There was something mildly unsettling about how quickly Cassie had taken to Storm. There was a smell of conversion to it. That was an exaggeration of course. Steve Singleton wasn't some kind of guru who had founded a cult; he was just a wealthy preppy who knew how to play politics the same way his father knew how to play the stock market, but still. . . . Lucy pondered, considered, reconsidered, and decided that if she didn't tell Cassie what was on her mind, she wasn't going to get much sleep that night. There were organizations you didn't want your best friend to be connected with. Storm might be one of them or it might be what Cassie said it was, but in any case she had to know. Looking around to make sure that no one was within earshot, she leaned forward. "I'm glad you're happy in Storm," she said in a low voice, "but there's something about your involvement in it that worries me."

"What's that?"

"Bang, bang," she said, "you know: target practice."

Cassie laughed. "Lou, what in the world are you talking about?"

Lucy paused and looked around again, feeling a little silly at her own paranoia. At the counter a heavyset man in a plaid jacket was choking down a cup of coffee; across the room two elderly ladies in hats were drinking glasses of something that looked like orange soda. No one was likely to overhear her, but she still felt nervous about saying what she planned to say next. What the hell, she decided. She lowered her voice even more. "Remember that phone conversation we had, the one about Ann and Steve?" Cassie's face was blank. "You remember, you told me they were learning how to use guns. I guess what I'm trying to ask you is, are they still—?"

"Oh, no." Cassie shook her head vigorously. "Absolutely not; they did go through a stage of thinking that maybe violence was the solution to everything, but they came to their senses. They both openly admit that. They say they were crazy ever to have considered such a thing. Storm is completely committed to peaceful protest; if it weren't, I wouldn't be in it."

Lucy was immensely relieved, but her relief was short-lived. Cassie's smile had faded, and she was looking down at her hands with a troubled expression on her face, one that was all too familiar. Lucy recognized that expression: it meant that Cassie had doubts. "Cass," she said, "level with me."

"There's nothing to level about." Cassie picked up her cup and took a swallow of tea. She brushed her fingers through her hair, fiddled with her earring, and smiled. "Nothing much, anyway. It's all great, just like I told you, except . . . well, sometimes it isn't exactly." She laughed nervously. "The truth is, the collective isn't a perfect democracy. There's an in-group and an out-group: the in-group is Bryan, Ann, and Steve, and the out-group is all the rest of us. Officially, they're our steering committee, which is only fair because they were the ones who founded Storm in the first place. The three of them have meetings fairly often that the rest of us aren't invited to, and I suspect that they don't tell us everything that goes on in those meetings."

Lucy felt a twinge of foreboding. She put down her teacup and looked at Cassie, trying to read her face, but it was the same innocent, friendly face, a little sad, but not in the least shrewd or deceptive.

"It may all be my imagination," Cassie continued, "but I've been feeling a lot of tension in the house lately, as if the three of them are keeping some big secret they can't trust the rest of us with."

"What do you think it is?"

"Probably nothing new." Cassie shrugged. "The truth is, Steve does a few things that aren't strictly legal, and I suppose he and Ann and Bryan sometimes get nervous about playing it too close to the edge. For example, just between you and me, he spends a lot of time up in Bryan's room working on devices that will let him make long distance phone calls without triggering Ma Bell's billing system. I haven't actually seen one, but from what I gather they're just a couple of transistors wired together in some special way. I can't say that I feel entirely comfortable with the idea of him cheating the phone company, even though it's never been high on my list of favorite organizations, but Steve says he's only going to use the things to keep in touch with other peace groups, and that's a good cause. In any event, even though it's a little shady, it's nothing to worry about, and the technology is so new that I'm not even sure there's a law against it yet."

"I don't like hearing this." Lucy looked at Cassie, and suddenly she was concerned for her. She imagined closed doors, secret meetings, hidden agendas. She could see Steve, smiling and reassuring everyone that he was a man of peace and that the ends always justified the means. She didn't like Steve's smile, not even in her own imagination. "I think you should get out," she advised.

"But Storm's like my family," Cassie protested. She shrugged again and laughed. "You know, you're taking all this much too seriously, Lou."

"Am I?"

"Of course you are." Cassie relaxed. Crossing her legs, she sat back and began picking crumbs of sugar off the table. "These are good, decent people. Come see for yourself; come to dinner." She laughed again, from the belly this time, an infectious, pleasant laugh that made Lucy feel a little silly for worrying about her. "There's nothing like watching us try to eat Bryan's cooking to undermine any suspicion that we might be dangerous. Last time he served us boiled tuna fish and spinach with sand in it. The fact that we didn't rise up and rip him apart is a tribute to our pacifism."

Lucy declined the invitation, reminding Cassie that she didn't want to meet Steve and Ann face to face. "Then come tomorrow night," Cassie persisted. "Steve and Ann are going out of town for a couple of days." She smiled and flicked a crumb of sugar playfully in Lucy's direction. "Don't worry; I'm not cooking, Sally is. Sally's from Baltimore and she makes the best crab cakes on the East Coast." She leaned toward Lucy. "Slaw," she crooned, "real french fries, bread pudding with brandy sauce, and I'll buy some wine to celebrate. For two years you've been eating what? Curried goat, probably. Tomorrow night we'll welcome you back to America with a real feast, and afterward we can hang out in my room, play some records, and you can tell me what Louise Crest plans to do with herself."

"I'll come," Lucy agreed. The dinner menu made her mouth water, and she could think of nothing she'd rather do than spend an evening with Cassie. She really had overreacted. Cassie was entitled to live with whomever she liked. She should encourage Cassie in her political work instead of acting like a wet blanket. She was just thinking that if Cassie ever got tired of Storm, she'd ask her to be her roommate again, when she heard a car door slam. Looking out the window, she saw Steve Singleton emerging from a cab carrying a large cardboard box. "Oh my gosh," she cried, jumping to her feet.

"Sit down," Cassie advised. "He's not coming in here." Cassie was right, as usual. Steve wasn't going anywhere but up the front steps. Lugging the box to the landing, he stopped and dug his keys out of his pocket. Lucy watched him until he was inside the house, then said a quick good-bye to Cassie, and fled, promising to return the following evening.

Cassie's room was on the first floor looking out on Marlborough Street. It was a large, pale green space with odd little corners and pretentious woodwork that did its best to imitate Corinthian columns, but Cassie had put her own stamp on it as surely as if she had built it herself from a Cassandra Quinn Instant Home Kit. Piles of dirty laundry lay everywhere: slips hung from the backs of chairs; socks lay in all the corners; orange and purple dresses competed for room with gray skirts and plain, white cotton blouses. On the walls, black-and-white snapshots marched toward the ceiling: three children playing hopscotch, an old woman in a black coat sitting on a park bench feeding the pigeons, a smiling bus driver, a dancer bent over an exercise bar. Lucy noticed that there wasn't a plant in the series.

"Housework is the curse of womankind," Cassie proclaimed as she threw herself down on her bed. She kicked several mounds of towels, sweaters, and assorted tops onto the floor, and curled up cozily among the rest of her unwashed clothing.

Clearing off a space beside her, Lucy sat down on the bed and surveyed the effect, wondering if her stomach was going to pop. Dinner with the collective had been everything that Cassie had promised. Now, floating on the memory of the best meal she had had in two years, she was amused and relieved to find that despite all the rules, Cassie had not changed her housekeeping habits. She looked around the room, wondering what surprises were lurking under the dirty laundry. In the far corner an old-fashioned record player sat among piles of empty Coke bottles. Suddenly she was seized by the desire to hear music. "Let's play some records," she suggested.

"What did you have in mind?"

"Mozart maybe?"

Cassie shook her head. "Sorry, but Mozart's not on the program. I gave all my records away. At present I'm borrowing stuff from Sally, and she's heavy into acid rock." Jumping to her feet, she attacked the nearest bookcase and extracted a half dozen albums with psychedelic covers. "What's your pleasure? The Doors, Bob Dylan, Jefferson Airplane, Sergeant Pepper, Mississippi John Hurt, or—" she paused, "David's new album?"

"Spare me David; I must have heard 'Get Out of Our Way' forty times in the last three days, and on the flight from Detroit to Boston I read a four-page article on him in *Rolling Stone*. My curiosity about David Blake has been satisfied for the present; I'll take The Doors."

Cassie nodded. "A good choice." Positioning the record on the turntable, she turned on the power and gently lowered the needle into the grove. Suddenly the room was filled with the sound of Jim Morrison singing "Break On Through." The walls vibrated, the windows sang, everything danced to the beat including Cassie who kicked off her shoes and began to whirl around the room laughing. Her joy was infectious. Jumping to her feet, Lucy joined her, and the two of them danced on opposite sides of the room like mad women, happy and free, singing along at the tops of their lungs.

When the record was over, they fell back onto the bed exhausted. "That was great," Lucy said. "Let's do it again." A few minutes later they were dancing to Grace Slick, who was asking them if they needed somebody to love.

Outside on the street, a taxi pulled up and a door slammed. It was Steve and Ann coming home a day early.

Steve heard the music coming from Cassie's room as soon as he walked in the front door. Stopping on the stairs, he turned to Ann. "I wish she wouldn't play that thing so loud." He was in the mood for peace and quiet, and he didn't need Grace Slick singing at ten thousand decibels. Cassie never did anything halfway. He could even hear her dancing inside her room, and it sounded as if she had a guest.

"You could knock on her door and ask her to turn it down," Ann suggested.

Steve strode over to Cassie's door, started to knock, and then changed his mind. "It's probably just as well she's making so much noise," he said, "under the circumstances." He lowered his arm and looked at Ann lurking in the shadows. On any other occasion he might have found her air of secrecy funny, but tonight it seemed appropriate. He wanted to lurk too.

He suddenly noticed that his hands were trembling. Stuffing them into his pockets, he shrugged and tried to look casual. He was annoyed with himself. He wasn't frightened in the least, only excited. The music thumped out from under the door dominating everything in the vicinity. Turning away, Steve went over to Ann and put his arm around her for a moment. Then, moving silently up the heavily carpeted stairs, the two of them climbed to Bryan's room.

The room was dark and cold and Bryan was nowhere in sight, since he worked the night shift at the packing plant. Turning on a light, Steve placed his briefcase on Bryan's desk and opened it. Inside were two pages of handwritten notes. Steve loosened his tie. Picking up the notes, he inspected them, frowned, and turned to Ann.

"Are you sure you took down everything Remo said?" Remo had not been the contact's real name; no real names had been used at the meeting.

Ann nodded. "Yes," she said. "Of course his English was pretty bad, but I think I got everything important."

Steve inspected a carefully drawn wiring diagram and shook his head. "I'm not in the mood to fill in blanks," he said, "not when the stakes are so high."

"It's all there," Ann reassured him, "every word." She reached out and touched the pages lightly. "It isn't all that different from what we did before, and those worked just fine."

"The one we put in the lab at MIT was defective," Steve pointed out.

"It went off early and killed that janitor. Not to mention the one you got Sally to leave in the rest room of the state house, the one you told her was just a packet of leaflets. That one never went off at all."

"These will work perfectly," Ann promised. "Remo is the best. Like I said, I took down everything we need to know."

"Wonderful." Steve put the notes down on the desk, smoothed out the dog-eared edges, and placed a bottle of ink on them to hold them down. Walking over to Bryan's closet, he extracted a large metal toolbox and carried it over to the desk, opened it, and surveyed the contents. On the first shelf lay needle-nosed pliers, wire snippers, and screwdrivers; on the second an ohmmeter, a soldering iron, some solder, rolls of wire, and transistors; the large bottom compartment was completely filled by four expensive clocks that ran with almost inaudible purrs as they counted off the minutes. Each clock was set to a different time. It amused Steve to keep them in sync with various world capitals. Earlier today he had selected Washington, D.C.; London; Cairo; and Saigon. One clock was always set to D.C. time; the others he varied according to his mood.

Going back to the closet, he fetched the cardboard box that he had unpacked yesterday morning. Ann stood by watching him, feeling honored that he was permitting her to be present at such an important moment. "Are those the . . . special ingredients," she said in a hushed voice, pointing to the cylinders.

Steve nodded.

"Can I touch one for luck?"

"Of course." He cradled one of the cylinders in his hand and presented it to her. Ann touched it lightly and made a small, pleased sound. Steve was amused. His Ann was so impressionable; still, he knew how she felt. The rough sensation of the cardboard against the palm of his hands made him feel omnipotent. Some men might be tempted to take advantage of power like that, but he knew that he was beyond temptation. He stood for a moment, letting the excitement surge through him. Then, reaching for a screwdriver, he set to work.

Ann tapped Steve timidly on the shoulder. "Excuse me, honey," she said.

He looked up from the wiring, mildly annoyed. "What is it?"

"Shouldn't you be using a safety light?"

"I am."

"Not here," she said pointing to the wires, "but here."

Steve paused and thought for a moment. "No, I've got it right."

"But I remember Remo saying—"

"Relax," Steve advised. He picked up the ends of the small copper wires and twisted them into one large strand. Holding his breath, he leaned forward and made the final connection. "There," he said, "you see? There's no problem." He straightened up and turned to put his arms around Ann. She looked so nervous that he felt sorry for her. He was feeling satisfied and complete as he turned. He didn't notice the edge of his coat hitting the handle of the screwdriver; he didn't hear the sound of the screwdriver rolling; he didn't see it fall, bridging the two wires. The explosion was so sudden and so violent that he had no last thoughts. Death blew on him and he went out like a candle.

Fountains of wood and glass spewed up into the air with a roar that shook the entire neighborhood and cracked plaster two blocks away. The top of the house disappeared, and in its place rose a column of flame. As the third-floor windows broke from the heat, the flames leapt out sideways, dancing gaily in the cold night air, waving banners of red and purple at the shocked residents of Marlborough Street. An old man out to mail a letter was wounded by a piece of copper gutter that flew past, nearly decapitating him. Revolution, the birds screamed, taking flight. Revolution, the pieces of the house sang as they pattered into the street. Revolution, huffed the flames as they laddered their way up toward the moon. In an instant everything was changed. Soft things that had once been alive fell like bits of discarded puzzles. Oh, the joy and the terror! And what a pity Steve and Ann weren't there to see it.

Downstairs in Cassie's room, Lucy was dancing in front of the mirror when it blew up in her face.

A few minutes passed and the house burned. In the distance the sound of sirens filled the air. On the first floor, Cassie picked herself up, and stood for a moment clinging to the window sill. Her nose was smashed, her face covered with plaster dust; she was in pain, confused, and terrified. Something terrible had happened. She had been dancing when a giant hand had grabbed her by the neck and thrown her on her face. She had been dancing over here, and Lucy had been dancing over there where part of the wall had collapsed. She coughed and spat out plaster dust and tried to understand what had happened to Lucy. She was nowhere in sight, which meant that she must be . . . oh, no! She must be buried under the wall!

Staggering to the other side of the room, Cassie fell to her knees and began digging frantically through the rubble. "Lou!" she yelled, "Lou, where are you?" There was no answer. "Lou!" She began to sob. "Help!" she yelled. "Somebody come help me! Sally, Charlie! Come here!" But Sally didn't come and Charlie didn't come, and she wanted to run outside and get one of the neighbors to help, only she was afraid that if she took time to do that Lucy would suffocate. Clawing at the hunks of fallen plaster, she broke her nails and cut her hands. Lucy was under this shit somewhere, and she had to dig her out before she died. She burrowed into the rubble, but there was nothing at the bottom but floorboards and splinters. "Lou," she screamed, "where are you, for God's sake?" Blood filled her mouth; her nose hurt so much that she felt as if she might faint, but she immediately started digging into another pile of boards, throwing them to one side.

Her mind was going a mile a minute, putting bits of information together, things she had known or half known for months, a piece here and a piece there, all of it finally clicking into place. The boards fell in a heap, spewing up more plaster dust. There was only one thing that could have caused an explosion like this: a bomb. And if a bomb had gone off in the house, then she knew who was responsible. She remembered the steering committee meetings she hadn't been allowed to attend, the trips out of town that had never been explained, the box of electrical parts she had once opened by mistake, the whispered conversation between Steve and a stranger she had overheard one night when she picked up the extension to the phone, and she felt half-crazy with anger because she knew too late that she had been manipulated and fooled and deceived. She had bought Steve's explanation that he was only building phone devices, while all the while he and Ann and Bryan were building bombs right under her nose.

"You bastards!" she yelled. She raised her fists and shook them at the ceiling. "You idiots, you double-crossing traitors, you—" *Sober up.* The tiny shred of what was left of rationality reached out and slapped her. *Steve and Ann are probably dead, and Sally and Charlie too because they were up there where the fire is. Everyone's probably dead and you're in shock.* "Lou, if you can hear me, say something," she begged. "Talk, dammit, talk!"

"Get me out of here." Lucy's voice was muffled and indistinct.

"You're alive!" Cassie yelled. She leapt to her feet and plunged toward the sound of Lucy's cries, only to collide with another part of the collapsed wall. Swearing, she climbed over the beam and kicked pieces of lathe out of the way.

"Help me," Lucy pleaded. "I can't move. I'm trapped under something." There was panic in her voice.

"I'm coming. Hang on, honey. I'll get you out."

"Hurry up," Lucy begged, "before I burn to death."

"You're okay," Cassie lied. "You're safe." Her relief at hearing Lucy's voice was short-lived. She was getting more scared by the second. The room was filling with smoke; overhead the flames roared, consuming what was left of the house, and sparks were falling through the broken windows. She could hear Lucy coughing and moaning in pain. Cassie panicked. Lucy was going to die. She couldn't rescue her alone; she needed help, but there was no one to help her and no time to look for anyone. Half-blinded by the fumes, she tossed aside things that had once been familiar: shoes, books, broken cameras. One corner of the room was burning now; her photographs were shriveling on the wall. She threw aside a pile of books and suddenly felt the warm touch of flesh; she had uncovered Lucy's hand protruding from beneath the dresser.

"I've got you!" Seizing Lucy's wrist, she tried to pull her loose. Lucy screamed, but her body didn't move. Pieces of broken mirror lay all around her, glittering like small silver daggers. Swearing, Cassie seized the edge of the dresser and heaved it to one side. The dresser turned over, legs in the air, spewing out purple and gray sweaters. Putting her arms around Lucy, she pulled her to her feet and gasped: Lucy's face was covered with blood.

Lucy clung to Cassie, dazed. Coughing, she struggled to breathe, but the smoke was like oil. It stung her eyes and her face and filled her lungs, and it seemed that pain was everywhere. Her face hurt so badly; it was as if someone had stuck hundreds of knives in it, and she wanted to touch it, only she was afraid to. The room blurred; some kind of warm liquid filled her eyes, and she couldn't see. The agony was excruciating; she felt as if she might pass out. Grabbing Cassie's shoulder, she fought to stay conscious.

"Easy now," Cassie said, "easy. You're okay." She hugged Lucy. "Try to get a grip on yourself; we have to get out of here before the police arrive."

Lucy touched her eyes and the pain was red and gold, black and gray, pinwheels and floating things that didn't exist. "I can't see," she moaned.

At that Cassie nearly panicked. "Are you blind?"

"I don't know." Lucy began to panic too. Maybe she *was* blind. The liquid in her eyes was salty and red and she realized that it was her own blood, running down from her forehead. Wiping it away, she discovered she could still see. She clutched Cassie by the shoulders. "I'm not blind."

"Thank God."

"The blood keeps dripping down into my eyes. My face must be a mess." Cassie pulled Lucy toward the door, but Lucy still couldn't see very well. She stumbled and almost fell. Grabbing on to Cassie, she froze. "It hurts so much, like someone stuck knives in me. Oh, God, it hurts."

Through one of the broken windows, Cassie saw three police cars skid to a halt in front of the house; whirling blue lights filled the room. There was no time left. Swooping Lucy up in her arms, she staggered out into the ruined hall with her and fled into the backyard. Outside, the fire was casting a lurid light, turning the leaves of the forsythia bushes blood red. Sally's bicycle lay in a heap next to overturned garbage cans and hunks of plaster. Heading toward the back gate, Cassie guided Lucy through it. Lucy clung to her arm, moaning.

"My face hurts so much. Make it stop hurting, Cass."

Cassie spoke to her gently. "I know a doctor who lives about six blocks from here. He's sympathetic to the antiwar movement. He'll take care of you."

"I want to go to the hospital." She stumbled, and Cassie caught her.

"We can't take you to a hospital, honey. They'll arrest us if we do."

"I don't understand. Why would they arrest us? I'm in pain; I'm in such terrible pain, for God's sake. Please."

Cassie pulled Lucy closer, trying to take the pain away. "Listen, Lou.

Can you hear me? There's something you've got to understand. There's a good chance that this isn't the first bomb Steve ever made. Do you understand what I'm saying? A janitor was blown up over at MIT last month. He was cleaning a lab that was doing research on missile guidance systems. And before that someone bombed the Brookline police station. Two cops were killed and three ended up in intensive care. Steve was probably behind both bombings."

She pushed Lucy's bloody hair off her forehead. Her voice broke at the sight of her poor, dear ruined face. "It's all my fault," she cried. "Forgive me, please. I'm a sucker and a fool." She guided Lucy into the shadows, into a place where no one could see them. They were almost invisible now. "I've got to hide and you've got to stay dead. Otherwise we may both end up spending the rest of our lives in prison."

Lucy thought about bars across windows, high walls, barbed wire, guards. She remembered how she'd gone half-crazy shut up in the palace. Prison would be far worse. She couldn't take it; she'd die. Clutching Cassie's hand, she surrendered herself to the shadows.

Twenty minutes later they were knocking on the back door of a large brick house on a street Lucy never learned the name of because they had arrived by way of the alley. A middle-aged woman lifted the shade and looked out the window. When she saw them, she gasped and put her hand over her mouth. "My God." She opened the door and waved them into the kitchen. "Come in and sit down. The doctor is upstairs asleep. I'll go wake him up." She turned on a light, helped Cassie settle Lucy on a chair, and left without saying another word. The chair was hard, with a straight back and no arms. Lucy leaned back and let the rungs press into her spine. Her face throbbed as if someone were drumming on it. Reaching out, she took Cassie's hand and hung on. The room seemed to turn in front of her: stove and sink and refrigerator and the frosted light fixture, cold and high above her head. She wondered again if she was going to faint. She moaned and shook her head, but the drumming went on and on, scaring her, because it was getting louder.

A few minutes passed, and a man appeared carrying a black leather doctor's bag. He was about forty-five, tall and thin, and he had obviously just gotten out of bed because he was wearing a pair of wrinkled cotton pajamas. A pair of dark, horn-rimmed glasses were balanced on his nose, and his eyes were sharp and efficient.

"Hello," he said, putting the bag down on the table. "This looks like a bad business." He took Lucy by the chin and tilted her face toward the light. "Are you in much pain?" She nodded, too upset to speak. "I'll take care of your pain first," he promised, "and then I'll clean you up." He turned to Cassie. "How about you? Anything serious?"

"I can wait," Cassie mumbled. She had picked up a napkin and put it over her nose, and it was already stained with blood. She was in pain too, but she knew it was nothing compared to what Lucy was experiencing.

"Good," the doctor nodded. He turned back to Lucy. "I want you to understand what I'm going to do," he said in gentle voice. "First I'm going to give you a painkiller. Then I'm going to clean up those cuts, get the glass out of your face, and sew up anything that needs sewing. I can actually see fragments of glass from here, and you're lucky it didn't get into your eyes because if it had, we'd have had to get you to a hospital no matter what the consequences. Afterward, I'll give you a tetanus shot and some antibiotics."

Lucy knew there were questions she should ask, but she was in such pain that she couldn't think. Familiar things were starting to look unfamiliar. The rug in front of the kitchen sink seemed hunched and half-alive, and the patterns on the wallpaper were oscillating in front of her, making her feel nauseous. The doctor was opening his bag, taking out a sterile syringe, filling it with amber fluid, and then he was sticking the needle into her arm and it was burning, only the pain was minor compared to the pain of her face.

She felt the texture of the air around her change; it became warm and thick, soft like cotton. Her heart beat a few times, spreading the drug through her body, and then suddenly there was no pain at all, only a floating feeling as if she were suspended by strings a few inches above the kitchen floor. Her mind slowed down, her fear disappeared, and the throbbing in her face stopped. She wanted to cry from relief, only she seemed to have no tears and no energy.

The doctor bent over her and began swabbing her face with something that smelled like a swimming pool. He was cleaning her cuts, picking out bits of glass with a small pair of tweezers. This seemed to go on for a very long time. He worked from her chin upward. When at last he began to probe her forehead she jumped, feeling a deep stinging, and he gave her another shot.

After that she had no clear sense of what he was doing. Once she thought she smelled iodine, and once she clearly saw him holding something that looked like black thread, but it was all very dreamlike. Words floated around her. *Glass, couldn't get it all, she needs to sleep.* And then he was finished with her and starting in on Cassie. His wife was back, leading her into the living room and helping her lie down on the sofa, which was made up with cool white sheets and a blue blanket.

She learned many things that night and in the nights that followed. She learned that there were doctors who would take care of people for free without asking names or questions. She learned that there were networks of sympathizers who were willing to help people on the run. She learned of places called safe houses, where you could hide if you had gone underground, houses where you would be fed and clothed and given money and sent on your way with no questions asked.

She and Cassie stayed at the doctor's for less than twenty-four hours before they were moved to the next stage on the underground railroad. A young woman who looked like a college student drove them to Connecticut and handed them over to an elderly lady who, in turn, drove them to a minister's house where they spent the next two weeks recuperating in the attic of the rectory. By the time they arrived in Connecticut there was an all-points bulletin out for Cassie. A fifty-thousand-dollar reward was being offered for information leading to her arrest and the arrest of the "mystery woman" who had been seen fleeing the burning house with her.

Lucy had asked the minister's wife for a mirror, and now it was lying in front of her, facedown on the table because she was afraid to look at herself. It was the old-fashioned round kind of mirror, done in bone-colored plastic with the initials MTW on the handle. It had been thirteen days since the accident. Today the last of the bandages had come off. Today she was to see her face.

She was scared. Since the explosion, she had looked at herself several times, but her wounds had always been hidden by tape and gauze. Now her face was bare. She took a deep breath and tried to think positive thoughts. Maybe she would look okay—a little messed up, of course, with a lot of scratches, but nothing permanent, nothing . . . disfiguring.

Her hands were trembling. Reaching up, she touched her face with the tips of her fingers, feeling the long cuts on her forehead and cheeks, the scabs and sutures. Everything still felt tender and swollen.

Her heart turned over inside her chest, and she felt sick with anxiety. She wished that she hadn't told Cassie to go downstairs and leave her alone to do this in private. It would have been better to have Cassie beside her to give her courage, because without the bandages her face felt bad, like a rutted road, and no matter how much she tried to tell herself that she was going to look all right, she knew that it wasn't true. But Cassie wasn't there; and the longer she put off looking at herself, the harder it was going to be to face her own reflection.

Gritting her teeth, she picked up the mirror, turned it over, held it up to her face, and gave a cry of anguish. A stranger looked back at her, an ugly stranger with long red scars on her cheeks and forehead and . . . oh, it was terrible, she couldn't bear it! Dropping the mirror, she began to sob uncontrollably. She looked horrible, like a botched quilt. Where was her real face, the pretty one that Mila had loved? "Oh," she cried, "I'm so ugly. I'm so damn ugly."

Cassie came up to the attic ten minutes later and found her still in tears. She had her face down on the table, cradled in her arms, and she refused to speak or look up. "Don't cry, Lou," Cassie begged. "We'll go to Mexico. There's a famous plastic surgeon there who can fix your face. The doctor who helped us in Boston gave me his address. Don't cry, please. I can't stand it. I feel like it's all my fault."

Lucy didn't reply. She just went on crying as if her heart would break. Cassie sat down beside her but she didn't touch her. She began crying too because she felt so terrible and so guilty and so sorry for Lucy. "Look at me, Lou," she begged. "Please. I don't care what your face looks like. I'm your friend and I love you and you'll look okay again, I swear. You have plenty of money from selling those diamonds, so we can get your face fixed, and mine too if you're willing to float me a loan."

Cassie looked at the mirror lying on the floor, at Lucy who looked just the same when you couldn't see her face, at the attic with its two army cots, a hot plate, and two small dusty windows, and she thought of how she was going to be spending the rest of her life hiding. "Do you know what happened today? They put me up in the post office, right next to the bank robbers and murderers. I'm told the poster reads: *Cassandra Quinn Rabinowitz: Wanted for Conspiracy, Terrorism, and Murder.*" She paused and tried to smile and make a joke of it all, but she felt scared. "I'm famous, Lou. We've got to go to Mexico as soon as we can. We'll both get our faces changed there. Together."

The clinic of plastic surgeon Roberto Suarez was located in the Mexican state of Yucatan on a large, placid lagoon far away from the beaches that attracted tourists. Designed to give Dr. Suarez's patients complete privacy, it could only be reached by water. On a clear day late in the winter of 1968, some three months after the explosion of the bomb factory, the doctor stood at the window of his office watching two young woman get into the motor launch that was leaving for Chetumal to connect with the daily flight to Mexico City. One was tall and exotically beautiful with a small, pretty nose, lush breasts, and heavy straight hair that tumbled in a dark mane over her shoulders. Thanks to a pair of violet-tinted contacts, her watery gray eyes were now the color of the clouds on the lagoon.

He had been less successful with the blonde who had sustained multiple facial injuries, and he frowned as he watched her approach the boat, wondering as he always did in such cases, if there was anything else he might have done. She should have been rushed to a plastic surgeon right after her accident—whatever that had been. Dr. Suarez had never asked and she had never told him, but by the time he had operated, her face was already scarred. He had covered most of the damage with skin grafts, but despite his considerable skill, there were limits to what he could do for her. She had emerged from surgery looking pleasant but rather plain. Even from this distance he could see that her cheeks were a little too full, and her smile was . . . well, it was slightly crooked, not enough perhaps for anyone else to notice, but he was a perfectionist. She had wept when he removed the bandages, and he had gathered that she had once been quite beautiful, but then women often wept when they realized he could not perform miracles.

He observed that the two young women helped each other into the launch, steadying each other when an unexpected wave slapped the boat against the side of the pier. They certainly were devoted friends, and he wondered what catastrophe had brought them to him. He never asked for names or explanations if his patients paid him in cash, but he was always curious. In the past five years dozens of people had left their original faces at his clinic and gone out into the world with new ones. Some he saw later in the newspapers; others disappeared forever.

The motor roared, and the launch glided away from the pier, leaving a rainbow-colored wake behind it. Under the flapping green canopy embossed with the seal of the clinic, the two young women sat side by side. Dr. Suarez watched them until they were a speck on the horizon, then shrugged and turned away from the window. He wondered who they had been and who they were going to be.

BOOK THREE

San Francisco, California

October 1988

• 1 •

*A*t *nine o'clock one cloudless* Sunday morning near the beginning of October, Lucy sat in the kitchen of her North Beach apartment putting together a present for Cassie, who was going to be forty-four next week. Frowning, biting her tongue, and adjusting her glasses from time to time, she was assembling the present from a large straw basket full of snapshots, selecting the best and mounting them in an expensive leather album, which was tentatively entitled *The Book of Sue and Lou.* The "Lou" was for Louise Crest, and the "Sue" came from Susan Clark, the alias that Cassie had been using for the past twenty years. Its subtitle, the one that she would tell Cassie but which she was absolutely *not* going to write on the cover, was *Twenty Years Underground Together.*

Taking a sip of coffee from the mug at her elbow, she hummed to herself as she worked. She was in a good mood this morning. The photograph album had been an inspiration. For the last five years or so she and Cassie had gotten into the habit of making each other Christmas and birthday presents, which was easy enough for Cassie, who had become a professional photographer, but hard for Lucy, who had no craft skills worth talking about and no time since she was presently juggling a law practice, a flourishing political career, and volunteer work at a shelter for homeless women and children. For Cassie's forty-third birthday she had given her a purple tie-dyed T-shirt that had faded disastrously, turning all of Cassie's underwear pale violet, and last Christmas, in desperation, she had constructed a yellow beanbag chair out of a prefabricated pattern, which was just on the edge of violating the make-your-own-presents code.

Cassie, of course, had sent her two beautiful signed photographs: one was of Lucy standing on a cliff next to a wind-sculpted tree, hair blowing, flesh whorled by shadows like manzanita bark; the other was a hand-tinted shot of five black women dancing with their heads thrown back and their eyes closed. The women, who were dressed in turbans and white lace dresses, were practicing the African-inspired religion of Candomblé. Cassie had taken their picture on a trip to Brazil, paid for by MasterCard, which had hired her to encourage people to charge their vacations.

That was what made the photograph album so perfect. Cassie was *always* taking fantastic portraits of other people, getting them published in prestigious places like *Rolling Stone* and *Vanity Fair*, but she almost never took any pictures of herself, and she was famous for not liking to be photographed, which was a mystery to most people, but not to Lucy. When you were concerned about the FBI trailing you, it made sense that you'd be camera shy. The only person Cassie felt comfortable being photographed by was Lucy, which meant, Lucy figured, that she owned almost the entire visual archive of Cassie's life.

Reaching into the basket, she extracted another handful of prints and fanned them out in front of her. Spring of 1982: an era memorable for the birth of Cassie's daughter, Carla. She selected a picture of a very pregnant Cassie and tossed the rest of the snaps into the reject pile.

She worked with complete concentration for another half hour, and then she got up, toasted herself a couple of English muffins, and went out on the roof to eat them. The roof was a garden of sorts, composed of earthenware pots filled with basil, finocchio, tarragon, and roses, but her landlady, Mrs. Albergetti, tended it as lovingly as if it were an entire backyard, picking off every aphid by hand, getting up at five in the morning to water and cultivate. Lucy sat down in one of the white plastic lawn chairs, ate a muffin, and contemplated the view. The fog had burned off early this morning, and over the rooftops she could see San Francisco Bay, blue and choppy, and, riding it, several hundred small boats with sails so white they looked like birds' wings.

The apartment itself was nothing much; she could have afforded a much better place because she had a successful law practice: a mix of wealthy clients who paid steep fees, which financed the *pro bono* work she did for the poor. But if she had lived in a fancy condo or a house in the Berkeley hills, she would have had to give up Mrs. Albergetti's roses and the celebration of the sailboats. Besides, she liked being the only lawyer she knew who was renting a place where the neighbors strung their wash over the courtyards, old men sat on the steps talking in Italian, and BMWs were something you only saw on TV. Some of her colleagues had gone into law for the money or the prestige or the thrill of tearing apart their opponents in open court, but the decision had been harder for her. She hadn't wanted any of the things lawyers were supposed to want.

When she and Cass first moved to the Bay Area right after their surgery, she hadn't known what she was going to do with her life. For a while she had toyed with the idea of going back to school and getting a degree in social work or even in medicine, if she could make it through chemistry and biology. Finally, after a lot of soul searching, she had settled on law, partly because she seemed to have a knack for it and partly because, as Cassie had pointed out, there was no better way to defend the rights of people who were defenseless. But it was always good to recall that she might just as easily have been something else. She never looked at Mrs. Albergetti's roses without remembering that most of the best things in life could be had for the price of a little sunshine, water, and loving attention.

After she finished her snack, she went back inside and inspected her handiwork. The album was divided into six sections, each occupying from two to six pages, each spread entitled "Sue" (left) and "Lou" (right). The first section, "Genesis," had been the hardest. On the "Sue" side there was a faded, poorly focused photo of Dr. Suarez's clinic that Lucy had taken from the back of the boat the day they left. She had entitled it "The Womb," and she could have just as well have put it on the Lou side because the categories didn't work at this stage in their lives. In this section also were snaps of Cassie and Lucy in Mexico City, clutching giant piñatas, standing on a pyramid, having dinner with two handsome Mexicans who had turned out to be married. (Thank God they'd had enough sense to avoid getting involved with those two!) There was also a photo of the central plaza in a town that Cassie would instantly recognize as the place where they had bought themselves everything they needed to establish their new identities. Don Antonio, the seller of high-quality counterfeit documents, wasn't in the picture of course, but he had been most accommodating. "What state do you señoritas want to come from?" he had asked, ushering them into his office with a courtly wave of his hand, and when they told him that they were planning to move to California, he had nodded in agreement.

"California," he'd said. "Ah, good. That will be easy. I get many requests for California."

Don Antonio had turned out to be a perfectionist. For a mere three hundred dollars, he provided them with authentic California drivers' licenses, social security cards, birth certificates, and rent receipts ("Should you wish to go to the fine colleges of California," he had advised, "these receipts will permit you to pay in-state tuition—a great savings to you"). Then, compliments of the house, he had given them the address of one of his colleagues in the United States who specialized in fake transcripts.

"Roberto is a good man," Don Antonio had assured them, "very skilled. He can give you any grade point average you wish at several fine educational institutions. Do you wish to be doctors?" He snapped his fingers. "Roberto can make you them like this. Only," he winked, "you must not operate, señoritas, for this would not be *honorable*."

Roberto, who was known on the other side of the border as Bob, turned out to be a balding, red-faced Scot who dressed in dark suits like a banker or a college president. His prices were higher than Don Antonio's, but the special services he offered more than made up for it. Cassie, who claimed she never wanted to set foot in a university again, declined to buy herself an academic past, but for five hundred dollars, Lucy obtained a valid college transcript from a small but completely respectable institution in Illinois. The transcript proved to be good enough to get her admitted into U. C. Berkeley's Boalt Law School the following year, no questions asked. Evidently Bob had employees in the registrar's office, because her false alma mater's alumnae association wrote her for a contribution to their building fund.

Lucy looked at the faded snapshots, thinking what a big piece of their lives they represented. This had been a difficult section, and she spent a long time staring at it, trying to decide if she should revise it. There really hadn't been much to work with. She had been tempted to put in some old newspaper clippings: the headline that read EXPLOSION IN BOSTON BOMB FACTORY KILLS FOUR or the one that said RABINOWITZ AND MYSTERY WOMAN FLEE BLAST, or better yet Cassie's wanted poster, but Cassie wasn't going to thank her if she turned the album into an incriminating document, and besides, the whole point was to make it into something pleasant and enjoyable. What was being left out was as important as what was being put in.

There was a lot she wasn't putting in this book. She got to her feet again, went over to the stove, poured herself another cup of coffee, and stood there drinking it, thinking of some of the sad things that had happened over the past twenty years. In the spring of 1970, Cassie's father had been killed in a head-on collision with a truck on the road from London to Oxford. Ironically, he had been on his way to collect still another honor. To Lucy's surprise, Cassie was completely devastated by the news. She had not had any contact with Quinn for over two years, but from the moment she read the report of his death, she insisted on going to his funeral. Never mind, as Lucy pointed out, that the ceremony would be crawling with FBI agents; never mind that every relative she had would be waiting to see beyond her new face, recognize her voice, and blow her cover: Cassie began to stomp around their tiny apartment in Emeryville, weeping and hurling her clothes into her suitcase.

"I always thought I'd see him again, Lou," she cried. "Yes, I hated the son of a bitch, but I thought we'd reconcile. I thought some day he'd get old and weak and lose his teeth and quit screwing around, and then he'd wish to God he hadn't been such a bastard to his daughter. I thought that sooner or later he'd be filled with remorse over Andy and want my forgiveness, and when that happened I figured I'd call him up and say, 'Daddy, it's me, Cassie—'" Her voice had broken, and she had heaved another pair of shoes in her suitcase with a curse.

That had been the second worst day of both their lives. For hours Lucy had pleaded with Cassie not to go to the funeral where she would almost certainly be recognized and arrested. Finally, around midnight, Cassie had at last come to her senses. Taking a Valium, she had retreated to the loft where she spent the next week in bed alternately crying, eating chocolate, and listening to Rolling Stone records at a volume that would have driven their neighbors crazy if they'd had any. Fortunately she and Lucy were living in a converted warehouse that year, so presumably only the rats went deaf as Mick Jagger told them over and over again that he couldn't get any satisfaction.

Sometimes, with the wisdom of hindsight, Lucy wondered if she should have encouraged Cassie to go to her father's funeral after all. There was a slim chance that she wouldn't have been recognized, and maybe if she'd had that moment of closure, it would have put her guilt to rest, and they could have avoided some of the trouble that came next.

A few weeks later, consumed by remorse, Cassie had had what Lucy could only call a nervous breakdown, not an ordinary nervous breakdown because Cassie never did anything in the ordinary way, but a nervous breakdown nevertheless. Within less than a year of her father's death, she had gotten herself pregnant, married, and divorced in whirlwind succession. The diamond money had run out by then, and the tiny apartment in the warehouse in Emeryville turned into a jungle of wet diapers and empty Gerber's jars as the two of them struggled to raise Renny, pay Lucy's law school tuition, and keep Cassie in unexposed film, a financial juggling act that often had them eating lentils and brown rice by candlelight when the electricity was turned off for failure to pay the bill. Still, there had been good times. Take Renny, for example. What a pleasure that child had been.

Lucy took another sip of coffee and remembered how relieved she and Cassie were each time Cassie's babies were born without any sign of birth defects. She thought of Renny, the way he had looked eighteen years ago, curled up in the dresser drawer they had used for a cradle, placidly sucking his thumb while she sat beside him studying. The memory was sweet, but painful. As much as she had loved Renny, he hadn't been enough. She had wanted children of her own, but with the exception of that one time in Patan, she had never been able to conceive. Over the past two decades she had gone from one clinic to another, had tests, taken hormones, gotten prodded, and X-rayed and analyzed, made herself sick on fertility drugs, taken vitamins until they came out her ears, but nothing had worked. A few years before she had given up trying and did her best to convince herself that her life was complete without a baby, but sometimes when she saw small children playing, the sight moved her to tears, and she would walk away feeling empty and cheated. She would think of Mila, who was still living in Patan, waiting for his father to die and Arjuna to fall from power, and she would imagine what her life would have been like if they could have gone on being married and in love and happy, and she would feel a great silence pressing in on her from all sides.

The trouble with counting up your griefs was that one always reminded you of another. Lucy frowned and ran her finger around the rim of the coffeecup. The cup was smooth, but her thoughts were of sharp things: slivers of glass, tongues of flame. Not being able to have a child had been hard enough to accept, but there was something else that was even more persistent, something she had to confront every morning. She tried to think of Renny again, but it was too late. The old grief came unbidden, pursuing her as it always did, slipping into her mind like an unwelcome relative. Put bluntly: she didn't like her face.

She sighed, drank more coffee, and tried to convince herself yet again that it wasn't such a bad face and that she was lucky to have ended up with it. She knew that if she walked into the bathroom and looked into the mirror, she would see a middle-aged woman with faint scars around her eyes that were blessedly merging into wrinkles; a plain, pleasant-looking woman with long blond hair styled into a perm, full cheeks, pale skin, and fashionably oversize glasses. She could still recognize herself, but some subtle harmony of contour had been permanently lost. It made her sad, and sometimes on bad days, when she was feeling especially low or out of sorts, she would think of how she might have looked if there had been no explosion, and she would shut herself away from prying eyes and have a long, private cry over her lost beauty.

Lighten up, Constable, she commanded herself. What are you doing standing by your kitchen stove wallowing in regrets? You're making your best friend a birthday present. This is supposed to be *fun*. Returning to the table, she sat down and turned to section 2, which she had called the "Treasure of the Sierra Madre." The film was a favorite of Cassie's, and the two of them had watched it together on her VCR at least a half dozen times. The snaps on these pages recorded their adventures outdoors. Almost every year when they could afford it, she and Cass had taken a vacation together, usually to Wyoming or Utah or Colorado. Here was the cabin near Loveland Pass that they had rented for a week in 1974 and again in '76 and '78; Cassie on a horse squinting at the camera; Lucy lighting a campfire; Cassie slogging up a steep mountain trail; the two of them sitting with their bare feet in a mountain stream drinking cold beer and laughing at some long-forgotten joke.

This was more like it. Here were the good times, pure and unpoisoned with regrets. The past twenty years hadn't been all that bad when you looked at them from the perspective of a mountain stream and two ice cold Budweisers. They'd had to struggle at first, but it had been challenging to build two new careers from the rubble of their old lives; they had shared everything, right down to money for postage stamps, and even though they sometimes groused about not being able to afford things like pot roast and movies and new shoes, it had been fun raising Renny together for the first three years. And always there'd been the romance of being fugitives. When you were waiting tables in the International House of Pancakes, as Lucy had done for eight months back in 1972, you could always look at the customers and whisper to yourself, "If they only knew." Their lives might have been inconvenient and even tragic at times, but they had rarely had a dull moment; you could tell that from their faces, the way they were holding up their beers, laughing and saluting one more summer of successfully hiding out together. How many people in their whole lives got to have as good a friend as Cassie, Lucy thought as she turned the page.

"School for Scandal" followed. Lucy had titled it that because she figured that if anyone had known how fake her academic credentials were, there would have been a scandal indeed. Here, on the "Lou" side, were four shots of Lucy clutching her law degree from Boalt, absolutely classic graduation photographs taken by one of her friends since Cassie had been living in L.A. by then and hadn't been able to come up for the festivities.

On the "Sue" side was a picture Lucy was particularly proud of. After Renny's birth, Cassie had broken her vow never to go back to school, and for almost two years she had studied with Imogen Cunningham through the Mendocino Art Center. Lucy had snapped a picture of the two of them: Cunningham in her nineties, dressed in black, pointing to a large, old-fashioned-looking camera on a wooden tripod, and Cassie, dressed in one of those denim pantsuits that had been so popular in the early seventies, listening to her with a rapt expression on her face.

Lucy looked at Cunningham, wondering what she had been saying that morning. She had been a sharp-tongued, demanding woman who dished out more criticism than praise, but her students seemed to thrive on it. Working with her had been a watershed for Cassie. Not that Cassie had gone straight to the top. She had spent years struggling to support Renny—photographing weddings, bar mitzvahs, taking stills for industrial films—but from the moment Cunningham became her mentor, her photographs changed. Before she worked with Cunningham, Cassie was a competent, talented photographer who occasionally produced something remarkable. Afterward she was more than that. She seemed to be on her way somewhere. Everyone who saw her work had predicted that sooner or later she would make it in a big way, and ultimately she had, exploding onto the cover of *Rolling Stone* in the spring of 1981 and never looking back.

The following section, "Wild Women Don't Get the Blues," had been the most fun to put together. Lucy grinned wickedly as she examined it, wondering how Cassie was going to feel when she saw her complete collection of major love affairs spread out in living color. There was Cassie with her arm around Utah Hawks, the construction worker whom she had had a brief (but hot) time with right after she divorced Allen; Cassie with Jim Greer, the alcoholic set painter for MGM; Cassie sitting on the knee of a young man whom Lucy vaguely remembered as a designer of educational software. Her two husbands had also been included: Allen Burnett, Renny's father, whom she'd married in 1970 and divorced ten months later, and Lorenzo Villanueva (1981–1988), with whose help she'd produced Carla. Lucy hoped Cassie would be amused to discover that she had painted a small arrow through Lorenzo's head.

The "Lou" half of "Wild Women" was a lot less wild, but the collection was respectable. There were five photographs of Lucy with five pleasant, kind, solvent men, three of whom had proposed marriage to her. Cassie was always telling her that she had more luck than she deserved, but Lucy wasn't convinced. She liked men and she liked sex, but actually falling in love hadn't been easy over the past two decades. Maybe it was because she had still felt married to Mila, or maybe she had just never met the right man, but whatever the case she started off passionately enough but soon became—why not admit it?—bored. She looked at the picture of Keith Irwin, the artist she had broken up with only eight months ago. Great guy Keith—handsome, talented, intelligent—but no lasting zing.

Section 5, "The Muppets Take Over," was another problem area. It contained a great snap of Cassie holding Fran and Freida, the identical calico cats that she and Lucy had adopted in the fall of 1972 when they moved from the warehouse in Emeryville to a small cottage in Berkeley, and there were some wonderful baby pictures of Renny and Carla, but the "Lou" section was a bit sparse to say the least. The best Lucy could come up with was an old newspaper clipping that gave an account of Sala's wedding. In 1982 Sala had married the Patanese ambassador to France, and Lucy had followed the story religiously, cutting out every mention of it. She frowned, bit her lip, and studied the photograph of Sala, wondering if it was a downer, but she had nothing else to put in this section. She could hardly include the notice from the Women's Health Clinic billing her for her last artificial insemination, especially since it had failed.

The sight of Sala, dressed in her wedding sari, brought back memories of her own wedding: the elephant she and Cassie had ridden to the ceremony; the procession of chanting monks; Mila leading her around the fire, lifting her veil, feeding her rice from a small gold bowl to seal their marriage. Lucy stared at the words under Sala's picture without seeing them. Behind her, on the kitchen wall, a band of sunlight moved unnoticed across a shelf of blue china plates and Mexican glassware. Time passed. Finally she blinked and shook her head. She hadn't seen Mila for over twenty years, yet every time she thought of him, it was like saying "open sesame" to all sorts of regrets.

Strictly speaking that wasn't true. Remembering Mila was nowhere near as upsetting as it had been when she was younger. Time had softened the pain of losing him, but she often remembered their life together, and then for a few hours or even a few days, she would be filled with nostalgia. She would miss him all over again and wonder what he was doing and if he still thought of her, and then she would begin thinking of ways to contact him: new, ingenious ways that might work, although by now, after a number of failures, she was pretty well resigned to the idea that she was never going to hear from him again.

On the other hand, even if she had wanted to forget him, it wouldn't have been easy. His face kept appearing where she least expected to see it. She would be reading a magazine on an airplane, passing a newsstand, watching the six o'clock news, thinking about something else altogether, when suddenly his picture would flash before her, and she would learn some new detail about his life. In 1971, for example, all the papers were filled with news of his impending marriage to a Nepalese princess. She had been jealous, ridiculously so considering the circumstances, and for days she had wandered about unable to concentrate on her studies. She had tried to convince herself that he was being forced into the marriage by his father, which was a likely possibility, for suddenly, the Nepalese princess was out of the picture, and Prince Mila was said to be on the verge of abdicating his claim to the throne in order to enter a Buddhist monastery.

Abdicate, Lucy had thought. Ridiculous. He'll never do it, not as long as Arjuna is in power. She wondered what nasty bit of palace intrigue had prompted the story, but evidently there was at least a shred of truth in it because in the fall of 1972, when *Time* did a special article comparing the situation in Patan to the situation in Vietnam, it featured a picture of Mila with a shaved head, dressed in a saffron-colored robe, praying before two lighted sticks of incense. Abdication was no longer being mentioned, but apparently he had converted his private chambers into a religious retreat and was studying Buddhist theology and philosophy with a Tibetan lama who had been invited to Patan from the Dalai Lama's enclave in Dharmsala.

Was he trying to strike some kind of bargain with his father? Perhaps so, because by 1974 he was out of the saffron robes and back attending state functions. For the next four years, he appeared at every important occasion, standing beside Marpa like a dutiful prince, a pose that Lucy had trouble taking seriously. Then, in 1978, she chanced on an article in an obscure publication called *The Journal of Third World Nutrition* that explained everything. Evidently, over the years, Mila had been quietly founding a half dozen small nutrition centers where expectant mothers and mothers with small children could obtain protein supplements. These were a far cry from the well-stocked modern clinics that he and Lucy had envisioned, but she could imagine what a titanic struggle it had been to wring them out of Marpa.

Over the next ten years Mila must have gone on struggling with his father, because the number of nutrition centers increased and infant mortality statistics in Patan dropped a few precious percentage points. When Lucy read such reports, she was proud of Mila, but sometimes, when she compared what he had been able to accomplish with what he could have accomplished had his father not been such a stubborn fool, she would find herself having imaginary conversations with Marpa, conversations in which she told him that he had wasted the best years of his son's life and brought his country to the edge of ruin. "You proud, greedy old turkey!" she'd tell him, and then she'd realize that she'd spoken out loud on the bus or walking along Market Street, and she'd feel renewed sympathy for old ladies with shopping bags who argued with invisible opponents.

Taking one last look at Sala's picture, Lucy turned the page, putting away thoughts of Mila and Marpa and the whole mess in Patan. Life went on, and there was no use brooding over your failures, especially when there was nothing at all you could do about them. "Rich and Famous," the last section of the album, was a joyous celebration of Cassie's and Lucy's triumphs. Bending eagerly over the photographs, she allowed herself to drink them in, feeling warmed by them. Here was one of the portraits of Paul McCartney from the *Rolling Stone* series that had made Cassie into one of the most sought-after portrait photographers of the decade; here was one of the campaign brochures from Lucy's successful race to win a seat on the San Francisco Board of Supervisors. There was a snapshot of Cassie with Meryl Streep, and a snapshot of Lucy with Dianne Feinstein, but the shot Lucy liked most of all was the one that showed her standing proudly on the front steps of the Refuge, an old Victorian house in the Haight that she and six other women had remodeled and turned into a shelter for homeless women and children.

Lucy sat looking at the "Rich and Famous" section for a long time, enjoying it and feeling good about how far she and Cassie had come since 1968. Putting their lives back together had been a long, hard struggle, but they'd done it with courage, guts, and a sense of humor. Cassie was going to love this album. So what if most of the snapshots were gritty, out of focus, and amateurish. They made a great celebration of twenty years of friendship.

On Monday, Los Angeles was covered with the kind of smog that separated real Angelenos from imports. Palm trees glowed slightly in the brown air, their drooping fronds trembling like the paddles of giant windmills; passengers descending into Los Angeles International Airport saw a vast yellow plain stretching out solidly beneath them; playgrounds were deserted except for a few intrepid joggers who plodded along in time to the music on their Walkmans, inhaling carbon monoxide, lead, and tiny particles of synthetic rubber. On the Hollywood Freeway a double trailer had jackknifed, spreading a mysterious white powder over lanes one through four, tying up traffic for miles in both directions, but inside the large pink stucco building on Santa Monica Boulevard no one gave a damn about air quality. Sealed off from the outside world, Thompson, Greenblat, Karkovsky & Associates made deals, put together packages, and negotiated contracts for their clients, as the air conditioner hummed and the tinted windows made the world outside look rosy and wholesome.

Cassie shifted her camera bag to the other shoulder, jabbed at the elevator button, and decided that the whole place was a setup for Legionnaires' Disease. Whenever she came to see Fred Karkovsky, she found herself wishing that he'd conduct business around his swimming pool like agents did in the movies, but Fred had an aversion to the outdoors. If he'd been a plant, he would have died long ago for lack of sunlight; he had to be the only successful agent in Los Angeles without a tan.

The elevator doors opened with an almost inaudible hiss, exposing a cube of high-tech mirrors. Stepping inside, Cassie pushed the sixth-floor button and leaned back enjoying the privacy. There were only two places in the world where she could still be Cassandra Quinn, and one of them was an empty elevator. The other was alone in bed at night, but that wasn't as pleasant. Since her marriage to Lorenzo Villanueva broke up, she had been finding the nights hard to deal with. With a great deal of effort, she had recently managed to stop sleeping exclusively on the right-hand side of the king-size bed Lorenzo had left behind when he moved out, but she still lay awake for hours missing male companionship. Lucy had suggested she get a tape of a man snoring and play it at night to cure her insomnia. Cassie was considering it.

If bed were a trap full of old memories, an elevator was neutral turf. In an elevator she could be her old self, or at least as much of her old self as was left. Cassie looked into the mirrored walls and saw a woman in her early forties looking back at her. The woman was dressed in a bright orange jumpsuit with lots of zippers, and she had a camera bag slung over her shoulder. She was tall and slender, with full breasts, long dark hair, and the best nose money could buy. She was getting a few wrinkles around her eyes and a few gray hairs, but she was interesting looking, even attractive. She sighed and thought of the days when she had been homely and painfully skinny. Fat lot of good being beautiful had done her. More trouble than it was worth.

The elevator came to a stop. She took a deep breath and prepared herself to face the world as Susan Clark, photographer and feminist; Susan Clark, one of the best portrait photographers in the business. No one messed with Susan, not even producers. The name was a joke and a pretty good one, but only she and Lucy could laugh at it. The Clark came from Clark Kent, Superman's old double identity; Cassandra Quinn, rest her soul, had disappeared forever, not counting fleeting reincarnations in elevators.

She found Fred Karkovsky in his office reading the poems of Catullus. When he saw her, he snapped the book closed and put it upside down on his desk so she couldn't read the title. Fred was a very thin man with a very fat voice, which gave him quite an edge in L.A. where power and fitness ran neck and neck. He also had an extensive education, having been a Jesuit priest for ten years before he quit in the midsixties. His time with the Jesuits was something Fred didn't like to talk about; he felt it made people in the industry nervous to talk to an agent who used to be a priest; worse yet it inspired confessions which Fred was in no mood to hear.

"Hello there," Fred said, rising to shake her hand. Kissing had gone out recently due to the AIDS scare, which was fine by Cassie. She shook his hand and settled down in one of his marshmallow leather chairs. Fred strolled over to the refrigerator near the window, opened it, and took out a bottle of chilled vodka, a bucket of ice, and two frosted glasses. "Care for a drink before we get down to business?"

"I've given it up," Cassie reminded him.

"Right," Fred said. "Sorry, I forgot. Everyone seems to be cleaning up these days." He poured himself a shot of vodka and added two ice cubes. "Care for some orange juice?" Cassie nodded, and he presented her with a large glass of reconstituted orange juice with a maraschino cherry floating on top. "So," he said, settling back behind his desk, "what's new?"

"Empty nest syndrome." Cassie took a sip of the orange juice and wondered if it would be worthwhile asking Fred to open the curtains. He wasn't her regular agent—she was too stubborn and independent to have one—but he got her a lot of work, and she had decided long ago that it was probably best to bear with his eccentricities. "Renny's off to U.C. Santa Barbara and Carla recently started first grade. I'm a lady of leisure."

Fred shook his head. "It must be hard having one kid who's eighteen and one who's six, especially when you have to raise them all by yourself."

"It's a piece of cake." Cassie smiled and fiddled with the zipper on her left arm. "You just get them used to eating rice and beans at an early age, plus you convince them that wearing fashionable clothes is geeky."

"I take it Lorenzo isn't sending you any child support?"

"You take it right. He's in New Mexico living with a twenty-year-old. The last I heard he was working as a janitor."

Fred folded his hands and frowned, and Cassie waited, knowing what was coming next. "You could make a lot more money," he said. He put up his hand: "Don't tell me you hate doing advertising; I know that. You don't have to do any more commercials. I could get you gigs doing more album covers." He pointed to two large black-and-white portraits on his wall, one of Katharine Hepburn and the other of Meryl Streep. "Actresses come in here and see those and go crazy. They beg to know who did them, and when I tell them you did, they want to hire you on the spot to do their publicity photos. Then I have to tell them that you're eccentric, that you only work when you want to, that you have to feel inspired before you'll let anyone stand in front of your camera. I find myself in the position of admitting that you'd rather take pictures of unknown people with craggy faces than immortalize their million-dollar profiles. They always get offended at that point and walk out asking, 'Who does she think she is?' The smarter ones say, 'Who does she think she is, Imogen Cunningham?'"

"I like to think of myself as an artist." Cassie picked up the maraschino cherry by the stem and bit into it. "I was bullied into one career in my life, and I swore that I'd never be bullied into another. Starlets don't inspire me."

"Not even rich starlets?"

"Particularly rich starlets."

"Meanwhile you scrape by, supporting your two kids on God knows what, agreeing to take a job maybe every eighteen months." Fred sighed and shook his head. "Offering you work is an exercise in masochism. If you weren't so damn good, I wouldn't even call you, no one would. But you're the best portrait photographer in the business, outside of maybe Annie Leibovitz, and you know it."

"Right," Cassie agreed, "I'm the best. Also, you have to admit that I'm modest, cheerful, and easy to work with."

"Like van Gogh on a bad day." Fred put his face in his hands, and Cassie waited until he came up for air. She knew the signs: when he started moaning and miming despair, that meant he was about to offer her work. Emerging from his hands, Fred took a gulp of vodka and shook his head. "Let's get down to business," he said. "There's someone I want you to meet." Cassie asked who, and Fred admitted that it was another agent named Seth Flynn. Evidently Seth had a new client who was bankrolling his own movie, and the client wanted to hire Susan Clark to do the production stills. Fred had warned him that Susan was an impossible case and would probably refuse, but Seth had been adamant. At the moment he was waiting in the next room to meet her and try to convince her himself. "He made me promise," Fred concluded, "that I wouldn't tell you a thing about the project until he had a chance at you. He's afraid you'll get the wrong impression."

"Invite him in." Cassie snapped the cherry stem in half and threw it across the desk so that it landed neatly in the center of Fred's large cut-glass ashtray. "I'm always willing to listen to a good pitch." She needed the money, but she wasn't about to let on to Fred how desperate she was, or the next thing she knew he'd be offering her weddings and bar mitzvahs.

Fred was ecstatic. "You're in a cooperative mood. I can't believe it." He quickly pressed the button on his intercom before she could change her mind. "Send Seth Flynn in," he commanded.

Seth Flynn turned out to be a small, heavy man in his mid-sixties, with round, intelligent eyes and a thick mustache. As soon as he opened his mouth, it was obvious that he was a transplanted New Yorker. "I used to write comedy for the *Jackie Gleason Show*," he said, shaking Cassie's hand. "The *Honeymooners* bit, that was my idea. Before that I managed circus acts. I once booked a troupe of acrobats into Hungary in the winter, and they all got frostbite. I'm used to handling difficult situations, and I'm warning you right now, in a friendly way of course, that when Seth Flynn wants something, he gets it."

"Is that so?" Cassie wasn't surprised by Flynn's arrogance; more agents than she could count had told her they always got what they wanted. Obviously he was a liar, but an entertaining one. He sat down across from her and loosened his tie, or rather he started to make the motion of loosening his tie, and then remembered he was wearing an open-necked sports shirt. He leaned forward, confidingly.

"Miss Clark, my client has seen your work in *Rolling Stone* and he's crazy about it." He cleared his throat. "He's got an unusual project and he thinks you might be interested in it. It's classy. It's a biography, a period piece." He said the words *biography* and *period piece* with more enthusiasm than Cassie had heard in years. Everyone knew that period pieces and biographies were box office poison in Hollywood. She suddenly found herself getting interested. "The movie's called *Dharma Road*, and it's based on the life of a beatnik writer named Jack Kerouac. You ever heard of him?"

Cassie nodded, amused. "Of course."

"Now at first take this probably sounds like a pretty noncommercially rewarding type project, but let me tell you right up front that for reasons I'll explain in a minute, it can't fail to do big box office, and like I said, my client wants the whole thing to be classy, and he thinks you're the only one who can give him what he wants when it comes to still photography." He paused and tried to assess Cassie's reaction so far, but she was good at keeping her face unreadable. A tough broad, he thought, but the body's a knockout. He wondered why with a face like that she wasn't on the other side of the camera. He smiled at her warmly, thinking that it would be interesting to unzip all those zippers she was wearing. "My client not only wants you to take the production stills, he wants you to act as a consultant to a research team that will recreate the beatnik era accurately in every respect. He said I should mention Mathew Brady, the Civil War photographer, to you. D. W. Griffith evidently used Brady's work to construct the sets for *Birth of a Nation*. My client says to tell you that he wants to do for the 1950s what D. W. Griffith did for the 1860s." Flynn waved his hands enthusiastically and his mustache trembled. He looked, Cassie thought, like a tubby hummingbird about to settle into a blossom. "We're talking art here, Miss Clark. There will be a new edition of Kerouac's *On the Road* illustrated with stills from the movie; also a new edition of *Dharma Bums*. Plus my client would also like to retain you to do a photo story on himself for publicity purposes: not the usual schlock, but a hard-hitting bit with all the wrinkles left in. Finally, and here's the kicker, if this movie makes money—and it will, believe me—he's going to give twenty-five percent of his share of the net to charity."

"We're talking big money here, Susan," Fred interrupted.

Flynn waved at him to be silent. "I'll be frank, Miss Clark." He shrugged and smiled at her. "You've got me over a barrel. My client doesn't want anyone else to handle this job; he's made that very clear, and since he's paying all the bills, his word is law. You can name your own price, within reason, of course."

Cassie unzipped the zipper at her knee, zipped it back up again, and looked at Flynn with lifted eyebrows. One and one had not yet made two, and this was turning into a very odd conversation. "You haven't told me who this client of yours is, Mr. Flynn. Frankly, I find that a little strange. He must be richer than God to be bankrolling his own movie. Who are you asking me to work for? a Mafia don? Marcos? an Arab sheik?"

Flynn laughed uneasily and turned to Fred, who had on his oh-no-there-she-goes look. "Quite the kidder, isn't she?" He turned back to Cassie. "It's nothing like that. My client's gotten all his money honestly. His name is—" he paused for effect, "David Blake."

Cassie started, knocked over her glass, and sent orange juice all over Fred's white shag rug. The juice puddled in the hairs under Fred's teak desk, it crept into the creases of the marshmallow leather chair and dripped into her lap. Fortunately she was wearing orange. She dabbed at the juice with the end of her scarf and muttered apologies, trying to gather her wits. David Blake wanted to hire her to do the stills for his movie! Had he somehow found out who she was? No, impossible. No one but Lucy knew that Susan Clark was Cassandra Quinn. This was one of those crazy coincidences that happened every so often in life.

"You may only think of Mr. Blake as a famous rock star," Flynn was saying, "but the man is a lot more than that. He went to Harvard."

Do tell, Cassie thought.

"He also used to write poetry, good poetry some people say. For the last twenty years or so, he's been writing song lyrics and making a lot of money at it, but now Mr. Blake has achieved success and he wants to do something more—" Flynn groped for the right word, "something classy."

"Let's be honest," Fred said. "The guy is having a midlife crisis. He doesn't want to go down in history as the hippie in the black leather jacket who wowed them at Woodstock with 'Get Out of Our Way.'"

"So," Flynn said, "what do you think?"

"Think?" Cassie was having a hard time getting her mind to work at all. She closed her mouth and stared at Flynn, feeling like one of the contestants on that old game show "This Is Your Life."

"Are you okay, Susan?" Fred sounded worried.

Cassie managed to summon up enough presence of mind to reassure him that she was fine. She got to her feet and slung her camera bag over her shoulder. "I'll let you know soon," she told Flynn. "I'll call you. It's an interesting offer, very interesting." She knew she sounded like a fool, but she couldn't help it. She was flabbergasted, confused, and, why not admit it, tempted. David was part of Cassandra Quinn's life, not the best part, perhaps, but a part. Seeing him would be like having a look at a piece of her past. What would he be like after all these years? Would he recognize her? That was the real question. If there was the slightest chance that he might, then she couldn't afford the risk. The FBI wasn't looking for her very hard after twenty years, but she had no doubt that she was still in their files somewhere, and there was no statute of limitations on people who were wanted for murder. Flynn's offer might have turned her brains to mush, but she still had her survival instincts intact.

"So we'll be hearing from you?" Fred was following her across the room. Embarrassed, Cassie realized suddenly that she had been about to walk out without saying good-bye to him.

"Yes," she promised, "definitely, and I'm sorry about your rug."

"Forget the rug." Fred reached out to pat her on the shoulder, then reconsidered. "Take this job. You'll never get another one as good, Susan."

"I have to think it over. I need time." She fled out of Fred's office and plunged into the privacy of the elevator. David Blake, her mind kept saying. David Blake. It's too much. It's impossible. She had to find a phone; she had to call San Francisco and tell Lucy what had just happened. Only Lucy would understand.

Lucy sat in her apartment polishing off a plate of spaghetti and looking out at Mrs. Albergetti's roses which were busy soaking up the late afternoon sunshine. Finishing her dinner, she took a sip of wine and sat back content, or as content as she could manage to be considering what kind of day it had been. The morning had started off with two divorce cases: one for a wealthy couple who were fighting bitterly over who got the yacht and the English sheepdog, and one for a woman so poor that all she wanted from her estranged husband was fifty dollars a month child support. Then Maria Eglesias had appeared at her office to report that she and her two children were being threatened with eviction again from the sleazy hotel Welfare had put them into.

Lucy massaged her temples with her thumbs and thought that it was too bad that there wasn't room for Maria and her kids at the Refuge, but there were only twenty places, all full at present, and a waiting list of homeless mothers and children so long that sometimes she was tempted to nail it to the door of the mayor's office and invite the press in to take pictures, but as the youngest, least powerful member of the San Francisco Board of Supervisors, she had to watch her step. She was just trying to decide whether or not to pay a call on Maria this evening and see if she could smooth things over with the manager, when the phone rang.

Cassie was on the other end of the line, so excited she was barely coherent. "Lou," she exclaimed, "do I have news for you!" "Lou" had proved a convenient nickname. It stood for Lucy and it stood for Louise, and if the line were tapped no one would know the difference. Cassie was haunted by the fear that after all these years the FBI was still hunting for her, so Lucy was careful always to call her "Susan" on the phone.

"What's up, Susan?" she inquired, parking her wineglass on the table.

"What's up is that it looks like I might be coming up to North Beach in a couple of weeks to take some preproduction stills for a film about the Beat generation. It's called *Dharma Road* and it's a biography of Kerouac."

"That's great." Lucy was delighted. "You and the kids can stay with me if you don't mind camping out on the living-room floor. I've got three foam futons."

"Not kids. *Kid.*" Cassie chuckled. "You keep forgetting that Renny's off at college. I'm not bringing Carla with me either because she'd have to miss school. Thank God Marta, Lorenzo's mother, loves to look after her. My friendship with Marta was the only good thing I got out of that marriage. It'll just be you and me, like old times."

"I'll lay in some brownie mix for you to burn," Lucy offered, "and we can celebrate your birthday belatedly in style. Maybe I'll even go to an antiques store and buy some pink sponge hair rollers so we can recreate the ambiance of Holmes Hall. It's a cinch neither of us is going to the class reunion. We can sit up late, stuff our faces, and bemoan our lack of success with men."

"That brings me to the real news." Cassie paused dramatically. "Guess who's financing this movie and guess who's playing Kerouac?"

"Tom Cruise? Dustin Hoffman?"

"Try David Blake."

"Jesus, you have to be kidding." She sat down on the couch and stared at the receiver, feeling an odd mix of emotions at the mention of David's name: surprise, mostly, but something else too, something that was hard to put into words but that was unsettling and altogether unexpected. "You can't possibly be serious."

"I'm completely serious. David's evidently having some kind of crisis of artistic conscience. After twenty years of sex, drugs, and rock and roll, he's decided that he should have been Walt Whitman after all, or to be more precise, he's finally realized that he should have stayed a beatnik poet. If you ask me, Lou, our mutual friend has discovered that there's gridlock in the fast lane."

"But you can't possibly work with him. You'll have to be in the same room with him for hours at a time and, my God, suppose he—" She was going to say, *Suppose he recognizes you*, but she remembered just in time that they were talking on the phone. She was upset that Cassie could even consider taking such a risk.

"Why not?" Cassie grumbled, obviously peeved by her reaction.

"Because it's too high profile. He's liable to—" She stopped, feeling upset and annoyed. There was no way she could say this in code if Cassie kept refusing to get the drift.

"Look who's talking high profile. You're on the Board of Supervisors, and you worry about *me* blowing our cover."

"I've only agreed to run for the board to save the Refuge; programs for women and children were getting cut right and left. Besides it's different for me. I'm—" *Officially dead*, she thought, *unrecognizable, not wanted for murder, and it's unlikely that Arjuna's thugs are still looking for me after all these years*, but she couldn't say that until she and Cass were in the same room. "Be sensible," she begged. She knew instantly that that was the wrong thing to say. One of the perversities of Cassie's character was that she never knew exactly what she wanted to do until someone told her not to.

"Relax. This won't involve you at all, and it's perfectly safe. I need the money, and remember, Lou, we're no longer *les chickens de printemps.*"

Translated from Cassie's franglais, that meant that they were no longer spring chickens. Translated again, it meant that she was convinced David would never recognize her. All of which was probably true, but just the same Lucy wished that Cassie would forget the whole thing. She spent the next five minutes pleading with her to do just that, as Cassie grew more and more stubborn.

"I'm curious to see what David's turned into," she kept saying, "aren't you?"

Lucy denied it, but the truth was she was curious. Having completely failed to convince Cassie to turn down the job, she repeated her offer of a place to stay and hung up the phone. She'd have to work on Cassie in person and make her see that this was a completely crazy thing to do.

Three days passed, three uneventful days during which Lucy attended the weekly meeting of the Board of Supervisors, discussed a proposed increase in BART fares, met with clients, filed petitions, argued cases in court, and spent whatever spare time she had at the Refuge helping the volunteers paint the children's playroom blue. On Tuesday she packed up the photograph album and mailed it to Cassie by express mail, figuring that she'd open it early, remember her own past, and come to her senses, but the album had no effect. Cassie called to thank her on Wednesday, and although she was as enthusiastic about the present as Lucy could have wished, she didn't mention reconsidering her decision to work for David, and Lucy didn't bring it up. The more you tried to change Cassie's mind, the more obstinate she got.

By Friday Lucy was exhausted and looking forward to a weekend puttering around her apartment and maybe taking a short hike at Point Reyes to see if she could spot some of the migrating whales, but the week wasn't over yet. The moon, as Cassie would have said in her astrological days, was in Old Loves, and another surprise waited for her.

She was sitting in the lobby of a run-down hotel in the Tenderloin district when she heard the news, just sitting there, catching her breath among the rows of cheap plastic furniture and the pots of fake plastic plants, congratulating herself for having solved Maria Eglesias's housing problem. Negotiations with the manager had been delicate. He had turned out to be from New Delhi, a devout Hindu who was absolutely opposed to liquor of any kind. His hotel, he had informed Lucy proudly, never admitted anyone under the influence of alcohol. In a part of town where winos were the main customers, this was quite a claim, and it was clear that he meant what he said. Lucy had pointed out, as gently as possible, that it wasn't Maria who had the drinking problem, but her ex-husband, and that legally he had no right to evict her and the children unless *they* did something. She had promised to get Maria to sign a restraining order to keep her husband off the premises, pleaded with Mr. Prasad to think of the welfare of Maria's two homeless children, and softened him up with a few polite words of Hindi that she had picked up during her stay in India. Mr. Prasad had come around at the sound of the Hindi, and she had felt quite nostalgic at the sight of him standing there in his high-collared shirt, as if Mr. Kapur, her old friend and adviser, had stepped out of the past to pay her a visit.

Taking off her left shoe, she rubbed her foot and decided she would take a bus back to North Beach instead of walking as she usually did. She liked the exercise, but she was exhausted and seemed to be developing a blister. That was what you got for wearing high heels in the city. She would have gladly worn tennis shoes, but people expected their lawyers to dress conservatively and look prosperous. It gave them confidence.

Smothering a yawn, she looked up at the television set, chained to the wall as was usual in such places. The evening news was on, and Dan Rather was talking about Brazil's latest threat to renege on its foreign debt. At least that's what she assumed he was talking about since someone had been intelligent enough to turn down the sound. Ordinarily, televisions in the hotel lobbies off Market Street blared at deafening levels.

She started to put her shoe back on when suddenly, with no warning, she found herself looking at the streets of Sindhala. Up on the screen a Rolls Royce was burning in Kalpa Square. Leaping to her feet, she pounced on the set and turned up the sound. A riot was in progress. As she watched, the situation grew worse. Crowds of angry Patanese attacked another car. Swarming over it, they smashed the windows, pulled out a man in a business suit, threw him to the cobblestones, and began to beat him. Over the noise of the mob she could hear a reporter speaking in that excited on-the-edge-of-breaking tone that came with major disasters.

King Marpa was dead.

Patan was on the verge of revolution.

The military had taken over the government.

General Ajiti Karwit Arjuna, head of the new military junta, had assured the outside world that order was being restored.

Then came Arjuna himself, sitting at Marpa's desk behind a row of bonsai trees, still wearing sunglasses and gold chains, his face old and dry, wrinkled and turtlelike. Smiling coldly he announced that Prince Mila was in protective custody. The military, he insisted, had only intervened to prevent a communist coup d'état. Sound of shelling, screen trembling, bonsai trees swaying in an invisible breeze. Concussion after concussion. "No, there was no resistance," Arjuna insisted. End of interview. Horizontal lines, static. Dan Rather looking somber.

Lucy sat for a moment, staring at the screen as a vapid commercial for instant noodles replaced Dan Rather. Too upset to get to her feet, she put her face in her hands and tried to blot out the sound. This was terrible; it was a catastrophe. The thought of Arjuna seizing power was terrifying. He was a merciless son of a bitch, and it didn't take much imagination to figure out what he was planning to do to Mila.

For the next three days she clung to the television and radio as the news out of Patan grew worse and worse. Saturday and Sunday were endless. She drank dozens of cups of coffee, paced her apartment, and alternated between hope and fear. She had never stopped loving Mila, but over the years her feelings for him had moved from the front of her heart to the back. Now, she remembered with renewed intensity how tender he had been, how hard he had fought for her freedom. She remembered the sound of his laughter, the look of love that always came into his eyes when he caught sight of her.

On Sunday night she had a long, disturbing dream. She was back in Patan, sitting in the Hindu garden, lonely and afraid, when suddenly Mila appeared holding an ivory and gold box inlaid with swans and court ladies. The swans were black and ominous, and the ladies were dressed in mourning.

She leapt to her feet and began to push him toward the garden wall, thinking that if he could just climb it he would be safe. *Run for your life!* she begged. *Run, darling!* But instead of running, Mila took her in his arms and kissed her. *I've always loved you*, he said. *I waited for you for twenty years, and now I've come to say good-bye.* Pressing the box into her hands, he vanished.

The dream was prophetic. On Monday morning she woke, turned on the news, and learned that during the night the PLF troops had overrun the palace and General Arjuna had committed suicide. Arjuna's last act before he took his own life had been to order Mila's execution.

Cassie flew up from Los Angeles the next day and they held a wake in Lucy's apartment. The wake consisted in part of two large pizzas, Calistoga water for Cassie, and wine for Lucy, but mostly it consisted of the two of them sitting silently together, grieving. Every once in a while Lucy would reach out and grab Cassie's hand for comfort, and Cassie would squeeze it and pat it and murmur something kind. On the surface it didn't look like much, and if Mrs. Albergetti had come to water her garden she might have wondered what the two women were doing, but to Lucy, Cassie's presence meant everything. She felt so sad. Only Cassie could understand what a big hole Mila's death had left in her life. Finally, Lucy broke down and started crying, and Cassie comforted her.

"I miss him," she sobbed. "I know it's hard to believe that I could after all these years, but I do. I loved him a lot, Cass."

"I know," Cassie murmured, "I know." She thought of Andy and how lonely and sad she had felt when he died. "Time doesn't mean anything when you really love someone."

Lucy cried for a long time. At last she sat up and took the Kleenex Cassie offered her and wiped her eyes. The day was sunny and the boats were back out on the bay, but as she looked toward the Marin headlands, she saw everything through a fog of misery. She felt pale and heavy and old. When she was six she had felt this same heaviness, and again when she was fifteen. This, she thought, is the weight of death; it presses on us and bears us down, and sooner or later it will crush all of us, even Cassie, who is sitting here trying to comfort me. She wished she could believe in something, in God or even the divinity of nature, but all she could imagine on the other side of life was a blank. She imagined a telephone going dead, static on the line, a long silence.

"I know this sounds crazy," she said, "but I really feel widowed. I always thought I'd see Mila again. You and I used to talk about how someday things would change, and I'd be able to call him up on the phone and tell him who I was and what I'd been doing all these years. I'd go back to Patan, and he and I would do all the things we'd planned to do. Sometimes, after those conversations, I'd start longing to hear from him. I just wanted a few words, something to show that he was thinking along the same lines. I tried to contact him, you know, not just once but several times. I knew that under the circumstances it wasn't going to be easy, but for a long time—for years—I was convinced that if I just exercised enough ingenuity, I'd be able to get some kind of message through to him."

"You never told me you tried to get in touch with him," Cassie said. "Although, frankly, I'm not surprised." She wished that she could say something more to Lucy, something encouraging about Mila's death that would help her accept it, but all she had to offer was the flow of an ordinary conversation. "Sometimes I used to imagine that you two were writing to each other in secret, planning a reunion in Brazil or Mozambique or some other out-of-the-way place. I used to think how romantic that would be, and then I'd get freaked and think that if you did meet Mila on the sly, maybe Arjuna or the FBI or Interpol would track the two of you down and it would blow our cover, and I'd be tempted to ask you if you *were* writing to him, only I didn't want you to think I didn't trust you, not after all we'd been through together."

Lucy nodded and drank more wine. She would have been glad to obliterate herself with it, but she knew that if she tried, she would only end up feeling sick, so she took small, measured sips, rationing the comfort. "I used to be afraid of that too," she confessed, "so I was very discreet, maybe too discreet because nothing I did ever panned out." She fell silent for a moment, studying the wine in her glass. "The first time," she continued, "I tried writing him an anonymous letter. I thought, why not be simple and direct? Who knows; it could work. But it didn't, of course. I rented a mail box in south San Francisco—don't laugh—to use as a return address, but I might as well have saved my money. I never heard a word. The second time, I got smarter. I wrote the American ambassador in Sindhala, just like I did when I was in

India—a new ambassador, by the way, because good old Willis Elderby was history by that time." She smiled sadly and shook her head. "I told the ambassador that I was a college friend of Mila's and asked him to give Mila my address so we could correspond. In return, I got a travel brochure inviting me to 'See Scenic Patan, Land of Enchantment.' I can't tell you how many times I cried over that stupid thing. The ambassador must have thought I was just another dizzy, royalty-crazed American looking for the prince's autograph. I don't imagine he even passed my letter on to Mila. After that came the Tibetan Buddhists."

"What Tibetan Buddhists?" Cassie plucked a bit of fennel off of a nearby plant and twirled it between her fingers. She frowned, trying to remember some occasion when Lucy had been involved with Tibetans, but the only Buddhist she could recall was Mila himself. She thought of all the things she didn't know about Lucy's life and all the things Lucy didn't know about hers. Even when you were as close as they were, there were always secrets. Maybe no one ever got to know anyone completely. The thought made her sad. "Where was I when all this was going on?" she asked.

"You were in L.A., Cass, and besides, even if you'd seen these people, you would have thought they were Methodists or Episcopalians or something perfectly ordinary. They didn't shave their heads and jump around in orange robes. They wore normal clothes, except that under their shirts they had these little red strings around their necks that meant they'd taken vows from the Dalai Lama. One day I read in the *Berkeley Express* that a half dozen of them were going on a pilgrimage to Patan. Mila was famously into Tibetan Buddhism in those days, and I figured that there was a good chance he'd give them a personal welcome, so on a hunch, I went over to their center and persuaded them to take a message to him. They thought it was very funny, a lady lawyer sending a message to a prince, but they were accommodating people, very nice, and they didn't ask a lot of questions." She shrugged. "The only problem was that they never ran into him while they were in Patan."

She went back to her wine. "I'll spare you the story of my other attempts to get in touch with him. Suffice it to say they all failed. Of course in my rational moments, I knew it was highly unlikely that I'd ever be able to get through to him. If I had been able to come out in the open as Lucy Constable, it would have been a piece of cake, but as

Louise Crest, private citizen and fugitive in hiding, what chance did I have? Still, in some dark, irrational corner of my heart, I always hoped. Despite the rumors that he was going to marry that Nepalese princess, Mila never took another wife, and I thought perhaps he—" She stopped in midsentence, too upset to continue. "Oh, dammit," she said. "Am I a fool to think he was waiting for me, Cass?"

Cassie shook her head and plucked at the sprig of fennel she was holding in her hand. The fennel smelled warm and licoricelike, and she sat for a moment smelling that smell, thinking it reminded her of the curry she had eaten at Lucy's wedding. "No, you're not a fool," she said softly. "I understand how you feel. Whether you ever heard from him or not doesn't matter. I know he loved you, and he was waiting for you too, I'm sure of it."

"You are?"

"Yes."

She had expected Lucy to be relieved, but instead Lucy leaned forward, her face tight with controlled fury. "And what good did it do either of us to wait? Thanks to Arjuna, poor Mila was virtually imprisoned in Patan for the last twenty years. *Twenty years*, Cass. Who would have ever thought Marpa would live that long? And all that time Arjuna was manipulating him, scaring him with threats of a communist revolution, turning him into the very sort of king whose people would do *anything* to get rid of him. You know, I hate Arjuna. Even now, when he's dead and I'm finally free from the fear that he's going to have me killed, I still hate him. Maybe another twenty years will wash that feeling out of my heart, but I doubt it. Mila and I could have stayed married if it hadn't been for him."

There was nothing Cassie could say to that, no comfort she could offer. They sat for a while in silence. Lucy glared angrily at the cuff of her sweater, and Cassie went on picking at the fennel. Gradually, Lucy grew calmer. She ate some pizza, let the sunlight soak in, and tried to understand her life and why it had turned out as it had. "Has it ever occurred to you," she said at last, "that you and I have had some particularly rotten luck with men?"

"Yes," Cassie agreed, "it has, but no worse than most women of our generation. Love has been a mess for all of us."

"You think so?"

"I'm sure of it." Cassie waved at the flowers, the bay, the sky, indicting all of them. "We blew it somehow. It's not just the herpes and the AIDS—that's bad enough—it's the mistrust between men and women that's been the worst part of the eighties. And don't get me wrong. I don't think the Women's Movement is to blame. The mistrust was there when we were in college. It came out of the fifties and it kept getting worse and worse, like some kind of plague, until no one could connect to anyone or commit to anyone anymore. Look at the state we're in: I don't know more than four or five people who haven't been divorced at least once; men walk off and leave their children and don't pay child support; and as for finding someone undamaged enough to love," she shrugged, "forget it."

"Maybe it was our own fault." Lucy sighed and shook her head. "We had such great expectations; we were going to remake the world; we were such merciless idealists. Look at me. I've spent the last twenty years looking for someone as good as Mila. I wasn't going to take any inferior substitutes, not me. I'm not saying that's the reason I was never able to get pregnant with any of the men I slept with, but I'm sure that's why I could never love any of them. I could never be with any of those men, even when we were lying together in bed, because part of me was always with Mila, and what was left over was still with David. I only loved twice in my life, and each time it was total. That's what I thought love should be. And where has that idealism gotten me? All I ever wanted in life was to do some good for other people and have a family of my own. Well, I've managed to do a little good. I'm proud of the Refuge, but I'm lonely, Cass."

"I'm lonely too," Cassie admitted.

"But you have your children."

"That's true." Cassie leaned forward and her eyes hardened. "But it's not the same. I love Renny and Carla, and I'd walk through fire for them, but it's not easy being a single mother. Sometimes when I see them perfectly healthy, I think of Andy and what a goddam waste his suicide was. I'm still mad at him, Lou. Not a week goes by that I don't want to yell at him, *Look! These could have been our kids! They came out just fine; your compound had no effect on me!* And I'll tell you something else: I haven't had an orgasm since Andy died. Believe me, I've tried, but zip, nothing." She shrugged and sat back. "I don't know why. Sometimes I think it's because I can never be myself. This face isn't mine. It belongs to Susan Clark. When Susan climbs in bed with a man, Cassie Quinn, the real me, gets left behind. Maybe I can't have a decent relationship because I can't talk about my own past. Maybe I can't be intimate because I always have a secret voice whispering in my ear that no one is to be trusted. Whatever the reason, I feel like something defective."

"You aren't defective, Cass. You're a good friend and a wonderful person."

"Am I?" Cassie frowned. "I wonder."

"Look at it this way." Lucy poured herself a glass of wine and lifted it to Cassie, toasting her. "No matter what has happened, we still have each other."

"That's true." Cassie brightened. "We do."

"Do you know what one of the women at the Refuge said to me the other day?"

"No, what?"

"She said, 'Husbands come and go, but friends are forever.'"

Cassie threw back her head and laughed. "Ain't it the truth."

Lucy began to laugh too, so hard she choked on her wine, and Cassie had to pound her on the back, and in the confusion they forgot everything except the fact they were alive and together and still friends after so many years.

When they finally sobered up, Cassie opened her purse and took out her wallet. "I have something I thought you might like to see," she said. "It doesn't fit in the birthday album you gave me, but it's another piece of our mutual past. I had it stuffed in my shirt pocket the night of the explosion because I'd been sorting through some old photos just before you came over, and I haven't shown it to you until now because it was the only bit of Andy I had left, and I couldn't bear to share it. It's a snapshot that I took of all of us on that day we went rock climbing and Bill Bishop got himself stuck. I used an automatic timer so I'm in it, too, for once." She extracted the snapshot from her wallet and handed it to Lucy. "I call it 'Season of Shadows.'"

Lucy took the photograph, spread it out in front of her, and looked at it for a long time without saying a word. There they all were—Andy, Cassie, Lucy, Mila—muffled in ski parkas, smiling like crazy at the camera: four college students in their early twenties looking like they didn't have a care in the world. Like all Cassie's photos, this one caught something essential. Lucy pondered it, trying to figure out exactly what made it so touching. The snapshot had been taken near the end of the day; if you looked closely, you could see four shadows, long and exaggerated, stretching out behind the group to the ragged edge of the quarry pit. Beyond that there was nothing but a dark crescent that represented the inside of the quarry. Suddenly she understood Cassie's genius: that cliff was their future. Andy and Mila had already gone over the edge. She and Cassie were the only ones left.

· 2 ·

On Wednesday morning Lucy drove Cassie to the airport and said good-bye until the following week when Cassie would return to begin preproduction work on *Dharma Road*. Then, feeling particularly sad and lonely, she went to her office to find a delegation waiting for her. At the sight of the three women and two men standing in the reception area clustered together like a flock of well-dressed birds, her heart sank. It wasn't as if she didn't like them: she did. On some level they might have even qualified as friends, but when they appeared out of nowhere without an appointment it meant that a political problem had cropped up. She wondered wearily what water main had broken, what ugly multistory skyscraper had made it past the Planning Commission, what city park had been taken over by crack dealers. Usually she enjoyed pouncing on corrupt developers and harassing the mayor about keeping the streets safe, but this morning she was in no mood to jump back into the political fray. Mila's death hung over her like a gray cloud; she wanted to sit in her office with the phones unplugged, drinking tea and grieving, but there was no way she could explain that to anyone except Cassie, so she put on the best smile she could muster and shook hands all around.

"Good morning," she said. She imagined fleetingly what they would think if she suddenly sat down on the floor, put her head between her knees, and started sobbing and tearing her hair. That was the way widows expressed grief in Patan: they rent their clothes, threw themselves on the cremation pyre, and clasped their man in their arms one last time. In Patan a woman who had lost her husband got to carry on for hours, raging at the top of her lungs, cursing the gods and fate and everyone else in sight.

"Good morning, Louise," they chorused, pumping her hand. They were liberal people of good conscience, rich and powerful and decent. They had been the mainstays of her campaign to get elected to the Board of Supervisors, and she owed them a great deal, but she couldn't help wishing that just for once they would suffer simultaneous heart attacks and leave her in peace.

"What can I do for you?" she asked guiltily, glad none of them could read her mind.

"Invite us into your office," Hanson Millwright suggested. Bald and tubby, Hanson looked like a stunted teddy bear, measuring, Lucy had calculated, only a little over five foot two, but he was a genius at creating something out of nothing. At the age of fifteen he had bought himself a shrimp boat and started taking tourists on cruises of the Bay, charging them a dollar and feeding them lunch. Now, at fifty, he owned a huge fleet of tour boats, several hotels, and a major hunk of Ghirardelli Square. Hanson winked and nudged her with his elbow. "Invite us in, unless of course you've got a hot date stashed under your desk."

"Hanson!" Paula Johnson, a slender black woman, directed a withering glance at him. She was the head of the Human Rights Commission and was always on the watch for anything that smacked of sexism. "He doesn't mean that," she said to Lucy. She turned on Hanson. "Do you?"

Poor Hanson shrunk down to something under five feet beneath Paula's glare. "No, of course not. Just kidding."

Lucy decided that to prevent further bloodshed she'd better invite them into her office. They came in willingly, and there was an awkward silence. Hanson inspected her paperweight; Paula looked up at the ceiling; Sandra Hauge, a successful trial lawyer, fiddled with the strap on her purse; and Stan Sikes, who owned a high-tech computer company in Silicon Valley, stared off into space. Something big was definitely in the air, and she wondered what the hell it was. Only Liz Cardullo seemed to be functioning normally, which was hardly surprising since it would have taken a combination of bubonic plague and atomic war to throw Liz off stride.

"You've done a great job on the Board of Sups," Liz observed. Liz, a state senator, was a white-haired, matronly looking woman in her mid-fifties who had authored a half dozen child-care bills, some pioneering legislation on custody rights, and who had, on more than one occasion, completely dismantled her opponents with a tongue so sharp that her enemies claimed she honed it on a whetstone. When Liz started speaking softly and paying you compliments, you were in big trouble.

"Thanks," Lucy said through clenched teeth. Now she knew what they had come for. They weren't going to support her for reelection. Well, the hell with them. She wanted to keep that position on the Board of Sups, and she would, with or without their help. There were other people she could go to for campaign funds, people who thought she had been doing one hell of a good job. She was so sure they were going to dump her that what Liz said next took her completely by surprise.

"We know how hard you've fought to get funding for programs like the Refuge," Liz continued, "and we want you to know that we're all behind you. You've built quite a power base in this community, Louise. No one has a better reputation for defending the rights of mothers and children. You draw votes from men and women of all races and all social classes, and that brings me to why we're here today." She cleared her throat and looked at Hanson, Paula, Sandra, and Stan. "We want you to consider running for mayor next year."

"Run for mayor?" Lucy had an irrational image of herself in a jogging suit doing the Bay to Breakers Marathon. The words *mayor* and *run* wouldn't go together in her mind. "Huh?" she said. "What?" It wasn't one of her most articulate moments.

"We want you to run for mayor," Liz repeated.

"Me?"

"No, Sylvester Stallone. Of course you."

For a few seconds Lucy let herself imagine all the things she could do if she were mayor: build new low-income housing, set up city soup kitchens, improve the schools, stop downtown from becoming a lightless canyon lined with ugly skyscrapers. But all of that was pure fantasy. If she so much as considered running, she'd be exposed to the kind of public scrutiny that would more likely get her into Santa Rita Women's Prison than into city hall. "I'm sorry." She shook her head. "I couldn't possibly. I'm touched, I'm flattered but—"

"What!" Liz interrupted.

"I can't," Lucy repeated. Running for the Board of Sups had been risky enough; running for mayor would be insane. The risk of having reporters snooping into your past went up exponentially. Sups were low-profile workhorses. Mayors, on the other hand— My god, only a few years ago Dianne Feinstein was being seriously considered as a vice presidential candidate. She cast around for some acceptable excuse. "I'm not qualified." It was a lame reason, and Liz pounced on it.

"Don't be ridiculous, Louise. What's gotten into you? You're at least as qualified as the present mayor and a lot more qualified than many we've had in the past." Her face colored slightly, and she leaned toward Lucy. "You're too humble," she admonished. "Let's talk facts: this city faces another major budget deficit. The next mayor is going to have to make some hard decisions, and we want those decisions to be made by *you*, not by some flunky who's sold out to big business interests."

"Think of the good you could do." Sandra Hauge moved in for the kill. She was a small woman, tidy and quick, with a chin like a knife blade and eyes as sharp as tacks. She had been one of Lucy's professors at Boalt. What would she say if she knew that Lucy had bought the undergraduate transcripts that got her admitted? What would any of them say if they knew the truth? Lucy had a crazy urge to laugh. It was all so disappointing. She could have had a shot at being mayor of San Francisco except for one tiny little hitch: Louise Crest had a past that wouldn't bear scrutiny.

"It's an open secret that the Refuge is in bad financial shape and may have to close," Sandy was saying. "Nearly every decent program in the city is in the same boat, just hanging on from week to week. If you were sitting in the mayor's office, you'd be the one setting budget priorities. You've got to run, Louise."

"No."

"What do you mean no?"

"I can't do it."

"I'm not following this," Hanson complained. "Why won't she run?"

"She's going to," Liz snapped. "Just hang on, Hanson. We've surprised her, that's all. She needs some time to assimilate the idea."

"No, I don't." Lucy was beginning to panic; her excuses sounded hollow and unconvincing, and the truth was so bizarre that if she so much as mentioned it, they'd probably think she was having a nervous breakdown. *Believe me,* she felt like telling them, *you don't want me as your candidate. If you think there were problems with Gary Hart, just wait.*

"I'm a very private person." She groped for some kind of graceful exit and only succeeded in making things worse. "You may not believe this, but I'm shy."

"Bull," Liz snapped. "You're about as shy as a Doberman. Don't talk nonsense, Louise."

"I'm serious: I'd hate having my face on billboards. I'm not good at slinging mud. I'm—"

"You're the only woman for the job," Liz interrupted. She turned to the others. "Let's get out of here," she said, "and let her think it over."

"But—" Lucy protested.

"But nothing." Sandra grabbed Lucy's hand and gave it a good brisk shake. "We're going, Louise, but we're coming back. The election is in '91, and it's not any too soon to get moving on this. In case we haven't made it clear yet, we want *you*. You may not recognize it, but you're made for campaigning."

After they left, Lucy walked over to the window and stared at the view, trying to sort out her feelings. Mila's death and now this. It was too much. She felt overwhelmed by contradictory emotions: grief, elation, disappointment. It was enough to make a person crazy. In front of her a crimson-and-cream-colored cable car labored up the Powell Street hill, passengers clinging to the sides. She pressed her forehead against the glass and watched it struggle toward the summit. There was so much beauty in this city, so much pain, such a mixture of wealth and poverty. What would it feel like to have the power to shift that balance, to make the beauty more beautiful, the pain less painful? She had failed to do just that in Patan, and now she was being given a second chance. Second chances were rare. She took a deep breath and forced herself to turn away from the sight of the city toiling beneath her. San Francisco was just going to have to get along without Louise Crest.

At 10:25 on Thursday morning David Blake was sprawled flat on his back on his Sharper Image aquarium water bed, snoring softly through his nose. Beneath him, lapped in tepid greenish water, neon tetras darted in and out of a fake rock garden chased by rare red-and-purple Tunisian fighting fish. He had bought the bed back in the days when he was still doing a lot of coke, before Ronnie Craft, his drummer, died freebasing and put the fear of God into everyone in the band. Now that

David was totally off coke, he rarely watched the fish, but he kept the bed because on the increasingly rare occasions that he brought a groupie home to sleep with him, it gave him something to talk about. Over the past three years, faced with the threat of AIDS, David had started to sleep alone more often than not, and sometime in the last nine months or so he had started to prefer it that way. Besides, when he had the whole water bed to himself, he dreamed better.

The dream he was having at the moment was a particularly pleasant one. He was at Woodstock, dressed in his favorite black leather jacket, stoned on Mickey Mouse blotter acid, playing dueling guitars with Jimi Hendrix while the crowd went wild. At the same time—and this was the best part—he was reciting his own poems at the top of his lungs. The poems were from *Living in the Volcano*, and appropriately enough Bill Bishop was looking on jealously while Sandy Roberts, his old nemesis from the *Advocate*, sat at the edge of the stage with his head in his hands, beaten at last. Out in front of him, in a psychedelic blue haze, the crowd was going wild. *Poet! poet! poet!* the hippie old ladies yelled, ripping off their shirts and flashing their breasts at him as they screamed for him to come down and sock it to them. He was just about to do just that when the alarm clock went off, shearing through his skull like a knife.

Swearing, David reached out and beat the clock into submission with the flat of his hand. The clock, also from Sharper Image, was one of the fancy kind that projected the time on the ceiling. Opening his eyes as little as possible, he saw that it was 10:26 A.M. Shit, he thought. His dream was blown, completely humpty-dumptied with no hope of putting it back together.

Reluctantly, he sat up, swung his legs over the edge of the bed, and contemplated the wreck of another day. Through the double French doors that led to the deck, he could see the beach, a long curve of oatmeal-colored sand, smooth as a sheet without a bottle or a cup or a hunk of Styrofoam in sight. La Vista Beach was always unnervingly clean, a lot cleaner than the beach at the Malibu Colony, but then the houses were bigger at La Vista, the average income of the residents astronomical, and no one thought twice about paying a full-time cleaning crew to pick up the flotsam.

Yawning, he stretched and his joints popped like corn. Was he getting arthritis in his fingers? His dad had had it. He strummed a few phantom guitar notes, feeling a rush of anxiety. His hands were insured by Lloyds of London, but that wouldn't be much consolation if the joints started freezing up from natural causes. Fish oil was supposed to be good for arthritis, but it tasted rotten. He'd choke some down anyway and maybe it would help. Besides, the last doctor he'd gone to had told him he should be eating a lot of fish. His cholesterol level was high, 270 plus, and this after two years of brown rice, seaweed, and jogging. Running his tongue around his teeth, he wished he was back in his dream. It was a drag to wake up in a forty-six-year-old body. He tried to recall exactly what had been happening, but it was all a vague blur. There'd been music, of course. There was always music in his dreams.

A few disconnected bits remained, throbbing at the back of his mind like a drum track. By the time he got out of the shower, he remembered that he wanted to have a look at *Living in the Volcano* to see if the poems were as good as he remembered. Unfortunately, they were. He sat for a long time reading and rereading them, wishing like hell he could write something as honest and intelligent and powerful as he had when he was at Harvard. He should never have given up poetry; he knew that now, about twenty years too late. Except for being able to support his mother and sisters and tell his father to go to hell, selling out hadn't been worth it.

The drum track in his head picked up speed. Leaning back in the chair, he put his feet up on the desk and began to massage his temples, clockwise and then counterclockwise just as his polarity therapist had taught him to do when he went to her complaining of tension headaches. As usual, the trick worked. The pain began to recede, growing fainter and fainter until it was only an echo somewhere in the center of his skull. Too bad he couldn't fix his life as easily, he thought glumly. The last two decades had given him enough headache material to last a lifetime.

He sat for a few minutes with his eyes shut, thinking of all the wrong turns he'd taken: not the healthiest form of mental exercise for a man to perform in the morning, but one that he had been doing a lot lately, especially since Ronnie died. Putting Ronnie in Forest Lawn had been one of the most depressing experiences of his entire life. There had been piles of flowers from Ronnie's agents and producers and managers and groupies, and even a wreath from his coke dealer that had said Rest in Peace, but not even a dandelion from any of Ronnie's three ex-wives or his kids who had all hated his guts for turning their lives upside down with his crazy coked-out adventures. Like everyone else in Nickel Lid, Ronnie had had it made: the money, the imported cars, the big house, the whole bit. But in the end, all Ronnie got was the regulation box in the ground, and maybe, David couldn't help thinking, that was all he was going to get too. Before that happened, he intended to figure out what he really wanted in life and to get it; only the problem was he didn't know exactly what he wanted. Once he'd thought he had, but he'd been wrong.

When he'd been a kid, back in Somerville lying in bed at night listening to his father bat his mother around, he'd thought he wanted money, so much that no one would ever be able to touch him or her again. Of course, he'd also wanted to be free, but most of the time money seemed like the solution; it was like having your own private bodyguard or your own personal island, and he'd imagined himself sitting on a big pile of it giving the world the finger. Going to Harvard had just made the get-rich desire stronger: all the put-downs, all the snide remarks about shanty Irish drunks, the snobby way those preppy bastards let their ties turn over to show the Brooks Brothers labels. Every morning when he'd gone down to breakfast to face the lifted eyebrows and condescension of his classmates, he'd felt bitter and driven. He promised himself that someday he'd make enough money to buy and sell those Harvard assholes.

And he'd done it. Not that it had been easy. From the summer of '64 until the fall of '66 when "Ask van Gogh" went gold, he'd damn near starved. He'd had his freedom at last, but he hadn't been able to enjoy it or stick with it like he might have been able to do if he'd been born rich. He worried all the time about where his next meal was coming from, and that first year in the Haight, when he was trying unsuccessfully to persuade other people to sing his lyrics, before he realized he could sing them himself, he had survived on food stamps and shoplifting. It had been a crazy life: eating shrimp and imported cheese three times a day because the only store without a security system was a fancy deli. He'd never felt good about that, and later in the early eighties when he was in his straightening up and making reparations phase, he had looked up the deli, which was still in operation, and sent them a certified check for five hundred dollars, which he figured was at least twice what he'd lifted from them plus interest.

Then in '66, when all the guys in Nickel Lid were about to give up and get jobs waiting tables, "Ask van Gogh" had made number one on *Billboard* magazine's top singles chart, and their days of standing outside the Print Mint begging spare change from tourists were over forever. That November they'd appeared on the Ed Sullivan Show, and—standing right where John, George, Paul, and Ringo had stood only two years before—they played their way into stardom. David had sung "Get Out of Our Way" for the first time that night, and the TV audience had gone wild. Within the next week the network got over fifty thousand letters: half of them demanding that David Blake be banned from the airways as a threat to God, mother, and the flag; and half (the younger half) begging Ed to book him for another appearance.

David gave his temples another workout, thinking that '67 had been a wild year. For the first time he'd had money, so much of it he couldn't keep track, and he'd gone on a giant spending spree: a Ferrari, twenty antique jukeboxes, an eighteen-room house in Bel-Air with a pool and six bathrooms. In May their first album, *Spare Change*, came out, rocketed to the top, and they started touring: Paris, Germany, Australia. For nearly four years they traveled almost nonstop, doing one-night stands, charging more and more for each appearance until you'd have thought nobody would be willing to pay such outrageous prices, only somebody always was.

By the time he appeared at Woodstock in '69, the stream had become a river. Only five minutes of him was in the movie, but that had been enough. The day after the premiere, some guy had called his agent and tried to negotiate for the subsidiary rights to his face. To his *face*, for chrissake! They wanted to put out new posters of him, make him into jigsaw puzzles, sell him to little girls as a wind-up doll that played a tin guitar, and he'd said "yeah, sure" to the whole thing, and more money had come pouring in faster than he could ever spend it. And for maybe ten years, he'd just surfed on the crest of that money, hanging ten and giving the world the finger whenever he felt like it, touring a little less, having all the women he wanted whenever he wanted them without ever getting himself tied down. Oh, he'd done other things, of course, besides spend: he'd put together Van Gogh's Ear, one of the best sound studios in the country; produced a lot of records; lost himself in the fabulous technology of noise; gotten so good he could mix his own tracks better than the best. But mostly, he'd spent those ten years making money, spending it, and ultimately investing it.

But at the center there had been something off-key, something playing a sour note, singing to him that it wasn't enough. He'd be standing on the beach at Monaco, maybe, or some other fancy place he never thought he'd see, and he'd hear a little voice inside him saying, *So what, man?* At first he thought maybe it was guilt, so he decided to give some of his money away to worthy causes the way Lennon was doing. Those were the days when John and Yoko were doing their famous bed-ins in Amsterdam and Canada to promote world peace, but Mississippi had soured David forever on politics, so he took another tack. In the morning he'd pick up the newspaper and look for a disaster: drought and famine in Africa, floods in Bangladesh, earthquakes in Burma, air crashes in Italy. Five or six times a year, he'd send an anonymous check to the relief effort, usually in the range of ten thousand dollars, sometimes more.

But it didn't help. The cosmic *so what?*, the fly in the sweet honey of his success, continued to get louder. He paid a shrink a hundred dollars an hour, and all it did was make the voice enunciate the words a little clearer, like someone was turning up the volume: *SO WHAT?* Finally, he realized that what was missing wasn't anything he could buy or touch. It was something much more subtle, a piece of himself that he'd left behind, the whole rebel-Kerouac-beatnik-poet part of his identity. Now that he had money, he saw that money was not all he'd wanted. He'd wanted respect too; he'd wanted to be free; and he'd wanted to be a poet. He'd forgotten that in the scramble, he'd sacrificed it, and now his talent was neglected, rusted out like an old car left in a garage for fifteen years, and when he tried to start it up again he got nothing, zip, a big blank.

And there was something else he'd also lost along the way, something he didn't even like to think about because it was too painful. That something belonged to the part of himself he never showed in public. It was something quiet and intimate and vulnerable, something he had thrown away the way a fool throws away a diamond thinking that it's only a piece of coal. He didn't know what to call it because by then he didn't believe in love anymore. He wasn't alone. Almost all the men and most of the women he knew had decided that love didn't exist; that it was just another fantasy, like the kind you had when you took a hit of acid and thought you could talk to God or walk on water. Everyone had been burned enough times by then to agree that what the sixties had called love was all hormones and romantic illusions promoted by soap writers and women's magazines, and anyone who took it seriously was going to wake up one morning to find out that the beloved had sued for palimony or divorce.

And yet . . . it had felt like something you'd have to call love whether you wanted to or not—not sex, because God knew he'd had enough of that over the years, and not even affection because that had been offered to him too—but love: passionate, warm, real love. He'd had it once with Lucy, who was dead and gone and irretrievable, or maybe he'd only imagined that he'd had it, but real or imagined, the lack of this nameless thing was painful.

He had to admit that this whole train of thought felt depressingly Catholic, even though he'd chucked any belief in anything long ago. What would Father Harrigan back in Somerville have called his state of mind? An examination of conscience? A dark night of the soul? David didn't know, but sometimes he suspected that maybe it wasn't anything so noble. Maybe he was just another middle-aged jerk having a midlife crisis, spared the obligatory young chicks and red sports cars because he'd had those in his twenties, but ridiculous nevertheless.

Yet as time passed, he found himself remembering Lucy more instead of less, because he never found another woman who even came close to moving him the way she had. He would remember the day he had left her, that stupid argument in the kitchen and what a young, arrogant fool he had been. On those days, he would wish that his money could buy him one more thing: a time machine that would take him back to Matoon so he could apologize and make amends.

But there was no time machine: only more gigs, more money, more third-rate song lyrics, more blank paper with no poems on it, more beautiful ladies who kept his body warm but left his soul out in the cold, and the *so what?* kept getting louder and louder. In the spring of '79 something inside him finally snapped, and he spent the next two years coked up to the max, into drugs heavily for the first time since the mid-sixties. He flew from one continent to another, singing and screwing and partying his way around the world, trying to still that voice, by the end of which he was a physical and mental wreck, too screwed up even to realize it. Because when you had money and did a lot of drugs you didn't suffer like ordinary people; you didn't bottom out and find yourself on the street standing around trash can fires shivering and hungry and dying for a fix. You could carry your miniature silver vacuum cleaner in your shirt pocket and hoover the white stuff up your nose and even buy off the cops when you got stopped for DUI, and if you got too fucked up, you could check into a spa and spend a few days on orange juice and health foods, kidding yourself that the craving was gone forever. And all the time your brain was experiencing minor hemorrhages, and your heart was on the verge of bursting, and you couldn't remember if it was Tuesday or Thursday and neither could Ronnie or any of your other friends, until one night—July 15, 1982—Ronnie went to Palm Springs and pulled a John Belushi, and the whole house of cards had come down.

Three days after the funeral, David had cancelled all public performances, paid off his dealer, signed up for Coke Enders, and gone into seclusion for nearly two years. When he emerged in the fall of '85, clean and sober and humbled, he found himself once again facing the thing he'd been running from for nearly twenty years: back in '64 he'd made a wrong turn. Two roads had diverged in the woods, but instead of taking the one less traveled, he'd taken the goddam L.A. freeway, leaving behind everything that had ever really mattered to him.

This time instead of trying to do a U-turn into oncoming traffic, he decided to take life slow, a day at a time. He started performing in public again, but not too often; he sold his fancy house and bought himself a place at La Vista Beach where he could sit in his living room and contemplate the sea gulls. He wrote some poetry—bad poetry compared to the old stuff—but he tried not to be too hard on himself about it. And whenever he started feeling bored with this new, calm life, he would think of Ronnie and be grateful to have gotten out alive.

And then, one night at a party in Beverly Hills, a quiet party with lots of mineral water and boiled shrimp and low cholesterol snacks that would have struck him as hilariously straight in the old days, he found himself talking to a short twerp who started pitching him an idea about a movie based on the life of Jack Kerouac. The guy's name was I. I. Rogers—no first name, just the double initials, which was a major turn-off. Rogers, who talked nonstop at a furious rate, insisted that David should invest in this movie because "hey, you were a poet once, right? I mean everyone knows that, David. You don't mind if I call you David, do you? And this is a great script."

David had been rude enough to Rogers to send him away pale with humiliation and fury, no small trick when you were dealing with a Hollywood producer, but in the first place he did not like to be called *David* by every money-hungry little rat on the West Coast, and second he felt set-up, since he'd obviously been invited to the party so that Rogers could bend his ear. Also he resented the line "you *were* a poet." He resented it a lot. As a matter of fact it stung. Screw you, fellow, he'd thought. Movies are a rotten investment, especially historical biographies. If I want a hole to pour my money down, there's always dry oil wells and pork belly futures.

But to his surprise, he couldn't forget the encounter. The idea of making a movie about Kerouac kept floating around in his mind, gaining momentum. Drop it, he kept telling himself. It's just another one of the thousands of lame ideas that people come up with when they're trying to extract money from the rich and famous. Remember the guy who wanted you to finance his electrically heated toilet seats or that group of nuts from Sunnyvale who claimed to have invented a computer program that would predict lottery numbers?

Then one morning, when he was sitting on the deck looking out at the ocean and thinking of nothing in particular, he heard a new voice at the back of his head, one that didn't say *so what*. It was a familiar voice, one that he hadn't heard for a long time, and later he wondered if maybe it wasn't the voice of his Muse, although his Muse was probably long dead by that time. *You could play Kerouac*, the voice had suggested. At first he had dismissed the idea, because what did he know about acting in movies? But it seemed to have a life of its own. A few months passed, and gradually he became convinced that this was it at last, the positive thing he'd been trying to think of, the thing that might give him a foot back in the door. If he couldn't be a poet, then he could play one; he could live out in front of the camera the life of the man he had wanted to be before he lost himself.

Calling up Seth Flynn, he told him to find Rogers and tell him that David Blake might be interested in investing in *Dharma Road* if, and only if, he played the role of Kerouac. According to Seth, Rogers had almost wept with joy when he heard the news because the project had come to nothing so far. The deal was negotiated in record time, and the contracts were signed giving Blake Enterprises such complete control that Rogers couldn't even take a leak without getting it cleared and approved in triplicate.

For the first time in years, David found himself really excited by a project. He kept telling himself not to get his hopes up too much, but he did anyway. He kept thinking that maybe some of Kerouac's magic would rub off on him, that maybe he'd be able to write poetry again. And even if that never happened, there were other possibilities. Maybe he'd prove to be a great independent filmmaker like Robert Altman. In any event, it was a new start, a way of getting his life back in hand.

Still, for all his newfound optimism, when he read the poems in *Living in the Volcano* they made him want to cry; they were so beautiful and fierce, and he longed so ardently to write new ones that would have the same power. Picking up the book, he began to reread his favorites. What film, he thought, is ever going to get inside people's heads and souls the way poetry does? And for a second he felt that old *so what?* gnawing at him again, but he knew how to live with it now, how to have mercy on himself and even on other people.

He was just finishing the poem about his sister Theresa—the one who had run away from home and never come back—when the doorbell rang. He waited for his housekeeper, Conchita, to answer it, and then he remembered that he had given her the day off to go to her niece's first communion.

Getting to his feet, he pulled on a pair of jeans and plowed barefoot toward the door, reciting the poem to himself. He knew he had an appointment this morning, that was why he had set his alarm clock, but who was it with? Damned if he could remember. He wondered if all the drugs he had taken over the past twenty years had given him a premature case of Alzheimer's. Give yourself a break, man, he thought, even twenty-year-olds forget things. He suddenly realized that he had also forgotten to shave. The hell with it; whoever was at the door would just have to take him as he was.

The doorbell rang again impatiently. Annoyed, David grabbed the knob and threw the door open. There on his doorstep was a tall, dark-haired woman wearing a bright purple jumpsuit with about a thousand zippers. On her face was an expression of stunned awe that David knew only too well. Oh, no, a fan. How had she managed to get past the security guards? He paid those losers thirty thousand dollars a year to keep him from going the way of John Lennon, and this was the result. Heads were going to roll, he thought grimly. There were other security services in L.A., ones that did their job.

At least this fan looked harmless. That jumpsuit was so tight that there was nowhere she could be packing a gun, but that didn't mean she wasn't going to be a nuisance. David knew what was in store, having been through it all a hundred times. The next thing he knew she would be lunging for his buttons, offering to hop into his bed, pursuing him into his own house, and begging for his autograph. There had been a time, not all that long ago, when the sight of a beautiful woman on his doorstep wouldn't have been entirely unwelcome, a time when he would have been up for anything no matter how crazy. That time was over. "Go away," he snarled and started to slam the door.

"But Mr. Blake, I'm Susan Clark." The woman grabbed for the edge of the door, and David found himself in the embarrassing position of wrestling for it. She hung on tight and didn't give an inch when he shook her. She's a fucking pit bull, he thought.

"I don't care who you are," he yelled, "get out of here and leave me in peace."

"But Mr. Blake—"

"Scram, lady. I've got all the Fuller brushes I need and I'm not handing out autographs." The woman was strong, and he was shaking her back and forth now, trying to dislodge her. This was getting ridiculous. He wondered if he should go back inside and call the police. He always felt like a fool asking them to dispose of women for him. "Let go," he roared. He tried a quick jab to the outside, trying to catch her off balance, but she must have studied karate or something because she didn't move an inch.

"Dammit, David Blake," she yelled, "cut it out! I'm Susan Clark, the photographer. You hired me."

The word *hired* stopped him dead in his tracks. Startled, he let go of the door, and she pulled it wide open and stood there on the porch with her hands on her hips glaring at him. "I hired you?" he said. It was all beginning to come back.

She wiped off her hands and nodded at him, looking as if she'd like to slice him up and make him into a sandwich. "I'm your photographer, remember? You invited me over here this morning to do a photo essay on you."

He noticed for the first time that there were cameras hanging around her neck. Oh, Christ, what a mistake. She wasn't a fan. She was Susan Clark, the lady photographer that Seth had had so much trouble hiring. Jesus, and he'd nearly knocked her out cold with the front door. He was sorry and he told her so.

"Forget it," she said, but she didn't look like she was going to forget it. He invited her in, and she came warily, looking around her like she was entering a madman's lair. Not that he could blame her. He decided to turn on the charm.

"I'm delighted to meet you," he said. "I've seen your work in *Rolling Stone*, and I think it's terrific." He reached out and shook her hand and gave it a small extra squeeze for good measure. Usually a squeeze from the hand of David Blake reduced women to putty, but this one wasn't in a melting mood. She looked him up and down and took the lens cap off one of her cameras.

"So you want me to do a photo essay on you?" she said.

"Right." David nodded. He found her failure to respond to him intriguing. "When would you like to start."

"Now."

"Now?"

"Why wait?" She squinted at him through the camera and made a few adjustments. "You have an interesting face," she observed.

"Thanks." That was more like it.

"But you haven't aged very well."

"What!" He was astounded. This woman had just insulted him. He had had her in his house less than three minutes, and she had had the temerity to tell him that he looked like shit. He stared at her, not knowing whether to laugh or throw her out on her ass.

She lowered the camera and looked him over again as if she were taking him apart and putting him back together. "When you were younger your face had more tension in it—not the kind of tension you get from anxiety, you've got plenty of that now, but the kind you get from the underlying tone of the muscles. It's gone lax and a little sad. Also your eyes have changed a lot. You used to look angry and full of energy, but now your lids have started to droop and you have a kind of hangdog, disappointed look. Fortunately," she chuckled, "you still have all your hair."

"How do you know so damn much about what I used to look like."

"I've studied your old pictures." She lowered the camera again. "Don't pose, please. It never works."

"What do you mean, 'Don't pose'?"

"I can tell that you're used to being on stage. You've got a public personality. Most stars do. Well, forget it, please, and try to be yourself. We'll get the best pictures if you just go on doing what you usually do and forget I'm here as much as you can. What do you usually do this time of day?"

He resisted the temptation to tell her that this time of day he usually banged arrogant lady photographers while they pleaded for seconds. "I eat breakfast," he said through gritted teeth. He had to hand it to her; she was absolutely right about his public personality act. She was smart, talented, and a bitch to the core. He hadn't been put down by a woman so thoroughly since he left Cambridge. Against his own better judgment he was starting to find her sexually attractive. She reminded him of all those beautiful, rich, tight-assed 'Cliffies he'd spent so many years trying to get in the sack. "Where did you go to school?" he asked.

"I didn't." She pointed the camera at him and clicked the shutter.

"Seriously?"

"Seriously."

"It doesn't fit."

"Maybe not, but that's the way it is. I never graduated from college, but I took courses with Imogen Cunningham through the Mendocino Art Center. We used her old cameras with the wooden film holders, and at the end we showed her the stuff we'd shot, and believe me, she didn't mince words. After Imogen finished demolishing my ego, I decided that I had better study design, which I did at San Jose State. Other than those two dips into formal education, I've taught myself everything I know, including the fact that a middle-aged man standing still looking straight at a camera is one of the most uninteresting objects on the face of the earth. Could you move around a little, go in the kitchen and eat your granola, floss your teeth, manifest some sign of life?"

"Maybe I should take a leak for you."

"Anything you want," she said, not shocked in the least, "as long as you do it where the light is good. I never use artificial lighting."

Okay, David thought, if that's the way you want to play it, that's the way we'll play it. "How long are you going to be doing this?" he asked.

"Who knows," she said. "Probably about a week."

"Suppose it takes longer?"

"Then you pay me for longer." She pointed the camera at him and clicked it like a gun. "Any problems with that?"

"No problems." He'd see to it that this took more than a week. He was going to get her into bed; he was going to peel that ugly purple jumpsuit off her and find out what made her so sure of herself. Something about her intrigued him. He couldn't quite put his finger on it, but whatever it was, it made him want her. He hadn't really wanted a woman for a long time.

He went into the kitchen to make himself a cup of coffee, and she trailed after him, taking pictures that as far as he could tell were a total waste. She complained about the fluorescent lights, switched them off, and opened the drapes.

"That's a strange-looking camera," he observed. She was using the motor drive now, snapping one shot after another as if she intended to put out an animated short film entitled *David Blake Eats His Breakfast*.

"It's a Hasselblad, top of the line." She patted her camera affectionately. "You get a much bigger negative with one of these babies, and it has exchangeable backs so I can change from color to black and white without having to go through the trouble of winding off the film."

"What kind of film do you use?"

"That depends on what I'm shooting." She grinned. "Today I thought I'd bring along some Ektachrome. It's strong on blues, and I thought it would pick up the blue tints in your eyes. If I were using Kodachrome the reds would be emphasized, and you'd probably end up looking like you'd been smoking a lot of grass." She went on explaining the technical aspects of photography to him and he began to relax, lulled by her chatter, which was no longer aggressive. He was impressed by how well she knew her trade, and once he got over feeling irritated by the way she kept circling around him, it was interesting to watch her work. *People* had done a photo essay on him a few years ago, and their photographer had gone out of his way to get slick, flattering shots. Clark, on the other hand, was going to a lot of trouble to capture something spontaneous. He could see that she really cared about her work. She had already used two rolls of film, and if she was getting bored or frustrated, it didn't show. That was the sign of a true perfectionist, he thought, and he began to feel the kind of respect for her that he always felt for artists who weren't willing to compromise.

"How about a smile," he suggested when she was halfway through roll number three.

She lowered her camera and pursed her lips, and he noticed that her eyes were pale violet. Colored contacts, no doubt. He wondered what her real eye color was. "A smile?" She raised the camera and adjusted the focus and the violet eyes were replaced by a glass cyclops ringed by F-stop numbers. "Why? Are you in the habit of smiling in the morning?"

"Not really," he admitted.

"So why fake it?"

"Because I'd like something to send to my mother. She's seventy-two, and if I'm not smiling, she'll call me up and tell me to eat more vegetables."

She was obviously taken by surprise. "You really want a picture for your mother?"

"Why not?"

"Because you don't seem like the kind of person who has a mother."

"I do though," he said, "and I'd like to have a picture for her, a smiling picture if it's all the same to you."

"Well, why not?" she shrugged, repositioned the camera and closed in on him. She waited while David positioned his lips in his best, most charming smile. It was a great smile, a smile that had sent two decades' worth of teenage girls into sexual frenzies; it was a ten-million-dollar smile, and he could turn it on and off like a faucet. "How's that?" he asked.

"Looks terrible."

"What!"

She lowered the camera. "It's fake; you look like you died and some amateur mortician got hold of you. Say 'bromeliad.'"

"Huh?"

"Bromeliad, say 'bromeliad.' It's a tropical epiphyte like a pineapple, but that's not important. What's important is that the *brom* part relaxes your lips and the *eliad* part makes you smile. Now say it."

"Bromeliad," David said. The camera clicked, recording a pleasant, smiling David Blake. It was a picture to warm a mother's heart.

Cassie called Lucy that evening. "I've seen him," she announced breathlessly. She was so excited she nearly dropped the phone. "I've seen him in the flesh."
"Seen whom?"
"David, of course. Who else?"
Lucy sat down on her couch and closed her eyes. The news made her feel weak-kneed, which was ridiculous. "What does he look like?"
"Aha!" Cassie pounced on the question with delight. "I knew you were curious!" She wound the phone cord around her arm, stepped over Carla's Legos, and threw herself into the large yellow beanbag chair Lucy had given her last Christmas. "He looks—" she paused dramatically, "great."
"Great, huh?" Lucy thought of the album covers she had seen of David over the past twenty years: David tied to the roof of a 1954 wood-sided station wagon, David skydiving with his guitar; David looking out from the shadows like Bogart, sneering and sucking on an actual, three-dimensional rubber cigarette that you could take out and suck on yourself. There had always been some gimmick. "Does he still have his own hair or is he wearing a toupee?" Cassie was right: she was curious.
"You bet he has his hair," Cassie exclaimed, "and that's not all. He's been lifting weights or something because his shoulders look terrific. I got some great contour shadows when I was shooting him without his shirt on."
"What do you mean 'without his shirt on'? What have you gotten yourself into?"
"Don't panic. It was a purely professional observation. You aren't jealous are you?"
"Don't be ridiculous," Lucy snorted. "It's been what? nearly twenty-five years? I can barely remember that I ever had a relationship with someone named David Blake. Jealous? Don't make me laugh."
Cassie poked at the beanbag chair with her free hand, forming the yellow canvas into a range of miniature mountains. She stared at the phone, trying to imagine what Lucy's face might look like, but only a row of anonymous white buttons stared back at her. "Too bad you don't

care anymore, Lou, because I went out of my way to even up the score. You know, I never have forgiven David for the way he jerked you around."

"What did you do?" Lucy demanded. "Good Lord, can't I let you out of my sight?"

"Forget it," Cassie chuckled. "You wouldn't be interested."

"You bet I'm interested. What did you do? I wouldn't put anything past you. You're the Leonardo da Vinci of revenge when you set your mind to it. I still remember how you got even with Kathy DeVelt when she ate that chocolate pudding you made."

"You mean the Ex-Lax?"

"That's exactly what I mean." Lucy rose to her feet and paced across the room. "What did you do to David? Blind him with your flash? Put fixing solution in his coffee?"

"Nothing so dramatic. I just told him he looked like shit."

"You didn't!"

"I did." Cassie laughed wickedly. "You should have been there to enjoy the effect. You know how insecure he always was about his looks. Well, I burst into his living room, pointed my camera at him, did a quick visual survey of his face, and informed him that he'd gone flabby and wrinkled. There was some truth to it, but not much. Actually, he looks pretty good."

"How did he take it?"

"He turned about six shades of red. I thought I might have to give him CPR."

"You know sometimes you're completely out of control."

"Admit it, you're pleased."

"I am not. I think it was unkind, and unnecessary, and . . . how could you even care about evening scores after all these years?"

"I don't forget it when someone messes with my friends. Come on, Lou, confess: it gives you a charge to think of David taking it for once instead of dishing it out."

"Well, it does give me a little charge," Lucy admitted.

"That's more like it. Now I can confess something: I felt guilty afterward. He's changed a lot."

"Changed how?"

"Oh, I don't know." Cassie settled back in the beanbag chair, frowned, and twirled the phone cord. "I asked him to tell me about himself—you know, like I had no idea who he was. I expected him to lay a whole lot of garbage on me about how he's a combination of Mick Jagger and Bob Dylan, but he hardly mentioned his singing career. Instead he talked a lot about Kerouac and how he wishes that he'd lived like him. He says that nearly every morning he wakes up wishing he'd dedicated his life to poetry instead of wasting it on rock and roll. He claims that he started writing lyrics for money partly because he was so insecure about being poor and lower class and partly because he needed the cash to support his mother and sisters, but that selling out wasn't worth it. Then he started talking about a friend of his who'd overdosed on coke and heroin and how the experience had turned his life around. He didn't mention any names but I got the impression that it was his drummer, Ronnie Craft. You remember the story; it was all over the papers. When I said with my usual tactless devotion to the truth that he himself had been rumored to be one of the biggest coke heads in Hollywood, he said that it wasn't just a rumor, that he'd had a real fight with drugs, but that with the help of Coke Enders and some first-rate therapy he'd managed to clean up. He claimed to have been straight for a long time now and said—with real passion—that he was never going back. This movie, he said, was a positive step toward a whole new life, but even if it flopped, even if he couldn't write poetry anymore, he was grateful most days just to be alive. I started out being cynical and ended up being touched by his doubts about himself. I'd expected him to be a lot more arrogant, but he surprised me. I hate to admit it, but he seemed almost humble at times, like he was finally turning into a vulnerable human being. Can you imagine David being humble and vulnerable? Like I said, I think he's changed a lot."

They spent the next ten minutes arguing about how much David had changed. Lucy wasn't convinced that he had, but Cassie was adamant. "You had to be there," she kept saying. "You had to hear him talk. I almost called up my shrink afterward to get a reality check. I was actually starting to like him."

"Are you sure he didn't recognize you?" Lucy hadn't wanted to raise the question again until she saw Cassie in the flesh, but under the circumstances she had to make sure. So David had been humble, had he? So Cassie had started to like him. She smelled a rat. "Maybe he figured out who you were and started stringing you along to see how you'd react."

"Not a chance."

"You're absolutely certain?"

"Absolutely." Cassie poked at the beanbag chair again, thinking that Lucy was far too uptight about what was obviously an impossibility. David had looked straight at her and talked to her for hours, and there hadn't been even a flicker of recognition on his face. She knew, because she'd been looking at him through the lens of her camera the whole time. "Relax," she advised. "He didn't know me, no way."

Lucy gave a sigh of relief. "Good," she said. "Keep it that way."

If Cassie could have seen David at that moment, she might not have been so quick to tell Lucy to relax. David was sitting in his living room looking out the picture window at the beach. To his left an old Vietnamese man in waders was raking the beach; to his right a flock of sea gulls was picking at something that had washed up on the sand. But David wasn't seeing the sea gulls or the man or the surf or much of anything because a word kept going through his mind. The word was *bromeliad*, and he knew he'd heard it used before to make people smile. He also knew that if he thought long enough he'd remember when.

• 3 •

"Get out of our way!" David yelled, banging on his guitar and rocking down the ramp of the Oakland Coliseum into a screaming crowd of middle-aged fans. Colored lights played on his red silk jacket as he strutted over their heads, thrusting his pelvis in their direction Elvis style, singing the same goddam song he had been singing since 1968, the song they would never let him put on the shelf. Sometimes he thought if he sang the words to "Get Out of Our Way!" one more time he would go out of his mind.

Performing always made him recall how much fun it had been at first to be a star; the applause of the crowd had been a great high that had gone on and on until he got so lost in the ozone that he couldn't find his way back. The best moment had come just after "Ask van Gogh" had gone gold, and for the first time in his life he knew beyond a doubt that he was going to be rich. The day after the record topped the charts, he had flown back to Boston, driven over to Somerville, and kidnapped his mother. She'd been hanging up clothes in the backyard, wearing an old housedress that made her look like a hag, and he had picked her up in his arms, tossed her, laughing and protesting into a cab, taken her to Jordan Marsh, and bought her a full-length mink coat. He still remembered her crying from joy as she petted the fur, telling him how proud she was of him and what a good son he was.

"We're the future and you know it!" he sang, reaching the end of the ramp and leaning toward the thousands of bodies that swayed beneath him like some great, dumb animal. He shouldn't think of his fans so contemptuously because they had made him a millionaire, but often he did. Half of them were wearing Blake T-shirts with his face silkscreened on the front, which made it odd to say the least to look at them because it was like looking into ten thousand distorted mirrors. There were Blake mugs, Blake surfboards, even Blake bathmats, for chrissake, and they bought them all. He knew for a fact that he had fans who hadn't missed one of his concerts in twenty years. What kind of life was that? They might once have been groovy kids with nothing to do but dance to his music, but now most of them were adults. How could they afford to keep coming and coming? Where did they get the energy to scream and clap and nearly riot every time he walked out on a stage. Didn't they have anything better to do? Didn't they have to work for a living?

"Get out of our way before you blow it!" He straightened up and smiled his famous smile, and a collective moan went up from the female half of the crowd, a moan that sent a shudder up his spine. Still smiling he turned and danced his way back up the ramp, wondering what would happen if he ever tripped and fell into the crowd.

Probably they'd eat him alive.

The next day he was still brooding about his career, having a kind of relapse into old doubts that made taking life one day at a time hard going. He was thinking as he drove across the Golden Gate Bridge that he should have noticed the point where his life had stagnated, but instead the disillusionment had crept up on him, and he found himself wondering how many other things were also creeping up, hiding out there in the underbrush waiting their turn to pounce. After all, if the fun of being rich and famous could vanish into thin air, then anything was possible. A person could have a fatal disease, cancer say, and not even suspect it, or . . .

Give yourself a break, Blake, he thought. You're becoming a hypochondriac. The real problem was that he no longer enjoyed performing. For years now he'd wanted out of the rock music business, or at least that's what he told everyone from his agent to his shrink. Take his hair, for instance. He'd originally grown it long as a symbol of rebellion, and now he was trapped with the style. He couldn't cut it if he wanted to. He supposed it might have been worse: he might have been bald by now.

Thinking about his hair always made him irritable, so when he pulled into Sausalito and saw the extravagant, isolated house his own manager had rented for him—directly contrary to his express orders—he lost it entirely and did a stupid thing that later he couldn't remember without embarrassment: He leapt out of his car and started yelling at Cecil.

"I told you I wanted to be in the city!" he screamed. "This place is a fucking castle. All it lacks is a moat!"

Cecil, who had come to the front gate to greet him, observed the attack calmly. Probing at his front teeth with a wooden pick, he spat in the direction of the gardenia bushes and shrugged. Cecil was a Harvard Business School graduate, class of '82, but standing there in his acid-washed jeans, he looked more like a displaced cowboy. "Don't exaggerate," he advised, "and remember, it's tax deductible."

David pointed at the house and his face grew red and his whole body seemed to swell a little, as if his blood volume were doubling and redoubling, inflating him into that early heart attack he was always worrying about. "I don't care about the damn tax advantages! Think beyond the bottom line for once. Look at it, will you. It's completely isolated from everything."

"What's the problem?" Cecil said in his mild, I'm-only-an-accountant voice. "It looks okay to me." *Okay* was hardly the right adjective to describe the house. Set into the hillside just below the Golden Gate Bridge, it was composed of five curved, sweeping stories flung into space with twenty-foot leaded windows, six fireplaces, four separate terraced Japanese gardens, a fish pond, two spas, a small swimming pool, and what appeared to be a miniature grape arbor, although Cecil wasn't sure about that because he hadn't had time to check it all out. "The view is nice."

"Nice!" David yelled.

"Yeah, nice." The view was a two-hundred-and-sixty-degree panoramic view of San Francisco Bay framed by carefully planted flowering trees. The vista point at the north anchorage of the bridge was poor in comparison.

David made a noise of snarling discontent. "I told you I wanted to live in an apartment in North Beach where I could get up in the morning, look out the window, and see some other human beings. I'm tired of living in places where you have to launch a safari to buy a loaf of bread. I'm not a lighthouse keeper by temperament."

"The herding option just wasn't viable."

"What's that supposed to mean?"

"It means," Cecil said as he picked out one molar and moved on to the next, "that although all of us appreciate your desire to return to the human community, it just doesn't make sense securitywise."

"I want that apartment." David paced around Cecil's car to the far side and stood with his back against it, glaring at the house and Cecil and the world in general. "If I let you imprison me in that," he said as he waved contemptuously at the house, "I'll be cut off from the soul of the city. I won't be able to write or think or create. Jesus, you yuppie idiot, do you know what it's like to write a poem? You need inspiration, and I get my inspiration from *life*. No, you don't understand, do you? You couldn't. So try this on: I'm tired of being packed in cotton like some kind of golden egg that you guys are afraid of breaking. This film is a new start for me, and I want to enjoy it to the fullest. I want to live around other people. That's spelled p-e-o-p-l-e."

"Right," Cecil nodded. "I understand. I already got you a place in the city just off Union Street. It's a great apartment. All the conveniences." He opened the gate and motioned for David to step inside, but David stood stubbornly backed up against the car glaring at him. "What more do you want? You can spend eighteen hours a day there—which should be enough urban life even for you—but you can't live there. Living is the bottom line. Our insurers will cancel if you try to live there on a twenty-four-hour basis." He decided to try a lighter touch. "Think of the apartment as a woman. You don't want to move in with her, or you may get slapped with palimony, so you go back to your own place to sleep. Get it?"

"No," David said.

Cecil's patience was wearing thin. He had seen this syndrome before, especially in baby boomers. They were a crazy generation, always longing to go back to the days of communal living when they were involved in "meaningful" activities, which in Blake's case had probably meant screwing and blowing dope. Cecil didn't understand their nostalgia and didn't want to. What could David Blake possibly expect to get out of life that he didn't already have?

"Let's go over it all again." Dropping his toothpick into his vest pocket, Cecil folded his arms across his chest. It was a closed posture, a posture that said Cecil was the manager here and David had better let him manage. "You can't be provided with proper security in that apartment." This was old territory; they'd been over it a thousand times. "This place," he said, waving his hand in the direction of the house, "is like a fort. It's got motion detectors, lasers, sirens, a direct line to the cops, and a twenty-four-hour security guard, not to mention that it's surrounded by a fence that's virtually impenetrable. The only way for some nut to get to you would be for him to scale the cliff or drop out of the sky." He could see the anxiety rising in David's eyes, which was reasonable considering the volume of crazy-fan mail he got. This was more like it. Compassion, Cecil thought, was the next thing on the agenda. He put his hand lightly on David's shoulder, buddy to buddy, letting him know that he really cared. "You don't want to end up like John Lennon, do you?"

"No," David admitted.

"And you don't want the insurance on the film cancelled, do you? Because you know the only thing that's going to make *Dharma Road* work is you, and if you get popped—"

"Okay, okay, I get the point." David shook off Cecil's hand and took a grudging step forward, giving in. "But I'm going to hate this place."

"Make it your own." Cecil followed David through the gate, feeling relieved and triumphant. "The rugs look great for screwing on and the fridge is full of sushi. This is Marin County, remember. The place where people stroke each other all over with peacock feathers, drink fine wine, pass out, and cook to death in their hot tubs."

"Sounds delightful." David pounded up the front steps and stood on the lower balcony looking out at the bay. The sun was turning everything pink and purple and apricot. Alcatraz seemed to float at the exact center, gray and remote like an island of ghosts. Behind it, the skyscrapers were lighting up one by one, each capped by a thin streamer of fog.

It was beautiful, he thought, obscenely beautiful. Behind him he could feel the house looming like Godzilla.

When Cassie showed up that evening for a photograph session, she found him drinking margaritas and looking glumly into the fireplace. He was wearing a bathrobe, and his face was pinched and unhappy. Around him, occupying every spare inch of the coffee table and rug, were books of poetry. There were fat, leather-bound editions of Whitman and Keats; paperbacks filled with the poetry of Elizabeth Bishop, John Ashbery, and Adrienne Rich; small exquisitely printed chapbooks with less familiar names stamped on the covers. He looked up as she came in the room, and she saw that he had been writing or perhaps trying to write. Wads of yellow paper surrounded him, and the wastebasket was overflowing. They'd had an appointment, but she felt as if she were interrupting him.

"I can come back later," she said, "if this isn't a good time," but he waved her in and made her sit down on the couch.

"Keep me company," he begged. "I feel like hell."

"What's the matter?" She fingered her camera, wondering what F-stop she should use to get the different textures of his skin. She liked the look of his face tonight: it was human and unguarded. He looked humble and tired. It's a suffering face, she thought, one he doesn't let out very often. She wondered what had provoked it.

David rubbed his forehead and pinched the skin between his eyes. "My head feels like six guys with jackhammers are remodeling it from the inside out." He paused and sat for a moment, massaging his temples with the balls of his thumbs. "You don't happen to have an aspirin, do you?"

"Sure." She opened her purse, took out a bottle of tablets, and handed him two. Thanking her, he washed them down with a swig of margarita. "Looks like you're having a rough night," she observed.

"I'm made out of glass." He fixed her a margarita without the tequila, squeezing the lime expertly between his thumb and index finger. She accepted the drink, and they sat silently for a while. David stared off into space, presumably waiting for his headache to go away. Finally he seemed to come back to life. "I'm going to try to finish that poem I was working on," he announced.

"Are you sure you don't want me to leave?"

"No. Stick around. It won't take very long."

"Would you mind if I took some pictures of you at work?"

"Help yourself. I probably won't even notice. When I'm writing, I'm on another planet. I put together the lyrics to 'Ask van Gogh' sitting on a couch next to a guy who was learning to play a base guitar. He was driving everyone else in the room crazy, but I didn't even hear him."

He was wrong about it not taking very long. They sat in silence for a good forty-five minutes as he stared at the half-finished page in front of him, scribbling and crossing out and scribbling again. The fire crackled in the fireplace, and through the huge leaded glass window Cassie could see the fog rolling in from the ocean. Every once in a while, she would lift her camera and take a picture. It was an exciting series from her point of view, but not one he was going to want to send to his mother. Finally he threw down his pen and sat back.

"It's not working."

"What's not working?"

"The poem." He drank off his margarita and frowned. "It's complete garbage."

"Maybe it will work tomorrow."

"No." He shook his head. "I don't think so. The truth of the matter is, if I ever had any talent, I lost it a long time ago." He tore off the sheet, crumpled it, and sent it to join the rest. "I'm a big zero." He smiled bitterly. "Come on, take a final picture of me now sitting here amid the wreckage. You could call it 'Portrait of the Artist as a Washout.'"

Cassie drank her margarita slowly, thinking that he was right, the expression of despair on his face would make a good photo, but for once she wasn't in the mood. "I think you're being awfully hard on yourself," she observed.

"Is that so?" He seemed surprised that she hadn't said something sarcastic.

"I really liked *Living in the Volcano*, and I'm not ready to buy the idea that once having written that well you can't do it again, and—" She stopped in midsentence, horrified with herself. She hadn't meant to mention his book, but the title had just slipped out of her mouth. Jesus, Lucy was going to kill her.

David did a double take. "You've read my poetry? My God, what a surprise. I wouldn't have taken you for someone who liked poetry."

"Oh, I do," Cassie stuttered. "I always have." She tried desperately to think of some way to change the subject, but nothing came to mind.

"Well, well." He was delighted that she had actually heard of *Living in the Volcano*. He hadn't met more than a handful of people in the last twenty years who knew he was a published poet. "How did you get hold of it? It's been out of print since 1965."

"I stumbled on it in a used bookstore." Actually David had given her an inscribed copy. She wanted to talk about *anything* but his poetry, but she didn't dare change the subject too abruptly because that would just bring attention to it, and besides, she could tell by the look on his face that it wasn't going to be easy to steer him in another direction.

"Which poems did you like the best?" he asked eagerly.

She decided that she had no choice but to continue. "I'm not good at remembering titles, but I liked the one about your sister, and the one about growing up in Somerville."

He rose to his feet, his face glowing. "You actually have read them!"

"Sure."

"This is absolutely amazing." He walked over to the couch and sat down beside her. "Thank you." He took her hands in his. "I can't tell you how much it means to me to find someone who's read my poetry." He was filled with gratitude and desire, all mixed up together. It had been years since a woman had seen him as anything but a rock star. It was a real turn-on.

"Forget it." She pulled back her hands, feeling embarrassed and anxious. The thrill of skating on thin ice was highly overrated. She hoped now that he'd thanked her, he'd start talking about something else, but no such luck.

"No, I can't forget it."

"Look, they're good poems. More people should read them." She lifted her camera defensively, positioning it so that it was only inches from his face. She meant to record this moment, take that glowing, satisfied face away with her and put it next to the suffering face, but he was too fast for her. Catching the camera, he pushed it aside, drew her to him, and kissed her. She was so surprised that she nearly slugged him.

"Dammit," she snapped, "you wrecked a great shot."

"Susan . . ."

"Don't call me that."

"Why not?"

"Because . . ." She realized that there was no way she could explain. "Just because," she said. She got up and started for the door. "I think I'd better leave." That was an understatement. She should have left fifteen minutes ago, before she opened her big mouth. Better yet, she should never have come, at least not tonight when her unconscious seemed to be leaking out all over the place.

"Why?" he followed her and tried to put his arm around her waist. "Don't you like to be kissed?"

"Not by you."

"Why not? I've been told that it's not a bad experience."

"You've been told wrong."

"Oh, come on," he said, "give me a chance." He made another grab for her, not meaning to hurt her or anything, but she must have misinterpreted his intentions because the next thing he knew he was flying through the air straight toward the coffee table. He landed on his ass with a sickening crash, sending glasses and books flying in all directions. For a moment he just lay there, dazed, trying to get his mind around the fact that she'd heaved him over her shoulder.

"Are you okay?" She was standing over him in her red jump suit with her hands on her hips, looking down at him with an embarrassed expression on her face. She looked like a cross between a worried mother and a paratrooper, and he was seized with an insane desire to laugh, only it hurt too much.

"I'm in great shape," he gasped, "humiliated, injured, back dislocated, ribs broken, but don't let that bother you, ma'am. I count myself lucky that you didn't rip out my heart with your bare hands." He sat up and looked at her with respect. "Where the hell did you learn a trick like that?"

"In school," she said.

"What school? Our Lady of the Green Berets?"

"Look, I'm sorry. I didn't mean to flip you. It's just that I took judo once, and when you tried to kiss me, I went into a defensive posture. It was instinctive, and I really am sorry if I hurt you."

"Think nothing of it." He got to his feet and examined himself for damage, but except for a sore ass, he seemed to be intact. "Susan," he said, "I'll be frank. I had every intention of seducing you tonight, but now I'm not sure I could come out of bed alive, so if it's all the same to you, why don't we just adjourn this session."

"You're mad? You want me to leave?"

"Mad? Me? Heavens, no. I'd love to stay up and spar with you. We could throw one another across the room until dawn, break a few cement blocks with our bare hands, crush iron bars with our teeth and have a jolly time of it, but unfortunately I have to get up early in the morning." He limped toward the door and held it open. "In other words, Ms. Clark, get the hell out of here." He paused. "But don't make the mistake of thinking that I'm firing you. Oh, no. You're due back at four-thirty tomorrow for our last photo session, and I expect you here at four-thirty on the dot, or I may sue for breach of contract not to mention assault and battery."

"That's low," Cassie snapped.

"Right," David agreed. "It is low, but then I've always been a low kind of guy."

"What's on your mind?" Lucy asked the next day. They were having lunch together at a Hunan restaurant on Grant, sharing a plate of tofu and red peppers.

"Nothing." Cassie lied.

"David giving you any trouble?"

"No."

"You're awfully quiet today."

"Can't a person be quiet sometimes without having it made into a matter of public inquiry?" She hadn't slept all night and she had a headache and her emotions were jumping up and down like a mob of demented kangaroos, and she was in no mood to be civil. She knew she should tell Lucy about last night's fiasco, but what she had done was so embarrassing that she could barely face it herself. Throwing David on his back—what the hell had gotten into her? The poor guy had only tried to kiss her, and she'd treated him like a rapist. Worse than that, she'd responded to his kiss. She hadn't wanted to, but she had, only thank God he hadn't suspected. Her body had betrayed her and she'd wanted him, and the very thought made her feel a little crazy. Tell Lucy that, confess that the Quinn lust level was on the rise and aimed at the world's most inappropriate target, and there'd be hell to pay. *You thought about having sex with David!* Lucy would yell. *You must be out of your mind!* She'd worry herself sick, even though there was nothing to worry about. Cassie wasn't going to sleep with David. Absolutely not. She was a mature woman with a great deal of self-control, and she knew a disaster in the making when she saw one. Sleep with David Blake? Certainly not. The photographic sessions were almost over, and besides, the bastard had threatened to sue her, her a single mother with two kids to support.

"How many more times do you have to go over to his place?" Lucy asked out of the blue, as if reading her mind.

Cassie flinched and dropped her chopsticks. "Once more," she said through tight lips. "This afternoon at four-thirty."

"Well, that's a relief." Lucy picked up a piece of tofu, examined it, and then popped it into her mouth. "I suppose you'll still be working on the production stills, but you won't have to have so much personal contact with him."

"I never did have any personal contact with him," Cassie snarled. She fished her chopsticks out of the sauce, perversely ate a red pepper, and began to cough.

"Well, excuse me." Lucy was annoyed. "I didn't mean to pry, but as you know our mutual welfare happens to be at stake, so I have more than a passing interest in this folly of yours."

"Pass the water," Cassie ordered. She clammed up for the rest of the meal, and Lucy left feeling upset. It was definitely one of the worst lunches they'd had in a long time, and if Cassie hadn't been scheduled to go over to the Refuge that night to help her cook dinner, she would have had it out with her immediately. She wondered what the hell was going on that had Cassie so on edge. Maybe it was something to do with Lorenzo.

A half hour later Cassie stood in the darkroom bathed in cherry-red light, washing the prints of David's face in fixing solution: David, bent over his poem, biting his lower lip; David, looking defeated; David, angrily crumpling his work and throwing it away. Everything had been right last night: the light, the shadows, the timing. What the camera had revealed was a man fighting for some part of himself that he'd lost long ago. Shot by shot you could see him struggling to hang on, refusing to accept that he'd been defeated. It was the best series of photographs she had ever taken. Why?

Because you're sexually attracted to him, part of her mind argued.

No, another part said, *admit it; there's more to it than that. You've been sexually attracted to men before, but you never took shots like this.*

David lay in her hands, looking up at her with a dozen expressions, each one complex and impenetrable. Although his suffering was clear, the source of it was an enigma. She washed the photos carefully, taking much longer than usual. Why had she done so well with him?

Because he's a piece of your past.

What did that mean?

It means that you feel attached to him because he knew you when you were Cassandra Quinn, and you miss Cassie. You're always looking for some sign that your other self existed.

That was ridiculous. David didn't even know who she was.

Or was it so ridiculous after all? She thought of the men she had known since Andy's death: a professor from UCLA; a construction worker; a reporter; Allen, Renny's father; a computer programmer; a nice guy who taught nursery school; an alcoholic artist who painted sets for MGM; Lorenzo; tall men; short men; rich men; poor men; men with jobs and men without; intelligent men; fools. She'd tried every possible combination and nothing had worked. No lover had been right. Fiasco, disaster, pain. What had she been looking for in those men? What had she wanted? What had gone wrong?

None of them ever knew you.

Yes, they did, she protested.

No, they didn't. You changed your name, your face, your entire identity. When they loved you, they loved Susan Clark, but you never were Susan and you always knew it.

She put the photos of David in the rinse tray and watched the water flow over them.

You purchased beauty, success, and safety at the price of loneliness.

She picked up the best photo of David and held it carefully by the edges. He was looking straight at the camera, and it would have been an ordinary close-up except that she had caught him in transition between two thoughts. What the thoughts were, she had no idea, but you could see two faces: the young face of his past and, over it, the mask of age and disillusionment.

"David," she said softly, "it's me, Cassie. You remember me, don't you, David? I'm alive and Lucy's alive. Andy isn't alive though. I really loved Andy, David. I never got over him killing himself. Why do you suppose that is?"

It was crazy to stand there in the darkroom having a conversation with David's photograph, but it would have been a lot crazier to have a conversation with David himself. She stared at his face for a few more seconds, and then dropped it back in the rinse tray.

She arrived at David's house promptly at four-thirty, confident that she had worked out her feelings about him and made peace with herself. She understood that it wasn't him she wanted; it was her own past, and he couldn't give her that. But she hadn't counted on David. He came to the door barefoot, wearing white jeans and a white open-necked shirt, and to her surprise she felt such longing that it was painful. I'm hopeless, she thought.

"Hello." David leaned against the door frame and surveyed her warily. "Back for round two?"

Cassie planted her hands on her hips and did the best imitation she could of a woman in control of herself. "Look, I apologized for flipping you, and you refused to accept my apology, so what more do you want?"

"How about a friendly 'good afternoon'?"

"Good afternoon."

"That wasn't very friendly."

"Sorry, but it's the best I can do."

David sighed and straightened up. "Come on in," he said, "and let's get this over with." They went into the living room, and he sat down on the couch and put his feet up on the coffee table. Books of poetry were still scattered all over the floor, but there were changes. For one thing, the light was different. Sunlight streamed through the great window with such intensity that when she looked through the lens of her camera the walls and carpet glowed. But the most striking change was that a long, handwritten poem lay on the coffee table.

"You wrote!" Cassie exclaimed. She took a step forward, intending to pick up the poem and read it, but he stopped her.

"It's not ready for public consumption."

"But it's a poem?"

"Yes, it is." He smiled. "I don't know what happened, but for some reason last night I had a breakthrough. As much as I hate to admit it, I suppose I should thank you for tossing me on my ass. I think it stirred things up."

Cassie looked at the poem, lifted her camera and took a shot of it. Then she moved straight toward him with the intention of capturing the expression on his face, but she never pressed the shutter. Instead, she kissed him. She hadn't meant to kiss him, but it was as if something grabbed her from behind and threw her toward him, and once she started she didn't want to stop. She felt his surprise and then his response and then he seized her in his arms and began making love to her. Her last coherent thought was, Go for it.

David's lovemaking was fierce and passionate and silent, and later she remembered very little of it, only that he had taken off her clothes very quickly, and that they had ended up rolling on the floor across the books, screwing on the history of poetry, as the pages came off and stuck to her skin. She moaned and clawed at his back, but he was going on too fast, almost without her. She felt him inside her, but he wasn't with her in any way, and even though the smell of him and the touch of him and the quickness of his breathing and the force of his pelvis grinding against her were all exciting, there was no mystery, no loss of self or union with another, only a kind of sexy, wild wrestling match that left her breathless and wanting more.

Then it was over and she knew that she had made a terrible mistake. She hadn't even had the forethought to ask him to use a condom—but when had there been time for that?—and now she could be pregnant or have AIDS. She was a fool. He hadn't known who she was and never would. Like all the other men in her life, he'd made love to Susan Clark and had a damn good time, while Cassie Quinn sat on the sidelines. She sat up, feeling ashamed of herself for being so impulsive. Lucy was never going to forgive her. The only thing good about this whole mess was that no one had walked in on them. In a house this big there must be a maid and a cook and God knew how many other servants. David probably didn't care about screwing in front of the help. He probably did it all the time.

David smiled and yawned. "Are you all right?" he asked.

"Fine." She couldn't meet his eyes. Getting up, she gathered her clothes and fled to one of the upstairs bathrooms, praying that she wouldn't meet anyone on the way. Closing the door, she locked it and spent five minutes scrubbing herself with hot water and soap, trying to wash away the folly she had just committed. As she stood there, naked, holding the sponge in one hand and the soap in the other, she realized that she had two choices: she could either bury this incident and never think of it again, or she could confess what she'd done to Lucy.

Bury it, the voice inside her advised. *Forget it. You did something completely neurotic and out of line. Why should Lucy ever have to know? It would only cause her pain.*

She put on her clothes quickly, combing her hair so hard that it brought tears to her eyes. When she was dressed, she went back out to face David. On the way to the living room, she passed a wall phone and remembered that if she didn't call Lucy at once, she was going to have to show up at the Refuge to help her cook dinner. She seized the receiver and then hesitated. Could David hear her? Not likely. He was downstairs with the record player blaring. Casting caution to the winds, she quickly dialed Lucy's office.

"This is Susan Clark," she told the secretary. "I need to talk to Lou if she's still there." The secretary told her to hold on, and a minute later Lucy was on the line.

"Hi," Lucy said, "what's up?"

"I can't make it to the Refuge for dinner tonight, Lou." Just the sound of Lucy's voice paralyzed her with guilt, and there was no way she could face her until more time had passed.

"Too bad, what happened?"

"Look, Lou, something came up, okay? It's complicated."

"Okay, fine. But if there's something wrong I wish you'd tell me. You looked frazzled at lunch. Maybe you're working too hard."

"Lou, listen. I'm perfectly okay. I'll call you tomorrow." Cassie hung up, feeling that she might as well have sent Lucy a telegram. Lucy wasn't stupid. Keeping the truth from her wasn't going to be easy. When she got back to the living room, she was relieved to discover that

David was nowhere in sight. Gathering up her cameras, she left. Maybe she should have at least stayed to say good-bye, but she didn't want to see him again, and she imagined that he probably felt the same way.

David watched her leave from an upstairs window as she walked down the long driveway and climbed into her car. He saw her slam the door and start the engine. He saw her car climb the hill and disappear into the trees. He knew.

I need to talk to Lou if she's still there. He had been coming to see what was taking her so long in the bathroom when he'd overheard her talking on the phone. It seemed ironic now that, at the time, he'd been worried about her, afraid that maybe the sex had been a bad idea and that she was upset or having regrets.

I can't make it for dinner tonight, Lou. She'd been speaking in a whisper, but the hall—like all the rest of the house—was curved, so he had been close. *Look, Lou, something came up, okay?* It was Cassie's voice and as soon as he heard it he wondered why he hadn't recognized it before. There had been a snapping sound inside his head, and all the pieces had flown together in a perfect fit. He knew now why Susan Clark had seemed so familiar, why she had read his poems. "Say bromeliad," Cassie had ordered one day when he and Lucy were standing on the bank of the Charles, and they had said "bromeliad" and Cassie had snapped their picture.

Cassandra Quinn, Radcliffe class of '66, former Storm member. Cassie Quinn, terrorist, wanted for murder, underground for twenty years. The day after the bomb factory explosion her face had been on the front page of every newspaper in the United States, which was no doubt why she'd had it changed. He wondered where she'd had the plastic surgery done and how much it had cost her. She was as famous as Bernardine Dohrn, as famous as Abbie Hoffman. He had seen her wanted poster hanging in the post office for several years every time he went to buy stamps or mail a package. The FBI had hunted her but never found a trace. Cassie had given herself a new face and a new name: Susan Clark. But that wasn't the half of it.

Lou, listen. I'm perfectly okay. I'll call you tomorrow.

David stared out the window at the place where her car had disappeared into the trees. He stood there, motionless, for a minute or two, lost in thought. Then he slammed his fist into the palm of his hand, muttered something to himself, and rushed downstairs to the phone Cassie had used. The phone, like all the other phones in the house, had a redial button. Any number that had been dialed could be redialed hours or weeks later as long as no one had used it in the meantime.

For a second he stood with his finger poised over the redial button, afraid to touch it. He remembered the Catholic funerals of his boyhood: the widow in black; the draped altar; the priest looking sober; the cold, final sound of earth hitting a wooden coffin. Out of the depths, he thought. It wasn't really a prayer, but it was the closest he had come to one in years. He wished suddenly that he really could pray because he needed all the help he could get. He had a superstitious feeling that he was about to resurrect the dead.

• 4 •

"Ms. Crest's office," an unfamiliar voice said. David leaned his forehead against the wall, closed his eyes, and swallowed a pang of disappointment so strong it made his throat burn. He'd been crazy to think that Lucy would answer the phone in person. He had an old Carter family record with a song on it entitled "No Telephones in Heaven," and he heard it now, playing sadly in the back of his brain, complete with the steely drone of a Dobro. One of the bitter truths of life was that when people you loved died, you couldn't just dial them up and charge it to your AT&T card. "Hello?" The woman on the other end of the line persisted. "Who's calling, please?"

David turned off the lamenting music and forced himself to come back to the world where there were no miracles. "Is Lou there?" he asked. His voice was gruff and full of emotion, but if the receptionist noticed it, she made no comment. Perhaps she often took calls from people who could barely speak.

"No, Ms. Crest just left for the Refuge, and she won't be back until tomorrow morning. Would you like to leave a message?"

"No, thank you." He gripped the receiver and repressed an urge to give a whoop of triumph. Success! "Lou" was a *her*; not "Louis" but a *female*. This was like tripping, like being on some kind of strange acid where your whole life flowed and changed and came back to you transformed. A dozen thoughts spewed through his mind, and it was all he could do not to demand to know at once if "Lou" was Lucy, but twenty years of performing had taught him how to keep his cool. "However, I would appreciate it if you could give me her address; I need to mail her something."

"Certainly. Mail for Ms. Crest should be addressed to: Zeitling, Griffith, and Crest; 824 Powell Street; San Francisco 94119."

Give me her first name! he wanted to beg, but if he said that it would sound suspicious, and he didn't want to make waves. When a woman had faked her own funeral and gone into hiding for twenty years it was reasonable to assume that she might be skittish. If Lucy was alive the last thing he wanted to do was scare her into skipping town before he had a chance to find her. "Thank you." He hung up the phone and stared at the wall as if it were a blank piece of paper. Don't hope, he told himself; don't be a fool. She's dead. You've got her obituary in your scrapbook, a morbid little piece of your past pasted up next to the reviews of "Get Out of Our Way." She died in 1968, the year your singing career peaked, and you've always believed there was a connection. You felt at the time that you'd sold your soul to the devil, paid him a nice little demonic retainer in the form of Lucy. Don't hope. There could be a thousand "Lous" in San Francisco, none of them her. Lucy is dead, man, and the only way you're ever going to get to talk to her again is to hire some table-tapping medium at seventy-five dollars an hour to fake it for you.

All the way upstairs, he tried to make himself listen to the voice of reason, but by the time he had his portable computer unpacked and plugged into Infonet, his heart was beating like crazy, and he was feeling like he was eighteen again and about to do his first poetry reading. He put his face in his hands and tried to calm himself, but calm was another country and he no longer had a passport. Drunk with anticipation, he took a deep breath and typed in the information he had so far. This Ms. Crest, whoever she was, was a professional woman of some kind who had an office on Powell Street. He tried the phone listings first, but there were Crestas and Cressittos and Cruzes, but no L. Crests, at least not in the white pages. Too bad he didn't know what heading to look under in the yellow pages. He remembered that her uncle had been a doctor, so he searched doctors next with no success. Then he tried calling up the membership lists of business and professional organizations, but once again Crests were in short supply.

Feeling frustrated, he sat back and tried to figure out a better way to track her down. Maybe she was in one of those Who's Who books, the kind they always offered to sell you leather-bound copies of for fifty bucks when they listed your name. There was a press in England that churned those things out by the boxcar loads. Sure enough, he actually found a volume in the series entitled *Who's Who in California.*

Give me the Crests, David commanded. The computer screen glowed like the sky before a big storm, green and bright, and he could feel his heart pouring out into it, running over all the chips and wires into the place where she was hiding.

Crest, Lacy. (1918-). Playwright. Female but too old.

Crest, Lawrence. Male.

Crest, Lloyd. Male.

Crest, Lois Brightwater. (1948-). Nuclear Engineer. He looked up this one even though it didn't seem likely. Lucy had never been good at math. Once she'd admitted to him that she'd only gotten a 520 on the math half of her SAT's. She was convinced they had only let her into Radcliffe because she'd promised to major in English. Lois Brightwater Crest claimed in her biography that she was a full-blooded Sioux, educated at Cal Tech, and David believed her.

Crest, Louis.

Crest, Louise. (1949-). Lawyer. He punched in the command that would bring up the complete biography, and the screen blinked. Two seconds later he was sitting in front of his computer crying, which was a goddam stupid thing to do, just sitting there bawling like a kid because he had found her. She'd made herself four years younger, but he had no doubt that it was Lucy. She was no fiction writer: she'd kept her real birthday, her parents' first names, and had herself born in her grandmother's hometown. And as if that weren't enough, she and Louise Crest shared the same initials.

After a minute or two he stopped crying. Rubbing his eyes on his sleeve he grabbed a Kleenex, blew his nose, and looked around, glad that Cecil hadn't been there to witness him cracking up. The little yuppie son of a bitch would never have let him live it down. I'm a living relic, he thought, wadding up the Kleenex and throwing it on the floor.

The Refuge was located in an old Victorian in the Haight Ashbury district near Panhandle Park, and there was a legend that Janis Joplin had once lived on the third floor when she was an unknown singer, but what Lucy saw as she walked up the front steps was not a monument to the sixties but a spread sheet. The house had a lot of space, which was why Children's Aid had bought it in the first place, but it always needed repair, and there was never enough money to complete the job. Today she noticed with despair that the paint was peeling from the entire south side and that one of the drain gutters had come loose. The peeling paint was particularly disheartening because they had redone the house only two years ago, but evidently the south side hadn't been prepped properly, which was no wonder when you considered that all the labor had consisted of inexperienced volunteers—women mostly and a few of the older children. As for the drain gutter, that could turn into a real disaster.

She put her hands on her hips, looked up at it, and sighed. It was already October, and the winter rains could come at any time. A bad storm would equal a leaking roof, falling plaster, buckets on the floor, and more expenses, and where was the money to come from? Cassie had once pointed out, only half in jest, that the trouble with the Refuge was that it rarely had rich alumnae. You could hardly ask single mothers who had fought their way off the streets and into minimum-wage jobs to contribute to the upkeep of the place, and who else was interested? She knew for a fact from working with Project Hunger that it was easier to raise money for children in Bangladesh than San Francisco. The rich preferred to help the exotic poor, not the shabby, home-grown variety. If the women in the Refuge had been Patanese, it would have been a lot easier to get that gutter fixed.

She was just wondering if maybe she ought to scare up a couple of dozen saris, when a four-year-old girl came running out of the front door and threw herself into Lucy's arms with so much force that she nearly knocked her over backward. "¡Ola, Lou!" the girl yelled happily.

Lucy picked her up and gave her a kiss. "Hi, Consuela, what's happening?"

"Ty ate a houseplant and barfed all over the rug, but he's okay now." Ty was Consuela's one-year-old brother Tyrone, and there seemed to be nothing he wouldn't eat, including the rug itself. Lucy made a mental note to recheck all the houseplants to make sure that nothing poisonous was lurking within reach of the toddlers.

Laughter and screams came from within the house, followed by the sound of running feet. Lucy braced herself for the onslaught, thinking that this was always the best part of her day.

"Lou!"

"Hi, Lou!"

Within seconds she was surrounded by half a dozen small children who were jumping up and down, hugging her, begging for kisses, and demanding to know if she'd brought them candy. Laughing, she raised her hands above her head, surrendered, and allowed them to rummage through the pockets of her coat where she had providently stashed a whole bag of miniature Tootsie Rolls. From that moment on, she didn't have a spare second to brood over peeling paint, loose storm gutters, or anything else.

When Children's Aid founded the Refuge, the board had been determined not to make it into either a poor house or a holding pen for homeless women. Lucy had suggested, and everyone else had agreed, that instead of being organized from the top down, the shelter should be run communally, like a cooperative dormitory. This meant that as soon as each woman was admitted she became a full, voting member of the House Committee and was expected to take part in all the chores necessary to make the place run smoothly. Many of the women had never had power before in their lives, had never been listened to, and were awestruck by the idea that they were not only equal to Lucy and the rest of the board but could outvote them. It would have been much easier, of course, to run things by executive fiat, but the added dignity that a democratic structure gave to the women made it well worth the inconvenience. Slackers usually left after discovering that no one was willing to tolerate their scams, and the place was probably cleaner, better kept, and more peaceful than it would have been if an army of social workers had swarmed around directing things.

The only real problem was that some of the new women lacked that most basic of survival skills: the ability to cook. After several years of eating things like limp turnips and underdone spaghetti, Lucy had made it a habit to volunteer for kitchen duty when she paid a visit. Tonight, even without Cassie's help, she managed to transform what was destined to be greasy fried chicken into crisp baked chicken, and she was sitting at the kitchen table feeling quite satisfied with herself, when Doris appeared to announce that there was a man outside asking for her. Men often came to the Refuge, so Lucy wasn't particularly surprised, but Doris, who was a tough, streetwise mother of four, looked awestruck.

"You'll never guess who it is," she said breathlessly.

"Who?"

"He said that all I should tell you is that he's an old friend of yours."

"What does he want?"

Doris shrugged, pushed up the sleeves of her sweatshirt, and grinned. "I don't know, but whatever it is, I'd give it to him."

"Well, send him in." Lucy was mystified. Doris wasn't an easy person to impress. She couldn't think of any "old friend" who could put a look like that on her face.

"Okay."

Still wondering who it could be, Lucy bent over the fern in the middle of the table and began picking off dead fronds. That was the problem with Boston ferns, no matter how healthy they were you had to give them a monthly haircut. She pushed her glasses onto her forehead so she could get a better view of the plant. Lately the print on menus and the directions on medicine bottles had been getting smaller and smaller. Soon she would be farsighted as well as nearsighted and have to go to bifocals. She'd heard that they could make glasses now so that you couldn't tell. She attacked another dead frond, thinking that if she could just convince someone to mist the fern every night, it would hold up better.

"Lucy."

The sound of her name brought her straight up out of her chair. She whirled around and found—oh, Jesus—David Blake, standing in the doorway. She was horrified. Cassie must have screwed up; she must have let their secret slip out. I told her, she thought incoherently, I warned her, but she wouldn't listen, and now, oh, this is beyond bad luck, this is terrible. "There's no one by that name here," she stammered. She threw the dead fronds down on the table and backed away from him. She could feel Louise Crest melting, peeling off her like old paint.

"Lucy," he said as he took a step forward, "it's me, David." He looked older, but his eyes were still the same, pale gray with blue tints that reminded her of the ocean. His hair was dark, worn long with only a few strands of gray, and his chin was square and stubborn, and he looked nothing at all like his album covers, no rhinestones or black leather or even trendy denim, just a pair of gray slacks and a gray-and-violet shirt made out of soft cotton that fell open at the neck. And even though she was freaked out at the sight of him and wished he was anywhere but where he was, she thought, He's aged well, and then she thought, You fool, you fool, what do you care how good David looks? This is a disaster.

He stood there, not flinching under her gaze, as if he actually imagined she might be happy to see him, and she knew that he had recognized her and that no amount of protesting was going to convince him that she was Louise Crest. She could see him taking in her face as she had taken in his, comparing it to the memory of what she used to look like, and she saw herself as he must have seen her: a forty-four-year-old woman with full cheeks and a few faint scars that the years had turned into wrinkles, pale skin, glasses, a slightly crooked mouth. Her hair was still blond the way it had always been, but that probably only made the changes in her face more painful by contrast. He was shocked and making no attempt to hide it. Go ahead, she thought defiantly, stare at me. I'm plain, David. I'm not beautiful anymore. It hurt to see how surprised he was by the change in her appearance. Shaken and upset, she held her ground. She had too much pride to throw her hands over her face and run.

"Hello, David," she said. "This is quite a surprise." Her voice shook slightly, but other than that she gave no sign of how distraught she was. I'm being brave, she thought, and was proud of herself. She experienced a wave of vertigo as if the room were tilting. The kitchen felt close and hot, and she thought of the door behind her and how easy it would be to turn around and walk through it without saying another word, but it was too late to escape. I'm going to have to talk to him, she thought. She swallowed her panic, took a deep breath, and forced herself to walk up to him and shake his hand as if he were an ordinary visitor. "It's been a long time, hasn't it?"

"Yes," he said. His grip was hot and damp, and she realized that he was at least as upset as she was, which was encouraging. They stopped shaking hands and an extremely awkward silence ensued. David shifted his weight from one foot to the other, and she looked down at the toes of his boots, wishing passionately that he would go away. No matter what happened next, she was going to have to persuade him to keep his mouth shut, and David's mouth, as she remembered all too well, had a momentum of its own. If he blew her cover, she would probably lose her seat on the Board of Sups, not to mention be disbarred. There would be a scandal; she wouldn't be able to practice law and she would have to start all over again and she was too old for that. She thought of the Refuge and the four years of hard work she had put into it and how he could kick it out from under her like a pile of sticks. I won't let him destroy my life, she thought. I don't know how I'm going to stop him, but I'll think of a way.

David took a deep breath. He was panicking. He hadn't expected her to look so different, and he knew she had seen the surprise in his face. She was probably hurt and insulted on top of everything else, which was about the worst possible way to start off with her that he could imagine. How the hell could he explain that now that he was over the first shock he didn't give a damn? She was still Lucy, and he still wanted to take her in his arms and kiss her and tell her how much he'd missed her, but he knew if he so much as laid a finger on her, she'd run. He felt like a man about to jump off a bridge into a raging river. Lucy was that river, and he had no idea what was waiting for him under the surface of her greeting: rocks maybe and snags, or a cold current of indifference, or even a whirlpool of anger and resentment. That was the trouble with being a poet, you thought in goddam metaphors when all you wanted to do was speak from your heart.

"You're alive," he said, and immediately felt like a fool because of course she was alive.

"Yes," she agreed, "I am."

"For all these years—" He paused, too upset to go on. "For all these years I thought you were dead." *Get a grip on yourself, Blake.* "And I guess that was the way you wanted it, so I'm sorry to surprise you this way, only I had to . . . I wanted to . . . see you again." He ground to a halt, paralyzed by the look she was giving him. It was the strangest look. He couldn't read it at all. He tried, failed, tried again; and then he lost it entirely and his cool collapsed. "Lucy," he pleaded, "I had to see you, do you understand? I had to."

She turned very pale and gripped the edge of the table. The emotion in his voice was washing the floor out from under her, and she could feel herself being swept away by it. She tried to stay calm but she couldn't, and all at once there were two people out of control in that kitchen and one of them was her. "Oh, why are you here?" she cried. "Why? What could we possibly have to say to each other after all these years?"

"Lucy—"

"Just leave. Please, please, go away. Forget you ever found me. This is a terrible mistake."

"Lucy, I—"

"Please don't call me 'Lucy.' Doris might overhear, anyone might. My name is Louise. I haven't been Lucy for over twenty years. You messed up my life twice. Do you want to do it again?"

"No, please, listen," he begged. "I've changed. I don't want to hurt you in any way. I'm not going to give you away. No one else knows who you are. You're safe. I'm not the same person I used to be. I was a—"

"Louse," she supplied. Desperation made her tactless. She willed him to go, but he wasn't moving. He seemed rooted to the kitchen floor.

"Call me anything you want. I probably deserve it. But at least give me a chance to tell you that I'm sorry for what I did to you."

"Sorry?" She couldn't have been more surprised. The word *sorry* clanged around in her mind, making no sense whatsoever. "Did you say you were *sorry*?"

"Yes, sorry."

"After twenty-five years you've hunted me down to tell me that you're *sorry*?" If all this weren't so terrible, she'd laugh. In fact she might laugh anyway. She was definitely on the verge of hysteria. This was like one of those bad dreams where you wandered around trying to make sense out of the world and it kept changing too fast for you to keep up with it. "Are you telling me that you've come back to apologize for screwing around on me back in 1964? Is that what you're telling me?"

"Right."

She let go of the table. "I don't understand what's going on here." There had been a time in her life when she would have cried with relief at the idea that David cared enough to apologize, but this was a bit late to say the least. She didn't want it or need it, and all it did was make her feel even weirder than she did already if that were possible. All she wanted him to do was go away and forget that he'd seen her. "Why are you telling me this? What do you want from me? Are you working one of the steps of AA? Have you become a born-again Christian?"

He shook his head. "No . . . that is . . . it's simple." He swallowed hard and clenched his fists, ashamed of himself for going to pieces in front of her. "I've just come to apologize."

"Well, well." It was an inane response but as good as any other under the circumstances. This was most amazing. Sitting down on one of the kitchen chairs, she tried to gather her wits. "Is that all you've come for?"

"No," he said, "there's something else."

"What?"

"Nothing, never mind." To her surprise his face turned bright red. "I shouldn't have mentioned it. It's nothing. I can tell you some other time. It might," he fumbled for the right words, "it might shock you."

This was indeed a different David Blake from the one who had left her in Matoon twenty-five years ago. "David." She leaned forward, past the fern and the salt and pepper shakers, encouraging him. He looked as if he might be about to have a heart attack, and she remembered that he was forty-six and she didn't know CPR. "If I didn't keel over when I first saw you standing in the doorway, nothing you can say is going to be all that shocking. What are you trying to tell me?" She wondered fleetingly if he was about to announce that he was gay.

He knew he should keep his mouth shut, but she was so close that he could almost touch her. *Be cool, Blake.* He pleaded with himself, tried to stop himself from making a full confession, Catholic style, a poet's confession, but the battle was lost before he began it. "I—" he said, "I—I." He had never stuttered before in his life.

"What is it, for heaven's sake?"

"I'm trying to tell you that I"—he nearly choked—"still love you. In fact I've never loved anyone else."

"Oh," she said. "Oh, no." She would have been less stunned if he'd announced that he was the reincarnation of Krishna or Superman or E.T. This was terrible. He must be drunk. He couldn't possibly mean it. "You can't still feel that, not after *twenty-five years!*"

"I don't blame you for not believing me." He paced across the room, to the counter where glass bottles of grains and beans sat in neat rows, and his love for her poured out, and he couldn't have stopped it any more than he could have turned back the sea or stopped electricity from running down a wire. "I treated you rottenly." He turned toward her. "I cheated on you, I didn't appreciate you, I was arrogant and cruel and vain and heartless the way only a twenty-year-old twerp can be heartless, but in my own way I loved you. I wasn't very good at showing it, I admit, but I loved you passionately, I really did."

My God he really meant all this. His eyes were bright, and he spoke with such ardor that even now, twenty-five years older and supposedly saner, she could hardly resist the force of the fantasy he was creating: that she had been the love of his life, that not a day had passed when he hadn't thought of her; that he had had a whole lifetime of regrets. She wanted to stop him from digging himself in deeper, but she was speechless with amazement.

"You made me *feel*! Do you understand what that meant to me? Can you possibly know? Men are so damn reasonable, so trained to believe in the holy power of logic, but you made me throw reason out the window. You freed me from my mind, from all those dead, numb thoughts they'd stuffed in my brain at Harvard. You stirred things up in me. I loved you—oh, how I loved you. I'd never loved anyone like that before, not even my mother. So what did I do? To get you out of my system I cheated on you and made sure you knew it. I walked out; I left. I betrayed you. I played Judas to you and to myself, because I was young and dumb and scared and terrified of the force you represented."

"David, please stop."

"No, let me tell you. I know I'll never get another chance so let me finish. *Mea culpa*, Lucy. I was the one to blame. I blew it. I lost you and I've regretted it ever since, because when I took off I didn't just leave you behind me; I left my poetry and my creativity . . . maybe even my soul if such a thing exists." He laughed a low, harsh laugh. "My soul— that's a good one—I'm not sure I have a soul, but I am sure of one thing: when I didn't ask you to marry me, I made the biggest mistake of my life."

"David don't say any more. You're going to regret this tomorrow. You're going to hate me for confessing all this." Against her will, she was moved by his declaration. She felt pity for him, embarrassment even—why not confess it?—satisfaction. So David regretted the day he'd walked out on her, did he? She wished that she could call up her nineteen-year-old self and tell her the good news. But when she looked into his face her sense of triumph vanished, and she felt only sadness and even regret that his confession of love had come too late to do either of them any good. "You shouldn't be telling me all this."

"Lucy—"

"Please, stop. I mean it. I can't listen to another word."

"Lucy, darling—"

"David, I'm not your darling. This is a fantasy you're having. Do you understand? A fantasy. We can't just take up where we left off. I don't even understand how you can call up these emotions after so many years. Try to understand: we're two completely different people than we were when you were twenty-one and I was nineteen. If we'd married, we'd probably have torn one another apart, but what does it matter? It all happened a quarter of a century ago."

"For me it's like yesterday." He put his hands lightly on her shoulders and she could feel them trembling. "You're my Muse." His voice was rough and passionate, and it sent chills through her. "Go ahead, laugh, but it's the truth. "You're my love and my—"

"Look at me, David." She had to make him face reality. "Look at me: I'm not anyone's Muse but my own. I'm a plain, middle-aged woman with wrinkles around her eyes that barely hide the scars. Even my smile is a little screwed up. The Lucy Constable you knew doesn't exist anymore. I'm sort of her distant cousin, her elderly aunt."

"You still look beautiful to me."

She was touched by that; in fact it brought her close to tears. "Thank you," she said softly. "It's been a long time since anyone's said something that kind to me."

"I'm not being kind. I mean it. The first night I saw you in the Dunster Common Room, I was attracted to your body—I admit that. Jesus, Lucy, you glowed like something made of gold and fire; you filled up the whole place, and no man in the room had a chance to resist you, but after I got to know you, your looks didn't matter anymore. I fell in love with what's inside your head or your heart or wherever the real you is located, and nothing can change that."

He was moving her and she didn't want to be moved by him, not now, not ever again, because she knew how changeable he was. At the moment he was in love with a piece of verse drama entitled "The Poet Meets the Woman He Should Have Married," and he probably believed every word he was saying, but as soon as he came to his senses he'd see that she was plain, or at the very least that some young, pretty woman was more attractive. Opening up to him would be sure disaster. She had had all the heartbreak and trouble she needed from David Blake. "You're talking like a poet," she said, detaching his hands from her shoulders. "Life isn't a sonnet."

"I mean what I'm saying."

"Then prove it."

"How?"

She leaned back, putting some space between them, thinking that if she kept listening, he was going to suck her into his fantasy world against her will. I could even love him again, she thought, and the idea made her question her own sanity. After all this time, after so many years? She wondered what there was inside her that made her long for the impossible and fall in love with disasters. Maybe it came from losing her mother when she was so young, or maybe it was something else, something deep and compelling that she would never be able to understand. Whatever the source, she had to get rid of David before he tempted her to make a fool of herself for a third time. Go and take all your romantic, passionate, poetic bullshit with you, she thought, because I love it, David, and I respond to it and that scares the hell out of me.

He bent over her, so close that she could smell the old familiar scent of his skin. "What do you want?" he said softly. "I'll do whatever you want, Lucy. I swear it."

"I want you to . . . go away." She saw the words hit him and he flinched, but she went on, determined to make him understand that there was absolutely no hope. "Forget that Louise Crest has anything in common with Lucy Constable." She sat there, not taking the words back and not regretting them. She felt sad, but it was better this way. If growing older had given her one thing, it was the ability to see trouble in time to avoid it. And this was more than trouble; this was a recipe for disaster.

He swallowed hard, straightened up, and stood for a moment in silence. "Is that what you really want? Do you really want me to go?"

She nodded. "Yes, David." Her voice was firm and clear. She wasn't so firm on the inside, but she didn't show it. "That's what I really want."

His face turned very pale and he bit his lower lip. He was so wounded by the ease with which she seemed to be dismissing him that he could hardly speak. Twenty years' worth of groupies had idolized him, fought for the chicken bones that had touched his mouth and the buttons from his shirts, and now the one woman he had ever loved was ordering him to get out of her sight. "This is hard to take. I lose you; I find you; and then I lose you all over again." He walked over to the window and stood staring out at the backyard, feeling hurt and abandoned and bitterly disappointed. All the pain and loneliness of his life seemed to roll itself into a ball that lodged in his throat.

Finally he got himself under control. "Well, thanks." He walked back to the kitchen table and stood in front of Lucy, looking down at her, defeated. "I mean it. You've been straight with me. You don't feel anything for me anymore and all you want from me is my absence. And you know what: I actually love you enough to give it to you. Isn't that amazing? David Blake caring enough about another human being to give up the one thing he wants most in the world?" He smiled a painful smile that fell off into a grimace. "I think I've just grown up, and it hurts like hell."

"You're a good man, David." She meant it; she had more respect for him at that moment than she'd ever had before, and she wanted to tell him as eloquently as he had told her, but she was no poet. "I wish you a good life."

"Thanks." He stretched out his hand, took hers, and shook it. "Goodbye. Don't worry, I'll survive. And I'll never tell anyone who you are." He paused. "If you ever change your mind, you can give me a call." He pulled a card out of his pocket, wrote something on it, and held it out to her. "Here are my phone numbers: the 415 is the place I'm renting in Sausalito and the 213 is L.A. They're both unlisted. I still don't know where you've been all these years or why you went into hiding, and if you ever want to tell me or need help or—" He stopped. "No, huh? Well then, I guess that's about it. Good-bye, Lou."

Five minutes later Doris came into the kitchen and found Lucy with her face cradled in her hands, sobbing as if her heart were about to break.

"What happened?" Doris demanded. "Did Blake lay a hand on you? I recognized him right off, you know, from his album covers, and I don't care if he is a rock star; if he hurt you, I'll chase the sucker down, whittle his famous head to a point, and pound him into the sidewalk."

"No," Lucy protested. "I'm okay. I'm okay."

Doris wasn't convinced, but she had been at the Refuge long enough to know that when a sister wanted to have a good cry, the least everyone could do was leave her alone. Planting herself outside the kitchen door, she kept everyone away until the sobbing stopped. Then she went back into the kitchen.

"How's it going?" she asked.

Louise seemed in much better shape. She said that she was just fine and asked to borrow a quarter so she could use the pay phone on the corner to call someone. The Refuge didn't have a phone because too many people had racked up anonymous long-distance calls.

• 5 •

Cassie usually camped out on Lucy's living-room floor when she was in San Francisco, but on the odd occasions when someone else paid for her hotel room, she removed herself to the luxury of room service and a bed that didn't have to be folded up in the morning and stashed in the closet. At present she was staying at the Fairmont, courtesy of Blake Productions. The Fairmont had always been one of her favorite hotels; the view from Nob Hill was spectacular, the rooms were pleasant, and the management always supplied you with two terry-cloth bathrobes, one trimmed in pink and one trimmed in blue. Terry-cloth bathrobes, however, did little for a person sunk in a slough of guilt and regret, so when she got back from Sausalito she called room service, ordered a bottle of Chardonnay, and sat in her coat on the edge of the bed, drinking from the bottle and watching television with the sound turned off. She got as far as the top of the label when she realized that she was going to make herself sick, so she put the bottle out in the hall for the bellhop, lay down on the bed, and went to sleep or passed out, you could take your choice.

When she woke a few hours later, it was dark outside, and she felt like someone had been rummaging through her stomach with the business end of a vacuum cleaner. The look on David's face just before she kissed him kept rising up in front of her like a concrete bridge abutment. Great going, Quinn, she thought. You seduced *him*, you idiot. You hurtled toward him at 90 mph like a car out of control, and now you'd give anything to go back and repeat the sequence at 55, omitting the kiss and everything that followed, but tough luck. What's done is done, and you've got no one to blame but yourself.

Staggering out of bed, she made her way into the bathroom, turned on the shower, undressed, and sat down in the tub, letting the water patter off her head. She occasionally took showers this way, especially when she was in a foul mood. The sound of water hitting her skull was soothing, and if she closed her eyes she could sometimes convince herself that she was caught in a spring rainstorm in a tropical jungle, but tonight the jungle fantasy went nowhere. *You screwed up*, the water said as it bounced off her, *and it's going to take more than a sit-down shower to put this folly behind you.*

She was just stepping out of the tub when the phone rang. Swearing softly, she threw on the blue-trimmed robe, padded into the bedroom, leaving puddles of water in her wake, grabbed the receiver, and balanced it between her chin and chest as she dried her hair with one of the Fairmont's thick white towels.

"Uh," she said, which given the mood she was in was the closest she could come to "hello."

"Susan, this is Louise." It was Lucy's voice, tight and angry. "I want to see you at my place in half an hour."

"Is something wrong?" Cassie felt horribly guilty and then incredulous. Lucy must know that she'd slept with David! But wait a minute, how could she? That dreary scene on his living-room rug had happened only a few hours ago. Dropping the bath towel, she clutched at the receiver. Calm down, she ordered herself. The woman isn't psychic. *Oh, yes she is*, another voice said. *Lucy can read your mind as if it were a newspaper, and you know it.*

"You know good and well that something is wrong," Lucy snapped.

"And you know exactly what it is. I don't care to discuss it on the phone. Just be at my place in half an hour." Slam.

She'd hung up on her. She'd actually hung up on her. This was serious. Lucy had never hung up on anyone in the thirty years Cassie had known her. Grabbing one of her jumpsuits out of the closet, she threw herself into it, zipping up the zippers so fast she nearly removed all the hair from her crotch. Consumed with anxiety, she paced back and forth in the elevator all the way down to the lobby. Lucy *must* have found out about David. There was no other explanation for the way she'd sounded on the phone.

She made it to Lucy's apartment in twenty-six minutes flat to find Lucy out on the roof armed with a pair of large wooden-handled shears, pruning Mrs. Albergetti's roses by the light of a large floor lamp. One look at her face and Cassie's last shred of hope vanished. It was a pale, angry face; a face that said, *You've hurt me terribly.* Launching into a bush of white roses, Lucy hacked it into shape in something under four seconds—an impressive performance, but not one designed to instill feelings of security. Cassie contemplated the remains of the bush, thinking that it was a good thing Lucy had always been a pacifist.

"You're pruning them too early," she said. "You're supposed to wait until February."

"You don't say." Lucy attacked another bush, scattering roses in every direction. Snip, slash, snip, slash. "Always the expert, aren't you?"

"I was a botanist, remember?"

"I remember everything. I wish I could forget some of our mutual past, but it's seared into my mind." She opened the jaws of the shears, caught a rose stem between the blades, pruned it back, and moved on to another.

Cassie collapsed on the redwood bench next to Mrs. Albergetti's basil, dropped her purse onto the tar and gravel, and watched the massacre of the roses progress. There was a short silence. "You know," she said.

"Right." Lucy nodded, kicking piles of stems out of the way and opening her shears for her next attack. "I know." Snip, slash. "Why the hell did you do it, Cass?"

Cassie stared at her, trying to think of some excuse, but all she could think was that she didn't have one. "I'm sorry," she mumbled. "I didn't know you'd care so much."

"Didn't know I'd care!" Lucy straightened up and tossed aside the shears. They hit the roof hard, bounced, and settled at her feet like a pair of exclamation marks. "What did you think I'd do? Rent a hall and celebrate?"

"I'm sorry."

"Sorry!"

"I'm not saying I'm innocent," Cassie protested, "but give me a break: a couple of weeks ago you told me on the phone that you could barely remember you'd ever had a relationship with David. Those were your exact words, Lou. So what was I to think? I know it was a bad idea, but I was attracted to him, I admit it. I even told you that, but if you'd made it clear that you were going to be this jealous, I swear to God that I would never have considered sleeping with him. If it's any consolation to you, it was a completely rotten experience, I feel horrible about it, and I'm certainly not planning to do it again."

Lucy opened her mouth and closed it again. The look on her face was so odd that Cassie wondered if maybe she'd inhaled a rose thorn or something. "You slept with him?"

"Of course. What else are we talking about?"

"You *slept* with David?"

"Lou, what's wrong with you? Yes, I slept with David, and I'm sorry."

"Aggh." Lucy picked up the shears and began pruning everything in sight.

"Aggh?" Cassie was completely bewildered by her reaction. "Does that mean you're so jealous that you're never going to forgive me? Speak English, please. I can't stand to—"

Lucy stopped pruning and wiped the sweat off her forehead. "This is horrible," she moaned.

"Right," Cassie agreed. "You've pruned off too much. Mrs. Albergetti is going to have a seizure when she sees what you've done to her roses. But you're upset. It's understandable. Why don't you come inside, we'll have a nice cup of tea, and you can calm down a little." She laughed weakly. "Frankly I don't like the way you're wielding those shears."

"That's not what I mean. I mean it's horrible that you slept with him. I didn't know that."

"You didn't?"

"No, I only knew that you'd blown our cover by telling him who you were, who I was, and"—she threw the shears to the ground again—"I am jealous. By God, I am. How the hell could you sleep with him, Cassandra Quinn? You knew I was lying when I told you I didn't care about him anymore. You knew I was just trying to save face. So despite that, you jump into bed with him, spill your guts, tell him who you are, put us both in his power, and—"

Now it was Cassie's turn to be astonished. "Are you crazy? I slept with him, yes, but I didn't tell him who I was or who you were. I may be horny, but I'm not insane."

"Then how do you explain the fact that David showed up at the Refuge tonight?"

"He didn't!"

"Oh, yes, he did, Cass. He not only showed up, he cornered me in the kitchen and told me I was the only woman he'd ever loved." She laughed mirthlessly. "It was like a Jane Austen novel rewritten by the Marx Brothers, and evidently I have you to thank for it."

"Oh, my God. He couldn't have."

"Of course he did. What did you expect him to do after you informed him that Louise Crest and Lucy Constable were one and the same?"

"Lou, I swear to God, I never told him anything. I may be guilty of jumping on his bones, but I'm not—"

"Try Benedicta Arnold," Lucy suggested.

"That's not fair."

"Not fair maybe, but expressive. I'm mad at you, in case you haven't noticed. You've done something so idiotic and irresponsible that—that you've risked everything, dammit, just to get yourself laid. Didn't it even once cross your mind that the FBI is still looking for you? Didn't you even think of *me* and how I might feel? No? Well, let me tell you. I feel hurt; I feel betrayed; I feel like you've played roulette with my life. The Refuge could go under. I could lose my place on the Board of Sups and my law practice and everything I've spent the past twenty years putting together. I don't have a legitimate law degree, remember? I don't even have a valid passport, and it didn't occur to me to apply under the new Amnesty Act for illegal aliens by the cutoff date because I didn't know you were going to turn me in to the INS. That's what you've done, you know, potentially at least. It should be a lot of fun to be deported to the People's Republic of Patan. I'm sure, as the ex-princess, I'll get a warm welcome from the PLF."

"Lou, calm down, please. It isn't that bad."

"Oh, it isn't? How do you know that? How can you possibly predict the consequences of what you've done?" She pointed to her chest. "Your betrayal hurts me, Cass. It hurts me right here in the heart. Maybe you think that's melodramatic, but it's true. My heart aches over your betrayal. I'd cry, but I ran out of tears about an hour ago."

"Lou, I'm sorry you feel so bad, and I'm sorry you're so worried, but I'm not to blame. I kept my mouth shut, I swear I did. I have no idea how David tracked you to the Refuge, and I'm as upset as you are that he showed up. The idea that he knows who we are scares the hell out of me."

"You expect me to believe that!" Lucy narrowed her eyes and folded her arms across her chest. "Oh, no, Cassie, not this time. I'm not buying it. You've always gotten me into trouble. When we were in high school in Colorado you nearly got me expelled for cooking spaghetti on a hot plate in our closet, not to mention the time at Radcliffe when you chained yourself to that tree, and I was the one who had to plead with the dean not to have you arrested for criminal trespass. But those were trivial things compared to your idiotic involvement with Storm. You know what, I'm going to tell you something I should have told you twenty years ago. I don't think you're innocent. I think you're guilty of criminal stupidity if nothing else. You knew Steve was making some kind of illegal device, and you *knew* he was a fucking maniac, and you went on living in that house anyway."

Cassie's face turned white and then red. "How can you say that! How can you even suggest that I'm guilty when you know that I had no—"

"It's easy, and I'm not done. I've got a lot more to say. You know, we've talked about this maybe a hundred times, but I never let all the stops out. I never told you how I really felt about that night because I was afraid of losing you. You were all I had left of my past, so I hung on to our friendship by keeping my mouth shut. Well, screw the past. I lost my looks thanks to you. Do you know how painful that was? how hard it was for me to look in the mirror? For months I cried myself to sleep at night. Even now when I dream, I dream of myself as I was before the explosion. For twenty years I've struggled to piece my life back together. Without you I would have had money, but almost all I got from the diamonds Mila gave me went into our new faces; without you I might have been able to go back to being Lucy Constable. After a few years maybe I could have come out in the open again and told Mila where I was without trying to use a pack of Tibetan Buddhists to carry the message. But you were there. You were my friend and my responsibility, and I took that responsibility. I manufactured a person called Louise Crest and did a damn good job of it, and then: enter Cassie Quinn. How many times are you going to kick my life apart?"

"Lucy, stop it. Stop it right now. You're blaming me for everything that ever happened to you."

"You think I'm overdoing it, huh? Well, look at it from my perspective. In 1968, thanks to you, my life went to hell. I put it back together. Now you've blabbed out our secret to David—who knows when or how? In the middle of an orgasm maybe—and—"

Cassie rose to her feet and drew herself up to her full height. Her zippers sparkled in the moonlight, and she towered over Lucy. "I didn't blab out our secret in the middle of an orgasm because I didn't have one and furthermore—"

"You want a sympathy card? A year's supply of Dr. Ruth tapes? I don't know how it happened; it happened. You're impulsive and unreliable and self-destructive. Everyone you get close to ends up getting screwed. Look what happened to Andy."

"You leave Andy out of this, dammit!"

"Fine, we'll leave Andy out of it. We'll push that one under the rug again. We'll just stick to the present. We'll stick to the fact that you've hurt me and betrayed me; you've put my career at risk, you've put the Refuge at risk, and as if that weren't enough, I've been thinking about trying to adopt a child. Now, thanks to you, I'll be lucky if I'm considered qualified to adopt—"

"Lucy, shut the fuck up." There was a stunned silence. Cassie picked up her purse and slung it over her shoulder. "Now it's my turn. First let's get one thing straight. Has David threatened to tell anyone what he knows?"

"No," Lucy admitted, "but that doesn't mean that he won't change his mind and—"

"But at the moment we're in no danger?"

"No, but—"

"Good. That's a load off my mind. Now I've got some things to say and I'd appreciate it if you'd let me say them without interrupting me with more accusations. Number one: I did not—repeat *did not*—tell David who you are, but I suggest that we had better work together to find out who did. Number two: I did not wreck your life in 1968. You were already on the run from your own past. Number three: I'm sorry about your face, but I can't do anything about it. Number four: If you ever mention Andy to me again in that tone of voice, I'm going to walk out of your life forever. And number five: I'm sorry you're in such pain, but I don't intend to stand here and listen to you rave at me. Our friendship has lasted for nearly thirty years and I fully expect it to last thirty more, so when you come to your senses, give me a call." She picked up the pruning shears and placed them in Lucy's hands. "Meanwhile I think you've left some signs of life on this roof."

It was a great exit line, but by the time Cassie got down to her car she was so upset she could hardly get her keys in the ignition. This was the worst fight she and Lucy had ever had, and every time she thought about the cruel things they had said to each other, her eyes filled with tears and she had to wipe them on the sleeve of her jumpsuit so she could see where she was driving. It wasn't my fault, she thought. One look at David, and Lou went bananas. She was out to get me before she heard my side of the story, and she wouldn't listen to reason. It wasn't fair. I didn't tell him anything. She always was slow to anger but when she gets going she has the meanest tongue of anyone I ever knew. She doesn't just say mean things; she says *memorably* mean things. Babbled it all out when I was having an orgasm, did I? For your information, Constable, I'm too busy when I'm coming to speak in full sentences. Of course you're probably different. You probably provide footnotes.

She drove past Washington Square, muttering to herself, protesting her own innocence, but it was a downhill battle because somehow David knew. There was no way around that. And if he knew, she must have told him—not on purpose, but told him just the same. She must have let something slip, but try as she might, she couldn't imagine what it had been. And then suddenly she remembered the phone call. Oh my God, she thought. He must have overheard. She felt guilty and then angry with herself and Lucy and the world in general because how could life be set up so rottenly?

I hate San Francisco, she thought petulantly, as she turned onto Columbus Avenue. It's cold and desperate and sleazy, and relationships die here. The whole place is a goddam elephant graveyard of friendships. Except for the lack of drive-by shootings, it's worse than L.A.

At the corner of Columbus and Broadway hustlers lounged outside the topless joints, their faces striped red and green by the flickering neon signs, urging pedestrians to come on in and see the live sex acts. An old woman in an orange ski parka and bright purple socks was pushing a shopping cart full of rags and wet newspapers into a wino, banging him on the heels and yelling something incoherent in a high, irritated voice that grated on Cassie's nerves like chalk on a blackboard. It was nights like this that drove otherwise mild-mannered people to shoot up shopping malls. Urban stress. Screw it. She and the kids should move to the Sierras, get a shack and some chickens and . . .

She turned from Columbus onto Broadway and headed toward the freeway, thinking of a new life where she could turn her car into a planter, tomatoes coming out of the front seat, corn in the trunk, a couple of zucchini plants where the motor had been. *Lucy is the only person who connects me to my past, and if she gives me up, then what? Who will ever know me again?* Sad thought. The car garden disappeared to be replaced by more tears, and she was just pushing them angrily out of her eyes when she looked into the rearview mirror and saw a whirling red light.

Oh, no. A cop. Just what she needed on top of everything else. She was going to get a traffic ticket, and her insurance rates were going to go through the ceiling. Pulling over to the curb, she breathed a silent prayer that he was after someone else, but no such luck. The police car cruised to a stop behind her, and a black woman got out. Rolling down her window, Cassie waited for the inevitable.

"May I please see your driver's license, ma'am?" the woman said politely. About twenty years ago, in the wake of the Watts riots, the cops in California had all been sent to charm school or something, and they tended to sound like graduates of the Emily Post Academy of Criminal Justice.

"What did I do, Officer?"

"Illegal left turn, ma'am. May I please see your registration and proof of insurance?"

Cassie handed her the whole shebang and waited while she went back to her cop car to run them through the computer. An illegal left turn was how many points? Two? Three? Maybe she could go to traffic school and keep the points off her record. What with Renny in college, she could hardly afford to fork over another six hundred dollars a year.

The police officer came back accompanied by her sidekick, a young, mustached white male who looked as if he had been issued a uniform two sizes too big. "Would you please step out of your car, ma'am?" he said.

"I beg your pardon?"

"Please exit from your vehicle."

Grumbling, Cassie climbed out of the car and stood on the sidewalk, staring down curious passersby who probably thought she was being busted for dealing crack. "I'm not drunk," she said. "I'm cold sober." She waited for them to put her through the routine of walking a straight line or blowing into the breatholator, but they didn't seem interested.

The white officer scratched his head and consulted his notebook. "Ma'am," he said, "I'm afraid we're going to have to ask you to come along with us."

"What do you mean?"

"We're putting you under arrest, ma'am," the black officer said so politely that Cassie thought at first she must have misunderstood her. Suddenly she did understand and she went cold all over. Putting her under arrest! She'd been caught at last. They knew she was Cassie Quinn. She tried to breathe and swallow, but she couldn't. Fear choked her and she looked around wildly. Maybe she could make a run for it. Would they shoot at her if she did? Wasn't that what they did on TV, shoot escaping felons?

". . . for two unpaid traffic fines," the policewoman continued.

"Traffic fines? You're arresting me for unpaid *traffic tickets*?" She was so relieved that she could have hugged them both.

"That's right, ma'am. Under California law failure to pay the fines for moving violations is a criminal offense, and there is an outstanding warrant for your arrest."

"But I don't have any unpaid fines; I always pay everything right away, even parking tickets."

The policeman consulted his notebook. "I'm sorry, ma'am, but according to the computer you have a 22350VC and a 22405oVC, both delinquent."

"Could you translate, please. What's a 223 . . . whatever?"

"One's for speeding, ma'am, and the other is for running a stop sign. The first citation was made 1/13/83 and the other 8/26/83, all in the greater Los Angeles area."

Now Cassie remembered. Nineteen eighty-three had been a bad year for traffic tickets, in fact it had been a bad year for almost everything. That was the year she and Lorenzo were beginning their long, painful breakup, the year he started yelling at her all the time. Lorenzo had specialized in starting fights while she was driving and couldn't get away from him. She had gotten those two tickets in the middle of shouting matches and had written out the checks for both of them right away. "But I paid those," she protested. "Check again. Your computer must have made a mistake."

"I'm sorry, ma'am, but it isn't up to us to determine whether or not a computer error has been made. When a warrant has been issued, we have no choice but to arrest the party named therein. You'll have a chance to tell a judge your side of the story. Meanwhile you have the right to remain silent." The policewoman read Cassie her Miranda rights.

"Well, take me away then," Cassie said when she was finished. This was annoying, but it was so much better than what she had expected that she couldn't help feeling miraculously reprieved. "I feel like Arlo Guthrie. Are either of you old enough to remember *Alice's Restaurant*?"

The police officers looked at her as if she were out of her mind, which in a way she was. They could have arrested her as an accessory to a murder, and they were only arresting her for traffic tickets. Maybe they'd even let her use her MasterCard to post bail.

But when she got down to the county jail she discovered that her bail wasn't going to be set until morning. "Just let me go to an automatic teller," she begged. "I've got fifteen hundred dollars in my savings account."

"Sorry," the matron said, "that's against regulations and anyway money isn't the problem. Your bail hasn't been set yet, and no judge is going to get himself out of bed to hear a traffic citation case." She was a beefy woman with short hair and a small, hard mouth. "After we finish processing you, you can make your phone call and get a friend to bring over the cash first thing in the morning. My guess is that you'll be looking at about three hundred bucks, but then I'm not the judge. It could be more; it could be less. Meantime, it's after ten o'clock and you've been arrested on a criminal warrant, so we're going to have to keep you for the night." She turned to the officer behind the desk. "Larry, would you pull an inventory form for me?"

Cassie was alarmed. "You mean I'm going to have to spend the night in jail for two traffic tickets that I already paid just because your computer screwed up?"

"Right," the matron said. "Now empty out your purse."

"But this is ridiculous. I'm not a criminal."

"You want to empty your purse, or shall I do it for you?"

Cassie began to empty out her purse, thinking that the matron had obviously never been to charm school.

"One lipstick," the matron said, tossing Cassie's lipstick into a plastic Ziploc bag.

"Check," said the clerk.

"Fifty-three dollars cash."

"Check."

"Three Tampax." She examined the unopened wrappers and then handed the Tampax back to Cassie. "I think we'll let you keep these."

"Thanks. Your generosity is overwhelming."

The matron was not a woman finely tuned to irony. "You're welcome," she said. She continued until all of Cassie's possessions were stowed in the plastic bag, and then handed her the inventory form. "Sign here."

Cassie signed. "What next? You spray me for lice maybe?"

"No," the matron said. "We only do that to the males. Consider yourself lucky that you're going to the women's wing." Retrieving another form from the clerk, she began to fill it out.

"What are you doing now?"

The matron sighed. "Jesus, you traffic-ticket types are the limit. Always asking questions. I'm booking you, of course."

"Booking me!" This was like something out of *Miami Vice*. Cassie began to panic all over again. If they were booking her, then they were probably going to take her picture and fingerprint her. The picture part was okay, but the fingerprinting! She couldn't let them take impressions of her hands because they were Cassandra Quinn Rabinowitz's hands and somewhere in some FBI file there might be matching prints and . . . She felt cold, then hot, then very, very frightened.

The matron finished filling out the form and handed it back to the clerk. She seemed to be doing everything in slow motion. I'm going to freak out, Cassie thought. The vomit-green walls danced up and down and in and out around her, closing in until she could hardly breathe. She tried to stifle her panic, but it was growing, coming up bitter in the back of her throat like a hairball. She dug her nails into the palms of her hands and looked down at the tiled floor, brown and nasty and covered with cigarette butts and scraps of paper. The whole place smelled of mildew, disinfectant, and bad trips.

"This way." The matron was pointing at the door. I should try to escape, she thought, but there was nowhere to run to. Sober up; calm down. You've got to think of some way to keep them from fingerprinting you. Maybe you could claim that it's against your religion. Maybe you could . . . Thanks to two traffic tickets she was going to end up spending the rest of her life in places like this. *Don't think like that. Be positive.*

She walked down the hall trying to make a plan. Maybe the FBI didn't have her prints. She'd never been booked before. Arrested, yes, one time back in Ann Arbor when she and a group of women staged a protest outside her father's lab, but not fingerprinted, at least not to her recollection. As for the Storm house in Boston, it had burned to the ground, so they couldn't have dusted it for prints. She would have to play it cool, let them do what they wanted. I'm safe, she kept telling herself. They'll never find out who I really am. I'm Susan Clark, remember. Susan Clark.

The room at the end of the hall was completely bare except for a camera mounted on a tripod and a table that contained an ink pad and a pile of white cards. Standing Cassie up against one of the walls, the matron hung a number around her neck and took two pictures of her, full face and profile. The light was so harsh and flat that every pore and wrinkle was going to show. It was all Cassie could do not to tell her how to make the snap look better, but this was a mug shot, for chrissake, so she just stood there, glowering at the camera, thinking that no wonder people on wanted posters looked like hardened criminals.

The matron fiddled with the camera for a few seconds afterward, making sure that the tripod was perfectly lined up with three pieces of dirty silver duct tape. Then she coughed, wiped her nose on the back of her hand, and pointed to the table. "Over there," she ordered.

Cassie started to walk toward the table with every intention of going through with the fingerprinting, but when she saw the white cards with the little squares on them, one for each finger, panic took hold of her again, and she stopped dead in her tracks.

"What's the problem, Clark?"

"I can't let you fingerprint me." She folded her arms behind her back and locked her hands together. "I simply can't permit it. I can't consider—"

"I knew you were going to be trouble," the matron said. "I can always spot it. So I can't fingerprint you, huh?" She made a grab for Cassie's wrist, and Cassie executed a perfect judo escape maneuver, pulling against the weak hinge of her thumb.

"Shit!" the matron yelled. "That hurt."

"I'm sorry," Cassie babbled, backing away from the table. "I didn't mean to hurt you, but I can't let you—"

"Shut up," the matron suggested. Stalking out of the room, she locked the door behind her. A minute later she was back with two male police officers. Before Cassie realized what was happening they had grabbed her and were forcing her toward the fingerprinting table. Cassie begged, raged, told them they were violating her civil rights, cried, and threatened them with a lawsuit, but they were unimpressed. Forcing her hands into the ink, they took ten neat fingerprints, each one centered in the middle of one of the little white squares.

The matron stood to one side, rubbing her injured thumb and watching the whole procedure with grim satisfaction. These middle-class types always thought they were above the law, but in the end they had to knuckle under like everyone else, and the sooner they realized that, the better. Still, this one was making an unusual fuss. She decided that when they had Clark stowed away for the night, she'd ask Allen to fax her fingerprints to the FBI to see if maybe she was in the main computer as a wanted felon. Ordinarily she wouldn't have bothered, but she had a gut feeling about this one. Any prisoner who tried to break your thumb just to keep you from taking her prints had to have something to hide.

· 6 ·

Lucy subscribed to the *New York Times*, the *Sacramento Bee*, and the *San Francisco Chronicle*. She usually managed to get through the editorial pages and the most important articles by the time she finished breakfast, but on the day after her fight with Cassie, she slept late and woke up feeling too miserable to go through the hassle of making herself anything to eat, even instant coffee. Collecting the newspapers from the front steps, she tossed them into the entryway without even bothering to take off the rubber bands, and went out to get herself a sweet roll and a cup of strong espresso at the Café Trieste.

It was nearly eleven o'clock before she noticed the *Chronicle*'s banner headline. She had just emerged from the Cost Plus Garden Store lugging replacements for Mrs. Albergetti's roses when she happened to glance at one of the automatic vending machines on the corner, a glance that gave her a sense of disorientation and déjà vu comparable to being taken up in a small plane and dropped without a parachute.

Dumping the rose bushes on the sidewalk, she fished through her pockets, came up with a quarter, and tried to buy herself a *Chron*, but she kept dropping the money, getting down on her hands and knees, retrieving it from the gutter, and dropping it again. On the third try she managed to line the coin up with the slot, and within seconds she was sitting on the curb, breathing through her mouth, trying not to pass out as she read some truly horrible news.

BOMB FACTORY TERRORIST ARRESTED AFTER TWENTY YEARS IN HIDING

San Francisco—Early this morning San Francisco police announced that they had arrested Cassandra Quinn Rabinowitz, wanted by the FBI since 1968 for her involvement in a Boston bomb-factory explosion that killed four. Rabinowitz, who has been living in Los Angeles under the alias Susan Clark, was stopped in North Beach late last night when she made an illegal left-hand turn. Taken into custody for two previously unpaid traffic citations, she was booked and fingerprinted. When Clark's prints were cross-checked with FBI files, San Francisco police were astounded to discover that they had in custody none other than the notorious   See page 6.

On page 6, two photographs of Cassie had been mounted side by side, one captioned "Rabinowitz in 1968" and the other, "Rabinowitz after plastic surgery." Lucy looked at Cassie's two faces and felt a terrible pang of regret. How had their lives gotten so hellishly screwed up?

Closing her eyes, she sat for a moment holding the paper, biting her lips, and trying not to make a public spectacle of herself. She wanted to yell and tear her hair at the idiocy of it all. For twenty years Cassie had been hiding successfully, raising her children, working, building a new life, only to have all of it destroyed by two unpaid traffic tickets. She should have known it would happen this way. She shouldn't even be surprised. You spent your life worrying about the FBI, but it was never the FBI who caught you. It was the neighbor who called the police because your stereo was too loud; the traffic cop who stopped you for going 30 mph in a 25 mph zone; the department store clerk who didn't like your looks. Life underground wasn't noble or romantic; it was a string of petty dangers and two-bit disasters.

Folding the newspaper in half, she forced herself to read the rest of the article, but it didn't tell her anything she didn't already know except that Cassie was being held temporarily in the San Francisco county jail. She was evidently refusing to talk to the police, which was a good sign because it probably meant that she didn't plan to tell them about . . .

My God. What a selfish thought. She dropped the paper into her lap and took herself to task. She had been thinking that Cassie wasn't going to tell the police about *her*—not only thinking it, but actually feeling relieved that she wasn't going to be directly involved. What kind of friend was she, anyway? Cassie was going to need her testimony to clear herself. No one else knew the facts.

Testify? A small, uncharitable voice inside her objected. Are you crazy? You aren't implicated in this and you should stay out of it. Cass will keep her mouth shut. She won't expect you to throw your life away to save her.

She was disgusted with herself. How could she be thinking this way? Cassie was her friend. She couldn't let her go to prison. She turned back to the front page and began to reread the article. Cassie had been arrested within blocks of her apartment, distraught about the fight they'd just had, crying maybe, making that illegal left-hand turn without noticing it because she was so upset.

Well, she should have been upset, the voice insisted. Remember how she spilled her guts to David? Was that a friendly, responsible act? It put both of you at risk. And now this. She could have paid those tickets, and then she could have made all the illegal left-hand turns she wanted without getting herself arrested. You wouldn't have wished it on her, but it's her own fault. She always has been irresponsible.

She turned to the photos again, to Cassie's homely old face and her beautiful new one, and she thought of all the years they had kept each other's secrets, of the changes they had gone through together; she remembered how they had always been there for each other no matter what happened; how they had comforted each other when relationships with men turned bad, listened to each other cry and complain and rejoice. They'd called each other up in the middle of the night when they were afraid, sent each other money when they were broke. Sure she was angry at Cassie, but that was no excuse for abandoning her. It was cowardly to sit here rationalizing away almost thirty years of friendship.

Get real, Constable, the voice whispered. Your ethics are museum pieces left over from the sixties. Friendship has its limits and Cassie has just stepped over the edge. If you come forward to testify for her, you're going to cause the biggest scandal since Gary Hart was caught with his pants down. Your political career will be finished; you'll have to resign from the Board of Supervisors; the Refuge will go down the drain. She's your friend, yes, but you don't owe her your entire life. You've got her on one hand and homeless women and children on the other. Which deserves your devotion more?

Are you finished? she asked the voice angrily. Are you quite through? Wadding the newspaper into a ball, she rose to her feet and stuffed it into a wire trash basket, mumbling to herself. She was so tempted to go on being Louise Crest that it made her thoroughly ashamed of herself. How easy it would be to slide away, take a vacation, disappear until all this blew over. Even if she testified on Cassie's behalf, there was a good chance that no jury would believe her. Well, so what? If you couldn't be loyal to your friends, who could you be loyal to? Sure, she wanted to keep the Refuge going, but Cassie was the closest thing she had to a family, not to mention that—

There's something else you have to consider, the voice said. Take a deep breath and try to imagine what it's going to be like when you inform the world that the princess of Patan didn't die in 1968. You're going to be hounded by reporters for the rest of your life. Look at poor Christina Onassis. She couldn't gain ten pounds without every sleazy newspaper in the world informing the public that she was a pig with no willpower, and now that she's dead they're starting in on her three-year-old daughter. Cassie's created enough headlines. Why be a martyr? Why not just shut up and let her take the consequences? Besides, don't forget there's a good chance that instead of helping her you'll only get yourself arrested once you admit that you were in the house the night the bomb went off.

Gathering up the rosebushes, Lucy walked to the Cost Plus parking lot, locked in a struggle with herself. It wasn't a dramatic struggle, and it wouldn't have made a good movie. There were no shoot-outs or car chases to let the world know that the conflict was going on, but it was an important struggle all the same because it dealt with one of the only questions worth pondering in life: Who comes first?

Me or her? Lucy kept thinking. Her or me? By the time she had the rosebushes stowed in the trunk of her car, she was more or less convinced that she knew the answer.

Cassie was in deep trouble, and she had no idea how she was going to get out. Some time around two in the morning, she had been pulled from the women's dormitory and placed in solitary confinement. The dormitory had been bad enough, crowded and rank, with pillows so thin they looked like hunks of cheap carpet, and not enough bunks so she had to sleep on a mattress on the floor, but the cell was infinitely worse. Two iron beds hung from the wall, the sink was small and grimy, and the toilet lacked a seat. She could have handled all that if she hadn't known the second they put her by herself that they had found out. She wasn't sure how she knew: maybe by the look on their faces, maybe by the way they isolated her as if she had some kind of contagious disease, maybe by the way no one would meet her eyes. But she knew in her gut that the game was up, and the knowledge made her scared and angry because she deserved better than this, because not only had she lived for the past twenty years as a peaceful, law-abiding citizen, she was innocent in the first place, completely, entirely innocent.

She spent the better part of three hours pacing back and forth, thinking of things that she had been trying to put out of her mind for nearly two decades: of Ann and Steve Singleton and their crazy political views; of her own stupid naïveté; of that fatal night when everything in her life had literally been blown to hell, and all the time the word *innocent* beat in the back of her mind. She wasn't here because she had tried to murder anyone or bomb anyone or even because she hadn't paid those damn tickets. She was here because she was cosmically unlucky. That was an important point, and scared as she was, she didn't intend to forget it.

It was a long night that faded out slowly into a morning that was as gray and gloomy as a roll of fogged film. Some time around five, a trusty brought her a plate of oatmeal, two pieces of limp toast, and a cup of surprisingly good coffee, and shortly afterward the matron returned, accompanied by a detective and the two male guards who had fingerprinted her by force. Triumphantly they read her her Miranda rights again, and advised her that she had the right to remain silent.

"Cassandra Quinn Rabinowitz," the matron had said, chewing over the syllables as if they were chocolate caramels, loving the sound of them by the look in her eyes. At the sound of her real name, Cassie experienced a strange sensation: the air was sucked out of her lungs and replaced by fear, and she knew that she might be sick, but she was too proud to get sick in front of the bastards who had caught her, so she just stood there, tall and proud and more frightened than ever, not answering to her name or anything else, taking advantage of her right to remain silent. Maybe she'd never say anything again, and if she did, it certainly wouldn't be to the four of them.

When they were done telling her that if she couldn't afford a lawyer the court would appoint one for her and all that sort of legal garbage, and when it was clear that she wasn't going to talk to the detective, the matron stepped forward and wagged her bandaged thumb at her. "You screwed up, Rabinowitz," she said, and you could tell that she was happy and on top of things, plump and vulturelike, ready to pick Cassie's eyes out if she had the chance. "You shouldn't have done this. I had your prints run personally, and we all had a little party downstairs when they came back. My bet is that the feds are going to put you away for about fifty years." She grinned and waved her thumb again with its dirty brown banner edged with adhesive. "Enjoy the scenery, and as we like to say here in friendly San Francisco, have a nice day."

After she and the others left, Cassie could have collapsed on her bed and sat there, looking at the wall, because her life was over just like that, only she wasn't the collapsing kind. She started pacing again, thinking with each step how she was going to get even and get out and clear herself, walking a mile every twenty minutes or so if you counted the turns. It was important to keep looking at the up side. She'd get a lawyer and fight this. There had been six people in the Storm house the night the bomb went off; four of them were dead, blown to bits instantly, and one of them, Lucy, shouldn't be involved at all, which left no one to testify on her behalf. Still, the evidence that she had known anything illegal was going on was circumstantial, and if no one was alive to testify for her, no one was alive to testify against her either. She could honestly claim to have been ignorant that Storm was doing anything but organizing peaceful antiwar protests. She really was innocent; surely that counted for something.

In a pig's eye. More likely she'd end up getting fifty years for terrorism and conspiracy. Renny would be able to visit her in prison, but Carla would be put in a foster home or given to Lorenzo, who wouldn't know how to take care of her. The loss of her daughter was more than she could bear to think about. She couldn't take it. She'd do something really crazy to prevent herself from going to prison if it meant that she wouldn't get to watch Carla grow up, pay some underground group to rescue her in a helicopter like the Weather Underground rescued Timothy Leary. Sure, sure and where would she get the money for that and who would she ask? Times had changed since Leary was flown over the wall. All you had now were the Libyans and the Mafia and she didn't relish the idea of contacting either. No, she had to get out legally. She absolutely had to prove she was innocent.

Which of course brought her back to the question of Lucy. Could she ask Lucy to testify for her? No. She rejected the idea out of hand. She couldn't. Bad enough that one of them was going to be sacrificed. What good would it do to get her up there on the witness stand? And yet . . . what harm could it do? Lucy was a persuasive person. Juries were supposed to be irrational; she might move them, grab their sympathy with her story of twenty years as a princess in hiding. She'd be a glamorous figure and a great character witness.

Cassie paced over to the wall and stared at the graffiti and peeling green paint. I definitely should ask Lucy to testify for me, she thought, but I'm not sure I can because if she refuses, it's going to destroy something inside me—call it whatever you want—my faith in humanity, I suppose. If she says she won't, it will injure my dignity irreparably; I'll feel undervalued and worthless, as if our entire friendship has been a farce. She might very well refuse because it's a great deal to ask and she's angry with me and practically told me to get out of her life the last time we spoke, if you can call two women yelling at each other "speaking," so I can't ask her.

At noon a trusty brought her lunch, wieners and baked beans, but she didn't eat it. She watched the window above her head grow brighter, like an overexposed negative, and slowly the dialogue in her mind slowed and then stopped entirely and a strange kind of peace settled over her, and to her surprise she began to feel something close to relief. Being caught was terrible, but it had some compensations. For the first time in twenty years, she could be herself. She was Cassie Quinn again, not just in elevators or in bed alone, but twenty-four hours a day from now on for the rest of her life.

She was just thinking how ironic it was that it had taken jail to give her her freedom back, when a new matron appeared—the day shift, no doubt. She was a tall woman with deep-set eyes, and Cassie decided that no matter what the provocation, she wouldn't sprain her thumb, because the price of thumb spraining was much too high. My God, she was getting her sense of humor back. She was going to survive after all. The thought cheered her, and she stopped pacing. The new matron coughed and eyed Cassie as if she were a dangerous commie mad bomber, which was undoubtedly what she thought. "You got a visitor," she said.

That must be Fred Karkovsky, her agent. When she'd called him last night, shortly after her first arrest, Fred had promised to fly up from L.A. this morning with the cash she needed to spring her out of jail. Now it was going to take a hell of a lot more. She should have contacted Fred and saved him the trip, but he'd been the last thing on her mind. She wondered if he'd heard the news yet. Knowing Fred, the first thing he'd think of was a movie deal. She could just picture him walking in, contract in hand, to sign her up for a five-part miniseries called *I Was a Teenage Terrorist*. Fred was a nice guy, but he saw every disaster as a chance to put a package together. "Who is it?" she asked the matron. She wasn't sure she could take Fred today.

"Your attorney."

Cassie was puzzled. "I don't have an attorney yet."

"Well, according to her, you do. You want to see her or not?"

"Her?"

"Right: female, age approximately forty, height five two, weight approximately one sixteen. Like I said, you want to see her or not?"

Despite her situation, Cassie was amused at the description, which the matron seemed to have read off a wanted poster. Probably if you worked in the county jail long enough you saw everyone that way. "What's her name?"

"Louise. The last name is Crest."

"Oh my God!" Cassie yelled. "Send her in!"

"You don't see her here; you get taken to a conference cell. If she weren't your attorney you'd be talking to her over a telephone behind four inches of bulletproof plastic."

Five minutes later Cassie and Lucy were locked in a giant bear hug, crying and consoling each other, and generally making sentimental fools of themselves, but fortunately for their image as tough women who could take whatever knocks came their way, there were no witnesses. It was clear from the first second they laid eyes on each other that the bad feelings between them were gone.

When they calmed down a little, they sat on opposite sides of the table, and Lucy told Cassie the only news worth hearing. "I've come to tell you that I'm going to testify for you, Cass."

Cassie was so relieved that she didn't know what to say. She grabbed Lucy's hand and squeezed it and opened her mouth, but no words came out. Lucy lifted one finger and put it over Cassie's lips. "Don't thank me, Quinn," she ordered, "and don't fall apart and get all sentimental. It's the least I can do."

Cassie found her tongue. "No, it isn't," she yelled. "It's wonderful of you!" She pulled Lucy to her feet and danced her around the cell laughing, grateful and relieved, and Lucy started laughing too, and it was lucky that the table and chairs were bolted to the floor because otherwise they would have knocked them over. When they stopped, breathless and a little embarrassed by their own excess, they found a guard standing in the doorway glaring at them.

"What's going on in here?" she demanded.

"Nothing," Cassie said with as much dignity as she could muster.

"Nothing at all," Lucy agreed.

"If I were you," the guard said, jabbing her finger in their direction, "I'd take life more seriously." She was right, of course. There were many problems ahead: they needed to raise a lot of money that neither of them had, because Cassie's defense was going to cost a fortune; they needed to find her a good lawyer because Lucy couldn't take the case; they were going to be hounded by the press, interrogated by the FBI, and God knew what else, but at the moment it was hard to take life seriously, because they had just proved beyond a doubt that their friendship was so strong that nothing could destroy it.

· 7 ·

Lucy went straight from the county jail to her office to call Liz Cardullo, tell her the bad news, and have her set up a press conference. Liz had seen plenty of political careers crash, but this scandal was going to set a new record even in her book. As she stood waiting for the elevator, she suddenly had a failure of nerve. Her hands shook as she pressed the button, and she felt light-headed. For a split second she had an urge to turn and run. Hang on, Constable, she told herself. This isn't going to be so bad. But it felt bad; it felt terrible. She put her forehead against the wall, ignoring the curious stares of the other people who were waiting for the elevator, closed her eyes, took several deep breaths, and reminded herself that Cassie was counting on her. She could do it. She had to. One phone call to Liz, that's all it would take.

When she walked into the reception area of her office, she was surprised to find her secretary, Vinnie, sitting idly at her desk, looking off into space with an enraptured expression on her face. Vinnie noticed Lucy and gave a little start. "Hello, Louise," she said. She gazed nervously at Lucy and then at the door to Lucy's office, which was closed. "There's a Mr. Sullivan waiting to see you." Vinnie seemed out of breath and disoriented. She had fluffed up her hair and put on lipstick. The last time Vinnie had put on lipstick was just after she accidentally erased part of the hard disk, blotting out five months of accounts receivable. Lucy hoped there wasn't another computer disaster in the works, and then she remembered that it really didn't matter anymore.

"Sullivan?" She frowned at Vinnie and ransacked her memory, but no Sullivans of any kind came to the surface. Damnation. Why this? Why now? She was anxious to go into her office, call Liz, and get the press conference set up before she lost her nerve again. The last thing she needed was to deal with a new client who hadn't even made an appointment. "Do I know anyone named Sullivan?"

"He says you do."

Lucy gave a sigh of frustration. It wasn't like Vinnie to let someone in her office when she was out, but now that it had happened she could hardly toss Mr. Sullivan down the elevator shaft. "Since he's here, I'll see him," she told Vinnie, "but please, don't let anyone else in and hold all my calls."

"Sure thing." Vinnie gave her a weird, conspiratorial grin that made Lucy wonder if she was having some kind of nervous breakdown. Troubles seemed to be piling up right and left today. Wondering what new disaster Mr. Sullivan might have in store for her, she tossed her coat on the rack and headed toward her office.

"Bon voyage!" Vinnie called after her. Now what in the world was that supposed to mean? Opening her office door, Lucy froze in astonishment on the threshold. The whole room was filled with daffodils. Yellow blossoms nodded on her desk, lifted their heads along the windowsill, stood in glorious profusion along the walls, and cascaded from her filing cabinet. Dancing a slow ballet in the invisible draft from the ventilator, the flowers spread the scent of spring, so sweet and overwhelming that it made her dizzy. At her desk, his face half hidden by daffodils, sat David Blake.

"Hello, Lucy," David said, rising to his feet. He stepped out from behind her desk, rocking the nearest daffodils into motion. "I'm sorry about telling your secretary that my name was Sullivan, but I couldn't have used the name 'Blake.' You might have gone away without seeing me, and I didn't want to chance that, not with all these flowers to keep watered." He waited for her to say something, but Lucy was speechless. She looked from David to the daffodils, trying to get her mind in gear, but it kept grinding in neutral. The blossoms closest to the window were swaying lazily, like dancers in a chorus line. She opened her mouth, swallowed hard, and closed it again, not knowing whether to laugh or cry or turn around and walk out.

David saw how upset she was and cursed himself for being a fool. This wasn't going to work. In about three seconds, she was going to toss him out of her office. He gestured desperately at the flowers. "Do you remember the daffodils? I made you a chain of them a long time ago. Do you remember?" Her face turned pale and then all at once went red, and he knew she remembered. His relief was so great that it was all he could do not to give a cry of joy.

Lucy stood among the flowers, remembering everything: the garden behind Lamont library, pale spring moonlight, their bodies pressed together, desire running through them like sap, the exuberant arch of the yellow daffodils, the endless kissing, the excitement she'd felt at the chance they might be discovered. Making love in that garden had been an insanely reckless thing to do, but she'd never regretted it. They'd had the best of each other that night; it had been a perfect, innocent, golden hour. She had trusted David and he had trusted her, and no shadow of the pain to come had spoiled one second of their love.

Closing her eyes, she found herself reliving the moment as if no time had passed. Twenty-five years dissolved, and again she smelled the dampness of the earth; again she felt the soft grass beneath her head and saw David above her, his face bright with love.

When she opened her eyes, she was trembling. "Oh, David," she said, "why?" She meant, Why did we throw it all away? But she couldn't say the words. Her voice broke and she began to cry, because it was all too much: the flowers and Cassie and her whole life falling apart at once, and him coming back to remind her of the past. She tried to wipe the tears away on the sleeve of her blouse, but they kept coming, and she was too overwhelmed to stop them.

"Lucy," David said. "Lucy, don't, please. I'm sorry. I didn't mean to make you cry. I only meant . . ." He no longer knew what he had meant. He came up to her and stood in front of her, wanting to put his arms around her, but afraid to touch her.

She saw how awkward he was, how vulnerable, and that only made her cry harder because it seemed to have come twenty-five years too late.

"Don't cry," he begged. He couldn't stand it any longer. He put his arms around her to comfort her and felt the old, familiar feel of her and smelled the sweet scent of her hair. Taking her chin in his hand as gently as if it were an open blossom, he tilted her face toward his. He hadn't meant to kiss her, but when he saw her looking up at him, her eyes swimming with tears, he forgot everything except how much he loved her, and leaning forward, he kissed the tears from her cheeks and then put his lips to hers.

"No," she protested, pulling back, alarmed. "This is crazy; you can't just . . ." She was going to tell him that he couldn't just expect her to fall into his arms, not after twenty-five years, not after all they'd been through, but to her surprise the reasonable speech she was about to make went completely out of her head. "I—I" she stuttered, "oh—!" Throwing her arms around his neck, she kissed him back and forgave everything. This is not what an independent woman is supposed to do, she thought. And then she stopped crying and laughed at herself and went on kissing him, because she was happy and she didn't give a damn.

They stood for a long time, wrapped in each other's arms. When the kiss finally ended, Lucy laid her head on his shoulder. "Help us," she murmured, meaning Cassie, meaning the trial and the money, but most of all meaning that she wanted him beside her through the hard times to come.

"Yes," he promised. "I'll help. I'll be there for you, now . . . as long as you'll have me." Brushing her hair away from her face, he lifted her mouth to his and kissed her again, sealing the bargain. A poem was beginning to form in his mind, a short, clean poem about Lucy and luck and how close he'd come to losing both of them.

EPILOGUE

In March 1989, thanks to Lucy's testimony, Cassie was cleared of all charges stemming from her involvement with Storm. Although formally admonished for practicing law under the name Louise Crest, Lucy was not disbarred. Her loyalty to her friend and the story of her flight from Patan aroused public sympathy, and by late summer the Refuge was receiving so many unsolicited contributions that the newly incorporated Refuge Foundation was able to establish two more shelters for homeless women and children. In September, David published his first book of poetry in twenty-five years. Dedicated to Lucy, it was entitled *Homecoming*.

ABOUT THE AUTHOR

MARY MACKEY is a poet, novelist, and film script writer. In 1966 she graduated *magna cum laude* from Harvard and in 1970 she received her Ph.D. in Comparative Literature from the University of Michigan. At present she is a professor of English and Writer in Residence at California State University, Sacramento, where she teaches creative writing and film.

Her published works include four volumes of poetry (*Split Ends, One Night Stand, Skin Deep,* and *The Dear Dance of Eros*), a novella, *Immersion,* and five novels (*McCarthy's List, The Last Warrior Queen, A Grand Passion, The Kindness of Strangers,* and *Season of Shadows*).

Mary Mackey's works have sold over one million copies and have been translated into eleven languages including Japanese, Hebrew, and Finnish. She reviews regularly for the *San Francisco Chronicle,* and has contributed to such diverse magazines as *The Saturday Evening Post, Ms., The New American Review,* and the *Harvard Advocate*. She is presently serving as chair of the Steering Committee of the West Coast branch of PEN.